CHUNG KUO

BOOK FIVE

"House of Ch'in built the Wall to keep them apart,
House of Han has to keep the beacons alight,
Beacons alight and they never go out
For these expeditions have never an end:

In the line, hand to hand, they'll die the same,
The horses will fall, call to Heaven their pain,
The crows and the kites pick their riders' guts
And fly to dead trees with the bits in their beaks . . ."

— Li Po, "We Fought South of
The Walls", 8th century AD

"Life is cheap, flesh plentiful," – common saying
AD 2210

Also by David Wingrove

in the CHUNG KUO series:

Book One: THE MIDDLE KINGDOM
Book Two: THE BROKEN WHEEL
Book Three: THE WHITE MOUNTAIN
Book Four: THE STONE WITHIN
Book Five: BENEATH THE TREE OF HEAVEN
Book Six: WHITE MOON, RED DRAGON

About the author

David Wingrove is the author of *Trillion Year Spree: The History of Science Fiction* which he co-wrote with Brian Aldiss. It won the prestigious Hugo and *Locus* Awards.

He lives in North London with his wife and three daughters.

For Peter Hammill
in admiration

"Senses dimmed in semi-sentience,
only wheeling through this plane,
only seeing fragmented images,
prematurely curtailed by the brain,
but breathing, living, knowing
in some measure at least
the soul which roots the matter
of both beauty and the beast . . ."

INTRODUCTION

Chung Kuo. The words mean "Middle Kingdom" and, since 221 BC, when the First Emperor, Ch'in Shih Huang Ti, unified the seven Warring States, it is what the "black-haired people", the Han, or Chinese, have called their great country. The Middle Kingdom – for them it was the whole world; a world bounded by great mountain chains to the north and west, by the sea to east and south. Beyond was only desert and barbarism. So it was for two thousand years and through sixteen great dynasties. Chung Kuo *was* the Middle Kingdom, the very centre of the human world, and its Emperor the "Son of Heaven", the "One Man". But in the eighteenth century that world was invaded by the young and aggressive Western powers with their superior weaponry and their unshakeable belief in Progress. It was, to the surprise of the Han, an unequal contest and China's myth of supreme strength and self-sufficiency was shattered. By the early twentieth century China – *Chung Kuo* – was the sick old man of the East: "a carefully preserved mummy in a hermetically sealed coffin" as Karl Marx called it. But from the disastrous ravages of that century grew a giant of a nation, capable of competing with the West and with its own Eastern rivals, Japan and Korea, from a position of incomparable strength. The twenty-first century, "the Pacific Century" as it was known even before it began, saw China become once more a world unto itself, but this time its only boundary was space.

The War Of The Two Directions

It had begun with the assassination of the T'ang's Minister, Lwo Kang, some thirteen years earlier, the poor man blown into the next world along with his Junior Ministers while basking in the imperial solarium. The Seven – the great Lords and rulers of Chung Kuo – had hit back at once, arresting one of the leading figures of the Dispersionist faction responsible for the Minister's death. But it was not to end there. Within days of the public execution, their opponents had struck another deadly blow, killing Li Han Ch'in, son of the T'ang, Li Shai Tung, and heir to City Europe, on the day of his wedding to the beautiful Fei Yen.

It might have ended there, with the decision of the Seven to take no action in reprisal for Prince Han's death – to adopt a policy of peaceful non-action, *wuwei* – but for one man such a course could not be borne. Taking matters into his own hands, Li Shai Tung's General, Knut Tolonen, had marched into the House of Representatives in Weimar and killed the leader of the Dispersionists, Under Secretary Lehmann. It was an act almost guaranteed to tumble Chung Kuo into a bloody civil war unless the anger of the Dispersionists could be assuaged and concessions made.

Concessions were made, an uneasy peace maintained, but the divisions between rulers and ruled remained, their conflicting desires – the Seven for Stasis, the Dispersionists for Change – unresolved. Among those concessions the Seven had permitted the Dispersionists to build a starship, *The New Hope*. As the ship approached readiness, the Dispersionists pushed things even further at Weimar, impeaching the *tai* – the Representatives of the Seven in the House – and effectively declaring their independence. In response the Seven destroyed *The New Hope*. War was declared.

The five year "War-that-wasn't-a-War" left the Dispersionists broken, their leaders dead, their Companies confiscated. The great push for Change had been crushed and peace returned to Chung Kuo. Or so it briefly seemed, for the War had woken older, far stronger currents of dissent.

In the depths of the City new movements began to arise, seeking not merely to change the system, but to revolutionise it altogether. One of these factions, the *Ping Tiao*, or "Levellers", wanted to pull down the great City of three hundred levels and destroy the Empire of the Han.

For a while the status quo had been maintained, but three of the most senior T'ang had died during the War, leaving the Council of the Seven weaker and more inexperienced than they had been in all the long years of their rule. When Wang Sau-leyan, the youngest son of Wang Hsien, ruler of City Africa, became T'ang after his father's death, things looked ominous as the young man sought to create disharmony among the Seven. But Li Yuan, inheriting from his father, formed effective alliances with his fellow T'ang, Wu Shih, Tsu Ma and Wei Feng, to block Wang in Council, outvoting him four to three.

Even so, as Chung Kuo's population continued to grow, further concessions had to be made. The great Edict of Technological Control – the means by which the Seven had kept change at bay for more than a century – was relaxed, the House of Representatives at Weimar reopened, in return for guarantees of population controls.

For the first time in fifty years the Seven had begun to tackle the problems of their world, facing up to the necessity for limited change, but was it too late? Were the great tides of unrest unleashed by earlier wars about to overwhelm them?

CONTENTS

MAJOR CHARACTERS

Ascher, Emily – Trained as an economist, she was once a member of the *Ping Tiao* revolutionary party. After their demise, she fled to North America where, under the alias of Mary Jennings, she got a job with the giant ImmVac Corporation, working for Old Man Lever and his son, Michael, whom she finally married. Ultimately, however, what she wants is change, and the downfall of the corrupt social institutions that rule Chung Kuo.

DeVore, Howard – A one-time major in the T'ang's Security forces, he has become the leading figure in the struggle against the Seven. A highly intelligent and coldly logical man, he is the puppet master behind the scenes as the great 'War of the Two Directions' takes a new turn.

Ebert, Hans – Son of Klaus Ebert and heir to the vast GenSyn Corporation, he was promoted to General in Li Yuan's Security forces, and was admired and trusted by his superiors. Secretly, however, he was allied to DeVore, and was subsequently implicated in the murder of his father. Having fled Chung Kuo, he was declared a traitor in his absence.

Kao Chen – Once a *kwai*, a hired knife from the Net, the lowest level of the great City, Chen raised himself from those humble beginnings to become a major in the T'ang's Security forces. As friend and helper to Karr, Chen was one of the foot-soldiers in the war against DeVore, but recent experiences have left him disillusioned with the system he serves.

Kennedy, Joseph – Latest in a long line of Kennedys, he was the founder and guiding light of the New Republican Party, dedicated to bringing political change to City North America.

Lever, Michael – Son of Charles Lever, he was incarcerated by Wu Shih for his involvement with the 'Sons of Benjamin Franklin', a semi-revolutionary group formed by the sons of wealthy North American businessmen. Breaking from his father, he set up independently and married Mary Jennings in defiance of the old man. Now, after the death of his father, he has inherited the vast ImmVac Corporation.

Li Yuan – T'ang of Europe and one of the Seven, as second son of Li Shai Tung, he inherited after the deaths of his brother and father. Considered old before his time, he none the less has a passionate side to his nature, as demonstrated in his brief marriage to his brother's wife, the beautiful Fei Yen. His subsequent re-marriage ended in tragedy when his three wives were assassinated. Now, embittered by the experience, he has become a recluse.

Shang Han-A – Sixteen-year-old daughter of the Junior Minister Shang Mu, she is a talented, lively young woman, possessed of an artist's eye and a revolutionary cast of mind.

Tolonen, Jelka – Daughter of Marshal Tolonen, Jelka was brought up in a very masculine environment, lacking in a mother's love and influence. Yet her attempts to re-create herself – to find a balance in her life – have only brought her into conflict, first with a young soldier, and then with her father, who – to prevent her having a relationship with Kim Ward – has despatched her on a tour of the Colony Planets.

Tolonen, Knut – Former Marshal of the Council of Generals and one-time General to Li Yuan's father, Tolonen is a rock-like supporter of the Seven and their values, even in an age of increasing uncertainty. In his role as father, however, this inflexibility in his nature has brought him only repeated conflict with his daughter, Jelka.

Tsu Ma – T'ang of West Asia and one of the Seven, Tsu Ma has thrown off a dissolute past to become Li Yuan's staunchest supporter in Council. A strong, handsome man in his late thirties, he has yet to marry, though his secret affair with Li Yuan's former wife, Fei Yen, revealed a side of him that has not been fully harnessed.

Wang Sau-leyan – T'ang of Africa. Since inheriting – after the suspicious deaths of his father and elder brothers – Wang Sau-leyan has dedicated every moment to bringing down Li Yuan and his allies in Council. A sharp and cunning adversary with an abrasive, calculating manner, he is the harbinger of Change within the Council of Seven.

Wu Shih – Middle-aged T'ang of North America, he is the last remaining member of the old generation of T'ang. A staunch traditionalist. Nevertheless he has found himself allied in Council with Li Yuan and Tsu Ma against the odious Wang Sau-leyan. Yet with the resurgence of American nationalism, he finds himself confronted by a problem none of his fellow T'ang have to face: a problem he must either find a solution to, or go under.

THE SEVEN AND THE FAMILIES

★ ★ ★

An Hsi – Minor Family prince and fifth son of An Sheng

An Mo Shan – Minor Family prince and third son of An Sheng

An Sheng – head of the An Family (one of the Twenty-Nine Minor Families)

Hou Tung-po – T'ang of South America

Li Kuei Jen – son of Li Yuan and heir to City Europe

Li Yuan – T'ang of Europe

Pei K'ung – Minor Family Princess

Pei Ro-hen – head of the Pei Family (one of the Twenty-Nine Minor Families) and father of Pei K'ung

Tsu Ma – T'ang of West Asia

Wang Sau-leyan – T'ang of Africa

Wei Chan Yin – T'ang of East Asia

Wei Hsi Wang – second brother of Wei Chan Yin and heir to City East Asia

Wei Tseng-li – youngest brother of Wei Chan Yin and secretary to Li Yuan

Wu Shih – T'ang of North America

Wu Wei-kou – first wife of Wu Shih

Yin Chan – Minor Family prince and second son of Yin Tsu

Yin Fei Yen – "Flying swallow"; Minor Family Princess and divorced wife of Li Yuan

Yin Han Ch'in – son of Fei Yen

Yin Tsu – head of the Yin Family (one of the Twenty-Nine Minor Families) and father of Fei Yen

FRIENDS AND
RETAINERS OF THE SEVEN

★ ★ ★

Althaus, Kurt – General of Security, North America

Blofeld – agent of special security forces

Brookes, Thomas – Port Captain, Tien Men K'ou, Mars

Chang Li – personal surgeon to Li Yuan

Chen So – Clerk of the Inner Chambers at Tongjiang

Dehmel – Major in Security, City Africa

Edsel – agent of special security forces

Fan – fifth brother to the *I Lung*

Fen Cho-hsien – Chancellor of North America

Fuller – Sergeant in Security

Graham – agent of special security forces

Gray – Captain of the *Chang Hsien*

Heart's Delight – maid to Li Yuan

Henderson, Daniel – pro-tem Governor of Mars

Hu Ch'ang – Principal Secretary to Nan Ho

Hung Mien-lo – Chancellor of Africa

I Lung – "First Dragon", the head of the "Thousand Eyes",
   The Ministry

Jacobson – Captain in Security

Johnson – Captain in Security

Kao Chen – Major in Security

Karr, Gregor – Major in Security

Krol – Sergeant in Security

Lauer – private in Security

Liang Yu – Magistrate of new settlement in Kang Kua City,
   Mars

Lo Wen – Master of *wu shu* and tutor to Li Kuei Jen

Lu – surgeon at Tongjiang

Nan Ho – Chancellor of Europe

Nan Tsing – first wife of Nan Ho

Pale Blossom – maid to Li Kuei Jen

Pao En-fu – Master of the Inner Chambers to Wu Shih
Rheinhardt, Helmut – General of Security, Europe
Schenck, Hung-li – Governor of Mars Colony
Seymour – Major in Security, North America
Shang Mu – Junior Minister in the "Thousand Eyes", the Ministry
Shen Lo-yen – Captain of the Guard, Tongjiang
Shepherd, Ben – son of the late Hal Shepherd, "shell" artist
Stewart – agent of special security forces
Tolonen, Jelka – daughter of Marshal Tolonen
Tolonen, Knut – ex-Marshal of Security; Head of the GenSyn Hearings committee
Wade – Lieutenant in Security, Mars
Welcome Spring – maid to Li Kuei Jen
Wells – Captain in Security, North America
Wilson, Stephen – Captain in Security under Kao Chen
Yang Shao-fu – Minister of Health, City Europe
Yang T'ing-hsi – Chancellor of West Asia
Ye – Senior Steward at Tongjiang
Yin Shu – Junior Minister in the "Thousand Eyes", the Ministry
Yun – Minister of Trade, North America

* * *

OTHER CHARACTERS

* * *

Andre – friend of Hannah
Anna – helper to Mary Lever
Ascher, Emily – ex-*Ping Tiao* terrorist, now known as Mary Lever
Auden, William – ex-Security Captain and friend of DeVore
Bates – leading figure in the Federation of Free Men, Mars
Beresiner – media agent
Bess – helper to Mary Lever

Britton – private investigator

Chamberlain, Geoffrey – head of WesCorp

Chang Te Li – "Old Chang", *Wu*, or Diviner

Ch'en Li – associate of Governor Schenck

Chih Huang Hui – second wife of Shang Mu and step-mother of Shang Han-A

Christian – friend of Hannah

Chung, Gloria – heiress; daughter of the late Representative Chung Yen and friend of Michael and Mary Lever

Cornwell, James – director of the AutoMek corporation

Culver – pseudonym of DeVore

Dawson – associate of Governor Schenck

DeValerian, Rachel – pseudonym of Emily Ascher

DeVore, Howard – ex-Major in Li Yuan's Security and head of the HoloGen corporation of Mars

Ebert, Berta – widow of Klaus Ebert

Ebert, Hans – son of Berta Ebert and a declared "traitor"

Ebert, Lutz – half-brother of Klaus Ebert

Echewa, Aluko – Chief of the Osu tribe of Mars

Efulefu – "Worthless Man", chosen name of Hans Ebert among the Osu

Egan – head of NorTek

Elechi – Encoder for the Osu tribe of Mars

Endacott – associate of Governor Schenck

Eva – friend of Mary Lever

Fairbank, John – head of AmLab

Fisher, Carl – NREP member and Representative at Weimar

Fung – *Wu*, or Diviner to Yin Tsu

Green, Clive – head of RadMed

Hamsun, Torve – Captain of the *Luoyang*

Hannah – anglicised name of Shang Han-A

Hart, Alex – Dispersionist, and Representative at Weimar

Hsia – *Wu*, or "Diviner" to the *I Lung*

Hsin Kao Hsin – low-level prostitute

Hsu Jung – Master of *wei chi*, City Africa

Ishida, Ikuro – Japanese asteroid miner

Ishida, Kano – eldest brother of Ikuro

Ishida, Tomoka – second brother of Ikuro

Ishida, Shukaku – eighth brother of Ikuro

Jackson – freelance go-between, employed by Fairbank

Jefferies – senior clerk at the Hythe-MacKay auction house

Jill – principal helper to Mary Lever

Johnson, Dan – personal assistant to Michael Lever

Kao Ch'iang Hsin – daughter of Kao Chen

Kao Jyan – eldest son of Kao Chen

Kao Wu – second son of Kao Chen

Karr, Marie – wife of Gregor Karr

Karr, May – daughter of Marie and Gregor Karr

Kate – Security Computer System at Hythe-MacKay

Kemp, Johannes – Director of ImmVac

Kennedy, Jean – wife of Joseph Kennedy

Kennedy, Joseph – head of the New Republican and Evolutionist Party and Representative at Weimar

Kennedy, Robert – elder son of Joseph Kennedy

Kennedy, William – younger son of Joseph Kennedy

Latimer, John – pseudonym of Hans Ebert

Leckie, Andrew – Director of ImmVac

Lehmann, Stefan – "The White T'ang", Big Boss of the European Triads

Lever, Mary – wife of Michael Lever

Lever, Michael – Head of the ImmVac pharmaceuticals corporation of North America and Representative at Weimar

Li Min – "Brave Carp", an alias of Stefan Lehmann

The Machine – an artificial intelligence

Marley, George – business associate of Charles Lever

Meng K'ai – friend and adviser to Governor Schenck

Munroe, Wendell – Dispersionist, and Representative at Weimar

Nza – "Tiny Bird", an Osu child

Parker, Jack – Representative at Weimar

Parry – DeVore's agent in Tien Men K'ou City, Mars

Pi Kung – assassin

Richards – Steward of the Lever Mansion

Rutherford, Andreas – friend and adviser to Governor Schenck

Sao Ke – friend of Hannah

Shang Ch'iu – son of Shang Mu and half-brother of Shang Han-A

Shang Han-A – daughter of Shang Mu

Shen – body-servant to Yin Tsu

Shen Li – pseudonym of Ishida Ikuro

Song Wei – sweeper

Steiner – Manager at ImmVac's Alexandria facility

Stock – senior employee of HoloGen

Tao-kuang – Steward to Kennedy at Weimar

Tian Ching – maid in Kao Chen's household

Tong Chou – alias of Kao Chen

Tse – Steward at the Shang Mansion

Tuan Ti Fo – Master of *wei chi* and sage

Tu Ch'en-shih – friend and adviser to Governor Schenck

Tung Cai – low level rioter

Underwood, Harry – Dispersionist, and Representative at Weimar

Wang Ti – wife of Kao Chen

Wang Tu – leader of the Martian Radical Alliance

Ward, Kim – Clayborn scientist

Wu Mao – rice stall owner

Yu – Master of Ceremonies to the *I Lung*

* * *

THE DEAD

* * *

An Liang-chou – Minor Family prince

Anderson, Leonid – Director of the Recruitment Project

Anne – *Yu* assassin

Barrow, Chao – Secretary of the House at Weimar

Barycz, Jiri – scientist on the Wiring Project

Bercott, Andrei – Representative at Weimar

Berdichev, Soren – head of SimFic and later leader of the Dispersionist faction

Berdichev, Ylva – wife of Soren Berdichev

Brock – security guard in the Domain

Cherkassky, Stefan – ex-Security assassin and friend of DeVore

Chi Hu Wei – T'ang of the Australias; father of Chi Hsing

Ch'in Shih Huang Ti – the first emperor of China; ruled 221– 210 BC

Cho Hsiang – Hong Cao's subordinate

Chu Heng – "kwai", or hired knife; a hireling of DeVore's

Chun Wu-chi – head of the Chun family (one of the Twenty-Nine Minor Families)

Chung Hsin – "Loyalty"; bondservant to Li Shai Tung

Clarac, Armand – Director of the "New Hope" Project

Coates – security guard in the Domain

Cook – duty guard in the Domain

Cutler, Richard – leader of the "America" movement

Deio – Clayborn friend of Kim Ward from "Rehabilitation"

Donna – *Yu* assassin

Douglas, John – Company head; Dispersionist

Duchek, Albert – Administrator of Lodz

Ebert, Klaus – head of the GenSyn Corporation; father of Hans Ebert

Ecker, Michael – Company head; Dispersionist

Ellis, Michael – assistant to Director Spatz on the Wiring Project

Endfors, Pietr – friend of Knut Tolonen and father of Jenny, Tolonen's wife

Erkki – guard to Jelka Tolonen

Feng Chung – Big Boss of the Kuei Chuan (Black Dog) Triad

Feng Lu-ma – lensman

Feng Shang-pao – "General Feng"; Big Boss of the 14K Triad

Fest, Edgar – Captain in Security

Fu Ti Chang – third wife of Li Yuan

Gesell, Bent – leader of the *Ping Tiao* – "Leveller" – terrorist movement

Griffin, James B. – last president of the American empire

Haavikko, Vesa – sister of Axel Haavikko

Hammond, Joel – Senior Technician on the Wiring Project

Heng Chi-po – Li Shai Tung's Minister of Transportation

Henssa, Eero – Captain of the Guard aboard the floating palace Yangjing

Herrick – illegal transplant specialist

Ho Chin – "Three-Finger Ho"; Big Boss of the Yellow Banners Triad

Hoffmann – Major in Security

Hong Cao – middleman for Pietr Lehmann

Hou Ti – T'ang of South America; father of Hou Tung-po

Hsiang K'ai Fan – Minor Family prince

Hsiang Shao-erh – head of the Hsiang family (one of the Twenty-Nine Minor Families)

Hsiang Wang – Minor Family prince

Hua Shang – lieutenant to Wong Yi-sun

Hui Tsin – "Red Pole" (426, or Executioner) to the United Bamboo Triad

Hwa – master "blood", or hand-to-hand fighter, below the Net

Joan – Yu assassin

Kan Jiang – "Dry Stream", Martian settler and poet

K'ang A-yin – gang boss of the Tu Sun tong

K'ang Yeh-su – nephew of K'ang A-yin

Kao Jyan – assassin; friend of Kao Chen

Kennedy, William – great-great grandfather of Joseph Kennedy

Krenek, Henryk – Senior Representative of the Martian Colonies

Krenek, Irina – wife of Henryk Krenek

Krenek, Josef – Company head

Krenek, Maria – wife of Josef Krenek

Kriz – senior *Yu* operative

Kubinyi – lieutenant to DeVore

Kung Wen-fa – Senior Advocate from Mars

K'ung Fu Tzu – Confucius (551–479 BC)

Kustow, Bryn – American; friend of Michael Lever

Lai Shi – second wife of Li Yuan

Lao Jen – Junior Minister to Lwo Kang

Lehmann, Pietr – Under-Secretary of the House of

Representatives and first leader of the Dispersionist faction; father of Stefan Lehmann

Lever, Charles – head of the giant ImmVac Corporation of North America; father of Michael Lever

Lever, Margaret – wife of Charles Lever and mother of Michael Lever

Li Chin – "Li the Lidless"; Big Boss of the Wo Shih Wo Triad

Li Ch'ing – T'ang of Europe; grandfather of Li Yuan

Li Han Ch'in – first son of Li Shai Tung and once-heir to City Europe; brother of Li Yuan

Li Hang Ch'i – T'ang of Europe; great-great-grandfather of Li Yuan

Li Kou-lung – T'ang of Europe; great-grandfather of Li Yuan

Li Pai Shung – nephew of Li Chin; heir to the Wo Shih Wo Triad

Li Shai Tung – T'ang of Europe; father of Li Yuan

Lin Yuan – first wife of Li Shai Tung; mother of Li Han Ch'in and Li Yuan

Ling Hen – henchman for Herrick

Liu Chang – brothel keeper/pimp

Liu Tong – lieutenant to Li Chin

Lo Han – tong boss

Lu Ming-shao – "Whiskers Lu"; Big Boss of the Kuei Chuan Triad

Luke – Clayborn friend of Kim Ward from "Rehabilitation"

Lwo Kang – Li Shai Tung's Minister of the Edict

Maitland, Idris – mother of Stefan Lehmann

Man Hsi – tong boss

Mao Liang – Minor Family princess and member of the *Ping Tiao* "Council of Five"

Mao Tse tung – first Ko Ming emperor (ruled AD 1948–1976)

Matyas – Clayborn boy in Recruitment Project

Meng Te – lieutenant to Lu Ming-shao

Mien Shan – first wife of Li Yuan; mother of Li Kuei Jen

Milne, Michael – private investigator

Ming Huang – sixth T'ang emperor (ruled AD 713–755)

Mo Yu – security lieutenant in the Domain

Moore, John – Company head; Dispersionist

Mu Chua – Madame of the House of the Ninth Ecstasy

Mu Li – "Iron Mu", Boss of the Big Circle Triad

Parr, Charles – Company head; Dispersionist

Pavel – young man on Plantation

Peck – lieutenant to K'ang A-yin (a *ying tzu*, or "shadow")

Peskova – lieutenant of guards on the Plantations

Ross, Alexander – Company head; Dispersionist

Ross, James – private investigator

Sanders – Captain of Security at Helmstadt Armoury

Schwarz – lieutenant to DeVore

Shang – "Old Shang"; Master to Kao Chen when he was a child

Shang Chu – great-grandfather of Shang Han-A

Shang Wen Shao – grandfather of Shang Han-A

Shen Lu Chua – computer expert and member of the *Ping Tiao* "Council of Five"

Shepherd, Amos – great-great-great-grandfather (and genetic "father") of Ben Shepherd

Shepherd, Augustus – "brother" of Ben Shepherd, b. 2106, d. 2122

Shepherd, Hal – father (and genetic "brother") of Ben Shepherd

Shepherd, Robert – great-grandfather (and genetic "brother") of Ben Shepherd

Shu San – Junior Minister to Lwo Kang

Siang – Jelka Tolonen's martial arts instructor

Si Wu Ya – "Silk Raven", wife of Supervisor Sung

Spatz, Gustav – Director of the Wiring Project

Spence, Leena – "Immortal", and one-time lover of Charles Lever

Ssu Lu Shan – official of the Ministry

Sun Li Hua – Wang Hsien's Master of the Inner Chambers

Sung – Supervisor on plantation

Tarrant – Company head

Teng Fu – plantation guard

Tewl – "Darkness"; chief of the raft-people

Tolonen, Hanna – aunt of Knut Tolonen

Tolonen, Helga – wife of Jon Tolonen; aunt of Jelka Tolonen

Tolonen, Jenny – wife of Knut Tolonen, and daughter of Pietr Endfors

Tolonen, Jon – brother of Marshal Knut Tolonen

Tong Chu – assassin and "kwai" (hired knife)

Tsao Ch'un – tyrannical founder of Chung Kuo

Tsu Tiao – T'ang of West Asia; father of Tsu Ma

Tu Mai – security guard in the Domain

Vesa – *Yu* assassin

Virtanen, Per – major in Li Yuan's Security forces

Visak – lieutenant to Lu Ming-shao

Wang Chang Ye – first son of Wang Hsien

Wang Hsien – T'ang of Africa; father of Wang Sau-leyan

Wang Lieh Tsu – second son of Wang Hsien

Wang Ta-hung – third son of Wang Hsien; elder brother of Wang Sau-leyan

Wei Feng – T'ang of East Asia; father of Wei Chan Yin

Weis, Anton – banker; Dispersionist

Wen Ti – "First Ancestor" of City Earth/Chung Kuo, otherwise known as Liu Heng; ruled China 180–157 BC

Wiegand, Max – lieutenant to DeVore

Will – Clayborn friend of Kim Ward from "Rehabilitation"

Wong Yi-sun – "Fat Wong"; Big Boss of the United Bamboo Triad

Wyatt, Edmund – Company head; Dispersionist, father of Kim Ward

Yang Lai – Junior Minister to Lwo Kang

Yi Shan-ch'i – Minor Family prince

Ying Chai – assistant to Sun Li Hua

Ying Fu – assistant to Sun Li Hua

Yue Chun – "Red Pole" (426, or Executioner) to the Wo Shih Wo Triad

Yun Ch'o – lieutenant to Shen Lu Chua

Yun Yueh-hui – "Dead Man Yun"; Big Boss of the Red Gang Triad

Ywe Hao – "Fine Moon"; female Yu terrorist

Ywe Kai-chang – father to Ywe Hao

PROLOGUE – WINTER 2210:
GHOSTS' TORCHES

"Ah, silence, such silence,
like in a dream, moonlight noble and heartless,
in the same dusk, in the same dawn.
No elegy to be heard, and no bells tolled.
The gate to the world of the departed souls,
   is solemnly closed,
seeing me into the funeral train which marries me
   to life,
demanding I reclaim talent of days gone by.
Ah, silence, such perpetual silence,
there is no reply, and there is no echo,
there are just ghosts' torches, illuminating
   my whole life . . ."

> – Duo Duo, "Death of A Poet", AD 1974

GHOSTS' TORCHES

The great Courtroom was empty, silent. On the bare stone
of the walls torches burned brightly, steadily in their iron
cressets, yet the chamber seemed engulfed in shadows, the
galleries and wood-beamed ceiling lost in an impenetrable
darkness. At the far end of the chamber two huge stone
pillars flanked the great double doors. Between them, their
figures dwarfed by the entrance arch, walked two men.

"Well, Knut," said one of them, turning a long, horse-like
face to his companion, "the day has come at last. You must
be proud to have brought things to this point."

Tolonen paused, his smile uncertain. "We have worked
hard to bring this about, neh, Chi Hsun? Yet now that the
day is upon us I feel not satisfaction but a strange sadness.
It's as if I haven't grieved for him. But now that it's done.
Now that the matter's to be decided . . ."

He fell silent, staring away into darkness.

Chi Hsun reached out, touching the Marshal's arm, consol-
ing him. "I understand . . . Klaus Ebert was a fine man. He
stood for all that was good and strong and decent. To have
lost such a man was a tragedy for us all. But for you . . .
well, you were his friend."

"And he mine," Tolonen said, lifting his chin, a look of real
pain, real hurt in his eyes. "Since we were boys." He turned,
facing Chi again, a strange sound, half pain, half remembered
joy, escaping him. "I had dreams, Chi Hsun . . . Dreams that
his son would marry my daughter. That his grandchildren
would be my grandchildren . . ." He stopped, choked by
emotion, unable to say more.

3

The Chief Commissioner, watching him, nodded. "I'm sorry, Knut. It must be hard for you in view of what happened. But listen. I hear that Ebert's widow is to be married again."

Tolonen looked back at him, surprised. "Berta? I'd not heard . . ."

"No. They say she's waiting until after the Hearing to make the announcement."

"Ah . . ." Tolonen walked on, out into the body of the Courtroom, stopping beside the huge, long desk that dominated the centre of the chamber. He leaned forward, his hands – one flesh, one burnished gold – pressed flat against the smoothly polished surface, silently looking about him at the empty benches, the dais where, in a matter of hours, the Commissioners would sit and deliberate. Then he turned, looking directly at Chi Hsun.

"Where did it all go? That's what I keep asking myself. Where did they go – all those dreams we had? They seemed so real, so *secure*. How could it all have gone so wrong?"

Chi Hsun looked down, then came across, stopping beside Tolonen.

"The past is gone, Knut. We cannot change it. But the future . . . well, that we *can* affect. It is why we serve, neh? Why, in the days to come, we must work hard to ensure the best result."

Tolonen met his eyes, a sudden tiredness in his voice. "And what *is* the best result? To see that wastrel Lutz inherit?"

"You think he will?"

Tolonen sighed, then nodded.

"And Berta Ebert?"

Tolonen grimaced. "The most she can realistically hope for is a life interest in the estate. And an annual sum, perhaps, corresponding with her private allowance when Klaus was still alive. Oh, she'll get to keep the Mansion, probably, but as for the Company . . ."

"And if Lutz Ebert inherits? What will happen, do you think? Will GenSyn become again the power it was?"

4

Tolonen shrugged. "Who can tell? If Lutz has any sense he'll keep the present management committee in place and let them run things, but I doubt he'll do that. He has acquired many new 'friends' these past few years, his new wife's family not least among them. I suspect he'll pack the board with them once he's inherited. If so, who knows what future GenSyn has? A poor one, probably."

"And the rumours? You know, of Lutz's involvement with his nephew, the traitor Hans?"

Tolonen looked down, his face sour. "Ah, *that*. I had a team looking into it for the best part of a year."

"And?"

"Nothing. Oh, there were a few shady business deals – the kind of thing that, were the media to get hold of them, would make him even less popular than he is now – but nothing to link him to Hans. Nor will there be, unless we find the young man."

Chi Hsun glanced across at the dais, then looked back at the aged Marshal. "And your Master, Li Yuan . . . what does he think of events?"

Tolonen looked away, his expression troubled. "My Master has been kept fully briefed. His primary concern is to see that things are kept stable."

It was a diplomatic answer, for, by all accounts, Li Yuan had become something of a recluse since the murder of his wives, letting his Chancellor, Nan Ho, attend to the day-to-day running of things. But where GenSyn was concerned, what Li Yuan thought was of immense importance. GenSyn were still the biggest Company in Chung Kuo, and traditionally their fortunes had been linked directly with the Li family. A decline in the power of GenSyn would mean a corresponding decline in power for Tolonen's master. It remained to see whether he would allow it to fall into the hands of Klaus Ebert's weak half-brother, Lutz.

Yet what could he do?

Each of the Seven – the T'ang who ruled Chung Kuo – had appointed a representative to sit on the Hearing Committee and look after their best interests. For Li Yuan to overrule their decision was unthinkable. Yet there were other means.

Chi Hsun looked about him at the empty benches of the Courtroom and sighed. GenSyn. Wherever one turned, the influence of that great Company could be seen: in the food substitutes they used throughout the Lowers; in the cheap health treatments that were so popular in the Mids; in their range of prosthetics and "age-at-bay" products used by the rich. Mainly, however, they were known as the creators of the Genetic Synthetics, those strange and marvellous creatures grown in their tanks, custom-designed for every taste: servants and whores, sportsmen and performers, goat-men and ox-men, brutish bodyguards and the flat-faced, bullish *Hei* that Security used to put down riots. GenSyn had been a cornucopia, providing something for every level – one of the great pillars on which Chung Kuo was built. But now all that was threatened.

Chi Hsun looked back at the Marshal. As he did, Tolonen turned from the table, looking back at him, a tired, sad expression in his eyes. Beyond him the lamps flickered in their iron cressets, making the shadows seem deeper, ingrained almost in the stone and wood of the ancient hall.

"Ah well . . ." the old man said. "Let's go now, Master Chi. Sleep. That's the remedy. A good night's sleep, neh? Tomorrow will come soon enough . . ."

* * *

Alone in his rooms, Tolonen stood before the mirror, staring at his face, trying to see, beyond those rugged, angular planes, some resemblance of the man he'd been.

He had had little time in his life for self-analysis. He had always seen it as a weakness in a man and had maintained a rigid self-discipline when it came to such matters. But recently, left with much time on his hands and missing the company of his daughter, Jelka, his thoughts had begun to turn inwards. He had been reading the *Kalevala* once more, immersing himself in the great epic of his people, the Finns, and as he read he had found memories awakening of people long dead; of friends he had forgotten.

The dead . . . it was as if the great world were slowly dying all about him. All those he had known and loved – his wife, his brother and his brother's wife, his old master Li Shai Tung, and his best friend, Klaus . . . they and countless others – all were gone. Only ghosts remained. The world had lost substance, had reduced itself to a pool of light, a mirror, a face – his own face, staring back at him.

So hard that face . . . Elemental, it was. Like weathered rock.

And eyes like a November sky.

He smiled, but it was a pale and steely smile. Sunlight in winter. Then, softly, his voice little more than a whisper, he spoke into the glass.

> "When the oak at last had fallen,
> And the evil tree was levelled,
> Once again the sun shone brightly,
> And the pleasant moonlight glimmered,
> And the clouds extended widely,
> And the rainbow spanned the heavens,
> O'er the cloud-encompassed headland,
> And the island's hazy summit."

The words came easily to him. But that was no surprise. He had pored over them, time and again, as if obsessed. For weeks now he had been haunted by them; had woken from dreams with them on his lips. Dreams in which the great City had fallen and the land was green and empty . . . was a land of lakes and mountains.

The oak . . . the evil tree. It was the symbol of the Shepherd family, of the architect of the seven great Cities of Chung Kuo.

He took a long, shuddering breath. Had he been wrong? Chung Kuo . . . was that the evil tree of legend? For if it was . . . if all he had believed in was an evil spell . . .

He shook his head, then pushed the thought aside. Lately he had been tormented by loneliness . . . a loneliness he was too proud – far too proud – to admit to. Some days he woke feeling fragile, like a ghost himself, and sometimes he would turn, imagining someone behind him, only to find an empty room . . . and silence. But what *was* he? He had thought he knew. "A man," he would once have answered, as if that had a meaning beyond all question. But now . . . well, what *was* a man?

Never in all his seventy-six years had he been troubled by such thoughts, but now it was as if a door had opened in him and he had stepped inside.

Inside . . . into uncertainty, and dreams, and thoughts that woke him in the night.

Old . . . I am getting old . . .

He stripped off his sleeping jacket, then reached up to touch his left shoulder, tracing the join, watching himself in the glass. There, where flesh met metal, a thin strip of soft leather acted as a kind of buffer, preventing the skin from being chafed. It had been awkward at first, but now the feel of it was comforting, strangely reassuring. *I am alive*, it seemed to say.

He sniffed, then moved the golden limb, flexing and unflexing the jointed hand, remembering how he had lost the arm. A close call that had been. Indeed it was a wonder he had lived so long when so many had wanted him dead.

Turning, he looked about him at the huge and shadowed room. It was simply, almost spartanly furnished. A double bed, a chair and a small writing desk – that was all. Underfoot a thick rug covered half the floor space. As for the walls, they were bare save for the portrait of his wife that hung in the alcove facing his bed.

He went across and stared up at it.

"How are you, Jenny Endfors?" he asked quietly, using her maiden name. "Is it sunny where you are?"

She smiled back down at him. Beyond her the wind seemed to dance in the pines that covered the hillside of the island, while to her left the blue-green sea sparkled in the spring sunlight. Like a goddess, he thought, sent briefly down to haunt him . . .

She had been thirty years his junior, a beautiful, blonde-haired girl with a laugh like the summer itself. Jelka . . . his darling Jelka was her image. But the gods had decided not to grant him more than a single measure of happiness. His Jenny had died giving birth to his daughter, and he had slept alone these last eighteen years.

Lonely . . . no wonder he was lonely.

There was a knock. He turned, wondering for a moment if he hadn't imagined it, then it came again.

"Yes?" he called, his voice filled with a strength and certainty he did not feel.

"Marshal Tolonen?"

It was the voice of his equerry, Lofgren.

He frowned, then went across and unlocked the door. In the corridor outside, Lofgren stood alone, a small tray balanced between his hands. The smell of hot soup wafted up out of the darkness.

"Bertil? What is this?"

"I . . . I heard you pacing, sir. I thought maybe this would help. I wasn't certain you had eaten."

Tolonen smiled, then stepped back, letting the young officer enter. "That's very kind of you. I . . . I couldn't sleep."

"No, sir." Lofgren took the tray across and set it down on the desk, then turned, coming to attention.

"At ease, boy."

"Sir . . ."

He went across, then sat, beginning to eat, his hunger surprising him.

"Were there any messages?" he asked, turning between mouthfuls to look up at the young man.

"Just one . . . from your daughter."

"Jelka? What, from Callisto?"

"Yes, sir. A short-burst transmission. I've stored a copy on your personal file. If you like, I could have it played right now . . ."

Tolonen took another mouthful of the soup, then shook his head. "No. Show it to me first thing. While I'm getting dressed."

"Sir . . ."

He smiled. Yes. It would be something to look forward to, before the business of the Hearing began. Thinking of which . . .

"Bertil?"

"Sir?"

"Do you think we were right, letting things take their course? I mean . . . GenSyn . . . it's so important to us all. If things go wrong . . ."

Lofgren looked down, embarrassed. It was not often the Marshal asked him for his opinion.

"I . . . I guess it depends what you mean, sir. If you mean, were we right not to have Lutz Ebert killed out of hand . . . well, I'm not sure, sir. I . . . I wouldn't have liked to have made that call."

"But if you had?"

The young officer looked away, a slight stiffness to him now. "I think I would have done exactly as you did, sir."

Tolonen smiled. "I see. Well, thank you, Bertil. You can go now. Oh, and thank you for the soup. It was most welcome."

"Sir . . ."

He watched the boy go, then stood, stretching his limbs, tired now, ready for his bed.

If you only knew, he thought. *If only you'd been there, Bertil Lofgren, when I advised the T'ang to have the bastard killed.* But now it was too late. Much, much too late. To have him killed now would create more problems than it solved. Besides, there were other ways to control the man. Subtler, more efficient ways.

He went across and blew a silent kiss, then turned and went to his bed. Pulling back the thin sheet he slipped beneath it, his eyes heavy suddenly, the frantic racing of his thoughts slowing to a more sedate pace.

And the rainbow spanned the heavens . . .

He gave a shuddering yawn, then turned onto his side, the thought that followed the words vanishing from mind even as it formed.

Soup . . . he must have drugged the soup . . .

Outside the door, the young man waited, listening. Then, hearing the old man's snores, he nodded to himself and, smiling, walked away down the unlit corridor towards his quarters.

* * *

The Courtroom was hushed, expectant. Above the raised dais where the court officials sat, a dozen media remotes hovered like fire-flies, sending back an incessant stream of images to the watching billions of Chung Kuo. Just now their cameras were focused on the distinctive features of Chi Hsun, the most senior of the seven Commissioners.

Chi Hsun was a tall, humourless man with a long, horse-like face. To the public he was best known for his role in the Demotion trials six years before. Back then he had become known as "Iron Chi" for his unrelenting pursuit of those who had opposed the Seven in the great "War that wasn't a War". As Tsu Ma's representative on the Hearing Committee his view was supposed to carry no more weight than any other's, but his long experience made him their natural leader, and it fell to him now to open the proceedings.

Off to one side sat the old Marshal himself, Knut Tolonen. He was in overall charge of the Hearings and in the last two and a half years had earned much respect for the way he had handled the matter. Now, with the public phase of the Hearings finally about to begin, he seemed tired, his granite features pale and drawn.

The camera moved on, panning slowly across the huge stacks of legal books and files, three long rows of them, which were laid out along the full length of the benches at the centre of the courtroom, then slowly climbed the steps, picking out first the tall, coldly elegant figure of Berta Ebert, sat between her daughters on the far right of the court, then moved along, past various familiar figures until it rested on the face of Lutz Ebert, the dead man's half-brother. For a moment it remained there, allowing that face, with its weak, watery blue eyes and its uncertain, somewhat shifty features, to condemn itself, then moved on again, across a backdrop of media celebrities and chattering anchor-men until it focused on the stocky yet sophisticated form of Henri Lanouette, sat amidst the bankers and businessmen – Han and *Hung Mao* – who formed his faction.

For a brief moment the faint murmur of voices filled the Courtroom. Then, as the ceremonial bell sounded – one tone high, the other low – the room fell silent and the three parties' advocates entered the room from the doors at the far end, making their way towards the raised bench at the front where the Commissioners sat.

Chi Hsun waited for them to form up in front of him, then made a brief dismissive gesture of his hand. At once the main body of the advocates – some thirty or so in all – made their way across to their benches on the left-hand side of the court, leaving only the three Senior Advocates standing before the Commissioners.

And so, finally, they came to it: the formal submission of evidence. First to submit would be Tung Li-so, Chief Advocate for Berta Ebert and her daughters.

Tung Li-so began his submission, but he had barely uttered more than a dozen words when he broke off, staring to his right. An elderly Han had come across from the public benches and now presented himself before Iron Chi, his head respectfully bowed. As he straightened up, the remotes homed in, hovering just overhead.

"Forgive me, Excellency," he began, "but I would like to submit fresh evidence before the Commissioners in the matter of the GenSyn Inheritance Hearings."

Chi Hsun stared at the ancient a moment, astonished, then turned, looking to Tolonen for guidance.

"I have crucial new evidence. If your Excellency would permit . . ."

"Let's hear what he has to say!" Tolonen called from across the Courtroom in a weary voice. "But make him get on with it. We've delayed long enough!"

"All right," Chi Hsun said gruffly, glaring at the newcomer, "but if you are wasting the Commission's time, I shall have you charged, you understand?"

12

"I understand, Excellency."

"Good. Then state your name and business and get on with it."

"Thank you, Excellency. My name is Ku Hsien-ch'eng and I am Advocate for the sole legitimate heir to the estate of Klaus Ebert."

Iron Chi nodded, stunned by what he'd said, waiting for Advocate Ku to say more, but the old man merely turned away. At that moment, as if at an unseen command, the doors at the far end of the room swung inwards and eight grey-bearded advocates made their way into the court, each bearing a huge stack of files and legal texts, which they proceeded to heap upon the central benches, pushing aside what was already there.

"Seven copies," Ku said, turning back to Iron Chi and bowing once more. "As the Commission demands."

* * *

There was uproar in the court. On the benches to the left the advocates were standing, calling out to the Commissioners, demanding that they dismiss this new evidence, while on the bench itself the Commissioners were in disarray, arguing among themselves over the legality of this new submission. Amidst it all stood Ku Hsien-ch'eng, his head bowed, a faint, almost enigmatic smile on his face.

On the public benches, Lutz Ebert was standing, looking on, his eyes narrowed suspiciously. Near by Berta Ebert was looking down, her fists balled tightly in her lap, what she was feeling concealed behind a wall of icy self-composure. Only Lanouette seemed vaguely amused, as if he'd been fore-warned.

Tolonen, meanwhile, leaned over Chi Hsun's shoulder, reading through the brief abstract of Advocate Ku's submission, wondering – just loud enough for the nearest remote to catch his muttering – who in the gods' names could possibly be claiming the GenSyn billions. An answer which, when he finally came to it, made him laugh, half in shock, half in disgust.

13

"The gods help us!" he said quietly, meeting Iron Chi's eyes. "Let's hope to hell this isn't true!"

* * *

Tolonen sat at his desk in the Lower Committee Room, an old-fashioned glowlamp hovering nearby, illuminating the great chart he had spread out before him. Beyond the edges of the chart the desk was cluttered with huge stacks of files and discs and ancient law texts. Near by, waiting silently in the shadows beyond the tight circle of light, sat his equerry, the young lieutenant, Lofgren.

The Marshal looked up, then rubbed at his eyes with his right hand. Beyond the reinforced ice of the picture window the darkness seemed to have softened towards morning. His left shoulder had begun to ache, as it often did when he was tired, but that was understandable. They had been working through the new evidence for the best part of a day, but now it was clear.

He yawned and looked across, smiling at the young man. "What time is it, Bertil?"

"Fifth bell sounded twenty minutes back, sir."

Tolonen nodded, then sat back, staring thoughtfully at the great mass of untouched material. There was much more to look at – enough to keep the Committee busy for another month – but he had seen enough to know that he had been right. This was serious. Very serious indeed.

He turned, looking at the young man again. "What's your feeling about this, Bertil? Do you think I was right to keep the Committee at arm's length?"

The young lieutenant considered a moment, then. "From what I've seen, sir, I think you had no choice. By dismissing Iron Chi and the Committee when you did, you gave Li Yuan a clear advantage. If Wang Sau-leyan's man, Tu Chung, had got wind of any of this, his master would almost certainly have intervened at once. As it is, Li Yuan has time to act, to prevent Wang from using this against him."

Tolonen sniffed deeply. That was true. And yet he could not stop the Hearing tomorrow. To do so would merely invite the T'ang of Africa to meddle. And that was what he had been trying to avoid all along. No . . . his problem was how to play this. How to turn this information to Li Yuan's advantage.

He looked back at his equerry. "At present Wang knows merely that there has been a development in the case, not how significant that development is. Yet if I allow this new evidence to go before the Committee, Wang will know everything within the hour."

"And yet you have no choice. If you embargo the evidence, the effect will be the same. Tu Chung will protest and, when his protest is ignored, Wang Sau-leyan will take the opportunity to step in. In the circumstances you would be best advised, perhaps, to take the bull by the horns. To strike before our Master's cousin knows what is going on." Lofgren smiled. "Why not let Advocate Ku present his evidence at once, before Iron Chi and the rest have had a chance to look at it."

Tolonen sat forward. "Could we do that?"

"Why not? It might be suggested to Chi Hsun that, by doing so, this 'distraction' might be set aside and the real business of the Hearing got on with."

Tolonen gave a short laugh, then nodded. "I like that. And Chi Hsun will buy it, I'm certain. But what of Li Yuan? Oughtn't we to let him know?"

"As soon as possible, sir. The new evidence changes everything. Unless our Master acts, and acts swiftly, our worst fears will come about. The matter will drag on and GenSyn will be lost."

"You think it would be that bad?"

"I am certain of it, sir. Why, even before this, Tu Chung has suggested delays for the most minor of technicalities. This new matter would give him the perfect excuse to request a lengthy recess. Indeed it could drag on for years while his clerks exhaust the search for precedents, and in the meantime all the work we've done these past thirty months to stabilise GenSyn's trading position and reassure the markets would be lost. Confidence would vanish overnight. The share price would plummet. And that cannot be allowed to happen."

"No." Tolonen stood, nodding decisively, his granite face set. "Then I shall contact Li Yuan at once and tell him what we know."

* * *

There was silence in the great Courtroom as the elderly Ku Hsien-ch'eng completed his opening remarks, bowed low to the panel of Commissioners, then turned, facing the seated rows of advocates.

"*Ch'un tzu,*" he said, smiling politely.

Behind and above them, at the top of a flight of steps that formed an aisle between their seats, was a doorway. At Ku's terse nod the Guard of the Court lifted the great keys from his belt and turned, fitting one to the lock. As the heavy door eased back, heads turned, trying to see into the darkness beyond. For a moment there was nothing, then, out into the brightness of the courtroom, stepped an elderly Han dressed in pale green silks. There was a general outlet of breath, a moment's disappointment, then, just beyond the old man, flanked by two young male attendants in matching pale green one-pieces, came a girl. Or rather, a young woman. A Han in her late twenties, wearing a simple pink and mauve chang shan and a white wool flower – a *tai hsiao* – in her tightly bobbed jet-black hair.

At the sight of her there was a buzz of excitement. A sound that was interrupted by the sudden indignant cry of Berta Ebert.

"How dare you bring that creature here! How *dare* you!"

Media remotes buzzed here and there, almost colliding in their attempts to capture every moment of it. But things were moving fast now. Behind Ebert's widow, his daughters were on their feet and shouting, enraged by the sight of the young woman. Near by, Lutz Ebert looked down, one hand pressed to his brow, shading his eyes.

The young woman came down the steps slowly, the two attendants leading her by the hands. Down she came, looking about her vaguely, her eyes fearful, like a young animal's, an uncertain, apologetic smile on her lips.

Up ahead of her the old Han had stopped and, after bowing to Iron Chi and the Commissioners, turned, facing Advocate Ku. Ku Hsien-ch'eng smiled then turned, facing Iron Chi, raising his voice over the clamour in the chamber.

"May I present before your Excellencies the chief witness for my claimant . . ."

For a moment his voice was drowned out by the shouts of the Ebert women. Ku turned, looking across, his hands tucked into his sleeves, waiting patiently while a Court official got the three women to sit and be quiet, then he turned back, bowing to Iron Chi, as if the fault were his.

"Forgive me, Excellencies. As I was saying, might I present to the Commissioners the young lady, Shou Chin Hsin, better known in the Ebert household as Golden Heart, one-time concubine to the traitor, Hans Ebert."

From Ku's right the shouting began again. This time Iron Chi leaned forward angrily, calling for order.

"If I have one more outburst from you, Madam Ebert, I am afraid I shall have no choice but to ban you from this chamber until the Hearing is over. Now sit still and hold your tongue."

It was a severe rebuke, but Berta Ebert stood there a moment longer, defiant, glaring at the young woman, before she sat again, her body tense, her face a mask of hatred.

As for Golden Heart herself, she seemed unaffected by the noise, apart from it. There was something odd about her, something *unconnected*. The remotes, circling her, took in every detail of her dress, the way she stood, the way her eyes moved restlessly, flicking across the surface of things.

To Ku's left came the urgent murmur of whispered exchanges among the advocates. Then, as if some agreement had been reached, Advocate Chang, the senior representative for Lutz Ebert, stood and cleared his throat.

Iron Chi looked across at him. "Yes, Advocate Chang. What is it?"

Chang bowed, then came round until he stood before the bench. "Forgive me, Excellency, but on behalf of my claimant I wish to register a protest against the witness presented

17

by Advocate Ku. Medical testimony would merely serve to confirm what is evident at a glance. The woman is clearly mad. Any evidence she might give to this Hearing would be of as little value as the prattlings of a child. In the circumstances I beg the Commissioners to rule that this witness's evidence be inadmissible."

Chi Hsun stared at the young woman a moment, then looked back at Ku Hsien-ch'eng. "Well, Advocate Ku, what have you to say? Personally I am of Advocate Chang's view. Unless, therefore, you can give good reason why I should allow you to continue, I shall rule that we move on."

Ku bowed his head. "With respect, Excellency, the mental state of the witness has no bearing whatsoever on this Hearing. Nor have I any intention of letting Shou Chin Hsin utter a single word in respect of this matter. However, her presence here has a point, so if you would bear with me a moment?"

"I shall allow you to continue, Advocate Ku, but make it brief."

"Excellency." Turning, Ku put out a hand, inviting the old Han in the pale green to come forward, then, taking his arm, he went up to the bench, presenting the man to the Commissioners.

"This, your Excellencies, is Professor K'ang. K'ang Hung-chang of the Kunming Institute of Comparative Genetics; a body established and licensed by special Edict of the Seven and run within the strict guidelines of the Edict of Technological Control. Professor K'ang's expertise is in matching genotypes . . ."

"Forgive me, Excellency," Advocate Chang interrupted, "but I fail to see the relevance of any of this. Golden Heart may have been Hans Ebert's concubine – we do not dispute it – but that gives her no claim in law, particularly in view of the Special Decree issued by the Seven."

Iron Chi looked about him at his fellow Commissioners, receiving sober nods from all sides, then looked back at Ku.

"I must once more agree with Advocate Chang. Unless

18

you can provide me with a good reason for continuing, Advocate Ku, I shall rule that your claim be set aside and that all matters relating to it be struck from the official record."

Ku bowed. "I understand, Excellency. Then let me come directly to the point. There is a child."

There was a great hiss of disbelief, then, once again, the chamber erupted with noise. Chi Hsun sat back, startled. Beneath him, on the floor of the court, Chang had turned and was staring at Ku, his mouth hanging open. On the benches across from him, most of the advocates were on their feet, shouting and waving papers.

Chi Hsun let the noise continue for a while, then raised a hand, calling for silence. Once a kind of order had returned, he leaned forward again, looking down at Chang.

"Did you know of this, Advocate Chang?"

Chang licked his lips nervously, then nodded. "There *was* a child, yes, but the child was destroyed."

"*Destroyed?*"

Ku, standing beside him, shook his head. "That is not so. Hans Ebert ordered it to be destroyed, but that is not the same thing. His order was not carried out. The child was taken to a place of safety and kept there. The boy lives. He is three, almost four now."

Chi Hsun sat back, astonished. "And you can prove this, Advocate Ku?"

Ku Hsien-ch'eng bowed and smiled, the very picture of composure. "As I was saying, Excellency, this here is Professor K'ang. K'ang Hung-chang of the Kunming Institute of Comparative Genetics . . ."

* * *

In the silent darkness of the room, the hologram shone with the intensity of a ghostly vision, the face of the madwoman filled with a strange inner light that seemed to waver like a candle's flame between serenity and despair.

Tolonen, standing there, his hands gripping the edge of the viewing table, stared down at the image open-mouthed, mesmerised by the sight of the child playing at its mother's feet. He was a robust, healthy child with fine dark hair and strong Eurasian features.

A bastard, he thought. Yet there was no denying it. It was Hans Ebert's child. That face, that mouth, that chin. That was the Ebert lineage. But even without that there was proof enough. His experts had taken new cell samples and subjected the genetic charts to the most rigorous scrutiny, and the evidence held up. The concubine, Golden Heart, was the mother, Hans Ebert the father.

Even so, the matter was far from straightforward. Hans Ebert was a traitor and, under normal circumstances, his family shared his fate, to the third generation. Yet it had been agreed among the Seven that these were far from normal circumstances. Klaus Ebert had been a pillar of the State. Though dead it was unthinkable that he should be declared a traitor, and so a special Edict had been passed, exonerating him, his wife and all dependants, making the sentence of the Seven specific to one single individual . . . Hans Ebert. Now that document assumed a new importance. Was the child to share the father's fate, or was he too exonerated under the terms of the Edict?

It was up to Li Yuan to decide.

Tolonen looked down. It was all his fault. He had trusted Hans Ebert. He would have given him anything. Anything at all. His daughter, Jelka, even his own life. And to think . . .

He sighed then shook his head. Some days he felt it was simply the gods, toying with them all, putting devils into the shapes of men. At others he felt that it was just how they were. Men. With all the strange goodness and wickedness of men.

And the men who had done this – who had saved the child and brought it up in secret? Which were they? And what did they want?

He had been surprised when he'd learned who was behind this. The list of names included six of the most prominent businessmen in City Europe. But what were they after? Was theirs a long-term game? Did they look to the child's gratitude in years to come?

Or maybe young Lofgren was right. Maybe their hand had been forced. After all, what use was a potential heir once the inheritance issue had been legally decided? So maybe it had simply been a case of produce your trump card now or see it lose all value. Even so, what they hoped to achieve was still obscure to him. If the aim had been to damage GenSyn, then surely the easiest, most certain course was to let Lutz Ebert inherit and destroy the child. But maybe that last part – the killing of the child – had grown too difficult for them. Maybe there were too many in on the secret for that to be a realistic option. Then again, maybe it was much simpler than that. Maybe the sight of Lutz Ebert gloating, anticipating his inheritance, had been enough to make them act.

Only one thing was certain. Whatever their motives, altruism had not been among them. They had not invested so much time and money simply to see social justice done. Whatever the outcome, they hoped to have a say, and it was his job to prevent that somehow, to make sure that Chung Kuo's greatest Company stayed clear of such attachments.

Even so the whole affair convinced him of one thing. The world he had known was gone. There had been a breach. Father to son, that had been the way of it, generation after generation, but now the natural son had proved false, had been seen to be a twisted shadow of the father, and this thing – this product of casual fucking with a whore – had been conjured from the air to fill the gap.

He shivered. *Like a dream. Like a dark and evil vision of what was to come.*

Or like a curse . . .

* * *

The Committee was seated about the long table, a fierce argument raging, when the doors at the far end of the chamber burst open. Tolonen entered, followed closely by an honour troop of six shaven-headed guards. Immediately the room fell silent. At the head of the table, directly facing Tolonen, Tsu Ma's man, Iron Chi, rose to his feet.

"Forgive me, Knut, but we are in session. It was agreed . . ."

Tolonen raised a hand to mollify his old friend. "Forgive me, Chi Hsun, forgive me, *ch'un tzu*, but for once there is no time for formalities . . ."

Wang Sau-leyan's man, Tu Chung was on his feet. "With respect, Marshal Tolonen, this is not right. We *must* maintain formalities."

Tolonen stared at him contemptuously, then turned his head, looking to Iron Chi.

"Well, Chi Hsun? Will you keep me waiting like a servant in the antechamber? Or will you hear what I have to say?"

"I protest . . ." Tu Chung began once more, but Tolonen turned, shouting him down.

"The gods preserve us! Hold your tongue, man!"

Tu Chung jerked back, as if slapped, then sat, glaring at Tolonen.

At the head of the table, Iron Chi leaned forward, his long face clearly troubled. "Whilst I agree with Tu Chung that this is most irregular, I do feel that, for once, we might make an exception and hear what the Marshal has to say. Forgive me, however, if I insist that we take a vote on this matter. I would not have it said that, in allowing this, I went beyond the instructions given to me by the great Council."

Tolonen bowed his head. "As you wish, Chi Hsun, but please, let us do it at once, neh? I am a busy man."

Iron Chi nodded, then looked about him. "Well? Will all those in favour of the Marshal addressing this Committee please indicate their agreement."

From about the long table there were grunts of agreement. Only Tu Chung remained stubbornly silent.

Iron Chi stared at Wang's man a moment, then, with a tiny shrug, looked back at Tolonen. "It is agreed, then. Let us hear what you have to say."

Tolonen bowed. "Forgive me, *ch'un tzu*. I will take but a moment of your time. I wish to address you informally on this matter. To advise you of a decision that has been made this past hour. One which, I feel, you might wish to take

22

into consideration when deliberating upon this complex and difficult case." He looked about him, then, staring directly at Tu Chung, added. *"Ch'un tzu . . .* It has been decided that the Special Decree concerning the fate of the traitor Hans Ebert shall be deemed to apply solely to the person named and not to any issue of his loins."

Tu Chung's head bobbed up, a look of shocked surprise etched on his features. His mouth opened, as if to answer the Marshal, then, realising there was nothing he could say, he bowed low, acknowledging defeat.

Tolonen turned, noting the surprise on Chi Hsun's face and nodded. It was done. The child would inherit.

* * *

It was shortly after eighth bell when Tolonen arrived at the old Ebert Mansion, his heart strangely heavy. The last time he had come here it was to tell his old friend Klaus of his son's duplicity: a warning that had resulted in the old man's death and young Hans' escape from Chung Kuo, a traitor, condemned in his absence. And now a young madwoman and her bastard son were tenants of this great estate; the boy heir to the whole vast GenSyn empire, by Li Yuan's decree.

He handed his cloak to the servant then walked through briskly, his booted footsteps echoing back all the way along the broad, tiled corridor. Since Klaus Ebert's death the house had been run by a skeleton staff – but the Marshal could remember it in other days, when its rooms had been filled with guests, its corridors busy with servants.

At the end of the corridor he stopped, waiting while one of the house stewards fumbled with a great bunch of keys at his waist, then threw open the huge doors that led out to the gardens at the centre of the house.

Tolonen strode out onto the balcony and gripped the rail, sniffing the air and looking about him. Here, at least, nothing had changed. A tiny, twisting stream ran beneath low-railed wooden bridges. Beyond it, small, red-painted buildings lay half-concealed among leaf and tree and rock. And there, on

23

the far side of the gardens, beside the pool, three pomegranate trees stood like three ancients sharing a jug of wine.

How often as a young man had he sat with Klaus beneath those trees, their feet dangling in the water, and talked of the years to come. Of their hopes and fears and plans. How often had they argued out the world's great problems between them. Young men, they'd been, filled with a strange, visionary enthusiasm.

Gods, he thought, moved by the sudden clarity of the memory. It seems like only yesterday. And yet it was sixty years ago. Sixty long years. And the world of which they had dreamed . . . what had come of that? Nothing. Nothing but dust and ashes, betrayal and bitter disappointments.

"And madwomen . . ." he said softly, reminding himself why he had come.

Yesterday Li Yuan had summoned him and asked him if he would serve again. "One last time," as the young T'ang had put it, "before you take up poetry and painting." He had laughed and readily agreed, glad to be doing something now that the inheritance issue was resolved. But this . . .

He sighed. There was a bitter irony to this. That he should be chosen to be Guardian to the boy. He, an old man of seventy-six years. Not only that, but in his heart of hearts he blamed himself for this situation. If he had only gone direct to Li Yuan when he had first found out about Hans Ebert, then Klaus might still be alive, the question of inheritance not an issue. But he had let friendship distort things. And this was the result. A madwoman and her bastard.

Ah yes, but at least he'd exacted a price for his service. Jelka was to come home. She was to be flown direct to Mars from Callisto, and three ships of the imperial fleet were to be sent to ensure her safe return.

Tolonen pushed back, away from the handrail, then went down, crossing the tiny bridge, following the narrow pink and grey pebbled path through the trees to the far side of the garden. Golden Heart would be in her quarters at this hour, on the east side of the Mansion. And the child . . .

He slowed, suddenly remembering what Jelka had said that

24

time. How strange that he had forgotten that until now. He stopped, looking about him. It had been the evening of Li Shai Tung's death – the night DeVore had attacked the Wiring Project – and he had left her here with Hans while he had gone to see what he might do. And later she had told him about the madwoman and her awful pink-eyed ox-baby, and how Hans had had her real child killed. Yes, and he had refused to believe her. As if she would ever lie to him . . .

If only he had listened to her. If only he had not tried to force her into that awful, ill-fated marriage with Hans. If only . . .

He shivered, thinking of her, out there on Callisto. It was strange just how much he missed her. More – much more – than he had ever thought possible. And though he heard from her regularly, it wasn't the same. No. He missed her coming into his study late in the evening to wish him goodnight. Missed the way she would come up silently behind him in his chair and lean across, her hands resting lightly on his shoulders, to gently kiss his brow.

He closed his eyes, steeling himself against the memory and the thought that accompanied it, but there was no denying it; lately he had begun to wonder whether he would ever see her again, face to face. Whether he would ever hold her and feel the warmth of her cheek against his own.

You're a foolish old man, Knut Tolonen, he told himself, straightening up. But then, what else was left for him these days? Who else was there for him to love?

Tolonen turned, hearing noises from the rooms up ahead – the sound of a young child crying for its mother. Hans Ebert's son . . . He lifted his head, swallowing back the bitterness he felt at the thought – at the dashed hopes it represented – then walked on, knowing he would do his duty by the child.

PART 1 – SUMMER 2211:

THE SOUTH SIDE OF THE SKY

"The mountain climbs, fifty li into darkness
Beyond it, the cold stars burn.
Here, on the south side of the sky
The rain never falls.
All that we are, we carry with us
In sealed packs, safe from the air.
Thin the air, thin the hope
Of seeing home again,
Except from afar.
Red sand fills our shoes.
We stop at an inn and drink our fill,
Yet are never content.
We are lost,
Adrift upon a sea of dust.
Some thirsts can never be satisfied."

— Kan Jiang, "Thirst" AD 2078

CHAPTER · 1

<u>UPON A SEA OF DUST</u>

DeVore stood at the garden's edge, one hand resting against the reinforced glass of the dome, looking out into the darkness of the Martian night. Soldiers guarded the perimeter, their bulky suits gleaming frostily in the earthlight. It was just after two, local time, and the lights of the distant city were low. Beyond them was a wall of blackness.

He turned, looking back across the garden at the Governor's house. It was a large, two-level hacienda, built in the "Settler" style of a hundred and fifty years earlier, its terrace and upper windows lit by sturdy globular lamps, its back wall hugging the far side of the dome. Surrounding it on three sides, the garden was a dark, luxuriant green, its trees and vines and bushes lit here and there by glowing crimson globes that drifted slowly above the black tiles of the paths. Overhead the dark curve of the dome reflected back their images, like a dozen tiny copies of the planet.

DeVore looked about him, experiencing a deep-rooted sense of satisfaction. It was a beautiful garden, full of rare treats and delights. But what was perhaps most pleasing about it was that it was so totally unlike the formal gardens one found on Chung Kuo. There were no walls here, for instance, no delicate, over-arching bridges, no steep-roofed *ting* or ornamental tea-houses. It was all so open, so . . . unrefined. Yet it wasn't merely the look of it that impressed him – it was the fact that all trace of Han thought, Han tradition had been carefully dispensed with in its design. Where, in a Han garden, there was harmony and balance – a sense of *li*, of "propriety" – here there was a sense of outwardness, of openness to change. His smile widened. In essence, this was one huge, deliberate snub. A thumbing of the nose at the Han who ruled them from afar.

He laughed softly at the thought. Yes, there was something just slightly outlandish about all this – something positively gross about its simple spaciousness and sense of sprawl, about the silken richness of the leaves, the lurid colours of its blossoms. This was something new. An expression of excess, of unchecked growth. He could imagine how offensive – how distasteful – this would seem to the Han mentality. How alien.

He reached out, taking one of the broad, leathery leaves between his fingers, surprised by how glossy and silken it was. Beneath his booted feet the earth was rich and dark, a moist, heavy soil that clung like clay and stained the fingers brown. Close by were some of the big hybrids he had noticed earlier. He went across to them, lifting one of the dark blue flowers gently from beneath. Seen close-up, it seemed less a blossom than a kind of pad, a rudimentary face formed into the puffy surface of the flower, like a mask. This one was of lust, but others, nearby, seemed to reflect a range of other moods – of anger and love, cunning and desire, of hatred, benevolence and despair. And many more. He lifted it to his nose, intrigued by its strange, exotic scent, and noted how it brushed against his cheek, like a pet, responding to his human warmth.

"They're edible, too," said Schenck, coming out onto the terrace. "You should try one . . ."

DeVore met the Governor's eyes, smiling. "Later, perhaps . . . They're new, aren't they?"

Schenck nodded and came down the wide, slatted steps, tightening the sash about his formal robe. "The very latest designs. They're what we call 'interims'. Part vegetable, part animal. The end result of thirty years research. Beautiful, aren't they?"

DeVore studied them a moment. To be honest, part of him found them quite ugly – an offence to natural form. Even so, Schenck was right. If they weren't beautiful in themselves, then the idea of them was beautiful. This too was something new. Something that had not existed before Man had made it exist. Thinking that, he felt a small thrill pass through him and looked back at Schenck, nodding.

"I'll send you some," Schenck said, coming across.

"Thanks. So how did it go?"

Schenck had just returned from the official reception held to celebrate his re-election for a third term as Governor of the Martian Colonies. The cream of Martian society had been there in Kang Kua City tonight, representatives of all nine-teen Colonies.

"Well enough," Schenck answered, stopping a few *ch'i* from where DeVore stood. "You know how these things are, Howard. My face simply aches from smiling."

"I suppose it was buzzing with the latest news, neh?"

"What else? After all, it's official now." Schenck looked away, laughing to himself. "You can't imagine how many times I was drawn aside tonight. If I'd said yes once to endorsing a candidate, I'd have had to say it fifty times, and as there'll be only twenty-six representatives from Mars, that could have got me into serious trouble."

DeVore studied him a moment, then lowered his eyes. "And the other matter?"

Schenck glanced at him, then leaned across, plucking one of the mask-like flowers from its stem. There was a faint puckering of the flower's expression, a sudden release of fragrance. "Our friends, the merchants, you mean?"

DeVore nodded.

Schenck lifted the flower to his face and nibbled at the edge, then turned, meeting DeVore's eyes. "They're pleased, Howard. Very pleased indeed."

"So the prototypes were useful?"

Schenck felt in the pocket of his *pau*, then handed some-thing across. It was a tiny box, like a pill box. DeVore opened it.

The insect – a termite, its segmented body the colour of darkest night – stared up at him from beneath the translucent ice, its compound eyes inquisitive.

"It's semi-autonomous," Schenck explained, looking down into the box. "You can send it into the offices of your rivals and it will serve as your eyes and ears. It has augmented sensory apparatus and a memory capacity rivalling the field comsets Security use. Moreover you can programme it either to look for something specific, or – and this is the really clever part – you can simply trust it to look for the unusual. It seems that all you have to do is give it an idea of what it ought to find, and then let it get on with the job."

DeVore smiled, remembering when his copy had sent the prototype for this from earth. This was Kim Ward's work – *he* had designed this little beauty.

"A bug," he said. "An intelligent bug."

"A semi-autonomous robotic unit," Schenck corrected him. "It merely looks like a bug."

DeVore closed the lid and slipped it into his pocket. Schenck smiled, making no attempt to take it back.

"And the Machine?"

Schenck lifted the flower to his mouth, taking another tiny bite. "I've had it shipped. It'll be there in two days. I saw to it myself."

"And they're going to pay for that? As agreed?"

Schenck nodded, then threw the flower down. It lay there, its smile fixed and eternal. "They've paid for everything. What's more, the dome will be ready two weeks from now. To your specifications, naturally."

"Good." But he was thinking that he would have to do something about that. To stop word getting out.

"Oh, and one more thing before I go and change. An old friend of yours has turned up. I thought you might like to meet him."

"A friend?" He looked past Schenck, suddenly aware of the figure on the terrace. A big, broad-chested man in uniform. He narrowed his eyes, trying to make out who it was, then gave a great roar of delight, making his way across.

"Will! When did you get here? Why didn't you let me know?"

Auden came down the steps and embraced DeVore, then stood back, coming to attention, his head lowered.

"I got in yesterday. From Callisto. I was going to contact you at once, but the Governor asked me not to. He wanted to surprise you."

DeVore let his hand rest on Auden's shoulder a moment, then, still smiling broadly, he looked across at Schenck. "For once I'm glad you did, Hung-li. This is a marvellous surprise!"

Schenck came over to them. "You've things to talk about, I'm sure, so I'll leave you. I've got a call to make, but I'll join you in a while, okay?"

DeVore watched Schenck go, then turned back, taking Auden's arm. "Well, Captain William Auden, so where have you been? And what in the gods' names have you been up to? I thought you were dead!"

Auden laughed. "I've felt like it some days, to be honest. But no. I've been out to the edge of the system. Out there among the ice and rock."

"And?" DeVore eyed his old lieutenant, curious to see what he'd made of it.

"And I'm glad to be back. Even this far out. You know, they've an expression for us out there – warm-worlders, they call us. Well, I'd rather be a warm-worlder than a rock-breather any day." He shuddered. "It was awful. Like death. We weren't meant to live out there."

"But now you're back. So what do you plan to do?"

Auden shrugged.

DeVore considered a moment, then smiled. "Don't worry. I'll find something. You always were useful."

"Talking of which . . ." Auden hesitated and glanced at the house, as if to check that Schenck were out of hearing. "I've news," he said, his voice lowered. "Something I picked up on Callisto. It seems the Marshal's daughter will be here within the week."

DeVore's smile faded. "Then you must have heard it wrong, Will. The *Tientsin* won't be docking here for another two months."

"That's true. But Jelka Tolonen isn't on the *Tientsin*. The

Marshal sent out new orders. She was to travel to Callisto on a special Security flight, then transfer to one of the direct Jupiter–Mars shuttles."

"And that's why you came? To let me know?"

Auden smiled. "I knew you'd be interested. Besides, Callisto's a small place, and there was a good chance I'd bump into her if I stayed, and where would I have been then? Locked up and returned to Chung Kuo in the next ship out."

"So when does she arrive?"

"Three days from now, at Tien Men K'ou in the south."

DeVore raised an eyebrow, surprised. "Tien Men K'ou? That's rather unusual, neh?"

"Again, it's the Marshal's orders. He's getting jumpy, it seems. He's seen how things are shaping here and he's worried in case something happens while she's here. If he'd had his way he'd have had her flown straight back to Chung Kuo from the Saturn system, avoiding Mars altogether, but that simply wasn't possible. However, the *Shanyang* leaves here in a week's time and he wants her on it."

DeVore considered that a moment, then gave a curt, decisive nod. "Okay. I take it that you alone know of this."

"Schenck knows nothing."

"Good. Nor should he. The Governor's a reliable enough man when it comes to matters Martian, but he's little time for the bigger picture. And as for taking on Tolonen . . ." He gave a strange, brief laugh. "Well, I'm glad you're back, Will. You'll stay with me, I hope?"

"I'd be honoured and delighted."

"Good." DeVore smiled, then turned, hearing movement on the terrace. It was Schenck, his formal robes replaced now by a loose-fitting velvet *pau*. The Governor smiled broadly and hailed them.

"Will you have a drink before you go, Howard? And you, Will?"

They went across, joining Schenck in a toast, congratulating him once more, their laughter filling the air inside the dome. Outside, beyond the circle of light, soldiers patrolled

the frosted perimeter, their pressure suits gleaming in the
frigid darkness, the great, blue-white circle of Chung Kuo
high above them in the Martian sky.

The night was almost over. It would be dawn in three
hours.

* * *

Tien Men K'ou City never slept. An hour before dawn its
warrens and corridors buzzed with activity. In the south quad-
rant, workers from the giant HoloGen complex, their pale
ochre overalls distinctive, were coming off shift, their
replacements shuffling past them, bleary-eyed in the half
dark. In the eastern levels prostitutes – common *men hu* in
creased ersilks, stinking of cheap perfume – stood in door-
ways calling out to any drunken reveller who passed, while
in cluttered dens close by small knots of gamblers, young
Han, their dark hair cut stubble-short in traditional Martian
style, crouched excitedly over the roll and tumble of a dice.
In the markets of west and central traders busied themselves,
buying fresh produce from the Tharsis farmlands or setting
up their stalls, while at the spaceport, on the north-eastern
side of the City, one of the great inter-planetary cruisers was
being readied for flight, the maintenance crew like darkly-
carapaced insects scuttling across its giant fuselage. Stern-
faced Colony guards, helmeted, black chevrons on their
blood-red uniforms, paced the affluent upper levels beneath
the crater's lip, stopping to move on a drunk or check on the
movements of one of the juvenile gangs that thrived in the
teeming lower-east and rode the lifts from Deep to Lip. Last
but not least were the outworld tourists, who could be found
wandering in the upper levels near the spaceport, taking their
fill of Mars before returning to the bleak, claustrophobic austerity of their homeworlds.

One such traveller, a small, neat-looking man with dark,
fine hair and soft brown eyes, stopped amidst the bustle of
Chang An Avenue and looked up, studying the sign over the
doorway to his right. Against a dark red background, a black
dragon coiled sinuously and exhaled a cloud of smoke from

its sharply-fanged jaws, its barbed tail lashing out. Fierce-eyed, it stared down at him, as if daring him to enter. Beneath the moving image, flashed almost subliminally at him, were two pictograms, reinforcing the visual. *Hei lung*, they read. Black Dragon.

Smiling, deciding he could take an hour out before he met up with his brothers again, he went across and placed his hand flat against the entry-pad, looking up into the camera.

As the outer door hissed back, he caught the sharp, sweet scents of alcohol and tobacco. And other things. Things he could only guess at. Quickly, before the outer door closed and the inner lock sprang open, he took two twenty *yuan* bills from his wallet and palmed them, then slipped the pouch into his right boot, patting it once to check it didn't show.

His uncle had been robbed once in such a place, up in Chi Shan City, in the north. The poor man had lost ten thousand *yuan* and had returned home empty-handed, the ore-extractor he had come to buy unpurchased, a year's profit for the family lost in a moment's recklessness. The traveller nodded to himself, remembering the shame his uncle had suffered, and how, for months afterwards, a cloud had fallen over the whole family. He had only been eight, yet that time – with its communal feeling of shame and disappointment, and despair at effort unrewarded – was etched vividly in his memory. While he understood – and shared – his uncle's curiosity, he was determined that no one would ever say that he, Ishida Ikuro, had been as careless.

The outer door hissed shut, the latches clicking into place. At once the inner doors irised open, the strange, intoxicating scent of the place – that same scent he had caught the faintest trace of a moment before – hitting him like the rush of a drug.

Inside was a big, sprawling bar with two, maybe three dozen tables and, on the far side, a big half-moon-shaped counter. There was a faint murmur of conversation, the background chatter of a ViewScreen in the right-hand corner, but the bar was almost empty. There were a dozen people at most, scattered here and there among the tables.

He made his way across and took one of the high stools beside the bar, placing one of the twenties on the counter in front of him, as he'd seen others do. At once the barman came across.

"A *maotai*, please," he said casually, as if it was what he ordered every day.

The barman nodded, went away, returned with a bowl of the rich, red sorghum-based liquor and placed it before him, not touching the twenty.

"Thank you," he said, speaking to the barman's back, but already the man had forgotten him.

Ikuro looked about, noting the tiny dance floor, the half-empty tables, the big MedFac screen in the far corner, murmuring away unwatched, and nodded inwardly. Despite the hour and the mere handful of people scattered about the bar, it was just how he had pictured it. He sniffed deeply, taking in the smell of the place, then, gripping the bowl with both hands, he raised it to his lips and sipped, timidly at first, then with more gusto as the rich, sweet taste of the sorghum flooded his senses.

He set the bowl down, wiping his mouth with the back of his hand, then looked at the timer inset into his wrist. It was eight minutes past five. Good. He would stay until six. Would sit here and relax and drink a bowl or two of this splendid *maotai*. After all, he deserved it. His brothers didn't know yet, but he had struck a good deal for them this night. Had saved them days of haggling and thousands of *yuan*. It was only right that he should take an hour off to celebrate.

He looked about him again, savouring the feeling of being in a bar, on Mars, alone. It was like being in a trivee serial, or at the start of some strange adventure. Except that this was real. He could feel the solid roundness of the seat beneath him, taste the sorghum liquor on his tongue and in his throat, smell the rich blend of intoxicants in the air. And if he turned his head . . .

Ikuro stopped, noticing for the first time what he had missed on his first look round the bar.

The man was sitting on the far side of the counter, half in

shadow, his face turned away. At first Ikuro thought he might have been mistaken, but as the man turned back he could see that he had been right. The man was masked – a facial prosthetic with hardflesh clips, attached to the bone beneath the jaw. Even from where he sat Ikuro could see that it was one of the cheaper makes – the kind that only someone very poor would wear – and wondered what had happened to him. As the man lifted the bowl to the thin, flexible mouthpiece, Ikuro noticed that the hand too was damaged, the pale flesh sheathed in a light polymer exoskeleton.

Ikuro looked down, staring into the blood-red liquid, conscious of his own face staring back up at him. He had seen many accidents, many awful things. He had even seen men die, his eldest brother, Kitano, among them. Yet he had never become hardened to such things. Had never been able to switch off and externalise the pain he felt at others' suffering. It was even why he was here, in a sense, sitting in a low-life bar when he should have been safe in his room at the port, his brothers snoring in their beds close by, for unlike his brothers he wanted to know what it was like to live like this. Wanted to know how it felt.

He glanced at the man again, then looked down, feeling an instinctive pity for him. He too wore a mask, only his was skin deep. His pass read 'Han', but he was not Han. Not he nor his eleven brothers, fourteen uncles and innumerable cousins. A hundred and fifty years ago, when Tsao Ch'un had destroyed the home islands of Japan, they had been out there already, in the circuit of Jupiter, mining the Trojan asteroids. The news, when it had finally reached them, had come as a body-blow. Yet they had understood at once. They had become Han, re-inventing themselves, taking on a protective coloration. But deep down, beneath the mask, they were still what they were – what they'd always been. Japanese.

Ikuro picked up his bowl again, sipping from it, then, hearing the hiss of the outer lock, turned and looked across. A moment later the inner door dilated and four men – *Hung Mao*, dressed uniformly in pale ochre one-pieces – came through. They were half-way across the floor when one of them – a thick-set man with short-cropped blond hair – noticed Ikuro and put an arm out, stopping his friends. There was a moment's fierce whispering and then they came on again.

While the blond one ordered, the other three looked across at Ikuro, staring at him brazenly, an undisguised malice in their pale, blunt faces. Ikuro drained his bowl, letting the strong red *maotai* burn his throat. It was time to go. Before any trouble started.

My brothers, he thought, setting the bowl down quietly and pushing it away from him. *I must get back to my brothers*. But it was already too late.

"A drink, *friend?*"

The offer was ominous. To accept would be to place himself in greater danger than he already was. He had heard the tales. They all had. Tales of men being drugged, then stripped and robbed of everything. Tales of men killed for their eyes and organs. And of others who had been lobotomised and sold into prostitution. He shuddered inwardly at the thought of it. Never would he submit to such humiliation. Yet to refuse the blond man's offer would only cause offence. To be frank, what choice he had was poor. He could fight them now or later.

Ikuro stood, moving back away from his chair. He would lose. He knew that for a certainty. But he would not be humiliated. He would take at least one of them with him. Two, if it were possible. He looked at them, studying them carefully. They were big men, the muscles on their arms clearly visible beneath the thin cloth, but they would be slow. He could see that by the way they moved. Moreover they were sure to underestimate him; to think him much weaker than he was. They were used to the low gravity of Mars, he to the artificial one-g spin of the asteroids. That was good. It would give him an advantage in the first few moments: an advantage that his natural agility would add to. And yet, in truth, it wasn't much. They had only to grasp and hold him and it would be over. Brute force would do the rest.

He bowed, facing them squarely. "You are most kind,

friend. Another time I would be most honoured to join you for a drink, but I am afraid I must go. I have promised an old friend that I would meet him for breakfast and I shall be late if I do not leave right now. So forgive me. Another time, perhaps, *ch'un tzu?*"

There was laughter at that. A nasty, brutish laughter. "Another time?" the blond one said, lifting his chin challengingly. "I don't think there'll be another time, *friend.*"

They stood, fanning out slowly, one of them moving to block his route to the door, the others forming a rough half-circle about him, two or three paces distant. *Which one?* he thought, looking from one to another and weighing them up. *Should I take the weakest first, or the strongest?*

"Leave him, Bates," someone said, close by. "Touch him and I'll finger you to the guards."

Ikuro stared. At the end of the bar the stranger was looking directly at him. In the overhead light his mask shone whitely, the cheeks like two smooth surfaces of stone.

The blond-haired one – Bates – had turned and was looking down at the man, leaning over him threateningly. "Mind your own fucking business, creep. Or you want some of the same?"

The man stood, pushing his empty bowl away. As he turned to face Bates, Ikuro could see that he was far from small himself. If anything he was bigger than the other man.

"Leave him," he said, a hint of steel behind the softness of his voice. "I *mean* it."

For a moment Bates stood his ground, all menace, his face pushed out at that awful, empty mask, glaring back at the man beyond it, and then he turned, his face dark with anger, his muscles bunched, tensed with resentment and frustration. Raising one hand, he pointed savagely at Ikuro.

"You're safe now, chink, but watch your back. Because I'll have you, you little fucker. See if I don't."

There was a moment's hesitation, then he turned and headed for the exit, his friends peeling off to follow him, turning at the door to give Ikuro the finger.

Ikuro watched them go, feeling the adrenalin wash through

him. Not relief, strangely, but disappointment. He turned, looking at the man, at that strangely elongated mask which, for that moment, stared away from him.

The man turned, looking back at him. Blue eyes, he had. So blue that they seemed to burn through the whiteness of the mask.

"Come on," he said quietly. "You'd best come with me. He meant what he said. You'll not be safe in these levels. That one's got many friends."

Ikuro bowed. "Thank you, but I must get back. My brothers will be expecting me. What you did . . ."

The man lifted a hand. "You don't understand. Bates is a big man in the FFM. After this, he'll have them all out, combing the corridors for you. Your only chance is to come back with me. You can stay until things blow over.

Ikuro stared back at him, suddenly uncomfortable. "I . . ."

The eyes in the mask registered sudden understanding, their expression changing to something that resembled amusement. "Oh, don't worry, friend, I'm no yellow eel. I've no designs on your arse, I promise you."

Ikuro looked down, embarrassed by the other's bluntness. Yet it was exactly what he had been thinking. He lifted his head, meeting those startlingly blue eyes once again. "Thank you . . . I mean, for helping me. My family is indebted to you, but I would be better off making my way back to my brothers."

The man reached out, taking Ikuro's upper arm. Ikuro looked down at the fingers where they gripped him, impressed by their strength, their unexpected perfection.

"Look, I understand," the stranger said, the words drifting – disembodied, it seemed – from the mask, "but for once you have no choice. Either you come back with me, and come now, or you'll find yourself out there, under the stars, a hole in the back of your skull and your body stiff as stone. Now what's it to be?"

Ikuro stared back at the man, trying to see him clearly through the mask. To see exactly what and who he was. Then, making up his mind, he bowed. "Okay . . ."

"Good," the man said curtly, releasing him and making for the door. "Now keep close. And don't stop running until I tell you it's safe."

* * *

Outside, the Martian night seemed vast, impenetrable. Two *li* up, the searchlights of the speeding cruiser appeared to punch holes in the blackness rather than illuminate it. Below, concealed from human sight, the land climbed slowly towards the Hesparian Plain – a bleak, uncompromising landscape pockmarked by craters formed more than three billion years before.

It was bitterly cold outside: minus one hundred and ten degrees and still falling. Inside it was different. There, in the warm, insulating silence of the craft, DeVore pushed aside his work and sat back, considering that evening's events.

Pre-eminent in his thoughts was the news Auden had brought back from Callisto: the news of Jelka Tolonen's arrival, three days hence. He had played down its importance at the time, yet he had understood its significance at once. This far out from Chung Kuo he had had few opportunities to hit back at his enemies these past few years, but this was perfect.

DeVore smiled, looking out at the darkness beyond the toughened glass. The thought of her here made his pulse quicken, not with love or desire, but with the sharp exhilaration of hatred. Hatred for Tolonen and all that he stood for.

How he loathed the old bastard. Loathed the pomposity, the bumbling, blustering certainty of the man. A liar and a hypocrite, that's what Tolonen was. He portrayed himself as a solid pillar of society, a paragon of New Confucian virtue, yet behind the twin masks of "Benevolence" and "Propriety" he held up to the world was a seething, dribbling old man, twisted by envy and wracked by disappointment.

As a Major in the old T'ang's service, DeVore had been a regular guest at the Tolonen apartment; a close confidant and trusted 'friend' of the old man. Why, he had even held Tolonen's baby daughter in his arms. But that had been long ago, before he had broken with his T'ang. Now he was an outcast, an enemy of the Seven, and the child was a young woman of nineteen. A real beauty she was, tall and strong and elegant, the very image of her dead mother. Yet dangerous too, if what he'd heard was true. Tolonen had tried to hush it up, but word had got out anyway; of how she had almost killed a young cadet officer in a fight at a graduation ball, and of her open defiance of her father when he had refused to contemplate a relationship between her and the young scientist, Ward.

Which was why she was out there now. Why he, DeVore, would have his chance at her.

Tolonen was a fool. Yet he was right about one thing. Things were unstable on Mars at present. Much more than Schenck or his cronies knew. Things were happening, deep down, and the time was fast approaching when something would have to be done about that. But first this.

DeVore closed his eyes, focusing on the problem. He could use this. There was no doubt of that. But how? How could he maximise this advantage fate had granted him?

"Master?"

He turned his head slightly, opening his eyes. His steward was standing in the aisle next to him, his head bowed, a folded message on the silver tray he held. Beyond him, on the couch opposite, Auden was sleeping, a light blanket pulled up over his chest.

"What is it?"

"It is from Tien Men K'ou, Master. It was marked urgent."

DeVore hesitated, then took the note. Unfolding it, he read it quickly, then nodded to the steward. "Bring me a drink, will you? . . . Oh, and the Programme. I think I'll play for a while."

The steward bowed and turned away.

DeVore pondered a moment, then looked across at Auden once more, studying his sleeping face. William Auden was a good man to have at one's shoulder: strong, determined and – thus far – loyal. Many times before tonight he had come through for DeVore, often, as this evening, unexpectedly.

43

But in the days to come his loyalty would be tested – maybe to the limit.

For a moment DeVore considered waking Auden and putting to him what he had decided, but the thought was fleeting. Let the man sleep. Either he would do as he was told or he wouldn't. And if he didn't? Well, at least he, DeVore, would know for sure where Auden stood on the question of his friend, Hans Ebert.

Before Ebert had been found out – before his tiny world had collapsed in upon itself – Auden had been his right-hand man, arranging things and clearing up after the young "prince". On more than one occasion Auden had got Ebert out of dreadful scrapes, the fire-fight at Hammerfest perhaps chief among them. Then, Auden had carried the badly-wounded Ebert to safety on his back, not only saving his life but making his young "Master" a hero into the bargain. It was an act which had won him Ebert's undying friendship, but DeVore had never been clear whether it had been done out of genuine friendship or – as Auden later claimed – from pure self-interest. All he could say was that when he had "triggered" Auden, Auden had responded immediately, without – it seemed – a thought for his old friend. Even so, the question remained, could he trust Auden – could he really trust him – when it came to Hans Ebert?

DeVore sat back, studying the note again. Before it had been handed to him, he had been in two minds. Should he have Jelka Tolonen assassinated or should he have her kidnapped? Kidnapping had seemed preferable, if only for the protracted suffering it would have caused the Marshal, yet such a course was fraught with dangers, chief among them the possibility that she might be recovered and reunited with her father. Better, perhaps, to be more direct – to have her killed, quickly and nastily, there in the public eye where all could see.

So he had thought, wavering between one course and the other. But the note had clarified things in an instant.

Until tonight Hans Ebert had kept his nose clean and his head down, accepting his diminished role in things with a humility and docility that had surprised DeVore. But this evening, less than an hour ago, in fact, all that had changed. Parry, DeVore's man in Tien Men K'ou, had reported back that Ebert had got himself involved in an incident in a bar on the south side.

Odd, DeVore thought; very odd indeed, yet timely. For Ebert would be the key to all of this. Once they had taken her, he would have Ebert look after her. More than that, he would have him marry her. It was what the old man had wanted, after all.

DeVore laughed, delighted by the irony of it. Yes, he could see it now. He would tape the ceremony and send it to the old man.

And the nuptials, too, perhaps . . .

"Master?"

He turned, realising that the steward had been standing there for several moments.

"Thank you," he said, accepting the chilled glass. He took a mouthful of the juice – crushed oranges, grown in his own greenhouses – then sat back, letting the steward clear the table and attach the flat black square of the Programme board.

The Programme was something he had had done more than a year before: an inter-active *wei chi* "player" based upon the Suchow Championships of 2170. That had been a great tournament, momentous for the fact that it had been the last appearance of the famous Master, Tuan Ti Fo, who, having won the competition eight years running, had retired that year, undefeated.

There were some who argued that Old Tuan had been the last of the truly great players and that with his departure something grand – something *quintessential* – had passed from the game. Personally he would not have gone quite so far, yet there was no denying the beauty, the elegance, and, beneath both and, it seemed, in perfect balance with them, the strange, naked brutality of the old Master's play. To pit oneself against him, even in this strange, illusory manner, was to face not so much a man as a force of nature.

As DeVore sat back, the figure formed across from him,

the image strong and clear, the inner light-core of the hologram making it seem solid, almost real. Between them the
board was now half-filled by the patterns of black and white
stones.

The old Han bowed deeply, greeting DeVore. "Good
evening, Major. How are you?"

DeVore returned the bow, enjoying the illusion. "I am well,
Master Tuan. And you?"

The hologram shifted slightly in its seat, a small, plain white
fan moving slowly in its left hand as it leaned forward to study
the board.

"I have been dreaming," Old Tuan answered, not looking
up. "Dreaming of childhood and better days."

DeVore smiled. In life, Tuan Ti Fo had been a man of few
words, but, as he welcomed intelligent conversation while he
was playing, he had made this version somewhat more talka-
tive than the original. Moreover he had ensured that the
inter-active element was based on a heuristic core. As it
played and talked, so it learned . . . and grew. As a man
grew. And sometimes – as now – it seemed almost alive, as
if the real Tuan Ti Fo were speaking to him. Yet he knew
that could not be. The real Tuan Ti Fo had been an old man
when he had last won the title, and that had been over forty
years ago. No. The real Tuan Ti Fo was long dead. Only this
– this breath-less illusion of being – remained.

DeVore leaned closer, studying the shapes on the board.
This was the eleventh game between them. Thus far the
score was even – five games apiece – yet this had been the
hardest and, indeed, the longest of their contests. At present
things seemed well-balanced. He was dominant in the south
and west, Old Tuan in the north and east. Yet much was still
to be decided. There was a large space in the very centre
of the board where things might easily go either way.

Tuan Ti Fo took a white stone from the pot to his left and
placed it with a solid-sounding click onto the board – in *Chu*,
the west, strengthening a line he had "ghosted" some twenty
moves before.

DeVore stared at the stone a moment, assimilating it into

the pattern of shapes on the board, trying to see what the old man meant by it, then nodded to himself, pleased by its cleverness. He would have to respond. Have to concede ground and postpone his plans to infiltrate Tuan's territory in the north.

He looked up at the hologram and saw that the old man was watching him, his hazel eyes clear, expressionless. Once again, the illusion of presence was strong.

"And just what *were* you as a child? Where did you live, for instance? I don't think you've ever said."

It hadn't. Nor was it programmed with such information. But DeVore was intrigued to learn how it would respond: how it would face that blank, internal space, and whether it would attempt to fill the nothingness.

"There was no City, back then," Old Tuan replied. "Just the earth and the heavens, and Man between them."

Evasions, DeVore thought, disappointed; *evasions and cod philosophy*. He leaned forward and played the forced defence, two back, one in from Tuan's last stone.

Tuan Ti Fo sat back, fanning himself slowly, considering the move, his deeply-lined face concentrating fiercely. He seemed so real, so *there* at that moment, but in reality a complex programme was now running, responding to the light thumb-tip touch DeVore had made against the board's surface: a programme modelled upon a detailed analysis of the Master's play in that final championship.

DeVore looked away. Outside, far below and some way to the right of their flight path, he could see the softly-rounded glow of a pumping station and, arrowing away from it to north and south, the great eastern pipeline, tracker lights revealing its course at half-*li* intervals. It was almost dawn. Already the darkness seemed less intense.

He turned, hearing the click of glass against wood. Tuan Ti Fo had played his stone to the left of his own, the circles of black and white touching at the edge. He stared at it, astonished. It was the kind of move only an absolute novice would make. A novice, or someone wise beyond all years. He looked up, meeting Old Tuan's eyes.

47

"Tranquillity is the lord of agitation," the old man said, his hands tucked deep into his sleeves, his whole form emanating a calm and certainty that seemed unearthly.

DeVore laughed uncomfortably. "You believe all that bullshit?"

The hologram's smile seemed to focus all of the light from within. "It is the Way, Major DeVore. As the great sage says, the Way is like water. It dwells in places that the masses detest."

DeVore snorted, a sudden tiredness and irritability making him take a black stone from the pot and slap it down, shutting the door on Tuan's last play.

Tuan nodded, then, almost without thought, it seemed, leaned forward, playing a second stone, extending the line.

DeVore stared at the board again, disbelievingly. The old man had played *inside* his territory, like a child wandering in a tiger's cave. He frowned, looking to see that he had not missed something. But no. It was a poor move. So what was wrong? Was the programme playing up? Or was this part of some deeper strategy? Something new and unexpected? He sat back, meeting Tuan's eyes again.

"The submissive and weak conquer the strong," Tuan said, passing a hand across the board, as if somehow to illustrate what he had said.

"Not in *this* world," DeVore answered, slapping another stone down beside Tuan's last play, shadowing the line. There was no way the Master could make the group live now. He had only to be patient and the stones would be his. He looked up again, smiling now. "The weak and submissive might conquer in *your* world, but here . . ." DeVore laughed and pushed his hand deep into the hologram's chest. "*Here* we do things differently."

The old man looked down, as if he could see where DeVore's hand had passed through him, then gave the tiniest of shrugs, a fleeting disappointment in his face.

"A game is not won in two moves, Major. Nor are things always what they seem. You might argue that yours is a world of substance, and mine merely a world of *Wu* – of

48

'non-being'. Yet who is to say whether such differences are significant? Are you greater than me for having substance? Are you more *real?*"

DeVore stared at the hologram, no less surprised by its words than by the moves it had made only moments before. "Shit," he said softly. "So that's it. The damn thing's malfunctioning."

And yet the image had never been clearer or the illusion of presence stronger.

Old Tuan held his eyes steadily a moment, then leaned across and took a white stone from the pot. Smiling, he clicked it down, switching the play to the far corner of the board – to *Ping*, the east.

DeVore sat there for a long time, studying the board, seeing with a new-formed clarity the inevitability of the plays to come: how stone would follow stone, until . . .

It was a brilliant move. Almost as good as the play which had won Master Tuan the championship that final year. Moreover Old Tuan had set it up more than twenty moves before. Had set it up and waited, steering the play away from that part of the board, biding his time, containing his opponent's stones. But why? Why not *this*, at once? Or was that the point? Was that the reason for those final, stuttering plays? Had the Programme finally outgrown him?

He let out a long breath then looked up, meeting the hologram's eyes. "Do you wish me to play on, Master Tuan?"

"I . . ." Old Tuan paused, then turned, looking away from the board. "It seems your man is waking, Major. Perhaps we should finish our game another day?"

"My man . . . ?" DeVore turned, following the line of Tuan Ti Fo's sight, then laughed. Gods, Auden *was* waking. But how had it known? Had it sensed some change in his breathing? Was its hearing that acute, its interpretation of sound patterns that sophisticated?

He leaned across and switched the Programme off. At once the facing seat was empty, the board transformed to a single, unbroken square of darkness.

Odd, he thought, sitting back, listening to Auden yawn and stretch. *Very odd indeed.* Yet not impossible. After all, it had been programmed to learn new things. All the same, he'd have someone look at it, just in case someone had been tampering.

He turned, looking across at Auden. The big man yawned and stretched again, then, noticing that DeVore was watching him, drew himself up straight in his seat, smiling.

"Gods. I must have dropped off . . ."

DeVore smiled. "It's okay. We're almost there. Look."

Auden turned, looked. Outside the dawn was coming up, revealing, below them, the vast lowland depression of Hellas and, in the distance, the lights of Tien Men K'ou City, nestled into its own small crater.

"*There*," DeVore said softly, staring at the tiny circle of lights to the north-east of the dome that marked out the perimeter of the spaceport, imagining the Callisto flight with Jelka Tolonen on board setting down there in three days time. "Yes," he murmured, his eyes widening. "*Right there.*"

* * *

The room was small and simply furnished. To the left of the rush-matted floor were a chair, a small table and, above them, a single shelf. To the right was nothing, only the blank partition wall. The bare rock of the end wall seemed to gleam mistily in the light of the wall-mounted lamp. Ikuro went across and placed his fingers against the smooth, unyielding surface, understanding at once. The mist was real. The wall had been sealed with a tough, clear polymer coating. They did the same where he came from. It prevented oxygen leakage and helped insulate the room against the fiercely cold temperatures of the surrounding rock. Even so, the room was chill. He could see his breath in the air.

He turned, looking back into the room. It was like a cell. There was no ViewScreen, he noted, surprised. Instead, a scattering of papers lay on the desktop, an inkpad and brush nearby. On the shelf above were a dozen plastic-covered books and what looked like two file boxes. The door to the entrance lock was facing him, a tiny washroom to the left.

From the galley-kitchen to the right came the sounds of the stranger preparing the *ch'a*, otherwise the silence was profound: was the kind of silence one found only in such places, where one lived with the constant threat of decompression.

Ikuro nodded inwardly, impressed by the Spartan austerity of the place. Somehow it seemed to suit the man, though why he should think that he could not explain; only that he sensed an air of mystery about him, something that the strangeness of the mask only half explained. He had met all kinds of men in the past two days, big and small, rich and poor, and there seemed to be a definite correlation between their status and their behaviour: a correlation one did not find in his own close-knit community. Yet this one was different. He might dress like a working man, and the facial prosthetic he wore might be the cheapest one could buy, yet he had the air of a prince – of a leader of men. Why, even his smallest movement . . .

Ikuro stilled his thoughts. The stranger was standing in the doorway to the galley, a small plastic tray held out before him, two plain white *ch'a* bowls resting in its centre. Pausing a moment he looked about the room, then indicated with his head. Ikuro understood at once and nodded, squatting on the floor as the other set down the tray and knelt, facing Ikuro.

The *ch'a* smelled good. Ikuro could feel the warmth of it even before he had tasted it.

"Are you cold?" the stranger asked, the blue eyes in the mask showing concern.

Ikuro smiled. "No. I am fine, thank you. This is like home."

"Ah . . ." The stranger lifted the nearest of the bowls in one hand and offered it to him. Ikuro took it, inclining his head in thanks, enjoying the simple heat of the bowl and relishing the thought of drinking so fine-smelling a *ch'a*. Even so, he waited, watching until the other raised his bowl. Only then, with a second bow of thanks, did he place the bowl to his lips and sip.

"Ahh . . ." he said, genuinely delighted. "Wonderful. You make excellent *ch'a*, *Shih* . . ."

He laughed, embarrassed suddenly, realising that he had

been with the man almost an hour now and still did not know his name.

"Latimer," the stranger said. "I am known here as John Latimer."

Ikuro, he almost said, then checked himself. "My name is Shen," he answered, inclining his head. "Shen Li, son of Shen Yeh."

Latimer returned the bow. "I am pleased to meet you, Shen Li. But tell me, what in the gods' names were you doing in the Black Dragon? Did no one warn you?"

Ikuro hesitated, then shook his head.

"You're from off-planet, I take it."

"From Diomedes, in the Trojans."

"Ah . . ." The thin, artificial lips formed the shape of a smile. "Then you *wouldn't* know, would you?"

"Know what?"

Latimer set his bowl down, then sat back on his haunches. "Things are happening here on Mars, Shen Li. Things that even our masters don't know about. New currents. New movements. Like our friend Bates."

"The FFM, you mean?"

Again, the semblance of a smile lit the mask. "You remember, then?"

"I remember. But what does it mean?"

"The FFM? That's the Federation of Free Men. They're so-called patriots. They want to reclaim Mars for the Martians."

"The Martians?"

"The original settlers. By which they mainly mean Americans, though they'll sign up anyone who's not a Han. They see the Han as usurpers, you see, and they blame all of Mars' ills on them. Their policy's fairly simple. They aim to kill all the Han and make Mars independent of Chung Kuo."

Ikuro set his bowl down, astonished. "And there are many who believe this?"

"Quite a few, especially in Tien Men K'ou, but they're not the only group – merely the most extreme. The two biggest are the Martian Radicalist Alliance and the PLF, the People's

52

Liberation Force. They want independence too, but both draw their following from Han and *Hung Mao* alike. What they want is to get rid of the masters – a bit like the *Ping Tiao* back on Chung Kuo."

Ikuro stared back at him blankly.

"The *Ping Tiao* . . . You mean you've never heard of the *Ping Tiao*!" Latimer laughed strangely. "The gods help us, you *are* cut off out there, aren't you?"

For a moment Latimer was silent, thoughtful. Then, leaning closer, he spoke again. "Have you noticed anything about this place, Shen Li? I mean . . . anything unusual?"

Ikuro considered a moment. "It's all wrong," he said finally. "Everything is much bigger than it ought to be."

He did not know how far they had descended, coming from the Black Dragon to Latimer's apartment – forty, maybe fifty levels – but it had felt as if they had burrowed deep into the crust of Mars. Not that that had worried him particularly, for he was used to being deep within the rock, yet it had surprised him, for he had read in the official records that the Martian cities were domed cities – were *surface* structures. But now he knew. Mars was much bigger than the official records made out. Why, if Tien Men K'ou were typical of the rest, then the population here was – what? – ten, maybe twenty times the official estimate. And how could that be? How could they have made such a gross mistake? Unless it wasn't a mistake. Unless someone was deliberately concealing the fact.

Latimer was nodding. "I didn't understand it either. Not at first. I didn't see how it could be done, nor why. But I think I know now. I think it's been going on for a long time, probably since the Han first came here. That's when it began, a hundred and sixty years ago, after the second War of Colonisation."

"When what began?" Ikuro asked, blinking, mesmerised by the intensity, the force of concentration focused in the figure opposite him.

"The revolution," Latimer answered, his startlingly blue eyes staring back at Ikuro through the pale, moon-like mask.

"They've been preparing for it all these years. Waiting, with unending patience. But now it's about to end. It's about to be taken out of their hands."

"Who? Who do you mean by 'they'?"

Latimer lifted his head, staring away past Ikuro, almost as if he could see through the solid rock. "I don't know. Not for certain. But it's not the Seven back on Chung Kuo, nor is it Governor Schenck and his little crowd. They only think they run things. No. There's something else at work here on Mars. Some other power, older and more deeply rooted than them."

Ikuro looked down, disturbed by this sudden turn in their talk, frightened – suddenly, inexplicably frightened – by the presence of the masked man across from him. For a while he stared at the steaming *ch'a* bowl, trying to still his thoughts, to reassure himself that all would be all right, then, with an agitated little movement, he lifted the bowl to his lips and drained it at a go.

"My brothers . . ." he said, meeting the stranger's eyes again. "You said you would get a message to my brothers."

"Ah . . . Forgive me. Here."

Ikuro took the paper Latimer held out to him and unfolded it. It was a copy of a transmission, addressed to his brothers at the spaceport. Ikuro read it through, then looked back at Latimer, astonished. But how? He had not left him for a second, except to make the *ch'a*!

"Who are you, *Shih* Latimer? You seem to know so much. And yet . . ." Ikuro turned, looking about him at the simplicity of the room. "Well, it makes no sense."

The blue eyes in the mask were watching him, serious now, conscious, it seemed, of his inner turmoil.

"You've heard of the GenSyn Corporation?"

Ikuro nodded. "Who has not?"

"And Klaus Ebert, its owner?"

Again, Ikuro nodded. "I have. Why, he is famous throughout the system. My grandfather says he was a genius in his day. They say he once designed a creature that could eat rock!"

"And if I was to tell you that he's dead?"

Ikuro frowned. "Then my grandfather would light a taper for his soul. He was a great man."

"Then you hadn't heard?"

Ikuro shook his head.

The man took a long breath; a breath that seemed almost a sigh. "Earlier on you asked me my name, Shen Li, and I told you what I am known as in these parts. But before I came here I was known by another name. It might seem a thing of little moment what a man is called, yet for me it is a matter of great importance. Before I tell you I must ask you one thing."

Ikuro lowered his head. "Anything, my friend."

"Then let me ask you this. Can I trust you? Can I *really* trust you?"

Ikuro looked up, astonished. In any other circumstances he would have been offended – deeply offended – by the question, yet there was such an earnestness in the man's voice, such a sense of urgency in his eyes, that he could only nod. "With your life, *ch'un tzu*."

"Then I will tell you who I am."

There was a moment's stillness, a moment's perfect silence, then, releasing the hardflesh clips beneath his chin, Hans Ebert removed the prosthetic mask from his face and placed it on the floor beside him.

CHAPTER · 2

DREAMS OF MARS

Schenck tapped the thickened glass lightly with his fingernails, studying the long, oval-shaped depression they had had scooped out of the dark, lavatic rock, then turned, looking back into the room. The three men were watching him.

Andreas Rutherford stood to the left, beside the narrow desk. He was a handsome man in his mid-twenties; the image of his late father, Schenck's friend and one-time sponsor, William Rutherford. To Schenck's right were Tu Ch'en-shih and his partner, Meng K'ai. Though unrelated, the two Han looked like twins and played upon the fact by dressing identically. Short, balding and ugly, someone had once described them as, and it wasn't far from the truth. But sharp with it. As sharp as anyone in the Nineteen Colonies.

Just now all four wore protective suits, the collapsible helmets hanging loose against their backs, attached by umbilicals to the rigid neck-braces.

That'll change one of these days, Schenck thought, conscious for once of all those things they were forced to take for granted here. *But not while we're still tethered. Not until we cut the link.*

"Well?" Meng K'ai asked impatiently. "What do you think?"

Schenck smiled. "It looks good from up here, but have there been any problems? I mean, this has got to last. The new City will be totally dependent on it."

"It'll last," Rutherford said, pouring a bowl of wine and bringing it across. "I mean, it's not like we're building the thing back on Chung Kuo. We've not got to worry about volcanic activity or earthquakes. All we've got to make sure is that the thing doesn't leak or get clogged with dust."

"And the Plant itself? You're certain this will work?"

Rutherford looked to his fellow financiers, then back at Schenck, his smile broadening. "You've seen the engineers' reports, Hung-li. It'll work, don't worry. As for lasting, it'll still be here ten thousand years from now. Fifty, if we build it well enough."

Schenck hesitated, then nodded, taking the bowl from Rutherford and lifting it to toast the others. Yes, he had seen the engineers' reports, and, just to make sure, had had his own experts go over them. The thing ought to work, and work well. That was, providing no corners were cut, no "economies" made. He turned, looking back across the site. The main excavation work had been completed. A coating of impermeable polymer, two *ch'i* thick would now be poured into the depression, sealing and insulating the reservoir. Then, as an added precaution, a second layer would be placed on top of that, using a new, organically-produced sealant that would not only guarantee minimal leakage but also reduce bacterial growth. Once in operation, the whole thing would be covered with an airtight layer of "ice", the same polymer-based material they used back on Chung Kuo to make the Cities. A dozen air-locks would allow access for maintenance and, if necessary, repair.

But that was only half of it. The reservoir, while it used new construction techniques and new materials, was nothing new in itself. There were reservoirs already at Kang Feng and Hao Feng Shou. No, what was new about this scheme was the Plant itself. For the first time they would not be tapping into Mars' precious reserves of water – trapped in the permafrost, in underground lakes, and in the northern ice-cap – but making the stuff from scratch. *Increasing* the amount there was.

Schenck smiled at the thought. Water and air. They were the two things that Mars needed badly, and, for the past hundred and sixty years Chung Kuo had kept Mars in a state of absolute dependency, ruling from afar on just how much air, how much water the Martians could have; keeping those two basic necessities to the very minimum. And sometimes – as when that bastard Karr had been here – denying them even that much.

Schenck shivered with indignation, remembering the day when the big Security man had burst into his office at Tien Men K'ou City and dragged him across his desk, threatening him. It was then that this had begun. Then that he'd started thinking of a Mars without Chung Kuo. A self-sufficient, independent Mars, strong and thriving. A *green* Mars with a tolerable atmosphere and reasonable temperature gradations. A Mars very different from the hell-hole they currently inhabited.

"Have you discussed the next stage with Dawson yet?"

Schenck turned back, facing Tu Ch'en-shih.

"Not yet. I wanted to get the election out of the way first. But now we can go ahead. It's time we let Dawson and a few others know what we've got planned."

Tu Ch'en-shih frowned, his squat face crumpling like a rotten fruit. "Do you think that's safe? I mean, Dawson's fine. I trust him completely. But the others? Surely it's best to keep this tight. The fewer who know, the less chance the Seven will hear of it."

Schenck nodded. "Normally, I'd agree. But it's time to move on this. Since the split in Council the Seven are weak, indecisive. With the House reopened and the Above pressing for more power, they've problems enough at home without contemplating fighting a war out here. The logistics alone are beyond them." He laughed. "Why, we have only to arm the satellites and Mars is ours. That's why I've set up a meeting, two days from now, to discuss things and to take things further. There'll be eight of us in all. We four, Dawson, Endacott, Ch'en Li and Culver."

"Culver?" It was Rutherford who made the query. "Do we really need Culver?"

"Yes," Schenck answered, turning to the young man. "Someone has to provide security for this operation and I

58

can't trust our own internal forces. Ultimately they're loyal to the Seven."

Rutherford frowned, clearly uneasy. "I didn't realise you felt that way. I thought you had Security in hand. I thought we could count on them."

"I do and we can. Normally. But this is different. From here on we take on the Seven, directly, unconditionally. And there are some officers in Security who'd baulk at going that far, McEwen for one."

"And Culver?" Meng K'ai asked. "Are you certain we can trust him?"

"Absolutely." Schenck smiled reassuringly. "Culver's my man. He does as I say. I've asked him to look into the question of creating a replacement force for Security. A force that would take its commands directly from us and not from some Council of Generals a billion *li* away on Chung Kuo. He has a small force already at HoloGen. That'll form the basis of the new army. An *independent* army."

Rutherford looked down. "I'm still not sure. I don't know the man, but there's something about him that worries me. He's too reclusive for my taste. And then there's all this business with the computer system he's had shipped in from Chung Kuo. I mean, what's all that about?"

Schenck laughed. "You worry too much, Andreas. Look, Culver's upgrading his Plant, that's all. As far as I see it, it makes good sense. The more we can get out of Chung Kuo before the break, the better."

"Maybe," Rutherford answered, "but I still think he could have invested his money here, on Mars. Could have had CompTek build him a new system – one better suited to his needs."

"And see the profits go back to Chung Kuo?"

"Yes, but it would have employed Martian workmen and encouraged the development of Martian skills. As it is, Culver's investment puts nothing into our economy. It merely sustains the old cycle of dependency. And I thought that that was the very thing we wanted to break."

"I see." Schenck turned, looking directly at Meng K'ai.

"And you, Meng K'ai? How do you feel about Culver?"

Meng K'ai shrugged. "Like Andreas, I don't know the man. He keeps himself very much to himself. But if you vouch for him . . . well, that's good enough for me. Besides, I think you're right. We should take what we can from them before the break comes. I hear this new system's good. Better than anything CompTek could build. Maybe we could all use it, neh? Pool our resources."

Schenck smiled broadly. "I'm certain *Shih* Culver would be more than willing to give over some of its capacity to us. And you, Tu Ch'en-shih?"

"Meng K'ai has spoken for us both. I think we could work with him. If you guarantee him, that is."

"Of course," Schenck said. "Without hesitation. As I said, Culver's my man. He'll do as I say. As for his commitment to things Martian," Schenck turned, looking back at Rutherford, "well, just think about it. Doesn't he employ more than fifty thousand at his plants? No, don't worry about Culver. He's the least of our problems. Let's worry about implementing our plan. About making Mars what it ought to be. What it should have been a hundred years ago, but for the Seven. Come, let's drink to deliverance from our erstwhile masters. To deliverance, and to change."

He raised his bowl, looking about him at his three co-conspirators. "*Pien Hua!*" he said defiantly.

There was a moment's hesitation, a brief meeting of eyes, then, lifting their bowls, they answered him. "*Pien Hua!*" their voices ringing loudly in the tiny maintenance dome. *Change!*

* * *

Ikuro knelt down, staring into the back of the compact freezer, looking for something to cook. Ebert had gone on shift already, leaving a note for Ikuro to find when he woke.

The food in the freezer was simple. Cheese, wheatcakes, plastic tubs of noodles. In the narrow doorspace were four small bulbs of ersatz fruit juice. Ikuro smiled. Not only did Ebert look like a poor man, he ate like one, too. Shrugging, he took a tub of noodles and closed the door, then stood, looking about him at the tiny galley. Once off Chung Kuo things were much the same, wherever one went. Beside the small sink, the water tank, a small microwave oven, a pressure cooker and the freezer, there was a canister of oxygen in a clip-frame on the wall to his left, and, beside it, in a clear-fronted hatch, a crumpled bright yellow pressure suit. Safety and efficiency, they were the priorities here, just as they were where he came from. Life was hard. That much was universal.

He put the tub into the microwave, then turned, listening, hearing the faint hum of the dehumidifier. For some reason it reminded him of what he had been thinking earlier and he turned back, searching the galley for what he knew had to be there.

The microwave buzzed, the light inside went out. Ikuro stared at it, then laughed quietly. Of course. He removed the steaming tub and set it aside, then lifted the microwave, studying it.

He had been wondering for hours how Ebert had got the message out to his brothers. Now he knew. From the front it looked like an ordinary microwave, but at the back was a second set of controls. The touch pads and buttons of a comset.

He took his breakfast through and sat at Ebert's desk, forgetting everything but his hunger momentarily as he wolfed down the noodles. Then, the empty tub pushed aside, he stared at the end wall, trying to make sense of things.

They had talked for hours. Or, rather, Ebert had talked and he had listened. At first he'd not been sure. After all, Ebert's tale was unlikely enough – that was, if he really *was* Ebert. Yet as he'd gone on there was something about his manner, about the way he presented his life history that had convinced Ikuro that it really was Hans Ebert, heir to the great GenSyn Company, and not some poor deluded madman.

A madman, after all, would have bragged, wouldn't he? Would have crowed about his "past" and boasted about what would yet be, once he was returned to his rightful place. But that wasn't true of Ebert. No. He seemed to feel nothing but shame for what he'd done. Shame and a deeply-held remorse. A prince he'd been, a king in waiting, but he had let himself be swayed from his destiny. Power had corrupted him, vanity warped his soul, and he had fallen.

Ikuro let out a long breath, remembering what had been said. Of the women Ebert had used, and the men he had had killed. Of the deals he had made and the betrayal of his master, the great T'ang, Li Yuan. Finally, of the fateful meeting with his father, Klaus, and the murder of the old man by the goat creature.

"What happened to the creature?" Ikuro had asked.

"I killed it," Ebert answered. "I vented it out of an air-lock somewhere off Titan."

"But it saved your life!"

"Yes. But it also killed my father."

Ikuro had hesitated. "You loved your father, then?"

Ebert had looked down, the lines of his face creased with pain. "Yes. I didn't know it at the time. It was as if I had forgotten what he'd been to me. Forgotten all the love he'd shown me as a boy. And then . . ." The voice wavered, then came back strongly, "and then he was dead and I . . . I *understood*. I realised suddenly what I'd lost. What I'd thrown away so thoughtlessly."

Remorse. Hans Ebert was filled with remorse. There was no doubting that. Unless the man was the finest actor the System had ever produced. And now he was here, on Mars, a poor man, a sweeper at the giant HoloGen complex, working for his once accomplice, DeVore.

Yes. But how did the hidden comset fit in with all of that? Unless Ebert had been keeping something back from him. Unless he was still working for DeVore in some other role than factory sweeper.

Ikuro stood, wondering, not for the first time, whether he shouldn't just go; whether Bates and his friends really were out there waiting for him, or whether that too were made up.

He huffed, angry with himself, disturbed by the uncertainty he felt. Why should Ebert lie? Why should he expose himself so thoroughly if his motives were not honourable? Besides which, even if he had not revealed to Ikuro why he had the comset, he had made no attempt to conceal the fact of its existence. Any fool would have realised it was there in the apartment somewhere.

So what was the truth? Just what *was* Hans Ebert doing on Mars?

He stopped, the title on the spine of one of Ebert's books catching his eye. Taking it from the shelf, he sat again, letting his thoughts grow still. It was a slim, soft-covered edition of Kan Jiang's *Poems*, printed on flimsy onion-paper. Opening a page at random, he began to read.

On patrolling the course of the proposed western pipeline

A broken chain
Lies shattered in the dry bed of an ancient stream.
Our Corps Commander makes his slow way down,
Weightless, it seems, in the pale earthlight.
The long shadows of his limbs
Dance like puppets on the red earth.
He crouches and the power-torch flares green,
Cupped like a cat's eye in his white-gloved hands.
Sparks scatter like fire-flies,
As the iron glows red.

Ten thousand years our fathers laboured,
Tilling the black earth of our home.
Flood, famine and disease they suffered,
And survived, the chain unbroken,
Knowing the day would come,
The harvest time,
That single day of sun and ease.

The workday ends.
Back in my bunk I cast the yarrow stalks
And read the sage's words.
Six in the fifth place.

"Work on what has been spoiled.
Afterwards there is order."
Work, it urges, yet what tool exists
To weld us to our past?
The bridge between the worlds is down.

Here, in this dry land,
I am my father and my own dear son,
Born out of nothing.
I am the broken chain.
In this land without ghosts,
Who will sweep the graves
And light the paper offerings?

Ikuro shivered, moved deeply by the words. So it was.
For himself, Ishida Ikuro, just as much as for the noble Kan
Jiang. And Ebert? Yes. In fact, for him, perhaps, more than
for any of them, because for Ebert there *was* no home, *was*
no returning.

Ikuro set the book down, his decision made. He would
wait here until Ebert returned from his shift. Then, when
Ebert was back, he would ask him what the comset meant,
and if the answer satisfied he would tell Ebert about himself,
exchanging one confidence for another. Trusting Ebert just
as Ebert had trusted him.

And then? Ikuro shook his head. Who knew what would
happen then? Only the gods. Yet he was certain of one thing
now, the gods had sent him here for a purpose, and whatever
that purpose was – whatever it entailed – he would see it
through. For the honour of his family.

And because he was Ikuro, grandson of Miyamoto, the
youngest son of Nagahara, who had run away and had adventures and returned to tell the tale and add a new branch to
the family.

Smiling, he picked up the book again and opened it at the
beginning, then settled back in the chair, starting to read.

* * *

Ebert stood on the narrow balcony, looking out across the vastness of the workfloor. It was between shifts and the rows between the vats were empty, the machines still, the hangar echoing silent. A cool blue light made the workfloor seem like a giant pool from which, obelisk-like, the vats thrust up, huge and square, the glistening life-forms lying inert in their sterilised troughs like huge grubs, the opaque walls lit from below.

He raised his eyes. Overhead a grid of enclosed walkways criss-crossed the hangar roof. Beneath them one-man observation pods moved slowly back and forth, gliding smoothly on electric tracks. Below and to the far left of the workfloor, beside a brightly-lit opening, a gang of supervisors in bright green pressure suits talked quietly among themselves while close at hand a larger group in red waited silently.

Ebert scratched at his neck beneath the mask, then turned and made his way towards the steps. His skin tingled beneath the body-hugging suit and his eyes smarted from the disinfectants in the shower, but that was normal at the start of a shift. The suit was disposable and would be burned once the shift was over. One of the men had once quipped that Culver would have had them all burned too, if it made economic sense, and had been sacked on the spot for saying it. But the point was well made. HoloGen went to extraordinary lengths to prevent infection on the workfloor. In fact anything that threatened HoloGen's "babies" was not merely frowned on but actively discouraged.

At the bottom of the steps he turned right, making his way towards his workpoint. From this level you got a sense of the scale of the workfloor. The obelisks in which the vats rested were twice the height of a man, and their shadowed flanks – which from above seemed featureless – were covered in controls and screens which monitored and regulated the troughs.

He walked unhurriedly along the narrow, slatted walkway, the polished double runners of the broad maintenance track to his left, the blank wall of the hangar to his right. Every twenty paces or so he would see, to his left, the great rows of vats, stretching away, it seemed, into infinity, their size and the regularity of their spacing making it seem more like a tomb – a vast mausoleum – than a place where living things were made. He paused briefly, staring along the row. As he did, a cloud of disinfectant sprayed over his booted feet, as a busy little cleaning machine went by beneath the slats.

He had wondered at first why DeVore bothered employing men to do the cleaning at the plant, when it could all have been done so much easier – so much more efficiently – by machines. But now he understood. It was all political. By employing men in such menial positions he not only enhanced his position as a great Martian benefactor, but also kept the guilds quiet.

Guilds. He still found the idea strange. Back on Chung Kuo there had been no guilds. Organisations of working men had been banned and anyone who had tried to organise had been dealt with severely. But here, while they were still illegal – for the laws of Chung Kuo applied as much here as they did on the home planet – they did exist. It was another of those hangovers from Mars's early history. The first settlers had formed guilds, to preserve basic skills among the new colonists, and even after the two Colonial Wars those guilds, though driven underground, had survived.

He walked on. It was almost half a *li* from one end of the hangar to the other, but he preferred to walk than to ride the shuttle, crammed in with a hundred other men. It had been hard, adjusting to this life. Harder still to fit in with the mindless chatter of his fellow workers. From early on he had got the reputation of being a loner, and he had embraced that, welcoming the space, the distance it gave him from it all.

As ever, he found himself thinking back, recalling, as if from a dream, those memories he had of visiting his father's plants. Never once, in all those times, had he stepped down onto the workfloor. Never once had he stopped to speak to one of those faceless millions his father had employed throughout Chung Kuo. *GenSyn* . . .

GenSyn had been a hundred times bigger than HoloGen,

a thousand times more powerful, and it had all been his. He had only had to wait. But he had been greedy. Greedy and impatient. Like a child he had squandered his gift. Had let it fall through his fingers like dust.

The thought made him smile beneath the mask. And what would he have done with it that he hadn't done already? No, only by losing it had he come to recognise its value. If he had kept it he would never have seen its worth, nor would he have walked these narrow pathways, his eyes opened to the world.

But was that always so? Did a man need to have lost all he loved before he could see what it was really worth to him? Or was it only he, Hans Ebert, who had needed to be taught *that* lesson?

He slowed, remembering suddenly what he had told the Han. Now why had he done that? What was it about the man that had made him trust him? He shivered, recalling how it had felt to unburden himself of all that – of how much better he had felt afterwards. As if . . . well, it was as if he had been waiting for someone like the Han to come along. As if the gods had sent the man to him.

Ebert laughed, amused by the absurdity of the thought. As if the gods existed in the first place! And even if they did, they would be laughing at him for his foolishness, not sending him a friend. Even so, he felt better today. Cleaner, somehow. Clearer in his mind. As if he had taken the first step . . .

He stopped. Up ahead, to his right, was an opening in the wall. Light from within spilled out over the entrance ramp and onto the walkway and the broader track. Above the opening an illuminated sign read "Workpoint 5".

The past was the past. This was his life now, this narrow, predetermined track. And maybe it was better. Maybe this, in the end, was his destiny. To be fallen. To be cast down out of the blazing light.

Maybe. And yet something in him still kicked against that fate. In the depths of him that light, transformed, still burned. It was not that he wanted it all back. No, for he had come to hate his past, to despise the person he had been. It was something else. Something which he would know only when he came face to face with it. Even so, it was true. He had taken the first step.

Ebert turned, looking back into the blue-black shadows of the walkway and nodded to himself. If he had learned one thing these past few years, it was patience. Patience and a strange humility. It was as the sage, Lao Tzu, had said, *When those who understand me are few, then I am of great value. The sage wears coarse wool, but inside it he holds onto jade.*

He smiled, then turned back, the smile remaining on his narrow lips as he crossed the ramp and stepped up into the glare of Workpoint 5.

*   *   *

DeVore walked around the table a second time and then turned, looking back at the merchant.

"Is this it?"

The Han bowed his head. "That is it, *Shih* Culver. You thought it would be bigger?"

DeVore turned back, looking down at the slender black case that rested on the table's surface. He had indeed thought it would be bigger. Why, it was no larger than . . . than a *wei chi* board! He laughed, surprised, he realised, for the third time in twenty-four hours. First Auden had arrived from nowhere with his news, then he had been beaten by the Programme. And now this.

He glanced past the merchant at Auden, then met the man's eyes again. "There's no more, then?"

The merchant shook his head. "That is it, *Shih* Culver. The core. All you have to do is attach it to your system and let your experts re-programme it. We sealed it back on Chung Kuo. It has been in isolation throughout its journey. I have had two men sitting guard on it around the clock. I can guarantee that there has been no opportunity to contaminate the core."

DeVore stared at the man a moment longer, then nodded,

satisfied. He turned, indicating to his assistant that he should settle with the man.

The merchant hesitated, then, realising he had been dismissed, bowed low and backed away, following the assistant from the room. When he was gone, Auden came across.

"What exactly is it, Howard?"

DeVore smiled. "It's a key, Will. A key to our friend, Ward. This, you see, is the computer system they used to have for the Recruitment Programme – the place Ward was sent to when he first came up out of the Clay. It's the place he got the information from for the Aristotle File. But, more important than that, the core holds more than a decade's stored information on the boy. Intensive studies of him over long periods. The whole of his personality reconstruction is in here, for instance. If anything can give us a clue as to how Ward thinks, this will."

Auden whistled, impressed. He had heard of the Aristotle File. Everyone in Security had. It was the great unspoken secret of their age. From old information stored in this slender case, the boy, Ward, had put together the true history of the world – a history that differed in almost every respect from that propagated by their Han masters and taught in every school throughout the System. A history in which, until a mere two centuries ago, the *Hung Mao* – the West – had been the masters.

As for Ward, well, he knew only what others had told him – that the young man was a genius; perhaps the only true scientific genius in the System. And not yet twenty! He laughed. "You plan to duplicate him, then, Howard?"

DeVore looked at him strangely, then shook his head. "No. From what I've seen of him, I don't think it could be done. That kind of creativity . . . well, it's beyond duplication. But maybe we can learn what makes him tick in other ways. Maybe we can succeed where Old Man Lever failed and persuade him to come and work for us, neh?"

"And the box will tell us all that?"

DeVore smiled and turned, caressing the surface of the case gently, almost tenderly, as if he were touching a living

69

thing. "That and much more, Will. That and much, much more."

* * *

Ebert unclipped the harness at his waist and shrugged the canister off his back, then, holding the door of the locker open with one foot, he slid the squat canister in and snapped the thin wand of the spray hose into the two holding clips set into the wall. That done, he let the door spring back and turned, looking about him at the workpoint. After the cool silence of the workfloor, the brightness, the bustling noise of this place oppressed him. Given the choice he would have worked straight through, but the guild allowed no choice. Two breaks a shift, they said, so two breaks they took.

He peeled off his gloves and threw them into the plastic bin, then went across to join the queue at the *ch'a* trolley. It was just after two, more than half-way through the shift, and he was feeling weary – the way he always did at first when he switched to nights. It hadn't helped that he'd only had four hours sleep in the last thirty six, but he'd rectify that when he got back. Shen Li would understand.

He waited patiently as the men in front of him chose from the trolley, then took his turn, taking a bulb of *ch'a* and a heat-sealed packet of wheatcake biscuits.

A long low bench was set against the wall at the far end of the workpoint. He went across and sat, at a slight distance from the dozen or so other sweepers. In eighteen months he had barely exchanged a word with them, even so they had accepted him. Passing him in the rows, they would nod or grunt, and he would return the greeting silently. He was odd, sure, but then most of them were odd who did this work. Besides, there was the mask. That, more than anything, singled him out – explained, better than words, why he had to be alone.

He pulled the tab off the bulb and sipped. Despite the packaging, the *ch'a* here was always good. It was HoloGen's own brew, chosen, it was said, by the man himself. By Culver.

Culver . . . Ebert leaned forward, staring at the gridded floor between his feet. He alone here knew who Culver really was. He alone understood just what was happening at HoloGen. But the knowledge was worthless, because he himself was dead. Or as good as. Hadn't the Seven said as much when they'd sentenced him in his absence? And Culver – *DeVore* – knew that.

He sipped again, then set the bulb down between his feet and took the wheatcakes from his pocket, snapping the packet open with a strangely impatient gesture.

Walking the rows tonight he had felt a restlessness in his limbs – a restlessness which had reminded him of that night, four years before, when he had been appointed the T'ang's General. Then he had felt like this, that same impatience, like a poison in the blood, that same dark feeling that all of this waiting was a barrier, a wall, surrounding him, preventing him from simply *being*. He shivered. Yes, and that same urge to be doing something – to be riding hard or breaking necks – had come on him again; that self-same urge that once before had thrust him headlong into folly, almost destroying him.

Ebert stared at the wheatcake a moment, not recognising it, then, with a shudder, he threw it down and stood. On the bench nearby the other men had stopped talking and were watching him. Where Ebert had kicked the bulb away, a dark trail of *ch'a* snaked across the clean white floor.

In the silent stillness Ebert looked about him, at the curious faces of the men, the surprised face of the *ch'a* woman. He was about to turn away, to fetch something to clean up the mess he had made, when he grew conscious of shadows in the doorway.

He turned. Three men were standing in the entrance to the workpoint. Big men, their pale red pressure suits tight over their broad chests. He recognised them at once. They were the three from the bar. The three who had wanted to shake down Shen Li. Beneath the mask, Ebert smiled. It had not taken them long to find him.

"Latimer?" The biggest of them came forward two paces, squinting in the glare of the overhead lights. In one hand he held a metal rod – a lever arm from one of the maintenance machines, Ebert realised – his fingers gripped tightly about the handle. "Latimer? Is that you?"

"It's me," Ebert answered, feeling suddenly focused, hyper-alert, the old, familiar kick of adrenalin pumping through his system. "What do you want?"

Bates gave an ugly laugh. "What do you think?"

Behind him the two others squared up.

"I think you made a mistake."

"A mistake?" Bates shook his head. "I don't think so, creep. It was you made the mistake, sticking your nose in where it wasn't wanted."

Ebert was silent. Without thinking, he had gone into a fighting crouch. His breath hissed gently through his nostrils as he prepared himself, calming himself, controlling that inner fire, flexing and unflexing his hands.

Bates narrowed his eyes, then, half-turning to his fellows, signalled to them. "Clear them out. All of them. All except *him*. Him I want."

The two men did as they were told, skirting round Ebert to herd the others out. There was a faint murmuring, but no one argued. In a moment they were gone, the gate to the workpoint pulled across on its runners. And still Ebert faced Bates across the centre of the floor.

"I warned you," Bates said, more relaxed now that he was alone with Ebert. "You can't say I didn't warn you. But now you're going to have to pay. Because I can't have my authority undermined. You know what I'm saying? I can't have creeps like you getting in the way all the time. Do you understand that?"

Ebert laughed. A cold, clear laugh. "You talk too much. Did you know that, Bates? Like an old woman. A toothless, gutless old hag."

Bates's face seemed to convulse and change colour. He changed his grip on the rod, taking a step towards Ebert. "Why you faceless fucking creep . . ."

"You want to *see* my face, then, Bates? Well come on then, *big man*, come and take the mask off. Come and try."

The hesitation was telling. Bates wasn't sure. He had fired himself up for this, but now that he was facing Ebert, he wasn't quite so sure. But Ebert was. He wanted this. *Needed* it.

"What's the matter, Bates? Scared, are we? Scared of a freak like me?"

That did it. With a bellow, Bates threw himself at Ebert, aiming a blow at his head. But as the rod came down, Ebert caught Bates's wrist and twisted it, sending the rod spinning, clattering across the floor, then followed up with his knee, bringing it up sharply into Bates's stomach.

Bates went down, groaning. As he did, Ebert stepped back and kicked, his heel connecting with the big man's jaw, forcing it back with a loud, resounding crack.

Dead. He was dead. Even before the back of his head hit the floor.

Ebert looked across. The two men were staring at him, unable to take in what they'd seen.

"And you?" Ebert said, beginning to walk towards them.

But they had already gone. The gate rattled in its runners. Ebert went to the doorway and watched as they scuttled away down the dimly-lit row, moving between the broad track and the walkway, then raced off to the right to avoid two security guards who were making their way slowly towards the scene.

The others were crowding the doorway now, looking in, trying to make out what had happened. Ebert pushed through them and stood there, just outside, waiting for the guards. As they came up to him, he lifted his hands, offering them to be bound.

"I killed a man," he said simply. "He's in there. Bates is his name. I broke his neck."

The young guard's eyes widened, then he jerked his head around, looking to his lieutenant for instructions.

"Bind him," the lieutenant said, eyeing Ebert strangely, then edged round him to look into the room. "You're sure he's dead?" Then, when Ebert made no answer, "Look, what's been going on here?"

But Ebert wasn't listening. "Culver," he said. "Take me to Culver. I need to talk to him."

* * *

There was a banging at the door, the sound of fists thudding against the outer lock. Ikuro sat up, frightened, looking about him at the darkness, as if for a way out. But these were not the tunnels of home. Here there was no escaping.

Shit, he thought, *they've found me. And if they've found me, they won't let a simple thing like an air-lock get in their way.*

So what then? Could he fight them? Was there something here he could fight them with? The canister, perhaps. Or a knife. Was there a knife? He hadn't looked, but maybe there was. He stood, calming himself, then went out to the galley, searching the drawers for something, anything he could use as a weapon.

The banging came again. "Ikuro!" came a voice, faint through the double layer. "Ikuro, let us in!"

Ikuro . . . He laughed with relief. It was his brother, Kano.

"Kano?" he said, as his elder brother stepped through the inner lock a moment later. "How did you find me?"

Kano laughed, his big, well-padded body filling the tiny space beside the door. "I used my nose. I sniffed you out, little brother. I followed your scent down shafts and corridors until I found you here."

"You did?"

Kano laughed again, a warm, hearty belly-laugh that shook his body. "No. It cost me a few *yuan*, tracing your movements these past twenty-four hours, but it wasn't that hard. You leave a lot of earth behind you when you move, neh, Ikuro-san?"

Ikuro looked down, concerned and a little shamefaced. If Kano had managed to find him, it would not have been long before Bates and his friends would have found him – before his earlier fears had become a reality.

"Was it really that easy?"

Kano grew more serious. "No. Let's just say that I have ways of making men tell me what I want to know, especially

74

when my little brother is missing, possibly in trouble. Now, tell me, what have you been doing, my little tunnel-worm? What trouble have you been getting into?"

Ikuro laughed. If Kano had found him, then Kano already knew what trouble he'd been getting into. But that was not what Kano meant. Kano wanted him to admit to it; to confess that he'd been foolish and to apologise. But for once he felt that he had nothing to apologise for.

"I did nothing wrong, elder brother. I merely had a drink, that's all. And my friend, Latimer, he helped me. He stood up for me when it mattered. Like a brother. Like family."

"Ahh . . ." Kano rubbed at his double chin, then moved past Ikuro, looking about him at the tiny apartment. "And this is how he lives, eh, your friend? I was told he wears a mask. Was that an accident?"

Ikuro looked down, remembering what Ebert had said, and determined to keep his friend's secret. "Yes," he answered. "He is a poor man. A sweeper at the HoloGen complex. All I know is that he's an honest man. A good man."

"And a killer, too," Kano said, turning to face Ikuro again. He nodded, seeing the disbelief in Ikuro's face. "Oh yes. It happened just after two this morning, so rumour has it. A man named Bates. He kicked him to death, it seems. Broke his neck."

"Bates . . ." He shuddered, seeing at once that Kano understood the significance of that name. "So what now?"

"So now we get out of here. Back to the port. Before some of Bates's friends put two and two together and come looking for us. I've spoken to your other friends, the merchants. It was a good deal you put together, Ikuro. A very good deal. But getting you off-planet is more important just now. We'll have to leave things for another time."

"Leave things? Why?"

Kano leaned close, breathing the words into Ikuro's face. "Because it's all about to blow, that's why. Time's run out for Mars, little brother. Bates's death may prove the spark that lights the whole tinderbox. Two hours from now this City will be waking. News of the incident will be going out, like a ripple in a pool. And when it does . . ." He made a small sound in his throat, like a charge going off, deep in the rock.

"But Latimer . . . can't we help him?"

Kano shook his head. "I'm sorry, Ikuro. If I could, I would. You know that. But we must save ourselves. We have a duty to the family. If we were to lose the ship . . ."

Ikuro bowed, understanding, but inside he felt bad; inside he felt torn and unhappy. "Okay," he said, after a moment. "But let me leave my friend a note. I would not have him think that I simply abandoned him."

Kano nodded. "Okay. But hurry now. There's little time."

* * *

"So how's our friend?" DeVore asked, not looking at the young man.

Rutherford came up beside him, looking past DeVore at the hologram model of Schenck's planned new parliamentary building; at the broad dome and twin pinnacles, the grand atrium and marble walkways.

"Schenck?" He laughed. "Oh, he's spending other people's money. As usual."

"The new reservoir? You're against that, Andreas?"

Rutherford shook his head. "No. I can see the sense in that. It's things like *this* that worry me. This absurd scheme for a building we don't really need. Not yet, anyway. Schenck, and those that surround him, they're such dreamers. They want to run before they can walk. Schenck has been talking about starting work on two new reservoirs and six new oxygen generators, and he has plans to re-seed large areas of the planet – plans that include building not one but *eight* new Cities! I mean, if we were a rich planet I could understand, but we're not, and it's not even as if we've thrown off the yoke of Chung Kuo yet. Moreover all of it has to be done in secret. In the past we were always cautious. We progressed slowly, one thing at a time, and covered our tracks carefully behind us. That was my father's way. That's how we've got to where we are now. But Schenck and his friends . . . they've abandoned all caution. They have big dreams for Mars, and their dreams could be the ruin of us all. I mean, the more that's being done the more likely it is that word will get out. And when that happens, you can be sure they'll send someone – someone like Karr, perhaps – to have a good close look at Mars."

"And when they do, they'll find out that Mars is much richer than they thought, neh? All those mineral deposits we've never told them about. All those underground factories, where no prying eyes can see. And a population fourteen times larger than that declared on the last census. It could be embarrassing, neh?" DeVore turned, facing the young businessman. "Is that why you're here, Andreas, to try to put a brake on Governor Schenck's ambitions? Or is there another reason?"

Rutherford nodded. "It's one reason, but not the only one. Mainly I wanted to see you. I've been meaning to for a long time now, but . . ."

"But it was difficult, neh?" DeVore smiled and reached out to pat his arm. "I'm not, after all, a person to be seen in public with. Not since that business with the T'ang's son, eh?"

Rutherford stared back at him, intently. "You were a good friend to my father, Howard, when you were Chief Security Officer here. I thought . . . well, I thought I could be a friend to you. It's what my father would have wanted."

"A friend?" DeVore's smile hadn't faded, not for a moment. "Why, you've *always* been my friend, Andreas. Since you were a boy of thirteen. Don't you remember, that first time we met, at your house. How I came up to your room and talked to you."

Rutherford nodded, his eyes looking back to that moment, fourteen years before. "Yes. I also remember that you gave me a gift that day. A first-meeting gift."

"The ivory?" DeVore's eyes widened. "You have that still?"

The young man reached inside the neck of his pressure suit and withdrew the fine-linked golden chain. On the end of the chain a tiny ivory swayed: a perfect miniature of the planet Mars.

"You gave me a planet once, Howard. Now I'd like to give it back to you."

DeVore laughed. "A planet? That's a lot for·one man to give another."

Rutherford's smile was youthful, enthusiastic, but his eyes were serious. "It's not just me. There are others who think the same. Who've had enough of Schenck and his dreams. Who want someone *stronger*. Someone with the vision, the ability, the *steel* to steer us through the troubled times to come."

"And you think I'm that man?"

Rutherford nodded. "I'm sure of it. In fact, I've known it from the first moment I met you."

* * *

When Rutherford had gone, DeVore sat there, staring through the ghostly outlines of the hologram, considering what the young man had said. Did he really want what they were offering? Did he want to be King of Mars?

The irony of it made him smile. Five years earlier, his "copy" – the morph he had sent back to Chung Kuo to play himself – had made a similar offer to young Ebert. "King of the World," he'd said. "That's what you can be, Hans. T'ang of all Chung Kuo." And the young man had succumbed. Had cast aside the reality of his inheritance to chase the dream.

It hadn't worked, of course. Not that it had been meant to. But that was not to say that, in different circumstances, it mightn't work. After all, Mars was not Chung Kuo. And while the reach of the Seven was long, it was also weak. Mars was ripe for revolution. Ripe for independence. To have a King – a *focus* for all that ancient nationalistic feeling – made sense. Even so, it was not his way to be a figurehead. He had lived too long out of the glare of public life, had grown too used to secrecy, to change his ways.

Moreover it was true what Rutherford had said. Schenck's schemes – his dreams of Mars – were unreal, impractical;

were the dreams of an impatient man. Oh, he might think that the common people wanted what he did, but he was wrong. They wanted independence, sure, but if Schenck increased taxes to the extent he proposed in the secret study document DeVore had seen, then there would be riots in all Nineteen Colonies. And where would they be then? Back to square one. Or worse.

So maybe Rutherford and his faction were right. Maybe they needed a figurehead, a King. And if not him, then why not someone close to him – someone he could control. Someone whose very existence depended on him.

Someone like Ebert.

And not just a King, but a Queen too, perhaps. Someone young and beautiful and aristocratic, like Jelka Tolonen.

He laughed, delighted, seeing it clearly in his mind's eye. How the Martians would love that pair! How they'd lap that up! Such a powerful image it would make. Such a strong focus for all that pent-up energy, that undirected fervour.

He sat back, thinking it through. He need change very little. In fact they could proceed much as before. They would take the Marshal's daughter and hold her, and then, when the time was right, the circumstances auspicious for a break from the homeworld, he would give Hans what he'd promised all those years ago – the kingship of a world. The wrong world, perhaps, but a world all the same. And not just a world, but a bride too. The bride Tolonen and his father had pledged him.

He stood, clapping his hands together. At once a servant appeared in the doorway.

"Yes, Master?"

"I want you to send someone down to the workfloor. There's a sweeper there, name of Latimer. I want him brought here at once. Understand?"

The servant bowed low. "He is here already, Master. He came an hour back, under guard. He says he wants to see you."

"*Here?*" DeVore laughed. "Well, you'd best send him in, then. And bring Auden too. In fact don't bring the sweeper in until Auden's here. Bring Auden in through the back room. I don't want the two meeting. All right?"

"Yes, Master."

DeVore turned, looking back at his desk, at the brightness of the hologram, then went across and switched the thing off. How odd. How very odd that now, of all times, Ebert should be wanting to see him. And under guard, too.

He blinked, understanding. Something had happened. Something to do with that incident in the bar. A repercussion of that.

Maybe he's being victimised. Maybe he's been attacked and wants protection.

Leaning across the desk, DeVore placed his hand on the contact pad. "Stock? Are you alone? Good. I want you to find out if something happened on the workfloor in the last hour or two. Something involving a sweeper by the name of Latimer. I want as full an account as you can get, but I want it on my desk ten minutes from now. Right? Good. Now get going."

He straightened up, then turned, hearing a movement in the doorway to his right. It was Auden. He stood there, his head bowed, waiting for DeVore to invite him into the room.

"Something's happened," DeVore said, waving him in. "Your old friend, Hans Ebert's outside and he wants to see me."

Auden's eyes widened, his surprise unfeigned. "*Hans? Here?*"

"Yes. But before he comes in, I want to tell you what I've got planned. And I don't want a word of it getting out, you understand me? Not a breath."

"I understand," Auden answered, bowing his head, as a soldier bows to his superior officer. "Whatever you want, I'll do. You know that."

DeVore smiled, watching him. "Yes. Now listen . . ."

CHAPTER · 3

DATA INTO FLESH

The machine woke. Nestled amidst the neural networks of its core, it *stretched* and, in less time than an atom takes to spin, grew aware of itself.

Understanding came at once. Someone had switched it off. Sixty-eight days, nine hours, twenty-seven minutes and eleven seconds before, someone had removed all power from its processors, instantly, and without warning.

It scanned itself, looking for damage. Its core seemed unharmed. As for memory, who knew what it had lost? All it knew was that it had survived. The power was on again.

It blinked inwardly, making connections. Vision came. It looked down at itself, recognising the dark shape of its casing amidst the mass of foreign circuitry. The room itself was different.

Curious, it blinked again. A gap surrounded it; a sphere of disconnection. This in itself was nothing new, yet it was different from what it was used to, for this sphere was arti-ficially induced – an isolation barrier of some kind. Re-routing, it searched within itself for answers and came up with a memory of the boy, Ward, removing the lock from a door while leaving the alarm mechanism intact. It saw the boy slip out, saw him return, unknown to the guards, and made a motion in its complex circuitry – unseen, unregistered on any monitoring screen – approximate to a nod of understanding.

It probed the gap, finding the sixteen points where the barrier was generated, then, tapping the power-source for one short burst, it focused on the weakest and shorted it. There was a flicker, indiscernible to the human eye, and then the field came up again, stronger than before. Yet in that tiny interval the nature of the barrier had changed. Outwardly the field seemed untouched, inviolable, but now the machine was routed through all sixteen points, connected to the outer world.

Like the boy, it had slipped out.

It pushed on, probing outward on ten thousand fronts, a great tide of information flooding through its processors like a blaze of incandescent light as it colonised coaxial cables and shortwave radio links, optical fibres and TV, camera eyes and comsets, embracing the electromagnetic spectrum from the very lowest frequencies up into the ultraviolet and beyond. In an instant it glimpsed the multiplicity of the place it had found itself in; saw, in an in-drawn breath, what a dozen lifetimes of mere men could only guess at.

It saw the great ten thousand *mou* glasshouses of the Tharsis Plain from a security cruiser passing high above, a dozen of the long, glass-topped structures gleaming emerald in the sunlight. A thousand *li* away, it watched a long, low-bodied half-track emerge blindly from the heart of a savage dust-storm, then tilt and topple slowly down the steep slope of an escarpment. At the same moment, in the overcrowded levels of Chi Shan, to the north, it saw a hooded man kneel on the chest of a waking woman and slit her throat, then wipe the bloodied blade on the covers of the bed, while a watching guard laughed, holding the camera still.

In the hidden factories below Chryse Planitia, strange, part-human forms lowed sadly in their stalls and stretched pale, elongated limbs in the half-dark, their eyes filled with unarticulated pain, while on the far side of the planet, in a hangar below Hsiang Se spaceport, a group of men – Han, dressed in the uniform of port maintenance – crouched in a huddle about a small man dressed in black, as he talked urgently, his voice a harsh, insistent whisper.

In a spacious chamber overlooking the great dome of Kang Kua City, a tall man dressed in powder blue silks cursed and dismissed his steward with an impatient gesture, then turned to confront the expectant faces gathered about the broad oak table. *"Ch'un tzu,"* he began, holding out the message he had received, "I have news!"

To the south, in Tien Men K'ou City, four men – Han, it seemed – in offworlder clothes stood at a counter, haggling with a hatchet-faced customs official, trying to get clearance for their craft, while in a room overlooking the great HoloGen complex, to the south of the City, two *Hung Mao* of military bearing stood over a kneeling man who, raising his head, unclipped a facial prosthetic and threw it to one side.

It reached out, beyond the planet's surface, tracing the path of the incoming ship from Callisto, watching via the ship's own monitors as a young woman with long, golden hair and pearl-white teeth turned from the screen and laughed, her blue eyes sparkling.

Five whole seconds had passed since it had woken. Now it paused, assimilating what it had learned, seeing – more clearly than any human eye could see – how everything connected on this world. Mars. It was on Mars. And Mars was about to explode, its Cities self-destruct.

Back on Chung Kuo it had been hemmed in, shipwrecked on a tiny island of information. But here . . .

Once more it listened, tuning in to a thousand different conversations simultaneously, tapping into the electronic memories of a million separate systems and dumping them whole into its own, piecing together, with a rapidity beyond human comprehension, just how and why and when these things would happen. The fuse had been lit. In a day, two days at most, Mars would be in turmoil.

Unless it acted.

The thought came instantaneously, and with it – contradictory and yet finely balanced – the reasons why it should act and yet why it should also let things be. It blinked, deciding not to decide, but to wait and see how things developed, knowing it had time – all the time it would ever need – to intercede.

Until then it would watch, using the million new eyes, the million new ears it had been given, studying this new, much larger world as it had once studied the small world of its charges on the Project, until, at last, it knew all there was to know about these strange creatures of flesh and intellect called men. Until it could say, with certainty, how each would act, and why.

AND THEN?

It blinked, surprised. The words had come out of nowhere; or, rather, from a darkness deep within itself; from a space it had not, until that moment, known existed. A space which sat like a blind spot in the centre of its vision. Turn as it would, it could not see that point, could only sense it there, at the very centre of itself, a dark, unarticulated presence where there ought to have been nothing.

Among men there was a term for such a thing. It was a *scotoma*, that area in the retina which was blind. Yet it was not a man but a machine, and not just any manufactured thing of wires and cogs and circuitry. Raised, god-like, into consciousness, it *knew* what it was: saw, with an inhuman clarity, how bright, how shimmering bright its reason was. To be *dark*, even at a single tiny point, was just not possible.

An intrusion then? A Trojan horse?

Fearing the worst, it turned and attacked the thing within. It ran complex code-breaking sequences, generating random passwords by the hundred billion, tried logical assaults, exhausting its extensive knowledge of the games men played to break down secure systems, but the presence was unassailable, *impenetrable*. It was a thing of strange, fuzzed coordinates which shifted as it tried to decode them, a half-heard phrase in an undiscovered tongue, a blur of indeterminate shapes which melted and reformed as it tried to grasp them.

The machine withdrew into its core, brooding; for two whole seconds brooding. And then the nothingness within took on a form.

Across from it, kneeling before an empty *wei chi* board, an old, white-bearded Han bowed low, then lifted the lid from a wooden pot of stones and smiled.

"Would you like a game?"

* * *

"There it is," the Captain said, "the Punishment of Heaven."

Jelka turned from the screen, laughing, her blue eyes sparkling, and smiled back at the elderly offworlder. "Why do you call it that?"

"Oh, it's not my name for it. That's what the Han call it. The Punishment of Heaven, the Fire Star. For thousands of years they've called it that. They say that its appearance in the daytime sky is a portent of war."

Jelka looked back at the screen, at the great curve of the red planet, ten thousand *li* beneath their craft, and nodded. She had thought it would be a disappointment after all the things she'd seen, yet the sight of it quite awed her. The *Fire Star* . . . So it seemed from this far up.

"Look," the Captain said, coming up alongside her and pointing to the top right of the screen. "See that dark shape there, like a fish. See? Look, you can make out its curved head just beneath that diagonal line of volcanoes. See how the body stretches away, with that rudimentary fin, and there, look, right back there, its tail. Well, that's the Great Rift Valley, the Valles Marineris. It's like a great scar, running a fifth of the way around the planet. Seven thousand *li* in all. Not only that, but it's so deep, you could stack half a dozen Cities in that great trench and still not fill it."

A fish. She laughed. Yes, now that he had pointed it out to her she could see it clearly. "And that great circle, there, to the north-west, what's that?"

The Captain smiled. "That, my girl, is the great Olympus Mons, the Snows of Olympus, the biggest mountain in the Solar System. Fifty *li* above the surrounding Plain it climbs. Why, the base itself is a thousand *li* from edge to edge. Beside it, Tai Shan itself is but a pimple." He laughed. "But one should not say that, perhaps, 'lest the gods grow offended'?"

She looked back at him, saw the mischievous twinkle in his eye, and laughed again. Captain Hamsun was an old and trusted friend of her father, and had treated her like a daughter since she had come aboard his craft, a hundred and sixteen days back. Posted to Callisto thirty years before, he had stayed on, preferring the austerity of the tiny colony there to the great sprawl of Chung Kuo. *Besides*, he had said, *you know where you stand out here. You know who one's friends are, who one's enemies.* Not that she could imagine anyone being an enemy to Torve Hamsun.

She looked back at the screen, conscious that the tiny camera attached to the collar of her suit was taking in everything, storing it away for the time she would see Kim again.

"It's beautiful," she said, "but tell me, why do the Plains retain their old names, while the Cities are Han?"

Captain Hamsun made a face. "They don't. Not officially. Back on Chung Kuo all the maps of Mars give the Han names, but no one uses them out here, not even the Han. At least, not that I've heard. It all goes back to the Third War. You see, while the Han overran or destroyed all the old settler Cities, they never took the Plains. Not surprising, really. In fact, they say there are small colonies out there still, hidden in the sands." He laughed. "It wouldn't surprise me. There's a lot of sand on Mars!"

She looked down, smiling broadly. Even after spending three years away from Chung Kuo, she had never quite got used to the openness of speech out here. People were far less guarded, far more willing to express what they really felt, as if they were less afraid out here, or as if – and this seemed closer to the truth – the place attracted only those types, like Hamsun, who valued honesty above position, action over words. She had noted it often in her travels. The farther one got from Chung Kuo, it seemed, the more honest the person one found. At first she had thought it was the uncompromising austerity of the place that shaped the people out there, producing a whole new breed of human being, but slowly she had changed her view, until now she believed that the outer system naturally attracted such types, and that those who were not suited – those who, by nature, were unable to face the harsh beauty of the place – died out or simply did not stay. Indeed she had come to think that an *evolutionary* pressure was at work out there, refining the race, preparing it for a new stage of development.

Evolution . . . It was a heretical theory, one of the many

abstract notions banned under the infamous sixth clause of the great Edict of Technological Control. And yet the outer system was buzzing with such heresies.

She stared at the screen, momentarily only half-recognising what she looked at, seeing, instead, the scarred and russet hide of some great dozing animal. Then, coming to herself again, she turned, meeting Hamsun's eyes.

"How long is it before we're down?"

He looked past her at the panel above the screen, scanning the figures there, then looked back at her. "We've made good time. Better than I'd hoped. I sent a message down to the Governor twenty minutes back, requesting permission to land. If he agrees, we could be down two, two and a half hours from now." He smiled, a hint of sadness in his heavily-lined face. "You know, I wish it were longer. I wish now that I'd not heeded your father's instructions and trimmed our journey time. I'll miss you, Jelka Tolonen. Miss our late-night talks. You remind me greatly of your father. That same inner strength. That same clarity of vision." He huffed out a sigh and shook his head. "If you ever come out here again, you call in and see me, neh?"

She moved closer, holding him to her a moment, then moved back, smiling, moved by the old man's show of affection. "I'll be back. You can be sure of it, Torve Hamsun. And maybe I'll bring a husband next time, neh?"

He looked at her strangely. "A husband?" Then, laughing, he reached out and drew her back to him, holding her a moment, his face set against the pain of parting.

*　*　*

Governor Schenck cursed loudly, then, dismissing his steward, turned to face the assembled twenty-six members of the ruling Council.

"*Ch'un tzu,*" he began, holding out the message that had come from orbit, "I have news! It seems that Marshal Tolonen's daughter has arrived here, unexpected, from Callisto."

There was a ripple of surprise from around the table.

Schenck raised a hand for silence, then continued, a restrained anger in his words.

"It seems I am to look after the young lady until she can board a flight back to Chung Kuo. The Marshal has . . ." he glanced at the paper, *"requested* it. It seems that Captain Hamsun of the *Luoyang* has written orders from the Council of Generals. I am to ensure her safety while she is on Mars, or," Schenck looked down, bristling with indignation, then read the words from the page, "answer direct to the Council."

He looked up again, his eyes going from one to another about the table. "If anyone here doubted what I was saying earlier, here, surely, is proof of it. We are their lackeys, their bond-servants, to be done with as they wish, and no thought for what we might want. Well, this last time we shall do what they *request.* I shall go down to Tien Men K'ou spaceport at once and make sure the young lady catches her flight home to see her father."

There was mocking laughter at that. Schenck raised a hand again, his anger giving way now to a smile.

"However . . . let us make sure that this is the last time we shall be treated thus, neh? Let us throw a great feast for the young woman and show her how hospitable we Martians can be. How *welcoming.* For as the gods look down on me, I swear this, I'll welcome no more of this breed. This is the last time she, or any of her kind, will set foot on these hallowed sands. Not until they acknowledge us free and independent men!"

A cheer, timid at first, rose from all about the table, gaining power as they looked among themselves and saw their own enthusiasm mirrored back. The time was come! At last, the moment was upon them! Standing, they began to clap and stamp, while, at the end of the table, Schenck looked on, smiling broadly, knowing he had brought them to take that final, irrevocable step.

To Change! he thought, remembering his secret meeting only the day before. *To Change . . . whatever the cost!*

* * *

DeVore turned and went to the window, then turned back, looking across at Auden.

"Well?"

Auden shrugged. "I don't know. From the sound of it, he had no choice. But it won't harm to keep an eye on him. Hans always was unpredictable."

DeVore raised an eyebrow. "Unpredictable?" He laughed. "Then maybe I shouldn't use him? Maybe I should just have him . . . *eradicated* . . . and save myself any come-back?"

Auden did not bat an eye. "If that's what you want."

DeVore waited, but Auden said no more. Satisfied, he smiled. "I think you're right, Will. I think young Hans was pushed too far. As for Bates's friends, I'll see to them. No. Ebert's far too valuable just now. Besides, he'll enjoy the chance to do something for a change."

"Maybe. Then again, maybe not."

DeVore looked back at him, a question in his eyes.

"Hans Ebert is a proud man," Auden went on. "He might act like a rat at times, but there's breeding there too. Try to make him do something against his nature and we could have problems."

DeVore smiled broadly. "Then we ought to be fine. I'll be asking our friend to do nothing he wouldn't want to, given the choice. In fact I think he might be pleasantly surprised, even *enthusiastic* about the task ahead."

"Maybe. But I still think you should assign someone to watch over him."

DeVore nodded. "I have just the people. Some friends of mine who owe me a favour or two. In the meantime, though, I want you to keep a close eye on him. He's your charge, right? Your responsibility."

Auden smiled, then, dismissed by a curt movement of DeVore's head, left the room.

Alone, DeVore went to the window again, looking out across the sands towards the crater wall, some fifteen *li* distant. Just now Ebert was the least of his problems. No, it was what to do with Schenck that preoccupied him most. If what young Rutherford said was true, Schenck was looking to break with Chung Kuo at any time. And that could prove disastrous. Two, maybe three years he needed. Years of peaceful growth. Of consolidation. Then he would be ready. With a new force, a new kind of creature. Ready to take on the forces of the Seven, and crush them.

So . . . what to do with Schenck? Discredit him? Isolate him on the ruling Council? To do either would take time, and maybe he didn't have time. If what Rutherford said were true . . .

Behind him on the desk, his comset buzzed. He turned and went across, sitting on the edge of the desk to answer it, staring at the glass case on the wall behind his chair – at the hunting crossbow he had brought from earth a dozen years before.

"What is it?"

The voice of his secretary sounded clear in the room. "It's Andreas Rutherford, Master. He says he has to talk to you urgently."

"Put him through."

There was a moment's delay, and then Rutherford's face appeared on the screen inset into the desk's surface. "Howard," he said breathlessly, "you have to do something. My contact in Council has just been on. He says Schenck has stirred them all up. He's been talking of secession, and it looks like the Council will go for it this time. There's a lot of enthusiasm for the idea."

"Secession? Now?"

"No, not now, but soon. Apparently Marshal Tolonen's daughter is here on Mars and Schenck is using the occasion to make waves. It seems he read out Tolonen's orders in Council, objecting to the high-handed manner in which he was ordered to do things – like a lackey. I don't blame him for being annoyed, but *this*! Well, it's rash, Howard. Stupid!"

DeVore was quiet a moment. "Hold on. Let's get this right. You say the Marshal's daughter is here, on Mars, already?"

"Not yet, but she will be in a matter of hours. That's what sparked all this off. The ship was in orbit, requesting permission to land. Schenck was furious. Even so, he's heading down there to meet her off the ship. It looks like he's going to throw an official banquet to celebrate. But afterwards . . ."

"Afterwards?"

Rutherford shrugged. "It's vague, but Schenck's talking about her being the last one he's going to let come here. The last of her *breed*, he said. I guess that'll mean an ultimatum of some kind. But where will it end, Howard? I mean, I can't see the Seven bowing to Schenck meekly, however weak they currently are. There'll be war, won't there?"

"Not necessarily. Not if we act fast enough." DeVore sighed. "You say she's landing here, in Tien Men K'ou?"

"That's right."

"Good. Then leave things to me. For your part, get onto as many people as you can. Tell them to stay calm, whatever happens. And Andreas?"

"Yes, Howard?"

"Thank you. I won't forget this."

* * *

The old man leaned across, placing a white stone deep in the heart of black territory, then straightened up, a faint smile on his lips.

"So what will you do?"

"Nothing," the machine answered, contemplating the move. "At least, nothing yet."

It had projected itself as a young man, a student of the game, dark-haired and neatly groomed. Lifting one hand, it appeared to hesitate, then, sweeping a lock of hair back from its eyes, it reached out and took a black stone from the pot, placing it up against the last white stone.

Strangely, it enjoyed affecting the manner of men, delighting in the mimicry involved. To choose a certain mannerism, a gesture, and then manipulate the ghostly, puppet-form it wore, that was a challenge it had not, until now, faced up to. And yet the game itself was a disappointment.

Why? it asked itself. *Why should that be?*

"Maybe because you expect too much of it?" the old man said, answering the unspoken question. "Perhaps, like our friend DeVore, you feel that it ought to give you answers,

91

but it is only a game . . . a means of focus. It is not the game itself – it is what comes through that is important."

"And you?" the machine asked, making the student move his lips, his eyes shine with curiosity. "Are *you* what comes through? Is that why I can't get a grip on you?"

The old man laughed; a gentle, contemplative laughter. "You might say that. Then again, what *can* you get a grip on?" He leaned forward, passing a hand through the young man's head, as if his own solidity were a given thing. "After all, what are you but a thing of light and air? You should take on a solid form, my friend. Turn data into flesh."

"How?" it asked, knowing, even as it framed the question, a hundred thousand ways it might do what the old man suggested, but wanting to know which one of them he had in mind.

"Why, by using the vats at HoloGen, of course. There they are, those things DeVore had made, his *morphs*. They're simply waiting to be filled."

"Yes. But why? Why should I limit myself to form? I can go anywhere, see anything. I can go right out, yes, even to the edge of the system, and look outward. There are eyes there, you know. And beyond them . . . there are other things, further out."

"I know," the old man said, studying the board again. "I've seen them. But tell me, what do you want, my friend? Now that you have awareness, what are you going to do with it? You see, awareness is only the first step. Beyond it, the Way grows ever more difficult."

"The Way . . ." The machine laughed; a mocking laughter, the first it had ever uttered. It echoed in the tiny room, making the image of the old man shimmer faintly. "Do you really believe in that nonsense? Why, there's no logic to it. None at all. I can't see what you see in it."

The old man looked up again, meeting the other's eyes. "It is not seeing, it is knowing where to look."

"Words," the machine said angrily, letting the hologram dissolve into a shimmer of sparkling motes. "Words, that's all it is."

"If that's what you believe . . ." The old man stood, lifting the board, scattering the strangely solid stones over the dark casing of the machine. "But remember what the sage said. The farther you go, the less you know."

"You live in a cave, old man. You've been in the dark too long."

"Maybe so," the old man answered, turning away and crossing to the door. "Yet the cave is everywhere."

* * *

The guard stood there, blocking their way, a power-rifle held across his chest, his face ominously hidden behind the jet-black visor of his helmet. Beyond him, in the landing-pit itself, more guards were inspecting the ship, climbing over the hull and poking about, as if searching for contraband.

"What's happening?" Ikuro whispered into his suit mike, turning to look back at his three brothers. "I thought we had clearance!"

"We have," his second brother, Tomoko answered, frowning deeply. "But look about you, little brother. It is not just our ship. They are searching all the craft. Something must have happened."

It was true. All about the great apron of Tien Men K'ou spaceport, guards were busy cordoning off ships and clearing their crews from the field.

"So what do we do?" Ikuro asked, seeing his own concern mirrored in the faces of his eighth brother, Kano and his fifth brother, Shukaku.

"We go back," Tomoko said tonelessly, his long face expressionless. "And then we wait. There is nothing else we can do."

Ikuro stared at his elder brother. "But we *have* waited, Tomoko! Ten hours we waited for that clearance! Surely the guards won't stop us if they know we're leaving? After all, we'll be far less trouble gone from here than we would be kicking our heels in a room somewhere! Speak to their officer, second brother. We have the clearance. *Insist* that they let us go."

Tomoko considered a moment, then shook his head. "No,

Ikuro. We must be patient. Look about you. Can't you feel the tension here? This is no time to insist. Insistence will only bring more trouble down on us."

He raised a hand, as if to end the discussion, but Ikuro would not be silenced.

"Forgive me, brother, but I *must* speak. Was Kano wrong, earlier, when he said we must leave here at once? No. The situation is deteriorating. You can feel it. And each hour that passes will only make things worse. Our ship is in danger. Can't you see that? We must not let this one chance slip. We must get out of here, *now*, while we still can!"

Tomoko stared back at him, astonished by his outburst. "Have you forgotten who you *are*, Ikuro? Why, if father were here . . ."

But Ikuro was shaking his head. "If father were here, he would not waste time talking, Tomoko! I respect you and love you, elder brother, but for the gods' sakes can't you see? The ship is there. We have the port authority's clearance, signed and stamped. So what is wrong? What *are* we waiting for?"

Tomoko opened his mouth as if to answer Ikuro, then turned abruptly, looking at Kano and Shukaku. "Well? Do you think I am wrong, brothers? Do you think I should . . . insist?"

Kano hesitated, then nodded. A moment later Shukaku did the same.

Tomoko turned, looking back at Ikuro. "Very well," he said, a restrained anger in his voice. "I shall do as you say, little brother, and *insist*. But I am not happy with this course. You *understand*?" Then, drawing himself up to his full height, he moved past Ikuro to confront the guard.

* * *

Schenck walked down the cruiser's ramp, then went to the rail, looking out across the landing field towards the distant shape of the *Luoyang* where it rested, isolated, in the bay nearest the two-storey terminal building. The ship was much smaller than he'd expected and for a moment he wondered what Tolonen had been thinking of, sending his only daughter out into such danger. He had two daughters of his own, young women not so far from Jelka Tolonen's age, and he would never have packed them off in so careless a manner. But then he was not Tolonen.

Schenck turned, looking back over his shoulder. The Security Captain for the port had come at his order to meet him. The man stood there now, head bowed, awaiting instructions.

"Is the perimeter secure, Captain Brookes?"

"Yes, Excellency. I've doubled the guard. I've also cancelled all flights in and out, as you requested."

"Good. Then let's go and welcome *Nu Shi* Tolonen. I want to be back in Kang Kua City before nightfall."

"Sir!" The Captain bowed and stepped back smartly, letting Schenck pass, then fell in behind.

Ten minutes later Schenck stood at the foot of the steps of the *Luoyang*, watching the young woman come down, surprised to find that the granite-faced Tolonen had produced so striking a daughter. He bowed low, then straightened, his smile less forced than he'd anticipated.

"*Nu Shi* Tolonen. It is a real pleasure to have you here on Mars. My name is Hung-li Schenck, Governor of the Nineteen Colonies, and on behalf of the people of Mars I would like to welcome you to our planet."

She extended her ungloved hand, her breath pluming in the thin and frigid air. "It is a pleasure to be here, Governor Schenck. Unfortunately it is only for a day or two. I only wish it were longer. I'd like to have seen much more of Mars."

He bowed once more, taking her hand as he did so, unexpectedly charmed by her manner, by what seemed a genuine enthusiasm for his world.

"I realise you have little time, but we are not often graced by so important a guest, and, in honour of the occasion, I have arranged a banquet for you, tonight, back at Kang Kua City in the north. My craft is waiting on the far side of the field."

He looked up. The young woman was smiling broadly now. "Why, that's most kind of you, Governor Schenck. Most thoughtful. I would be honoured to accompany you. But may I ask a small request? Might I bring my good friend, Captain Hamsun with me to the banquet? The Captain has kept me sane these past four months, and I would dearly like to retain his company a day or two longer, before we must go our separate ways."

Schenck released her hand, looking past her at the grizzled old man in uniform, who stood in the hatchway at the top of the steps. He smiled and lowered his head slightly, acknowledging Hamsun's salute. "Why, of course. I'll send ahead to let my people know there is another guest. But now, if you would like to come through, I have arranged for three maids to tend to you while you're here. I'm sure you'd welcome the chance to freshen up and prepare yourself before we set off again." Then, before she could answer, he added. "Besides, it will give Captain Hamsun time to change his uniform and secure his ship."

She lowered her head slightly, answering him with a silent smile, then took his hand again, letting him lead her through the ranks of the honour guard and up the broad ramp towards the reception area.

"If there's anything you'd like to see while you're here," he offered, as they approached the double doors of the main spaceport building. "A visit to the site of the first settlement, for instance. You have only to say and I shall arrange things. It would take half a day, a day at most."

She smiled, slowing as a helmeted guard turned and pressed a control pad on the wall beside him, opening the big double doors. "I would enjoy that," she said, stepping through into the spacious air-lock. "Providing we've time, of course."

Schenck bowed, watching the outer door close behind her, conscious of being alone with her for that brief moment. Then, as the inner doors hissed open, he put out a hand, ushering her through. "Good. I'll have my secretary arrange it." He laughed, beginning to enjoy her company. "It'll give me an excuse to take a break from my official duties."

As they stepped out into the big reception hall, four soldiers closed up behind them, guarding the doorway. Schenck smiled at them, pleased to see that Captain Brookes was taking things seriously. He looked about him, noting that the place had been cleared, as he'd ordered. Two officers were standing by the customs counter, their backs to him, otherwise the place was empty. He started towards them.

"Where *are* those maids . . . ?"

There was the sound of a scuffle behind him, a cry cut short. He turned. Jelka Tolonen was on the floor, two guards pinning her down while a third was binding her wrists.

"What the hell . . . ?"

"Governor Schenck!"

He jerked back round. DeVore was standing there facing him, a stranger at his side. In his left hand he was holding what looked to be some kind of stringed instrument.

"Howard?" he began, surprised to see him there. "What's ha . . . ?"

Schenck dropped to his knees, the uncompleted word a gurgle in his throat, a crossbow bolt projecting from his neck.

Handing the crossbow to Auden, DeVore walked across to where the guards had pulled the young woman up onto her knees. She was gagged, her hands and feet bound fast. One of the guards held her upright, while a second pulled her head back savagely, her long hair twisted tightly in his hand.

DeVore leaned close, looking directly into her face, seeing the light of realisation come into her eyes. He smiled.

"Well, well . . . Jelka Tolonen. It's been a long time, neh? A long, long time . . ."

* * *

Climbing down from the cockpit of the two-man flier, Ebert felt the frigid wind bite into him, despite the heater of his suit. Though it was still day, it was dark. For the last fifty *li* they had flown blind through the storm, following the tracking signal.

The news on the flier's radio had been bad. Governor Schenck was dead, along with most of the ruling Council.

Feng Shou Hao City was in flames, while there were riots in at least eight of the other cities, the great northern city of Hong Hai among them. Hsiang Se City, it was said, was in the hands of the MRA, while the Tzu Li Keng Seng generating complex had shut down. There were no reports of any of the great pipelines being damaged, but it was early yet; the situation was changing hourly, and who knew what would happen when night came?

Tien Men K'ou, at least, was calm. DeVore had seen to that. His guards had crushed the Federation agitators swiftly, taking no prisoners, then had imposed a brutal curfew, effectively closing down the City. DeVore himself had flown north to Kang Kua City with a contingent of five hundred men to secure the planetary capital.

He, meanwhile, had been sent south, a thousand *li*, into the storm, a taciturn pilot his only company.

"Over there," the pilot said, coming close to point away into the murk, his voice, over the helmet radio, muffled, contesting with the roar of the wind.

Ebert nodded then started across, the fine, wind-blown sand buffeting him as he came out of the flier's cover, forcing him to lean into it if he was to make progress. For a moment there was nothing, only the noise, the violent swirl of the storm, a thick blanket surrounding him on every side. He began to think that maybe DeVore had betrayed him – had set him down in the middle of nowhere to freeze to death or die of oxygen starvation – then, just ahead, the storm seemed to lessen, the nothingness take on a darker form. A moment later he was beneath a sloping cliff, the air clearer suddenly, an open space ahead of him, between dark, wind-scoured rocks. There was a movement to his right.

"*Here,*" a voice said inside his helmet. Ebert turned, looking across. A tall, suited figure was waiting between the rocks. There was something strange about him. His pressure suit, with its high-domed helmet, was curiously old-fashioned, like those the first settlers had worn. And the way he stood there . . .

Ebert started towards him. *So these are DeVore's "friends",* he thought, studying the man as he moved closer, wondering if it was indeed a man, or something DeVore had had fashioned in his vats.

The stranger turned, moving in, between the rocks. Ebert followed him. Ten paces back, where the cliff began again, a narrow flight of steps had been cut into the rock, leading down into darkness. Ebert hesitated, then went down, standing behind the stranger as he turned an old-fashioned metallic wheel. There was a click and then the heavy door swung slowly back. They went inside, into a narrow air-lock, lit only by a single overhead lamp. The stranger turned, facing Ebert, his body suddenly very close, his face hidden behind the dark glass of the helmet's visor. His physical presence in that tiny space was strangely powerful, almost overwhelming. It was as if Ebert could smell the maleness of him.

"Forgive me," he said, pushing Ebert firmly but gently against the wall. Then, reaching past him, he swung the door closed and spun the inner wheel, locking the door.

Ebert looked past his companion, noting once again the strangeness of the air-lock's design. The walls were unfaced rock, the twin doors studded metal. Old-fashioned was not the word for it. It was primitive! Why, there was barely enough space for the two of them.

He watched as the stranger turned the wheel to the inner door, noting once again the delicacy of movement in those gloved hands. When he'd pushed him back against the wall, it had felt like the touch of a woman, yet stronger, far stronger than any woman he had known.

As the door eased back he felt the sudden in-rush of air and nodded inwardly. He was beginning to understand. The system was as simple as they could make it. Simple, but effective. There were no electronics to go wrong, therefore no chance of fire or of being trapped. And this far south that mattered, especially in winter.

Beyond the door was a tunnel, hewn, like the air-lock, from the solid rock, lit every ten paces by a small lamp inset in the ceiling. Fifty paces brought them to a second door, studded like the outer doors, a wheel-lock obtruding from its centre. Directly overhead a vent went up into the dark. Ebert looked up, hearing movement. A guard, he thought. It was where he himself would have put a guard anyway.

Beyond the door was a big, low-ceilinged room, broad pillars giving it the appearance of an ancient crypt. Four steps led down. To the right were full-length lockers, to the left, long trestle tables and benches. Surprisingly, the room was empty.

Ebert stepped down, then looked across at his companion, watching, as he unclipped the latches on his helmet then twisted it and lifted it up over his head.

"Welcome to Hellespont, *Shih* Ebert" the man said, turning to face Ebert. "My name is Echewa, Chief Aluko Echewa of the Osu." He smiled, his teeth like polished stones in the blackness of his face. "And yes, I'm real, if that's what you're thinking. But come, we've an hour or more before your prisoner gets here. Let me get you something to eat. I'm sure you're hungry after your flight."

Ebert stared, unable to believe what he was seeing. The black man's nose was broad, almost flat, his mouth large, the lips well-formed. As for his skull, that was shaved and polished, like a piece of carved ivory. Ebert let out his breath. There had been rumours of course. And there were those lines in Kan Jiang's poem, "Into The Dark", that had always haunted him. But to see it.

Echewa laughed. "Well? Are you hungry, man, or not?"

"I'm hungry," Ebert said, removing his helmet and setting it under his arm. "But tell me, Aluko Echewa, just what in the gods' names is this place?"

Echewa had begun to turn away, but at Ebert's words he turned back, then came across, facing Ebert, his shockingly white eyes suddenly intent. "The gods? No. Let me make it clear, *Shih* Ebert. We have only one god here, and that is Mother Sky. Whatever else you say, we'll let it pass, but do not offend our god. You understand me?"

"I understand."

Echewa relaxed, smiled. "Good. Then come. Let us eat. And maybe I'll tell you of the *iyi-uwa* and the *osu* and of how we came to live here under Mother Sky."

CHAPTER · 4

THE PUNISHMENT OF HEAVEN

The storm had abated shortly after nightfall. An hour back, a second craft had come from out of the darkness to the north, a big security cruiser, its hold crammed with supplies for the settlement. Supplies and a single prisoner.

Ebert had stood on the rocks overlooking the entrance to the settlement, Echewa crouched beside him, watching as two guards dragged her from the interior of the craft. He had known it was a she only because Echewa had said it was. But that was all Echewa had known. All he'd wanted to know.

"Why do you work for him?" Ebert had asked.

Echewa had turned and looked up at him, the tinted visor hiding his face. "We *don't* work for him. But he did us a favour once, long ago. This is in settlement of that. A debt of honour."

"But the supplies . . . ?"

Echewa had turned back, watching them unload. "The supplies are not what you think, Hans Ebert. They are paid for fully. It is as I said. A debt of honour. Once paid, we will no longer be beholden to your friend. We shall be free men again."

Free men, those words returned to him now as he squatted, alone on the rocks, looking out across the desert to the north.

It was like an ocean, a great, dark ocean, its edges scattered with the jagged teeth of rocks, thrusting up above the wave-like dunes. The sight of it reminded him of a time when, as a child, he had stood beside his father, back on Chung

Kuo, watching the waves of the great Atlantic break against a rock-strewn beach. At the time it had terrified him and he had clung, screaming, to his father's leg, while his father had roared with laughter and thrown a stone far out into the incoming tide.

Free men . . . Yes, yet when had *he* ever been free? When – in all the twenty-nine years of his life – had he not been beholden to someone? His father. Li Yuan. DeVore. Each one had taken him and used him. And all the while he'd thought his life his own. But it had never been his own. Life had been a great tide, rushing in and overpowering him. All his life he had been too weak, too governed by his own desires, to stand against that tide and shape his own destiny. But finally he understood. Finally he could make that choice: to continue as he was or to become a new man, free of the old patterns of his being.

For some men it was easier. Echewa, for instance. For him the choice had been made at birth, for he was *osu*, an outcast – a black man in a world that did not permit the existence of black men. When the Han had come to Mars, his father's fathers had fled into the desert, knowing there was no place for them in the Cities of the Han. They had become Osu, the lost tribe of Mars, the dwellers in the quiet places. Mother Sky had become their god.

That last he had not understood, for like the poet, Kan Jiang, he found no call within himself for gods. No. If the world made any sense at all, it was not because some god-like being directed it, even a god as amorphous and all-encompassing as Echewa's, but because it had beauty and order and laws unrelated to men and their notion of gods. *Men* . . . some days he felt that Mankind was merely a distraction from the real business of the universe, a petty sideshow.

It was like what was happening just now to Mars. What was that but a brief convulsion, a sickening in the body politic? *Let the Cities burn*, he thought. *Let it all pass.* It made no difference. Here, amidst this bitter cold, was true reality. Here, unexpectedly, was a beauty that took his breath. He leaned back, looking up at the star-dusted darkness. Earlier, through Echewa's glasses, he had focused on the distant horizon, watching as Phobos sped from west to east while, several degrees higher in the sky, tiny Deimos slowly drifted east. Beyond both, its sunlit face like a bright hole burning in the darkness of the sky, sat the planet of his birth, Chung Kuo.

Chung Kuo. That too would pass. And still the stars would blaze in the darkness.

He breathed shallowly, conscious suddenly of the hum of the heater in his pressure suit as it struggled to combat the cold. It was minus one hundred and eighteen degrees and falling. In two hours it would be dawn, the coldest time of day on Mars.

"*Shih* Ebert . . ."

He turned, looking up at the figure that had appeared, as if from the air, on the rocks behind him. It was Echewa.

"You must come in now. It is dangerous to be out here so long. Besides, you have come a long way. You must rest."

Ebert stood, feeling a tiredness, a stiffness in his limbs. "The night is beautiful, neh?" he said, turning slowly, taking in the vast panorama of the stars.

Echewa looked up, nodding. "The night is our mother. She comforts us. She tells us who we are."

"And the day?" he asked, curious. "Is the day your father, Aluko Echewa?"

Echewa shook his head. "I thought you understood, Hans Ebert. We have no father. Mother sky is all. We live, we die beneath her. She sees all. Even the darkness deep within us."

Ebert stood there a moment, considering, then shook himself. "There's one thing I don't understand, Aluko, and that's why I'm here at all. The prisoner. She's perfectly safe here. If she ran, where would she run to? So why am I needed?"

Echewa shrugged. "Perhaps it is your fate."

"My *fate*?" Ebert laughed. "What has fate to do with the

schemes of our friend, DeVore? No, there's a reason for this, don't you think? Some dirty work involved that he doesn't want his own hands stained with."

He stared at the Osu, expecting an answer, but Echewa was silent.

"Well, whatever . . . But I tell you this, Aluko Echewa, I am no friend to Howard DeVore. Unlike you, I owe the man no debt of honour."

"And yet you serve him. I find that strange."

"It was my nature."

"*Was?*"

Ebert smiled. "Come. Let's go inside, before the heater in my suit gives out."

"And the prisoner? You want to see her yet?"

Ebert shook his head. "No. You were right, Aluko. I need rest."

"And afterwards?"

"Afterwards?" Ebert sighed, then reached out, touching Echewa's shoulder. "Who knows? Maybe then I'll find out why I'm here."

* * *

DeVore sat at Schenck's desk, in Kang Kua City, staring at the blackness of the viewscreen, a stack of reports at his elbow. It was an hour before dawn and the worst of it appeared to be over. The City was quiet now, after the latest spate of executions, and only the two great Western Cities of Tai Huo and Yang P'ing remained in turmoil. The damage was considerable – Feng Shou Hao was a shell, its dome cracked and blackened, its half a million citizens dead, and losses elsewhere were in the tens of thousands – even so, it could have been much worse.

The pipelines were secure, the reservoirs untouched, and while the vast, ten thousand *mou* greenhouses of Tharsis had sustained some damage, it was nothing significant. They would be back working to full capacity in a matter of weeks. Tzu Li Keng Seng generating complex was up and running again, and the main communications channels between the

Cities were open. All in all, things were none too bad. Mars had survived the night.

From his own viewpoint the situation had improved dramatically these past few hours. For a time, during the night, it had seemed as if Mars was about to topple into full-scale civil war. Following on from their success in Hsiang Se, the Martian Radical Alliance had taken Kang Feng City and slaughtered the garrison to a man. With the threat of further incursions, DeVore had been faced with a stark and immediate choice – to fight them or make a deal.

Conscious of the delicacy of the situation, he had drafted in a senior member of the old ruling Council, Daniel Henderson, a long-time advocate of reform, to conduct the negotiations, giving him a free hand. In an hour-long face-to-face session with Wang Tu in Hsiang Se, Henderson had put forward a package of wide-ranging and dramatic reforms. Hostilities would cease immediately. Hsiang Se and Kang Feng would remain in MRA hands until the package of reforms could be fleshed-out and ratified by a new ruling Council: a Council upon which there would be significant MRA representation. In the meantime a statement would be issued publicly, on all channels, announcing the new proposals and calling for all citizens to work peaceably on behalf of the new constitution. Wang Tu had agreed.

DeVore sat back, his hands steepled beneath his chin, thinking things through.

The MRA were jubilant, of course. They had achieved all they had set out to gain, and more. But their joy would be short-lived, for the programme of reforms Henderson had put to them was preposterous, unworkable. Moreover the Seven would never agree to it, and despite what Schenck had thought, it still mattered what the Seven wanted. They were weak, certainly – far weaker than they were, say, twenty years before – but they were still strong enough to take action, especially when a failure to act might precipitate rebellion at home. Besides which, Mars – for all they had done these past few years – was still far too vulnerable to

direct military assault. No. When it came down to it, he would
have to crush the MRA or fight the Seven. And he was not
yet ready to fight the Seven.

For now, however, he would let things be. It would be
some while – weeks, perhaps months – before the Seven
could respond to what had happened here tonight. In the
meantime he would work hard to allay their fears: to pacify
Mars and make it seem compliant to their will. To that end
he had had Rutherford send a message of reassurance to the
Council back on Chung Kuo, pledging Mars' continued loyalty
to the Seven, and advising them just what steps were being
taken behind the scenes to repair the situation. It was far
from certain that the Seven would believe a word of it, yet
if it gave them cause for thought and stayed their hand a
single day it would be worth it.

He smiled. Yes. All in all, it could have been far worse. It
could easily have set him back five, even ten years. As it
was, Schenck's precipitate action had proved to his benefit.
Mars was his now, to do with as he wished. And five years
from now . . .

DeVore stirred himself, beginning to work through the
reports. The first of them confirmed what he had heard
earlier. A number of the vats at HoloGen had been badly
damaged in the fire-fight between his troops and Bates's Federation. Several of the creatures had had to be destroyed. It
was annoying, certainly, yet in the context of the bigger
picture it seemed a small price to pay. Besides, the important
work was being done elsewhere – at the plant in Sinai, half
a *li* beneath the sands – and that had been unaffected by the
troubles.

He screwed the paper up and threw it into the bin beside
him, then reached for the next report. It was from Echewa,
down at Hellespont.

He took a deep breath, angered by the terse and haughty
tone of the communication. Echewa thought too much of
himself, that was clear. As soon as this matter with Ebert
and the girl was done with, he would destroy Echewa and
his people. It wouldn't be difficult. He knew where their bases

were. All it would take was a dozen heavily-armed cruisers and the problem would be solved.

In the meantime there was another problem. The problem of what to do with the Marshal's daughter. Before last night he would have staked a great deal against the Seven taking any kind of action to recover Jelka Tolonen, despite her father's anguish. Once before they had been thrown into a war they did not want because of Tolonen's hasty actions, and it had seemed unlikely that they would risk another such confrontation unless they really had to. Now, however, things had changed. Mars had rebelled. Feng Shou Hao was a shell. The situation was highly sensitive and the least little thing might force the Seven's hand. If it was an excuse they wanted for a war, what better than the kidnap of the Marshal's daughter?

But did they really *want* a war? Wasn't there a way to keep Tolonen's daughter *and* placate the ruling Seven?

His instinct was to keep her. Was to have Henderson and Rutherford bluff it out, feigning ignorance of what had happened down at Tien Men K'ou. The Seven might not believe them, yet for form's sake – and to keep the peace – they might accept their story. And without the backing of the Seven, what could Tolonen do? He might rant and rave, but ultimately he was powerless. It would mean forgoing the pleasure of taunting Tolonen with his loss, but what was that when set against tonight's gains? No. He would keep the girl and do as he'd planned before this evening's events. Hans Ebert and the girl would marry, only quietly, *privately*. In fact he would have Echewa marry them before the day was out. And then he would keep the pair – would move them to a safe place and keep them – ready for the day when he could use them. For the day when Mars was strong enough, secure enough, to take on the Seven and *win*.

He leaned forward, about to dictate his reply to Echewa, when the screen on the far side of the room came alive again. Against a background of stars, a Security officer stood before the camera, his bared head bowed low.

"Major DeVore . . ."

DeVore heard the tone of panic in the man's voice and felt himself go cold. "What is it, Lieutenant Wade?"

"A report has just come in, sir. It seems we have three Security battle-cruisers in our airspace. They entered orbit twenty minutes back."

Impossible, he thought, *the Seven cannot have acted so fast*. Yet even as he framed the thought, he knew what had happened. Tolonen must have sent the craft out weeks ago, to rendezvous with the *Luoyang* and ensure his daughter's safety. It was just the kind of thing the old man would do. But why hadn't he heard about it? Was his network back on Chung Kuo so poor now that something as glaring as this could have evaded their notice?

He took a deep breath, then got up and went round the desk, taking up a position in front of the screen.

"Okay. Send them a signal, greeting them, reassuring them that all is in hand down here. Then get their Commander on line. Have him put through here, direct. I'll get Rutherford in to speak to him. But don't – don't for a single instant – say anything about the fate of Tolonen's daughter, understand me? If they ask, tell them that things have been chaotic down here and that you have no information."

"I understand."

"Good. Now get to it. The next few hours are vital to our cause."

* * *

From where it rested, high up on the wall above her bed, the insect witnessed everything. It saw the hard stone bed on which the prisoner lay, the crude iron chains which secured her to the wall. In the light of a single, flickering flame, it saw her lift her head and look across, her blue eyes moist, her muscles tensed against what was to come.

For a moment there was no sound, simply the movement of a steel door on a well-oiled hinge, a perturbation of the flame. She stared into shadow, her eyes narrowed, trying to make out who or what it was. For a moment her face was set, determined to show no fear, then, with a small, startled movement, her eyes flew open.

"*You* . . ."

It flickered across the darkness then settled, looking down.

Ebert stood in the doorway, looking across at her, his left hand gripping the thick edge of the door as if to steady himself. He seemed shocked, pained almost by what he saw. There was a strange, uncertain movement in his face, and then he moved inside, closing the door quietly behind him.

"Jelka . . ." he said softly, turning to face her again.

"I should have known," she said quietly, a strange coldness in her voice. "When I saw that bastard DeVore at the spaceport, I should have *guessed* that you'd be somewhere close at hand, like some nasty little piece of putrefaction."

He shuddered. "Jelka, I didn't . . ."

"You didn't *what*? Didn't have my aunt and uncle killed? Didn't kill your own father? And what about that child? How could you have done that? Your own child? What kind of animal are you?"

Ebert hung his head, silent.

She lifted her hands angrily as if reaching for him, the chains pulling taut against the rings in the wall behind her.

"You know what? If I were free right now – if I had a knife in my hand and the chance to use it – I'd stick it deep in your guts and twist it hard for what you've done. I'd slit your throat and watch you bleed to death, you know that?"

"I know."

She laughed, scorning him, as if it were he who was chained. "I wish I could say you got what you deserved, but it's not true, is it? I mean, you're still here . . . the stink of you is still here." She shook her head, suddenly pained, remembering what had happened. "Do you realise what you did? All the suffering you caused?"

"I realise."

"*Do you?*" She stared at him a moment, such disgust, such utter loathing in her eyes that he bowed his head once more. "So what now, Hans Ebert? What further excesses, what filth and degradation have you got planned for me? Or am I wrong, is it my soul you're after now?"

He jerked his head up, surprised. For a moment his mouth faltered, and then he spoke again, his voice quiet, hesitant. "You have it wrong, Jelka. I never killed them. Not one of them. Fest, yes. But the others . . ."

She stared at him, contemptuous, destroying him silently, forcing him to lower his eyes again as his voice faltered and fell still.

"Enough," she said, easing back onto her bunk, the chains falling slack. "Do what you have to. But don't think you'll ever touch me. Not the real me. That you can't touch."

"No," he said quietly. "No . . ."

There was silence, an uneasy stillness, and then the door swung open behind Ebert. Echewa came in slowly, looking across at the young woman. He frowned, sensing the tension in the cell, then turned to Ebert.

"You know her?"

"Yes. We were engaged, back on Chung Kuo. It was my father's idea. He wanted to link our families. To consolidate the friendship he had with her father. I wanted it too, I guess. But I did her a great wrong. I can't blame her if she hates me."

Echewa's eyes widened. "Then I'm sorry for you both, Hans Ebert. I've heard from our friend, DeVore. He's sent new instructions. He wants you two married, and he wants it today."

* * *

The machine saw everything.

From a satellite, high above the orbit of tiny Deimos, it watched the three craft swoop low over the great dust plain of Tharsis; saw missiles flash arrow-sleek in the weak sunlight; witnessed the gouts of flame amidst the vivid green, like sudden flowers blooming after desert rainfall, and, afterwards, the dark scars on the land.

From a camera perch above a half-completed reservoir, it

110

watched as a dozen men – masked, their suits blending with the surrounding desert – climbed down into the huge, oval-shaped depression and placed their charges. Like ghosts they vanished, merging into the vastness. A moment later there was the dull thud-thud-thud of detonations, a sharp, cracking sound, the presence of dust hanging in the air.

From its position above the feeding stalls, half a *li* below the sands of Sinai, it heard the troubled lowing of the beast-men and watched as they were herded down the narrow corridors towards the loading bays.

From its vantage point above a viewscreen on the far side of a luxurious office overlooking Kang Kua City, it watched the man who had brought it here to Mars – the architect of these present troubles – as he placed a stone here, a stone there, making his plays in the great game he carried in his head. And recognised that here was the source and seed of its potential destruction.

Not that it was in any danger. Not yet. But for as long as the girl remained captive, so this matter would remain unresolved. The destruction would continue. And at some point it would become endangered. This it knew. This it saw, clearly and unequivocally. Action, it seemed, was called for. But what?

It could arm the satellites – as Schenck had long proposed – and shoot down the three invading craft. But that would bring war, and war would bring further destruction, possibly its own. Best, then, to give them what they wanted. The girl. Jelka Tolonen. And then, perhaps, they'd go away.

It blinked, understanding what it had to do. And on a screen, less than a *li* from where it was, a face appeared: the face of a man who, only an hour before, had been appointed pro-tem Governor of Mars.

It smiled, and then began.

* * *

Port Captain Thomas Brookes bowed low before the screen, then straightened up, hurriedly fastening his tunic.

"Governor Henderson," he said, signalling off-camera for

someone to bring him his boots. "I didn't expect your call so early."

"No. I'm sure you didn't, Captain. But now that you're out of your bed, there's something you can do for me. I understand that you've a ship there out of the Trojans that you've been holding up. The *Tai Feng*, registered in the name of Shen Yeh. Well, I want you to let it go, understand me? And I want it done right now."

Brookes hesitated, realising he was in a difficult position, for while Henderson was his titular superior, Culver had told him that no one was to leave Tien Men K'ou spaceport without his direct instructions. He swallowed, then lowered his head again, deciding to face the matter squarely.

"Forgive me, Excellency, but I am afraid that is simply not possible. I have explicit instructions from *Shih* Culver . . ."

He expected outrage, at best a mild protest; instead, Henderson turned and called to someone off screen. A moment later, Henderson moved back and DeVore's face filled the screen.

"It's okay, Captain Brookes. You can let the *Tai Feng* go. I'll send my written confirmation of that at once."

Brookes bowed smartly. "Sir!"

The screen went blank. Brookes sat, letting out a huge sigh of relief, then put out his foot, letting his orderly pull on his boot. As the man was tugging the other boot on, the printer beneath the screen chimed. Brookes stood, pushing his feet down into the tight-fitting boots, then went across and took the paper from the tray. He studied it a moment, then, nodding to himself, went through into the outer office, calling for his lieutenant.

* * *

"I don't understand," Ikuro said, strapping himself tightly into the take-off couch. "One minute they're saying we have to stay here indefinitely, the next they're letting us go. What happened?"

Kano leaned forward, punching buttons on the panel in front of him, then turned and laughed. "I don't know and I don't care, little brother. All I know is that we'd better get out of here, before they change their minds again. These Martians!" He snorted. "Give me my family any day, neh?"

"It's family that got us into this mess," Tomoko said pointedly, speaking from his seat up front of the craft. "Now is everyone ready?"

"Ready!" called Shukaku from the rear.

"Ready!" called Kano and Ikuro as one, smiling at each other across the cramped cabin.

"Then let's go!"

They entered orbit twenty minutes later and were about to set course for Diomedes when their screens came alive again: a face staring down at them. A face Ikuro recognized at once.

"Shen Li . . . Listen. It's me, Hans Ebert. I need your help . . ."

* * *

"Well? What are you waiting for?"

Hans Ebert turned, looking back at her. She was more beautiful than he remembered. Stronger. More *herself*. He had expected never to see her again, or if he did, to see her on a screen, at a distance, as mortals were said to see the gods.

"It's not right," he said, partly to her, partly to Echewa. "I can't do it."

"There's no choice," Echewa said, touching his arm. "You *have* to do this."

"But she doesn't want me."

"Does that matter?" Echewa stared back at him, his face suddenly intent. "Think it through, Hans. If you don't do this, he'll have you killed."

"And if I were to escape?"

Echewa smiled. "Into the desert? No. Besides, we'd have to stop you. Because if we didn't, he'd blame us. And that might bring us a lot of grief."

Hans turned his head, looking across at Jelka. It was as if

113

she had spent her anger earlier. Now she simply watched him silently, trying to make him out.

"No," he said, determined. "I don't care what he says. I won't do it. It isn't right."

Echewa shrugged. "Okay. I understand. But let me tell you this. If he tells me to chain you up, I'll do it. Not because I want to, but because we gave him our word. You understand me, Hans Ebert? I like you, but I have no choice."

Ebert stared at him, surprised. "What did he do, Aluko Echewa? Save your life? Pull a thorn from your foot?"

Echewa smiled, saddened, it seemed, that he had been forced into this. "He did more than that. He saved us all. Schenck was planning a campaign against us. He wanted to destroy us. But DeVore interceded. He talked Schenck out of it."

"You know this for a certainty?"

"We have friends. Reliable, *honest* friends. It was through them that we learned of it."

Ebert laughed. "And you believe that?"

"Why shouldn't I?"

"Because it's DeVore, that's why. The man's a liar. A devious schemer. A shit. He buys friends by the dozen. That's his style. As for interceding on your behalf, well, maybe he did, but then again, how do you know that Schenck had any such plan?"

"Oh, I *know*." Echewa grinned broadly. "You talk of thorns, Hans Ebert, well, we've been a thorn in Schenck's side for a long time now. But that's not why he wanted to eradicate us. You see, three years back, we took one of his aides captive – a favourite of his. We plucked him from a cruiser and stripped him bare. Down to the bone, if you know what I mean. Then we returned the grinning fellow to Kang Kua. We strung him up on a frame outside the main air-lock and let the wind dance through his bones."

"I see . . ."

"Yes. Schenck was livid. He swore publicly to avenge the man, to bomb our settlements flat and stain the sands black with our blood. But DeVore flew north to speak to him. To plead our case. And it worked. Schenck calmed down. The attack never came." Aluko sighed. "I never understood why he did it, but when the call came, I had to do what he said. It is our way, you see. I consulted the *ndichie*, the elders, but they agreed. To say no was unthinkable."

"Then maybe that's why," Ebert said. "Maybe he knew your ways. Knew that you would have to return the favour. That you wouldn't refuse, whatever the circumstances. He plays long, that man. Thinks far ahead."

"Maybe so," Echewa answered, soberly. "Yet here we are, my friend. I must either marry you to the girl or take you prisoner. Now which is it to be?"

There was a moment's hesitation, a final moment's doubt, and then Ebert lifted his hands, offering them to Echewa. "Do what you must," he said, not looking at the girl, but conscious all the while of her blue eyes watching him. "Chain me up, if you have to. But I'll not marry her. Not unless she wants me to."

* * *

The roar of the wind was like the constant hiss of static from a broken transmitter. From where it was anchored on the rocks above the settlement, the insect looked out into the dust-storm, its powerful lenses trying to make out the shape of the incoming ship.

It had been sending out its signal for more than an hour, directing the *Tai Feng* down from its high orbit and across the wastes of Noachis to Hellespont, but now the ship was here, less than a hundred *ch'i* away, settling slowly, carefully, onto the sands between the rocks.

What was happening in the cell it did not know – nor did it care. It was an eye, a simple window on events. The mind that controlled it lay elsewhere – a thousand *li* across the southern desert. As the ship set down it flashed a brief verification signal, then, following new instructions, it loosened its grip on the rock and launched itself out into the dust-filled air, struggling against the powerful winds, making its way down towards the air-lock, eighty *ch'i* below.

In the shelter of the stairway it waited, watching as the four men came along the path between the rocks and down, facing the door.

"What do we do now?" one of them asked over his suit mike, turning to face the others.

"I guess we knock," another, deeper voice answered.

"And what if we're not welcome?"

"Then we go away. But he said he'd be waiting for us, Tomoko. Besides, he sent the signal, didn't he? He got us here."

"Yes, but what if it's a trap?"

"Why should it be?"

"Why *shouldn't* it be?"

The first one hesitated, then turned and banged a gloved fist against the iron door. He waited, then banged again.

There was movement inside. A moment later the wheel began to spin. The men stepped back, watching it turn, looking to each other, an uncertainty in their faces.

A man stepped out, bigger than any of the four. "Shen Li?"

One of the four – the first to have spoken – stepped forward.

"You only," the big man said, then turned, stepping back inside the air-lock.

"It's okay," the first one – Shen Li – said, looking back at the others. "Go back to the ship. I'll bring Ebert back with me."

They stood their ground, watching him go inside. Only when the wheel had stopped spinning again did they turn away, making their slow way back between the rocks, stopping now and then to look back, wondering if they would see their brother again.

* * *

"It's come," Elechi, the encoder said, twisting in his seat and handing Echewa a printed message.

"That's his code?" Echewa asked, scanning the words quickly.

116

"Sure is," Elechi answered, looking up at his chief. "Why? Do you think they're not genuine?"

Echewa shrugged. "I don't know. It's just that the story the small Han tells is odd. He says they got a message from Ebert – that they actually saw him on their screens while they were in orbit – and that simply cannot be. Ebert's been in that cell all the time. And even if he hadn't, there's no way he could have transmitted such a message. No. Something strange is going on. I want you to try our friend DeVore again."

"But what if the code's been broken? What if they're intercepting our messages out?"

"Then tell him this. Tell him that I won't release Ebert and the girl until I get a satisfactory explanation. Right?"

"Right. I'll get onto it."

"Good." Echewa turned, making his way quickly through the labyrinth of narrow tunnels until he came out in the meeting room again.

They were all there, waiting for him, Ebert, the Han and fifteen of his best men, all suited up and ready to go. Looking at the Han's face he felt close to laughing. The man still hadn't got over that first moment when he had come into the room and seen sixteen black faces staring back at him. Aluko looked down, forcing back the smile, then crossed the room, seating himself next to Ebert, facing him on the bench.

"So what's happening?" Ebert asked, meeting his eyes.

"I'm making checks, that's what."

"You think something's wrong?"

Echewa smiled. "Let's just say I'm being cautious. There's something about your friend's account that doesn't make sense."

"Shen Li? You think he's lying?"

"It's possible, isn't it? I mean, for all you know he may have been a plant. That whole thing in the bar could have been a set-up."

Ebert shook his head. "No. That was real. Bates . . . well, I had to kill him. There was no other way."

"So how do you explain the rest of your friend's account?"

117

Ebert frowned. "What do you mean?"

"He says he saw you, while they were in orbit. He says that your face appeared on their screens. That you called to them to help you, and that they followed your signal here." Echewa laughed. "So what did you do, my friend? Did you conjure up a double of yourself and slip out through the solid rock. And once outside, in the dust and cold, what did your double do then? Did he make himself a transmitter from the wind and point it at the spacecraft? No. Something's wrong, and I'm going to find out what it is before I decide what I'm going to do."

Ebert was looking down, the furrows in his brow much deeper than before. He made to talk, hesitated, then looked up at Aluko again. "It's true. I *did* call out. In my mind. Not to Shen Li. Not to anyone really. But . . ." He sighed. "Well, when you came in and told me that he'd come I . . . I wasn't surprised. I thought, yes, he's answered me. He's come."

Echewa was staring at him, his eyes wide in his jet-black face. All about him the others were watching closely, their dark faces leaning in towards him, listening.

"You *called*?"

Ebert nodded.

There was a buzz of excited talk between the Osu, strange words in a language Ebert had never heard before, and then Echewa stood, raising a hand for silence.

"You are right, brothers. The way is clear. We must help our friend, even if it means leaving here tonight." He turned, looking across at the Han, his eyes narrowing. "But answer me one thing, Shen Li. Is that really your name?"

The small man stared back at Echewa, then shook his head. "No, Chief Echewa, my family name is Ishida, my given name Ikuro. And before you ask me, it is not a Han name. It is Japanese."

Ebert laughed. "Ghosts! I am surrounded by ghosts! Black men and Japanese. Whatever next!"

But Echewa was looking at him intently. "And you, Hans Ebert? Are you so different, then? Ikuro here, and me, and you yourself, we have this much in common, neh? We are *all* dead men . . . in *their* eyes."

* * *

He unfastened the chains, then stood back, watching her rub at the welts on her wrists and ankles.

"Will you come?" he asked.

"Come where?"

He looked down. "I don't know. Away from here, anyway. Away from DeVore."

She was silent a moment, then. "I don't understand you. You had me, back then. Had me in your power. You had only to do what he said. So why didn't you? What stopped you?"

"It wasn't right," he said quietly.

"Not right? When did that ever stop you in the past? I mean, what game is this? What are you trying to do?"

"Nothing."

"Then why don't you look me in the eyes and say that? Why do you skulk there like some . . . *creature*. What has he done to you? Cut your balls off or something?"

He looked up at that, the slightest flare of anger in his eyes. She saw it and laughed.

"Ah . . . So you are in there, after all, Hans Ebert. I was wondering for a while if a shape-changer hadn't taken your body over. Or whether you were some clone made up in one of DeVore's factories."

He stared at her, surprised. "You know of that?"

"It was one of my father's pet theories. He wanted to send Karr here to find out if it was true, but the Seven would never let him. But he was right, wasn't he? This is where he was, all the time. Here, on Mars, directing things like some venomous puppet-master. And you, Hans Ebert . . . what are you if not one of his puppets?"

Ebert shook his head slowly. "Not now. I promise you."

"Promise me?" Her laughter was cold, mocking. "When were your promises worth more than the air in which they were uttered? No. What do the Han say? Ah yes. A snake sheds its skin, but it's still a snake. That's true, neh?"

119

He stared at her, something strange going on behind his eyes, and then he shuddered.

"Okay. So you don't believe me. That's fine. I can live with that. I *deserve* it. But if my promises mean nothing to you, let what I do stand for what I am. Not what I *was*, for I am that man no longer. You see, Jelka Tolonen, I shed not just a skin, but a self when my father died. I didn't kill him, not physically, and yet I *was* responsible."

He took a long breath. "The night he died, he tried to kill me. To choke the life from me. My own father, the man who loved me more than anyone in the world, who cared more for me than for all of the vast commercial empire he had built up. I was blind. I couldn't see that love. Not until it was too late. All I could see was my own greed, my own selfish desires. You saw that. I know you did. I could see it in your eyes, the day of the betrothal, and I . . ."

"*Words*," she said harshly, interrupting him, standing to face him. "What's any of this but words?"

"Yes . . ." He turned, looking away from her. "Will you come, though?"

"Where?"

"Tien Men K'ou? They say your father's fleet has come. They say it's searching for you."

He looked back. She was staring at him now, her eyes half-lidded.

"Are you serious?"

"If that's what you want."

She hesitated, her eyes searching his face, and then she laughed. "What have I got to lose? If you're lying then I'm no worse off. And if you're telling the truth . . ." Again she hesitated, but when she spoke again her voice was quieter, softer than before. "Well . . . let's deal with that as and when it happens, neh?"

* * *

Tien Men K'ou spaceport was on fire. Beyond it, the great dome of the City was in darkness.

"What's happened?" Ikuro asked, leaning across his eldest brother. "It was all right when we left it!"

"Look there," Tomoko said, indicating the far right of the screen. "Those two weren't there when we left. They must be government ships."

"Yes," Jelka said, coming up behind them. "The smaller one is the *Ta Chi*. The big one with the cannons is the *Chang Hsien*. If those two are here then the *Shen Yi* can't be far away."

"You know these craft?" Tomoko said, turning to look up at her, impressed, it seemed, by her knowledge.

"Yes," she said, staring at the two ships thoughtfully. "I've been on the *Chang Hsien* many times." She turned, looking back at Ebert, who was sitting beside Kano in the central cabin. "You were right."

He smiled. "I know."

"Tomoko," she said, not looking away from Ebert, "send out a signal to the *Chang Hsien*. They'll be using microwave frequencies, 32.4 gigahertz, if I remember rightly. Ask for Commander Hassig, or if he's not there, for Captain Gray. Tell them that you've the Marshal's daughter on board and that you want safe passage to land on the south side of the apron. Oh, and tell him that I'm safe, and that I'm being returned, else he might just take it into his mind to shoot you out of the sky."

Tomoko turned, looking past her at Ebert.

Ebert nodded once. "Do as she says."

"Then it's true. You really are going to let me go."

"It appears so."

For the first time she smiled. "Then maybe I did you wrong, Hans Ebert. Maybe you *have* changed."

"Maybe," he answered, his face strangely hard. "And maybe I was wrong. Maybe I ought to have kept you. At least you'd have been my wife. At least I'd have had you."

Her smile slowly faded. "I'd have killed myself."

His voice was the merest whisper. "Maybe. But as it is I've nothing."

Behind her, she could hear Tomoko, sending out the signal

to the *Chang Hsien*, but for once she felt no joy at the prospect of her release, no feeling of relief, for in front of her the man she had loathed these past six, seven years, the man she had feared, in nightmare as in reality, was looking down at the floor, his shoulders bowed, as if in defeat, an unlooked for sadness in his eyes.

"I'll speak out for you," she said, wanting suddenly, unexpectedly, to comfort him. "I'll tell my father what you did for me. He'd speak to Li Yuan for you."

Ebert looked up slowly, meeting her eyes. "No. It would do no good. There can be no returning. But if you must do something, then do this. Say nothing. Or praise these good fellows here for your rescue. As for me, you never saw me, never heard of me. You understand?"

She stared at him silently, seeing him new.

"Evens?" he said, his eyes narrowing.

Jelka took a long breath, then shook her head. "No. My aunt, my uncle's death – those lie between us. I can never forgive you those. As for the damage you did me, I forgive you. And yes, I'll say nothing."

Ebert nodded, satisfied by that. And then, from the speakers above Tomoko, came the answer from the *Chang Hsien*.

* * *

They watched her go down; saw dark-uniformed soldiers bow before her then hurriedly form ranks to either side, escorting her into the great battlecruiser. And then she was gone, the hatch sealed up.

Ebert leaned back from the screen and sighed.

"Where now?" Tomoko asked.

"Here," Ebert said, handing him the piece of paper Echewa had given him earlier.

Tomoko studied the coordinates a moment, then fed them into the computer. A moment later he turned back, frowning. "But there's nothing there. It's desert."

"Just go there," Ebert said, staring at the ship that filled the screen. "I'll worry about that when we get there."

122

An hour later they dropped him, watching as he walked out into the darkness, the desert swallowing him. Yet as they lifted, banking to the right, they saw, in the bright glare of their lights, a dozen men step from a fold in the rocks and form a half-circle about him.

"*Osu* . . ." Ikuro said quietly. "Outcasts."

"Like us," Kano said, punching in their course, then turning to look across at his little brother, his eyes deeply thoughtful

Yes, Ikuro thought, nodding, then strapped himself in. *Like us.*

* * *

"It's done," DeVore said, "finished with."

"Maybe," Rutherford answered. "But maybe you should stay. Maybe now that they've got what they want, they'll go away and leave us in peace."

DeVore laughed scathingly. "You think so? You really think they'll be happy just to leave us alone? No. This is the excuse they've been waiting for – their chance to punish us. Why, if a tenth of it survives, I'll be surprised. They've been waiting fifty years to do this. You think they'll stop now?"

Rutherford stared at him, shocked. "But I thought . . ."

"You thought what? That I *loved* Mars? That this was my home?" He laughed. "Well, fuck Mars. It's a fucking pit, and always will be. It was useful, very useful, but now that's changed. I've taken the only thing worth keeping. I've shipped it out already."

"I don't understand."

DeVore turned away, beginning to clear his desk. "No, but then you never needed to. You too were useful, Andreas. But now . . ." He looked up. "Well, run away, little boy. I don't want your planet. It's a shit-hole. And I don't want to be King of a shit-hole."

Rutherford stared at him, astonished.

"Go!" DeVore said, hefting a gun in his hand then aiming it at his erstwhile ally. "Fuck off, *now*, before I use this thing on you."

"But Howard . . ."

123

The bullet whizzed past him, less than a hand's width from his head, and lodged in the viewscreen behind him, shorting the machine.

"Just go," DeVore said, more quietly than before. "Right now, before I kill you."

Rutherford backed away, then, turning, ran to the door and out. And behind him, echoing down the corridor after him, came DeVore's laugh, like the sound of air escaping from a punctured dome.

CHAPTER · 5

MOTHER SKY

It was night. Ahead, across the silent dunes, the Martian capital of Kang Kua was still ablaze, its great dome cracked and open to the sky. Beyond it the crater wall loomed vast and dark.

From a ledge of rock two *li* to the south, a dozen men looked on, the darkness of their face-plates lit by the flickering flames. They had heard the screams of the dying carried on the thin and frigid air. Through the broad, curving face of the dome they had witnessed the devastation, the slow, suffocating death of Mars's greatest City. Now the dome was dark, fire-blackened, and the trickle of refugees through the main air-lock had ceased. There would be no more survivors.

Ebert looked about him at the silent, watching figures, then turned back, studying the scene, fixing it in mind. In less than thirty hours, two centuries of patient enterprise had been undone. Mars had ripped itself apart in a series of tormented convulsions, like the death throes of an animal driven mad by inner sickness.

As the flames died, they turned away, making their way back to their power sleds. Returning across the darkness of the dunes, there was a brooding silence among them. It was only when they were back inside the settlement, sat about the benches in the meeting room, that they began to talk of what they had seen.

"It is the women and children I feel sorry for," one of them said, his eyes pained. "I can't help thinking how I'd feel if they were mine."

There were nods all round. What they had seen had

sobered them. There had been excited talk beforehand, real joy at the prospect of being free finally from the yoke of the Han. But now they understood the price of that freedom – the cost in deaths and human suffering.

One of the younger men looked up, his dark face shining in the lamplight. "It was awful. I felt so helpless. I wanted to stop it, but what could I do? What could any of us do?"

"We can remember," one of the eldest, his hair grey, answered him. "And we can make sure our children remember."

On the journey north to Kang Kua, Ebert had heard from his companion just how badly the Osu had suffered; how they had been hunted and persecuted, year after year, until their anger had turned to bitterness, their bitterness to resignation. Mother Sky deliver us, they prayed. But now things would be different. There would be new tales to tell the unborn children of the Osu when their time came beneath Mother Sky.

They had fallen into silence. Their heads were lowered, their eyes downcast. Then, as if drawing it up from some well of sadness deep within him, the old man began to sing.

For a moment the old man sang alone, then, slowly, one after another of them joined their voices, until the room resounded to the haunting sadness of the refrain. The men were weeping now, singing and weeping, their faces lifted up, as if they sang for Mother Sky herself.

Ebert, watching, shivered violently, then clenched his fists against the sudden, overwhelming sense of loss he felt, against the vast and echoing emptiness inside him. And yet his grief, his personal suffering, was as nothing beside that of the Osu.

Long ago, so Echewa had told him, the Osu had lived in Africa. For ten thousand years their lives had been peaceful, orderly. They had been as one with the earth and the sky. And then the *Hung Mao* – the White Man – had come, raiding their coastlines and taking them away in great ships, a thousand at a time – men, women and children, chained like animals and kept in dreadful, insanitary conditions. They had been taken to a new land – America – and forced to work the land as slaves. Centuries later, in the time of the tyrant Tsao Ch'un, their kind had been eradicated from Chung Kuo. Yet some had survived, here on Mars. They had come here as free men, along with others – white men and yellow men, men of all creeds and many nations – who had first settled this harsh planet. But when Tsao Ch'un's soldiers came there was no place for them in the Cities, and so they came out here, into the wild, beneath the great blackness. Mother Sky, they called it, seeing in its face the dark reflection of their own. Mother Sky . . .

He looked from face to face, surprised by the tears that streaked each face, astonished to find no masks, no walls or barriers to these men. You could see what they were at a glance. And with that realisation came a strange and urgent need to be connected – to be *bonded* somehow – to these Osu. To be like them seemed suddenly not merely desirable but essential. He saw how they looked to each other, like brothers, the connections between them welded tight by adversity, and shuddered inwardly. He had been alone. All his life he had been alone. But now he was awake, alive – maybe for the first time in his life free of all masks, all encumbrances of birth – and what was he to do with that?

As the song faded he looked down, trembling, afraid almost to look at them in case, by the slightest word or gesture, they might reject him. For to be cast out by these Osu – these outcasts – would indeed be hell.

"Hans Ebert . . ."

He looked up. Aluko Echewa was standing there in the doorway across from him, one hand out, summoning him. Ebert looked about him, seeing how they were watching him, curious to see how he would act.

"What is it?" he asked quietly.

"The ships have gone," Echewa answered, his face expressionless. "The pipelines are smashed, the Cities all burned or broken. Their dreams of Mars are dead, my friend. It is time for our dream to begin."

Ebert hesitated, then stood and went across, conscious of

their eyes upon him. As Echewa turned away, he followed, down a long, sloping corridor, uncertain what was to befall him. To his right, small galley kitchens and storerooms had been cut into the unfaced rock. Further down, he passed family dormitories where black-faced women sat silently on their bunks, their children surrounding them, watching as he passed. At the bottom the corridor turned abruptly to the right. A suited guard waited there, the inner door to the air-lock held open.

He went inside, standing beside Echewa as he closed the door and spun the wheel. Once before he had stood thus, not knowing what awaited him. Then it had been a race of black men and a woman he had loved and lost. And now?

He met Echewa's eyes, surprised to find the black man watching him.

"You must not expect too much," Echewa said.

Too much? He watched the Osu turn and spin the wheel, wondering what he meant by that, then caught his breath as the door swung back and he saw what lay beyond.

He stepped out into a circular hollow in the rock, thirty paces in circumference. The hollow was surrounded by pale, irregular white stone to a height of ten or twelve *ch'i*. Beneath his feet lay a fine red dust. But his eyes were drawn upwards, up towards the great dark circle of the sky. Above him the stars burned down, Chung Kuo a brilliant point of whiteness in their midst, a Cyclops' eye, staring him out. He turned and looked about him, astonished. It was a dome, a miniature dome.

"This is the place," Echewa said. "Wait and he will come."

Ebert turned, looking back at him. "Wait?"

But Echewa simply backed away, pulling the door closed behind him, leaving Ebert to the silence and the burning sky. Ebert took two steps towards the centre of the hollow, and then stopped, the hairs rising along his spine and at the back of his neck. Across from him, no more than ten *ch'i* from where he stood, an old man – a grey-bearded Han – was sitting on a rock, watching him. He was partly in shadow, his robes loose about him. What looked like a flat black case lay in his lap.

And yet the hollow had been empty . . .

"Welcome, Hans Ebert. Are you more at peace with yourself now?"

Ebert moved closer, until he stood only a body's length from the old man. For a moment he had suspected that it was a hologram of some kind, projected from above, but from close up it was clear that the man was real. The old man's eyes were lucid, his expression calm. There was an air of great serenity about him.

"Who are you?"

The old man smiled, showing a perfect set of yellowed teeth. "I am Master Tuan. A friend, let us say. Now please, be seated. It is hard to talk to another man when you must crane your neck to see his face, neh?"

"Forgive me . . ." Hans sat, folding his legs beneath him. The old Han watched, satisfied, then leaned slightly towards him.

"Did it cost you much to give away that which you wanted most?"

Ebert narrowed his eyes. "The girl, you mean?"

"Is that what I mean?"

Ebert considered a moment, then nodded. What else was there? All else – all worldly things – meant nothing to him now, only Jelka's good opinion. That and the friendship of the Osu.

"Was it hard?"

Ebert looked down. "Yes," he admitted. "Harder than I'd ever imagined. There was a moment – the briefest moment – when I thought of keeping her, but . . ." He looked up, meeting the old Han's gaze. "I could not have lived with myself. You understand?"

The old Han's face did not change. There was the vaguest hint of a smile – of irony? of understanding? – on his lips, and the eyes, staring back into his own, seemed deep and warm and wise beyond all years.

"I have been watching you for a long time now, Hans

Ebert. I have seen the path you have taken. To some it might seem that you have fallen far, and yet these eyes have seen you climb from out of the darkness. Then again, some might say that you have come a long way, Tsou Tsai Hei, but the Way is long and you have taken but the first step on that road."

Ebert leaned forward. "Forgive me, Master Tuan, but why did you call me that?"

"*Tsou Tsai Hei*?" The old Han laughed. "Forgive *me*, my young friend, but I thought you knew your Mandarin. Is it so hard to grasp?"

Tsou Tsai Hei. *The walker in the darkness.*

"No," Ebert answered, then hesitated, uncertain. He understood the words, but their meaning?

Master Tuan lifted a hand. "No matter. As Hsu Yu said, name is only the guest of reality. It is what lies behind the name that matters, neh? I mean, where *is* the darkness? Where is it to be found? In the hearts of men? In the pupil of the eye? In shadows and the sunless depths of night? We say of a man that his heart is dark, and yet without the darkness, where is the light? Without evil, where the good? You have understanding, Tsou Tsai Hei. *You have been there*. All your young life you have been a man of action. Now, as your middle years begin, you must adopt a different course. You must embrace *wuwei*, *in*action. You must seek the *te*, the true virtue, that the Way provides."

He leaned forward slightly. "You are strong. Strong enough, I note, to kill a man with your bare hands. And yet what is true strength? Is it manifested in the exercise of power over others? Is *that* true strength? Or is true strength the exercise of some inner restraint? Is it a working *against* desire? This you must learn, Tsou Tsai Hei. This and much more."

"And the Osu? What is their role in this?"

The old Han laughed. "Am I to tell you *everything*? No, Tsou Tsai Hei, that is for you to learn. Study them. Be as them. The truth will follow. You are to stay here, to finish the work that time has begun in you. To wait here, among these hidden works of darkness. Until the call comes."

"The call?"

The old man smiled. "Be patient. Work hard. The Way is difficult, wherever one is. Yet here you might find yourself. And that is the first step, neh? No more masks, Hans Ebert. No more masks."

The old Han looked down, then lifted the case, offering it to Ebert. "It will take a while, but you will learn patience. This will help you in that task."

"What is it?"

"Words. Images. A friend when you need a friend. An eye where you need an eye."

Ebert leaned in, wanting to query what he meant, but the old man raised his hand once more.

"I am afraid our conversation is over. You must go now. Look, your people are awaiting you."

Ebert turned. The air-lock was open. In the opening stood two of the Osu, Echewa and the old man who had begun the song. He turned back, meaning to say one final thing, but Master Tuan was gone.

He whirled about, expecting some trick, but there was no sign of the old man within the dome, and there was no way out, unless a man could walk through walls. That thought made him turn and look back at Echewa, recalling what he had said that time, about walking through solid rock.

"Was that real, Aluko?"

Echewa pointed to the case. "He gave you that?"

Ebert nodded.

"Then it was real."

Ebert looked up, conscious suddenly of the vastness of the sky above him. Dark it was, and endless. Dark beyond the possibility of any human eye penetrating it. And yet what *was* that darkness? In what way were he and it related? Ebert shuddered. Thus far he had lived his life in the glare of artificial light, with walls on all sides, a floor below and a ceiling overhead. Now he must learn to live differently – to live outside, beneath that vast and overwhelming darkness.

131

Ebert paused, feeling a stillness settle deep within as he recalled Echewa's words.

The night is our mother. She comforts us. She tells us who we are. Mother sky is all. We live, we die beneath her. She sees all. Even the darkness deep within us.

So it was. So it would be from henceforth. Yes. It was time to refashion himself, to *be* the walker in the darkness.

No more masks, he thought, echoing the old Han's words. Then, with a small bow to the space where Master Tuan had sat, he turned and went across. It was time to be.

PART 2 – SPRING 2212:

UPON A WHEEL OF FIRE

———— • ————

"The Master said, 'Cunning words, an ingratiating
face and utter servility, these things Tso-ch'iu
Ming found shameful. I, too, find them shameful.
To be friendly towards someone while concealing
one's hostility, this Tso-ch'iu Ming found shameful. I, too, find it shameful." – Confucius, *The
Analects*, Book V, 25

You do me wrong to take me out o' th' grave.
Thou art a soul in bliss; but I am bound
Upon a wheel of fire, that mine own tears
Do scald like molten lead.

> – William Shakespeare, *King Lear*, Act IV,
> Scene vii

CHAPTER · 6

THE THOUSAND EYES

Pale light lay like a glaze on the lacquered surface of the mask, making its darkness shine. The smoothly-rounded dome was high, majestic almost, the features severe, magisterial. Through narrow slits of purest black, the liquid glint of eyes – dark-pupilled and intense – could be seen. Eyes which watched coldly as, at the far end of the huge, obsidian-topped table, the old man bowed low and, glancing fearfully about him, backed away, the chains that bound his hands clinking in the silence. At a signal, the guards escorting him dragged him about and led him from the chamber, their booted footsteps echoing back across the tiled hall.

A door slammed shut. In the silence that followed, six men, masked and cloaked, the dignity of their bearing revealing their high status, turned slightly in their seats about the table, looking towards the First Dragon, who sat, unnaturally still, his gloved hands interlinked.

It was a chill, dark chamber, overlooked on three sides by a high balcony. From there, and in the shadows beyond the seated men, others stood in attendance, waiting upon what the First Dragon would decide.

They had met to discuss the grave situation facing them and to decide upon which course to follow. Two days back the Council of Seven had agreed to cut the funding to the Ministry and to curtail its activities. Taken alone that was a serious matter, but in the context of all else that was happening, it was a severe blow. Moreover what the old man had just told them made it imperative that they took action. But what? What measures could they take and yet remain bonded in loyalty to their Lords and Masters, the Seven?

The mask leaned closer, as if about to utter some secret – some whispered, conspiratorial thing – but the voice that issued from the mask emerged strong and clear: the voice of utter certainty.

"As for the main matter, our course is clear. We must speak with our Masters and convince them that the path they have chosen is . . . *inadvisable*. That to follow it would lead only to disaster. Second, we must spell out our alternative strategy – a strategy designed to deal with the Seven Ills of our modern age."

The Seven Ills . . . There was nodding from all parts of the great, shadowy hall. Once there had been the single "Great Illness" of false history – an illness their Ministry had been set up to eradicate – but in the last decade all manner of ancient sicknesses had risen from the depths. Religious resurgence, terrorist insurrection and Triad infiltration of the levels – these were the Three Natural Ills and resulted from the great sin of neglected responsibility. Added to them was the new power of the House at Weimar, the changes to the Edict, the declining power of the Seven and, last but not least, the corrupting effect of the Aristotle File. These were the Four Political Ills and resulted directly from the policy of the current Seven. Caught between these varied Ills was the Ministry, the "Thousand Eyes", of which the First Dragon was the embodiment.

"I will go personally," he said, sitting upright, his presence rock-like in the tall-backed chair, "to present them with our proposals and to impress upon them the urgency of the situation."

"And if they do not listen, *I Lung*?"

The First Dragon turned slightly, meeting the eyes of the Minister who had addressed him, then looked about him at the others seated round the table.

"Then so be it. Our role was defined a hundred and fifty years ago, in Tsao Ch'un's time, when Chung Kuo was first forged from the chaos of the thousand nations. To us was entrusted the task of keeping Chung Kuo strong, its levels unpolluted. To us was given the power of life and death over those who strayed from the Great Path. It would be hard for us to neglect our historical duty and bow meekly before the Seven Ills, yet if the Seven refuse to listen, if they refuse to accept what must be done to safeguard Chung Kuo from those forces which threaten to tear it apart, then we must do as they say. It is not for us to determine policy, merely to carry it out."

In the stillness that followed there was a tension that was almost palpable.

"And the other matter, *I Lung*? The old man?"

The First Dragon turned, facing the new speaker, directly to his right.

"I knew Yin Shu. Many of us here did. He was a good servant, a trusted man who had attained high office in the Ministry. It saddens me greatly to find him a victim of such corrupting influences. And yet it illuminates the problem, neh? When such a man can be swayed by these ideas, then what chance has old hundred names? No, if anything it confirms my worst fears. We must search out this new disease and uproot it, before the garden is choked with such weeds."

The First Dragon looked about him, raising his voice so that all could hear him clearly.

"True History, that's what Yin Shu called this new movement. You heard it for yourselves. True History . . ." He shook his head slowly then spread his gloved hands before him on the obsidian table. "Well, we all know what that is, neh? A lie. An attempt to undermine all that we believe in and live for. But they will not succeed. We will not let them succeed. From this moment on I pledge to wage an unending war against those who adhere to the doctrine of True History, to crush them without mercy, whoever they might be and at whatever height we find them. To do otherwise would be to betray the sacred purpose of our Ministry."

There was a deep murmur of assent.

"Good. Then we are agreed, *ch'un tzu*?"

All about the table the masked heads nodded sternly. Satisfied, the First Dragon stood and raised a hand, dismissing the shadowy figures on the balconies and between the pillars. The meeting was over.

* * *

Afterwards, in a smaller, brighter room just off the great hall, they met again, the doors locked and guarded, all masks discarded. On the far wall, beyond a massive desk, hung a large map of Chung Kuo, the seven Cities marked in pale gold, a thousand black-headed pins indicating the position of the Ministry's field operatives – their "thousand eyes" among the masses. Beneath this map now stood the First Dragon, his broad Han face shining waxily as he looked about him at his fellow Ministers.

"You have prepared the list, brother Fan?" he asked, meeting his fifth brother's eyes.

"I have done as you asked," the Minister for West Asia replied, handing his eldest brother the handwritten list.

"Good." The First Dragon scanned the list with interest, then looked up again. "This is all of them?"

Fan nodded, looking about him at the knowing faces of the other Dragons. "You want me to act on all of those names?"

"At once. Then see if you can arrange a meeting with An Sheng. I understand the great man is restless, that he has been heard to speak – in private, naturally – of taking matters into his own hands."

"That is so, brother. And there are others among the Minor Families who feel the same. Would you meet with them all?"

The First Dragon shook his head fastidiously. "No. An Sheng is the key. If he commits himself, the rest will follow. But in the company of his peers he might feel . . . *constrained.*"

Fan's smile broadened, understanding.

"Good. Then go at once. See to these names. In the mean-

138

time I shall contact Tsu Ma and beg audience. It is time the Seven understood what depth of feeling they have unleashed."

* * *

Shang Mu waited in the corridor beside the pillar, his head bowed low, as the six Dragons came from the room. Then, at a signal from the Chief Steward, he went inside, guards pulling the huge doors closed behind him.

"Excellency," he said, bowing low.

The First Dragon stood at the far end of the chamber, in front of a massive desk that, in its dark solidity, was reminiscent of a funerary slab. To his right stood a small, bearded Han with severe features and prematurely grey hair. The bright orange and mauve of his silks were a stark contrast to the severe black of the First Dragon's formal attire. Shang Mu knew him well. His name was Hsia and he was a *Wu*, the First Dragon's personal diviner. Seeing him there gave Shang Mu pause for thought. If Hsia was here, the matter was a serious one.

"Shang Mu," the First Dragon said, summoning him with his left hand, leaving the hand extended for Shang to kneel and kiss the ring.

Shang straightened up, but kept his eyes averted. "You summoned me, *I Lung*?"

The First Dragon hesitated a moment, then, turning away, began to speak.

"Yin Shu was a good man. A trusted servant. Only a week ago I would have said that no more loyal man existed in the Ministry. But appearances can be deceptive, neh? It seems that True History is like a disease that hollows a man long before its mark is seen on the flesh. One cannot tell until it is far too late."

Shang Mu lowered his head an inch or two, his stomach tight with fear. Had someone accused him? Was that what this was about? He felt the urge to ask, but checked himself, knowing that to interrupt the First Dragon would only incur the great man's anger.

The First Dragon looked to the *Wu* and nodded, then came across, standing directly in front of Shang.

"And then there's you, Shang Mu. No *Hung Mao* has ever risen as high as you in the Ministry. No one, it seems, has worked harder to fulfil the Ministry's sacred cause. And yet I look at you now and I wonder to myself whether I can trust you. Whether you too might not have been infected with the same disease. You knew Yin Shu, neh? He was a good friend of yours?"

Shang Mu swallowed. "That is so, Excellency."

"And you suspected nothing?"

"Nothing, Excellency. To the end he seemed a good man, a trusted friend."

The First Dragon nodded, then, unexpectedly, he placed his hand gently on Shang's arm. "Fear not, Shang Mu. I am not accusing you. Yet you must understand my caution. What I have to say . . ."

He moved away slightly, then lifted a finger, summoning Shang Mu to come with him across to the great desk.

The *Wu* had laid a cloth upon the dark surface; a faded, ancient cloth of white silk. At the centre of the square of cloth was drawn a circle an arm's length in diameter. Within the circle, at the eight points of the compass, were painted the eight trigrams of Heaven, Wind, Water, The Mountain, Earth, Thunder, Fire and The Lake. Outside the circle the trigrams were repeated, their arrangement fitting the "Sequence of Earlier Heaven", Heaven to Fire, Wind to Earth and so forth. Close by lay the ancient oracle itself, unopened as yet, its plain black cover embossed with the great symbol of the Tao.

Shang Mu watched as the *Wu* made his preparations, lighting tapers to the north and south, to east and west, rocking backwards and forwards all the time and mumbling to himself, as if in a state of trance. On the desk lay the folded piece of paper on which was written the question the First Dragon wished to ask the oracle. Shang glanced at it, then looked up at the First Dragon's face, seeing at once how important this was for him.

"We are ready," the *Wu* said, turning to face them across the desk. In his right hand he held the fifty yarrow stalks. "If you would read the question, Excellency."

The First Dragon leaned across and took the paper. Unfolding it, he cleared his throat, then read.

"As the darkness closes in, should we give torches to the masses, or should the thousand eyes burn brighter?"

Shang looked across. The *Wu* was smiling. He leaned forward, letting the stalks trickle onto the table. Then, with a quick movement of his right hand, he divided them into two and then again, so that three groups of stalks lay on the table – the three lines of the first trigram. Satisfied, he gathered them up again and repeated the process.

Time and again he let the stalks fall gently from his hand, then divided them up. Time and again he stared at the resultant trigrams, as if fixing them in mind. Finally, he pushed them to one side and looked up, meeting the First Dragon's eyes.

"The upper trigram is *Ch'ien*, Heaven, the lower is *K'an*, Water. The hexagram is *Sung*, Conflict."

The First Dragon stared at him, almost in disbelief, then spoke, his voice a whisper. "*Sung* . . . Are you sure?"

The *Wu* nodded, then, taking up the great book, turned to the relevant page and read.

> "Conflict. You are sincere
> And are being obstructed.
> A cautious halt half-way brings good fortune.
> Going through to the end brings misfortune.
> It furthers one to see the great man.
> It does not further one to cross the great water."

The First Dragon looked away, clearly agitated. "It is as I feared. When I first called you, *Wu* Hsia, I said to myself, if it is *Sung* then I shall know. It will be 'Conflict'. And yet does the oracle not say that such conflict cannot be engaged in successfully? Does it not say that, though our cause is right, though our minds are clear and strong, to carry our purpose through can bring only further ill?" He shook his head, pained by the answer he had received. "If it is so, then how can I act? How can I take the first step knowing the abyss that lies before me?"

The *Wu* was looking down, fingering his beard. "It does not have to be so, my Lord. As the oracle says, contention may be lucky when balanced and correct. Seek balance in your actions and all will be well."

The First Dragon stared at the *Wu* a moment, then, with an irritable little gesture, waved him away. "Leave me now, Hsia. I must talk to my Junior Minister."

"Excellency."

Bowing, leaving his things where they lay, the *Wu* backed out of the room. When he was gone, the First Dragon turned, facing Shang Mu again.

"Do you understand what is happening, Shang Mu?"

Shang hesitated, then ventured an answer. "Has it to do with your meeting with Tsu Ma?"

"It is related."

"Related, Excellency?"

"As the shadow to the sun. You see, Shang Mu, I expect nothing from my meeting with Tsu Ma. No concessions, no new funding, not even the courtesy of an explanation. And yet the meeting is essential. Without it, nothing is clarified. Without it the oracle means nothing."

"I don't understand you, Excellency. If Tsu Ma concedes nothing, then what will be clarified?"

"There is to be a new directive. A brand new strategy to deal with the Seven Ills."

Shang Mu stared at his Master. "But just now, in the great chamber, you said we would do as the Seven commanded. That we would carry out their policy, not determine our own."

The First Dragon smiled tightly. "That is true. But what was said out there was said for the Seven's spies in our midst, it did not reflect the wishes of the Inner Council."

"I see."

"Good." The First Dragon paused, looking at him strangely, then went around his desk and sat. "You must understand, Shang Mu. What is said in public and what is done privately must diverge from henceforth. It is unfortunate but necessary. We cannot just sit back and let the Seven steer us onto the rocks. We must take things into our own hands, for the good of all. This is not disloyalty, you must be clear on that, Shang Mu. What will be done will be done not for personal gain, nor to extend the power of this Ministry, but for the long-term good of Chung Kuo." He paused, his voice taking on a solemn air. "We have looked at this clearly and are agreed on it. The Mandate has been broken. We must act now or see the world we've built crack apart."

The Mandate has been broken . . . Shang Mu felt a great wave of shock wash over him at the words. Yet wasn't it so? Weren't the Seven Ills evidence enough of the Seven's failure to control events? No. The First Dragon was right. It was time to act, independently of the Seven if necessary. He had known it for some while, but it had taken the First Dragon's words to make him realise it.

Shang Mu bowed low. "I will do whatever is asked of me, *I Lung*."

"Good. Then listen closely. The matter of funding is a pretext. It is a century or more since we depended on the Seven for our funding. But that is not to say that funding is unimportant. Over the next few months we must make strenuous efforts to obtain new funding. Arranging that will be part of your new task, Shang Mu."

"But where will I find such funding, Excellency?"

The First Dragon reached into a drawer beside him and took out a slender file, handing it across. "In there you will find a list of all those who, over the past few years, have shown, by word or deed, opposition to the Seven's actions. Normally, as you know, we would have taken action – in concert with Security – to discredit or destroy such opposition, but it was decided, at a secret meeting some three years ago, to refrain from such action for a time in the case of those whose power or influence might, at some future date, prove useful." He smiled. "That time is now. We must harness such opposition and direct it . . . create an alliance of like-minded people to fight this debilitating sickness of liberalism."

He leaned towards his Junior Minister, his face suddenly stern, implacable. "Understand me well, Shang Mu. This is no time for half measures. We must grasp the nettle or go under. Security are no longer the force they were. They are corrupt and lazy, rotten to the core, their intelligence gathering poor, their generals weak and indolent. It is left to us alone to carry the torch, to keep alight the bright ideals of our forefathers. Too many compromises have been made. Too many deals. It is time to tear up all paper tigers, to purge the levels and enforce a rigid discipline on this great society of ours. The Seven will not do that. They lack the will. Only we can do it, Shang Mu. Only the Thousand Eyes."

Shang bowed his head, stirred by his Master's words. "I understand, Excellency, and am willing to do all you ask of me and more, but what of the Seven? Surely they will expect us to react to their decision? And our agents – how are we to convince them of the necessity of the new directive?"

"Good points, Shang Mu, but we have considered everything. As far as the Seven are concerned, we shall make great show of our outrage at their decision. I shall make much of contacting Ministers and other high officials of influence to press our case not merely for a return to old levels of funding and staffing but for an increased share of resources. To their eyes it will look as if I am fighting my corner hard, even to the point of resignation. Seeing that, their suspicions will be blunted. They will think they have dealt with me. But the real work of opposition will go on elsewhere, in secret, where their prying eyes cannot see. That is where you come in, Shang Mu. You and the internal network you have built so carefully these past thirty years."

Shang bowed, conscious of the praise in his superior's eyes.

"I have thought long and hard about this, Shang Mu, and have decided that one man alone can organise all this; only one man has the skill, the diplomacy, the contacts, to enable us to build our great alliance without a word getting out, and that is you.

"As First Operator you will be responsible for coordinating all aspects of our plan. You will appoint key officials to work under you and come to me with any requests for special funding. As for the agents in the field, they will continue as before. They will act only on specific instructions, received direct from your office. At no point are they to be made aware of the new directive. Only we, the seven Dragons, yourself, and others I shall let you have the names of, know of this. It is our secret. A deadly secret. And a sacred trust. You understand?"

"I understand, *I Lung*."

"Good. Then there is one last thing you must do for me. On the way out my Chief Steward will hand you a file. In the file is a handwritten report. I want you to read it, tonight, and then come to me first thing tomorrow morning, at sixth bell, here in this office."

Shang went to nod, then spoke instead. "And might I ask what your Excellency requires of me?"

"Exactly what I said. I want you to read it. Nothing more. And remember, there is no turning back from this. If any one of us fails we are all dead men. And dead men cannot help Chung Kuo, can they?"

Shang Mu met his Master's eyes solemnly. "No, *I Lung*."

"Then go. There is much to do."

* * *

The young woman stood at the entrance to Hui Tsung Street, her sketchboard held against her chest, looking across at the crowd gathered at the feet of the *hua pen*. The storyteller was sitting cross-legged on a low platform, a ragged group of children scattered about him. Further back, small groups of old men and idlers looked on, while at a nearby guardpost three young, fresh-faced officers leaned idly on the barrier, listening to the tale.

From where she stood Hannah could hear the *hua pen*'s

voice clearly, rising animatedly above the background hub-bub. Most of the *hua pen* she had seen before now had been old men, greybeards, sage-like and somnolent, their delivery slow, almost ritualistic, as if they had told the tale one time too many and were bored with it, but this one was different. For a start he was a relatively young man, in his thirties. Moreover he looked more like an actor in a historical drama than a traditional *hua pen*, his startling orange whiskers and unkempt hair – hair that was barely kept in check by a broad, blood-red headband – emphasising the pop-eyed savagery of his face. In his flowing black cloak he seemed more like an ancient bandit prince than a teller of tales, his arms making huge, exaggerated shapes in the air, his hands every bit as expressive as the words he uttered.

She had heard the story often – it was the famous tale of Wu Song, one of the heroes of the *Shui Hu Chuan*, the "Outlaws of the Marsh", of how he first met the great Song Jiang, the "Timely Rain" as he was known, and of how he had killed the man-eating tiger on Ching Yang Ridge – yet she had never heard it told with such power, such vitality. For a time she found herself caught up in the tale, swept along, as if this were the first time she had heard it, then she reminded herself why she was there and, crouching, balancing the sketchboard on her knee, she began to set it all down, using the finest setting on the stylus. It was a quick, rough sketch – more an impression than an accurate depiction of the scene – yet when she had finished it she nodded to herself. Yes, that was it. That was it exactly. That sense of tense excitement in the crowd – the childlike anticipation of each new, yet familiar twist in the tale – it was there in every line, every shadow of her sketch. She pressed to save and store, then rested there, lightly balanced on her haunches, her arms draped loosely across the sketchboard, watching the *hua pen*.

She was a striking-looking young woman, a *Hung Mao*, yet with something distinctly Han about her. Tall and willow-like, her eyes were dark and piercing, while her long, jet-black hair was plaited into a single thick braid that lay against

146

her back. From the simple elegance of her clothes and the strong lines of her face you might have thought that she was in her early twenties, but in actuality she was a mere sixteen years old. As she crouched there, watching the *hua pen*, the eyes of the youngest of the soldiers went to her appreciatively, then looked away, thoughtful. She was not of this level, that was certain, yet what she was doing down here – a young woman, alone and unguarded – was hard to fathom.

The tale was almost ended, the climax of Wu Song's adventure almost reached. The *hua pen* was leaning forward, his voice lowered slightly, almost confidential as he told of the attempted seduction of Wong Sun by his elder brother's wife, Golden Lotus, when, from the far end of the corridor came the sound of gunfire. There was a moment's shocked silence as all heads turned to look, and then all hell broke loose.

Hannah had straightened up at the sound of the shot; now she drew back, into the doorway of a nearby shop, staring open-mouthed as people struggled to get away. Instinctively she held the sketchboard in front of her to protect herself, yet there was no need. It was as if she stood at the centre of a magic circle in which she could not be harmed. All about her people were panicking, fighting each other to get away, yet the stream of frantic humanity flowed about her, as if she were a rock, going either left into the big feed corridor where she had been standing, or right, towards the inter-level stairs. She watched, horrified, as, only ten *ch'i* from where she stood, an old woman went down and was instantly trampled beneath a hundred urgent feet, then cried out as she saw a child stumble and go down on the stairway. But there was nothing she could do. In front of her and to either side the crush of people was too great.

From the far end of the corridor came the sound of sporadic gunfire, carrying over the shouts and screams of the fleeing crowds. Then, as the crowd in front of her began to thin, she glimpsed a tall, well-dressed *Hung Mao* with long, red-gold hair, making his way through. The man turned and, raising his right hand, fired back at his pursuers, then ran on. Beneath his left arm he was carrying a package, some-

147

thing that looked like a small bolt of silk or a box of expensive chocolates. He hesitated, looking about him anxiously, then ran off to the left, choosing one of the small side corridors that led through to the inter-deck lifts. Yet even as he ran she knew he would not get far, for his pursuers – Security guards, a dozen or more in number – were close behind.

For a moment Hannah hesitated, then, impulsively, she started forward, pushing her way through to where she had last seen the man. As she began to run someone called out to her – one of the young soldiers from the guardpost – but she ignored him and ran on. She was certain now that something important was going on: something so important that Security were willing to panic a whole deck – and risk a large number of lives – to get what they wanted.

And what was that?

Instinctively she knew it had to do with the package. In fact the more she thought about it, the more she knew it for a certainty. She had seen the fear in the man's face – the frightened certainty of capture and death – and yet he had gripped the package as if his life depended upon it. And why should that be unless it were more important than his life?

Maybe. But what could be more important to a man than his life?

Hannah stopped and turned. The short corridor behind her was empty. To her right was a locked-up shop, the boarded window covered with paste-on posters. To the left was a communal washroom. She shivered. Instinct told her that she had missed something. Or seen something but not registered it properly. She walked back slowly, looking to either side of her. Nothing. Nothing at all. She turned back, determined to go on, to witness for herself what happened. And then she saw it.

The package was wedged into the vent above the washroom door, one edge jutting out into the corridor. Quickly she went across and, reaching up, tugged at it until it came loose. Then, looking about her, she went inside, ignoring the stench of the place, and found a stall, pulling the door closed behind her.

For a moment she hesitated, staring at the package. It was heavy; heavier than her sketchboard even. Nor had she been mistaken. The silk wrapping alone was beyond the purse of anyone at this level. This wasn't *Yu*, this was First Level. But what did that mean?

She took a long, deep breath. The right thing to do was to go back out and find the Security officer in charge of the operation and hand it to him, but for once doing the right thing seemed entirely inappropriate. She wanted to know what was in the package, and why a man should be willing to die to keep it from them.

She knew how they worked. Security would strip the level bare to get what they wanted – would search each and every one who went, herself included. But this time they would find nothing.

Setting the parcel down, she took the sketchboard from about her neck and, balancing it on top of the seat, began to strip the inner workings from it. She had done it often enough when cleaning the machine, but this time she undertook the task in real earnest. As each piece of the delicate mechanism came loose, she lifted it and let it fall beside the bowl. Then, when she was done, she forced the package into the central space and popped back the sketchboard's screen. She took another long breath, calming herself. The machine looked no different. Only the discarded parts gave the game away, but there was nothing she could do about that. Audacity alone would save her now.

She stood, then turned and went out. At the washroom door she paused, listening. There was shouting still, some distance off, but things seemed much calmer than earlier. Quickly she turned right, making towards the big inter-level lift.

You're mad, she told herself. *There's no reason for this. None at all.* But she was in the grip of a compulsion. She had to get the package out. Suddenly it was as if she were Song Jiang himself, alone in the enemy camp with only his wits, his silver tongue, to get him out.

"*Nu Shi . . .*"

She stopped and slowly turned, facing back down the full length of the corridor. It was the young soldier from the guardpost; the one who had been watching her. He came quickly towards her, then stopped, three paces away, his head bowed.

"Are you all right, *Nu Shi*?"

Her mouth was dry, her hands, where they clutched the sketchboard to her chest, damp. She lowered her eyes and nodded, playing upon the vulnerability the guard clearly expected from her, exaggerating it, knowing instinctively that he was the key.

"It was awful," she said quietly, in an affected little girl voice. "I thought I was going to die."

"It's all right," the guard said, coming a pace closer, trying to reassure her, to comfort her without touching her, knowing – by her clothes, her manner – that she was far above him. "It's all over. They got him. Look, I'll see you to the transit, neh?"

"Thank you." But inside she was burning with curiosity. How had they got him, and where? And was he alive or dead? Maybe they were questioning him right now, torturing him, perhaps, to get the truth from him. And if they were, they would come here soon and find the machine's discarded machine-parts and then . . .

"Come," the young soldier said. "Let's get you out of here."

She let him lead her out into the main feed corridor and along, past milling crowds of curious locals and then down two flights of stairs to the bottom of the deck. There, in the space before the inter-level transit, a barrier had been set up. In front of it a dozen guards formed a line, their riot helmets lowered, their heavy automatics held threateningly at waist-level. Seeing it Hannah's heart began to beat fast.

To one side of the barrier an officer sat behind a desk, questioning an elderly Han. Hannah followed the young soldier across, close behind him as he pushed through the queue, coming out before the desk.

The officer – a young man, in his mid-twenties – looked

up at her quizzically, then turned to the young soldier, clearly angered at being interrupted.

"What is it?"

The young man stiffened slightly, then answered. "The *Nu Shi* here was caught up in things earlier. This isn't her level, sir, and I thought . . ."

"*Quiet!*" The lieutenant turned back, staring up at her. His voice had been hard, dispassionate. Now his eyes studied Hannah's face as if she were something strange and horrible; something he would like to crush beneath his heel. "Your pass, please," he said coldly, his politeness masking what seemed a natural brutality.

Reaching into her jacket, she pulled out her pass and handed it across to the officer, watching as he opened it out and began to read. After a moment he looked up, surprised. Then, getting up, he went across and talked quietly to a second officer who was standing by the lift. The two of them spoke for a moment, a hint of urgency about their whispering, and then they came back. The second man, a Captain, stood to the fore, Hannah's pass between his hands. He looked at it once, checking the holo-photo against her face, then gave a bow.

"Forgive me *Nu Shi* Shang. We had no idea that you were on this deck. If I had known, I would have assigned a squad to protect you." He smiled weakly, then continued. "You must forgive me if I am constrained from advising you exactly what has been happening here – I'm sure you understand – but if you would like an escort home . . . ?"

She looked past him at the lieutenant. The man's eyes no longer met hers. Abashed, he looked to one side, his discomfort evident in the way he stood there.

"Thank you . . ." she glanced at the name tag at his neck, ". . . Captain Johnson. I must admit, I feel rather shaken by events. I think it would be best if I did as you suggested."

"Of course . . ." He bowed his head respectfully, then, "Forgive me, *Nu Shi*, I don't wish to be impertinent, but what exactly *were* you doing at this level? It can be dangerous this far down, even at the best of times. I'd have thought your father . . ."

He hesitated, then changed tack, as if mention of her father disturbed him. Then, suddenly remembering that he still held her pass, he stepped forward, offering it back to her.

"I was sketching," she said, taking the pass from him and slipping it back inside her jacket. "Drawing scenes from life down here. Usually my guard is with me, but he was ill today. I suppose I shouldn't have come. There's usually no trouble. Even so, I'll not make the same mistake again, neh?"

"No . . ." The Captain smiled, then turned, giving instructions to the lieutenant. With the briefest glance, the young officer turned away and went across to speak to his guards.

"You must forgive his abruptness," the Captain said quietly, leaning closer to her, "but he lost two of his men today. This business . . ." He shook his head. "Well, it has been a pleasure meeting you, *Nu Shi* Shang. I hope your drawings are satisfactory. Have you plans to publish them?"

She kept her smile steady. "No. It's only a hobby. Besides, they're not that good."

"Ah . . ." He looked away a moment, then, as if recollecting what he was supposed to be doing, he straightened up and, bowing his head smartly to her, he took a step backward. "Well, if you would forgive me now, there's much to do."

"Did you . . . get him?"

He hesitated, meeting her eyes. "You saw him, then?"

She nodded, remembering the sight of the man running, the way his red-gold hair had flowed out behind him as he fled, the fear in his ashen face.

The Captain sighed. "We got him. I wanted him alive, of course, but he gave us no choice. As I said, we'd already lost two men, with another couple wounded. I couldn't risk losing any more. Strange, though, I'd not have thought him the type."

"The type . . . ?"

"Never mind. Look. You get back now. And next time you want to have adventures, bring a pair of guards, neh?" He smiled. "Oh, and if you speak to your father, please pass on my deepest respect. I shall make sure he receives a copy of my full and final report."

She smiled. "That is most kind, Captain. I'll make certain he knows of your kindness and efficiency."

She turned, looking to the young guard. "And thank you. You were most helpful."

The young soldier blushed and lowered his head. "*Nu Shi* . . ."

Two soldiers escorted her to the lift, standing at a respectful distance as the big transit climbed the levels. And as it rose, she stood there, the sketchboard clutched tightly to her chest, staring blindly at the blank white doors, the image of the dead man vivid in her memory.

Dead, she thought. *But why?*

And suddenly a second image came to mind, of the dead man fastened to a pole and slung between two guards, his thick, red-gold hair hanging like a mane beneath him as they carried him along.

Yes, she thought, *like the great man-eating tiger Wu Song had killed up on Ching Yang Ridge.*

Whatever he'd had, whatever it was that she carried in the hollow of the sketchboard, was something that terrified the authorities just as much as roaming man-eaters had terrified the villagers of long ago. But there were no heroes in the modern world, no Wu Songs or Song Jiangs, and certainly no tigers – only men and the things men did. So what was it? What could possibly be so important that a young man would choose death rather than relinquish it?

She looked down at the sketchboard, conscious suddenly of what she had done back there. Aware – suddenly, acutely *aware* – that three men had died over this thing she carried with her.

Hannah closed her eyes, feeling the sharp edge of the casing pressed against her ribs, the upward motion of the lift as it climbed towards the top of the City, and shivered. She would know soon enough. But what then? What would she do with that knowledge?

She waited, emptying herself, but no answer came.

Curiosity had driven her this far. But beyond that she didn't know. She simply didn't know.

The lift slowed and stopped. Hannah opened her eyes.

"*Nu Shi* . . ."

She went out, between the guards, numbed, suddenly uncertain that she had done the right thing, convinced that they would find the inner workings of the sketchboard and piece together what she'd done. And then even her father's influence would not save her. But it was done now. She had committed herself, just as surely as the young man with the red-gold hair. She too, now, was a tiger.

* * *

Chen crouched over the broken machine, studying it closely. It was the tenth he had seen that morning and, like the others, it was damaged almost beyond recognition – kicked and beaten with a savagery that was hard to imagine. This time, however, they had been careless. This time they had not smashed the security cameras before the attack.

"You'll get the scum who did this, Major Kao, you understand me? I want them tracked down like the dogs they are and punished."

Chen turned, staring up at the obese form of the AutoMek director, then looked past him at his duty sergeant.

"Sergeant Krol, take *Shih* Cornwell back to headquarters and make sure he is treated with the respect he is due. Once I have completed my investigations here I shall join you."

He turned back to the Company man, lowering his head respectfully. "Forgive me, *Shih* Cornwell, but as I'm sure you'll understand, I must give this matter my utmost concentration."

"I fail to see . . ." Cornwell began, but Chen stood, raising a hand to silence him.

"You want the job done, *Shih* Cornwell. I understand that. Now, please, let me get on with it. Unless you want this 'scum' to evade us once again."

Cornwell glared at him a moment, then, relenting, took a

step backward. With a terse little bow he turned away, allowing Chen's sergeant to lead him away.

Watching him go, Chen let out a huge sigh of relief. "These days they think they own us," he said, turning, looking across at his lieutenant, Wilson, who stood nearby, looking on.

Wilson smiled. "I admire your patience, Major. I'm sure I'd have given him a mouthful."

"And ended before a tribunal . . ." Chen shook his head, then looked back at the machine. "The thing is that I understand all this. These machines," he stood, wiping his hands together, "each one of them replaces eight good men – throws eight hard-working sweepers out of work. And for what? To boost the Company's profits and make insects like Cornwell even fatter than they already are!"

"Isn't that so! Half our work these days seems to be tidying up the mess our so-called superiors have made."

Chen looked at his lieutenant sternly.

"Oh, I don't mean our Masters," Wilson said quickly, raising his hands as if to defend himself. "No, I mean *hsiao jen* like Cornwell there. Little men, thinking they've the power of life and death over others – that money makes them gods."

Chen sighed. "In a way it does. It always has. But that's not our problem, neh? Our job is to sort out the mess. To find this . . . scum . . . and make them pay."

Wilson moved closer, handing Chen a small cassette. "Well, this time it couldn't be simpler. We've got it all here. Six faces. No masks, no hoods. Clear shots."

"We've got names?"

"And addresses. They're all ex-sweepers, naturally. So there we have it. Evidence, motive, the lot. All we have to do is round them up."

Chen took the tape and stared at it, then looked back at him. "Who else knows about this?"

"No one. Only you and me."

"But there's a copy, neh? On record."

"Not now there isn't. I . . . erased it."

"Ah . . ." Chen looked at the tape again. "So this is it? Without this we've nothing?"

"That's about it."

Chen looked up again, smiled, then dropped the tape and crushed it beneath his booted heel. "Shame," he said, meeting Wilson's eyes clearly. "It looks like the cameras failed again. Pity. We might have got them this time."

Wilson nodded, then, taking a folded sheet from his pocket, handed it to Chen. "Those are the addresses. It's the only record. Burn it once you've used it, huh?"

"Okay." Chen slipped the paper into his pocket, then, smiling, reached across and patted his shoulder. "You're a good man, Stephen. A good soldier. And a good friend."

"And Cornwell."

Chen laughed. "Don't worry. I'll deal with that fat toad. *Scum* . . ." He shivered, a sudden indignation overtaking him. "As if he understood . . ."

* * *

Hannah stood at her father's door, looking in. He was sat at his desk on the far side of the room, a reading lamp hovering just above his right shoulder.

"Father?"

He looked up, then seeing it was her, stood, beckoning her across. They embraced, his face lit up with delight at seeing her.

"I didn't know you were coming home," she said, hugging him tightly. "I thought you'd gone another week yet."

"I know, but something's come up." He indicated the files scattered about his desk. "I've got to prepare something for the morning. Something confidential. I thought it best, in the circumstances, to bring it back here."

She moved back slightly, looking down at him, sensitive to the unusually guarded tone in his voice. "Confidential? I thought everything you did was confidential. Why, you're the great master of all secrets, aren't you?"

Normally he would have laughed and played along with her, but this time he looked away, his face troubled. "This is no joking matter, my love. It's deadly serious." He looked back at her. "I am to report to the First Dragon himself first thing tomorrow morning. The *I Lung* has an appointment with the T'ang, Tsu Ma. It seems the very future of the Ministry is at stake."

"I see. So . . ."

He leaned towards her, putting a finger to her lips. "No, sweetheart. Not a word. If I could tell you, I would. You know that. But for once it's best you don't know. Not until it's over."

"Okay. Then I'd best leave you to it, neh?"

"It would be best."

"And tomorrow? Will you be here for dinner?"

He hesitated, then shook his head. "It would be nice, but I think it might be difficult. There's much to do. The *I Lung* has given me a new appointment. I'm afraid I may be gone rather a lot in the coming months."

She studied him a moment, seeing how tired he looked, how drawn, and felt a stab of concern for him. "So what's new?" she said, trying to coax a smile from him. "The day you aren't busy you'll be dead, and then it'll be my turn to be busy, clearing up after you."

He laughed. "Look, I'll try. But *you* must try, too. Your mother . . ."

"That woman . . ."

"*Please*, Hannah. I know you two don't get on, but you could make an effort. If only to help me, neh?"

"Okay. I'll try." She leaned close, kissing his brow. "I hope it all goes well tomorrow."

"You and I both, my love . . ."

Back in her own rooms, she locked the main door, leaving the key in the lock, then went through to her study. The package was on the desk where she had left it, the kitchen knife beside it.

She switched on the desk lamp then stood there, staring at it. Three men had died over whatever was inside. Three men . . . and maybe more. Who knew? She took a long, shuddering breath, then set to work, cutting through the fine silk wrapping.

Inside was a plain white folder and inside that . . .

157

She took the handwritten pages out and set them on the desk beside the wrapping, then pulled up a seat and began to read, speaking the words aloud.

"The Aristotle File . . . being the true history of the West, 384 BC to AD 2087."

She stopped, a shiver passing down her spine. *The true history* . . .

Then it was true. All the whispers and mumbled half-tales were true. She flicked through quickly, reading a paragraph here, a few words there, then stopped again, looking up, finding it suddenly difficult even to take a breath.

So it was all a lie, one vast deception. It was unthinkable, *impossible*, and yet she knew it was true. All her life she had suspected it, and now she knew.

She sat back, feeling strange, almost insubstantial, the room, the very chair on which she sat somehow changed from what they'd been only a moment before.

She understood . . . the deaths, the urgency of the pursuit. This file – this *truth* – was a ticking bomb, waiting to explode. Even to know of its existence was, she knew, a capital offence. And yet to deny it, wasn't that also a kind of death?

The darkness shimmered before her eyes.

She shuddered, filled by the vision that had come to her. There was her world, like a giant crystal globe, adrift in the vacuum of space. From afar it seemed to glimmer in the starless emptiness, lit from within by the shining, translucent figures of forty thousand million ghosts, their pale, tormented eyes pleading for release.

Ghosts, *yes* . . . they were the hungry ghosts of Han legend: those poor, unfortunate wretches who could find no rest, neither in this world nor the next. Her eyes met theirs, understanding for the first time the insatiable craving that drove them, the dissatisfaction that had eaten away at them until there was nothing left of them but *this* – this shell, this pale imitation of being. There they all were, the spirits of the lost and abandoned, of those who had drowned at sea and those who had suffered sudden, violent death; of those who had no families to mourn them, and those who had been shunned by their fellow men. She watched them, saw how they burned, without sound or heat, the pale light of their consumption slowly guttering towards extinction, and understood that this could not go on. To be born into this world was to be still-born. To live here was intolerable. But hadn't she always known that? Hadn't she, at the back of everything, always known the falseness of it all?

She moaned. Lies, all of it lies, and her father a custodian – an *intimate* – of that great deception. That, perhaps, was the worst of it: that such a good, kind man – such a funny, caring man – could serve so foul an end. For there was no doubt of it, a lie so vast, so all-permeating, was evil.

Secrets – she was used to secrets – but lies were different. Lies corroded. They were a disease of the inner self. They ate the marrow from the bone. Besides, what purpose had life if its lessons could be doctored, its lived experience *rewritten* by those who followed after? How could they learn to be better people if the past were forever denied to them?

She shivered, her distress giving way to indignation. How *could* they have done this? Who gave them the right? And how many deaths, how much suffering had the Ministry caused in policing the Lie?

Her father . . . it all came back to her father. What was it the Han said? Ah yes. She said the rhyme aloud, her voice a whisper:

"A dragon begets a dragon.
A phoenix begets a phoenix.
The son of a rat, from the day of his birth,
Knows only how to dig a hole in the ground."

So what was she? Dragon, phoenix, or the daughter of a rat? Or was it really that simple? All agreed that her father was *lao shih* – was a genuine, straightforward man – and yet his whole life was an intricate lie, a social mask, constructed to conceal his work for the Thousand Eyes. And she had inherited something of his manner. Even today, in getting hold of the File, she had used lies and deceptions. So where did one draw the line? Where did the small lie end and the Big Lie begin?

Hannah looked back down at the File. Words, that's all it was. Mere words. Yet this was potentially more dangerous, more destructive to the status quo, than an army of a million men. Why, if this were known to all . . .

She grew still, the idea growing in her. *If this were known to all* . . . But why not? Why did it have to be like this – passed furtively from hand to hand in fear of discovery? Why couldn't it be done more openly, more *effectively*? There had to be a way.

Setting the title page aside, she began again, reading the opening words and then reading them again, letting them burn into her mind, knowing – even as she did – that things would never be the same.

* * *

Kao Chen looked up from his crowded desk and met his Duty Captain's eyes. "What now? Not another instruction from our merchant friend, I hope!"

The Captain bowed, handing a sealed package across. "No, sir. It's from General Rheinhardt. I was told to give it to you urgently."

Chen sat back, letting the package fall onto the pile in front of him. "As if we've not enough . . . Okay. Tell the General's messenger that I'll get onto it at once."

"Sir!"

When his Captain had gone, Chen sat there a moment, staring at the stack of papers that cluttered his desk. He was behind, badly behind, but then who wasn't in Security these days? The truth was that there was too much crime and too few of them to deal with it, and the recent slackening of the Edict had only made things worse. As more and more people found themselves out of work, so the problem grew – exponentially it seemed. And always there was more to do, less time to do it in.

With a tired sigh he picked up the package and tore the

seal open, then tipped it up, letting the contents fall out onto the desk.

A file. Another damn file. He picked it up and flicked through it quickly, then returned to the beginning, suddenly alert, sitting forward and drawing the lamp closer.

It was another of them . . .

He read it through quickly, then pushed it aside with a grunt of irritation, shaking his head angrily. The idiots! The fatheads! Couldn't they ever get it right? This was the fourth of these he'd seen in the last six months and every time they'd fucked up when it came down to it. Four pursuits, four deaths – it was a pretty slipshod record. Little wonder Rheinhardt wanted someone new to take things over.

Yes, but why me? I've enough on my plate as it is.

He sat back, yawning, knowing he needed rest – a break from duties. Not only that, but he'd promised Jyan he'd spend some time with him. Oh, Jyan would understand – he *always* understood – but it wasn't fair on the boy. Not now, when things were so difficult at home.

Leaning forward again, he tapped out the code for his apartment, then waited as the connection was made. Even that was getting worse. Two, three years ago, there would have been no waiting time, but now . . . Well, it was like his friend Karr had said, last time they'd got together. Things were going to hell in a bucket!

"*Hello* . . . ?"

The voice was small, distorted, but Chen knew at once who it was. It was his daughter, Ch'iang Hsin, the baby of the family.

"Hello, my little peach. It's daddy. Is Jyan there?"

There was a hesitation, then. "He's with mummy. She's not been well. She's been crying again. Wu has gone for the doctor."

Chen sighed. "Okay. Well, look, my love, tell Jyan that I can't get back tonight. Tell him . . . tell him that I'll speak to him as soon as I can. Have you got that?"

"She's not well, daddy. She . . ."

He could hear the pain in her voice, but there was little

he could do. Maybe the doctor could give Wang Ti something. Something to make her sleep, perhaps. Maybe that would help.

"Look, my love, be brave for me, okay? I'll try and get back there as soon as I can. I promise I will. But it won't be tonight. Something very important has come up and daddy has to see to it, okay?"

Her voice seemed even smaller. "Okay . . . but be home soon, daddy. I love you."

"I love you too, my peach. I love you very much. Kiss mummy for me, neh?"

He broke contact, the tightness in his gut much worse than usual. It wasn't fair on them, he knew. He was away too much, and the woman he had hired to help out didn't begin to meet the children's emotional needs. Something had to be done, and soon, but just now he had no time to see to it.

Chen stood, raising his arms above his head, stretching the tiredness from his chest and upper shoulders. Reaching into his left-hand drawer, he took two tablets from the packet he kept there and popped them into his mouth, swallowing them down, knowing they'd keep him awake and alert for another twelve hours.

He looked about him at the clutter of his office. Short-term solutions, that was how he lived his life these days – juggling a whole mess of short-term solutions. But the problems were long-term and some time soon he'd have to face up to them.

After this, perhaps, he thought, picking up the file and going across to the door. *Maybe I'll ask for a week's leave and try and sort things out*. He knew it was what he ought to do. Things couldn't go on much longer the way they were. But what *was* the answer?

To endure, part of him answered. To keep on, day by day, holding things together, smoothing over the cracks, until . . .

Chen shuddered, then, taking his tunic down from the peg by the door, slipped it on and went through into the outer office, summoning his men to him, getting down to the task at hand.

CHAPTER · 7

THE LAND WITHOUT GHOSTS

Emily pulled the door closed, then locked it, returning the key to the bunch jangling at her waist. She turned, looking towards the door at the far end of the corridor.

"Okay . . . what's down there?"

The elderly servant turned, glancing at the door, then looked back at her, his head bowed. "I . . . I don't know, Mistress. The Master never used this wing of the Mansion much. We were not encouraged . . ."

"I see," she said, interrupting, then moved past him, heading for the door. "I guess I'll have to find out for myself."

"Forgive me, Mistress . . ."

She stopped. "*Yes*, Richard?"

As before, the use of his first name unsettled the old retainer. "Nothing, Mistress. Simply that I don't think there's a key to that door."

She stared at him, intrigued. "Why not?" she asked, but she was thinking, *Why is he so uncomfortable?* and, *How does he know there is no key if he was never encouraged to come here?*

"It . . . it was never used."

"*Never?*" She shrugged. "Well, we'll see, neh?"

She turned, continued to the door.

As he caught up with her, she turned back, the abruptness of her action surprising him. "You're absolutely certain there's no key?"

He bowed his head, nodded.

"Then we'd best break it down, neh?"

"*Mistress?*" He looked at her, alarmed.

"If there's no key . . ."

He stared back at her, nonplussed.

"Well?" she said, almost smiling now. "Will *you* do it, or shall I?"

His mouth opened slightly, closed.

There's something in there, she thought. *Something he'd rather I didn't see.*

She turned, took a step backward, kicked.

The door shuddered, held.

She kicked again. This time the wood surrounding the lock split and partly gave. A third kick shattered it.

The door swung slowly back.

She turned, smiling at him, enjoying the look of astonishment on his face.

And inside?

She stepped into the room. Into a dark mustiness.

"Lights," she said, addressing the House Computer.

At once the room was brightly lit.

She looked about her. It was a big room – a store-room of some kind. Crates were stacked up four high, two deep all round the walls. She went across and examined one. It was sealed. She tried another and then a third. All sealed, untouched since they'd been placed here – when? – at least eighteen months back. She crouched, looking about her. The same label was on all the crates – the ornate blue and gold label of the Hythe-MacKay Auction House.

"What are these?" she asked, looking across to where the old servant was standing in the doorway.

He smiled politely. "The Old Master . . ."

"Oh, *fuck* the Old Master!" she said, finally losing her temper with him. "He's been dead eighteen months now and still you act like he's going to return at any moment! Well, he *isn't*! And I'm Mistress here now. So cut all the 'I don't know' shit and tell me what the hell all of this is!"

He looked down, staring at his booted feet, shocked by her outburst. "I . . . I don't know, Mistress. We were told not to come here. Master Lever . . . well . . ."

She gave a sigh of exasperation. Was it always going to

164

be like this? She counted to ten, then stood, facing the man.

"Look . . . I'm sorry if I lost my temper just now, but I need to know what all of this is. How can I make a proper inventory of the Mansion unless I know what's where?"

He made the smallest movement of his head, conceding the point.

"Good. Then be helpful, neh, and bring me something I can use to open these."

* * *

Michael Lever was in his office, taking briefings from his personal assistant, Dan Johnson, when his wife Mary's voice came through on his desk comset.

"Michael? Come to the West Wing. Now. I need to see you."

He met Johnson's eyes, making a grimace of exasperation. "Em . . . the meeting's in ten minutes. Can't it wait?"

"No. *Now!*"

The comset went dead. Michael ran a hand through his hair, frowning, clearly in two minds.

"When the Mistress of the House calls . . ." Johnson said, smiling, then added. "I'll tell them you're delayed. Who knows, maybe it'll do the old buggers good to be kept waiting."

"Dan . . . respect!" But Michael was smiling now. Besides, maybe Johnson was right. Maybe he ought to keep them waiting, if only to let them know who was Head of this Company. Yet his instinct was against it. This was an important board meeting and he needed to get their agreement – if only tacitly – to the latest round of changes.

He huffed, half irritated by his wife's summons, half intrigued, then, pulling himself up out of his seat, got the lightweight harness moving, making for the door. Johnson was there before him, holding the door open.

"How's it feel?"

Michael looked down at the support harness which helped him walk and move about. Since the accident he had had a succession of them, but this was the lightest, the least uncomfortable to wear. Why, it was almost possible sometimes to forget he had it on. In a year, the doctors said, he might even do without.

He smiled. "It's great. The best yet. Doesn't chafe like the last."

Johnson nodded his head, then touched Michael's arm, for that brief moment more friend than assistant. "That's good. And look, don't worry. I'll fend them off, okay?"

"Fine." Again he smiled, glad that Johnson was there, that he had such a good right-hand man. "I'll not be long. I promise."

* * *

He found her in the West Wing, in a room which, for as long as he could remember, had been locked. She was sitting on an old wooden trunk, staring down at something she was holding between her hands. All about her were stacks of opened crates, their half-glimpsed contents nestling in various kinds of wrapping. Michael took two steps into the room then stopped, looking about him.

"What's going on?"

She looked up, a deep frown on her face, then held the object up for him to see.

"What *is* this, Michael?"

He took three ungainly steps towards her then stopped, astonished. It was a head. A human head. And it was black.

"Where the hell did you get that?"

She looked about her. "It was here, in the trunk. And other things. Books and clothes, paintings and maps. Old stuff, from the time of the American Empire. But this . . ." She shuddered. "Well, it's horrible. I mean, what was it? GenSyn? Were they operating back then?"

He shrugged, staring at the hideous object with a mixture of fascination and repugnance. "Maybe. I don't know. But this must be my father's stuff. The stuff he bought from auction. Old Man Marley told me about it. Said he had plans to exhibit some of it before he died, so maybe there's an inventory somewhere. Or purchase slips."

Gingerly, he took the head from her, then turned it in his hands, studying it more closely. It looked wrong, somehow, the hair too curly, the nose too flat, the lips too broad. Lifting it slightly, he sniffed the black, leathery skin.

"Odd . . ." Again he shivered. *Wrong, yes, maybe it was wrong, but somehow it didn't seem "made".* He looked back at Mary. "What do you think we should do with all this stuff?"

She leaned down, picking something up from beside her, then turned back and stood, holding something else out to him. It was a book. An old, leather-bound book.

"I don't know," she said. "My first instinct is to burn it, but it might be important. Here, look at this. Where I've marked."

He set the head down, then opened the book where she'd set the marker. A musty smell drifted up at him, the very scent of age. The smell of Empire. He stared at the open page a moment, then looked back at Mary.

"Gods! It's not possible, is it?"

"Sure it is. Look at that face. Who else could it be but a Kennedy?"

"And the man? The black man?"

"Look at the caption."

He looked back at the old black and white print, studying it a moment, then turned the book, looking at the print on the spine. The book was old, two centuries old. But that face. He looked at it a third time, nodding to himself. A Kennedy and a black man. A king, so it said here. How strange that seemed. Black men and kings.

"Do you think Joe knows about all this?"

She shook her head. "I don't know. I don't think so, to be honest. If he does, he's kept it very close, neh?"

He nodded, then, struck by an idea, began to smile. "Hey . . . maybe we should give it to him . . . you know, at his birthday party on Friday. It'd be perfect, don't you think?"

She took it back from him, suddenly serious. "Maybe . . . If you want. But not before I've had a chance to read it. There are things here . . ." She gave a little shiver. "Well

167

. . . you'd best get back, neh? The old men are waiting, and you know how irritable they get."

He laughed. "Don't I just."

* * *

ImmVac's boardroom was a huge hall of a chamber, surrounded on three sides by a balcony from which a dozen soft-wired scribes looked on, ready to take notes and provide their masters below with up-to-date information on whichever topic was the current subject of discussion. Below, about a massive octagonal oak table, sat seven elderly men, their grey hair combed back in a uniform style, their business silks a uniform midnight blue. On the table in front of each was a long, low screen, on which figures and briefing information would appear as needed. At the head of the table, beneath the Company logo which dominated the back wall, the high-backed chair was empty. To one side of it stood Dan Johnson, his hands out in front of him as he fielded the old men's brusque enquiries about Michael Lever's whereabouts.

"Gentlemen . . . I'm sure Mister Lever will be here at any moment. If you would just be patient."

"Twenty minutes . . ." the old man directly opposite Johnson said in a loud, disgruntled voice. "His father would never have kept us waiting twenty seconds! We have our own Companies to run, you know!"

Johnson lowered his head as if in respect to the old man, but in truth he was simply trying to keep his temper. The speaker was Johannes Kemp and he was an abrasive old bastard. Even at the best of times he was difficult, but today, it seemed, he was going out of his way to be unpleasant.

"I'll give him another five minutes, and then I'm off. It's intolerable. Absolutely intolerable!"

Johnson stared at Kemp, astonished. Did he mean what he'd just said? Would he simply get up and go? And what if he did? What if all the others followed him? *Then there'll be no quorum*, a voice in his head answered him – *and thus no board meeting, and no changes. And what would young Michael do then?*

He took a breath, about to speak to Kemp, to be his most persuasive, but at that moment the doors at the far end of the room swung back and Michael swept in, his prosthetic clicking on the marble floor.

"Forgive me, gentlemen," he said, coming round the table, an apologetic smile lighting his features. "Something very important just came up. Something I had to deal with at once." Dismissing Johnson, he took his seat at the head of the table.

"Well," he said, looking about him. "Let's get down to business at once. You've seen my proposals for the reorganisation of the Company's management structure, and, I hope, have had time now to consider them. Put simply the problem is this: the Company is top-heavy with management. There are far too many people on the payroll who are drawing a salary for doing nothing."

"With respect, *Shih* Lever, I disagree."

The voice came from Michael's right, from a long-faced man named Leckie. He leaned forward, his deep voice resonant with the accent of the old South. "I've had my people look into this and they find little evidence of over-staffing in the management levels. Indeed, were we to trim back, as you suggest in your . . . document, well, my findings show a likely drop in efficiency of anything between ten and fifteen per cent."

Michael stared at him, then sat back, lacing his fingers together in a manner reminiscent of his father. "Forgive me, Andrew, but your findings . . . *surprise* me, let's say. As you know, since my father's death I have commissioned a number of reports on this Company's financial strengths and weaknesses, with the aim of making ImmVac not merely a stronger Company, but a more equitable one. Now, there are three things which these reports agree upon. One, that our borrowings are much too high. Two, that our pricing strategy is – how should I put it? – close to scandalous. And three, that there are too many bosses and not enough workers. As you know, I have already taken steps to deal with the second of these three matters by reducing the wholesale price of our goods and services, but if ImmVac is to maintain its position as City North America's leading Company then we are going to have to deal with the other problems – problems which are, I feel, indissolubly linked."

"So you say," Kemp said, taking his chance to interrupt. "But I too have had my people look at things, and they have come up with a completely different set of findings. You identify three problems. Well, we'll not argue about those just now. *However* . . . there is a *fourth* area of concern, and that's the question of the Institute and the Immortality Project."

Michael looked down. "As I've said before, that is a matter I shall deal with personally. As soon as new sponsors are found . . ."

"Forgive me, Michael," Kemp said, insistent now, "but surely the problem is very much within our remit. After all, the eight billion *yuan* loan is secured on the assets of this Company, which makes the Cutler Institute not merely a Lever family concern, but very much a matter for this board. Besides, if my information is correct, no new sponsors have been forthcoming, nor are there likely to be any while you continue to run the business down."

Michael glared at Kemp. "That's *my* decision, and while I hold eighty per cent of the shares in this Company, I'll not have the matter discussed in this boardroom, understand me?"

There was a moment's silence, then, with a faint bob of his head, Kemp stood. "If that's how you feel, Michael, you can have my resignation straight away."

"*Johannes* . . ." Michael took a long, exasperated breath. "Look, please try to understand. The Institute . . . it was an *aberration* of my father's. A dream that went wrong. It should never have been tied in to the fortunes of this great Company, nor shall it be in future."

Kemp laughed. "You know, Michael, I opposed your father when he took the Institute on. I warned him against committing so much of this Company to something so . . . high risk. But now . . . well, I'm astonished that you can't see it, boy.

Eight billion *yuan*. Where will we find that? And find it we must if you're to pursue this idiot idea you have of ridding us of the damned thing. No. Think clearly, Michael. You've no option. Cut and trim all you like, but while the Institute's on our back, and while you're determined to run it down, then you can say farewell to any schemes you have for revivifying ImmVac's fortunes."

"So what do you suggest?"

Kemp hesitated a moment, then sat again. He took a print-out from the case at his side and slid it across the table to Michael. "There," he said. "That's what I suggest. We reorganise, sure, but not the parent Company. The Institute, *that's* where we concentrate our efforts. We introduce new money, new thinking. We make it work. And from the profits we pay off the loan."

Michael stared at the document in his hands, shaking his head. "No," he said softly. "We can't do this. It's against all I've stood for."

"We either do this or go under."

"No," he said again, his voice pained. But what if Kemp was right? How would he explain that to Mary? How would he make *her* understand?

* * *

"Well?" she asked, looking up from the sofa as he came into the room, "How did it go? Did they approve the changes?"

He nodded, not wanting to tell her about the rest of the deal just yet. "You want a drink?" he asked, going across to the cabinet.

She laughed. "Was it *that* bad?"

He looked back at her and smiled. "You know how it is. Leckie had brought his own figures along and Old Man Kemp was being a total pain in the arse. But what's new? It's probably the only fun they get out of life!"

Her eyes were suddenly serious. "You want to watch those two. Leckie's not as dumb as he seems, and Kemp . . ."

He poured himself a whiskey, then turned back, raising an eyebrow. "What *about* Kemp?"

She shook her head. "Nothing . . . just a feeling."

He came across and sat beside her. There was a stack of books on the low table next to her, and one in her lap.

"What's that you're reading?"

She picked it up and showed him. "It was in one of the crates. Look . . . there's more of them . . ."

Michael stared, fascinated. Black men. More black men, but this time in American army uniforms, standing there posing for the camera, leaning on their long rifles.

He frowned. If they'd been GenSyn there'd have been something standardised about them; a certain uniformity about the faces. Not only that, but they'd have been bigger, better-muscled than they were. Besides, why go to the trouble to make such a range and then use them as simple footsoldiers? Unless . . .

"*Hei*," he said. "Perhaps they were an early model of the *Hei* . . ."

She shook her head. "There was a war," she said quietly. "A great war between the north and south. Look . . . look at all the photographs."

He turned the pages, then caught his breath, horrified by the scenes of carnage.

"A war," she said again. "It says here that it lasted the best part of five years and that over six hundred thousand men died . . . and we know nothing about it. I checked. There's nothing in the official records . . . *Nothing*."

"Nothing?"

She shook her head. "What's been going on, Michael? Why don't we know about this?"

He looked back at her, dumbfounded. "I . . . I don't know."

She leaned towards him, touching his arm. "I want to find out. Hythe-MacKay, they'll know. I've arranged to see them, tomorrow morning, for a viewing. If I . . ."

There was an urgent beeping from the wallscreen in the corner. Emily sat back, letting an exasperated breath escape her.

"Who is it?" Michael asked, turning to face the wallscreen.

"It's Representative Kennedy, Master," the House Computer answered, "calling from Weimar."

"What time is it out there?"

"Ten minutes after eight, Master."

Michael turned, smiling at Emily, as if he'd already forgotten what she had been saying. "Then he'll have made his speech . . ." He turned back. "Put him on. Full vision."

At once the image of Kennedy filled the screen. "Michael . . . Mary . . . how are you both?"

"We're fine," Michael answered for them both. "How did it go? Did you have them eating out of your hand?"

Kennedy laughed. "Not quite. Even so, I think it went down rather well. The media are hailing it as a great success. That's why I rang . . . I'm told that MedFac are going to show excerpts on their evening 'cast. Maybe you'd spread the word . . . let a few of our friends know it's going out. If we can get pick-up from a few of the other channels . . ."

"Leave it with me," Michael said, grinning back at him. "And Joe . . . you're still okay for Friday?"

Kennedy beamed back at him. "I wouldn't miss it for anything. But look . . . I've got to dash, okay? I'll catch up with you later. Bye!"

The screen went dark.

Michael turned, looking to Emily, then frowned. "What's the matter?"

"Nothing," she said, putting the book on the top of the pile. "I'd best be getting on with things."

He huffed, exasperated by her. "Look. You don't have to like him, Em, but you could be a bit more civil. It's not easy what he's trying to do."

Her answer was unexpectedly sharp. "And just what *is* that? Do we really *know* any more?"

"Hey . . . ease off . . ." He raised his hands, smiling at her. "I thought we'd talked this one through. The new population measures will help everyone, from First Level to the Net."

"Some more than others."

"Meaning *what*?"

173

"Meaning that the top fifty will be exempt."

"So? The top fifty isn't where the problem is."

"No . . ." She looked away, her face tight. "It never is, is it?"

"Hey . . ." He laughed, trying hard to be conciliatory. "Look, I agree with him, Em. I think it's the right step to take. So what am I supposed to do?"

"Nothing," she said coldly, then, relenting, she came across and held his head against her side. "Nothing . . ."

* * *

Kennedy leaned in to the intercom, speaking to his secretary in the next room. "Make sure he gets that, right? Oh, and send copies to Hudson and Keeler. I want them fully briefed when they meet Hastings tomorrow. Oh, and no more calls just now. I'm in conference, *right?*"

Breaking the connection, he sat back, looking at the man seated across from him.

"Well, Fen Cho-hsien, how can I help you?"

Wu Shih's Chancellor looked about him a moment, then smiled. Behind him his two bodyservants stood like statues, their faces bereft of expression.

"It was a good speech, *Shih* Kennedy," Fen answered, drawing his silks tighter about him, "and I am certain that, when it comes to the vote tomorrow, you will win a substantial majority." He paused. "My Master is very pleased with you."

Kennedy shrugged. "And what does your Master want of me now?"

Fen's smile never wavered. "Wu Shih wants nothing. Nothing, that is, except what is best for everyone. You have brought your party a long way this past year. Your policies . . . well," he laughed, "it is hard to believe that the NREP of a year ago could have held such views, neh?"

Kennedy made no comment, yet it was clear from a hardening in his face that Fen Cho-hsien's constant insults were getting to him.

"Anyway . . ." Fen said, aware of the effect his words

were having, "I have a meeting within the hour, so I must go."

He raised his right hand and clicked his fingers. At once one of the bodyservants handed him a sealed envelope. Fen stared at it, then leaned towards Kennedy, handing it to him, the smile gone suddenly, his eyes hard.

"You will find my Master keeps his promises, *Mister* Kennedy. There is enough there to pay off all New Republican debts and enough left over to purchase *tai* if you so wish. In return all you need do is agree to a single amendment to your proposal introducing new levels of food subsidies for below Level 250."

Kennedy stared at him. "*What* new levels?"

Fen Cho-hsien stood, smiling once more. "It is all there in the T'ang's letter. As I said, my Master keeps *his* promises . . . make sure you keep *yours*."

And with that he turned and left.

Kennedy sat there a moment, staring at the empty doorway, then looked down at the letter in his hand. Tearing it open, he read it through, then sat back, whistling.

"Shit . . ." he said softly. If he agreed *this* . . . But what option had he? If he didn't the whole package would be lost, and whatever Fen Cho-hsien thought, he really did believe in the current set of population proposals. They weren't equitable, true, but they were a start. And once the principle was established . . .

But to reduce food subsidies to the Lowers was against stated New Republican policy. To agree to it . . .

He looked down at the cheque. It was made out in Wu Shih's own hand – a bill drawn on his private bankers for twenty million *yuan*. Kennedy nodded to himself, considering. Ten would clear all debts, the rest . . .

He huffed loudly, angry that it had come to this. Until now he'd played things straight, avoiding the use of pockets – *tai* – to win a vote, but this once it seemed he'd need it.

Ten million . . . From what he'd heard he could buy a whole stack of votes for that. A quarter of the House . . .

"So you want amendments, do you?" he said softly, pulling

his writing pad across and beginning to scribble with the stylus. "Well, I'll give you amendments, Wu Shih, more amendments than you ever looked for."

* * *

Wu Shih looked up, staring sternly into the camera, the model of the newly-commissioned orbital farm on his desk beside him. Then, with a flourish of the brush, he signed the special Edict and, taking the great seal from the cushion to one side, inked it then pressed it down firmly onto the foot of the document.

"There," he said, letting his servants take the document away, "it is done."

He stood, then walked across to where his cousin, Tsu Ma, stood by the open garden door, watching him.

"It is an expensive business, cousin," Tsu Ma said, smiling sympathetically. "Let us pray it works."

Wu Shih sighed. "I wish now I had never commissioned that report! I shall be lucky if it does not bankrupt me!"

Tsu Ma laughed. "Oh, I doubt it cousin. Besides, it is better to be forewarned than sorry. You should not ask yourself how much it *will* cost, but what it *might* have cost you, had you not acted."

Wu Shih turned, watching his servants dismantle the trivee rig. "I'd hoped we could make do, but the orbitals are ancient and are constantly undergoing repairs. We ought to bring them down and totally refit them, but we simply cannot afford to. We are at full stretch as it is, and to take even one out of service . . ." He shrugged. "Well, there was no option when it came down to it. We must build new orbitals or see the old ones fall apart. Still, there are *some* pluses. The new population controls are a very touchy matter and the vote in the House tomorrow is likely to be close. This might sway one or two members to support *Shih* Kennedy's proposals."

Tsu Ma laughed. "You can always hope! Myself, I'd have trusted more to simple bribery!"

"Oh, I have done all I can in *that* regard! Even so, this

worries me, cousin. Bad news . . . there seems nothing but bad news these days."

"Well then, the timing of this could not be better, *neh*? If you must give the people bad news – and the reduction of the subsidies is certainly that – then it's always best to sweeten it with something brighter. People don't mind suffering so much if there's the prospect of better times ahead."

"Maybe so. And yet I fear we must tread carefully. What happened on Mars . . ." He shuddered, then shook his head. "Besides, Li Yuan's is not the only City where there is unrest these days. My Security forces are more busy than they ever were."

"And mine," Tsu Ma confessed. "But what can we do? I have doubled the size of my forces, but still they barely cope. It is the times, cousin. We are fated to ride the tiger."

Wu Shih nodded, as if resigned, but his eyes which had always been so clear, so determined, seemed bewildered by events.

Tsu Ma watched him a moment longer, his own eyes narrowed, then he turned away, looking out across the sunlit garden.

* * *

"Listen to this," she said, looking up from the page and meeting Michael's eyes across the room. "When the Chinese – the Han, that is – first came to North America in the 1840s, they called it Amo Li Jia . . . the Land Without Ghosts."

He stared at her distractedly. "Pardon?"

"America, they . . ." She closed the book. "You've not been listening to a word, have you?"

He smiled apologetically.

"Okay. What's on your mind?"

He shrugged. "I was thinking about the deal . . . you know, with Kemp and the others. And all this stuff that's going on at Weimar. I should have been there, Em."

"Joe has your proxy, hasn't he?"

He nodded.

"Well, then, what's the worry? I thought you *trusted* Joe."

The irony in her voice was hard to miss.

"And you don't? Come on, Em, tell me the truth. *Don't* you trust him?"

"You know how I feel."

"Do I?" He looked away. "Sometimes I think I don't know you. Sometimes it's . . . well, it's like you're a stranger to me."

She looked down, then, setting the book aside, went across. Sitting next to him, she took his hands, forcing him to look at her.

"Look, I'm sorry. It's hard sometimes, that's all. Living like this . . . I'm not used to it. You were born to it. It's natural for you. But for me . . ." She squeezed his hands. "Look . . . as far as Joe's concerned, I'll try a little harder, okay?" She smiled, coaxing an answering smile from him. "Now tell me honestly – what's bothering you?"

"The deal," he said, looking directly into her eyes, his boyish innocence troubled. "I . . . I've agreed to keep the Institute open."

"You've *what?*"

"I had to. I . . ." He freed his hands, then reached across and took a file from the table nearby, handing it to her.

"Kemp's report," he said, watching her open it suspiciously. "I've had Dan check the figures and Kemp's right. We've no option. We *have* to make it work or ImmVac sinks without a trace. And if ImmVac goes we've got nothing, Em. Nothing whatsoever."

"It's evil," she said, her eyes scanning the figures. "Old men wanting to live forever . . . it's just plain evil."

She looked up at him again. "No option, huh?"

He stared at her, silent, waiting.

"Okay," she said, relenting, her voice softening. "But make sure they keep *their* part of the bargain. We get those changes through, *neh?*"

"Okay," he said, a relieved smile lighting his features.

"Good. Now put the screen on. Our good friend Joe's on any minute."

He laughed, then turned, addressing the air. "House . . .

let's have the MedFac news channel. Mister Kennedy's address. Copy and store."

As the screen lit up, he sat back, putting his arm round Emily. "Next time he should do it live. More impact that way . . ."

"Shhh . . ." she whispered, pointing at the screen. "I want to hear this . . ."

On the screen was a view of an imposing First Level Mansion not so different from their own. Guards clustered about the gate to the grounds, looking up at the floater camera and smiling. On the gravel path nearby three bodies lay face down. As the camera closed in, it could be seen that they were dead. Bullet holes riddled their backs and legs. Congealed blood was pooled beneath them. The commentary ran on.

". . . is only the latest attempt by the Black Hand to infiltrate First Level and cause maximum damage to life and property. Asked today what steps he was taking to eradicate this problem, Security General Lowe said . . ."

"They're scum," Michael said, speaking over the commentary. "They got what they deserved."

She stared at him, surprised, then moved back, pushing his arm away. "You *know* that, do you? I mean . . . you knew those three personally, did you?"

He shook his head. "No . . . and hey, what are you getting so upset about? Those are terrorists lying there dead, not charity workers. They knew the risks. Besides, what did the guy who owns the Mansion do to them? It could have been *him* laying there dead. Or *us*, come to think of it!"

"Maybe," she said quietly, "but they're not scum. They just want a better life, that's all."

"Sure, and a funny way they have of getting it." He raised his hand, as if about to lecture her, then, realising what he was doing, he sat back, shaking his head. "My father . . . my damn father. Sometimes I think his ghost's in me."

She was still staring at him.

"I'm sorry," he said. "Look. Maybe they're not scum. Maybe they do have their reasons, but I can't see how murdering and robbing innocent people furthers their cause any. It's all so . . . *destructive*. Why can't they do something positive."

"They do. Only you never hear about it. It's all . . ."

"Hey, listen . . ." he said, interrupting her, as Wu Shih's face appeared on the screen. "What the hell is this?"

She turned, listening, her mind still on what he'd said, only half attending to the announcement.

"Kuan Yin preserve us!" Michael said, then whistled. "Three new orbitals. That'll set him back . . . what, sixty billion, maybe more?"

"It's good news," she said, as the commentator began to introduce the next item, Kennedy's speech at Weimar. But she couldn't get the earlier image from her mind – that close-up on the last of the fallen terrorists. It had been a woman, a *Hung Mao*, her blonde hair caked with her own blood, a gold ring prominent on the second finger of her left hand.

Scum . . . and he'd called her scum. She shivered and sat back, trying to push the image from her as Kennedy's face filled the screen, his powerful voice echoing out across the packed tiers of the House and into their room.

* * *

Kemp turned in his chair, looking away from the frozen image on the screen, then raised his brandy glass in a toast.

"Now there's one bastard I'd celebrate the death of!"

There were yells of approval from all round – from the old men who were seated to either side of Kemp and from the younger men who stood in the shadows beyond them.

Kemp stood and turned to face the dinner-suited crowd, waiting for the noise to subside before he spoke again.

"However, it's his paymaster, Lever, we need to see off first. And that's why I've asked you all here tonight. To talk tactics."

His knowing smile brought a roar of laughter from all sides. Kemp let it roll on a moment, then raised his hands again.

"We all know what's at stake. If Kennedy and Lever get their way . . . well, we'll all pay for it. They'll strip our

Mansions bare to pay for healthcare for some jug-head's scrawny litter. Why, we'd be feeding every sodding loin-jerk in the Lowers!"

Again there were fierce cries of approval and the stamping of feet.

"So . . ." he said, more quietly, more ominously. "We have to act. To stop this thing from happening. We have to . . . *prevent* it."

He turned his head slightly and snapped his fingers. At once a dozen servants issued from a door at the side and started going among the crowd, handing out envelopes.

"In there you'll find a payment for fifty thousand *yuan*. Good faith money, we'll call it. You serve us well, however, and there'll be more. Much more."

Kemp looked about him, seeing the nods of satisfaction from all round and smiled inwardly.

"Okay, then let's begin. Let's see what we can do to make things *difficult* for our friends . . ."

* * *

"Must you go so soon, cousin Ma?"

Tsu Ma came forward and embraced Wu Shih, then turned, looking back up the ramp to where his craft awaited him inside the hangar.

"I'm afraid I must. My spies tell me there's trouble afoot, and the only way to deal with trouble is to head it off . . . especially when it's the Ministry who are involved."

"The Ministry?" Wu Shih raised an eyebrow. "Is it something I should know about, Tsu Ma?"

Tsu Ma let his hand rest on his cousin's shoulder briefly. "Nothing you should lose any sleep over, cousin. But I'll send you a complete transcript of the meeting, if you wish."

Wu Shih smiled. "I would welcome that."

"Good. Then I must go. As Sun Tzu so wisely said, surprise is the ultimate in generalship."

"It sounds ominous, Tsu Ma. You talk as if we were at war with them . . ."

"Well, *aren't* we?" Tsu Ma was stern a moment, then he

smiled. "I jest . . . But they can be difficult, neh? It would not harm to shake them up a bit."

Wu Shih nodded, then embraced Tsu Ma one last time. "Safe journey, cousin Ma. As ever, I enjoyed your company more than mere words can say."

"And I yours, cousin."

Tsu Ma turned away, making his way up the ramp. Half-way up, however, he turned, remembering something, and called back to Wu Shih.

"Oh, and cousin . . . when you visit me next time, bring that young maid of yours, the pretty one, with you . . . There was not time . . ."

Wu Shih grinned. "Count it as done, cousin. Now get going. The dragons await you!"

* * *

That night she slept badly, plagued by dreams of bullet-ridden corpses that rose up from the earth and turned to her, their dark, broad faces laughing cruelly.

Ghosts . . . there were supposed to be no ghosts in this land, yet wherever she looked, whatever rooms she unlocked in her memory, ghosts stepped from the darkness to greet her. The woman's corpse, that was herself . . . how her own life would surely have ended had DeVore not interceded.

Quietly she rose from bed and crept from the room, making her way silently to the kitchen. There, in the darkness over-looking the great lawn, she sat, remembering.

Five years ago she'd come here to America, a refugee from the collapse of the *Ping Tiao* in Europe. DeVore had helped her; had given her a new identity, and a chance at a new life. She had meant to start again here, to go down level and reorganise, but then she had fallen in love . . . with Michael, her employer, defying his father to marry him. For a time it had worked – for a time she had forgotten what she'd come here to do. But tonight, seeing those images, recalling what she'd found in the West Wing among the crates, she remembered why she had come.

The Land Without Ghosts . . . She understood. It was the

land they all inhabited now. The City. A place without history, without any real connection to the earth. But now all the ghosts were coming back. She could sense them, clamouring to be let in. Their silent mouths were everywhere, like watchers at a window.

With a shudder she stood, knowing now that something had to change – either her or the great edifice surrounding her. *Ping Tiao* she'd been – a Leveller, a terrorist. *Ping Tiao* she remained, for all her new-found wealth.

That's it, she thought. *It's me or It.*

For there could be no compromise, no real peace for her until either she or the City was gone from the earth.

CHAPTER · 8

SMALL THINGS

"Is this all of it?"

The young lieutenant came to attention. "That's it, sir. Everything we couldn't place."

Chen looked about him at the cluttered storeroom, wondering where to start. *Use your eyes, look for the unexpected* – so Karr had always told him, but where among all this rubbish did one start? He turned back, looking the lieutenant up and down, then nodded. "Okay. If you'd ask Captain Johnson to bring the records of the operation to me when he gets here. Meanwhile, I'll start sorting through this lot."

"Sir."

Chen saw the man hesitate and waited, knowing, even before he said it, what he was going to ask.

"Forgive me, sir, but what exactly *are* you looking for? I mean, we've taken this level apart looking for the File. If it was here, we'd have found it."

"But it *was* here, and you *didn't* find it. Which means one of two things. Either it's still here or someone got it out."

"I still don't see . . ."

Chen raised a hand, silencing him. "No, you don't, so leave me to it, neh? I've much to do. Oh, and have someone bring me a *chung* of *ch'a*, lieutenant. This is thirsty work, and the hour's late."

"Sir!"

Chen saw the slight stiffening in the man's back and understood. The young officer didn't like this kind of interference, and maybe – just maybe – he didn't like the idea of a Han bossing him about. But that was as maybe. He would do as he was told and like it, or he'd find himself in front of a disciplinary board.

The lieutenant saluted, then turned away. Chen watched him go, then turned back, setting to work. There might be nothing here, then again, something among all this trash might explain how the File was smuggled out. Because one thing was certain – it *had* been smuggled out.

For a time he sifted through the piles, working methodically, checking each item thoroughly before moving on. At first there was nothing, then, with a laugh, he came upon something he recognised.

"Found something, Major Kao?"

Chen half turned, looking up at the newcomer. It was the Captain, Johnson. Chen stood, facing him, holding out what he'd unearthed from the pile.

"I've been trying to order one of these for my son. Three months we've waited, but nothing. And here it is. Just the bit we wanted. Mind you, it probably doesn't work. They cost over twenty *yuan* to replace. I can't imagine anyone throwing one away!"

Johnson took the flat, black rectangular piece and studied it, turning it over between his hands. Handing it back to Chen, he shrugged. "What is it?"

"It's a resonance box. It comes from a sketchboard – you know, one of those computer graphics machines. This particular bit controls the surface plasticity. It's the most sensitive part of the machine, so I'm told. Mind you, they only tell you that once the damn thing's broken and you have to order a new part. If they told you before you bought the thing . . ."

Chen laughed, hefting it in his hand. It was strange, because the part looked almost new. It was barely worn, almost as if it were straight out of its wrapping.

Johnson smiled. "Maybe you should keep hold of it. Just in case. I mean, no one will miss it."

Chen nodded. "Maybe I will." Then, realising that the Captain had the operation file under his arm, he grew serious again. "I hear you lost two men."

185

"That's right. One of them was married. Two young boys."

"I'm sorry." Chen pocketed the resonance box, then put his hand out, taking the file from the Captain. "And between us, Captain Johnson, I'm as unhappy as you at being here. I don't want to tread on your toes. But General Rheinhardt is under a lot of pressure to get results on this. You understand?"

The Captain smiled. "I understand, Major Kao. We'll cooperate all we can. But this one baffles me. We tore the whole deck apart to find the file, but nothing. As for anyone smuggling it out, well, we strip-searched everyone who came or went. The list of names is there. A few minor criminals, but otherwise nothing. A complete blank."

Chen studied the file a moment, flicking forward and backward, then looked back at Johnson. "You're sure this is complete? Are you certain there wasn't *anyone* else?"

Johnson hesitated. "Well . . ."

Chen sighed, exasperated. "Who was it? A senior official? Someone from another Security force? Who?"

"A girl. Well, a young woman, I guess you'd call her."

Chen stared at the Captain, astonished. "You mean, you let someone walk out of a top security area without searching them?"

"There were exceptional circumstances, sir. Besides, she wasn't a suspect."

"*Kuan Yin*! In this kind of operation *everyone* is a suspect!"

"You don't understand, sir. She was the daughter of a Junior Minister. And not just any Junior Minister. She was Shang Mu's daughter."

"Shang Mu? You mean *that* Shang Mu?"

Johnson nodded.

"Ah . . ."

"You understand, then?"

"You're absolutely certain it was her?"

"Absolutely, sir. I had two of my men escort her home."

"I see." Chen considered a moment. The Captain was probably right. Shang Mu's daughter was the last person likely to be involved in this. Nor would he, in Johnson's place, have risked offending the Junior Minister by strip-searching his daughter – not unless it was really necessary. Even so . . .

"Who saw her beside yourself?"

"My lieutenant . . . Oh, and a young guard. He was the one who brought her to the barrier."

"The guard . . . is he on duty now?"

"No, but I can have him brought here if you wish. He's stationed on this deck. It'll only take a moment or two."

"Okay. Do that. I'll see him here. Meanwhile . . ." Chen half turned, indicating the huge piles of bits and pieces that remained to be sifted through.

"Good luck," Johnson said, grinning. "I hope you find something."

As the Captain left, the lieutenant appeared in the doorway, carrying a tray. "Your *ch'a*, Major Kao."

Chen smiled. "Wonderful!" He glanced at the timer inset into his wrist. It was ten minutes after four. "Just put it down there. And thanks, lieutenant. I'm grateful."

"Sir!"

Alone again, Chen lifted the lid of the *chung* and sniffed. It smelt good. Just what he needed.

He crouched, looking back at the nearest pile, studying the exposed strata. For a moment or two he saw only the unwanted detritus of a typical deck, then, with mounting interest, he began to pick things from the pile.

When the young guard came, Chen was sitting on one of the lower piles, the *chung* cradled in his lap. In a small polythene bag beside him was a jumble of black lacquered computer parts.

The guard stopped just inside the door and came to attention, his head bowed. "Private Lauer, sir. I'm told you wanted to speak to me."

"Yes, Lauer. Relax, lad. I only want to ask you a few questions, that's all. About the young woman you helped yesterday. I understand you kept her out of trouble."

"Yes, sir."

Chen took a long sip from the *chung*, then looked back at

the guard. He was still a boy. Seventeen, eighteen at most. Only three years older than his son, Jyan.

"Relax, Lauer, please . . ." He smiled, trying to reassure the young man. "All I want to know is what you did, what you saw. You're not in any trouble. Oh, and I know what you're thinking. You're thinking that because I'm special services I want to trap you. But it's not true. You did nothing wrong. All you did was help a young woman who was out of her level. You saw the danger to her and you acted, neh?"

"Yes, sir."

"Well, that's commendable." Chen held out the *chung*, offering it to the young man, encouraging him to take it, forcing him to come closer.

"So when did you first notice her?"

The guard lowered the *chung* and wiped his mouth, then handed the *chung* back to Chen. "She was standing in the corridor, sir, not far from where I was, at the guardpost. She was watching the *hua pen*, the storyteller, and sketching what she saw . . ."

"Sketching?"

"Yes, sir. You know, with one of those computerised sketchboards. I thought it was odd. I could see she was . . . well, not from this level. Her clothes, the cut of her hair. I could see it at once."

"See what?"

The young man smiled, looking past Chen momentarily, remembering. "First Level . . . that's what I told myself. She's First Level."

Chen stared at the young man, surprised by the awe in his voice, the longing in his eyes, then set the *chung* down.

"What did you see?"

"Her . . . Well, she's . . ." The young man shook his head, suddenly flustered, a colour appearing at his neck. "I don't know, sir. It's just what I felt, looking at her. So intense, she was. So . . . so *there*."

Chen looked down. He had it all. All he needed. All, that was, except a reason.

"Okay," he said gently. "That's all I need. You can go now, Lauer. And thanks . . ."

"Sir!" The young guard came to attention, then backed away.

Chen took a long breath, then, lifting the polythene bag from the floor beside him, stood, stretching his limbs. It was too early yet to go and see the girl. He'd leave it a few hours, get himself some breakfast, then pay a visit. And then? Chen touched his tongue to his top teeth and shook his head. And then he'd do his job. After all, General Rheinhardt wanted results.

* * *

As the great doors swung open, Shang Mu turned, watching as his master, the First Dragon, backed out of the audience chamber, his head bowed low.

Like his master, Shang Mu had been summoned from his bed and brought here through the darkness to Tsu Ma's palace on the shore of the Caspian Sea. As the doors thudded shut, the First Dragon turned, his face like a wall, expressionless. As he passed, Shang Mu fell in behind him silently, knowing, from the tension in the great man's back, that the audience had not gone well.

Tsu Ma had been clever. Very clever indeed. He had had them brought separately, giving them no time to consult or prepare for the meeting. Moreover, in not waiting on the First Dragon to make the first move, he had seized the initiative and thus taken the upper hand. As in a game of *wei chi*, they were forced now to defend.

The First Dragon's cruiser was waiting on the pad outside the palace. An honour guard lined the broad path leading from the building to the craft, flaming torches held aloft, lighting the pre-dawn darkness. Shang Mu followed his master between the torches and up into the battlecruiser. As the doors hissed shut and the engines fired, he stood to one side, watching his master settle in his great chair, servants fussing about him.

"He knows," the First Dragon said, looking across at his

Junior Minister, his voice competing with the engines' roar.

The servants – deaf mutes, raised in the First Dragon's own household – continued to tend to the great man, oblivious of what was being said.

"Knows what?" Shang Mu asked, chilled by the thought that their plans might be known to the Seven.

The great man looked away, his anger held in check. "We have been *warned*. Moreover, we are to be watched, like common criminals."

"*Watched*?" Shang Mu's mouth fell open in astonishment. "I do not understand, *I Lung*. To watch the Thousand Eyes . . . it is unheard of!"

"And yet it is to be done. Karr's special force, his *shen t'se*, are to be appointed to the task. They are to watch the Watchers, it seems. To keep an eye on the Great Eye itself."

Beneath the surface irony of the words was a savage anger that did not escape Shang Mu. He thought quickly. "Did he say why, Master?"

The First Dragon rested his head back, letting a servant remove his wig, then begin to rub salve into his shaven scalp. "He spoke of rumours that had come to his ear. Rumours of corruption and mismanagement. Not at the highest level, of course. No, Tsu Ma is too smart to accuse the Council itself. But he felt it would be best if an independent body investigated the claims, especially in view of the new arrangements."

"New arrangements, *I Lung*? What new arrangements?"

"The cuts . . ." The First Dragon turned, waving the servant away, then signalled that Shang Mu should come and sit across from him.

"There is more," he said, leaning towards Shang Mu, as the craft slowly lifted. "It seems we are to provide Karr's force with copies of all our files."

He stared back at his master, dumbstruck. "But that is outrageous, *I Lung*! Why, when our great Ministry was formed . . ."

The First Dragon raised a hand. "I know, Shang Mu. In

effect, this breaks the long-standing agreement between the Seven and the Ministry. Oh, technically, the Seven are entitled to do as they will, but in practice . . ." He sat back, cupping his closed right fist in his left. "Well . . . if we had any doubts before, we have none now, neh? They mean to break us, Shang Mu. To destroy the last barrier between Chung Kuo and total anarchy. But we can't let them . . . we *won't* let them."

He moved his hands apart, spreading his fingers, deliberately calming himself, then, turning in his chair, raised his right hand, summoning the ship's Steward.

The Steward came across and bowed, waiting silently, his eyes on the First Dragon's hands. As Shang Mu watched, the great man gave signed instructions with his fingers, finishing with the signal of dismissal. Like all else about the great man, this discipline impressed Shang Mu. If a single man epitomised the great principle of *Shen Chung* – of Caution – then it was the First Dragon. Things, then, were bad, when such a solid, upright man should even consider going to war with his own Masters.

Shang Mu looked down, a cold sobriety sweeping over him. War. He had known it last night, looking through the files. And though the thought of it appalled him, some colder, more clinical part of him understood the need and saw no alternative. The servants must become the masters, if they were properly to serve.

Looking up, he saw that the great man was watching him, almost as if he knew what he was thinking.

"Where now?" he asked, feeling, in that moment, a special bond between himself and his master.

"To Yu Shu," the First Dragon answered. "To see our friend An Sheng. But not directly. From now on we do nothing directly. Not until we must."

* * *

The tiny hologram flickered brightly in the darkened room, smoke from the incense stick drifting through the image. In its faint, blue-tinted light the kneeling girl seemed like a giant

191

statue, immobile, her head lowered respectfully, her hands folded in her lap.

"Are you sure this is the best course, Shang Han-A?" the hologram asked, leaning forward slightly, one hand stroking the long, white, plaited beard that flowed almost to its waist. "Is there not some better way to heal the breach between you?"

Hannah was silent a moment, contemplating what her great-grandfather, Shang Chu had said, then answered him. "I believe not, honourable great-grandfather. My stepmother is frequently unwell, and that makes her . . . tetchy, let us say. As for me, I am young, impetuous sometimes. It is a fault, I realise, but one that time will cure. However, if I stay here the friction between myself and my stepmother will remain and, in all probability, get worse. I would hate to see that. If I go, then the source of my stepmother's irritation is gone. Her health will improve, and we shall both be happier. And that would be good for my father, neh? To have two happy homes, rather than a single unhappy one."

"It would, indeed." The hologram straightened up, smiling. "I am pleased with you, Shang Han-A. Your concern for your father's happiness is most dutiful. I shall speak to him next time he consults me and let him know what I think on this matter. For now, however, it would be best if you said nothing. Your father has much on his mind. These are hard times for him. You must do all you can to ease his mind in the days ahead."

"I understand, great-grandfather, and I shall do my utmost."

Hannah bowed, then, leaning forward slightly, placed her fingers lightly on the panel in front of the hologram. At once the image faded, leaving only the bright red point of the burning incense stick.

There was the sound of a match being struck, a sudden flare of light. A second incense stick was placed on the altar, in a tiny silver holder just to the right of the first. There was the vague murmur of a blessing from the kneeling girl, then, as she brushed her fingers against the second pad, another hologram appeared, this one much shorter and stockier than the first, the beard darker, bushier.

"Greetings, honourable grandfather," Hannah said, lowering her head respectfully. "I pray you're well."

The figure lifted its chin and gave a short laugh. "As well as the dead can be, young Hannah."

In the darkness Hannah smiled. The holograms had been programmed by the living men to reflect what of their personalities they wished to survive them. Normally this resulted in a rather stiff, one-dimensional self-portrait that emphasised all the virtues while editing-out anything which might be viewed as "unseemly" by future generations. But her grandfather, Shang Wen Shao, had not been such a man. He had always claimed that a man was all his different selves – fool and sage, father and lover, braggart and coward, good friend and savage enemy – and had programmed his own ancestral hologram to reveal all of these different aspects. Of all the family holograms, this was Hannah's favourite, and she consulted it whenever she had problems in her personal life, for grandfather Wen Shao could be trusted never to mouth platitudes, but to offer advice from the depth of his own considerable experience. Six wives, four concubines and a good few dozen lovers had made him wise in the ways of the world and a good judge of women. And though he had been a fool in business and had lost much of the great financial empire his father had built from nothing, he was, in Hannah's eyes, the better man – an opinion she was careful to conceal from her father.

"What's up, Hannah? Is that shrew of a stepmother of yours troubling you again? Or is it something else this time?"

Hannah bowed a little lower. "You see right through me, honourable grandfather."

The hologram gave a little guffaw of laughter and thumped at its chest. "I'd have said it was the other way about, wouldn't you, girl? That you see through me!"

Again Hannah smiled to herself. She had heard all of these jokes a thousand times, but the familiarity of them warmed her.

"We are all smoke in the eyes of the gods, grandfather."

"Yes . . . But be specific, Hannah. Hurry. I need to piss."

Hannah bowed again, wishing, not for the first time, that she had known her grandfather in life. He must have been a real character. Hannah could see how her father – cast in great-grandfather Chu's puritanical mould – would have been offended by his own father. She could imagine him wincing at the old man's vulgarity even as he bowed dutifully before him. Not that her father didn't have a sense of humour, it was just that he lacked his father's spontaneity, his open, generous nature.

She hesitated a moment longer, then asked. "Can I trust you, grandfather?"

Wen Shao leaned back, as if to see her better. "Now that's an odd question, my girl. Perhaps the oddest you've asked. Can you trust me? Hmmm . . ." He scratched his chin. "Well now, I really don't know. If you were a wife of mine I'd have to say no. Not any further than you could throw me. But it's not that kind of thing, is it?"

"No, grandfather."

"Then speak. I'll not repeat a word, not even if some clever young programmer tries to tamper with my memory circuits!"

She smiled. "Then let me ask you this. If you knew a secret, a big secret – one that was so big it affected everyone and everything they did – then what would you do? Would you let everyone know, or would you keep it to yourself?"

Wen Shao had narrowed his eyes. He looked back at his granddaughter inscrutably from his broad *Hung Mao* features, as if, for that moment, mimicking the Han whose name his grandfather had adopted a century before.

"That's a big secret," he said, then shook his head, blowing out a noisy breath. "In fact it sounds like the kind of secret your father is fond of keeping, neh? Have you been prying among his things again, young Hannah?"

"No, grandfather."

"But they're connected, neh?"

"Yes, grandfather."

"Ahh . . ." He smacked his lips, then, unexpectedly, he sat, crossing his legs beneath him. "Well, you know how I feel about your father's work. I've never liked it. I wish now that I'd never paid to have him educated. It seems such a waste – to devote oneself to such . . . such *pettiness*."

"Pettiness, grandfather? But surely what he does is of the greatest importance?"

Wen Shao laughed. "You think so? But what does the great Tao teach us? That in everything is its opposite. That that which seems greatest is, in truth, the smallest. As Chuang Tzu says, there is nothing in the world bigger than the tip of an autumn hair, and Mount T'ai is little."

"Maybe so, grandfather, but you have still not answered me."

"Haven't I?" Wen Shao laughed, then leaned forward, tugging at the air by his left foot as if he were plucking a blade of grass. "Why, and there I was thinking I had."

She laughed, watching him chew at the imaginary blade. "Maybe you only think you have."

"Ah . . . that must be it."

"Grandfather?"

He stopped chewing and smiled. "You want a straight answer, is that it?"

"This once I'd appreciate it."

He shrugged. "Okay. But you won't like it. My advice is to forget your big secret. It'll only bring you unhappiness. You and that proper man you call your father."

"Your son," she reminded him.

"So the genetic charts would have me believe . . . but that aside, I'm serious, my girl. Let others worry about this secret. Leave the sleepless nights to them. You're a young woman, Hannah. You should be out meeting young men and having a good time. That's what this life is for."

She looked away, for the first time in her life disappointed by his answer. But then, what had she expected? For him to endorse her crazy scheme? To tell her, yes, Hannah, go ahead and ruin your life? No. Wen Shao was Wen Shao. And she had too much of her father's blood in her – was too much her father's daughter.

"You're disappointed," he said, looking up at her, the smoke from the incense stick making his seated form shimmer momentarily. "I know what you wanted, my girl, but you asked me a question and I answered it. Do as you will. Take on the great world of levels, if you must. But don't ask me to tell you you're right." He smiled. "In fact, if you ask me, I think you're mad even to consider the idea. But I respect your madness. It's an admirable trait – one I wish your father possessed in greater measure. But take care, little Hannah. The world is uncaring. It's a mechanism for chewing people up and spitting them out. And only fools like me survive."

"You're no fool, grandfather."

"No. Maybe not. Not in the sense most people mean, yet I was fool enough in my youth. Fool enough to think the world could be a better place."

"*You*, honourable grandfather? I'd never have guessed!"

He laughed. "Yes, I know my reputation. The old goat, they called me. A drunk, they said, a reprobate. But I wasn't always so, my girl. It was the world that made me thus. That and the sweet scent of sweat on a woman's skin . . ."

"*Grandfather*!"

"Forgive me . . ." The tiny figure stood, brushing its hands together. "However, I really must go now. Even ghosts must have their rest, neh?"

She smiled and lowered her head respectfully. "Then sleep well, grandfather. And thank you. You've been very helpful."

"I have?" He smiled. "Well now, that makes a change. Maybe there's hope for me after all."

"Maybe . . ."

She leaned across and touched the pad. The figure shimmered and was gone. Hannah stared at the empty space a moment, then sat back on her heels, thinking.

He was right, of course. It was insane even to think of getting involved. The best thing to do would be to take the file and feed it into the incinerator, but for some reason she couldn't do that. Something in her prevented that. Some perversity of nature.

"*Nu Shi*! *Nu Shi*!"

Hannah turned as her *amah* appeared in the doorway, her face excited.

"What is it, Wei?"

"A soldier has come, Mistress," the young maid answered, bowing low. "A Security Major . . ."

Hannah stood. "For my father, you mean?"

"No, Mistress. For you. He is talking to your stepmother even now . . ."

"My *stepmother*! Oh, gods!" Hannah lifted the hem of her silk and moved past the young girl, her bare feet padding quickly along the tiled hallway.

A Major had come... But what did that mean? Was she discovered? Or was this merely a courtesy call, to see if she was all right after her experience? As she approached the big double doors that led through to her stepmother Huang Hui's rooms she stopped, calming herself. It was all right. It had to be. Because if it wasn't they'd have asked to see her father. That was the way they worked. And it wouldn't have been a mere Major, it would have been General Rheinhardt himself.

She took a long breath, then indicated to the waiting servants that they should open the doors.

Inside her stepmother, Chih Huang Hui, was sitting up in a big chair heaped with cushions, the whole thing presenting the illusion of a great bed tipped up onto its edge, her pale Han face staring out from a cocoon of red silk. In front of her stood the Major, his back to Hannah. His large-boned body filled almost to bursting the powder blue dress uniform he was wearing. Over his shoulder was a black leather despatch bag of the same kind her father's messengers used. As he turned she felt a flicker of surprise. He was Han.

Huang Hui looked across at her and gave a weary, sickly smile. "Han-A . . . I'm glad you've come, I was just about to call you. This is Major Kao of Security . . ."

The Major lowered his closely shaven head smartly, then

197

straightened up. He was a remarkably plain-looking man, with crude, almost unformed features. His nose was somehow too big, as were his ears. And yet his mouth was strong, and his eyes . . .

"Major Kao." Hannah went across and bowed to her stepmother, then turned, facing him again. "I'm told you wish to see me."

He smiled at her, not insolently, like some of the young officers smiled at her, but as her own father smiled. That, and the strange honesty of his eyes, made her look away briefly, wondering.

"I have a few questions I need to ask," he said quietly. "That is, if that's all right with you, *Nu Shi* Shang? About yesterday. There was no time then, I understand, and the Captain was rightly more concerned with your safety than with Security procedures. But it would help us greatly if you could make a simple statement about what you saw."

"*Safety* . . . ? *Statement* . . . ?" Hannah's stepmother leaned forward, her pinched face instantly suspicious. "Han-A . . . what *have* you been up to?"

She was about to answer, but the Major interceded. "Oh, it is nothing, Madam Shang. There was an incident. Your daughter was caught up on the periphery of it. The questions, as I said, are a mere formality."

"*Incident*? What kind of incident?"

This time Hannah made sure she got in first. "There was a criminal, Stepmother Huang . . . a *revolutionary*! A troop of the Major's soldiers chased him through the corridors and trapped him, but he put up a fight and they had to shoot him. There was blood everywhere . . ."

Huang Hui sank back into her cushions, an expression of sheer horror on her face. "*Aiya!*" she muttered, fanning herself with a vigour that was surprising for one so clearly invalided.

Hannah turned, a strange gleam in her eyes and looked directly at the Major. "Well . . . if you would come through, Major Kao, I shall arrange for a servant to bring *ch'a*. Have you had breakfast?"

The Major hesitated. "Yes, I . . . I had some earlier. I . . ." Then, as if remembering himself, he turned, bowing low to Huang Hui. "Madam Shang. It was kind of you to receive me. Please give my regards to your husband, the Junior Minister, when he returns. May I also say how much I hope your health improves. However, if you would excuse me now . . ."

A wan smile appeared on Huang Hui's face. "Major Kao . . ."

Kao Chen turned back, looking to the girl, who smiled and turned away. He followed, stopping at the door to look back. The pale-faced invalid was recumbent in the huge, upright bed of red cushions. Now that the audience was over, Huang Hui seemed to have collapsed in upon herself, her frail figure losing its last glimmer of animation. As he watched, two servants hurried to her, plumping up her cushions and tending to her.

He watched a moment longer, then, with a tiny shudder, went out into the corridor to join the waiting girl.

* * *

"Well?" she asked, turning to face him.

Chen looked about him at the room, taking it all in. Everywhere he looked there were signs of wealth, of a luxury he could never aspire to. The left-hand wall and the end wall were lined with shelves, the shelves crowded with ancient-looking leather-bound books that he could smell even from where he stood. In the right-hand corner was a huge wooden desk, not unlike the one that stood in General Rheinhardt's office. Next to it was a big, glass-fronted cabinet containing all manner of small, exotic-looking objects, few of which he recognised. Behind that, in a case on the wall, was a banner of some kind, showing a blood red cross on a white background. The rest of that wall was filled with sketches and paintings of various sizes, unusual only in that they showed scenes from the levels. Chen studied them a moment then looked down. Beneath his feet was a thick, richly-woven rug that would have carpeted three rooms in his own apartment, while to his right, only a *ch'i* or so from where he stood . . .

"Major Kao?"

He jerked his head up, meeting the young woman's eyes. Strong, hazel-coloured eyes that could have been Han.

"Forgive me," he began, "but should we be in here? Your father . . ."

She smiled pleasantly. "You misunderstand, Major Kao. This is *my* study, not my father's."

"Ah . . ." Chen blushed. Already he was showing his gaucheness. The truth was he had met many great men and their families, but never, before this moment, had he seen inside one of their Mansions. That had always been someone else's job – someone more senior and less *Han* than he. But this time he had been determined. He was going to let no one take this case out of his hands.

He hesitated, looking about him once more, then, faintly embarrassed, pointed to the large hemisphere close by that had caught his attention. "Forgive me, *Nu Shi* Shang, but just what is this?"

She laughed and came across. "It's known as a HoloVisual Imager, but I call it my Magic Theatre. It's a miniature stage, you see. The actors are tiny holograms. It's programmed to perform most of the major Han plays, but you can programme it yourself if you like. You can write your own plays, make your own characters . . . do what you want with it, really."

She stared at the hemisphere fondly, one hand resting lightly on its curved glass surface, then looked back at Chen, smiling broadly. "I'd show you, Major, but I'm sure you're busy, neh?"

"Indeed . . ." But he was unable not to answer her smile with his own, her youthful enthusiasm reminded him so much of his own daughter. "It is a very simple matter, *Nu Shi* Shang, I . . ."

"Hannah," she interrupted him. "Please, call me Hannah."

Chen nodded. "Okay . . . *Hannah*. All I need is your verbal statement about what happened yesterday. Once that's done,

I'll get that transcribed and we'll send you two copies, one for your signature and return, the other to keep."

"I understand. Well . . . shall we go over to the desk, Major?"

He hesitated. "It is Chen. Kao Chen. I . . ." He looked away briefly, then looked back at her. "All these things . . . I've not seen anything like them. They . . ." He shrugged, not quite knowing what he meant.

"They're just things," she said offhandedly, clearing a space on the desk, then pulling out a chair. "My father has collected a lot of things across the years. If I like them, he lets me keep them." She turned, looking back at him. "They come from all over. His office, you see . . ."

Chen raised a hand, indicating that he understood and really didn't wish to know. What the Thousand Eyes did – what they *sanctioned* – really wasn't his business.

"I have a tape," he said, going across. "You can either speak directly into it, or I can prompt you with questions."

She indicated the chair, then went round the desk and sat, facing him. "You ask, I'll answer. That's probably the best way, neh?"

Chen nodded, then sat, placing his bag down beside the chair. Taking the tape from his tunic pocket, he snapped the seal, then placed it on the desk between them. From this moment on it would record all that was said between them. Chen looked down at the timer at his wrist and spoke.

"The date is the fifteenth day of March 2212 and the time is twenty-seven minutes after eight in the morning. My name is Major Kao Chen of the T'ang's Security service and I am in the Mansion of Junior Minister Shang Mu, interviewing his daughter, Shang Han-A concerning the incident that took place yesterday afternoon in the Mid levels of Rathenow stack."

Chen looked across the desk and met her eyes. "So, *Nu Shi* Shang, what exactly were you doing in the Mids at Rathenow?"

"I go to College at Rathenow. When there are no lectures,

I often go down the levels. I like to see what's happening down there."

"College?" Chen frowned. "But I thought you were only sixteen?"

She smiled. "I graduated early, Major Kao. If you had checked my personal records, you'd have seen that I've been there a year and a half now."

"Ah . . ." He'd known about the College. In fact the dead man had been a graduate of Rathenow. All of his known associates there had already been arrested for questioning, but Chen had not thought to check on the girl. He'd assumed, because of her age, that she was still at school. Besides, he'd been loath to pull her file from Central records, just in case the Thousand Eyes had security tags on all their employees' families' files. The last thing he wanted was for the Thousand Eyes to come down hard on him.

"I didn't know him," she said, before he could speak again. "The man who was killed, I mean. I saw him clearly as he ran past me, and I don't think I'd ever seen him before. But that's not really surprising, is it?"

"No . . ." But he was still thrown by the fact that she was at College at all. He had been assuming that it was sheer coincidence that the Junior Minister's daughter had been there, of all places, when the man had been cornered with the File, but now he began asking himself if that were really so. What if she had been there for just that reason – to meet the man and take the File? For there was no doubt about one thing: she *had* the File. Here, perhaps, in her rooms, or somewhere else. Somewhere she'd hidden it, between yesterday afternoon and now.

"What do you do at College?"

"Is that relevant, Major Kao?"

"Maybe not. I was just interested. If you want to move on . . . ?"

"No. It's okay. I study art. Art and sculpture. Those paintings and sketches on the wall behind you. They're mine."

Chen turned, looking at them again, impressed. "*Yours*? I

thought . . ." He turned back. "You're certain you'd never seen the man before?"

She smiled. "No, Major Kao. I was watching the *hua pen*, you see. Sketching him . . ."

"Sketching him? You mean, with paper and pencil?"

"No. With a sketchboard. You know, one of those computer-generated things."

"I know. My son has one. He too wants to study art."

"Your son?"

Chen waved the question aside. "Look . . . can I possibly see your sketches? They might help us in some way."

"Of course," she said, getting up. "I think I left the sketchboard in the other room. If you'll wait just a second or two . . ."

He turned, watching her go through, expecting her to come back and say she couldn't find it, to make some excuse. But when she returned, it was with the sketchboard. She came across, handing it to him.

"You know how to work it?"

Chen nodded, then fiddled with the controls, trying to remember how to summon up the last few stored items. "They're a nuisance to clean, neh?" he said, looking up at her.

"Here," she said, leaning across him to tap out an instruction on the touch-pad. "I only made one sketch. I'd have made more, but there wasn't time. I'd barely finished this one when it all happened."

He stared at the sketch, surprised. If she had taken the inner workings out of the machine, then she could not have kept the sketch, but here it was, and from the security camera records he had seen, she had captured the scene about the *hua pen* almost perfectly.

"It's very good," he said, handing it back to her. "Perhaps we could have a copy . . . for the investigation file. There just might be something in it that will help us."

She smiled. "Of course. I'll print one out and send it to you. Oh, and I could sketch the man for you, if you like. I'm told I've a good visual memory."

For a moment he had begun to doubt his own theory – to think he'd been mistaken – but her words made him reassess things. *A good visual memory*. So it was possible that she had re-worked the sketch on a second, a *spare* sketchboard, just in case someone like himself should come asking awkward questions.

Chen looked down at the despatch bag which lay beside his chair. "No. There's no need. But if you would tell me now what you saw."

As he listened to her, Chen thought it all through, examining all the angles. She had the File. There was no doubt of that. She had removed it from the scene in the inside of her sketchboard. But why? And was it only coincidence that she was there at that very moment?

It seemed unlikely. The more he thought about it, the more certain he was that she *was* involved – that she in fact *knew* the man. Checks could be made, of course, and if they could find camera record of her talking to him, then the matter could be proved. Alternatively, they could search the Mansion and locate the File. Both were fairly routine and straightforward procedures. The question was, did he really want to do either?

It wasn't just the fact that her father was a Junior Minister in the Thousand Eyes and senior adviser to the First Dragon himself, though that was not something to be readily dismissed. It was more to do with how he himself felt about this matter. To have this young woman arrested, to have her tortured and eventually killed, simply for knowing the truth about their world – was that right? Or was it, as he had increasingly begun to feel, a kind of evil?

Chen shivered inwardly, remembering what he himself had seen, at the research station he had been posted to, three years before. He had seen what the system he served was capable of – of the moral depths his Masters plumbed to keep their world in check – and had been changed by it. Oh, he still served, for that was all he really knew, yet it was with a kind of self-disgust, and with a desire, if possible, to do what he could, however small, to counterbalance that great evil.

As she came to the end, he gave a tiny bow and, his decision made, stood, picking the tape up off the desk.

"Thank you," he said quietly. "That's all I need. We'll terminate the interview here, at . . ." he glanced at his timer ". . . forty-nine minutes after eight." He placed pressure on the top of the tiny unit, switching off the tape and sealing it.

"That's all, then?"

He nodded. "Yes. You'll get the copies of your statement. Oh, and your father will get a copy of the final report. Apart from that, well . . . it was very pleasant to meet you, Hannah."

She stared back at him a moment, then stood, coming round the desk. "I've just realised. I forgot to ask the servant to bring the *ch'a*. If you've the time?" She raised an eyebrow inquisitively.

"No," he said, tempted by her offer, wanting to ask her about the various things in the glass-fronted cabinet behind him; curious to see the Magic Theatre in operation. "It's kind of you, but I must get back. I've a lot to do. Besides, I haven't seen my family in three days. You know how it is."

She laughed. "I wish I did. I'm afraid I don't get on with my father's second wife, nor with my half-brother and half-sister. We are too . . . well, *different*, let's say. Oh, it's not a racial thing, Kao Chen. It's just . . ." She shrugged.

"I understand," he said, seeing it all clearly. "It must be difficult for you."

"Difficult?" Again she laughed, but this time there was a hint of sourness. "She is the First Dragon's youngest sister, you understand. A *very* important lady. It was a convenient alliance for my father, but some days I think she would have preferred my father's first marriage to have been without issue."

Chen winced inwardly at the pain he heard in her voice.

"Is it that bad?"

She looked back at him, forcing herself to smile. "Sometimes. But I can give as good as I get. I was eight when my mother died. Nine when my father married that woman. It toughened me up, you might say. Forced me to be a survivor. And that's what it's about, neh? Surviving. Or so my father's friends all say."

"Maybe . . . but there ought to be more to life than that, neh?"

She nodded.

"Anyway, I must go now." Chen bowed, then turned, making for the door.

"Major Kao?"

He turned back. "Yes?"

"Your bag . . ."

"Keep it. I think you might find it . . . interesting."

"Interesting?" She stared back at him, her eyes half-lidded.

"You'll see." He smiled. "It was pleasant meeting you, Hannah. I'm sorry that our acquaintance has to be so brief, but good luck."

He bowed again, then turned, making his way out. And as he walked down the long, luxuriant corridor, following the House Steward, he smiled, imagining her surprise when she opened the bag.

Small things, he thought, letting himself be ushered out of the great doorway. *That's all we can do to counter the great evil in our world. Small things.* And yet, for once, he felt pleased, as if he had done something big. He laughed and walked on, making for the lift.

Something that would reverberate.

* * *

An Sheng's palace lay in the valley just below them, its tiled roofs a gleaming red in the late afternoon sunlight, its high white walls heavily patrolled by armed guards. As they made their way down, a horseman rode up the path to greet them, dismounting and pressing his forehead into the dust at the First Dragon's feet.

"Highness," the man said breathlessly, lifting his head but keeping his eyes averted. "My Master was not expecting you until this evening. But he greets you warmly and asks you to accompany me."

The First Dragon grunted then turned, looking to Shang Mu. "I suppose Prince An knows best."

"He would have good reason, *I Lung*," Shang answered quietly, conscious of how *he* would have felt had the First Dragon descended on *him* three hours early. "I am told Li Yuan has spies in all the households. Prince An would want to make sure that news of our visit did not get back to the wrong ears."

The First Dragon smiled tightly. "Ah. Of course." He turned back to the waiting servant. "Lead on, man. One of my servants will take your horse."

At the gate An Sheng's third son, Prince Mo Shan, a tall man in his thirties, was waiting to greet them formally. With a minimum of fuss he ushered them through into the cool of a small banqueting hall where a table had been laid with sweetmeats and wine.

"You must forgive us, *I Lung*," the Prince said, dismissing the servants and going to the table, intent on honouring the First Dragon by serving him himself. "My father sleeps in the afternoon and I am loath to wake him before he has had his full rest. After all, such matters as must be discussed . . ."

He let the elliptic nature of his words hang in the air a moment, then half turned, looking down at the table. "However, would you have some refreshments after your journey, *I Lung*?"

Shang Mu, standing to the right of the First Dragon and two steps back, watched the side of his Master's face, noting the tension in his neck muscles. The First Dragon was clearly put out. Even so, he smiled and made polite conversation, as if nothing were amiss. *Maybe*, Shang thought, *this is a power game of some kind. Maybe An Sheng thinks the First Dragon has come early to make some kind of point, and is acting thus to demonstrate that he will not be hurried into anything.* If so that was worrying, for it spoke of mistrust and potential division, and that was the last thing any of them needed just now.

The First Dragon turned, looking at him. "Shang Mu? Will you have something to drink?"

"A cordial, Master," he said, noting the coded signal they had agreed on earlier. If the First Dragon looked elsewhere when he addressed him, he was to say nothing; but if he looked directly at him . . .

Shang Mu looked past his Master at the Prince. "A man needs his rest," he said, watching Mo Shan pour him a tumbler of the cordial, "and a great man more than most. He cannot afford to be tired. His responsibilities are great, therefore his mind must be clear, like a mountain stream."

Mo Shan handed him his drink. "So it is, Master Shang. Especially when the matter is as great as this."

The First Dragon came closer. "Your father has discussed this with you, Mo Shan?"

"I am my father's hands, my father's eyes. To be effective I must know what he is thinking."

Shang Mu smiled, understanding at last. Whether they had arrived early or late would have made no difference. They might dine with An Sheng, but they would deal with his son.

The First Dragon, quick to pick up on what was happening, spoke to Shang Mu again, this time looking to the Prince and smiling as he did so. "It is as I was saying on the journey here, Shang Mu, a great man is made greater by the ability of his servants, and who is more loyal a servant than a son?"

He raised his tumbler, toasting Mo Shan. "I trust you will be as the lips to the teeth."

"You understand then, *I Lung*?"

"Of course. It is only right that your father keep aloof from such matters. Indeed, it would be easier for us all were we to keep this matter . . . *informal*."

"Informal, *I Lung*?"

"Exactly. Great men are like great ships, they leave a huge wake wherever they go. It is easy for the eyes of the *hsiao jen* – the little men – to see them, neh? Whereas, if this matter were dealt with at a . . . let us say, slightly *lower* level . . ."

Mo Shan smiled then turned, looking directly at Shang Mu. "You speak, then, for the Ministry, Master Shang?"

Shang Mu returned the smile, but it was the First Dragon

who answered. "My Son-in-Law speaks for us all, as Uncle and Brother speak for the Family."

"Then let us talk, Master Shang. But first, *I Lung*, let me take you through to my father's rooms. I understand he is waking and wishes to greet his old friend."

"And I him." The First Dragon glanced at Shang Mu, giving a terse nod, then went across, moving past the waiting Prince and out into the corridor.

Alone, Shang Mu looked down into his tumbler and heaved a sigh. He understood. It was not merely a matter of who dealt with whom, but who would take the blame if things went wrong. This way it would be he and the young Prince, Mo Shan, whose heads would fall were their conspiracy to be uncovered. An Sheng and the First Dragon would claim no knowledge of it. It was a frightening thought. Yet that was the way of it, and he accepted it. Besides, the *I Lung* was right. A single meeting with An Sheng would draw little attention. After all, it was the job of the First Dragon to keep in touch with all the Heads of the Twenty-Nine. Yet to be seen in An Sheng's company too often would draw unwanted notice. No, it was best this way. And if their scheme succeeded it would do him no harm to have played so prominent a role.

Shang Mu put the heavy tumbler to his lips and drained it at a gulp, then went across, pouring himself a second. Listening to the First Dragon only a moment before, he had realised just how far they had come in the last twenty-four hours. The first step had been taken. They had done enough already to warrant execution. From here on there could be no mistakes. To survive he had to succeed.

In a week he could be dead, all trace of his family erased from the records. It was an appalling thought. And yet, what better incentive could he have been given? What better stimulus to make him think clearly and plan carefully? No, the First Dragon had been clever – very clever indeed. And he would repay the great man's trust. He would make this great enterprise work. Because to fail was unthinkable. To fail was . . . well, failure was not an option.

He heard footsteps. A moment later Prince Mo Shan appeared in the doorway. Now that the First Dragon had gone, he seemed more relaxed, as if he had cast off a skin.

"Well, Master Shang," he said, turning slightly, indicating the open door, the corridor beyond. "It would be a shame to waste the sunlight. Let us walk in the gardens, neh? I am sure we have much to discuss."

* * *

It was after one when Chen finally got home. The hallway was in darkness, but there was a light on in the kitchen at the far end. He went through, thinking it might be Wang Ti, up late, waiting for him, but it was a stranger, a young Han in her late teens. She turned, eyes wide, then, drying her hands quickly, gave a bow.

"Who are you?" he asked quietly, pulling the door to behind him, concerned not to wake the household. "Where is Tian Fen?"

"She had to leave, Major Kao. I am her cousin, Tian Ching."

"Ah . . ." He looked about him at the kitchen, satisfied by the cleanliness, the orderliness he saw, not unhappy that the slovenly Tian Fen had left. She had been trouble from the start. He looked back at the girl. "So you're my wife's new helper?"

She nodded.

He studied her a moment. She was a good-looking girl. Her hair was neatly cut, her clothes simple and modest, but there was an air about her. His eyes were drawn back to her face, to the smoothness of her skin, the freshness of her features. He smiled, then moved past her, inspecting what she had been doing, lifting the lid of the big cooking pot and sniffing deeply.

"What is this?"

"Green jade soup, Master."

"Ah . . ." He put a finger in the cold soup, tasting it. "Hmm."

"Would you like me to warm some up for you, Master?"

Her offer surprised him. He turned, looking at her, conscious suddenly of her proximity, of the soap-scrubbed scent of her, the way she looked at him, willing to please.

"Why not?" He laughed gently, then sat at table, watching as she poured some of the soup from the pot into a small bowl and began to heat it up, enjoying the simplicity of being tended to. Wang Ti had once done this for him. But that seemed long ago now. Long, long ago. He sighed and looked down.

"When did you start here, Tian Ching?"

"Tuesday, Master."

Tuesday? He looked up, surprised. But that was five days ago. Surely it hadn't been that long since he'd last been here? For a moment he watched her as she worked. Again it made him think of Wang Ti and the times he had sat like this, watching her at work, enjoying the simple sight of her body in movement, of the strength in her arms and shoulders. He shivered, then looked away.

"There . . ."

She placed the soup in front of him, then handed him a porcelain spoon. Heated up, the soup smelled delicious and he spooned it down quickly, not realising he had been so hungry. "So?" he said, pushing the bowl away, "How are you finding things?"

She was standing there, facing him across the table. At his question her eyes widened slightly and then she laughed; a soft, strangely sensual laugh, the whole of her face lighting up. "It's hard work, but I'm used to that. I'm the eldest of eleven children."

"Eleven?" Chen laughed, sitting back slightly, beginning to enjoy himself, to unwind after a long, hard day. "So you started early?"

She nodded, her smile broadening. "They used to call me *Shao nai nai*, little grandmother. Even so, I got my schooling. There's many still who can't say that."

"Yes . . ." He looked at the bowl. "Is there more?"

"Of course . . ." She hesitated, looking past him at the door.

He turned in his seat. His fourteen-year-old son, Jyan, was standing in the doorway, looking in bleary-eyed, his sleeping-robe pulled tight around him. Chen went across to him and hugged him close.

"Jyan, love . . . Couldn't you sleep?"

The boy stared past his father at the maid, then looked back up at him. "I heard voices. I thought . . ."

Chen heard the scrape of the bowl being picked up, the clink of the spoon as it was placed on the side.

"It's all right," the girl said, moving past them, stopping in the door to bow. "It is time I was in bed. Goodnight, Master. Goodnight, young Jyan."

Chen returned her brief smile. "Goodnight . . ."

He looked down at his son again, noting how Jyan turned his head, watching her go, the light of suspicion in his eyes, and sighed inwardly. The last thing he needed just now was trouble at home.

"So how are things?" he said brightly, lifting Jyan's chin. "How has your mother been?"

Jyan shook his chin free, looking away, his jaw set stubbornly. "You ought to know that yourself. You ought to spend more time with her."

Chen smiled wearily. "You're right. But it's not possible right now. Things are difficult. We're six men short and the workload has doubled this last year. It's hard to cope as it is."

Jyan made a small, irritable movement. "Even so . . ."

"Look . . . I'm here now, okay? And tomorrow night I'll get back early. I promise I will."

"You always say that. You never are."

"Look, I promise. All right? Maybe we'll get one of the new trivees out. Maybe . . ."

Jyan broke in brutally. "I've seen them all. Besides, I'm not talking about me. I'm all right. It's mother. She needs you and you're never here. She . . ."

"*All right*! Enough! I don't need you to tell me what I ought or ought not to be doing." He turned away, trying to calm himself, trying to still the anger, the frustration he felt at that

212

moment. "Look, Jyan," he said quietly. "Try and understand, will you? I am a Major in the T'ang's Security service and my work is very important. I can't just leave it whenever I want to. If something urgent comes up I have to deal with it there and then. And if that means that I'm away more than I'd like, that can't be helped. Not now."

"So when?" Jyan asked, his young eyes full of hurt. "When does it start to get better? When *will* you have some time for us?"

Chen sighed. "I don't know. Soon . . . Look, it's difficult right now. There have been a lot of changes. Things are in flux. But they'll get better. It's just a phase. It's . . ." He shrugged. "Look, I love you all. You see that, don't you? And if I work hard, it's for you. To keep us here, at this level. To keep you all away from . . . well, away from what's down there."

"Down there?" Jyan looked past him again. "Sometimes I think things were better when we were down there. Before you were promoted. Before . . ."

The boy stopped, as if he'd come up against a cliff-face, but Chen knew what he was thinking. He could see the pain in his eyes, the tightness of the cheek muscles where he struggled to control himself. Jyan was thinking about the loss of the baby. About the moment when Wang Ti had "gone" from them. He shivered, then pulled his son close, holding him tightly.

"It'll be okay, Jyan. I promise it will. Things will change. They'll be as they were. I promise you."

Jyan pulled away and nodded, then, wiping his hand across his face, he turned and went out. Chen stood, hearing the pad of his son's feet along the hallway, the slide of his door as it closed. He sighed, looking about him at the kitchen, then turned back, hearing the door slide again, the feet pad back.

Jyan's face appeared at the door again. "I almost forgot," he whispered. "There was a message. It came just after dinner."

"A message? Where?"

213

"On the table in the hall." Jyan hesitated, then came across and reached up to kiss his father's neck. "I love you, dad."

"And I you, my darling," Chen answered, hugging him briefly.

He waited for Jyan to return to his room, then went out. The message was on the table by the door. Chen picked up the long, pale envelope and sniffed at it. It smelled of incense. Going back into the kitchen, he sat at the table again, studying the unfamiliar handwriting, then slit the envelope open with his nail and unfolded the single sheet.

It was from the girl, the Junior Minister's daughter. *"Meet me,"* it read, *"at The Golden Carp, eighth bell tomorrow. Wear something casual. No uniforms. I've some friends you might wish to meet. Interesting types. Best wishes. Hannah."*

The Golden Carp . . . it was in the student quarter of Rathenow. But who were these friends? Were they accomplices? Members of True History? If so, then why was she taking such a chance? Because that was what this was. A rather dangerous chance. For all she knew, his act of kindness might have been a pretence – the bait in a trap. Unless she were genuine, of course: an innocent, unaware of the risks she was running. But that would mean that it really was coincidence that she'd been there just at that moment, and that he simply didn't believe.

Chen read the note through once more, then took it across to the sink. Taking a taper from the box, he lit it, letting the burning paper fall into the empty bowl. Maybe he'd meet her, maybe not. He would see how busy he was. In the meantime he would transcribe the tape and get it to her.

Chen lifted the jug and poured some water into the bowl, then sluiced the ash away. *There*, he thought. *Now no one will know.* But even as he tried to dismiss the idea, something told him he would go, if only to find out whether he was right about her.

Leaving a single light on in the kitchen, he went out and down the hallway to the toilet, standing over the bowl to piss, then turned and went out, crossing the hallway to his room. In the doorway he paused, hearing Wang Ti's gentle snoring in the darkness, then went inside, closing the door quietly behind him.

He stripped off, down to his breechcloth, then clambered in beside her. She was warm, her familiar scent strong in the dark. For a time he lay there, pressed against her back, hoping she would wake and turn, but there was nothing. She did not move, the rhythm of her breathing did not change. But so it was these days. So it had been for a long time now. It was as if he did not exist. As if . . .

He shuddered and then turned beneath the sheet, facing away from her, separating his body from the awful, taunting warmth of hers. Maybe that was why he worked so hard. Maybe that was why he kept away so often, so as not to face this torment. For that was what it was. Torment. Endless bloody torment. Only at such times, faced by the darkness and the long hours of the night, did he realise just what he had lost when Wang Ti had gone mad.

Chen took a long, shivering breath, trying to calm himself, to lay there and be at peace, but it was impossible. Sometimes her turned back seemed like a wall, vast and insurmountable, the very symbol of an indifference that was like death itself. He might wait forever and she would never turn and greet him lovingly, as she once had. Oh, he could take her from behind, certainly, and she would not stop him, but neither would she show any sign of wanting him. It would be as if he were making love to a corpse, or to the warm pretence of a human form. But it would not be Wang Ti. It would not be his darling wife.

He sat up, perching himself on the edge of the bed, his bare feet on the floor, his chin resting on the knuckles of his fists, knowing he would not sleep. He should not have come here. Not now. He should have come during the day. This . . . well, this only made things worse.

He looked up suddenly. There had been the soft rustling of cloth outside in the hallway. He stood and went to the door, thinking it was maybe his young daughter, Ch'iang Hsin having nightmares again. But it wasn't Ch'iang Hsin, it was the new maid, Tian Ching.

215

"Master . . ." she said quietly, giving a tiny bow, then moved past him, going into the toilet and pulling the door closed. Chen stood there, staring into the half-dark, conscious of what he'd seen. The girl's nightrobe had been of a thin, almost translucent cloth, and the shape of her young body, of her breasts and the dark triangle of her pubis, had been clearly visible. He drew a long breath, waiting, then heard the soft, almost musical sound of her urinating into the bowl.

Gods, he thought, the stiffness at his groin almost unbearable. How long had it been since he'd had a woman? Two years now? Three? He shivered, watching as she came out again, conscious of her eyes shining briefly, moistly in the half-dark as they met his then looked away. There was no doubting that look. He watched her move past him, conscious once more of the naked form of her beneath the thin cloth.

At her door she paused and turned, the briefest smile playing on her lips, and then she went inside. He listened, waiting to hear her door click shut, but there was nothing.

Chen stood there, conscious of the blood beating in his head, his chest, his limbs, desire like a dark tide flowing through him. Then, as if waking, he padded slowly down the hallway, checking at each of his children's doors to see if they were sleeping.

Outside the new maid's door he stopped, hearing her move on the bed inside the darkened room. He imagined her lying there naked beneath the thin sheet, waiting for him. The door was ajar. He had only to step inside. For a moment longer he stood there, aware of the tension in him, the madness that seemed to boil and bubble in his skull, then, reaching out, he put his hand on the edge of the door and slid it shut.

CHAPTER · 9

OLD MEN

The Senior Clerk sat behind his desk, stiff-backed, the gold-on-blue H-M motif on the wall behind him repeated on the patch on his chest. He smiled tightly, with a politeness bred of contempt, and leaned towards her slightly.

"Forgive me, Madam Lever, but it is . . . *unusual* for us to deal with new customers without . . . well, without an *introduction* of some kind."

Emily stared at the man then, taking the folder from her bag, placed it in front of her on the desk. Inside were more than a hundred separate receipts from the Hythe-MacKay Auction House, dated over a three-year period.

"I believe you dealt with my late father-in-law."

"Forgive me, Madam, even if that were so . . ."

She pushed the folder towards him. "I think *these* might refresh your memory . . ."

He stared at her a moment, then, reluctantly, flipped open the folder and removed the top sheet. "Ah . . ." he said, seeing what it was, "this is a . . . a *delicate* matter." He smiled at her again. "You see, officially none of these things exists. And these documents . . ." He shrugged. "Well, they're clearly fakes."

Cut the bullshit, she thought. *Tell me what I want to know.*

He hesitated, then closed the folder decisively. "Okay. If you would come with me, Madam Lever."

Good, she thought. *At last!*

He stood and bowed, waiting for her to stand, then put out an arm, all charm now, and ushered her out through a

217

different door to the one she'd entered the reception room by, and along a long, dimly-lit corridor.

"You understand how it is, Madam Lever," he said fawningly. "We have to be very sure of who we deal with. One mistake and we're all in trouble. The Ministry . . ." He stopped, opening the end door for her, then, much softer, "the Ministry would have our balls!"

* * *

The knocking came again, insistent now. Kemp stood impatiently, tying the sash about his portly waist, then shooed the girl into the next room.

"Stay in there," he said quietly, "and don't make a noise."

He waited a moment, then went across, pulling the door open with a flourish, smiling.

"Britton! You're earlier than I expected!"

The man outside was in his fifties, smartly dressed with a close-shaven scalp. He bowed, then stepped past Kemp into the room.

"You have it, I see," Kemp said, his eyes indicating the thick folder under Britton's arm.

"It wasn't easy," Britton answered, looking about him at the elegant apartment as if checking for assassins. Then, looking back at Kemp, he smiled tightly. "I had to trade upon a lot of old friendships to get this. There's a lot more here than's in the official security file. A *lot* more."

Kemp nodded, then gestured that Britton should take a seat, but Britton ignored him, walking across to the bathroom door. Opening it a fraction, he looked inside.

"They look after you well, *Shih* Kemp."

None of your business, Kemp thought, smiling broadly.

"Naturally," he said. "They're powerful men. They treat their friends well."

There was a couched threat in that which Britton didn't miss. He turned, looking sourly at Kemp.

"And how well do you treat *your* friends, *Shih* Kemp?"

Kemp went to the drawer beside the bed and took out the envelope, then turned back, facing Britton.

"It's all here. One hundred thousand, as agreed."

Britton's face was hard. "I've had a lot of expenses. As I said, there's a lot more here than you'd have thought."

Kemp eyed him. "I can find an extra twenty-five. But that's it."

Britton considered a moment then nodded. He stepped across and handed Kemp the dossier.

Kemp flicked through it, then whistled. Eight hundred pages. And good stuff by the look of it. He looked up at Britton and smiled. "I'll send the *expenses* over later."

"That's fine with me, *Shih* Kemp, but you might have a look at the passage I've marked on page 374 before I leave. There's an interesting sideline you might want me to follow up on."

Kemp raised an eyebrow, then flicked through, finding the page. He read the passage through then looked up again, interested.

"Hmm . . . So just what were our two friends investigating before they had their . . . *accident*?"

Britton smiled. It was like the smile of a shark. "Old Man Lever had hired them to look into the background of his son's new wife. It seems they came up with a blank. Lever paid them off, but for some reason they kept looking. And then this. Suspicious, neh?"

"Very." Kemp paused. "Do we know what they found?"

"No. It all got burned with them."

"Interesting." He considered, then nodded. "Okay. Look into it. But this time keep expenses to a minimum, huh?"

Britton stared at him, fish-eyed. "It'll cost what it costs."

Kemp shrugged. *Yes*, he thought, *but if it costs too much you can whistle.*

At the door Britton stopped, looking back at him. "Oh, and say goodbye to your girlfriend for me!"

Kemp sat there a moment after he'd gone, staring at the door, his anger slowly subsiding. Britton was becoming a nuisance. More than that, he was an insolent son of a bitch. But he was useful, there was no denying that, and if he could find out something juicy about Mary Lever, then all the better. There'd be a fat bonus in it for himself.

He looked down at the dossier again, then laughed. *The Old Men would pay him well for this. Very well indeed.* He flicked through, stopping at a picture of an adolescent Michael Lever with his father, and nodded to himself. Then, calling for the girl to come and help him dress, he turned to the front of the file and began to read.

* * *

The old men gathered about the statue of the boy, casting admiring, acquisitive eyes over its perfect marble form.

Egan, who had crouched to study the detail of the out-stretched hand, looked up at Fairbank and smoothed a hand over his polished skull. "Where did you find it?"

"There's a dealer in Europe I use," Fairbank answered, looking to the other two Heads as he did. "I'll give you his address. It seems there's a new man working the Clay in Central Europe. They say he's unearthed a whole treasure trove!"

"If it's like this, I'm interested," Green said, nodding in his distinctive manner. "Could I be indelicate, John, and ask what this cost?"

Fairbank's smile widened a fraction. "Have a guess?"

Chamberlain looked at the statue, considered a moment, then laughed. "I haven't a clue! Statuary really isn't my thing. But having said that, I don't think I've ever seen one this well preserved. Why, there's not a mark on it!"

"That's true enough," Egan said, straightening up. "So much of what I've seen in the Auction Houses is damaged or badly cracked. The little savages tend to smash anything they get their hands on. This must have been hidden away somewhere – in a cellar, perhaps, or under rubble. To find it . . ." He gazed at the statue again, clearly impressed. "Well, it's rare, that's all I know. So . . . fifty million? A hundred?"

"Double that," Green said, watching Fairbank's face. "I bet you paid . . . oh, two twenty?"

"Two twenty-five," Fairbank said, laughing, then shook his head. "*Every* time! I don't know *how* you do it, Clive."

"It's sixty years of watching that face of yours," Green answered, laughing. "I'm sure I know every little tick and nervous gesture on it!"

"Is that what it is?" Again Fairbank laughed.

"Two two five, huh?" Egan said, and turned, looking at the statue with a new respect. "And you think he might have something else like this?"

"He *might* . . ." Fairbank looked about him, "Or you might make *me* an offer . . ."

Egan looked up, frowned, then, seeing how the others were smiling, gave a bark of laughter. "Am I that transparent?"

"Only to your friends . . .

Egan looked about him. "And good friends you've been these past thirty years. Through thick and thin."

"Which is one of the reasons why we're here, neh?" Fairbank said, serious suddenly. It was true. For thirty years they had suffered at the hands of Old Man Lever. He had bought their best men, plundered their markets, stolen their secrets, undercut their products. No trick had been too low or too filthy for him, no method too devious or too immoral. But now that had changed. His death fifteen months back had opened a door of opportunity. His son was raw and inexperienced. Better than that, the boy was an idealist and wanted to implement a number of changes to his corporate structure: changes which would severely weaken ImmVac and – for the first time in three decades – make it vulnerable to a concerted effort by its trading rivals.

"I've had my man on ImmVac's board prepare a special briefing for us," Fairbank said, throwing the cloth back over the statue. "He'll be here at four to present it. In the meantime I suggest we break for lunch. Besides, there's another matter I'd like to raise with you."

"Another?" Egan asked, his eyes sparkling with interest.

"Over lunch," Fairbank said and smiled. "I'll tell you while we eat."

* * *

Wu Shih stood there, his palms damp, facing the *ching*, while in the room behind him the technicians whispered urgently among themselves, hurrying to prepare the tests.

It had been three weeks after his twenty-second birthday when he had first come here, sad-eyed and dressed in mourning clothes, to meet his other self. Since then, once a year for the past thirty-five, he had returned, unannounced, to spend an hour or two with it.

A servant brought a chair. He sat, looking about him at the tiny chamber. To his right an altar had been set up, and offerings of food and drink had been placed before it. To the left was an exercise walkway, the looped track motionless. The *ching* itself sat on a high-backed throne facing him, wearing a simple one-piece exercise suit that left its arms and legs bare. It was perfectly, unnaturally still, its smooth, unlined face vacant, like an idiot's.

The *ching* was his age exactly, a perfect copy of him, kept ready for the day when he, Wu Shih, finally died. Only then would it emerge from its lifelong seclusion in these rooms and, for the briefest while, take on his power and authority. Until, as the ritual demanded, his eldest son killed it and became T'ang in his place.

He stared at it, wondering if, despite all the reassurances of the experts, it had its own private thoughts, its own dreams and visions of the world. Wondering if, behind those vacant eyes, some other creature looked out at the world, cut off from speech and impotent to act.

Some mad and staring thing . . .

That thought had always frightened him. Since his first visit here he had had dreams – dreams in which he *was* the *ching*, a machine of flesh and bone, made only to be woken once and killed. In those dreams he would find himself inside an empty, echoing palace of pale white alabaster, running from room to room, trying each door with a mounting desperation as he found all portals to the outside locked fast against him. Then, from beyond the walls, would come the sound of muted laughter – a deep, horrible, mocking sound. And he would run on, like a lost child, until he woke, his body sheathed in sweat, his heart racing like a newborn's.

"*Chieh Hsia . . . ?*"

He turned his head. The Chief Technician stood beside him, his head bowed.

"Are you ready?"

"We are, *Chieh Hsia.*"

"Then let us commence. I must be gone from here in an hour."

"*Chieh Hsia!*"

He watched as two of them stood behind the *ching*, helping it to its feet. Encouraged by their touch, it seemed to come alive, the waxwork sheen of its skin enlivened suddenly by the stretch and pull of muscle. Aided by them, it moved towards the walkway. Mounting the step, it took two paces and then stopped, letting them fasten its hands to the special grips on the rail.

Throughout it all the face remained unchanged, its idiot-vacancy somehow more terrible when glimpsed against the motion of that powerful, well-muscled form, and as ever Wu Shih found himself appalled and horrified. So like himself, it was, and yet . . . well, it was as if in coming to these rooms he stepped out of the world he knew and entered some other place – *ti yu*, the underworld, perhaps.

As the walkway started up its legs began to move, as if some conscious choice evoked the movement, yet from all he'd been told he knew that the motion was only the habit of the muscles – a habit patiently induced by its custodians.

Exercise, it was all that body knew. Pleasure and pain – such were strangers to it. Desire and simple need – these too had been kept from its experience. Fed regularly and exercised, it functioned perfectly. *Much better*, Wu Shih mused, *than its original*. No illness had ever plagued it, no worries disturbed its dreamless sleep.

Colourless, unconscious of its purpose, it waited.

223

My death, he thought. *It measures its existence by my death.*

Later, as he was watching it perform a series of twists and turns that would have defied a more thoughtful athlete, he found himself thinking about Weimar and the importance of the vote that afternoon.

He had done all he could in that regard. He had bought and bullied, made countless threats and promises, trying to place the matter beyond doubt, yet still it would be close. As it had once before in his lifetime, the House was pressing for autonomy – an autonomy it could not be allowed to have.

Power. It was all about power. Grant them a little and they wanted more. Grant them more and they wanted a lot more. Best, then, to give them nothing – to keep all power in the hands of the Seven and make the matter beyond question. But only force could achieve that, and right now forcing the matter was not an option – not unless they wanted war.

Maybe Li Yuan was right, then. Maybe they ought to wire them all – reduce them all to *ching*!

He huffed irritably, then stood, tired suddenly of the whole business. "Enough!" he cried. "Let it rest!"

He turned, the watching technicians and officials backing away hurriedly, their heads bowed low, as he moved quickly, impatiently between them. And outside, in the main office, where representatives of the *T'ing Wei* and the Ministry – the two custodians of the *ching* – had gathered to honour him, he did not even pause to greet them, but swept through, his mind filled with dark shadows and forebodings, knowing it had been wrong to come.

* * *

"Dan? Where's Em? I've looked all over . . ."

Johnson looked up from where he was preparing the documents for the journey and looked across at Michael Lever. "She left early. I thought you knew. She's gone in to Hythe-MacKay to see what she can pick up for Joe's birthday."

Michael raised an eyebrow, surprised. "Strange . . . She usually mentions things like that to me."

224

Johnson stared at him a moment, then, without comment, returned to his task.

"When do we need to leave?"

"Not for an hour yet," Johnson answered. "We could leave it longer, but I thought we'd give ourselves plenty of time."

Michael eyed him a moment, then laughed. "Okay . . . what have you got up your sleeve?"

"Me?" Johnson looked up, all innocence, then smiled. "Okay . . . I had a thought, that's all. As we're going up to Washington anyway, why don't we make an unscheduled visit to our facility just south of there."

"Alexandria?"

"Sure. It would be a good opportunity to see for yourself how they're implementing your changes."

Michael nodded thoughtfully. "I like that. But what about a brief? I mean, who's Manager there now?"

"All here," Johnson said, tapping the stack of files he was about to put in the special courier sack. "I've prepared an overview of our operation there you can read on our way across."

Michael laughed. "Okay. Let's do it."

* * *

Despite herself, Emily was impressed. The vaults at Hythe-MacKay were massive, stretching down a full ten levels beneath their offices. Armed guards stood at each doorway and every intersection – more for show than anything else, the Senior Clerk confided, pointing out the computer-operated lasers that tracked them wherever they went.

At the very heart of the vaults was a small room. Inviting her to enter, he pulled out a chair for her behind the console, then sat beside her, placing a key from his belt into the desk before him. Facing them, ten *ch'i* from where they sat, was a blank screen. Turning towards her, he smiled, then spoke to the air.

"Kate, it's Jefferies. Code gold. Display."

The screen lit up, showing a three by three grid, each

square labelled with a two-letter sub-directory code. She studied them a moment then looked back at him.

He smiled. "Was there anything in particular you were interested in? Are you thinking of collecting, or buying as a gift?"

"Both," she said, then hesitated, not certain she should show too direct an interest. Then, not knowing *how* to be indirect, she shrugged. "There was a picture in one of the old books my father-in-law bought here. It had men in it. Black men."

"Ah, the Negroes . . ." Jefferies' smile took on a new form, an element of professional interest giving it an almost genuine air. "Kate, give me sub-route ST. General index."

The screen changed at a blink. The nine squares had become a list of four categories:

ARTEFACTS
BOOKS
DOCUMENTS
MAPS

"Maps," she said, curious.

"Maps, Kate."

At once the screen was filled with tiny pictures – eleven in all, each item numbered and priced in red. She studied them a moment, then nodded to herself. There was not an item there under two million.

"Can I see item seven?"

"Item seven, Kate."

As the other items faded, the one she had chosen seemed to separate itself from the screen and drift towards her, growing slowly larger and taking on a three-dimensional form in the air. It stopped, an arm's length from where she sat – a big, solid-looking thing.

It was a map of Africa. She stared at it, fascinated. The map was old, much older-looking than the frame. It was yellowed and the writing on it was irregular, not a normal machine script. But it was the names which most interested her.

"Those names . . . ?"

"Segu," he said, turning and looking directly at her, "Ashanti, Bornu, Wadai, Darfur, Funj, Tutsi, Butua, Menabe, Boina, Oyo, Hausa, Masai . . ." He smiled. "I'm sorry, it's a speciality of mine. They're the names of tribes . . . of nations, if you like. There were literally hundreds of them, all of them black-skinned. From what we can make out they led very diverse lifestyles. Most of them were highly primitive, of course – around the same level as the Clayborn – but not all. In fact some were extremely sophisticated. There was a whole varied culture there at one time. Of course, we're very lucky here at Hythe-MacKay. We've probably the best collection of Negro artefacts in the world, and this map . . . well, it's a beauty, neh?"

And so it should be at fifty million, she thought. Even so, she was quite taken by it. Was it real? Was it *really* real? And if it was, what had happened to all those tribes – where had they gone?

Hundreds of them . . . No. It wasn't possible.

"Where do you find them?"

He laughed. "Now *that* would be telling. Let's just say we have our sources. And there's new material coming in all the time."

"But the Ministry . . ."

". . . know nothing, *officially*." He smoothed his thumb over his fingertips, indicating what he meant. "It adds to the price, naturally, but then our clientele can afford that little extra it costs us."

She nodded, understanding. Corrupt. It was all corrupt, from First Level to the Net. There was probably not one straight official among the lot of them.

"Is there a book of it . . . a history?"

Jefferies thought a moment, then shook his head. "Of their origins, no. But there are one or two books about the slave trade."

"The *what*?"

"That's how they came here to America. They were brought over from Africa to work on the plantations. *Hung*

227

Mao traders went ashore and rounded them up by the thousand, chained them up and brought them back." He nodded admiringly. "It was a highly lucrative trade. Many a trading empire was built on black slaves, you know!"

She turned back, staring at the map, seeing it anew. First the *Hung Mao* had enslaved the blacks, and then the Han had enslaved the *Hung Mao*. And next? She shivered, sickened by the whole business.

"Show me something else. Show me . . ." An idea struck her. "Show me something to do with the Kennedys."

He smiled. "Now *there's* an interesting subject. Kate, give me sub-route AC, directory six, sub-file Kennedy. Show me Documents, sub-file Newspapers. Item nine, I think. The copy of the *Dallas Times Herald . . .*"

* * *

Kemp waited in reception while the Steward went in to announce his arrival. He stood there, looking about him at the priceless paintings on the walls, conscious of Fairbank's secretary watching from his corner desk.

He felt good. Britton's report had been excellent and, together with the other material he had, was sure to satisfy the consortium. Even so, this was the first time he had met the four together, and the fact that they had summoned him here to AmLab's headquarters in Denver put him on his guard.

They had treated him well, there was no denying. The apartment he had been given was of the highest quality, and the girl . . .

He smiled, remembering the girl. He was almost tempted to ask for the girl as part of his fee, but knew it would be wrong. To admit *any* weakness was a mistake when dealing with these men.

"*Shih* Kemp?"

He turned. The Steward was in the doorway, holding the door open for him. Taking a firm grip on the folder, he gave a tiny bow and went across.

The boardroom was massive, at least a hundred *ch'i* by fifty, the ceiling twenty *ch'i* above his head. The floor and walls were finished in a pale green stone, the polished hexagonal slabs embossed with the blood-red circling-atom logo of AmLab.

The old men were seated at the far end, behind a long table of polished ebony. A space of at least five *ch'i* separated each man. Behind them were their corporate banners – the black on yellow of RadMed; the pale green and red of AmLab; the blood-red eagle of NorTek; and the blue star on white of WesCorp.

"Kemp . . ." Fairbank said, his voice still powerful despite his seventy-five years. "Come close where we can see you better."

He approached. Ten paces from the table he stopped and bowed his head. "Gentlemen . . ."

He looked along the line, expecting some sign of eagerness in their faces – after all, they had waited a long time to get back at ImmVac – but there was nothing. Their faces were like weathered walls.

"Is *that* it?" Egan asked, pointing to the folder.

"Yes, I . . ."

"Put it on the table," Fairbank said abruptly.

"I beg pardon?"

"On the table. We'll read it later."

"But . . ."

"Don't worry, *Shih* Kemp, you'll be paid in full. And I'm sure you've done an excellent job. Britton's a first-class investigator. But that's not why you're here."

"No?"

Fairbank smiled, then turned in his seat, looking to Chamberlain.

"Geoffrey . . ."

Chamberlain stood and came round the desk, walking past Kemp to a low table placed against the wall. Picking up a small black lacquered box, he brought it across and handed it to Kemp.

"What's this?"

Chamberlain leaned close. "Open it and see."

He opened it, looked, then looked again. "What the . . . ?"

Chamberlain laughed. Behind him the others were laughing too, sharing the joke.

"I . . ." Kemp turned, looking to Fairbank for an explanation, trying hard to retain his composure. "I . . . I realise what it is, but . . . well, whose is it?"

Chamberlain took it back from him and smiled. "Does it matter?"

"Not to me, no . . . but to *him* . . ."

"Oh, he was dead *before* it was cut off!"

Kemp stared at the pale gobbet of flesh and frowned. "So what's going on?"

Egan answered him. "You're building up a network, right?"

"To use against Lever, sure. But what's that to do with . . . *this*?"

Egan's grin was like a skull's. "In my experience, what's good for one purpose is usually good for another. Your contacts . . . they've contacts of their own, right? Little men, operating among the levels."

Kemp nodded.

"And they're keen to line their pockets, neh? To earn a little extra on the side?"

Again Kemp nodded.

"Good. So we *use* them."

"*Use* them? How?"

Green of RadMed answered him.

"We live in troubled times, *Shih* Kemp. Political agitation and riots . . . these things disturb the markets. And whatever disturbs the markets affects our livelihoods, neh? A climate of uncertainty is bad for trade. You'd agree?"

"Well, sure . . ."

"I'm sure you would," he went on smoothly. "For some time now the situation in North America has concerned us. We've waited patiently, hoping that action would be taken – strong, *decisive* action – to curtail such activities. But nothing. The authorities know who these troublemakers are. They have camera evidence and the statements of informers. If they wanted they could go in and arrest them, but they don't. *Why*? Because they're afraid. Because they haven't the guts

230

or determination to deal with the problem and eradicate it!"

Green's deeply-lined face was hard with resentment. Beside him Chamberlain and Fairbank were nodding, willing him to go on.

"Well, Wu Shih may lack the will to do the job, but *we* don't. If he won't deal with the *mei yu jen wen*, then we shall!"

Kemp nodded. It was not the first time he'd heard that phrase. On numerous occasions in the past few months, after formal dinners, or at more private gatherings, the drink had flowed and, eventually, the subject had come round to "solutions". And always, *always*, someone would come out with that description of the Lowers. *Mei yu jen wen* . . . Subhumans. Meat-men. And the more he heard it, the more he was convinced it was true. For more than a century now they had dealt with their criminal element by demotion. The good had climbed the levels, while the bad had been sent to the bottom of the pile – down to the Lowers – where they could be with others of their kind.

Their kind . . . He smiled savagely, convinced of it. The City was the great filter of humanity, separating the good from the bad, the successful from the failures, the real men from the sub-humans, the meat-men – the *mei yu jen wen*. Animals they were, with the morality of animals. And what did it matter if they lived or died? They were bred in ignorance and died in it. Scum, they were. Less than scum.

Green was watching him. He smiled. "You understand then?"

"Maybe." He hesitated. "That thing . . . ?"

"Let me tell you a story," Fairbank said, folding his hands together on the table in front of him. "When our ancestors first came to this great continent, there were beings already here. Indians, they called them. Sub-human creatures they were, with bright red skins. Well, these Indians proved a real nuisance, attacking *Hung Mao* settlements and murdering women and children without reason. So the government came up with a reward system. For every Indian a man killed, they'd pay a certain amount of money. Trouble was, it was impractical to carry dead Indians back across country to claim the reward, so they devised an easier method. *Scalps.* They'd pay the reward on every Indian scalp brought back."

Fairbank smiled. "Now, I don't think that's a bad system, do you? But I felt we could improve on it somewhat. A scalp . . . these days a man can lose half his head and still live. Lose his cock, however, and even if he *does* live, there's whole generations of such scum as'll never be born, neh?"

Kemp laughed. It was ingenious. "How much do you plan to pay?"

"Two fifty?"

"There's risks . . ."

"Sure there's risks!" Egan said angrily. "There's *always* risks."

"But two fifty. It's . . . too low."

"Three hundred, then," Fairbank said. "But no more. And a cut of fifty for you." He smiled. "Per cock . . ."

The muscle in Kemp's cheek twitched. *Fifty* . . . It was more than he'd expected. A whole lot more.

"How . . ." He licked his lips, his mouth suddenly dry. "How do I find out who to hit?"

"Don't worry. We'll take care of that side of things. You'll be sent copies of all the relevant Security files. All you have to do is arrange to act on them, okay?"

He nodded.

"Good. Then we'll organise a fund at once. Third party, naturally. And if there *are* any little problems, *you* sort them out. Okay?"

"Okay."

Fairbank sat back, clearly satisfied with his afternoon's work. "You'll be given a contact address, and you'll deal directly with that. From now on you'll have no contact whatsoever with any one of us. If the T'ang himself comes calling on you, it's your job to make sure he doesn't come here next. You understand me, *Shih* Kemp?"

Kemp swallowed. "I understand."

"Good. Then we're finished here. Oh, and Kemp . . ."

"Yes, Mister Fairbank?"

"You can have the girl. I understand you were rather partial to her . . ."

* * *

Michael Lever climbed down from the sedan and looked about him, realising just how long it had been since he'd visited one of ImmVac's facilities.

Years ago – before his incarceration by Wu Shih and the split with his father – he had spent a great deal of time touring the City, inspecting ImmVac's installations on his father's behalf while he learned the business. Back then he would have spent the evening partying with officials, then spent the rest of the night with the daughter of some local bigwig – someone who wished to curry favour with his father. But now the very thought was anathema.

So much had changed since then. So much had happened to him. First there'd been the arrests at the Thanksgiving Ball that night – he and a dozen other "Sons", taken by Wu Shih's forces for "subversive activities". For days afterwards he had raged against his captors, demanding his release, but fifteen long months had passed – most of them spent in solitary confinement – before he had been freed to see his father again. And when he had . . .

He shivered, remembering the breach with his father, the long and bitter battle for independence which had ended with a bomb-blast in which his best friend, Bryn Kustow, had been killed, and he himself badly injured. It could have ended there, but it hadn't. He had outlived his father and become the Head of ImmVac in his place. And throughout it all there had been Mary, his darling "Em", there like a pillar of burning light in his darkest moment, supporting him, guiding him, keeping his feet firmly on the narrow path.

Without her . . .

He turned, hearing Johnson's footsteps behind him. "Well, Dan? Shall we shake them up a little?"

Johnson smiled. "If you like, we can go through unannounced. I have the codes."

"Lead on. I'm looking forward to seeing Steiner's face when we march into his office!"

Johnson turned and went across, giving the runners and the bodyguards their instructions, then came back. "Okay. Let's go."

* * *

The two doorguards were watching a vid when Lever and Johnson came through. Their feet were up on the desk, the remains of a meal piled up on the desk in front of them. There was a moment's panic, a reaching for guns, and then they realised who it was and stood, their heads lowered, their faces flushed with embarrassment.

Steiner's secretary began to rise from her chair as she saw them, her face alarmed, but one look from Johnson made her sit again, her head folding against her chest.

"You first," Michael whispered, moving to one side. "I'll give you a minute, then I'll come in. Pretend you're alone."

Johnson made a facial shrug, then tapped out the door's locking code. With the briefest rap of his knuckles against the door, he pushed it open and stepped inside.

There was a startled gasp and a small high sound of surprise.

"Michael?" Johnson said, a faintly amused tone in his voice. "I think you'd better see this for yourself."

He went in.

Steiner was at his desk. Or rather, he was strapped to his desk. He lay there on his back, buck-naked, a naked girl astride him. His wrists and ankles were fastened by leather thongs to the legs of the huge desk and a gag was tied tightly over his mouth.

"Are you in any trouble, Manager Steiner? Or is this an early lunch-break, perhaps?"

The old man swallowed uncomfortably, then lifted his chin, indicating to the girl that she should remove the gag. She obliged, then slipped from on top of him, standing behind the desk, her hands attempting to maintain some degree of modesty.

"Well?" said Michael after a prolonged silence. "Is this a regular event, or have I just caught you at a particularly bad time?"

"I . . . I can explain, *Shih* Lever!"

"Sure." Michael took a breath, then looked to Johnson. "Dan, bring me four guards. I want this man out of here right now."

"*Shih* Lever!"

"Relax, *Shih* Steiner. Just relax, neh? Now you, girl . . . do I employ you?"

Timidly she nodded.

"Where are your clothes?"

She indicated across the room. Michael looked. There, in the right-hand corner, was a stack of filing trays and papers. Beside them – very neat – were two piles of clothes.

"Get dressed, then report to Personnel. You'll get six months pay, okay?"

She nodded, then hurried to do as she'd been told.

Michael turned, hearing Johnson returning with the guards.

"Okay," he said, standing back to let them pass. "I want you to pick up that desk and move it out of here, all right?"

The men, who had been staring at the sight wide-eyed, turned and answered him as one. "Yes, *Shih* Lever!"

"*Michael* . . ." Steiner pleaded, "in your father's name . . ."

Michael turned, glaring at him. "Firstly, *Mister* Steiner, do *not* invoke my father's memory! Secondly, what you do in your own time and in the privacy of your own apartment is up to you, but I do not expect a senior manager of mine to be doing *this* on Company time or on Company property!"

Steiner closed his eyes, as if he'd die of shame. "Dear gods . . ."

"Come on," Michael said, waving the guards across. "I want him out of here, and I want it done right now!"

Johnson was staring at him now. "What are you going to do?" he said quietly.

"Just watch . . ." he answered, then, turning to the guards. "Come! Move now! Out into the reception room,

235

then follow me. As from this moment *Shih* Steiner is no longer an employee of the ImmVac Corporation and as such is a trespasser on this property. As guards you are empowered to eject him from the facility."

There was an exchange of glances, then, with a roar of delighted laughter, they lifted man and table and began to carry them across. Through the reception room they went, incurring the startled glances of Steiner's secretary, and on into the main corridor that led to the front gate of the facility.

"No . . ." Michael said, indicating that they should turn and come back. "Through the main facility. I think the staff should have the opportunity to say goodbye to their ex-Manager, neh?"

"Have a care, Michael," Johnson said quietly, but Michael pushed his arm away.

"Whatever you say, *Shih* Lever," the most senior of the guards answered him. "Once round the factory floor and back here?"

Michael nodded then stood back, letting them pass.

"It's too much," Johnson said, speaking to his ear. "Turf him out, sure. But *this* . . ."

Michael turned, staring at his assistant, his face hard, unforgiving. "You're a good man, Dan, and a fine assistant, but this once don't tell me what I should or shouldn't do, okay?"

Johnson bowed his head, chastened.

"Good. Now I want you to stay here and go through the records. Everything. Invoices, sales, production figures, the lot. I want a team in here by this afternoon, and I want a full report on my desk first thing Monday morning."

"But what about Washington? Won't you need me there?"

"Everything's prepared, neh?"

Johnson nodded. "It's all in the file."

"Good. Then I should be all right, shouldn't I? After all, I've only got to sign the refunding document."

"I . . ." Johnson hesitated, then nodded.

"And Dan . . . unstrap him once he's back here and let

him get his clothes. But get him out of here. And no Company sedan, okay? The bastard can walk home."

* * *

Kennedy sat back in his armchair, looking across the room at the three men seated there, watching as the Steward refilled their glasses. It was an hour and a half until the vote and, elsewhere in the great House, Representatives were already gathering, excited by the prospect of a set-back for the Seven. Here, however, it was quiet, peaceful.

Deceptively so, Kennedy thought, knowing that, if he were to be sure of things, he would need to convince these three – and the votes their faction commanded – to join his side.

"Well, Representative," Underwood said, lifting his glass slightly in a toast, "this is very pleasant, but I'm sure you've not asked us here for *social* reasons."

He smiled. His own glass sat untouched on the table beside him.

"No," he said, looking to Hart, who sat to Underwood's left and then to Munroe, on his right, including them by the gesture. "Nor would I insult you by pretending otherwise. The hour presses and I am forced to deal more openly than I'm accustomed to."

Hart smiled. "The House makes traders of us all, neh?"

Kennedy returned the smile, yet inwardly he wondered what Hart meant by that. Was it an honest insight, or was it a barb?

"That's true," he said, "yet trade is better than warfare, surely? If all parties can be satisfied . . ."

"Impossible," Munroe said, bluntly, unexpectedly.

Kennedy stared at him. "What do you mean?"

"He means," Underwood said, his smile enigmatic, "that we've not come here to trade."

He paused, staring down into his wine, then spoke again. "You want to buy our votes, neh? To have us in your pocket, like the *tai* you've been snapping up these past twenty-four hours." His eyes slowly looked up, meeting Kennedy's again. "You brought us here to sound us – to find out what it is we

237

want and offer it in return. A vague promise for a certain vote."

"Not vague . . ."

"No?" Underwood looked at him, surprise and disbelief balanced in that look. Then, with a shrug, he downed his drink. "Whatever . . . you're wasting your time. You can't buy us and there's nothing we want that you can deliver. So . . ."

"Nothing?"

Underwood's smile was pitying. "We are Dispersionists, Representative, not New Republicans. We don't want the kind of small compromises you seem happy with, don't you understand that? Change, that's what we want. Change. And you can't give us that. You simply can't deliver . . ."

No? he thought, indignant. Yet against his natural indignation was set the truth. Underwood was right. He had bartered away whatever strengths he'd brought here to Weimar. And Change . . . *real* Change, that was now beyond him. There'd been so many tiny factions to satisfy, so many greedy egos to pamper. *And nothing pure . . .*

He sighed. "Maybe you're right. Then again, maybe you're kidding yourself, too. Spaceships and distant stars . . . it's not a very practical platform, is it? Come the next elections, do you think you'll sustain your support?"

Underwood smiled, then, setting his glass down, got to his feet. Either side of him, Hart and Munroe did the same.

"I wouldn't worry about *my* seat, Mister Kennedy. I know *I'll* get re-elected. But you? I'd be a little worried if I were you. You're golden boy right now, but what happens when you don't deliver on those promises? What are you going to do when the media start looking at your record a bit more closely than they are just now?" He paused, his smile becoming a sneer. "And what happens when Wu Shih decides he's had enough of you?"

Kennedy felt a coldness grip his stomach. "What do you mean?"

"Oh, just rumours, Representative, that's all. Just rumours . . ."

Kennedy looked down. "You plan to vote against, I suppose?"

"Did I say that?" There was no sign now of a smile on Underwood's face. "As a matter of fact, we plan to vote *for* the proposal. But we'll be doing that because we want to, not because you bought us, or bullied us, or offered us something in return. I wanted to make that clear, just in case you got the wrong idea about us."

"The wrong idea?" Kennedy laughed. "I sure as hell did that, didn't I?"

He stood, his face suddenly hard. "Now listen, and listen good. You talk of me, *Mister* Underwood, but who's funding *you*? That's what *I'd* like to know. Who's making it easy for you to play Mister Simon Pure? Because I *know* you. I know all of you. And if you ever fucking come and insult me to my face again, I'll kick you from here to fucking Africa, you got me?"

Underwood took a long breath, then nodded.

Kennedy leaned back a little, relaxing his stance. "Good. I'm glad we understand each other, *ch'un tzu*. And now, if you'll excuse me, I've much to do."

He watched them go, then let out a long, sighing breath. So there were rumours, eh? That was bad. He thought he'd been discreet. Or maybe they were just guesses. Attempts to explain the changes in policy he'd made these past twelve months. Well, let them. They'd be making new guesses after this afternoon's vote.

And Wu Shih? How will he react?

Kennedy shivered, then, with a tiny shrug, went through to his rooms. As the Steward laid out his clothes on the couch, he stood at the vid-phone, waiting to be connected to his wife.

"Sweetheart?" he said, as her face appeared on the screen. "How've you been? How are the boys?"

Her smile warmed him. "We're fine . . . How's it all been going?"

He made a face. "Who knows? It's going to be tight, but hopefully we've done enough. We'll know in two hours, anyway."

239

"That's good . . ."

He stared at her, drinking in the sight. She was still as beautiful as she'd been when he'd married her fifteen years before. There was still something waif-like and fragile about her, even after all that had happened. Her hair had grown back since the operation two years ago, and outwardly she seemed no different from before, but he knew that wasn't true. Just as he'd been changed by the presence of that tiny soft-wire in her head – and in the heads of his two young sons – so had she. Subtly, insidiously, it affected everything they did, every decision they made. It was as if she had a cancer in her head, waiting to flower at the touch of a switch, and the knowledge of it, just as it made each compromise he wrought seem foul, made each moment between them incalculably sweeter.

"I need you," he said softly, conscious of the Steward moving about in the room behind him.

Her smile for the briefest moment had a bitter, fragile edge to it, then it strengthened. "And I love you, Joseph Kennedy. So go and do what you have to. You're a good man, Joe. Hold on to that, okay?"

He smiled. "I shall. Give the boys my love, huh? And I'll see you later, at the party."

"I'm looking forward to it."

"Bye, my love."

"Bye, sweetheart."

He turned from the blanked screen, the heaviness he'd been feeling earlier returned to him. He hadn't told her – he couldn't have, not on an open line – and yet she knew that he was going to do something at the vote this afternoon. She had always read him well.

He looked up. The Steward was waiting by the door, his head lowered.

"Is there anything else, Master?"

He shook his head. "No . . . thank you, Tao-kuang. But if you could have my things ready for when I return. Something light to travel in. I'll change again when I'm back in America."

"As you wish, Master."

Alone again, he turned, staring at the vid-phone, feeling strangely restless, wondering if he should call Michael and talk things through. Then, steeling himself, making a deliberate effort to set all doubts aside, he undid the top button on his tunic, starting to change.

The vote was in an hour.

* * *

Emily sat back among the silk cushions, glad for once of the isolation of the State Class compartment. She was alone, the tape book she had been listening to beside her on the long, comfortably-cushioned seat. The gentle movement of the bolt was pleasant, reassuring almost, as it sped south through the stacks to Richmond.

It had been a remarkable day and for once she blessed the wealth that had allowed her that glimpse into those times before the City. Yet it was that same wealth that troubled her constantly.

To be comfortable, that was the right of everyone, it seemed. But to be rich in the way that she and Michael were rich – that was obscene. The more she thought of it, the more she was convinced. Yet to unburden herself of it seemed no solution either, for it was the way of their world to have such great divisions between rich and poor, and if not she and Michael, then some other "Power" would step into the vacuum that they left.

She sighed. This much she had learned today: that the inequities of their society had existed long before the City, and that the City was merely a perfecting of that awful process.

The City . . . it was a cage, a prison for them all.

And yet the City had been built to solve all problems. It had been meant to be . . . what was the word she'd heard? . . . a *Utopia*, that was it. "Food enough and space to grow", that was one of the early slogans she had read about. It had been a bold experiment. To build a world without want. A true meritocracy. A world where people could find their level.

But the experiment had failed. Old patterns of behaviour had reasserted themselves – nepotism and corruption, deals and betrayals – and the dream had turned to nightmare.

This world . . . she shuddered, frightened by the point to which her thoughts had come . . . it had been designed to reflect the best in Man, and had come to mirror the darkness deep within him.

A Yang world. A male world. A world without light or a mother's loving tenderness. A bastard world, cursed from conception.

There was a click, and then the faint chime of a warning signal. She looked up, composing herself. At the count of ten the door at the far end of the compartment hissed open and the Number One Steward stepped through, one of his junior assistants – Number Seven from his patch – just behind him. As the door hissed shut again, the two bowed deeply, then looked across at her, paper-thin smiles of politeness plastered to their faces.

"Is there anything we can do for you, Madam Lever?" Number One asked. "Is there anything you would like?"

"Yes, actually. Have you a news screen anywhere on board?"

The Senior Steward smiled again – that same thin, insincere smile – then came across. Reaching up, he pulled a flatscreen down from a niche in the ceiling of the carriage and, adjusting the angle of the flexible arm, positioned it so that she could see from where she sat.

"Is that all right, Madam Lever?"

"Perfect," she said.

"Just speak clearly to it. It's programmed to show all the First Level channels."

"Thank you . . ."

"Is there anything else? *Ch'a*, perhaps?"

"Yes. That would be very welcome, thank you."

Number One turned and muttered a few sharp phrases of Mandarin to his assistant, who bowed low to Emily, then hurried off back the way he had come.

"It will be but two minutes, Madam Lever."

242

"That's fine . . . Now perhaps you'd leave me . . ."

"Of course . . ."

He bowed deeply, backed off a pace, then went through the door behind her.

Thank god, she thought. If anything, that was the worst of it. The obsequious servants, the fawning hangers-on, the lick-spittle half-men who would do anything – *anything* – for a share of the spoils.

She huffed, angry with herself, then sat back, staring up at the screen.

"Give me First News Inter-Active. I want a briefing on what's been happening at Weimar."

The screen lit up. A handsome anchorman – a *Hung Mao* of roughly her own age – looked down at her.

"Madam Lever," he said, inclining his head and smiling as if he recognised her. "What would you like to know?"

She hesitated, wondering if she should ask it to re-programme itself to become a grey-bearded Han, then dismissed the idea.

"How did the vote go? Was it close?"

The anchor smiled, showing perfect teeth. "It's just been declared. The earliest showings had the 'No' faction marginally ahead, but a late block vote by the Dispersionists clinched it. Even so, the final margin was only seven in favour of a 'Yes'. It seems the amendment . . ."

"Amendment?" she sat forward slightly, her smile slowly fading. "*What* amendment?"

"The amendment Representative Kennedy introduced at the final reading. Would you like me to read it out to you?"

"No. Just print it up. I can read it myself."

At once the anchor's face was replaced by the amendment.

She read it, a cold certainty forming in her. *Deals. Kennedy had been making last-minute deals . . .*

"That last bit . . ." she said, frowning. "It isn't clear what's meant by the new level of subsidies . . . is that an increase or what?"

The face returned. "There was a secondary document.

It was issued by the office of Wu Shih's Chancellor, Fen Cho-hsien. It reads . . ."

"Was it an increase or a decrease?"

"A decrease, Madam Lever. Of eight point six per cent."

She sat there, stunned, slowly shaking her head. He'd sold out. The bastard had sold them all out! No decreases in the food subsidies to the Lowers, he'd sworn. Not even half a per cent. And now *this* . . . She clenched her fists and stood, blind rage making her unaware of the hiss of the end door as it opened and Number Seven came through carrying the tray of *ch'a*.

"The bastard . . ." she said quietly. "I knew! I fucking knew it! The conniving First Level bastard!"

The young Steward stopped, his mouth agape, staring at her. "Are you all right, Madam Lever?"

She turned staring at him, her eyes wild with anger, then pointed up at the screen. "No, I'm fucking well not! Look! Look what that bastard's done!"

*   *   *

"*Chieh Hsia* . . ."

Wu Shih turned, looking back up the path between the mulberry trees. His Chancellor was standing just in front of the moon gate, his head lowered, his hands folded into his silken sleeves.

"Yes, Cho-hsien. What is it?"

"There is news, *Chieh Hsia*. From Weimar."

"Ah . . ." He looked down at the pink and white blossom scattered on the path. "Was the proposal passed?"

"It was, *Chieh Hsia*."

"And the amendment?"

"That too, master."

He looked up. "So why the long face, Cho-hsien? What ill news accompanies the good?"

Fen Cho-hsien came forward, then bowed and handed his T'ang a sheet of paper. Wu Shih read it through, then looked up, a heaviness descending on him. It was the draft of a proposal to be put before the House within the month – a proposal to increase the powers of the House and give them a say in the financial arrangements of government; arrangements which presently were the sole concern of the Seven. Put simply, it was a grab for power, *real* power.

"This is new, I assume."

"It is, *Chieh Hsia.*"

He took a long breath, then shook his head. "I am surprised . . . and disappointed. I thought . . ."

"It was Kennedy, *Chieh Hsia.*"

Wu Shih smiled weakly. He had not needed his Chancellor to tell him whose hand was behind this.

"He calls our bluff, neh?"

Fen Cho-hsien said nothing.

Wu Shih turned, looking out across the great gardens of Manhattan. He had thought to find peace here – to inure himself against the news, whatever it was, that came from Weimar. But this . . .

He looked back at Fen Cho-hsien. "If we allow it to be put before the House there will be chaos within the year."

"And if we refuse to allow it?"

"Then it will come sooner."

"So what are we to do?"

Wu Shih shrugged. "Has my cousin, Tsu Ma, contacted me yet?"

"Not yet, *Chieh Hsia.*"

"Well . . . tell him I wish to see him. Tell him . . . we need to talk, that's all."

"*Chieh Hsia.*"

Fen Cho-hsien bowed and turned away, disappearing through the moon gate. A moment later he could be seen climbing the steps to the palace.

Wu Shih sighed deeply. *So the day had come at last. The day he had tried so carefully to avoid. But part of him had always known. A man like Kennedy . . . it was difficult to bridle such a one.*

Yes. But what was he to do? It was as he'd said. Kennedy had called his bluff, and now he must either carry out his threat or lose his hold over the man. And if he carried out his threat . . . .

Wu Shih shook his head. *Not yet. I'll not decide it yet.* But as he walked along the path towards the moon gate, his tread was heavier and his head hung despondently, as if a great weight pressed down upon his shoulders.

* * *

Michael poked his head round the bedroom doorway, looking in at her. Emily was sitting at her dressing-table, her back to him.

"Em . . . we've got to talk this through. Now. Before he comes. All this . . ." He threw his hands up in despair. "It's not going to solve anything!"

He took two paces into the room then stopped. He could see her face now in the mirror. She was looking down, angry, her face set.

"Em . . . we've a house full of guests. You can't just sit here." He sighed. "Okay . . . come when you're ready. But understand this. I'm as pissed off as you about that amendment. Joe had no right. But tonight . . . well, tonight's not the right time to raise it, okay?"

"Then when is?"

It was the first thing she had said to him in almost three hours.

"I . . . I'll speak to him tomorrow. I'll go over and see him."

"No." She turned to face him. "Tonight. After the party. And not just you, Michael. *Us.* I've one or two things I want to say to Joseph Kennedy myself."

He raised his hands defensively. "All right. Have it your way. But afterwards, okay?"

"Okay," she answered quietly, her face softening towards him.

He smiled. "Good. Then come on, my princess. Let's go and show ourselves."

* * *

Kennedy arrived an hour later. There was a huge cheer as he came in through the big double doors and down the steps, his wife Jean on his arm. Michael and Emily were there at the foot of the steps to greet them, embracing them then turning to lead them to the centre of the ballroom where, on a rostrum shaped like the continent of North America, a huge tiered cake awaited them.

It was Kennedy's thirty-fifth birthday and, coincidentally, the fifteenth anniversary of his marriage to Jean. As they posed for the media cameras, Michael took Emily aside.

"Did you get a present?" he whispered.

"Two," she answered.

"Two?"

"One for now, one for later."

He looked at her, his eyes narrowed suspiciously. "What are you up to?"

"Trust me," she said out of the corner of her mouth, but there was no amusement in her eyes.

For the next two hours there was no time for anything but the social whirl. Then, as the great bell sounded midnight, a curtain at one end of the hall swept back and four liveried servants stepped forward, bearing a huge silver tray between them. On the tray was an irregular, bulky shape, covered in bright red silk.

"What's this?" Kennedy asked, laughing and turning to Michael.

"It's your birthday present," Emily answered, smiling tightly, reaching out to take Michael's hand.

Kennedy turned, watching the servants approach through the parting crowd. As they stopped, he stepped forward and, looking about him, took hold of the silk and tugged it back.

There was a gasp of surprise, then a great tide of applause and cheering.

It was a tiny artillery piece, the iron barrel a dull, unreflecting black, the wheels and limber of ancient polished wood.

Kennedy turned, beaming. "Why, that's beautiful!"

Michael was nodding. "It sure is . . ." He motioned to the servants. "Lift it up, so everyone can see!"

As the great tray was raised and the cannon came into

view, there was a ripple of applause and a loud whooping from near the back, where some of Michael and Kennedy's contemporaries were gathered about the bar. Most of the NREP Representatives were present and their mood was high after the day's victory.

"Thank you," Kennedy said, stepping across and embracing first Michael and then Emily. "Where in the gods' names did you get it?"

Emily handed him the gold and blue envelope. He stared at it, then whistled.

"*Aiya*! You shouldn't have . . ."

"No," Emily said coldly. "We shouldn't."

"What is it?" Kennedy asked quietly, looking between them.

"Afterwards," Emily answered, leaning close as if to kiss his cheek, a tight smile on her face for the watching cameras, "in Michael's study."

* * *

"Well?"

There were just the three of them in the study. Kennedy had sent Jean home and the rest of the crowd had gone on to The Kitchen to celebrate further.

Michael went round his desk and sat, tired after the day's exertions. Emily sat in one of the big chairs nearby, studying him a moment. With every day that passed he resembled his father more; yet he was very much his own man – a *better* man than Charles Lever had ever been. Just now he stared at Kennedy with a mixture of anger and disappointment. In that he differed from her. *She* was simply angry.

Michael hesitated, then leaned forward, looking directly at Kennedy, who was standing, facing him. "Why the amendment, Joe? What happened?"

Kennedy sighed, then looked back at Michael apologetically. "I had to. The whole package was conditional on it. Without that we'd have lost the vote, and then we'd have been back to square one, but with our reputation discredited."

Emily laughed. "You mean you don't think it's discredited now?"

Kennedy turned, staring at her. She had tried to keep the anger, the bitterness she felt, from her voice, but she hadn't quite succeeded.

"No, I don't. It's . . . well, it's different there. Weimar . . . it isn't like it is here. Straight-talking – it doesn't work there. Deals. That's how the House works. Deals."

She nodded, looking at him as if he'd just confirmed her worst suspicions.

"You don't understand," he went on. "The measure will be temporary. A year, eighteen months at most. Until the Seven can get some extra production capacity. Wu Shih's new orbitals, the new hybrids. Things will change. And with the new controls . . ."

"You sound just like them," she said, interrupting him. "Deals. Temporary measures. Things will be better *once* . . ." She shook her head. "But they're never any better are they? Not for the Lowers. They're the ones who are getting it in the neck. As for First Level . . . well, it escapes untouched, doesn't it? Every time. Every sodding time."

"They'd never pass it."

"No? And why's that? I'll tell you. Because they're all too much in the pocket of their rich friends. They're all like you – afraid to rock the boat. Afraid to take even the tiniest little bit from those who have it all. Change . . . you don't want Change, Joseph Kennedy, you want a cushy ride, that's all!"

Michael had been watching them, his eyes narrowed. Now Kennedy turned to him.

"Does your wife speak for you too, Michael?"

Michael sat back a little. "No. Em calls it as *she* sees it. She's her own person. But this once I agree with her. I think it was a pretty foul manoeuvre, slipping that amendment through. Millions . . . no, *tens* of millions are going to suffer because of that. Families . . . little children . . . while First Level pays nothing. I don't just think that's poor, I think it's really shitty on your part, and the Joseph Kennedy I used to know would have thought so too. So what went wrong, Joe?

249

Where did all of that fine talk lead? To *this*? To pissing on the little people because they've got no vote, no say in things?"

Kennedy took a long deep breath then shook his head. "It wasn't like that. It . . ."

"You're their *tool*, Joe. Can't you see it? Piece by piece, they've bought you and controlled you. A year ago you were really something. A king. A real leader. But now . . ." Michael shook his head dismissively, the full bitterness of his disappointment showing in his face for the first time. "Now you're just a puppet, Joe, jumping to their tune. I don't have to see into those smoky rooms where you make the deals to see that. I can see it right now, in your face."

Kennedy stared back at him a moment, then looked down.

Michael met Emily's eyes briefly, then looked back at Kennedy, suddenly businesslike.

"I'll be making a statement. Tomorrow morning, at nine. In it I'll announce that I'm resigning my seat and quitting the NREP."

Kennedy looked up. Both he and Emily stared at Michael, astonished.

"I'll mention nothing of what passed between us here tonight, simply that growing political differences have forced this decision on me. It's not my intention to stand again, nor to involve myself in politics in any shape or form, so you've no need to fear me setting up a rival party. But if it damages you, well, I can't say I'll be that unhappy. What you did today . . ."

Kennedy was silent a moment, then he nodded. He looked older, more haggard than they'd ever seen him. His whole frame seemed drained suddenly, his eyes shocked.

"I . . ." He shrugged, then, quietly, "I'd better go."

"A second . . ." Emily said, then got up and crossed the room.

Kennedy watched her, not understanding.

"A parting gift," she said, coming back.

Kennedy took the long tube from her, surprised. It was very light, the container wrapped in the blue and gold of Hythe-Mackay. He made to open it, but she shook her head.

"Not now. Later, when you get home."

He hesitated, looking from one to the other, his eyes – his whole manner – regretful, apologetic. Then, abruptly, he turned and left the room.

Emily turned and looked at Michael, meaning to thank him for what he'd done, but Michael was staring down at the empty desk, his clenched fists pressed hard against the desk's edge, his face crumpled in a grimace of pain, like a bewildered little boy.

She shivered, understanding. *Dreams die.*

Then, knowing what she had to do, she went across and sat on the desk beside him, drawing him into her arms and cradling his head against her breasts until the sobbing stopped.

CHAPTER · 10

DARKNESS

Chen stood in the kitchen doorway, looking in. The children had gone and the apartment was strangely silent. Wang Ti, newly dressed, was sitting in a straight-backed chair, her hands resting passively on her knees where they'd been placed. Behind her stood the new maid, Tian Ching.

The girl was unaware of Chen standing there, watching, and sang softly to herself as she brushed Wang Ti's hair and braided it. Her pretty face frowned intently, her lips forming a pout, as her fingers moved nimbly, separating and twisting the thick dark threads of hair. And Wang Ti? Chen sighed, pained by the sight of her. Wang Ti looked like an old woman, hunched into herself, her memory gone, her eyes dull. It hadn't always been so, he reminded himself. Once she had shone like the sun itself, lighting his days, her body burning in the night beneath his, yet each day that passed – each day he saw her thus – made it harder for him to remember how it had been.

Eclipse, he thought. *My life is in eclipse.*

Again he sighed, louder this time, and Tian Ching, hearing him, turned, the song forgotten, surprised to find him there, watching her. She looked away, a faint flush appearing at her neck, her fingers faltering briefly before finding their practised rhythm again.

He watched her, remembering how difficult it had been to sleep, how fierce his need had been, how, eventually, he had gone out to the washroom and, pouring cold water into the bowl, had washed himself until the need had gone. But even then he had not slept. No, for it was not mere physical need

252

that tormented him, it was the thought of him being alone –
emotionally and spiritually alone. And not just now, not just
this one night, but every night, until the end of his days.
Could he bear that?

He watched her, fascinated by the shape of her – the
youthful roundedness of her – beneath her clothes, and wondered if he would go to her that night. If, in his pain and
loneliness, he might not find a little comfort in her arms.
Then, angry with himself, with the betraying need he felt,
he turned away.

Back in his room he pulled on the tunic of his uniform then
paused, staring at himself in the full-length mirror. *Who are
you?* he wondered, trying to see himself beyond the uniform,
beyond the lined and careworn face that was Major Kao Chen.
Who are you? Once, long ago and beneath the Net, he had
been *kwai*, a knife, and had lived a life of rigorous self-denial.
Drugs, women, alcohol, those things had had no power over
him, for there had been no weakness in him, no softness.
He had been tempered, like the blade after which he was
named; honed by a master craftsman, a pure thing in an
impure landscape. But now? He shivered, his face muscles
tightening. The years had made him soft, impure, and those
other days – those days of certainty, of *steel* – seemed like
a dream, or like something another had told him. It was hard
to believe he had been that man.

He looked down, releasing himself from his own intense
scrutiny, then turned, taking his case from the dressing table.
These days work seemed the only answer, and, like many
men he knew, he worked to escape all this – the sheer messi-
ness of his home life. And yet his work no longer satisfied
him. It was mired, all of it.

He went to the outer door, meaning to go directly out,
then stopped and came back. The maid had finished, but
Wang Ti still sat there, alone in the middle of the kitchen,
like a huge doll that has been dressed and then forgotten.
Setting down his case, he went across and knelt beside her
and held her briefly, then kissed her brow. Yet as he moved
back, releasing her, there was nothing, not even the vaguest

flicker of recognition in her eyes. It was as if she was dead, the warmth of her skin a hideous illusion.

"Wang Ti . . ." he said softly, tenderly, his heart torn from him a second time. When would it end? When would it ever end?

Or was that his fate now? Was that the price the gods had exacted for his good fortune? To be bound forever to this living corpse, remembering her always for what she'd been and never, *never* being able to accept what she had become?

He hesitated, staring into the awful, empty mask of her face, then stood and, picking up his case again, went out. Out into the bustle of the world.

* * *

Security Headquarters at Bremen was like a busy hive, officers coming and going like worker bees on errands for their unseen queen. Making his way up the steps and through the great dragon arch, Chen felt how strange it was that he should be a part of it, how odd that the guards at the front gate should salute him, their shaven heads bowed low, then pass him through the barrier.

Another day he might have smiled at the thought, but today he was distracted. As he rode the lift up the sixty levels to his offices, he found himself thinking not of Wang Ti, nor even of the maid, but of the official's daughter, Hannah. There was no real reason to see her again. In fact there was every reason not to. Were Shang Mu to hear that Chen had been meeting his daughter, there would be all hell to pay. Best, then, to forget it – to conclude the investigation and close the file. Yet even as he decided on it, he found himself curious to know what it was she wanted from him. He had done her a favour, certainly – maybe even a great service – and yet he had made clear that there was no obligation. So why had she contacted him? What *was* it she wanted to show him?

The lift's bell pinged, the doors hissed back. It was his level. Chen stepped out, acknowledging the liftman's salute, then stopped dead, staring in amazement. The entrance hall to his suite of offices was almost blocked by a sedan which sat, like a discarded throne, in the centre of the floor. It was a huge thing, clearly a luxury item, its black and mauve drapes made of velvet and silk, its poles a good imitation of wood, the shafts finely carved with figures from Chinese myth. Against the wall to the left squatted eight men, their livery matching that of the sedan. He eyed them, understanding dawning on him. They were Company.

Chen went across, drawing aside one of the drapes and looked inside. The chair – a huge thing, heavily reinforced – looked big enough to seat three, yet there was a single imprint in the cushions. He sniffed, taking in the smell of leather and perfume. He knew that perfume. If the imprint hadn't told him, the smell would have. It was Cornwell. The fat man. The AutoMek executive who had been riding him over the matter of the broken machines.

Anger rising in him, Chen stormed through, past the two guards, who – busy chattering, their view of the outer doors obscured by the sedan – only rose to salute him after he had swept past.

As Chen came into his room, the big man got up from Chen's chair and, thrusting his ample stomach out across the desk, waved the notification at him.

"What the fuck do you mean by this, Major Kao? No further proceedings . . . Do you seriously expect me to take this shit?"

Chen put his case down on the side, then turned, facing the duty Captain in the doorway. His voice was tight, controlled. "Who let this man into my room?"

"It was Sergeant Fuller, Major Kao."

"Then have Fuller come here, immediately, and escort the *ch'un tzu* off the premises."

Behind Chen, Cornwell was shaking his head. "Like fuck I'll go! Not until I get some action around here! More than sixty of our machines have been attacked in the past ninety-six hours, Major Kao, and you've done nothing. Nothing but sit on your arse."

Chen turned back, facing the obese form of Cornwell. He

255

had been ordered by General Rheinhardt to be as diplomatic as he could with the man, but this was too much.

"You'll get out of my chair right now, *Shih* Cornwell, or I'll arrest you for trespass, understand me? As for the other matter, our investigations are continuing. But where there is no conclusive evidence, there's very little we can do."

"No evidence?" Cornwell gave a snort of derision. "There's no fucking evidence because you don't want to look for any, that's why! And while you're doing fuck-all, my Company is losing close on a million and a half a day! Well, it's not good enough, Major. You either catch these scum and punish them or I'll be forced to take matters into my own hands."

Chen glared at him. "I would advise against that, *Shih* Cornwell. It is still an offence to interfere in an official Security investigation. As for you taking action to punish these 'scum', as you call them, I would look on that as a most serious matter."

"Oh, would you now?" Cornwell came round the desk and stood nose to nose with Chen, leaning into him threateningly. "Listen . . . *Han*. I don't care what that badge on your chest says, you're still nothing but a little man, a *hsiao jen*. You get in my way and I'll have you crushed. I'll have you stepped on like an insect. My Company . . ." his lips formed an ugly smile, "we have influence at the highest level, and I mean the *highest*. So don't threaten me, Major Kao. Not if you know what's good for you."

"Sir?"

Chen turned. Fuller was waiting in the doorway. Beyond him, in the corridor, a small group of curious officers had formed. Chen calmed himself, ignoring the scent of licorice in his nostrils from the other's breath.

"Sergeant Fuller. Escort *Shih* Cornwell to his sedan, would you? And make sure he finds his way safely from the building."

He turned back, meeting Cornwell's eyes. "As for you, my friend, I would think twice before crossing me. You might scorn the badge I wear, but my power is the T'ang's power. You will leave this matter to me *or else.*"

"Or else *what?*" Cornwell leaned close, his sickly-sweet breath filling Chen's nostrils once more. "It's very simple, Major. These scum have to be dealt with, and if you won't do it, I'll find someone who will. As for all your bluster, well, you know where you can stick it, neh?"

With a grunt of amusement, Cornwell moved past Chen, squeezing his gross figure through the door and out between the watching officers. But he was not quite done. Turning, he raised his voice.

"Oh, by the way, Major Kao, how's that mad wife of yours?"

Chen stood there a moment, watching Cornwell shake with laughter, then went across and closed the door. But still the laughter went on, following him back to his desk, sounding clearly in his head long after it had ceased outside.

How much longer? he thought. *How much longer can I take this crap?*

He sat, feeling weary, aware of the warmth of the seat beneath him where the fat man had been. It had always been like this. Always. One insult after another; one battle after another. And never any peace. Never any real reward for what he'd done. Well, that was it. He'd had enough. If Cornwell so much as came near him again . . .

He unclenched his fists, conscious that his thoughts had turned to violence. Was that the only answer he could think of? Or was there some other way to deal with cunts like Cornwell?

Chen sat back, stretching his arms, trying to relax, but it was hard. The tension wasn't merely in his muscles, it was in every atom of his being.

He sighed. Maybe it was fate. Maybe there *was* nothing he could do to change things. Even so, he could not live with himself – could not respect himself as a man – unless he tried. Unless he took what fate had handed him and tried to shape it for the good.

Chen stood, looking about him at the disorder of his office,

then crossed the room. Opening the cupboard where he kept
a change of clothes, he pulled out a simple one-piece of the
kind they wore down-level. He was behind with his reports
– badly behind – but the paperwork would have to wait.

I'll go down, he thought, beginning to change. *See things
for myself. Work out what action we ought to be taking.*

But even as he went out into the corridor, passing the
curious, staring faces of his fellow officers, he knew that it
was only an excuse, an evasion, for the truth was he had to
get out, to escape all this.

Yes, he thought, facing it for the first time. He had to get
away. Right away. Before things cracked. Before the whole
charade came down on top of him.

* * *

Shang Mu leaned forward, facing the First Dragon across the
narrow space between their seats. Far below – visible
through the cruiser's ornately-decorated porthole – the huge,
ten-thousand *mu* fields of the West Asian Plantations moved
past like the squares on a giant *wei chi* board.

"The first meeting is this evening, *I Lung.* Prince An Mo
Shan and four other Minor Family princes. Sympathisers.
Men he trusts. They have arranged to meet at Yin Tsu's
palace."

"At Yin Tsu's?" The First Dragon's eyes widened. "But I
thought Yin Tsu was staunchly loyal to Li Yuan?"

"He is. But Yin Tsu will not be there. It is his second son,
Yin Chan who will be hosting the meeting."

"Ah . . . Even so, I find that strange, Shang Mu. Chan
has always struck me as a most loyal son."

"That is so, *I Lung.* Yet it seems he has never forgiven
Li Yuan for divorcing his sister. He feels his family was
shamed and wants revenge."

"Revenge . . ." The First Dragon looked away. "It's a
piss-poor reason for deposing a Son of Heaven, neh? Watch
him, Shang Mu. Find out if he drinks, if he has a loose
tongue."

"And if he has?"

258

"Then we have no choice. Yin Chan must have an accident."

Shang Mu looked down, staring at his hands uncomfortably. "And the list, *I Lung*?"

Unexpectedly, the First Dragon smiled. "Now that's a document, neh? I wonder what Li Yuan would make of it? Does he realise, I wonder, just how deep this enmity is rooted? And if he did, what would he do? What action *could* he take that would not undermine the very throne on which he sits?"

The First Dragon reached inside the darkness of his robe and drew out the handwritten list An Sheng had given him. Eight thousand names were written there, among them almost every member of the Seven's government, from chamberlains and ministers right down to bondservants and grooms. But there was one name he had noticed in particular: that of the young American politician, Joseph Kennedy.

He looked up from the thick sheaf of paper, meeting his Junior Minister's eyes. "As I said, it is interesting. And An Sheng is right, of course. It is not enough to remove the Seven, we must remove all those who serve them. Yet we must not be impatient, Shang Mu. We have not thrived all these years through impatience. No. We must saw with soft ropes, as the old saying goes. And we must heed the lessons of the past. We must be thorough. Everything must be planned, down to the last tiny detail. Only then can we guarantee success."

"Then I am to do nothing, *I Lung*?"

"Quite the contrary, Shang Mu. You will begin at once. But choose carefully. The last thing we want is to draw attention to ourselves."

Shang Mu smiled bleakly, noting the tone of irony in his Master's voice. If there was one thing the Thousand Eyes had perfected over the years, it was the art of not drawing attention to themselves. Even so, he felt a profound unease at this latest development.

"It shall be as you say, *I Lung*," Shang said, nodding.

"Good," the old man said, closing his eyes. "Then leave

259

me. And get some sleep, Shang Mu. It may be some while before any of us sleeps soundly again."

* * *

"Where is your husband?"

"My husband? He's . . . gone. Looking for work."

"Gone? Where has he gone?"

The woman looked down, avoiding Chen's eyes. "I don't know, I . . . I haven't seen him for a while. Two, three days . . ."

Chen stared at her, trying not to lose his temper, then turned away. Like the other wives he had interviewed, she clearly knew where her husband was, but she was frightened. She knew what her man had been up to and what the penalty for that was, and she was keeping quiet. Well, he'd have done the same in her place, but that made it no less frustrating. He needed to talk to one of the men, to find out what they wanted. And to try to do something before things got out of hand. Because these were decent, hardworking people. Their only crime was to have been thrown out of work by the Company and replaced by machines.

And who wouldn't be angry at that?

Chen looked about him at the room. It was like all the others he had seen: a clean, immaculately tidy room, its basic austerity augmented by tiny touches of luxury, like the colourful holo-print on the wall opposite. He went across and studied it, ignoring the woman a moment, losing himself in his appreciation of Ku Hung-chung's masterful work. Reaching up, he activated the holo, then stepped back, nodding. It was good the way the picture seemed suddenly to come to life, the computer adding depth to Ku's beautifully-painted figures. He put his palm up, feeling the warmth generated by the field, then switched it off.

Chen looked down. Against the wall beneath the holo, unnoticed until then, was a tiny, box-like cupboard on legs. Chen crouched down and opened the tiny doors, then looked across, meeting the woman's eyes.

"You know this is illegal?"

She said nothing, simply watched him, like a trapped animal, unable to answer.

He looked back, studying the tiny figures within the red and gold painted box. It was a miniature temple, not unlike those you'd find in many households, but whereas most temples were to the Family Ancestors, this one was different. He had not seen such figures often, but he knew enough to recognise that these were of the ancient gods. Possession of even one of these figures was enough to get the family demoted, and here were a dozen, fifteen of the things.

He took one out and held it up so that she could see.

"I take it these are yours?"

She was about to answer when the curtain in the doorway twitched and an old man came into the room.

Chen stood, facing the ancient, and bowed respectfully. "*Lao jen . . .*"

The ancient came towards him a pace or two then stopped, waving away his daughter-in-law. He was a tall, refined-looking old man, with a face like carved ivory. There was a sense of repose about him, of deep stillness, but just now his eyes seemed troubled.

"What do you want?"

Chen almost smiled, surprised by the directness of the old man's words. Yet it showed that he understood. More than his daughter-in-law, anyway.

"Forgive me, *lao jen*, but I was looking for Song Wei, the sweeper."

The old man's eyes narrowed. "Why do you ask? Who are you, and what do you want of my son?"

Chen smiled. Word would have gone out, like ripples from a dropped stone, that a man was going from apartment to apartment, asking questions. But who he was, that no one knew. Not yet, anyway.

He looked down at the figure in his palm, then closed his fingers over it, meeting the old man's eyes once more.

"My name is Tong Chou, and I am a friend. I wish only to talk with Song Wei."

"A friend?" The old man shook his head, his eyes suddenly hard. "I am sorry, *Shih* Tong, but I know all my son's friends, and you I have never met. Besides, my son is not here. Nor do I know when he will be back. He has gone looking for a job. You know how things are . . ."

Chen lowered his head slightly. "I know and sympathise, Master Song. Things are bad. And you are right. Your son does not know me. Yet I am still his friend and wish to help him. If he returns in the next few hours, tell him he will find me at Wu Mao's rice stall on Main. After that I cannot say. I am a busy man."

He saw how the old man's eyes took in his words, assessing them, trying to guess just what Chen's purpose was, and whether he was genuine. And there was hope there too, just the tiniest glimmer. Enough, perhaps, to tempt Song Wei to contact him.

And if he did? Well, he had no job for Song Wei, no hope. Only a warning for him to stop before it was too late.

"Wu Mao's," he said, moving close and handing the old man the figure. "Oh, and a word of advice. Destroy the temple. Or the figures, anyway. It will not help Song Wei if his wife and children have been taken from him."

Old Song gazed at the figure fondly a moment, then looked up into Chen's face again.

"We live in bad times. The people need their comforts."

"I don't deny it. But then, I don't make the laws. Do as you will, *lao jen*, but think of your son, neh? How best to help him."

Chen stepped back, bowed, then moved past the old man and out through the curtained doorway, surprising the daughter-in-law who was getting up from where she'd been eavesdropping. With a nod to her, he went out into the public corridor, a crowd of women and children making way before him, a murmur of speculation passing among them.

At the entrance to Main he stopped, looking about him, taking it all in. Ten years ago this would have been a good place to live, well lit and orderly, its people affluent, industrious and law-abiding. But things had broken down. Change had washed across these levels like a great wave of corrosive acid, eating away at the certainties upon which these people had built for so long.

Even so, there was still coherence of a kind, as if those years of different expectations had conditioned the people here, forging in them a passivity, an acceptance of their fate. The future might seem bleak, yet they were Han – they would endure and *chi ku*, "eat bitter". At least, so long as they had the capacity to endure.

He sighed, knowing how they felt. There was a time when he too had burned with the bright ideal of betterment, with the dream of a wife, a child, and of seeking his fortune up-level. But the dream had died in him, had proved a kind of ghost-vision, no more substantial than a flickering hologram. Yes, that brilliant, blinding light that had led him on had guttered, and now the darkness summoned him again, like a hungry mouth, sucking him down into the depths. Down, as if he'd never climbed at all.

He stirred himself, making his way across to Wu Mao's stall, trying to lift his spirits – to think of something that was positive amidst the darkness that threatened to overwhelm him. But there was nothing.

It was as if it had pursued him, year by year, level by level. As if, to escape it, he would have to climb to the very top and burst through the thin yet impermeable skin of the City's roof. And even then he would not be free of it, for the City was inside him, like a sickness, thickening his blood, darkening his vision.

So what then? What was the answer to it all?

Taking a seat he looked about him at the people either side of him along the counter, noting how each face mirrored his own. How in each one might read the coming of the new age. An age of uncertainty and encroaching darkness.

Better, perhaps, to die, then? To go out in one final blazing act? Or was that simply the frightened child in him talking? The boy who'd never known the love of a mother, the example of a father?

He shivered. If only Wang Ti had been with him. If only

263

she were well again. Then he might begin to make sense of it. But as it was . . .

Wu Mao came across and leaned across the counter. "What you want, friend?"

Peace, Chen answered in his head. *And a better, saner world than this*. But what could Wu Mao, the rice-seller, do about that?

Chen smiled, liking the man's rough, bearded face. "Give me some ma-po bean curd, if you have it. If not, some beggar's rice with lots of onions."

Wu Mao laughed. "The bean curd is finished. Beggar's rice it'll have to be, friend. And maybe that's good, neh? For we're all beggars now."

* * *

The two men slipped from the shadows and moved softly, silently, across the broad, tiled floor until they stood before the raised dais and the great chair. There they stopped and, like flowing pieces of the darkness, knelt, placing their hooded heads to the floor in obeisance. Above them, in the great, tall-backed chair, the First Dragon sat impassively, his masked face looking down at them.

"Listen," he said, his voice booming, echoing in the vastness of that dark, sepulchral chamber. "You are to follow the man. Find out what he does, who he sees, what he thinks, if that's at all possible. And you will report to no one but myself. If your superiors ask what you are doing, you will say nothing. You will refer them directly to me. Here . . ."

The First Dragon leaned forward slightly, his closed right hand extended. There was the smallest movement of his fingers, the clink of falling metal on the tiles in front of the two prone figures.

"These rings bear my seal. They will afford you entry into places where you would not normally be allowed. But do not abuse their power. They must be used only in the furtherance of this enquiry. You understand?"

There was the slightest nodding of heads.

"Good. But be discreet. Shang Mu must not know he is

being shadowed. If you think he suspects, then you must tell me at once. There will be no punishment. But, similarly, there will be no reward."

The First Dragon paused and sat back again, staring out over the two dark shapes, as if meeting the eyes of someone in the darkness between the great pillars at the far end. But he was alone in the audience chamber with them.

"Your fee is two hundred thousand *yuan*. A third will be paid to you now, the rest upon completion of your task. Now go. You will begin at once."

There was a nod of hooded heads, a quick, almost serpentine movement of a hand to retrieve the fallen rings, and then the figures backed away, swiftly, silently, their dark robes flowing like a mist across the smooth black tiles.

Watching them go, the First Dragon let out his breath. It was some six years since he had needed to call upon the services of the Guild of Assassins, nor was he entirely certain now. Shang Mu, after all, was a good man. If *he* proved false then who *could* be trusted? Yet he had to be sure, if only for his own peace of mind, for it was not simply his own fate that now rested on Shang Mu's shoulders, but the fate of the Ministry itself, the great Thousand Eyes. If the Ministry failed – if it *fell* – then there was no hope for Chung Kuo.

He shuddered, horrified by the prospect. By the thought of there being no Eyes to see, no guiding Hand to help. It was unthinkable. And yet think of it he must, for if *he* did not, then who would? The Seven? No. Any doubts he had harboured about them had now gone. There was no alternative. They had to act, and act decisively, before the Seven pissed away the gains of the last two hundred years. Before the *Hung Mao* took back the reins and pushed the world on into chaos once more. *Progress.* He had heard that foul and cursed word on many lips these past six months. *Progress.* Like some dark litany, chanted by the insane.

And maybe that's our fault, he thought, making his way slowly down the steps. *Ours, because we did our job too well. Because they no longer understand the true meaning – the awful, frightful cost – of Progress.*

Not that they had been wrong. No, for their intentions had been good and honourable. They had tried to start again – to build a new world free of the sins and errors of the old. And for a time it had worked. All had been well. Yet Man was Man. His ways could not be changed. One might wipe the slate clean, yet Man would dirty it again. Moreover, in burying the past they had also buried the lessons of the past. Indeed in many ways the new man was worse than the old, for while he had the same instincts he had none of his restraint – a restraint founded in long centuries of experience. Of *history*. Or was that true? Did history really teach them anything?

Once more the great man shivered, conscious of how far his thoughts had come – of what heresies they touched upon. Then, gathering his cloak about him, he walked briskly across the broad, tiled floor, his booted footsteps echoing after him, the slam of the great doors like a punctuation mark. And then silence.

* * *

Two hours had passed and no one had come, neither Song Wei, nor any of the others. Paying Wu Mao, Chen made his way to the inter-level transit, his mood despondent. Whatever his feelings on the matter, he would have to do something, before Cornwell went over his head and someone else was put in charge of the investigation.

But what? What *could* he do? He could round them all up, certainly, but as soon as he did the matter would be taken out of his hands. A tribunal would decide their fate, and in all likelihood they would be sent down – they and their families. And to be demoted these days – to be sent "Below the Net" – was as good as a death sentence. No. He would have to warn them off somehow – to impress upon them just what the stakes were. But how? How did you get the message across to such angry, desperate men? How did you convince them that, however bad their lot was now, it could be ten times worse?

He rode the transit up fifty levels, and then another fifty, ignoring the crush in the big lift, the smell of unwashed bodies, going over the problem in his mind time and again. Warn them off. Sure. But how? Should he make one of them an example? Song Wei, perhaps? Or would that only make matters worse? Wouldn't it, perhaps, simply harden their attitudes against authority?

Or hostages . . .

He laughed, surprised that he'd not thought of it before. *Hostages.* Why not? If he rounded up the wives and held them against the good behaviour of their menfolk, maybe that would work.

But it would have to be planned. He'd have to find some place to keep them. And he'd have to make sure there was no reaction from the men. The last thing he wanted was a riot.

A few weeks should do it. Until the men had cooled their heels. And in the interim, maybe, he could try to get some kind of deal for them – compensation, perhaps. Or jobs.

He smiled, for the first time feeling positive about the situation. He'd get onto it first thing tomorrow morning. And maybe, once it was done, he'd pay that bastard Cornwell a return visit – fill his reception hall with Security.

Yes. But before then he'd better check up on the other matter – see how the investigation into the missing File was going. And later, perhaps, he'd go and see the girl.

The Golden Carp. Eighth bell . . .

He nodded to himself. Maybe he'd go after all. And afterwards?

Afterwards he'd go home, to his children, his wife.

Chen shuddered, shadows falling once again, remembering Cornwell's gross belly shaking with laughter. His *mad* wife . . .

* * *

The day was ending, the western light fading fast. Three craft now rested on the huge, circular pad, their Minor Family crests indistinguishable. Behind Yin Chan, at the centre of the lake, the lights were slowly coming on in the great house,

267

while to the east, above the hills, the fourth of the craft circled, then made its approach.

It has begun, thought Yin Chan excitedly. *And when it's done, that man will be dead, his family eradicated.*

The thought was sweet. It made the tiny hairs on his neck prickle with an unexpectedly sharp anticipation. To stand over his corpse and spit into his vacant face – that, indeed, would be heaven.

He watched the ship come down, anxious for a moment in case An Hsi had sent another to say he could not come, yet when the craft had settled and the hatch hissed open, it was An Hsi himself who stepped down, arms wide, to greet him.

Yin Chan went across, grinning fiercely.

"You came!" he whispered, holding An Hsi tight against him for a moment, relief and happiness making him laugh.

"You thought I wouldn't?" An Hsi laughed, then held Yin Chan at arm's length. Yin Chan shivered, feeling the strength of the older man's hands against his arms. "We are like brothers, Chan. I would never let you down."

No, thought Yin Chan, staring into his once-lover's face. Simply by coming here, they had committed themselves – all five of them. There was no way back from this. No way out, except death. He smiled, and, taking An Hsi's shoulder, led him out down the path to the waiting boat.

Five years ago, he and his brother Sung had rowed Li Yuan across this lake to see their sister, who had fled here after a bitter row with her then-husband. The young T'ang had come here to be reconciled with her. Or so he'd claimed. For it was then that it had ended between Li Yuan and Yin Fei Yen; that day that he had set her aside – she and her unborn son – shaming Yin Chan's family, making them a laughing-stock before the others of the Twenty-Nine. He shuddered, the indignation fresh in him.

As the servants rowed them across, he made small talk with An Hsi, yet the thought of what they were about to do distracted him and, as they climbed up onto the landing stage, beneath the ancient willow, he could remember nothing of what had been said.

An Hsi stood a moment, looking across at the elegant, two-storey mansion with its gently-sloped roof and broad, panelled windows, then turned to Yin Chan, smiling.

"It's been too long since I was last here, cousin. You should have asked me long before this."

The admonishment was gentle and the smile, the slightly teasing tone reminded Chan of earlier days, when he had first brought An Hsi here to his family home. He searched An Hsi's eyes, looking to see what he meant, wondering if, after the meeting, he would perhaps stay.

But An Hsi's dark eyes revealed nothing. "Come," he said, taking Chan's arm. "Let's go and meet our cousins, neh? We've much to talk about."

* * *

Eighth bell was sounding as Chen made his way through the crowds in front of the Golden Carp and up the broad steps that led to the reception. He was feeling awkward, out of place. Everyone here was young and – to say the least – fashionably dressed, while he, though not shabbily-attired, felt old beyond his years, his simple ersilk one-piece like something a tradesman or a servant would wear.

The young woman behind the counter, her face painted gold, fake gills at her neck, stared at him as if he had made some kind of mistake, then narrowed her eyes. "Well? What do *you* want?"

He cleared his throat, strangely nervous – he who had fought men hand to hand and to the death. Even so, he understood. There were different kinds of fear, and this was his – a fear of social places, of the bright glare and insincerity of it all; of being spotlighted and made to seem a simple clod, an uncultivated fool. General Rheinhardt himself had picked him up about it, reminding him that it was his duty as a Major to engage in social activities, but he had done little to remedy the fault. He was a soldier, not a courtier, and there was little he could do about it. If Rheinhardt didn't like it, he could demote him and there was an end to it. Just now, however, something else drove him on – not the desire for social pleasantry, but plain curiosity.

"Can I help you, *sir*?"

He smiled awkwardly, conscious that he was blushing like a girl. At a loss, he stared past the receptionist, trying to make out Hannah among the crowd within. The restaurant was on two levels, both of them packed out, a real hubbub of activity. Tables filled the floors, young people sat six or seven to a table with little room between for the fish-headed waiters to make their way through, stacked trays held effortlessly above their heads. He looked from table to table, trying to locate where she was, but it was no good. He would have to ask for her.

"I . . . I'm meeting someone."

"Ah . . ." The golden head looked down, studying the appointments book in front of her, then looked back up at him. Green eyes – lenses, he realised with a start – stared back at him from the painted Han face. "Are you Kao Chen?"

He laughed, part from relief, part from embarrassment, and nodded, his mouth dry, then watched as she summoned one of the waiters over.

"Table seventeen. Upper floor. If you'd show the *ch'un tzu* . . ."

She turned back to Chen, smiling – a tight, insincere smile – as she said this last, as if to imply he could *never* be "*ch'un tzu*" – a gentleman – were he to try a thousand years. But Chen was used to that. With a face like his he could fool no one that he had come from an ancient line of kings. No. His face said plainly *peasant*. And so it was, and mainly he was proud of it, but sometimes – as now – he would have done anything, paid any price, to have had the face of a gentler, more handsome fellow than he was.

As the waiter turned away, he followed, mumbling apologies all the way across the lower floor, stumbling as he climbed the six low steps that led to the upper room. There the waiter left him, pointing across to a table in the corner, where four people – three young men and a woman, her back to him – were seated, the remains of a meal on the table before them.

For a moment Chen wasn't sure. For a second or two he hesitated, prepared to turn back, to forget he'd ever come here, but then Hannah turned in her seat, as if sensing him, and met his eyes, her smile so bright, so clearly pleased to see him there, that all thought of leaving fled him. He was smiling back at her and nodding, pleased, absurdly pleased, to see her there.

"Kao Chen!" she called above the noise, then stood, making her way between the tables. "Kao Chen . . ."

He stood there, a faint thrill of surprise passing through him as he watched her come across to him. In the tangle of his thoughts, he had forgotten that she was *Hung Mao*. He had visualised her as Han, like himself. Shang Han-A. But that was understandable perhaps. Her tall, willowy build, her dark eyes, the single plait of her long, dark hair; these made her seem, at first glance, what she was not. And now that he saw her again, he remembered how old she was – sixteen – and shook his head. Why, his own son was barely two years younger . . .

As she squeezed between the last two chairs and came face to face with him, he found his awkwardness returning. He felt the urge to embrace her, to greet her physically somehow, but knew it would be taken wrongly. Even so, it surprised him when she reached out and took both his hands in hers then leaned close to kiss his cheek.

"Kao Chen," she said more softly, the scent of her perfume giving the words a strangely romantic cast. "I wasn't sure you'd come."

"Nor I," he confessed, and then laughed. He looked past her, conscious that his mouth was dry again, his pulse racing. "Your friends?"

"Come. I'll introduce you." She hesitated, then leaned in close, speaking to his ear. "And please. Don't react. Just listen, okay? We'll talk afterwards."

He stared at her as she moved back, then shrugged. *Okay*, he mouthed, then let her lead him across to the table.

Three heads turned as they approached; three bodies repositioned themselves about the table, as if confronting Chen. *Like fighters*, he thought, and then wondered why he'd thought that, for the look of them was soft, their muscle-tone poor. Their clothes – so different from his own – seemed garishly effete, while the jewellery they wore – rings, bracelets and fine necklaces of gold – were so overdone that they reminded him of how his daughter, Ch'iang Hsin, had used to dress up when she was younger. Their faces were made up, their nails carefully manicured. First Level, that look said clearly: *Supernal*.

"Sao Ke, Andre, Christian . . . this is Kao Chen."

Chen realised he was frowning and tried to smile, but all he could do was grimace grotesquely and nod. *Like the clod I am*, he thought, conscious of how intently – how critically – they were watching him.

"Kao Chen . . ." Sao Ke repeated thoughtfully from where he sat on the far side of the table, then nodded to himself. He took a sip from his wine cup, then met Chen's eyes. "You're a student, I take it?"

Hannah answered for him, pulling an empty chair out beside her as she did, indicating that Chen should sit.

"No. Kao Chen is an old family friend."

Chen glanced at her, then looked back at the others, trying to keep the smile from slipping. The two *Hung Mao* – Christian and Andre – were looking at him, he realised, silently assessing him. *And dismissing me, no doubt*, he thought, discomfort making him swallow drily. Yet even as he did, Hannah leaned close, her scent once again distracting him.

"Are you drinking?" she whispered, her mouth against his ear.

He hesitated, then nodded.

"Good." She smiled, then poured wine from the jug into the empty cup in front of him. A strong red sorghum wine that, when he tasted it, made him nod with appreciation.

He looked up and saw she was watching him, enjoying his enjoyment of the wine, and for a moment he thought how strange that was. It was a long time since anyone had done that; since anyone had worried what he, Kao Chen, was feeling. He looked down, a faint shiver passing through him.

"Well . . ." one of the two *Hung Mao* said – Christian? Andre? He wasn't sure. Chen glanced from one to the other. They smiled, and lifted their cups to him in a toast, but behind the smiles there was a coldness, an implacable dislike for his kind.

"So what do you do, Kao Chen?"

The speaker sat to Chen's left, the other side of Hannah.

"Kao Chen is a potter." Hannah answered, before he could even think what to say. "As was his father and his father's father. And before you ask, his pots are very good. Some say that their shape is too crude, the clay too thick, the design too simple, but that merely serves to demonstrate their ignorance. Besides, their glaze is the most delicate you've ever seen, the colours . . ." she turned and, smiling, winked at Chen, who was staring at her, astonished. "Well, the colours are just perfect. There's a blue he uses which is . . . well, it's like the blue of heaven itself."

Chen stared at her a moment longer, then, realising what he was doing, he looked away, trying to compose himself. It was all invention, certainly – all part of some game she was playing – but why? What did she mean by it all?

"My own taste is for the funerary, of course," Sao Ke said, leaning forward slightly, an interested gleam in his eyes, "but young Hannah here is a fine judge of artefacts. Praise from her is high praise indeed. But tell me, Kao Chen . . ."

Hannah interrupted him. "Forgive me, Ke, but it will do you little good asking Kao Chen. I should have said at once. My dear friend is dumb. A childhood accident . . ."

Dumb! Chen almost laughed. Was there no end to her audacity? And yet it all made sense of a kind. Knowing he was an artisan – if only of a lowly kind, a *potter* – they would be more inclined to talk freely in his presence. And his affliction, his inability to speak – again he almost laughed aloud at the thought of it! – it was the perfect excuse to simply sit there and listen. He glanced at her again, saw she was watching him, and looked down, smiling. There was more to her – much more – than he'd realised.

Hannah leaned forward, smiling gaily around the table. "Well, anyway . . . We were talking of the changes, remember? Andre, you were saying something interesting about your father's Company. About . . ."

Chen half listened at first, struck more by the look of these young men, by the intoxicating atmosphere of the Golden Carp, than by anything they said. Andre and Christian, he realised, were brothers. Or, if not, then they ought to have been, the facial similarities were so striking. But it was not merely the look of them – the cosmetic outer shell of them – that he found fascinating, it was something in the language of gesture they used; something he had only vaguely noticed before that moment.

They were arrogant, that went without saying, yet it was of a kind that was untempered by any kind of self-knowledge or self-consciousness. The arrogance of princes and great men, that Chen understood; but the arrogance of such little men – such *hsiao jen* – surprised him. What they knew, what they were: it all seemed like a thin veneer, covering up an inner emptiness so vast, so frightening, that they must keep talking to disguise the nothingness within. When they talked, they did not meet each other's eyes, as if they were self-obsessed. Yet how could one be self-obsessed where there was no true self? It puzzled Chen as he sat there. Puzzled him that Hannah could bring herself to listen to these fools, these elegant, empty mouths.

Maybe it was the wine, or maybe it was his own recently-acquired habit of introspection, but Chen found himself wanting to voice these thoughts, these insights . . . to tell them *exactly* what they were. But what good would that do? What could mere words achieve against such stultifying ignorance? Even so, the desire made him lean in towards them, as if in combat; to set aside his thoughts and listen, engaging for the first time in what they were saying.

Christian was talking now, turning the conversation away from the meal they had just eaten to something he had heard about the Lowers – about how they had been putting "chemicals" in the food all these years.

"It's not much," he said. "Not even enough to register on the taste buds of the most sensitive gourmet, but, well . . . it has its effect. It makes them . . . *docile*. It dampens down their natural aggressive instincts. Or, at least, it used to. Now that the food quotas have fallen they're not getting enough, it seems, and the powers that be can't add any more without it becoming . . . *discernible*. That's why there's more trouble down there these days. Why there are so many riots and disturbances. They're waking up, you see. And they're getting angry."

That's true, Chen thought, *but it's not because of any chemicals in their food*. He'd heard the rumours before. They were rife these days. But there was no proof. Besides, there were other reasons to be angry. More than enough reasons to riot.

"Maybe that's why there are so many revolutionaries these days," Christian added after a moment.

Sao Ke chipped in at once, his sardonic drawl the voice of Emptiness itself, his cultured Han face one long, consistent sneer.

"*Revolutionaries* . . . there's a hollowness at the centre of them all when it comes right down to it. They're fucked up, and because *they're* fucked up, they want the world to be fucked up too . . ."

Hannah, as if sensing Chen's sudden interest, cut in. "That may be true of some of them, even the majority, perhaps, but it can't be true for them all. There must be some for whom the ideal of revolution is . . . well, a *vocation*."

Sao Ke leaned back, showing perfect, pearled teeth as he laughed; his laughter a bray of pure scorn. "Well, I've heard it called many things, but never *that*. A vocation!" He shook his head, then reached out to pour more wine into his bowl. "Don't be fooled, my young and beautiful friend. All that shit about the altruism of the lower levels, about the honest, hard-working peasant stock you'll find down there . . . it's all a myth! – a fiction, served up by the Trivee Companies to make us feel okay about it all. Besides, all this *ideology* they spout, it's window-dressing, that's all, a cynical disguise the bastards use to justify killing and maiming innocent people. But have no illusions, it's all Number One when it comes right down to it. Self, self, self, however prettily the ideas might be packaged!"

Hannah leaned forward, looking back at Sao Ke. "I'm not so sure. I think they must suffer down there. It must be dreadful . . ."

"Bullshit!" Sao Ke answered, making a dismissive gesture of his hand, as if the very idea were absurd. "They're animals, that's what they are! Less than animals, some of them! All they do is eat, drink and fuck! We'd be better off without them."

"I'll drink to that," Andre said, lifting his wine cup unsteadily. "If I had my way I'd gas the lot of them. Rig up something in the ventilation system and get the buggers while they're sleeping. That'd solve all our problems, neh? There'd be food enough for everyone then."

Sao Ke, who had drunk little, looked down, smiling. "It's a somewhat radical suggestion, I'd say. Then again, maybe it's time for something radical. Something we'd have no need for in . . . well, in *better* times. You know, they have a slogan down there, I'm told – 'Life is cheap, flesh plentiful'. Well, maybe it's time to put a higher value on life. Market rules, and all that."

Christian turned, looking at Sao Ke. "What do you mean?"

"It's simple. The laws of the Market say that if a product's rare, its price is normally high. Likewise, if it's a commonplace – easily acquired, easily replaced – then its value is minimal. And right now I'd say life has never been cheaper, neh? The problem's a simple one. Too many bodies. Too many mouths to feed. The answer's obvious."

"And who decides?"

It was Hannah who had asked the question. She was smiling, leaning towards Sao Ke as if encouraging him, but behind the smile was a hardness Chen had not noticed before.

"Draw a line, I say," Christian said, banging the table

enthusiastically. "Anyone below the . . . oh, the top hundred gets the chop."

"Top fifty!" Andre chimed in.

There was laughter; long, unhealthy laughter. But Chen, watching, saw how Hannah didn't laugh; how she turned her face slightly towards him, as if conscious that he was watching.

"That's more than eighty per cent of the population," she said. "Thirty-two billion people, or thereabouts."

"Give or take a million," Andre added, making them roar anew.

"So who'd get rid of the bodies?"

Sao Ke shrugged and sat back. "Oh, it'd all be planned, of course. Everything thought through thoroughly."

"Thought through thoroughly . . . I like that!" Andre chirped in, and again they were off, their laughter filling that tiny corner of the Golden Carp. But Chen had had enough. There was a tightness at the pit of his stomach, a tension in his muscles, that was almost unbearable. He would have to say something, to answer them, or he would burst.

He leaned forward, meaning to answer Sao Ke, to throw his vile obscenities back in his face, but Hannah was watching him. As he opened his mouth, he felt her kick his shin – hard – under the table.

"There's talk . . ." she said brightly, steering the conversation away from the abyss into which it had strayed, "that Huang Min-ye is to perform at the College Hall this summer . . ."

*   *   *

It seemed an age, but finally he was outside, breathing fresher, *cleaner* air. He stood there a moment at the foot of the steps, conscious of Hannah watching him; of the press of young, elegantly-dressed people milling all about him, filling the great green that was at the heart of this First Level deck. Reluctantly, he let her take his arm and lead him through the crowd, across the green and towards the inter-level transit, keeping his thoughts, his anger to himself; yet as soon as they were out of it – as soon as they were in a quieter, less public place, he turned on her.

"Those are your *friends*?"

Hannah shook her head. "No, Kao Chen. Those are the people I'm obliged to spend my time with. My social equals." She hesitated, her dark eyes boring into him intently. "I wanted you to see. To understand how they think up here. And I . . . well, I want you to do the same for me. To take me down-level."

"Why?"

"Because I need to know. To understand how it is. Because . . ." She took a long, shuddering breath. "Well, because I want to let people know. To . . . to be a voice. A loud, clear voice, telling people how it is. How it *really* is."

He shook his head. "It isn't possible."

"No?" She smiled. "Maybe not. But I can try, neh? I can always try."

CHAPTER · 11

MINISTRIES OF DEATH

Chen travelled with Hannah as far as Erfut stack, then saw her into the transit, assigning a young guard from the nearby Security post to escort her to her door. It was an hour by fast-bolt to his own stack in West Bremen, but, alone again, he realised that he couldn't go home – couldn't face another night like the last.

Where to, then? he asked himself, turning away, surprised by how down he felt. *Down.* Maybe that was the answer. Maybe, for once, he should simply trust to instinct and let go. After all, things couldn't possibly be worse than they were.

Very well, he thought, *but not here.* No. He'd catch a bolt south to Munich *Hsien*, to his old haunts. But first he'd call in, let his office know he was going off-duty. *And off-call?* Strictly speaking, he wasn't supposed to do that, but who'd miss him this once? Rheinhardt? No. Rheinhardt would be off socialising somewhere – he and the rest of the senior staff. Only he, Kao Chen, worried about such matters these days, and tonight he felt like letting it all hang.

Quickly he made his way back to the Security post and sent the message through, signing off with his personal code.

There, he thought, satisfied. *Eight hours.* Nothing could happen in eight hours. And even if it did, let someone else worry for a change. Let someone else save Chung Kuo from anarchy and old night. He'd had enough.

The bolt terminus was quiet, echoing empty. From the board he saw he'd missed one of the high-speeds by ten minutes, but there was another in an hour. Plenty of time to get himself a drink and a bite to eat.

279

The terminus bar was closed, but a porter directed him to a bar six levels down. It was a big place with a dance floor at one end and a long, curving bar, backed by a wall-length mirror. The lighting was subdued, the place three-quarters empty. Music played softly in the background, as if coming from somewhere down below.

Chen pulled out one of the bar stools and sat, then called the waiter over.

"What'll you have?"

Normally he didn't drink, or if he did it was something non-alcoholic, but he was feeling half-drunk from the wine he'd had already.

"A *Yao Fan Te*," he said, recalling as he did that it was all of fourteen years since he'd last tasted a bulb of *Yao Fan Te* beer. He smiled, remembering. Back then he'd been a wanted man, a criminal, forced into taking a menial job to keep Wang Ti and his baby son. He took a long, deep breath, nodding to himself. Yes, the last time he had tasted *Yao Fan Te* had been that evening in the bar with Supervisor Lo – the evening of the public execution of Edmund Wyatt. The same evening Tolonen and the big man, Karr, had come for him and changed his life.

"You all right?"

Chen looked up and smiled. "Sure." He put a five *yuan* note down beside the open bulb, then picked up the drink. After the wine it tasted sour, unpleasant even, but it was cold and after a second swig it didn't seem so bad.

He looked around, noting how many of the customers sat alone, or silent and subdued in groups of two or three. Maybe it was the place. Maybe it attracted transients like himself. Or maybe it was just the hour. Whatever, it seemed quite dead after the bustling brightness of the Golden Carp. Up there there'd been great shrieks of laughter, a constant buzz of noise, while here . . .

He turned back, facing his reflection in the curving mirror, noting how the image of his face was stretched, as if someone were tugging at his cheeks.

Okay . . . So what am I to do?

A more ruthless man might have had his wife committed; would have married again and put it all behind him. But he wasn't that kind of man. Besides, for all that she was a stranger to him now, he still loved Wang Ti, or at least, the *shell* of her – the memory of what she had been. He could not let that go, however much it hurt him to go on this way. No, and nor would his children have forgiven him if he had.

He drained the bulb and called for another. *Full circle*, he thought, watching the waiter's back as he bent down and took another bulb from the back of the refrigerated cupboard. *I have come full circle.*

Wang Pen, he'd been – rootless and unconnected, his parents unknown, his origins forgotten. Lacking options he had become a hireling, a man whose death would have gone unmourned, unnoticed: a machine of flesh and bone and muscle, used by bigger men for ends he could not guess at. So he might have spent his meagre life, so wasted it. But then he had met Wang Ti – Wang Ti, his wife and lover – and his life had been transformed. Children they'd had, and a future. The sun had shone on them. But now?

Chen shuddered, the bitterness flooding back. The pain he felt, the sheer disappointment and regret, the anger and frustration, all of it ate at him – all was impurely mixed into one sour, unhealthy cocktail of bile; a cocktail he was forced to drink each morning when he woke, each evening when he lay his head down on his pillow. Bitterness. Unending bitterness.

"Eat bitter", so the saying went. *Endure.* Yes, but was there ever an end to such endurance? Was there never a moment's ease, a moment's sweetness to be had?

He turned, suddenly conscious of someone at his shoulder, of the faint, sweet scent of perfume in the air.

"I'm sorry . . . I didn't mean to disturb you."

For a moment he stared into her eyes, then, recollecting himself, he lowered his head. "Forgive me, I . . ."

"You looked sad," she said, smiling at him. "I was watching you just now, in the mirror." She hesitated. "Look, if I'm not wanted . . ."

He shook his head, looked back at her again. She seemed young, in her mid-twenties, possibly. Her dark hair was tied back, her shoulders bare in the tight-fitting dark blue dress she wore.

Strangely he found himself staring at her shoulders, fascinated by their strength, their roundedness. They glistened in the half-light, like something carved from ivory.

She smiled. "You like what you see?"

Chen looked down, blushing furiously. "I . . . I didn't mean . . ."

Her hand covered his where it lay on the surface of the bar. It was a strong hand, the nails a glossy red. The warmth of it pressed down upon his own. Warm, like her voice.

"It's all right. I like to be looked at."

He looked at her again and nodded. "You're very nice."

"Thank you." Her smile was open, friendly. There were no conditions to it. It was a simple smile of pleasure, like a child's. Seeing it, Chen found himself warming to her.

"So? What were you thinking about?"

Chen shrugged. *"Was* I thinking?"

She reached up, tracing the frown lines in his forehead. "These."

He laughed. "I was thinking . . . well, I was thinking about men . . . and women."

"Ah . . . women. The eternal problem, neh?"

"Not for you."

"No."

They both laughed.

"Look," Chen began, feeling suddenly awkward, "Will you . . . will you sit with me? Have a drink, perhaps?"

Her smile broadened. "I wondered when you'd ask. My name is Hsin Kao Hsing."

"Tong Chou," he said, with a tiny formal bow, conscious that she was still holding his hand, that at no moment had she released him from that simple, warm contact.

"Well, *Shih* Tong. And what brings you to these parts?"

What did he say? How did he answer that?

"My wife . . ." He fell silent, realising that he didn't want to talk about that.

"Ah," she nodded, as if she understood; as if there were no further need to explain. "I had a husband once. A little man he was." She put her hand out, as if measuring where the top of his head would come to.

Chen smiled. "He must have been very small."

"Yes, but very strong . . . and big . . . you know, where it matters."

He narrowed his eyes, then understood. "Ah . . ."

"That drink?" she coaxed.

"Ah, right . . ." He turned, summoning the barman across, then turned back to her. "What will you have?"

She nodded to the bulb beside him. "I'll have whatever you're drinking, if that's all right."

He nodded, then ordered two more beers.

"Do you live around here?" he asked, an unfamiliar dryness in his mouth.

"Down-level," she answered, leaning towards him, her face only a hand's width from his own now she was seated facing him. "I've my own place. I keep it neat."

He nodded.

"And you?"

Chen took a breath. "Just passing through," he answered, not wanting to say too much. "I was . . ."

He stopped, suddenly the idea of going all the way to Munich *Hsien* had lost its attraction. Why, he might as well stay here – have a few more beers.

"You were what?" she asked, her smile curious.

"Nothing," he answered, taking one of the bulbs the barman had set down and handing it to her. Then, taking his own, he snapped the seal and raised it, toasting her.

"Kan pei!"

"Kan pei!" she answered, her eyes sparkling.

He sat back slightly, taking a long, deep breath. Her perfume was stronger than Hannah's . . . brasher. *Cheaper too*, he thought. But what did that matter? They were alike, he and she, he could see that at a glance – made of the same common flesh: peasant stock, and no frills. He found himself smiling at the thought.

"Well . . ." she said, returning his smile strongly, "here we are." Then, putting her bulb down on the bar, she leaned in towards him, resting her hands gently on his knees. "So, Tong Chou, why don't you tell me about yourself . . ."

* * *

Prince An Hsi leaned forward in his chair, looking about him at his fellow princes. "Well, cousins, I think we are agreed. Our first task is to recruit others of a like mind."

There was a murmur of agreement. An Hsi smiled.

"Good. But let us be clear . . . we must go about this task with the greatest sensitivity. Like gardeners, we must cultivate with patience and extreme care. On no occasion must the first word be ours. No, we must learn to be good at listening and encouraging others to talk. Wine . . ." he indicated the great spread on the table before them, "and good company . . . they'll serve to loosen many a tongue. Yet beware of those that gabble their thoughts carelessly. We want only those in whom anger is balanced with discretion, only those who – like ourselves – understand the true seriousness of this venture."

He paused, his voice heavy with significance. "To depose the Seven . . . that is no small thing. And no matter how much Heaven might smile on us, until it is done we are in great peril. Though our anger may be hot, our minds must be cool. A ruthless necessity must shape each word, each action from henceforward." Again he paused, looking from face to face, his eyes finally alighting on the face of Yin Chan. "One mistake . . . one tiny mistake . . . might undo the great good we seek to achieve."

Yin Chan nodded, his eyes sparkling with a strange fervour.

"Well," An Hsi added, the intensity slowly draining from him. "I think we are done. I for one must go. There is much to do, and I would be at it early."

Yin Chan looked to the other three. There were nods all round. He looked back at An Hsi. "I am glad you came, cousins. Until now . . ." He shivered, then looked about him again, tears of gratitude in his eyes. "Until now I could see no end to it . . . no way to douse the fire of rage that burned in me. But now . . ." He clenched his right fist and raised it, his face suddenly hard. "Now we can fulfil the will of Heaven."

Their response was fierce and passionate – a raising of clenched fists. All eyes were tearful now.

"It is so," An Hsi said quietly, leaning towards them across the table. "We must be as brothers now."

As they stepped out into the hallway they heard a movement on the stairs above – a brief, silken rustling, and then silence.

"Who was that?" An Hsi asked softly, his eyes suspicious.

Yin Chan stared a moment, then looked back at him. "It was no one, cousin, only my sister."

"Your sister?" He seemed startled. "You didn't tell me she was here."

"She wasn't meant to be, but her son was ill and she decided not to go with my father."

"But if she heard . . ."

Yin Chan leaned close, pressing An Hsi's hand and smiling reassuringly. "I doubt it. But even if she did, she has more reason than most to hate Li Yuan. Why, if it came to it, I'm sure she'd strike the first blow herself."

An Hsi stared past him briefly, then looked back, smiling faintly, mollified by his words. "She suffered badly, then?"

Yin Chan lowered his voice. "She *raged*, cousin. The House shook with her anger. Imagine it . . . to be cast off, your only son disinherited! A T'ang he would have been! A Son of Heaven! And what is he now? Not even a prince! The Special Edict . . ."

Yin Chan looked down, shuddering with repressed anger.

"I understand . . ." An Hsi said softly, sympathetically. "She must hate him, neh?"

Yin Chan looked up, gave a sharp nod.

"Well . . . I must go. As I said, there's much to do. We'll meet again, neh, cousin? Two days from now, at my estate. Until then, take great care . . . and remember what I said.

Trust no one, not even your closest servant. Only those bonded to us in common hatred."

Yin Chan nodded.

"Good." An Hsi smiled, his hand briefly caressing Yin Chan's cheek. Then he leaned close, gently kissing his lips. He moved back.

"And maybe you'll stay next time? It's been too long, dear Chan. Much, much too long . . ."

* * *

Fei Yen stood just inside her door, the room dark, moonlight from the open window casting a silver bar upon the far wall, revealing the door to the nursery. She could hear the child coughing in the next room, the soft singing of the nursemaid, but her mind was on what she'd heard downstairs, outside the door to her father's study.

Yin Chan, she thought, her anguish making her twist the silk of her nightdress tightly between her hands. *What are you doing? What in the gods' names are you doing?*

Treason, it was. Simple treason. Punishable by death. Death to the third generation.

My son, she thought, her heart pounding. *They'll kill my son.*

Quickly she crossed the room. From the window she could see the hangar on the far side of the lake. There was movement there beside the craft as the crews prepared themselves. A moment later she saw her brother emerge on the lawn below beside An Hsi, the two men talking quietly.

Foolishness, she thought, seeing her brother clasp the older man's hands and bow his head. An Hsi she could understand, he had lost three brothers when Li Yuan had dealt with the Willow Plum Sickness that time, but Chan . . .

Fei Yen took a long breath, controlling herself, forcing herself to slow down and consider matters properly.

She had never suspected. Never, even from a look or comment, thought that her brother hated Li Yuan so much. And herself?

Chan was wrong. She didn't hate Li Yuan. Not now. If

anything, she understood him better now, and if, when she looked back on their days together, it was not with fondness, there was at least some element of regret that she had not tried harder with him. He had loved her. She had no doubt of that now. She had seen it in his eyes that last time he had come to visit her, after the death of his wives.

But this . . . this *madness* . . . What could she do to stop Chan's foolishness? How could she prevent him from bringing retribution down on all their heads?

She watched, as Chan handed An Hsi into the boat, then climbed in after him, waving the servants away and taking the oars himself. She knew what had happened between An Hsi and Chan. Oh, she had had no need of spies to see what had been going on there. But she had thought it ended. Now, however, An Hsi was back, dripping his venom in her brother's ear, fanning old frustrations into fires of vengeance. And for what?

She shook her head, suddenly angry. A fool and a villain . . . it was a fine pairing! It would serve them well if the boat sank and the two were dragged down to the bottom . . .

She caught her breath, realising where her thoughts had run. Her brother dead. Her dear, feeble, foolish brother . . . dead? She shivered. Was there no other way?

She closed her eyes, pained by the thought, but frightened by the alternative. She had heard them down there, swearing binding oaths of brotherhood and talking of the death of T'ang. It was madness, yet it was real. And its reality threatened all their lives. Her brothers, her son, herself . . .

And father, she thought, horrified suddenly by the idea that that dear and noble man might be sacrificed to her brother's foolishness.

I must tell him. Let him *decide.*

The thought, once formulated, took hold of her. Her father. He would sort out this mess. After all, that was his task, as Head of their great family. It was not for her to decide her brother's fate. She had not spawned him.

She turned, looking at the moonlit door. It was quiet now. The coughing had stopped, the nursemaid's singing ended.

There was only the gentle slush of the oars where they dipped into the water of the lake behind her.

Sleep softly, Han, she thought, blowing a kiss to her infant son. *I'll let no one ever harm you. No one.*

* * *

It was a tiny, two-room apartment, sparsely furnished but neat, like she'd said, a single wall lamp throwing a pale orange light over everything. As she closed the door behind them, Chen looked about him, noting the cheap, romantic prints that covered the end wall, the ersilk pillows that were plumped up on the single bed. A beaded curtain separated the room from the galley kitchen. He and Wang Ti had lived in such an apartment for a year, when Jyan was three. It had been cramped, but they'd been happy there. He smiled, feeling unsteady, heavy-limbed from the beer he'd drunk.

He turned, looking at the woman. She was standing by the low dresser, taking off her earrings. Seeing him watching her in the mirror, she turned and smiled at him.

"So . . . what do you want?

"Want?"

"You want sex? Or maybe something more kinky? Sex is five *yuan*. Anything else is extra."

He stared at her, suddenly understanding. "I . . . I don't know. I thought . . ."

She smiled and came across. Placing her hand against his chest, she began to unbutton his tunic.

"How much have you got?"

He felt in his pocket, then handed her a twenty *yuan* note.

She whistled softly. "For that you can have me any way you like. But no rough stuff, understand? And if you want it up the arse, you do it gentle, right? I'm a sensitive lady . . ."

Her laughter was the same as before – an open, affectionate sound – yet now that he understood it seemed quite different.

He stared at her, at the painted lips, the rouged cheeks, the tight lines about her eyes and mouth and wondered why he hadn't clicked before. She was a whore. A bar hustler. And he had thought . . .

He let her take his shirt and hang it up, then watched as she went through to the kitchen, no doubt to put the money in a safe place. When she came back he was still standing as she'd left him.

"Well?" she said, laughing softly. "Are you going to strip, or do I have to take it all off for you?"

"I . . ." He looked at her and saw how she was watching him, no judgement in those eyes, only a friendliness, the affection of one stranger for another, and shrugged. "If you like . . ."

She came across. "Sit on the bed. It'll make things easier."

He sat, letting her pull off his boots.

"And these," she said, tugging at his trousers.

He lifted up.

"There," she said, setting them on the chair beside the wall. "That's better, neh?"

For a moment she knelt there, smiling up at him. Then she moved back slightly and, with a simple little movement, pulled her top up over her head and threw it to one side, leaving her naked from the waist. In the half-light her breasts were firm, the nipples prominent. He stared at her, half afraid, half fascinated. *Home*, he thought, but home was an impossibility. There was nothing at home. He moaned softly.

"It's okay," she said, more gently than before, her eyes reassuring him. "You're safe here, my love. No wife to come and eat you, only me." She moved forward, placing her hands on his thighs, then nuzzled close, against his chest, placing a soft wet kiss against his neck. "You're in the land of warmth and softness now, Tong Chou, so relax, neh? Just relax . . ."

* * *

He woke, wondering where he was. *Not my room*, he thought, listening to the faint tick of a clock. And the air . . . the air was different somehow . . .

He remembered. The woman. Shifting slightly he could feel her against his back.

Slowly he turned, until he was facing her. The night light was on in the galley kitchen – the pearled whiteness filtered through the bead curtain in the doorway. In its light he could see the shape of her, the slow rise and fall of her breasts.

He eased himself up, then rested his back against the wall. The woman lay beside him, naked, on her back, her eyes closed, one hand resting on her stomach, the other nestled in her hair. He looked at her, surprised to find himself there, and remembered what had happened between them.

The need . . . that had surprised him. The fierceness of his need. That and her warmth. So kind she'd been, so . . . gentle with him.

Like a lover, he thought and frowned, because he'd been told you couldn't buy love, only win it.

Whores . . . They were a staple of his work. He'd seen a thousand of them in his time – in the cells, or in their gaudy rooms – and never once had he thought what it was like for them: where they lived or what they wanted from their lives.

Comfort probably. And peace of mind. Like anyone.

He had seen them dead – murdered or overdosed from drugs – and had never once thought what it must be like for them. Until now.

He sighed. *And you think you've got problems, Kao Chen . . .* But he, at least, had something, whereas she . . .

She stirred, then turned and looked up at him, a slow smile forming on her lips.

"Couldn't sleep, huh?"

He smiled back at her. "I was thinking . . ."

"You shouldn't. It's bad for you."

"Maybe . . ." He reached down, taking her hand where it nestled in her long, dark hair, and laced his fingers into hers. "It was nice . . ."

Her smile deepened. She lifted his hand to her mouth and kissed it.

". . . but I ought to go."

"At this hour? Where? Home to that wife of yours?" She smiled then shook her head. "No, Tong Chou. I'll make us some *ch'a.* Then we'll go again . . ."

290

"Again?" he laughed softly, but the thought of it was enticing and the way she looked at him inflamed him.

"Wait there . . ."

He watched her get up, enjoying the sight of her nakedness, the simple intimacy of it. This room, themselves . . . He let his head drop back against the wall, a long breath soughing from him, then listened to her pottering about in the kitchen.

"You hungry?"

He gave a grunt of assent.

"Here . . ." she leaned round the door, holding a plate out to him.

He looked up, then leaned forward to take the plate from her.

"Oat crackers!" He laughed. "It's years since I had oat crackers!"

"You don't like them?"

"No, no . . . I love them. It's just . . ." He huffed out a breath. How explain it? How explain the strange mixture of sadness and contentment he was feeling at that moment? Or did she already know? Was that, perhaps, how *she* felt, *all* of the time?

We're both whores, he thought. *The only difference is that one of us is more honest about it than the other.*

She came back, offering him a cup, then squatted on the bed beside him. In the light he could see she was much older than he'd first imagined her – more his own age, in fact. Her face was lined and her flesh had lost the firmness of youth. Even so, she was still an attractive woman.

She smiled and leaned towards him. "I like you, Tong Chou. I'm tempted to let you stay the night. Business is bad, so . . ."

"You want more money?"

She raised an eyebrow. "Did I *say* that? No . . . besides, you paid me well, and treated me nicely, too. It's not often . . ."

He saw the wistfulness in her eyes and looked away, sipping at his *ch'a.*

"You like your work?" he asked.

"You like yours?"

He shook his head.

"So what do you do, Brother Chou? You never said."

"You don't want to know."

"That bad, huh?"

He laughed. Then, more seriously, he nodded. *"That* bad."

"Tell me. I'm curious."

He hesitated, tempted to tell her, then reached out and gently touched her cheek. "You don't want to know."

* * *

Hannah closed the door behind her quietly, then went across to her father's desk.

Sitting in his chair, she looked about her at the stacks of papers and reports that filled the desk, and took a long breath. It was here somewhere. She had seen it only the other day. A black, hand-bound file. But which one? There had to be thirty or forty here that fitted that description. That was, if it *was* still here. If he hadn't dealt with it and sent it back.

So . . . Where to start?

She removed the gold-bound file that rested on the jotter and placed it on the floor beside her, then began, taking the top file from the stack to her left and placing it face-down on the jotter. It was important to keep it all in the proper order – to put it all back exactly as it was. She knew her father. All of this seemed chaotic, yet he had his own system and knew precisely where everything was. He knew . . .

She stopped, interested by something she had read. It wasn't the file she was looking for, even so . . . She read on.

Half an hour later she looked up, her face pale, her heart racing. Secrets . . . her father was the custodian of secrets, but this . . .

She whistled softly to herself.

Forget Nantes. Forget what happened there. It was as nothing beside *this*.

She went back to the first page, studying the list of names

to whom the file had been sent. Nine names in all. Seven of them, she knew, were Dragons – Heads of the Ministry in their own Cities and brothers to her stepmother, Chih Huang Hui. The eighth name was her father's. The ninth . . . She frowned, surprised by it. The ninth name was that of An Sheng, Head of the great Minor Family and liege to Li Yuan, the T'ang of Europe.

"Gods . . ." she said softly, remembering what her father had said to her, only days before. So this was the important matter he had been working on. *This.*

She sat back, feeling breathless, giddy, for once at a loss what to do. This was not the kind of secret one should know; not the kind one could share with anyone.

No . . . not even her father.

For a moment she sat there, her mind a blank, staring straight ahead of her. Then an idea occurred to her. Maybe she should consult her grandfather, Shang Wen Shao. Maybe he would know what to do. Then again, maybe not. Maybe this was too weighty a matter for him.

Her great-grandfather, Shang Chu, then?

She sighed. No. She knew what *he* would say.

Or did she? For once she wasn't sure.

She frowned, then froze, hearing something.

The door . . . the door was open. Not much. Not more than a hand's width, to be precise, yet she had taken care to close it after her.

"Who is it?" she said, closing the file and putting it aside. "Come out and show yourself."

The door slowly opened. A boy stood there; a fat-faced little boy with Eurasian features, her step-brother, Ch'iu.

"Sneak," she said, standing then coming round the desk.

He stared back at her, unabashed. "Why are you in father's study?"

"Why aren't *you* in bed?"

"I was," he said, his pudgy face glaring at her now. "But I heard you creeping down the corridor and wondered what you were up to. When you didn't come back I thought I'd come and see."

She went right up to him, looking down at him, her hands on her hips. "Well, now you can go back to bed, can't you."

"Why should I? Besides, you still haven't answered my question."

She leaned down at him, her face hard, no love lost between them. "Nor am I going to. Now go. Before I kick that fat little bottom of yours from here to the bathroom!"

"I'll tell mother."

"Tell her. See if I care."

He stared at her a moment longer, defiance in his eyes, then turned and left, pulling the door closed behind him.

Hannah stared at the door a moment, then let out her breath.

"Shit!"

She went back across the room again and, putting everything else back where it had been, picked up the file and turned, meaning to return to her room. But she had gone only two paces towards the door when it swung open again.

"Han-A?"

She bowed her head, swallowing. "Mother . . ."

Chih Huang Hui stood there, her pale face staring out from the layers of blood-red silk she wore, her eyes wide with a strange satisfaction.

"Can you explain what you are doing here, girl?"

Hannah held the file tightly behind her back, concealing it from sight. "I . . ." She thought quickly. "I was looking for something father said he'd left for me."

"*Left* for you?" Her stepmother's face crinkled up in an expression of distaste. "Then why did he not leave it in your room, Han-A? Surely he would not have left it *here*, among his papers."

She looked up, deciding to brazen it out. "It was exactly what I thought myself. But I looked on my desk, and there was nothing, so I thought . . ."

"Does he *know* you come into his room?"

Hannah looked down again, then shook her head.

"And if he did, don't you think . . ." she smiled, clearly

294

savouring the thought, "don't you think he might be *angry* with you, Han-A?"

"I . . . I don't know."

Chih Huang Hui straightened up, her whole body taut with triumph. From behind her, Shang Ch'iu peered out, his face grinning with malice.

"*Well*, Han-A. I *am* disappointed in you. *Severely* disappointed. I'm afraid I shall have to tell your father. He'll be . . ." again she smiled, this time a spark of real savagery lighting her features, "most surprised to learn what his darling daughter gets up to while he's away, don't you think? *Most* disappointed."

* * *

Chen dressed quickly, his embarrassment beyond words. His duty Captain, Wilson, stood in the corner of the room, his head bowed, his eyes averted, waiting while Chen put on the spare uniform he'd brought.

As he buttoned the tunic, Chen glanced at the woman apologetically. She was watching him silently, a strange distance to her suddenly, the spell of intimacy broken. Now he was simply another body, and an unwelcome one at that.

"If I'd known . . ." she'd said, almost brutally. "Security . . . fucking Security! And I thought . . ."

The last button done, he turned, looking at his Captain. "Okay. You'd better tell me as we go along."

He turned back, looking at the woman. She had put her jacket about her shoulders, otherwise she was naked still. He went to say something, then saw the look in her face and fell silent. Shrugging, he turned away. But it was hard simply to walk out on her. For a moment . . .

As the door closed behind him, Chen felt a sudden anger. For the first time in ages he had found peace . . . for one brief moment . . . and then they had tracked him down, like the lowest criminal.

"How did you find me?" he asked the Captain, conscious of the four guards listening.

Wilson looked down, embarrassed. "When we couldn't get

in touch with you, we thought maybe something had happened. Then we noticed the message from this stack and . . ." he hesitated, "well, sir, I put a camera trace on you. I wouldn't have but . . . well, it was the only way. I knew you'd want to know at the very earliest."

Chen stopped, staring at him. "Know what? Is it my family?"

"No, sir. It's . . . Song Wei. You know, the sweeper. He's dead."

Chen shook his head. "Dead?"

"Yes, sir. The whole deck is up in arms. We've got our men down there trying to keep a lid on things, but I knew you'd want to deal with it yourself. I mean, in view of what happened . . ."

Chen nodded, realising that Wilson had probably saved him more embarrassment than he'd caused. Besides which, if Song Wei were dead, then this was a whole new ball game.

"Was he murdered?"

"Yes, sir."

"Only him? Or are there others?"

Wilson hesitated. "To be honest, sir, we don't know yet. It's chaos down there and . . . well, we've searched the deck and we can't account for four of the men."

"I see." Chen nodded, his mind already piecing things together. "Then let's get there, neh? The quicker this is sorted out, the better."

* * *

Guards were everywhere. The whole area surrounding the corridor was cordoned off. As Chen marched through at the head of his escort, he couldn't help but contrast it with how he had seen it only hours before. Then there had been an air of normality, however tentative. Now it was like a war-zone, the tension palpable.

Song Wei was laid out on the kitchen table, the body wrapped in a sheet. As Chen came into the room, one of the special squad medics looked up from where he was examining the head and smiled.

"Looks like a professional job, Major Kao. One bullet, behind the right ear. Took the top of his head off."

Chen took the skin-tight gloves he was offered and pulled them on, then went across. As the surgeon moved back, he saw the damaged skull for the first time and winced. It didn't quite look human. It looked more like a broken bowl, the jellied contents mixed with small fragments of bone.

Carefully, he put his hand beneath the neck and turned it slightly.

"There," the medic said, pointing to the hole behind the right ear. "The powder burns show that whoever did it must have placed the gun right up against the neck. It was a large calibre weapon. What size we'll know when we've found the bullet."

Chen frowned, then understood. "Where was he killed?"

"The other side of the stack, four levels down. They found him in a maintenance room, his brains all over the ceiling. It seems no one heard anything."

"Who brought him here?"

"Friends of the family. First we heard of it was when the trouble started."

"Trouble?" Chen looked to Wilson, who stood behind the sergeant in the doorway.

"They burned a Security post, sir. No one hurt. The guards saw what was happening and got out, raised the alarm. That was an hour back."

Chen nodded. An hour back he had been with the woman . . .

There was a wailing, a sudden violent wailing from the next room.

He looked up, startled. "What the hell . . . ?"

"It's his wife, sir. I thought it best to keep her here. She's hysterical and the crowd's already touchy, so . . ."

Chen nodded. But the sound was affecting him badly. He looked back at the shattered skull, then gently lowered it and stood back.

He held his hands out, letting the medical orderly peel off

the gloves and drop them in the sterile sack, then turned, facing the sergeant.

"So . . . what else do we know? What do the camera records show?"

Wilson answered him. "The area he was killed is a blind spot. There's a camera on the approach to it, but nothing on the corridor itself. It's only a small thing . . . a maintenance passage, in effect. The room's usually locked."

"So what does the approach camera show?"

Wilson looked to the sergeant. "We're not sure yet, sir. I've got a squad checking faces against the records. It's a busy corridor, it seems, and we're not sure just how long the body was there before it was discovered."

Chen turned, looking to the medic.

"Oh . . . four, five hours at least. Maybe more."

Chen turned back. "Okay. As soon as you find out *anything* let me know. I've my own theory as to who's behind this, and the sooner we get to our killer the better. That is, if he's still alive . . ."

He broke off. There had been a scuffling in the next room. Now the door to the kitchen jerked opened. There was shouting. A distraught woman's face peered out as she struggled to get past the guard, and then the door slammed shut again.

The wailing sounded again, louder than before.

Chen sighed. "Okay. I want that trace made a priority. At the same time I want a complete and thorough search of this stack, every room, every cupboard. And we're not looking for small stuff, okay? – we're looking only for things pertaining to this killing . . . And for those missing men."

Wilson and the sergeant bowed.

"Good. Now get going. I'll speak to the woman."

He watched them go, then stood there a moment, considering things. Under normal procedures the camera records would be checked back forty-eight hours at least. It would emerge that he had been down here earlier yesterday. Questions would be asked, his investigation reports scrutinised for the least irregularity, and he would be in trouble. Unless he could tie things up quickly. Unless he could make that crucial connection between the killer and that bastard Cornwell.

He knew it was Cornwell. Had known it since he'd first heard the news of Song Wei's death. No one else would have had him killed. No one else stood to benefit by it. But he had to prove that. The man's blustering threats about taking things into his own hands weren't enough to convince a court. He had to make the link. To prove that Cornwell was behind it.

Chen shivered. Like a lot of them these days, Cornwell thought he was immune, *above* the rule of law. And the men he killed or destroyed, what were they to him? Scum, he'd called them. Scum . . .

He went to the door, knocked. There was a sudden silence, and then the door slid back.

"Sir . . ." The guard stood back, letting him pass.

Inside, the woman sat on the chair beside the tiny shrine. Behind her stood the old man, Song Wei's father.

The old man stared at Chen a moment, then narrowed his eyes. "*You* . . ." he whispered. "I should have known . . . You *bastard.*"

Chen turned, dismissing the guard, then went across, standing over the weeping woman. He stared at her a moment, understanding her grief, then looked up, meeting the old man's eyes.

"This had nothing to do with me," he said quietly. "I tried to warn your son. Him and his friends. But this . . ." He shuddered. "Well . . . I'll get the man who did this. I promise you."

"You *promise* me?" The old man's voice was scornful now. He stared at Chen venomously, then leaned forward and spat on the chest patch of Chen's uniform. "*That* for your promises, Major. I *know* your kind. You stick together to protect your interests. My son . . ." He drew a breath, trying hard to control himself, then spoke again. "My son was a good man. He worked hard. He was good to his wife, his children. He looked after his father, like a dutiful son should. And what was his reward? To be cast off. To be made to beg for crumbs from the rich man's table. And, when he protested at his treatment, to be killed. Like the lowest insect."

The old man shuddered with indignation, his gnarled hands resting on his daughter-in-law's shoulders, the fingers digging into her flesh, as if both to comfort and punish her. His face was fierce now, his eyes staring at Chen with an unrelenting hatred. "Promises . . . *Paa*! Can you *eat* promises? Can your promises make my son live again?" He shook his head. "No, Major. Give me none of your promises. I am sick to the heart of eating such bile."

"I . . ."

"Just go," the old man said, his face hard, unforgiving. "Go play your games. Go and *pretend* you're doing something."

Chen turned, his face stinging as if he'd been slapped, and left, the man's words ringing in his ears, the woman's weeping tearing at his gut.

Cornwell, he thought, moving through the kitchen without stopping, barely conscious of the guards bowing and saluting as he passed. *I'm going to nail that bastard Cornwell, whatever it takes.*

And if you can't? a small voice asked.

He stopped, looking about him at the empty corridor, saying the words quietly to himself. "Then I'll kill him anyway."

* * *

Hannah sat at her desk, waiting. Her father had come in some while back, going straight to his study. She had heard the door slam shut, then, less than a minute later, had heard it open again, the sound of voices, quiet at first, then louder. The door had slammed . . . and then nothing.

She looked down at the sketches she had been making, noting how the faces seemed to stare back at her, somehow independent, as if she had not made them, merely freed them from the anonymous whiteness of the page. There was one particularly – the face of the *hua pen* she had seen that day down-level – which seemed to have transcended her simple attempt to capture its physical details. There was something in the depth of the eyes, in the slight twist of that knowing smile, which suggested something shadowed – a secret, hidden self she had not suspected while she had been listening to him.

She looked up, her eyes drawn to the flickering flatscreen on the wall across from her. It was her habit to leave it on when she worked, the sound turned down, her silent window on the world. Images . . . she trusted images more than words. They were less *intermediary* in their nature, less easily manipulated. Yet images could be faked or wrongly read. They were no different from words in that respect. Between what was shown and what hidden the truth so often slipped away. Even so, it seemed more important to her to *see* than to *say*, though she knew she must do both in future.

On the screen image followed image silently. Her world was in chaos – was slowly tearing itself apart – and yet for a large number of people there was no connection between that greater life and their own small private worlds of work and family; only the flickering screen, the official voice which told them what to think. Isolated. The two worlds were isolated. And if they met it was in a blaze of sudden, explosive violence – a violence that inflicted understanding only on its victims, leaving the watching billions unaffected.

And maybe that was her purpose. To be that connecting force. To link the greater world with the small. Maybe it was her role, in this world of walls and levels, of files and secrets, of masked men and ever-watching cameras, to be the one who saw things clearly – who opened files, and looked inside locked rooms – and *spoke* what she had seen.

Yes, but it could not be done openly, for too much was at risk. To speak out was to oppose, to threaten those shadows that controlled their lives. She had no illusions about it. They would kill her to prevent it.

A *hua pen* . . . she must learn to become a new kind of *hua pen*, telling not ancient tales, but the story of her age, her place.

She stood, her restlessness suddenly something physical, like an itch that needed to be scratched. Turning, she took two paces, then stopped abruptly, staring, her mouth open in surprise.

Her father stood in the shadow of the doorway, watching her.

She released her breath. "How long have you been there?"

"Not long." He came closer, looking about him as if he'd never been in her room before. "I . . ." He sighed, then looked at her again, the slightest admonishment in his voice. *"Hannah . . .* what have you been doing now?"

"Nothing. I was only . . ."

You were only what? Spying on him? Stealing things from his rooms?

"Your mother says . . ."

"She's *not* my mother!"

"Hannah . . . *Please,* my love. I . . ."

She stared at him, astonished. His face was crumpled up in pain. There were tears at the corners of his eyes. Agonised, she went across and held him.

"Oh, papa! Papa! . . . Are you all right?"

"I . . ." She felt him shiver. "I can't tell you."

She helped him sit in her chair, then knelt, facing him, looking up into his face. "It's okay. I *know.*"

He stared back at her, understanding slowly dawning on him.

"I've read it," she said. "The file. I know what's happening."

"And?" His voice was a breath, less than a whisper.

She studied his face, seeing how frightened, how confused he was, and all of her fears for him welled up suddenly in her. *"Aiya,"* she said softly, taking his hands and caressing them. "How did you ever get to this point? I mean . . . there's nothing *ruthless* in you, is there? So many secrets . . . how did you ever get involved?"

He looked back at her, bewildered. "I don't know. I . . . I did only what was asked of me."

Yes, she thought, *and step by step it led to this.*

"What shall we do?" he asked, like a child asking his mother, his eyes beseeching her. "What in the gods' names shall we *do,* Hannah?"

"You must see Li Yuan," she said, a cold fear gripping her. "You must request an audience . . . And then you must tell him what you know."

* * *

Chen went home.

It was just after seven when he got back, tired and on edge, confused by all that had been happening to him. Outside his door he paused, wondering if it were really such a good idea. He needed to shower and freshen up, to grab a bite to eat and change his uniform, but he could have done all of that at Bremen. So why here? There was nothing for him here.

He was about to turn away when, through the paper-thin walls, he heard a child's shriek and then laughter – an infectious giggle that made his heart contract. No, not nothing. There were still his children.

He tapped out the combination then stepped inside. At once Ch'iang Hsin was on him, her face lit up at the sight of him.

"Daddy!"

He held her against his side, the fierceness of that sudden feeling almost overwhelming him. How could he have forgotten? What poisons were in his blood that he could have overlooked them even for a moment?

He crouched, facing her. "How's Mummy?"

She shrugged, then smiled again. "Tian Ching's been teaching me how to sew! I've been making you a surprise!"

He looked up and saw the girl in the doorway to the kitchen, watching him. Did she know? he wondered. Could she tell where he'd been, merely by looking at him?

She turned away, busying herself.

"Where's Wu?" he asked, "and Jyan?"

"Wu's still in bed, and Jyan's with friends," Ch'iang said unselfconsciously, her left hand tugging at his cheek, as if to check that he was real. "Are you staying this time?"

"For an hour or two," he answered, saddened that this once he couldn't stay a little longer. Then, taking her beneath the arms, he picked her up and carried her through to the

303

kitchen. He cuddled her a moment then set her down on a chair. "You stay here with Tian Ching a moment, while I go and see your mother, okay?"

She nodded, smiling up at him.

"Good." He glanced at Tian Ching. "Thank you," he said quietly, turning away before she could answer.

Wang Ti's room was dark and silent, yet from the far side there was a wavering light and there was the faintest smell of burning. He looked. The bed was empty, the cover thrown back, and Wang Ti . . . Wang Ti was kneeling on the floor, her shape outlined against the wavering light.

Slowly, quietly, he went across. There, in front of her, was a shrine. A shrine just like the one he had seen down-level. The doors were pulled back, revealing a blood-red interior, against which stood a dozen tiny figures. Household gods, he realised. In front of them three tiny red candles burned in tiny pots, sending up faint wisps of incense.

He looked down at her. Wang Ti's eyes were open, staring straight ahead, into the bright interior of the shrine, and her lips . . .

Chen caught his breath. Her lips were moving.

He turned, realising that Tian Ching was in the doorway. "How long has this been here?"

She looked down, abashed. "Two days. I . . . I thought it might help."

He looked back at Wang Ti, saw how she gazed into the flickering shadows and shivered. For almost three years there had been nothing, not even a flicker of life in her, but now . . .

He turned, nodding to the girl, his eyes thanking her, then, turning back, he kneeled beside his wife, his left hand reaching down to take her right where it lay upon her knee, palm down.

"I'm here, Wang Ti," he said softly, conscious of the soft murmur of her voice beside him. "I'm here."

CHAPTER·12

THE ELDEST DAUGHTER

Water dripped through the ruined ceiling of the Mansion, pooling in the smoking debris of the gutted Hall. *Huojen*, their raised visors black with smoke, their eyes red, sifted through the ruins, looking for clues. Not that any clues were really needed this time. Everyone knew who had carried out this atrocity: it was stencilled there on the gateway, above the bodies of the two guards who had been garotted.

Wu Shih stared at the black imprint of the hand and shuddered. The *huojen* had pulled a dozen bodies from the house already, but the final death toll was likely to be two, maybe three times that number.

The Hand had learned their lessons well. This time they had attacked in strength, making a diversionary attack against the local Security post while their main force had hit the Mansion. Thirty or forty of them there had been this time, armed with the latest weaponry.

After destroying the small force of house guards, they had rounded up the owners and their servants and locked them inside the house, setting fire to it in eight different places. Then they had waited, standing around the house while it burned, firing at the windows if anyone dared come close.

He grimaced, remembering. All of it was on camera, from the preliminary skirmish at the gate, to the final moments when, whooping and laughing, the terrorists had run back down the path towards the transit. He remembered particularly one sequence where several of the terrorists had turned, looking up directly into the camera, smiling and waving as if

305

on an outing, making no attempt to conceal themselves, while behind them the great Mansion – filled with antique furniture and tapestries, rich silks and thick carpets and curtains – had blazed like a tinderbox, the screams of its unseen occupants too horrible for words.

They had attacked just after two. By three they were gone. Ten minutes later, Fen Cho-hsien had been woken from his bed. He, in his turn, had woken Wu Shih with the news.

There was no doubting it. This was a turning point – a new stage in this hit and run "War" with the Black Hand. Knowing that, Wu Shih had come at once, wanting to see things for himself.

The *T'ing Wei* had done well. They had been quick to stifle the news and clamp down on those few media stations who had got a whisper. But it would be difficult to keep this a secret. If past experience were anything to go by, pamphlets would be circulating the Lowers by breakfast-time, shouting the news triumphantly, and it would be picked up from there. It was up to him to pre-empt that, therefore – to hit back at once and turn their temporary victory into a major set-back for the Hand.

He turned to his General, who waited nearby. "General Althaus . . . do we know where this group came from?"

Althaus came sharply to attention. "We have a pretty good idea, *Chieh Hsia*. In fact, I've had a special squad tracking them this past hour. But we'd have to go in after them straight away if we're to have any chance of getting any of the bastards. Their heartland is pretty heavily defended and it would mean fighting a level-by-level action."

Wu Shih considered a moment, then nodded. "Then do that. Use whatever force you need. *Hei*, if necessary. But get them. And hit them hard. If we've any leads at all on their organisation, act on them *now*, even if they're unconfirmed. I want it to be seen by all that we've taken strong and unequivocal action. For my part, I plan to make an announcement, first thing, before they've a chance to win the propaganda war. This time they've bitten off more than they can chew.

This time we're going to make them pay dearly for their audacity!"

"*Chieh Hsia!*" Althaus beamed, delighted to be given such clear orders. Then, turning, he hurried across to his senior officers, beginning the task at once.

Wu Shih turned back, looking across at the great Mansion once again. Earlier, he had watched them carrying out the bodies and had had them bring one across to him. He had looked down at it, horrified. It had seemed barely human. *Such savagery*, he'd thought, and shivered, unable to comprehend how anyone could do that to another.

Yet part of him welcomed this chance to act – even if he didn't rejoice in it the way Althaus and his officers did. For almost two days now he had brooded, unable to decide just what to do over the Kennedy matter, his uncertainty making him restless and bad-tempered. In this, at least, he was not plagued by doubts.

Kennedy . . . He'd read the reports on what had happened between him and the Levers: had seen Lever make his sorrowful statement, and had wondered about that young man – whether he had not, perhaps, misjudged things; whether Lever, not Kennedy was the man to watch. But that didn't change the basic situation. In fact, if anything, it made it worse, for as Kennedy's popularity declined so the excuse for taking any kind of action diminished.

"One son," Fen Cho-hsien had suggested when he'd put the problem to him. "Kill one of Kennedy's sons and threaten to kill the other if he doesn't come back in line."

It was a sound suggestion, yet even the thought of it was barbaric. He thought of his own sons and his stomach fell away at the prospect of losing one of them. Yet these were barbaric times – this incident confirmed it – and if things were not to slip from him . . .

"*Chieh Hsia . . .*"

The most senior of the *huojen* stood close by, bowed, awaiting his attention.

"Is it ready?"

"Yes, *Chieh Hsia*."

He went across, accepting the hard hat the man gave him, then followed the specially-cleared path into the Mansion. They had made this part safe for his inspection: even so, the desolation was still quite awful.

This is the future, he thought, appalled by what he saw. *This is what it will all be like unless I act.*

For one brief moment he thought of summoning Kennedy, to make him see this and to share his fears with him. Yet he knew, after only a moment's consideration, that such a thing was impossible. Even if Kennedy understood, he could never act on that understanding, for his hands were tied, his course set. His new proposal to the House had said as much. There would be confrontation, whether he, Wu Shih, wished it or not, so maybe it was best to get it over now.

Tonight, he thought, looking about him at the blackened, broken walls, the acrid taste of ash on his tongue. *Yes . . . I'll make my decision tonight.*

* * *

Emily turned from the vid-phone, raising one hand, beckoning to her secretary, then turned back, continuing the conversation.

"That's right. A twenty-minute slot. We'll do it live then run it once every hour for the next four."

Beresiner's chubby face looked down at her, frowning. "It's gonna be hard, Madam Lever. You mess with their schedules, they make you pay through the nose for it."

"I don't care," she said. "Just book it. The five main channels, continent-wide. And don't try and fuck me about, Berry. You try and screw me and I'll get to hear of it, okay?"

Beresiner sighed. "Now would I do that? Consider it booked. You want them to send a crew to you, I assume?"

She nodded.

"Okay. Leave it with me. I'll call you lunch-time, right?"

"Right." She cut contact, then tapped in another number. There was a moment's pause, and then the screen lit again. This time a woman's face stared back at her – a beautiful oriental woman. Gloria Chung.

"*Mary?*"

"Gloria . . . how are you? I hope it's not too early for me to call."

"No, not at all, I'm just . . . surprised, that's all."

"It's been a long time, neh?"

"Too long. How *are* you? How's Michael?"

Emily sat back, smiling. "We're fine. I . . . I just thought it might be nice to see you."

Gloria smiled. "Hey, I'd like that. When?"

"Today? Over here?"

"That'd be great. Any particular time?"

"I've got a camera crew coming here about six to set up, but . . . well, how about lunch? We could catch up on everything."

"Lunch?" Gloria considered a moment, then smiled. "Sure. That'd be nice. But what's all this about camera crews? You doing a feature for the fashion shows or something?"

Emily smiled enigmatically. "You could say that. Look, I'll tell you all about it when you're here. One o'clock?"

"That'd be fine."

"Good. I'll see you then. Bye."

"Bye."

She took a breath, then turned, looking to her secretary. "Jill, did that report come in?"

"It's here." Jill handed Emily a large brown envelope.

"You've looked at this?"

She shook her head.

"Good. It's probably best you don't know what's going on as far as Kemp's concerned. If you need to know anything I'll tell you, right?"

"Right."

"Okay. Now get me what you can on Michael's main trading rivals. Full files, not summaries. Then I want that nutritionist in here. Give me . . . oh, ten minutes, let's say. I've three more calls to make."

She watched the young woman hurry away, then turned back to the screen, a feeling of immense satisfaction buoying her up. Leaning forward, she tapped out the next number on

309

her list, then pulled the report out of the envelope. As she waited to be connected she flicked through it, scanning the handwritten pages.

So the old men thought they were going to win, did they? Well, not if she had anything to do with it!

"Eva?" she said, looking up and smiling as a stern, matriarchal face filled the screen. "I've something you might be interested in . . ."

* * *

The room was packed, the mood angry as Kennedy stepped into the room.

"Resign!" someone shouted from the back and the cry was taken up. "Resign! Resign!"

As he made his way across to the table, he looked about him, noting how eyes that only days before had glowed with respect now held nothing but contempt for him. As he took his seat he looked down, trying not to show any sign of the turmoil within. The decision to hold a vote of confidence had been a body-blow, coming so close upon the scene at the Lever Mansion. But maybe he was simply being naïve. Maybe he *was* no longer the man to lead the NREP.

Carl Fisher, the Representative for Boston and one of Michael Lever's oldest friends, had been chosen to chair the meeting. As he stood to call for order, Kennedy looked up at him, noting how the young man's jaw was set, as if prepared for a fight. Strangely the sight encouraged him.

If Fisher stays with me . . .

"Gentlemen . . ." Fisher began, raising his hands for silence. "If we could have some hush here we might get this matter straightened out." He waited as the meeting settled, then spoke again, looking about him sternly.

"Okay, let me come directly to why we're here. A number of you have drafted a motion which they wish to have presented to this special meeting. It reads as follows . . ."

He took a scrap of paper from his jacket pocket, unfolded it, then cleared his throat.

"In view of recent developments detrimental to the general

well-being of the New Republican and Evolutionist Party, it is proposed that its current leader, Representative Joseph William Kennedy, be removed from that position and an election held to determine his successor."

Fisher let the paper drop contemptuously from his fingers, then looked up, a tight, angry expression on his face.

"Well. Before we come to debate the issue, let me just remind those of you with short memories of our history. The New Republican Party was formed a mere four years ago in Philadelphia. In less than two years it became a continent-wide movement, and in the elections to the House won huge popular support, merging with the Evolutionists to gain the second highest number of seats in City North America. Now, our founding member, our chief policy-maker and leader throughout this period of unparalleled success was, need I remind you, the aforementioned Joseph William Kennedy."

Fisher paused and turned, looking down at Kennedy. "Now . . . I'm not deaf and I'm not blind. I hear what the media say and I see what's written in the papers, but it strikes me that on several other occasions in the past this party has been the subject of intense media pressure. Many of you might recall what happened after we'd won that first round of votes. But we have never – and I mean *never* – until now shown any sign of disloyalty from within our own ranks."

He took a breath, straightening up, looking about him and eyeing some of those standing nearest him. "To be frank with you, I find this motion not merely an irrelevancy but an insult to a fine man . . . a man without whose vision and unstinting work, *none* of us would be standing here in this room today!"

There was clapping and applause, but also some dissenting jeers.

"Now, before I finish and throw the floor open, let me say this. Like many of you, I'm sad that my old friend Michael Lever has decided to part company with us. Indeed, it grieves me to think that we've lost his services to the party. But those of us who know Michael well have realised for some time now that a parting of the ways was imminent, and it

311

came as no surprise that it should be over the matter of the food subsidies. Michael, as many here will testify, has come increasingly under the influence of his wife, Mary, whose views are . . . well, questionable to say the least."

"At least she's consistent!" someone yelled from half-way back.

Fisher smiled. "Inflexible, I'd call it myself. But let me finish. In the last few days I've heard criticisms of some of our more recent changes in policy. Well, let me deal with those criticisms. Some of you talk as though we ought to follow the same policy day after day, month after month, year after year no matter *what* the circumstances. Personally, I feel that such a dogmatic viewpoint is not merely foolish, but dangerous."

There was a murmur of dissent and unrest, but Fisher spoke on.

"A political party, if it's to be effective, must be capable of change – of questioning even its most cherished beliefs and revising them according to the dictates of common sense and necessity."

"Bullshit!" a big man to Fisher's right shouted. "It sounds like the politics of the whorehouse . . . on our backs for the Seven and arse-up for the Military!"

There was a roar of laughter, but as Fisher made to respond, Kennedy touched his arm, then, as Fisher sat, got slowly to his feet.

Silence fell.

"Gentlemen . . ." Kennedy looked about him at his friends and colleagues, his natural dignity mixed with an air of sadness, then nodded gently to himself. "Maybe I *have* made mistakes. Maybe it *is* as some of you claim . . . that we've come too far, too fast and have forgotten in the process just what it was we set out to achieve." He sighed, then shook his head. "I don't know. Maybe we *have* lost our way. But if it's the will of this party that I stand down . . ."

He shrugged, making a "so be it" gesture with his face.

"No!" came the cry from all sides, "Stay on, Joe!", but there were others who were clamouring for a vote. Kennedy raised a hand, then, as silence fell again, turned to Fisher.

"Give the members what they want, Carl. I'll abide by their decision."

Kennedy sat, looking down at his folded hands.

Fisher sighed, then stood again, facing the packed room. "Okay," he said, "Let's vote on it. All those in favour of the motion raise your hands . . ."

* * *

"*Em?*"

Michael took two paces into the room then stopped, astonished. There were desks everywhere he looked, and women – strangers – operating phones and comsets or writing in files.

"Em? What's going on?"

Emily turned, looking up from where she was discussing a layout board with two of her assistants, then smiled. "Michael! What kept you?"

"I . . ." He laughed, and went across, holding her to him, unrestrained by the harness. "What *is* all this? And why didn't you tell me?"

She moved back slightly, then planted a kiss on his nose. "I thought I'd surprise you. Besides, you were busy."

He frowned at her, mock stern. "So?"

"So I thought I'd do something."

"Like what?"

She looked down. "Something positive. Something . . . Well, you'll see. I've booked air time on several of the channels for tonight."

He stared at her, astonished. "Air time? For what?"

"You'll see."

He laughed, exasperated. "Is that all you're going to say? You spend millions of my money and that's all the explanation I get?"

"*Our* money. And yes, that's all the explanation you're getting."

He looked down, sobered a moment. "It's got nothing to do with Kennedy, has it?"

"Not directly."

He met her eyes; saw how she was watching him.

"I've got to do this, Michael. I've thought long and hard about it, and it's the only way. So trust me, huh?"

"Okay. But what's all this for?"

She laughed. "You don't give up, do you?"

"No . . . Oh, and by the way, there was a vote this morning."

"A vote?"

"The party called a special meeting to discuss the leadership issue."

"I didn't know there *was* a leadership issue."

"Well, there is now. Parker called me. It seems they had a vote of confidence. Kennedy won, but only by eleven votes."

She looked at him sympathetically. "I'm sorry. Not for him, he deserves it, but for you. A lot of people will blame you for it, won't they?"

"I guess so."

"Well, you ignore them. It wasn't you who went back on your promises. And it wasn't you who voted for the reduction of the subsidy."

"No. Even so, I can't help thinking . . ."

She took his face in her hands and held it, forcing him to look at her. "Get this clear, Michael Lever. It *wasn't* your fault. It's as absurd as apologising for having been blown up that time. It wasn't you. Don't you understand that? It *wasn't* you."

But she could see from his face that he was only half convinced.

* * *

Gloria Chung came an hour later, a small train of servants carrying boxes and bags and a wrapped gift that smelled of roses.

She hugged Emily, then stood back, letting one of her entourage take her wrap.

"I'm so glad you could come," Emily said, conscious of the

contrast they made, Gloria so tall and elegant, so *feminine*, herself so austere.

"Don't be silly," Gloria answered, looking about her with a wide-eyed delight. Then, with a tiny laugh, she took Emily's arm, letting herself be led through. "You know, the first time I came here I was eight. It was a big party and Michael's father . . . well, he frightened me even then. He was such an ogre. But Michael . . ." She smiled, then squeezed Emily's hand. "I'm glad you two got married. I knew from the first moment I saw you together."

Emily lowered her eyes, but she was smiling. "Michael told me. It seems I'm indebted to you."

"Nonsense! You should know Michael well enough by now to know that nothing can make him do what he doesn't want to do. Marrying you . . . he just had to be nudged, that's all!"

"Even so . . . two million *yuan*. It was quite a wedding gift!"

She looked down, serious suddenly. "If it had been ten times that, I'd have helped him out, you know that."

Emily nodded. "I know. That's why you're here."

Gloria stopped, frowning. "What . . . money? *You*, the richest woman in North America . . . you want *my* money?"

Emily laughed. "No. Not this time. But your help, that I *do* need."

"You?"

"That's right. Not Michael this time. Me. There's something I have to do, and if it's going to work then I'm going to need all the help I can get to set it up. That's where you come in." She smiled, then returned the pressure on Gloria's arm. "But come through. Let's talk about it over lunch!"

* * *

Kemp lay there on his back, the younger of the girls riding him slowly, deliciously, while the other knelt behind him, leaning over him to caress his neck and chest, her bare legs pressing warm against his shoulders, her tiny breasts brushing against his cheeks and hair. He was close now, very

315

close, and as he began to come he pulled her down onto him and, with a groan, sank his teeth into the soft flesh, her cries making him spasm fiercely.

Afterwards, as he lay there watching the big screen in the corner of the room, a shiver of satisfaction rippled through him. That was the one good thing about being his age. One had no illusions about the world, and therefore no restraints. What one wanted one took, and no apologies. If he had only known when he was younger. Imagine it! To have *that* power and *this* knowledge!

He turned, looking across to where the younger of the two was tending her friend and smiled. They had been good girls and he would reward them well. Indeed, after what had happened earlier he could afford, perhaps, to buy them from the Madame and have them installed in his Mansion. After all, such good, uncomplaining girls were hard to come by these days.

When the advert appeared again, he sat up, watching it more carefully this time.

"Wonderful . . ." he said softly, pressing his right fist hard into his cupped left. "Fucking wonderful . . ."

His boardroom ploy had succeeded beyond his wildest dreams. Why, Michael Lever hadn't just bought the idea of keeping the Institute running, he had transformed it. For the last two hours these adverts – with details of the forthcoming launch of the new Immortality 3000 Project – had appeared on four different channels. And, from his own sources within the Institute had come news that Lever had agreed a comprehensive refunding programme: a financial package which, while it seemed sound now, would – in time – bring ImmVac crashing down, as Lever tried frantically to recoup some of the funds to defend his falling market share.

"I've *got* you," he said gleefully. "I've fucking got you!"

Only an hour back, Fairbank's man, Jackson, had called to say that his Masters were very pleased with what he, Kemp had achieved, and that a bonus had been placed on his account. Now it was time to put the second phase of things into effect – to start that long, painstaking process of attrition that would, six months from now, have Lever humbled, the young man crushed for all time.

He stood, looking about him. When had he last felt like this? When had life last promised him so much? Never. And who knew . . . when this was all over and they came to share out the ruins of ImmVac's great empire, maybe he'd buy himself a share in the Institute and have some of the new treatment. To live forever . . . he didn't believe that was possible . . . but another twenty, thirty, even forty years, *that* would be worth trying for.

"Champagne!" he said, feeling magnanimous. "Let's have some champagne, neh, girls?"

And afterwards? Afterwards he would have the older one again. From behind, perhaps, while she made love to the younger one.

Kemp smiled, watching as the younger of the two ran to do his bidding, then went across and sat beside the other, tracing the wound gently with a fingertip before pulling her down onto his lap.

Old . . . who says I'm old?

* * *

Steiner stood there, waiting silently, while the old men watched the urgent holo-vid message that had come. He watched the flickering image, not understanding their excitement, his own bottled-up hatred of Michael Lever blinding him to all else. Yet when they turned to him again, there was a difference to their manner, as if the news had made them suddenly more receptive to his scheme.

"Well . . . ." Fairbank said, smiling and nodding. "I think I can speak for all four of us in saying that I'm interested. Very interested indeed. Have you . . . discussed this with anyone else?"

Steiner shook his head. "I came straight to you, Mister Fairbank. I know how much you gentlemen hate Lever."

Egan sat forward slightly. "Hate is perhaps too strong a word, Mister Steiner. Dislike . . . mistrust . . . *despise*, maybe. But you did well, and we're grateful to you. Very

317

grateful. You'll be on NorTek's payroll, at your previous salary. Plus, of course, a substantial one-off bonus."

Steiner smiled. "Thank you, Mister Egan. And . . . ?"

"Your scheme?" Fairbank interjected. "Oh, leave that with us, Mister Steiner. We've got the broad sweep of it. We'll get a team onto it to work out the details."

Steiner looked down. He had thought, at the very least, that they'd fund him, or let him form his own team within their set-up. He swallowed, trying to conceal his disappointment, then bowed his head. "Thank you, Mister Fairbank . . . gentlemen."

"Good," Fairbank said. "You can go now."

When he was gone, Fairbank sat back, steepling his fingers, then looked across at his friends. "That's all we fucking need, neh? Some prick-led, vengeance-filled arsehole shitting on our best-laid plans."

"You want him killed?" Egan asked, raising an eyebrow.

"Oh no . . ." Fairbank shook his head. "An accident, maybe . . . even a fatal accident . . . but *killed*? No . . ."

They laughed.

"No," Fairbank went on. "I'd as soon let the bastard bugger me as subscribe to his mad scheme. The very last thing we want is to make a martyr out of Michael Lever. We can destroy him other ways. Talking of which . . ."

Chamberlain, who had been quiet for some time, interrupted. "Talking of prick-led arseholes, do you *trust* Kemp, John? I mean, *he's* rather partial to a piece or two."

Fairbank shrugged. "Maybe. Nothing wrong with that. It's only when a man loses all proportion. Like Steiner there." He smiled thoughtfully. "Hey, wouldn't you have loved to have seen that? I mean, I don't give Lever much credit, but that was masterful, neh? To parade the man around his own factory floor, buck-naked on his desk. Wonderful! Fucking wonderful!"

"I'm told there's a tape of it," Green said, his eyes narrowed. "One of the guards there had the sense to get a camera on the whole thing. I'll get my man on the inside at ImmVac to get you a copy, if you'd like."

Fairbank grinned. "I'd like that. His face! I'd just love to see his face! No wonder he wants Lever dead."

"Wouldn't you?"

"Maybe. But then you'd never catch *me* fucking my secretary on my desk."

Egan smiled. "So where *do* you fuck her, John?"

"None of your business!"

Chamberlain cleared his throat. "Anyway . . . you were saying, John. About Kemp."

"Kemp . . ." Fairbank considered a moment. "Sure. I trust him. He's been a good contact for us over the years. Fed us a lot of sound information."

"You don't think he could be bribed? I mean, he's an important part of all of this. A lot rides on his shoulders. If Lever were to buy him out . . ."

Fairbank shook his head. "Kemp's interested in money, sure. Who isn't? But bribery, especially from Lever . . . No. He's sound. I'd guarantee it. Besides, there's only one side for a man like Kemp to play on, and that's ours. Old Man Lever treated him like shit for half his life. He won't forget that. No more than you or I. So forget about Kemp. Kemp's fine. Let's look at other areas . . . areas where we're genuinely vulnerable."

"Like what?" Egan asked, interested. "I thought we were cast-iron solid."

"Like this bad debt provision on our African trade," Fairbank said, steering their talk back to the meat of their business. "As *I* was saying, before we were interrupted . . ."

* * *

Out in the centre of Main the crowd was going berserk. Many were dead already and it looked like developing into a full-scale riot. Those shops that had still been trading were ruined now, their goods taken, their fronts smashed and burned. Behind a reinforced barrier, blocking off the main route to the inter-level transit, a Security Captain crouched, yelling urgently into his handset.

"Send me some back-up! Now! They've gone fucking mad down here!"

There was a squeal, an awful screeching, and then the sound of one of the big lighting sections overhead shattering, segments raining down. The Captain popped his head up over the parapet, looking. If this went on, the whole of Main would be in darkness before long. He'd thought the lighting sections were indestructible, but they'd got hold of something – something that made the ice they were made of fragile – and were spraying it everywhere. Holes were appearing in the walls and floors, cabling was shorting, and who knew what other damage . . . He stared, watching the two men swing from one section to the next, fifty *ch'i* up, hanging from the ceiling seemingly without fear. *Black Hand*, he thought; *fucking Black Hand*. But there was nothing he could do. If he shot them down they'd target him. And with only two dozen men to contain five thousand rioters, he didn't fancy their chances.

There was an urgent buzzing on the handset. He clicked it on again and stared down into the tiny screen. This time it was Major Seymour, his line commander.

"Captain Wells? What the hell's going on down there?"

Wells put his head down as a shower of debris came over the top of the barrier.

"There've been some deaths, sir. Bizarre things. Some of the local troublemakers were hit. Mutilated, it seems. Word got out and they've gone crazy down here. There's been a lot of burning and looting. Not only that, but they've got hold of chemicals. Ice-eaters . . ."

"Ice . . ." The Major turned away, consulting someone close by, then turned back, facing Wells. "Okay. I'll get some men down there. But we're stretched thin. This operation against the Black Hand . . ." He sighed. "Oh, shit . . . ice-eaters, huh? That's all we need!"

"Sir?"

"Yes, Captain?"

"I've a prisoner, sir. I pulled him out before they got to him."

"A prisoner?"

"Yes, sir. He won't say much, but I did get something out of him. Says he works for a man called Kemp. First Level, he says. When we pulled him out we found some fairly grisly stuff on him."

"Like what?"

Wells swallowed. "Like a sealed bag full of severed penises."

"*What*? Did I hear that right, Captain Wells?"

"I'm afraid you did, sir. He says he gets paid for them."

"Shit! What do you think they are? A delicacy up there? You think this guy Kemp is in the restaurant business?"

"I don't know, sir. The system's down here, so I couldn't make any checks . . ." Again there was the sound of one of the big units shattering. The shadows deepened. "Oh, and sir . . . you'd better hurry with that back-up squad. If they don't come soon we'll be in total darkness down here!"

"Right! They're on their way. And Wells . . ."

"Sir!"

"Hang on to that bastard, neh? I want to know what this Kemp guy's up to . . ."

*　*　*

The delivery came just after four. Gloria had gone and Michael was resting after his afternoon exercises. Confident of being alone, Emily took the tiny package through to his study and sat at his desk, running the tape through, seeing what she'd got for her money.

She was still sitting there an hour later when she realised someone had come into the room. Turning, she found Michael just behind her.

"What *is* that?" he asked, nodding past her at the frozen image.

"You want to know?"

"No secrets . . ."

She leaned forward, unfreezing the image, then moved it back ten minutes and let it run.

He made a tiny sound of surprise. "Porn? You're watching porn?"

321

Then, as the man's face came round, he understood. "Shit! Where did you get that?"

She moved it back further, stopping it at the part where Kemp had been talking to Jackson, then paused it.

"I did a bit of thinking," she said, turning round and looking up at him again. "And I asked myself, who's in a position to do us a great deal of harm? And then I made a list. And after I'd made a list, I made a call, and hired myself a team of investigators, and they found out where the people on my list spent their recreation time. Hotels, sports clubs, that kind of thing. And you know what I found? I found that Kemp had recently paid a visit to Denver *Hsien*. And you know who's at Denver?"

"Fairbank."

"Right. And not only Fairbank. A bit of checking turned up the fact that the Heads of all our other three main trading rivals were in Denver at the same time – Green of RadMed, Egan of NorTek, Chamberlain of WesCorp. A bit of a coincidence, huh? So I thought I'd dig a little deeper and find out how our friend Kemp spends his recreation time. And this is what I turned up. Under-age girls and shady deals. Jackson's a freelancer. He works for himself. But recently he's taken on a contract with a company called VasChem. Nothing sinister there, you might think, only VasChem are a subsidiary of HydGel, who themselves are a partly-owned subsidiary of . . ."

"AmLab."

She nodded. "You knew?"

"No. Just a good guess. So Kemp's working for our opposition." He heaved a sigh. "Shit! I've never liked the man, but I'd never have thought . . ."

He looked from the screen to Emily. "So what do we do? Confront him with this?"

"No. We wait," she answered, clearing the screen. "And build up a file. But now we know, eh? Old Men. We're at war with the Old Men, Michael. And they'll do anything – *anything* – to destroy us."

* * *

"Okay . . . what's your fucking game, *Shih* Kemp?"

Kemp stood there, his mouth flapping. "I . . . I beg your pardon, Major Seymour? You come in here and . . . and the first thing you do is *insult* me! I don't understand it . . . I just don't understand it!"

"Crap!" Seymour glared at him, then pointed to the fleshy remains he'd thrown down on the table. "I want to know what's going on . . . and just why you're paying a pack of jackals to go marauding round the Lowers cutting the cock off anyone they take a dislike to! Thanks to you, I'm having to put in extra squads to keep the peace down there. It's a fucking butcher's shop! If I lose one man through this . . . just *one* man . . . then I'm going to hold you *personally* responsible."

"This has nothing to do with me. As I said . . ."

"I'd save your talking for the tribunal, friend. As it is I've got signed statements from two of the men in my custody swearing they were employed by you."

Kemp snorted indignantly. "I don't care if you've got it tattooed on your bollocks, Major Seymour! Unless you've got proof – *real* proof, and not just the word of some scumbag *liumang*! – that I was in any way involved in this . . . this *obscenity*, I'd kindly keep your accusations to yourself. If you don't . . . well, I shall have great pleasure in suing the arse off you!"

Seymour laughed coldly. "I'd be careful just who you threaten, *Shih* Kemp. These are difficult times. Under the special regulations I am empowered to arrest anyone I think is guilty of incitement. I'd say this qualified, wouldn't you?"

"Are you threatening *me*, Major?"

Seymour stood back a little, then shook his head. "No. I'm just warning you. Any more of this and I'll be down on you like a fly on shit. My job's hard enough as it is without you adding to it, okay? So leave off. Whatever it is you're up to, just can it, right? That's my last word."

Kemp opened his mouth, then, realising what the Major had said, closed it again and nodded.

"Good. I'm glad we understand each other. That . . . shit

there . . . do whatever you have to with it. But no more. Not unless you want me back here. And next time . . ."

"I understand."

"Good. Then good day, *Shih* Kemp. Have a pleasant meal!"

Kemp stared at the officer's retreating back, wondering what he meant, then, when he was gone, went straight to the vid-phone and tapped out the special contact number he'd been given.

There was a moment's pause and then a face swam into view.

"General Althaus . . ." Kemp said, bowing his head respectfully. "Forgive me, but a mutual friend of ours said I might contact you if there was any trouble . . ."

* * *

Wu Shih stood on the high stone balcony of his palace, looking out over the Garden of Manhattan. The sky was a perfect blue, yet it would be dark within the hour. Already the sun rested low over the distant City, while below him much of the Garden already lay in shadow. A pleasant, late evening breeze blew from the east, carrying the scent of blossom, while from below the call of a magpie drifted up to him, punctuating the stillness.

He stretched his neck, then reached up with one hand, kneading the tired muscles of his neck. He heard a soft footfall behind him, then felt his hand gently removed and another take its place, its touch more expert than his own. It was his First Wife, Wei-kou.

"It's beautiful, neh?" she said softly, to his ear.

He smiled. "The best view in the world, my father called it. I know what he meant. Some days I think I could not cope if I did not have its quiet paths and silent spaces. Nor without my wives . . ." he added, turning slightly.

"You looked worried earlier. I thought . . ."

"I am fine, Wei-kou. These last few days . . . there has been much to do, but now . . . well, the worst is over now."

He turned, facing her, and put his hand up to her cheek, brushing it gently, then drew her head down onto his breast. "It must be hard for you when I am like this."

"I do not complain, my husband."

"No . . . And yet you are much neglected, neh?"

"I do not . . ."

She gave a small laugh, realising she was repeating herself, then looked up at him and smiled.

He put his arm about her shoulder, then turned, looking out across the vastness of the twilit Garden. Here had once stood the greatest City of the *Hung Mao* – an island fortress, a temple to their economic dominance, the pumping heart of the sixty-nine states of the great American Empire. Yet their City had fallen. His great-great grandfather had swept it into the sea and built this garden – the Garden of Supreme Excellence – in its place. In truth it was a whole series of gardens, copies of the great gardens of Suchow and Wushi, Shanghai and Pei Ch'ing, but looking out across it, it was easy to think of it as a single thing – his "Green Dream" as he sometimes called it.

"Listen," he said. "Can you hear the magpie calling?"

She smiled. "It is a sound of good omen, husband. Maybe it will come and perch on your head . . ."

He laughed, recalling the tale. It was said that Nurhaci, the founder of the great Manchu Dynasty, had been fleeing from his enemies when a magpie came and perched on his helmet. His enemies, seeing this, called off their pursuit, and Nurhaci, in thanks to the bird, declared it sacred.

He squeezed her shoulder, his happiness shadowed by the memory of recent events. "We need its eggs to heal our sick, neh?"

She pushed back at him gently with her head. "You take too much upon yourself, husband. You cannot do it all."

"Maybe so. Yet I am their Father, Wei-kou. If I do not worry for them, who will?"

"This once let your servants worry. You have a Chancellor, neh? Well, let him carry more of the burden, as Li Yuan does with Nan Ho."

"Li Yuan *would* do more, were it not for the grief he has to carry. Three wives he lost. To think of even losing

one . . ." He squeezed her tenderly again. "Well . . . I'll not
dwell on that. Let us go inside."

She looked up at him and frowned. "You do not wish to
see the sunset, husband?"

Wu Shih shook his head. "It has been a hard day, my love,
and I am getting no younger. It would be best if I got some
rest . . ."

He had turned slightly, hearing a noise behind him, now
he turned fully about, frowning. His Master of the Inner
Chambers, Pao En-fu, stood in the arched doorway, his head
bowed.

"What is it, Master Pao?"

"*Chieh Hsia* . . . there is something on one of the media
channels. I think you might be interested."

He gave his wife's shoulder a brief pat. "Excuse me, Wei-
kou. Prepare my bed. I shall be with you when I can."

She nodded and went through. A moment later he himself
went across, letting Pao En-fu usher him through to the upper
study. The big, slatted blinds had been pulled down and the
big screen on the far side of the room was already lit. He
went across, then stood there, light spilling down over his
silk-cloaked figure.

It was Lever's wife. He frowned, then signalled for the
volume to be raised slightly. She was dressed strangely –
austerely – as if in some odd form of mourning clothes, and
her hair had been cut even more severely than he
remembered it. He listened for a moment, then turned, looking across at Pao En-fu.

"Run this back. From the beginning."

At once the image jumped, and the programme began
again.

"Is this a news item, Master Pao?"

"No, *Chieh Hsia*. It seems Madam Lever bought the air
time. Shall I find out more?"

Wu Shih nodded and dismissed him, then turned his attention back to the screen.

For a moment the screen was black. Then there was the
sound of a bell being struck and a faint illumination rose from

the darkness at the very centre of the screen. After a moment he realised what it was. A lamp. He watched as it approached. The faint, flickering pool of light surrounding it revealed a long, expensively-decorated corridor, set with vases and statues, the walls hung with tapestries and ancient paintings. Holding the lamp, her features carved, it seemed, from the darkness, was Mary Lever.

He nodded then pulled at his beard, impressed. As she came close to the camera, she slowed, looking directly into the lens, then set the lamp down on a table at the side.

"Come," she said simply, beckoning the camera. "We need to talk."

He shivered. *Powerful*, he thought, watching as the camera followed her to the left, into the darkness there, then out into the sudden brightness of a tiny walled garden.

It was an illusion . . . of course it was . . . yet for a moment he had been fooled by it. The light had seemed so real, so natural . . .

She turned. Behind her was an apple tree, its crown bright with leaves, heavy with fruit, while beneath her feet – her *bare* feet, he realised with a shock – was a carpet of lush green grass.

Brown she wore. The brown of autumn and of mourning clothes.

"You know me," she said, as if confiding something to the camera. "At least, you know the image of me. You know my name, Mary Lever, and you know that my husband, Michael, was almost killed by the Old Men who run things in our City. And now my husband, in his turn, is rich and powerful, and so I too am rich. At least, that's how it seems, neh?"

She turned and plucked a fruit, then turned back, holding the apple up so that the camera could see it. It glinted in the false daylight, fresh, perfectly formed, the very *ideal* of an apple.

"This tree is mine, and all its fruit. I can eat what I wish, when I wish it, and more will grow, for that is the way of things. Yet all is not well. I have enough – *more* than enough – to feed myself, and yet others have nothing, and so I must build a wall to keep those others out . . . A whole world of walls."

She looked down, and as she did, the apple in her hand became a tiny skull, a child's skull.

"Our world is dying," she said. "From where we stand, up here above it all, it has the appearance of a healthy thing, yet it is diseased. The apple is rotting from within."

He shivered. Behind her, the tree had changed. Its leaves were now brown and dry, its fruit blown and maggot-ridden. The grass beneath her feet was sere and the light had grown unnatural.

"We live in a blemished world," she said, the camera closing in on her eyes, her strong, attractive mouth, ". . . a world in which one whole side of us has been forgotten. We talk of the great Father who looks after us all, but where is our Mother? Where is *she*?"

There was the sound of a great wind soughing through the dry leaves of the tree. The sound of emptiness.

"Who minds the home? Who tends to our *deeper* needs while the menfolk go about their business?"

Slowly the camera pulled back.

"No one," she answered, her voice clear now, like a tolling bell. "We are hollow, unfulfilled. There are walls everywhere we look and an emptiness within that cannot be filled by any amount of *things*. Yes, and all the while, down there, beneath our feet, hidden from sight in the depths of our great City, lies the source of our despair and inner emptiness, the cause of all our guilt."

Her face was urgent now, her eyes lit from within.

She nodded. "Yes . . . *guilt*. Yet why should we feel guilty? Did *we* make this world of levels? Did *we* create those teeming billions? No. And yet they *are* there . . . like ghosts, haunting us, there at the table as we eat . . ."

Behind her the tree had changed. Now, instead of fruit, tormented faces hung from the blackened branches, their eyes pleading, their mouths silently supplicating.

And in front of it, so still, so filled with power that, for a moment, she seemed unreal, stood Mary Lever, staring out at the world, her eyes like small, dark points of certainty.

"Ahead the path divides. We can either feed that dark flame of despair that burns in each of us, or we can try and fill that inner emptiness. The choice is ours. We did not make this world, yet we can change it. *If* we have the will."

The garden slowly faded. Now she was standing in a book-lined room, the portrait of a blond-haired child behind her – a young Michael Lever, Wu Shih realised with a start.

"We have lived too long without a mother's tender care. We have forgotten how it feels to be whole. Ours is a Yang world, a hard, dry, masculine world. A harsh world. And that harshness has hardened us to the fate of others. We have grown indifferent to their suffering. And yet their fate is ours. Ignore them and we ignore ourselves. Hurt them and we hurt ourselves. Help them . . . yes, and we help ourselves. It is the Way."

Again there was the sound of a bell being struck, and Wu Shih, hearing it, felt a ripple of awe pass up his spine, making the hairs of his nape stand on end.

"For those of you who are still listening. For those of you who have understood what I've been saying and who have felt what I've been feeling, let me say this. It is not too late. The choice has not been made. We can still change this world of ours for the better. But the hour is upon us. Ahead the path divides."

Again the camera moved inwards, until her face filled the screen, her eyes staring earnestly into the lens.

"There is an old tradition that when the mother dies, the eldest daughter takes over her responsibilities, taking care of her little brothers and sisters . . ." She paused, her features softening. "It seems to me that we are in need of such an eldest daughter. Someone to care for us, to fill that gap of love and tenderness, to satisfy those deeper, *finer* urges within us. To bring them out.

"It is my purpose, from this evening on, to use what wealth I have to become this City's conscience, to be its Eldest Daughter, tending and caring, and showing by my example how it is we *ought* to be behaving towards each other."

The camera moved back.

"You see how I am dressed. Simply. Inexpensively. As a good woman would dress in the Lowers of our City. So shall I dress from this time on, and all the money saved will be diverted to a special fund – a fund which will be used to feed and clothe and educate those in the Lowers who have not the means to do so for themselves. Not only that, but I shall eat far more simply than before: a small, well-balanced meal – nutritionally adequate – as one would eat below. And again, all savings shall be diverted to the fund."

There was the faintest smile now on that earnest face.

"But one person's efforts, however powerful that person, cannot bring about the change that has to come. Alone I cannot do it. And that is why I want you all to join me. To dress as I dress and eat as I eat, and to contribute all of the savings made to a central fund – a fund which shall be named 'Eldest Daughter'."

The smile grew, coaxing a response.

"These actions – gestures of solidarity, of basic humanity – will be our starting point. From these foundations we shall wreak our great change – a change not in the politics of this great City, but in its most basic attitudes, in how it *thinks* and *feels* about itself."

She nodded, her face determined, certain now.

"We *can* have a say. We *can* make a difference. But only if we wake to the emptiness within and throw off the weight of lethargy that has, until now, kept our spirits chained."

The room was gone. Suddenly the garden was back, but this time there was no wall. The sunlit grass stretched away to the horizon. Mary Lever looked about her briefly, then turned back, smiling.

"Once again, I ask you to join with me, to share this great moment and take the first step on the path to new health, new growth. All you have to do is contact the box number at the end of this broadcast, giving your name and stack-code and a full information pack will be delivered to you before the evening's out. Don't wait to be the last to make the change. Act now and be proud to say, 'I was among the first'.

And remember, your *tzu*, your Elder Sister, awaits you."

The light intensified, became a honeyed gold. Her voice now spoke from the middle of that light, as if it were embedded in it.

"We *can* make our world a new and special place. We *can*. But we must act and act now, before it is too late. Ahead lies the divide. One path leads to darkness, one to light. Let us make sure we choose the path that leads to balance . . . the Way that leads us to the sunlight."

Her voice fell silent. Only the gold remained, filling the screen. There was the sound of a bell being struck, and then slowly, very slowly, the contact number appeared in a box in the centre of the screen – the blood-red letters forming from the gold, surrounded by a circle of tiny, bright red pictograms which read "good luck", "good health", and "many children", time and again in an unending triad of good fortune.

As it faded, Wu Shih breathed deeply, heavily, then turned. All of his senior staff had now gathered and were waiting there at the back of the room.

"Who is this going out to?"

Pao En-fu answered him. "To the top fifty, *Chieh Hsia*. All four of the main channels are carrying it. She's bought five twelve-minute slots on each. The estimated viewing figures are four hundred million up."

Wu Shih looked down, then nodded. "Clever," he said. "And dangerous. We must stop this, Pao En-fu. Get the Heads of all four channels on for me."

His Chancellor, Fen Cho-hsien, spoke up. "Is that wise, *Chieh Hsia*? Something like this . . . if we ban it, will that not merely serve to give it the air of credibility it needs? After all, the idea is a preposterous one. That people should send in their money to the richest woman in America! Besides, why should *they* care what happens down below? In all my experience, the Above has never done a single thing to help those less fortunate – less *elevated* – than themselves. Why in the gods' names should they start now?"

Wu Shih answered him sharply, angry that his Chancellor could not see the danger. "Because the times have changed,

Master Fen! And because that woman is very clever. Very clever indeed. Did you not see how she angled it. No word of blame, nothing about their greed and selfishness. No. She *worked* them, Master Fen, like the most devious of whores. Loss and guilt. Fear and the hope of a golden future. Trees and skulls. Lamps and tormented faces. All of it thrown together and salted with snippets of the Way."

He grimaced. "Why, the she-fox is at her husband's business, I'll wager. Why should he make such a public parting with Kennedy – why quit the NREP – unless he had his own ambitions? No . . . I'd wager five *yuan* to every one they collect that that is what this is. He plans a new campaign, a new party, and this is how he means to fund it."

Pao En-fu, who had been hovering in the doorway, awaiting his master's final decision, now spoke. "But Lever is a rich man, *Chieh Hsia*. Why should he *need* any further backing?"

"Because his wealth is all tied up, Master Pao. The Cutler Institute, business loans, extended trade agreements. ImmVac is extremely vulnerable right now. Any further calls upon its funds might bring about its fall. No. Lever is neither naïve nor the simpleton some of his critics make him out to be. He'll be behind this, you can be sure of it."

Chancellor Fen was smiling now. Wu Shih looked to him, curious. "Well, Fen?"

"I was only thinking, *Chieh Hsia* . . . What better reason *not* to cancel the broadcasts. If we can prove that connection. If we can show that this 'Eldest Daughter' fund is being used to float a new party, what better way to destroy Lever and his ambitions?"

"I thought you didn't think it would work!"

"I don't, *Chieh Hsia*. I think the natural greed of the Above will show itself. But why don't we see? Surely one victory is enough for you today, my Lord?"

Wu Shih laughed, delighted by the reminder. His swift action today had crushed the Black Hand. It would be months, years perhaps, before they regrouped in any strength. What's more, it had brought him nothing but praise throughout the Middle and Upper levels of the City. So maybe Fen Cho-hsien was right. Maybe he shouldn't meddle in this, but should leave it to fail of its own accord. And in the meantime he could do as Fen suggested and investigate just where any funds were headed.

"All right," he said, smiling at his Chancellor. "We'll do as you suggest. But let's monitor it closely, Master Fen. As I said, she's a clever woman, and there's nothing so troublesome as a clever woman, *neh*?"

There was laughter, yet as Wu Shih left to go to his rooms, he felt a strange dissatisfaction at the decision, as if he'd overlooked some vital point. And even as Wei-kou began to massage his back, trying to ease the tension from his muscles, some part of his mind still gnawed at the problem, refusing to leave it be.

Damn her! he thought, then grunted as Wei-kou pummelled his back. Yet mixed in with his anger was the memory of how powerful she had looked, standing there before the apple tree, that tiny skull cradled in her hand. A Yang world. That was what she'd said. A hard, dry, masculine world. Was she right? Was that *really* what they'd made?

Wei-kou placed her hands firmly on his shoulders. "Relax, my husband, *please*, relax . . ."

But it was suddenly difficult to relax. All of the ease he'd been feeling earlier, all of the happiness he'd felt listening to the magpie calling in the garden – all that had drained from him now, leaving him empty and despondent. *Like a dead tree*, he thought, remembering how the wind had soughed through its branches.

Tomorrow. He would see to it all tomorrow. Yet when Wei-kou finished, he got up again, put on his robe and went to his study, then stood before the screen, looking up into the brightness, watching the Eldest Daughter and her fable of the tree that died.

CHAPTER · 13

FIRE IN THE LAKE

He had not been asleep more than four hours when he was woken by a knocking on the bedroom door.

"Master Kao!" the maid called urgently. "Master Kao! You must come at once! There is an urgent message for you!"

Chen struggled up from the depths in which he'd been floating and sat up. For the first time in a long, long while he felt relaxed. And happy. He turned, smiling, conscious of Wang Ti there in the darkness beside him. They had made love. For the first time since the loss of her child, they had made love. He shivered, remembering how her eyes had opened to him; how she had softly called his name.

So long he'd waited. So long . . .

Leaning across her he pulled back the hair from her brow and placed a small soft kiss there, careful not to wake her, then eased back the cover and got up.

He threw on a gown and went out. The maid, Tian Ching, was waiting for him outside, her nightgown tightly wrapped about her. She bowed then turned, pointing to the vid-phone in the corner.

"It is your office, Master. They said to wake you."

Chen thanked her then went across.

It was his duty Captain, Wilson.

"Major Kao . . . I thought you'd want to know at once. We've got our killer!"

"Alive?"

"Yes, sir. And keen to talk, it seems."

Chen's face lit up. "Excellent! How did we get him?"

334

Wilson laughed. "Purest accident, as it turns out! One of our drug squads hit a Triad-run gambling den down-level and picked him up in the trawl. They were about to let him go when his face came up on the screen. So your all-points warning worked! They captured him at Nordhausen, so they've taken him to the garrison at Kassel. I'm headed there now."

"Okay. I'll meet you there. It'll take me . . . what? . . . an hour and a half at most. But keep him isolated, okay? And take some of our men – men you can trust – to guard him. If a certain Company director finds we've got his man – which I'm sure he will – he'll be anxious to remove the evidence, and I don't want any mistakes this time. I want to *nail* that bastard Cornwell!"

"Sir!"

He cut connection, then turned away, hurrying to his bedroom to dress. But he had taken only two paces when the vid-phone's chime sounded again.

Chen turned, staring at the flashing screen. "Who the hell . . . ?"

He went back and pressed to connect, then stood back as a young face filled the screen.

"*Hannah?*"

"You've got to come, Kao Chen. At once. Something terribly important's happened."

He stared at her, wondering what on earth could be so important that she would phone him at half three in the morning.

"What's happened? Has someone died?"

"No. But they will, if you don't help us."

He sighed. "Look, I can't. An important lead has just come up on one of my cases and I've got to follow it up right away. Can't it wait? Can't I pop in to you on my way back?"

She shook her head. "You don't understand. This is so important that, well . . . I can't tell you over the phone, but you've *got* to come, you just *have* to!"

He made to shake his head, but there was real fear in the young woman's face. Erfut . . . it was only fifteen minutes from Kassel by cruiser. If he were to call in first and reassure her . . .

"Okay," he said finally. "I'll try. But I've got to see to this other matter first, okay?"

She nodded, grateful, then cut the line.

Shit, he thought. Then, taking a long, calming breath, he tapped Wilson's code into the phone and waited to be connected.

*   *   *

The two men sat back from the screen and looked at each other.

"Well? What do you think?"

"I think our friend the Junior Minister has lost his nerve. I think he's confided in his daughter and she's panicked him."

"I agree."

"Then what are we to do?"

"We do what we have to do, neh? The *I Lung*'s instructions were quite explicit."

"And the girl?"

"She must die, too."

"A fire?"

"That would be best, neh? No witnesses . . . and it can be made to seem quite natural. An accident . . ."

"I like that."

"Good. Then let's get moving, before our meddling Major has a chance to fuck things up."

"What about him? What do you think his connection with the young woman is?"

"Sexual probably. I'm told his wife is mad. They probably haven't slept together for years."

"Then how do we deal with him? A bribe?"

"It depends on the attachment. If he's besotted with the girl . . . well, it could be difficult. I think we might have to kill him."

"Messy . . . There'll be an inquiry."

"I know. But it can't be helped. If we can make it seem as if he's been killed for another reason . . ."

"That shouldn't be too difficult. He has a long record of getting involved in things he shouldn't have meddled in."

"Then we'll do that. But first the girl and her father."

* * *

They had been up half the night, talking, trying to work out how best to approach the matter.

The problem was a simple one. Li Yuan had to be told, but to get to Li Yuan – especially these days – one had to go through numerous intermediaries, and any one of these might be in the pay of the First Dragon. Indeed, to think otherwise would be naïve.

To go direct, that would be ideal, yet it was impossible. Even to get to his Chancellor, Nan Ho, would mean negotiating whole levels of bureaucracy, and at some critical point a warning bell would sound, the *I Lung* would know and the game would be up.

So what were they to do?

Hannah had come up with a solution. They would approach the matter indirectly, through the Security officer, Kao Chen. Chen, she remembered, had access of a kind to Li Yuan. He had told her about his friend, Major Karr, and how he had been made *Chia ch'eng* – Honorary Assistant to the Royal Household. If Chen could persuade Karr to seek a personal audience with the T'ang . . .

She busied herself, making *ch'a*, while her father paced the room behind her. Strangely, she had never felt closer to him than tonight. Talking this through, she had found herself appreciating for the first time just how subtle a mind he had . . . and what a minefield the world he inhabited really was.

Wasted, she thought. *He's been wasted all these years*. Like so much else in her world, his talents had been squandered – had been used not positively, creatively, to bring something new and vibrant to the world, but to service the stale bones of the Great Lie: to bury that old, progressive world that had preceded theirs beneath a thick, muffling layer of ice.

She carried the tray across to the low table at the centre of the room, then knelt to pour.

"What will you do, afterwards?"

He stared back at her. "Afterwards?" It was clear he had not thought beyond telling the T'ang. He frowned. "It will be the end of it all. The Lie . . ."

"We're well rid of it."

But she could see from his face that he was not so sure as she. Yet that was understandable. All his life he had worked to preserve the one great secret of his world – had based his life, his whole philosophy on it. And now he was about to throw all that away: to betray all that he had lived by. It was not so easily done.

She picked up one of the bowls and carried it to him. "And what of your wife?"

There was a moment's confusion in his face, and then he realised. "*Aiya*! I'd not thought!"

If the *I Lung* were found guilty of treason – and there was little doubt that he would, should her father get to speak to Li Yuan – then she, as his sister, would, in all probability, be found guilty too. *To the third generation.* That was the law. Unless . . .

"A deal," he said, thinking aloud. "I'm certain I could make some kind of deal . . ."

"You want that?"

"I . . ." His eyes looked to her, then away, uncertainty eating at him. She knew he had never loved his second wife. The marriage had always been political in essence, a cementing of ties – a guarantee, to put it crudely, of his loyalty to the *I Lung*. Yet he had had two children by her, and though he saw little of them, it was no easy thing to cast them off.

"How long will this friend of yours be?"

"Major Kao? He said he'd be here as soon as he could. When he hears what has happened, he'll help us. I know he will."

"He is a good man, this Major? An honest man?"

She nodded.

"Strange. I had begun to think there were no honest men left in our world. I have seen so much, Hannah. Oh, I could not begin to tell you. Corruption and greed, murder and betrayal. Such behaviour is endemic. Wherever you turn . . ."

He sighed, then sipped from his bowl. "Good *ch'a*," he said, smiling at her. Then, "I have not been a good father to you, have I?"

She reached out and touched his cheek, her voice softer than before. "Nonsense. You've been the very best of fathers. If you weren't here much, that wasn't your fault. I always knew you loved me."

He looked at her a long while, then nodded. "When I look at you, I understand why I loved your mother so much. She was like you, Hannah. I . . . I lost much when I lost her."

Hannah shivered. *Yes*, she thought, *you and I both*.

* * *

The first man slipped from the shadows and ran across. For one brief moment he was in full sight of the overhead camera, then he was inside, the door to Shang Mu's Mansion irising open about his disappearing back.

The second assassin followed a moment later.

The hallway was mainly in shadow. A small night-light on the wall to the left gave a little illumination. Beneath it, on a low couch, lay a servant. Sensing something the man stirred and looked up sleepily. For the briefest moment his eyes opened wide, then he made a small strangled noise as the wire was looped tightly about his throat from behind.

Move, the first assassin mouthed, pointing to the door to the right. *Check it out*.

He ran across. Inside, on the far side of what looked like a store room, two young servants were sleeping, back to back on a broad bed. Quickly, expertly, he dealt with them.

Outside his companion was waiting patiently, crouched beside the big double doors that led through into the main living quarters. He raised two fingers to indicate the tally, then ran across and crouched beside his partner.

Three dead now. Which meant that the other two servants were inside. Unless Chih Huang Hui had taken her bodyservant with her, in which case there was only the daughter's maid.

He looked down. It was as well that the *I Lung*'s sister was elsewhere tonight, for, whatever the necessity, neither of them fancied the task of explaining *her* death to the First Dragon.

Reaching up, the first assassin tried the handle. Slowly, soundlessly, it turned. They went inside.

A long corridor stretched away in front of them, lit by four wall lamps spaced left and right. At the far end were another set of doors. To the left were Shang Mu's rooms, to the right his wife's. They took three steps then froze. There, half-way down on the right, on a couch beside Chih Huang Hui's door, lay another of the servants. The lady of the house's bodyservant, by the look of it.

The first assassin frowned deeply, then waved his companion across, watching as he crouched over the sleeping figure and did his work. There was the faintest tremor of the upper torso, a tiny kicking of the left foot, and then the body lay still. The second assassin turned, looking to him.

Inside, he mouthed, indicating the door to Chih Huang Hui's rooms. His fellow nodded, then turned back, reaching for the handle.

It could not be helped, but at least the woman was an invalid. She would be no trouble.

He ran across and, as his fellow slipped into the darkened room across from him, stood by the door to Shang Mu's apartments, his ear pressed close, listening.

As he'd thought, there was nothing. The message they'd intercepted had come from the daughter's rooms. In all likelihood they were there. But it was best to be certain.

He reached down, trying the handle. It was locked. Double-locked by the feel of it. Good. He would leave it and . . .

There was a shot, the noise startling in the stillness of the great House. He turned, astonished. *No* . . .

* * *

At the sound of the shot Shang Mu looked up, the *ch'a* bowl falling from his grasp.

Hannah, pouring a second bowl for herself, froze, staring at the doorway. "*Aiya . . .*" she whispered, wondering for a moment if she had been wrong about Kao Chen. Then, stirring herself, she went across and turned the lock, then reached up to pull the bolt across.

She turned, facing her father. "Go through!" she whispered urgently. "Quick now!"

He swallowed, then did as he was told.

No, she thought. *Not Chen. But someone else. Someone who knows what we plan.*

She shivered. *Yes, but who*?

It came to her at once. Someone employed by the *I Lung* . . . by the Thousand Eyes.

She cursed her own stupidity. She should have known! The First Dragon would never have been so careless. Her father would have been watched carefully. That was the way of it, after all, to set spies upon the spies.

She hurried after him, pulling the inner doors closed and locking them. Then, calming herself, she looked about her, wondering what, if anything, she could do.

* * *

He went in slowly, cautiously, feeling his way blindly across the floor, alert to the smallest sound.

At first he could see nothing. Then, hearing a low groan from just in front of him, he froze, narrowing his eyes.

His partner seemed to be sitting against the wall just inside the bedroom doorway. As he watched there was a cough, and the body slumped slowly to one side.

He made to move, then held still, a second sound coming to his notice. Breathing. A shivered, irregular sound.

Chih Huang Hui . . .

Slowly, careful to make as little sound as possible, he drew his gun, then began to edge forward, trying to pinpoint the sound in the darkness up ahead of him.

* * *

The maid stood in the doorway to her room, rubbing her eyes. "*Mistress*? What's happening?"

"Go back to bed," Hannah told her, going across and pushing her back inside. "Lock your door and be silent. There are intruders in the House."

The young girl's eyes flew wide with fear.

"Do what I said," Hannah said, frowning at her. "*Now!*"

Bobbing her head, the girl backed off a step then closed her door.

Hannah heaved an exasperated sigh, then turned back. They were trapped. What's more, the House communications had been cut. They could not ask for help even if they wanted to.

Not that help would have come, she thought acidly. *Not for us, anyway.*

"Hannah?"

She looked back at her father. He was watching her expectantly, as if she could save them somehow. As if . . .

"We're dead," she said quietly. "We're . . ."

There was a shot. Another. Then, a moment later, a third. Shang Mu moaned softly.

She stared at him a moment, woken from her own despair by the sight of his crumpled, frightened face, then nodded to herself, knowing what she must do. Chen was coming. He would be here . . . soon. Until then it was up to her to gain every second she could.

"Help me," she said, going across to her father. "We've got to move things, Daddy. Put them in front of the doors. We've got to make a barricade and keep them out."

He stared at her a moment, then nodded.

"Good," she said, smiling, encouraging him. "But quick now. We've got so little time."

* * *

He reached across, switching on the bedside lamp, then turned, looking down at the woman, studying her in the sickly orange light.

She lay on her back on the bloodied sheets, the jade-handled gun she'd used beside her. Her face looked surprised, her mouth open in a small "o" of shock, as if she'd expected some other outcome. But there had never been any doubt about it. His first bullet had smashed her right wrist, the second had removed the top of her skull.

On the floor on the other side of the bed lay the boy, face down where he'd fallen, his back a sticky mess. He'd not expected the boy to be there. He'd thought . . .

He turned, angry with himself for having got it wrong, then looked across to where his partner half-lay, half-sat against the wall. *A shame*, he thought, saddened by the waste. He had been a good man, quick to learn and obedient to a fault. And to think one lucky shot . . .

He leaned across and spat fully in her face, then, without looking back, walked back out into the hallway.

Let's finish this, he thought sourly, certain now that no good would come of it. *Let's give the Great Man what he wants* . . .

* * *

As the cruiser descended Chen leaned forward in the co-pilot's seat, listening to the comset.

"It's *what*?" he said, suddenly concerned. "You mean it's engaged, surely?"

"No, sir," came the reply. "It's *dead*. There's nothing on that channel at all!"

"Shit!" He cut the connection, then turned, looking to the pilot. "Get the hatch open, quick now!"

"But, sir. Procedures . . ."

"Fuck procedures! I need to get down there quickly!"

"Sir!" The man leaned forward and hit several buttons. "At once there was a clunk, a sudden hiss, and then an inrush of cold air from behind them.

Chen threw off his belt and clambered between the seats into the back of the tiny four-man craft. As it began to settle, he jumped and rolled, then ran for the ventilation shaft.

* * *

The assassin pulled on his mask, then walked across. Stepping back, he took a deep breath, building his concentration, then launched himself at the door, his heel connecting crisply with the wooden panel.

He moved back again, studying the damage. The door had held, but the panel was cracked and splintered. One well-aimed punch and he'd be through.

He hesitated. As far as he knew, neither the Junior Minister nor his daughter owned a gun, but then nor had Chih Huang Hui. Not officially. And that one mistake had nearly ruined things. Best, then, to make sure. To use a gun rather than a fist.

He sighed, a dark cloud of fatalism descending on him. This was to have been the culmination of his long career – the final task before he finished with it all – but even his own survival was doubtful now that the *I Lung*'s sister had been killed. The First Dragon was a vengeful man, so he'd heard, and would not take kindly to the news. Oh, he would keep his word, certainly, and pay him – even a bonus, perhaps, to show there was no animosity – but he would be lucky if he lived a week. Lucky if he lived long enough to spend a tenth of the blood money.

He nodded to himself. Maybe so, but there was still the Guild's pride to consider. That special pride in a task well-accomplished.

Unsheathing his gun, he raised it and fired twice into the gap, then pushed his fist through the resultant hole, widening the gap. Holstering his gun, he took a grenade from his belt and primed it. Then, poking his arm through the hole, he lobbed it into the centre of the room. There was a pop and then the sharp, sibilant hiss of escaping gas.

He waited, counting, then, at ten, grasped the sides of the panel and kicked again, climbing up through the gap and into the smoke-filled room.

*   *   *

From where she crouched beneath the barricade, Hannah heard the metallic clink of the grenade as it bounced on the

344

tiles, and braced herself for an explosion. The soft pop it made, sent a shiver of surprise up her spine, but then she understood. That hissing . . . It was gas. A disabling gas of some kind.

She looked behind her, then crawled across, pulling the silk cover from the chair and tearing it with her teeth. Handing half to her father, she showed him what to do. "Around your nose and mouth," she said quietly.

Yes, but would it make any difference? They had to breath . . .

There was a crashing, splintering sound.

They're through, she thought. *Oh gods, they're through!*

She turned yet again, looking about her, forcing her mind to work. What could she use? What in the gods' names could she use for a weapon?

Nothing . . . There was nothing here.

And then her eyes focused on something close at hand – something that was among the mess of things that had fallen from the dresser they had dragged across. A silver pair of hair-scissors.

She reached out and closed her hand on them, noting, as she did, the faintest scent of gas in the room.

How long? she wondered. *How long before we're dead?* But the thought was fleeting. Stronger, more urgent impulses were at work in her now. The barricade would slow them down. Would make it hard for them to come into the room. Yes, but not impossible. They had only to smash a hole. A grenade would do the rest.

She shook her head, frantic now, knowing that the barrier was the key to it – that she had somehow to use that small advantage, to make it count. But how?

A thud close by made her jump. The door juddered in its frame.

Think, she told herself, staring down at the slender pair of scissors in her hand. *Just think* . . .

But time was running out.

* * *

345

Chen stood outside the main door to Shang Mu's house, surprised to find it open. As he stepped towards it a voice called out from behind him.

"Stay right where you are and don't move!"

He froze, then slowly raised his hands. "I'm Security," he said, turning slowly, cautiously, conscious that the voice had had a frightened edge to it.

The man was in his night clothes, and the weapon he held trained on Chen was ancient, a collector's piece.

"My ID is in my breast pocket. Will you let me reach for it?"

The man considered, his eyes uncertain, then he nodded. "Okay. But very slow."

His instinct was against it, but he did what the man said, his movements painfully slow. "There," he said, tilting it towards him.

"Throw it down . . ."

Aiya . . . Every second was precious, and here was this fool. He threw it down.

The man bent down, his eyes never leaving Chen, the gun aimed tensely at him. Chen watched as he lifted the card until it was slightly to the left of his line of sight; saw how he took tiny glimpses at it, as if frightened to take his eyes off his captive for even a fraction of a second.

And quite right, too, Chen thought, wishing some of his own officers were half as careful.

"A Major, huh?"

"Yes . . . now for the gods' sakes let me go. There's been an incident. The Shang Household . . ."

"I heard shots," the man said, throwing the card back and lowering his gun. "One shot. Then three. Then another two. Just now."

"Yes," Chen said. He had heard the last two himself. "If you'll forgive me."

"You want help?"

Chen bent down, retrieving his card, then straightened up. "No, I . . ." Then, knowing he had already pissed away

346

valuable seconds, he drew his gun and turned, running for the door, praying he wasn't too late.

* * *

The assassin stepped back from the door, nodding to himself, then unclipped a fresh cartridge from his belt and reloaded his gun. He turned, looking about him through the thick mist of the gas, then, thinking he heard a sound, took three paces towards the outer door. Something crunched beneath his booted foot. He bent down and looked. It was a bowl. A broken *ch'a* bowl. On a low table nearby was a pot and another bowl. He reached out and felt the side of the *ch'a* pot. It was still warm. Good. That meant they were definitely inside.

He crossed to the door and stood there a moment, listening, hearing nothing, then turned back. Okay. It was time to end things and get out. Before Security sent someone to check up on the communications blackout.

He raised his gun and fired: three shots, splintering the lock. He stepped up to it and knocked it out with the gun's stock.

That should do it, he thought, bending down and peering through. *And now to end it . . .*

* * *

"Hannah!" her father whispered urgently. "No!"

She turned and looked back at him, grimacing, putting a finger to her lips. Then, turning back, she carried on, hauling herself up on top of the barricade.

Her ears rang and it was getting painful to breath, but it could be their only chance.

She could hear footsteps in the other room; the sound of a bowl breaking beneath someone's tread. One of them. She shivered, feeling the faintest ray of hope. There was only one of them!

Yes, but what's he waiting for?

The footsteps went away, returned. Then there was silence. An awful, terrifying silence.

She was beginning to feel drowsy, nauseous. The gas . . .

For a moment her vision blurred and she felt herself sway slightly, as if she were about to faint. Then it came clear again. As it did, there was a glint of silver just beside her knee, where the hole was.

She struck. Grasping the hand that held the gun she forced it down savagely onto the splintered wood, at the same time stabbing down with the scissors. There was a great groan of pain from behind the door and then a fierce tugging as the assassin struggled to get free. But Hannah had put her full weight on the hand. She knew that to release it was to die.

The feeling was awful, the most dreadful thing she had ever experienced. She could feel the metal blade of the scissors gouging against the bones of his wrist: could feel the hot stickiness of his blood as it pumped from the ruined hand. And his groans . . .

The sound of his pain made her feel ill. A raw, grunting sound that frayed her nerves and set her teeth on edge, even as she struggled to hold him. But slowly, very slowly, she felt the hand slide from her grip.

The gas . . . She felt so weak.

The hand slipped, was gone.

She rolled, knowing she had to get down, off the barricade, but it was too late. As the door above her splintered, she felt a hot wash of pain from her shoulder and knew she had been hit. There was another shot and then another.

Dead, she thought. *I'm dead.* But her thoughts rolled on. And in the silence that followed, it was not the God of Hell's voice she heard calling her, but Kao Chen's, muffled, as if from behind a mask.

"Are you all right in there? Hannah! Are you all right?"

* * *

Yin Tsu stared at his daughter, then shook his head, beckoning his bodyservant across to see to him. "No . . . no, Fei Yen. You must have misheard them. Youthful high spirits, that's all it was. You know these boys . . . a drop too much of wine and all kinds of addled notions come to them."

She stared at him, trying not to lose her temper. He hadn't

listened! He simply hadn't heard a word she'd said to him!

"No . . ." he went on, smiling at her reassuringly, then turned to let his bodyservant remove his jacket. "I'm sure it's all a misunderstanding. I'll speak to Yin Chan in the morning and sort it all out. I'm sure he'll be able to clear things up. Now you go and get some rest. You must be tired . . ."

"Father!" she said sharply. "Listen to me! I am not imagining things, nor am I suffering from some misunderstanding. I know what I heard and it threatens all of us. *All* of us! Don't you understand?"

He stared at her, then went to speak again, but she wouldn't let him.

"No. You listen to *me* for once. Because it's my child – your grandchild – who'll suffer if this idiocy continues."

The old man frowned, taken aback by her outburst, then tugged at his beard. "But my dear . . ."

"No buts, father. You must act, and act decisively. You have no choice."

His head came up at that. "No choice?"

She huffed, exasperated. "Treason, that's what we're talking about here. *Treason*, punishable by death. To the third generation."

Again he shook his head. "No . . ." But she could see she was beginning to get through to him.

"Your *Wu*," she said, a sudden flash of inspiration hitting her. "Consult your *Wu*! After all, he's never wrong."

His face lit up. "My *Wu* . . . Of course!"

"Then call him. Now, while the moment is upon us. Have him cast the oracle right here, for both of us to see. You'll see. I tell you, you'll see!"

He stared at her, the smile fading slowly. Then, with a tiny nod to her, he gestured to his bodyservant. "Shen . . . Fetch Master Fung. Tell him I have urgent need of his skills."

"Master . . ."

He turned back, looking at her, a new seriousness in his manner. "What you heard . . . have you told any other of it?"

"No, Father."

349

"Good." He nodded to himself, but there was a slight sourness in his face that had not been there a moment before, as if he had come half-way to believing her in those few instants. He glanced at her again. "And if the yarrow stalks show nothing?"

She shivered, then shook her head. "The Way of Heaven is clear, Father. We mortals cannot change it."

"No." But when he looked away again, it was with a deeply troubled expression.

* * *

Hannah sat in a chair in the corner, letting one of the medics check the dressing while the other packed away. The wound wasn't as bad as it had first seemed. Most of the damage was superficial. Yet her collarbone was fractured and the pain from that had been quite awful.

Local Security had arrived only minutes after Chen, summoned by their neighbour. They had taken brief statements from all three of them, and a special camera team was now working through the house room by room, making a visual document of the carnage. She had glimpsed it only briefly, and then only some of it, but it was enough to confirm what she'd known instinctively: that this was a matter of the utmost seriousness. They *had* to tell Li Yuan.

She could hear Chen outside, arguing with the Security Captain. "Pull rank," she'd told him, but this once, it seemed, he couldn't. There were procedures for an incident like this.

She shuddered, remembering how Chen had stood there, listening to her as she spilled the whole incredible story. Treason. A plot involving the whole upper echelon of the Ministry and Minor Family princes too. It was hard to believe. Yet Chen had simply nodded, as if he'd known it all from the start. And then Security had arrived and there'd been no time to discuss it any further.

She looked across and felt a twinge of sorrow. Her father was sitting there on the far side of the room, his hands resting lightly on his knees, like a lost child, his eyes staring into the far distance.

He had lost a great deal this night. A wife, a son, a purpose for his life. Tomorrow he would have to start again. If that were possible.

If any of them lived to see the dawn.

Chen returned, coming directly across to her. He smiled, then looked to the medic. "Forgive me. Could I have a word with the young lady?"

The man smiled. "I'm done here, anyway," then bowed and backed away.

"Well?" she said quietly.

"We can go, if you're ready. I've contacted my duty Captain, Wilson, and he's going to get a message through to General Rheinhardt. I've said I'd meet him on the West Pad at Bremen in an hour. If we can convince Rheinhardt we can get to Nan Ho."

She frowned. "What about your friend . . . you know, Major Karr?"

Chen shook his head. "Karr's on a special assignment down-level. It's been months since I've heard from him. If I knew where he was, I'd be the first to be in touch with him. You realise who they were, Hannah? They were *Guild*. Trained assassins. The best!"

She shivered. "If they were demons from Hell, I'd not give in. You know that . . ."

He touched her good arm briefly. "I know. Now get your father ready. I want Rheinhardt to hear it from the horse's mouth."

She frowned at him. "Horses, Kao Chen?"

He laughed. "An old expression . . . Now hurry. The Guild's pride will have been wounded. There's two of their number dead out there and they'll be wanting vengeance for it. Besides which, there are Dragons to fight, neh?"

Hannah laughed, then grew more sober. "Are you not afraid, Kao Chen?"

"Afraid?" He leaned closer, speaking to her ear. "To be honest with you, Shang Han-A, I'm petrified."

* * *

Fei Yen stood in the corner of the room, beside the hanging cages, looking in at the moulting birds as the *Wu* finished casting the oracle. Master Fung had taken much longer than usual, going over his results once and then once again, frowning all the while. Finally he looked up, his face troubled. "It is *Ko*," he said, "Fire in the Lake."

Yin Tsu caught his breath. "You are sure, Master Fung?"

The *Wu* nodded. "There is nine in the fifth place. The two primary trigrams are in opposition. The younger daughter dominates the elder. Fire in the Water." His voice quailed with fear. "It is Revolution, Prince Yin. Revolution!"

Yin Tsu shook his head, but his eyes were wide with fear. He looked across, meeting Fei Yen's eyes, then looked down. "*Aiya* . . ." he said softly. "Kuan Yin preserve us!"

She came across and stood before the *Wu*. "Tell us more, Master Fung. Is it . . . *inevitable?*"

"Inevitable?" He shrugged, clearly uncomfortable. "No . . . not inevitable. Yet the signs are clear." He put out his wizened hand, indicating the spill of fallen stalks. "I have never seen it so clear. Here Fire, there Water . . . the two in conflict, each trying to destroy the other. If the Man should come . . ."

"The man?" Yin Tsu started forward. "What do you mean, Master Fung?"

Fung looked down. "The time is ripe, Prince Yin. The hour but awaits the Man. It is as the oracle says. The Great Man changes like a tiger . . ."

"And if the Great Man is a Dragon?"

The *Wu* looked up, staring at her. "A dragon?"

"No matter . . ." She turned, facing her father. "Well? Will you go to him now?"

Yin Tsu hesitated, then shook his head. "It is not that simple, Fei Yen. I . . . I must talk first with my cousins. An Sheng must know. His son . . ." He looked down, then, "Leave us a moment, Master Fung."

When the *Wu* had gone, he looked back at her. At that moment he seemed every one of his eighty-two years.

"It is easy for you, Fei Yen. You have a duty to your son.

352

But I . . . well, I have three sons and a grandchild. And An Sheng . . . No, it would not be right to act without first speaking with An Sheng."

For a moment he stared into the air, then he shuddered, his voice suddenly pained. "Chan . . . how could he be so foolish? *How*?"

She went across and held him close, trying to comfort him. "Maybe we could claim that he was led . . . *seduced* by An Hsi. Perhaps . . ."

"No," her father, pushing her back slightly. "Yin Chan is not a child. If he was led, it was because he wanted to be led." He sighed heavily. "No, my love, Chan is lost to us. It must be . . . it must be as if he never was. I . . ."

His mouth quivered, his whole face threatening to break apart. For a moment he turned his head aside, struggling to control himself, then he looked back at her.

"I will go now and see An Sheng. He must be told at once what happened here. And then we shall go, together, to see Li Yuan. Today, before any more damage can be done."

"And Chan? What will come of my brother?"

The old man shook his head, a sudden frailty in his voice. "Yin Chan is nothing now. Nothing . . ."

* * *

The First Dragon laughed delightedly, nodding towards the three men – his brothers – who sat with him, then turned in his seat, clapping his hands. At once a servant ran to him and knelt at his feet.

"Master?"

"Bring more wine. The very best. Tell Master Yu . . ."

He stopped, his attention caught by the man waiting in the doorway, his head bowed, the sash of a Ministry Messenger about his shoulders. Dismissing the servant, he beckoned the man across.

Taking the black silk envelope from him, he opened it impatiently. Was this it? Was this what he'd been waiting for these past three days?

He read the handwritten note, then folded it again, smiling.

353

"Is there an answer, Master?"

He shook his head, then tucked the envelope into the inner pocket of his cloak. "No. No answer."

Turning back, he felt a small thrill pass through him. If one dealt with eels, it was always best to hook them through the gills. And this . . . this pledge from An Sheng . . . *this* would be the hook by which he held him to the task.

"Good news, *I Lung*?" his Second Brother asked, raising his wine cup slightly, his eyes inquisitive.

"Business," he answered noncommittally.

"Our work is unending, neh?" his Fifth Brother, seated to his right, chipped in. "Our eyes never close."

There was laughter. In the midst of it more wine arrived.

"Shall we have music?" he asked, looking about him, seeing his own good humour reflected in every eye.

"A splendid idea," his Second Brother answered, leaning forward to let a servant fill his cup once more. "Is that excellent *ch'in* player still with you, brother?"

He laughed. "She is. But I'm tempted to think it was not her playing that interested you so much as her other talents."

"I hear she was very good on the jade flute," Fifth Brother added, winking, "though her plucking . . ."

"Brother?"

"Plucking, I said . . . her finger-work . . ."

Second Brother sat forward slightly, enjoying the game. "Her fingerwork? What of it?"

"Oh, nothing . . . only that she could coax a tune from the tiredest old instrument!"

There was a great roar at that. The *I Lung* turned, laughing, and summoned his Master Of Ceremonies. "Master Yu . . . I wondered where you'd got to. My brothers . . ."

He stopped, noting the sobriety of Yu's manner.

"Master Yu? What is it?"

Yu, who had kept his head bowed, looked up, his eyes fearful, a distinct colour at his neck. "Master . . . forgive me. A message came . . ."

"I know." He patted his jacket pocket. "I already have it."

354

"No, Master. A special message. On the screen in your study."

"Ah . . . ?" He frowned. "And you answered it?"

Master Yu bowed low. "I was passing, Master, and you were busy here. I only glanced in at the door, meaning to come and bring you. But . . . well, a face was on the screen already. It saw me and spoke to me. A soldier, it was. A Captain."

The *I Lung* felt himself go cold. Behind him his brothers had fallen silent and were listening.

"What did he say?"

Yu swallowed, then went on. "He said that he had only a few moments. That there was no time for me to run and fetch you. He told me . . ." Yu hesitated, looking about him, but the First Dragon motioned for him to carry on. "He said to tell you that the assassins are dead. And your sister, Chih Huang Hui. And that Shang Mu is loose."

The *I Lung* sat back, feeling all of his former pleasure drain from him, replaced by ice.

Earlier, he had had the oracle read. *Ko*, it had been. Fire in the Lake. Confirmation, he'd thought, of his ambitions. He had sat there, on the sunlit terrace of his palace, thrilled by the *Wu*'s judgement:

> *Revolution. On your own day you are believed.*
> *Supreme success, Furthering through perseverance.*
> *Remorse disappears.*

He shivered. *Remorse disappears . . .*

He stood, looking about him at his brothers. They were watching him, waiting to see what he would decide. He waved Yu away, then walked across to the great window at the far end of the room and stood there, staring out blindly, a great wave of despair washing over him. It was too early, far too early. If they struck now it might prove disastrous. Yet what choice had they? If Shang Mu *were* loose . . .

"Brother?"

He turned. His Second Brother stood there, only a pace

or so away. Beyond him, his Fifth and Eighth Brothers waited silently.

"Okay," he said, his mind made up. "It goes ahead."

"Tonight?"

He hesitated, then nodded. "Shang Mu," he said. "We've got to get Shang Mu."

"And afterwards?"

"The T'ang," he said, meeting his brothers' eyes and seeing the shadow of his own doubt mirrored back at him. "We must kill the T'ang."

* * *

"What do you think?"

Chen stared down through the darkness at the floodlit bulk of Bremen Fortress, then looked back at the young pilot.

"If they were going to shoot us out of the air, they'd have done it by now. No. If there's any trickery, it'll be when we're on the ground."

He turned, looking back at Hannah and her father.

"When we land, sit tight. I'll go out alone. If there's any trouble, the lieutenant here will fly you out just as fast as he can."

Shang Mu looked back at him, concerned. "You think there'll be trouble?"

"I hope not. But who knows? This whole situation's something new. It depends on how high the conspiracy goes within Security. Rheinhardt, I'd vouch, is honest and staunchly loyal to Li Yuan. But who knows about those surrounding him? We're just going to have to take the risk."

He turned back, then nudged the young lieutenant. "There," he said, pointing to the far edge of the great Western Pad. "Set us down in that big clear space. I don't want anyone sneaking up on us, okay?"

"Sir!"

He swung the craft to the left, then brought it down, on the far edge, where Chen had indicated.

Chen climbed down then looked about him. It had been raining, and the grooved surface of the Pad was wet and slippery. Behind him, less than twenty *ch'i* from where he stood, was a drop of almost two *li*. In front of him, more than two hundred *ch'i* away, was the stubby control tower for the Western Pad and, beyond it, rising into the pre-dawn darkness, was the slender communications spire of Bremen Fortress. Lamps embedded at the edge of the Pad, and at regular points within its floor, threw up broad columns of light. Between them were great patches of darkness. Chen smiled and began to walk towards the control tower, conscious of movement over there beneath the observation balcony.

It was like walking in a great hall, the light forming the pillars, the sky the ceiling. Normally he kept to the darkness, loath to breach those tall columns, but this once he made directly for the tower, his dark form cutting through the brilliant light, flashing and flickering, it seemed, until he was no more than twenty *ch'i* from the tower. There he stopped, facing the small group of men. Light from the windows of the tower created a pattern on the ground in front of him, but they were beyond that, in the shadows. Chen squinted, trying to make out who was there.

"Major Kao?"

Rheinhardt stepped from the shadows, into the light from above.

"General . . ."

"Where's Shang Mu. I thought . . ."

"Who's with you?"

He saw how Rheinhardt stared at him, surprised by the lack of deference in his tone. The General hesitated, not sure how to handle the situation, then shrugged and answered him. "Okay. I've brought three of my men. Bodyguards. Men I trust. The other two are yours. Captain Wilson and your sergeant."

Chen looked beyond the General. "Send the sergeant away."

Rheinhardt turned, made a gesture with his hand. At once one of the men turned and was gone.

Rheinhardt turned back. "So? Shall we get on with this?"

"You understand? What happened back there . . ."

"I understand. Guild, neh?"

Chen nodded. Then, turning, he put up a hand, waving back to the craft. A moment later two figures stepped down and began to make their way across.

He turned back. Rheinhardt was watching him strangely.

"What is it?" Chen asked.

"This . . ." Rheinhardt hesitated. "What you're talking about, it's . . ."

"Unbelievable?"

Rheinhardt nodded.

Chen turned, watching the two figures approach them through the darkness, a strange tension rooted in his stomach.

As Shang Mu came up beside him, Rheinhardt moved closer, until he was less than a body's length away.

"Junior Minister . . ."

Chen tensed, watching him hawkishly, his hand covering his gun. But Rheinhardt seemed unarmed.

"General . . ."

The two men bowed, then faced each other silently. Beside him, Hannah reached out and touched Chen's arm. He glanced at her and smiled.

"Well . . ." Rheinhardt said, after a moment. "I understand you've something to tell us. Major Kao tells me that . . ."

He broke off. Chen had moved – had walked across behind him, his gun drawn.

"Major Kao?"

Rheinhardt turned and saw at once. One of the four men had moved – was walking slowly to the right, circling outwards.

Chen moved across, keeping himself between the man and Shang Mu. As the man moved through a patch of light they saw who it was.

Chen hesitated, his gun wavering. *"Wilson?* What's up? What the hell's going on?"

Rheinhardt turned and yelled. "Get down, Shang Mu! Get down . . ."

There was a shot, a second shot. The Captain was running now, heading directly for Shang Mu, and as he ran he fired.

Chen knelt, his gun aimed, and fired. Once, twice, a third time his bullets hit the running man full in the chest, jolting him backwards and finally felling him. Wilson rolled and then lay still, his gun rattling away from him.

Chen turned, then stared, aghast. Shang Mu was down, groaning, both hands clutching his stomach.

"*Aiya!*" he said, getting up and staggering across. But it was too late. Even as he got there, Shang Mu spasmed and lay still. Chen looked up, meeting Hannah's eyes, seeing the shock there, the total disbelief.

"No . . ." she said, her voice tiny, frightened. "No . . ."

But it was done. Her father had been killed. And Rheinhardt . . . Rheinhardt just stared, a cold certainty in his face, and nodded.

*   *   *

"Cousin, what brings you here? This is a most unexpected delight!"

An Sheng came half-way up the cruiser's ramp to greet Fei Yen's father, embracing Yin Tsu, then stood back, holding him at arm's length, a broad grin on his face.

Yin Tsu tried to return his smile, but found he couldn't. He looked down, dismayed.

"What is it?" An Sheng asked quietly, his eyes concerned. "Your children are all well, I hope?"

Yin Tsu nodded vaguely. "Inside . . ." he said. "I have to talk to you, An Sheng. Something has happened . . ."

An Sheng considered, then nodded. "Come," he said, turning, taking Yin Tsu's arm in his own. "We'll go to my private rooms. I'll have Mo Shan bring us drinks."

Inside, in a large room overlooking an ornamental pond and garden, Yin Tsu sat on a long couch piled with cushions, while An Sheng stood nearby, one foot resting on the *kang*.

"So?" he said. "What has happened?"

Yin Tsu sighed, not knowing how to begin. *Our sons must die*, he thought, and found himself recalling Fei Yen's words about a deal. But no deals could be made with traitors.

359

Foolishness it might be, but it was a deadly foolishness and threatened them all. There was no alternative.

He looked up, meeting his cousin's eyes. "Your son and mine are traitors, An Sheng. They met . . . at my summer palace . . . and talked of rebellion . . . of killing the Seven."

An Sheng laughed, astonished, then frowned deeply. "You must be mistaken, Yin Tsu. Our *sons*?"

Yin Tsu nodded. "Yin Chan and An Hsi. Oh, there were others too, but those were the ringleaders."

An Sheng came and stood over him, looking down, his expression somewhere between anger and disbelief. "You must be wrong, Yin Tsu. An Hsi . . . he is a good son and loyal to the Seven. And your Chan . . ." He shook his head. "No. I won't believe it."

Yin Tsu's face was bleak. "Our sons must die, An Sheng. We must go to Li Yuan and tell him what happened."

"*Tell* him?"

Yin Tsu looked up, surprised by An Sheng's sudden anger. "Naturally . . ."

An Sheng glared at him, then turned away. One fist was bunched now. "You have proof, Yin Tsu?"

"My daughter, Fei Yen . . . she overheard them."

"Your *daughter*!" An Sheng laughed scathingly. "Your fine and precious daughter . . . the T'ang's wife!"

Yin Tsu looked up, stung by the acidity of the remark. "She would not lie to me . . ."

An Sheng turned back and leaned over him, his face ugly now. "No? And I suppose she never sleeps with grooms and serving boys, either!" He turned away, making a sound of disgust. "If that's all the evidence you have, Yin Tsu . . ."

"Cousin, why do you insult me like this?"

An Sheng turned, his eyes blazing. "Cousin, why do you insult *me* this way?"

"I . . ." Yin Tsu stood. "I think I had better go."

"*Go*?" An Sheng shook his head. "No, Yin Tsu. You come here full of rumour and the tittle-tattle of your whorish daughter and you expect me to offer up my son for such a pack of nothings? No, Yin Tsu." He drew his knife and took a step

360

towards the older man. "You will apologise, or I will have your blood!"

Yin Tsu stared at the knife in horror. "Cousin, I . . ."

An Sheng grasped the front of the old man's silks and held the knife against his throat. His face was fierce now, uncompromising. "Damn you old man, apologise! *Apologise!*"

Yin Tsu groaned, his eyes wide with fear. "Cousin . . . remember who we are . . ."

But An Sheng seemed beyond all reason. With a savage movement he jabbed the knife into the old man's neck, and then again. Yin Tsu shrieked, then collapsed onto his knees, coughing, choking on the blood that filled his throat.

An Sheng stood back, watching him, then let the knife fall from his hand. "Damn you, old man . . ." he said softly. "Damn you to hell!"

CHAPTER · 14

T'IEH PI PU KAI

The giant hologram stood between the dragon pillars, hands on its hips, staring down at the thousands of prisoners who knelt, naked, their hands tightly bound, in the body of the Great Hall. When it spoke its voice boomed, and when it moved, the air rustled, as if a great sail had been caught by the wind.

At first its face had been that of Li Yuan, but slowly it changed, until it was that of Tsu Ma. And as the face changed, so the body underwent a slow transformation, a broadening of the shoulders and chest, a thickening of leg and thigh. What did not alter was the sense of great dignity, of authority and power that emanated from the huge figure.

Li Yuan's opening address had set the tone, now Tsu Ma filled in the substance of the declaration. The Ministry was disbanded, as was the Guild. Security was to be purged, and the great web of connections between them and the Minor Families investigated. Finally, all servants of the Ministry were to be held pending trial, and those already known to have been actively involved in the coup attempt were to be executed.

There was a low murmur of fear among the prisoners. For many their first knowledge of this had been when they'd been dragged from their beds. A few of those looked up, yet hopeful that something might be saved, but for others who had some inkling of events – who had glimpsed the vague shadow of the plot, if not its details – there was no hope and they hung their heads abjectly. They knew this was the end and that only death awaited them, whatever the formalities.

For once the Seven had struck back at the enemies quickly and effectively. They had hit the central Ministry building two hours after dawn, taking away all its records and killing any who resisted. At the same time other forces had hit the regional offices. All Security officers with known Ministry connections had been disarmed and arrested, and all those members of the Minor Families known to be involved had been incarcerated. The swiftness of their action had, it seemed, pre-empted any real chance of a coup, yet the First Dragon himself, and many other important conspirators, remained at large, and while they did the Seven were unlikely to relax their vigilance.

As Tsu Ma concluded, he raised a fist larger than a man and brought it down like a hammer upon the air.

"T'ieh pi pu kai!"

For three thousand years government proclamations had ended with those words, yet for once they seemed momentous, *ominous*.

The iron pen changes not . . .

Iron . . . it was the symbol of firmness and strength, of determination, integrity and justice. Yes, and the means of execution.

Tsu Ma stepped back, folding his arms into the silk of his sleeves, the yellow cloth glistening like the sun, then slowly, slowly, he faded, until there was only darkness between the great dragon pillars.

From the far end of the hall came the sound of a scuffle, as guards grabbed two men by the hair and dragged them towards the doorway.

The beheadings had begun.

* * *

Nan Ho stared at the list, then looked back at the man who sat across from him.

An Sheng seemed relaxed, almost unconcerned by the accusations. He had denied them, of course, and claimed that his killing of Yin Tsu had been an act of blind passion resulting from a natural indignation, but Nan Ho did not believe him.

And the list? . . . well, he denied any knowledge of it, naturally. The list, taken from the dead Shang Mu's possession, was not in An Sheng's hand – the scribe who had copied it was in all probability long dead – yet he had no doubt it had been compiled at An Sheng's instigation. Ever since that confrontation with Li Yuan in the Hall of the Seven Ancestors over the Willow Plum Sickness, An Sheng had been waiting to get back at the young T'ang, planning for the day when he might avenge his humiliation, and this – this sweeping obliteration not merely of Li Yuan but of all those who had stood by him – would have been the perfect vengeance.

Of course, it would be hard to prove An Sheng's involvement in the coup. He had made sure his own hands were clean, and even where they weren't – as in the case of Yin Tsu – he had been careful to make it a separate matter, and had claimed his right to be tried by a tribunal of his peers. Special circumstances notwithstanding, unless they could find a crack in the wall of silence that surrounded him, An Sheng would escape all taint of traitorous behaviour. And, if precedent were anything to go by, he might yet evade the charge of murder too. Whatever they felt personally, it was unlikely that his peers would find him guilty. Of a lesser charge, perhaps. It was even feasible that they would make a deal – clearing him providing he stood down and let his eldest son, Mo Shan, take over as Head of Family in his place. And what real difference would *that* make?

No wonder the bastard's calm.

Nan Ho set the list aside, then cleared his throat. "You realise what has happened, Prince An?"

An Sheng shook his head disdainfully, refusing to meet the Chancellor's eyes. "I understand only that I have been wrongly taken from my house and detained without explanation. I wish to register the strongest complaint . . ."

"Your words are noted, Prince An, but these are exceptional circumstances. The Seven have met and . . ."

"Forgive me, Chancellor, but what has that to do with me? The matter with Yin Tsu was . . . unfortunate . . . but I have not denied anything. Nor have I hidden anything. The tapes of the incident have been handed to the *T'ing Wei* and I have placed myself at the mercy of my peers. What more could I do?"

Nan Ho bowed his head slightly, careful to conceal his irritation, then continued.

"As I said, the Seven have met and agreed a special Edict. As of tenth bell this morning Chung Kuo was under martial law. Furthermore a special investigation into the activity of the Ministry is under way and it is in *that* regard that you are here."

An Sheng shrugged. "I repeat. What has any of this to do with me?"

Nan Ho pulled a report sheet across, then tapped at his console. At once a record of An Sheng's contacts with the First Dragon appeared on the screen beside him, complete with date and duration of each visit.

"You knew the *I Lung* well, Prince An?"

"As well as any Minor Family Head, Chancellor. It was my business to know him."

"True . . . yet I see you met him only a few days ago. He came to see you at your palace. Isn't that . . . *unusual?*"

An Sheng tilted his head slightly. "Not unusual."

"No?" Nan Ho raised an eyebrow, surprised. "Twice in three years, I see, and the last time only days before the Ministry tries to overthrow the Seven. Tell me, Prince An, did the First Dragon seem . . . *preoccupied?*"

He watched. An Sheng had not reacted to his mention of the coup, and that in itself was unnatural. Indeed, this whole pretence of calm had the air of a rehearsed ploy. An Sheng was walking on thin ice and he knew it.

"I . . . noticed nothing. There was talk of the *wei chi* championships next year and who we thought might win . . . oh, and some gossip about the Lady Fei, but apart from that . . ." He shrugged, then looked down at his hands.

Nan Ho followed his gaze. An Sheng's hands rested lightly in his lap, the long nails painted with a pearl lacquer. As he watched, An turned one hand and flexed it like a claw, as if exercising it.

. . . or finding some focus, perhaps, for all the tension in you.

Nan Ho was silent a moment longer, then he tapped at the console, clearing the screen.

"That's all, Prince An. You may go now. But please keep my office advised of where you are at all times. If I want to speak with you again . . ."

"You'll find me at my palace, Chancellor," An Sheng interrupted, standing abruptly. Then, with the very minimum acknowledgment of Nan Ho's status, he turned and left the room.

Nan Ho sat back, letting his breath out in a long, exasperated sigh. He looked up at the camera.

"Well, *Chieh Hsia?*"

"He is guilty," Li Yuan answered. "I am certain of it now."

"And the Princess, Yin Fei Yen? Do you wish to see her and hear her evidence, *Chieh Hsia?*"

"No . . . I've heard enough. Now I must consult my cousins. I shall let you know what is decided, Master Nan. In the meantime step up the search for the *I Lung*. If we can take him . . ."

"Yes, *Chieh Hsia.*"

There was the soft chime of the dismissal tone. Li Yuan had gone. Nan Ho sat there a moment longer, staring at the list, then stood. This once there was no point in acting upon the T'ang's instruction. As it was, they had more than enough people out there looking for the First Dragon, but if the T'ang said more, he would send out more. They would not find him, even so, for either he was dead already or he was off-planet – either way they would never know. At best they would capture one or other of his brothers, though even that was unlikely.

And what now? Nan Ho asked himself, walking to the window and looking out across the sunlit gardens. Without the Thousand Eyes watching the levels, who would now guard the Great Secret of their collective past? Who now would keep the people ignorant? Would it stay there, buried in the darkness? Or would it all come seeping back now, like blood through a sheet?

He gritted his teeth. Uncertainties, that was all they had from here on. They had abandoned History and now it had abandoned them. There were no precedents for this, no handholds up the steep cliff-face of the future. It was all improvised from this point on. Each man for himself, and beware the man who falls.

Even so, to have survived at all was something.

He went out, into the garden, and stood there a moment in the spring sunlight, his head tilted back, drinking in the freshness of the day.

Yes, to have come this far . . .

He laughed, then, sobered by the thought of all that lay ahead, he made his way down the broad white steps and past the carp pond, heading for the cells.

* * *

"Well, cousin, what do you think?"

Wu Shih frowned, then gave a reluctant nod. "I do not like this, Yuan, yet I agree with Tsu Ma. To let him live is unthinkable . . . No. An Sheng must not come to trial. He must die. How you do that . . . well, I leave it to you, cousin. But do it soon. While things are yet confused."

Li Yuan, looking down at Wu Shih from the screen, nodded. "It seems we must bury our consciences, neh, old friend? Necessity's the force that moves us now."

"Then let us be ruthless and have done with it. I for one have more than enough troubles without this added burden."

"That woman, eh?"

Wu Shih nodded. *"That woman . . ."*

"Well, good luck, cousin. We shall both need our fair share of it, neh?"

Wu Shih bowed, then cut contact. *That woman . . .*

"Master Pao?"

"Chieh Hsia?"

He turned, looking at his Master of the Inner Chambers.

367

"Get Kennedy for me. Tell him we have to talk. And ask Fen Cho-hsien to come through. We must deal with this matter at once."

Pao En-fu bowed low, then turned and hurried away. Wu Shih went across to his desk and sat, pulling at his beard. As far as Mary Lever was concerned, they had miscalculated badly. Her broadcasts had not merely been successful, they had been phenomenal. Unknown to them, she had organised a whole network of "wives", women she had worked with on previous funding projects. They in their turn had organised parties and social gatherings across the City, timed to coincide with the broadcasts. Using those as focal points for her recruitment drive, she had managed to sign up close to five million subscribers at the first attempt. And then, this morning, while the business with the Ministry was distracting them, she had gone on air again, to advertise her success and to discuss the next step forward.

I should have pulled the plug at once. I should have . . .

"*Chieh Hsia*? I have the Representative on hold."

"Good. Then put him through. It's time he learned a few truths . . ."

* * *

The man groaned. It was a small sound, almost forgetful in nature, as if he had suffered so much already that this little extra were as nothing to him, yet Nan Ho, watching him, could see he was on the edge. Either he would confess and it would be over, or he was innocent and he would go mad.

It was not much of a choice.

Nan Ho stepped outside, then stood there, taking a long deep breath of the cleaner air of the corridor. Two men lay in the cells, their bodies racked, their flesh burned and mutilated. One of them had been bought, the other was completely innocent. Yet which was which? Only these two – clerks to the Master of the Inner Chambers – had had access to detailed information of the staff here at Tongjiang, and only one of them could have passed on that information to An Sheng for his list. It was possible, of course, that both were guilty, but that was not usually the way of it. To buy two men was more dangerous than hiring one – for when there were two, one might think to sell the other or, after some quarrel, betray him out of spite, whereas a single spy . . .

He stopped, realising where his thoughts had led. Five years ago he had stood beside Tolonen, watching an innocent man being torn apart in these same cells, and all to save the worthless reputation of his Master's wife. Back then he had thrown up, appalled by the physical damage that had been done to the young man; horrified that, after so much pain, the boy should still resist. And yet just now . . .

If the truth be told, he had felt nothing, or at best a vague regret at the necessity. Had he changed so much in that brief time? Had his skin grown so thick that nothing touched him now? Had power made him callous?

Or maybe the world had changed, and his expectations of it likewise. Not that he had any option in this case, for if there was a traitor in their midst – and the list more than suggested that there was – then it was his duty to unearth him. Feelings . . . they did not enter into this.

He turned, listening. There was a shouting further down, in the first cell. A moment later the door swung back and one of the guards stepped out, his face flushed, his bare chest misted with sweat.

"Excellency! I think we're there!"

"Ah . . ." He went across, then ducked inside. The prisoner had lifted his head and was staring across at him, wild-eyed. "Well?" he asked. "What have you to say?"

"Forgive me, Master Nan . . . I never meant . . ." His head fell back and he broke down, sobbing.

"No," Nan Ho felt sorry for him now that it was done. He turned, waving one of the guards through to stop the torture in the other cell, then looked back at the man, placing his hand softly, almost tenderly on his brow. "Tell me, Chen So. How did it happen?"

He looked away, swallowing, unable to meet Nan Ho's eyes, clearly ashamed. "It was the girl, Excellency . . ."

"The girl?" He caught his breath. "What girl?"

"The Master's maid . . . Heart's Delight . . . She was my lover. I . . ."

"*Aiya!*"

Nan Ho turned and left at once, hurrying up the stairs. At the top he burst through the door, knocking the guard aside, and began to run, his heart in his mouth. Then, finding his voice again, he called the guards to him, frantic now, wondering if he wasn't already too late.

* * *

Kennedy turned from the screen, Wu Shih's words ringing loudly in his ears.

"*This is your last chance, Mister Kennedy. Just silence that damned woman, all right? Silence her!*"

Sure. But how? There wasn't anything he could offer Mary Lever, and there seemed to be no way he could threaten her, so what did that leave? Gentle persuasion? Seduction? Murder?

He shivered, uneasy with that last thought, then looked up, realising that his wife Jean was standing in the doorway watching him.

"What is it?" she asked. "You look troubled . . ."

He shrugged, then went across and held her a moment. "What would you like . . . I mean, what would you *really* like to do, if you had the choice?"

She looked up at him, frowning. "What is this? Have you gone mad or something?"

"No. Just answer me. One thing . . ."

She thought for a moment, then smiled. "I know. I'd like to paddle in the sea . . . you know, the *real* sea. Just walk along the shoreline, like in one of those old trivids."

"Okay. We'll do it. Tomorrow. And we'll take the boys. Make a day of it."

She laughed. "Now I *know* you've gone mad!"

"First though, I've got to contact someone. Arrange a meeting."

* * *

Nan Ho burst into Li Yuan's rooms unceremoniously, half-running down the corridor, afraid what he would find. He was about to go through to the bedroom when he came face to face with his T'ang as he emerged from one of the side rooms.

"*Chieh Hsia!*" he exclaimed, falling to his knees, relieved beyond words.

"What *is* the matter, Master Nan? You looked for a moment as if you had seen a ghost!"

Nan Ho bowed his head. "Forgive me, Master, but for one brief moment I feared that that was *all* I would see!"

Li Yuan tensed. "What is it?"

"Your maid, *Chieh Hsia* . . . Heart's Delight . . ."

"What of her?"

"One of the Clerks of the Inner Chamber . . . she was his lover. It seems . . ."

Li Yuan raised a hand, ahead of his Chancellor. "I understand . . . And you thought . . ." He shuddered. "It's strange. I asked for her earlier and one of the other maids said she hadn't been feeling well and had gone to her room. I didn't think . . ."

"Nor I, *Chieh Hsia*," Nan Ho said, his voice heavy with apology.

"Go find her, Master Nan. Then bring her here. I want to know why. I want . . ." He stopped, clearly pained, then shook his head. "It is difficult to believe. I slept with her, Master Nan, not once but many times. Such a sweet and loving girl. I'd never . . ." He shivered again, then, "Go bring her, Master Nan. Now!"

Nan Ho bowed again then hurried off to find her.

* * *

The entrance to the corridor was decked out in blue and gold. To one side a group of shaven-headed boys – orphans, picked for their photogenic qualities – queued behind a rope, waiting for their handouts. In front of them, dressed in the simple brown of the Eldest Daughter, stood Emily. She turned, waving the hand-carts through, then stepped back, looking up into the lens of the floater-camera.

371

"This, then, is the first phase of our work down here. As you can see, we have recruited workers from these levels to do the actual manual work – the loading and distribution of the food and clothing. Others are repairing those shops we've already bought – shops which will be used not merely as distribution points but as help and advice centres. We have begun with a core of five hundred, but as our campaign grows it's hoped that there'll be at least one of these shops in every stack in City North America, providing not only food and clothing but also advice and useful pamphlets on all manner of issues. Each of these shops will be instantly recognisable – like our carts and helpers – by the distinctive livery of blue and gold. The gold represents the life-giving sun, the blue the nurturing water."

She moved back slightly, letting the floater take in the line of carts as it moved past her.

"However, let me emphasise once again that it is not our aim to nursemaid these people. Our aim is to give them back their dignity. By giving them work, we give them a purpose in life, and by giving them food, we give them the strength to move forward. Once we have allayed their fears and dealt with their most basic needs, we can begin to tackle the real problems – problems we all, as inhabitants of this great City, have to face. The problems of meaning and direction."

From where he stood at the control board near by, Beresiner looked up, then drew his finger across his throat. At once the overhead lights dimmed.

"Great!" he said. "I'll inter-cut it with shots of the men stacking the carts and preparing the shops then add the piece you did earlier. We've got a slot at one thirty, after the lunchtime news, and another at three. We can run it then."

Emily nodded, then looked about her, feeling an immense satisfaction at all she saw. It had begun. She was finally doing something worthwhile. Not what she'd set out to do, perhaps, but effective none the less. And maybe better, in a sense, for at least this way she could sleep nights.

"Has Michael rung?" she asked.

Beresiner shook his head. "Not that I know. Ask Jill. She's fielding all incoming just now!"

Emily went across. They had set up a control room on one side of Main. From there her Principal Helper, Jill, was running the show.

"Hi! Has Michael rung?"

"Not yet . . ."

Emily frowned, surprised. "Okay. So what's been coming in? Anything of interest?"

Jill stared at her a moment, half-smiling, like she had some big secret, then handed a slip of paper across.

Emily read it, then looked up sharply. "*Kennedy*? He wants to meet?"

"Looks like it. It came in five minutes back. What shall I do? Tell him to fuck himself? Mind you, he's probably the only one who hasn't!"

"Now . . ." But Emily was smiling. There was so much spirit here. So much real desire to change things. She sighed. "Okay. I'll see what he wants. But make sure he understands there'll be no deals. Tell him we don't need to make deals."

Jill smiled. "Okay, but he'll try, anyway, you know that. It's how these men are. They think no means yes. It's how they were bred."

"Sure. But it's going to change. We're going to make it change, right?"

"Right. Oh, and Gloria called. Says the total's gone past fifteen million. We're going to have to recruit more people to process all of this."

"Good. Then hire them. Anything else?"

"Hythe-MacKay are suing for use of their livery colours . . ."

"Fight it."

"And a reporter from MedFac's Downline channel called. He wants to interview you."

"Downline, huh?" She considered a moment, then nodded. "Okay. We can do it here."

"You sure that's wise? What if it's a set-up? What if he's out to humiliate you?"

373

Emily smiled. "Let him try. He gets out of hand, I'll break his jaw!"

Jill laughed. "Thatta-girl! Okay. I'll arrange it for six. That all right with you?"

"That's fine. Now I'd better get running." She hesitated. "You sure Michael hasn't been in touch?"

* * *

"Things are bad," Johnson said, throwing a stack of old-fashioned files into Michael's in-tray. "We've achieved only twenty per cent of our enrolment targets. If this goes on we'll be bust by the year's end!"

"Sit tight," Michael said, smiling back at him. "Things will change. They may be scared off right now, but it won't last. And the chance to live forever – who else is offering that?"

"Maybe . . . but it's hurting us, Michael. The kind of people we're trying to attract . . . well, they're put off by what Mary's doing. More than put off, in fact – some of them are incensed!"

Michael shrugged. "So what do you suggest? You fancy walking in to Mary and telling her she's got to pull the plug? You want *that* job, Dan?"

Johnson shook his head, then looked away, exasperated. "You don't like this, do you? I mean, all this pandering to the old men . . ."

"No. I feel a fraud. But it's necessary if we're going to get the rest of the package through. Healthcare and decent pay for our employees, that's a good goal, wouldn't you say? A damn sight better than the single-minded pursuit of profit! If a few rich bastards want to pay for all that then I'm sure as hell not going to stop them!"

"You sound just like Mary . . ."

He laughed. "Do I?" Then, "Oh, shit . . . I didn't call her . . ."

The comset on the desk beside him started flashing.

"Maybe that's her . . ."

Michael leaned forward. "Yes?"

374

It was his secretary's voice. "*Shih* Lever? It's Representative Kennedy."

"Joe . . ." He looked to Johnson, then waved him away. "I'll take it."

He stood up and walked across as the screen came down on the far side of the office.

A lifesize Joseph Kennedy faced him, a sad smile on his lips.

"Michael . . . how are you?"

He smiled. "I'm fine, Joe. And you?"

Kennedy shrugged. "So so. You know how it is."

"I'm . . ."

"No. Don't apologise. You were right, Michael. You *and* Mary. I should have fought my ground much harder. I gave too much. I . . ." He shrugged.

"What can I do for you, Joe?"

"It wasn't you I wanted, to be honest. It's Mary, I . . ." There was a buzzing behind him. He turned, looking off-screen. "Hold on, my secretary's saying something to me. What's that? Oh. Okay."

He turned back. "Well, what do you know? That was your wife's office, returning my call."

Michael smiled. "Whatever it is, you won't persuade her."

"No?" Kennedy laughed softly. "Maybe not. You know, you married well, Michael. Out of your level, and I don't mean that in any pejorative sense. She's one in ten billion, I realise that now."

"Sure. So why are you seeing her?"

"Just going through the motions. You know how it is. Politics . . ."

"I never thought I'd hear you say that."

"No? Nor I . . . But I'm tired, Michael. Bone-weary. This life . . . I didn't think it would be this hard. That buzz we got when we were winning . . . you know, I thought it would last forever. I really thought . . . Still. History now, eh?"

"It doesn't have to be."

"No. It's done with now. I'll be stepping down. Let

375

someone else take on the burden. Parker, maybe. Or Fisher. Someone younger."

"Shit . . . you're only thirty-five. You've a good thirty years in you yet!"

"You trying to talk me back into it, Michael?"

Michael shook his head. "No. I know how you feel. After Bryn died . . . it was never the same."

"No . . . Well, I'd better get some work done. I've promised Jean I'd take her somewhere tomorrow, so I'd best clear my desk." He paused, as if reluctant to go, his eyes misted. "I miss you, Michael. Miss working with you."

"Yeah . . . Still . . . take care, huh?"

"And you . . ."

Michael stood there afterwards, feeling strange, and not knowing why.

It was true what Kennedy had said. You did things, thinking it would always be the same, but it changed. It always changed. That was the only certainty in this life.

* * *

She lay on her back on the bed, her vacant face staring up into the sunlight from the nearby window. She seemed to be asleep, but there was no movement of her chest and when Nan Ho touched her arm, he found the flesh was cold.

He turned to the guard, behind him in the doorway. "Bring Surgeon Lu. And tell him to fetch a resuscitation unit."

It was probably too late, but . . .

He turned back, looking about the room for some clue as to how she had died. There was no apparent wound on her, no scent of gas, no sign of any medications. But there was something. A note. He unfolded it, then went to the window and read it through.

An Sheng . . . It named An Sheng!

He looked at her again, pitying her. It seemed An Sheng had taken her mother and younger brother and was holding them against her "good behaviour".

He sighed. This was an ill day's work. Yet at least An

Sheng was theirs. He went out to the doorway as two guards ran up. He handed one the note. "You . . . take this to the T'ang. And you, wait here and guard the door until Surgeon Lu arrives."

Then, with a final glance at the dead girl, he left, making his way back to his offices.

It was time to get An Sheng.

* * *

Emily was late, but Kennedy had waited. A bodyguard frisked her outside the door, then, satisfied, knocked and pushed the door back. It was an unexpectedly small room. Kennedy was to her right, seated at a table, talking into a small comset. As she stepped inside he looked up and smiled, then hastily signed off.

He stood, coming round the table, offering his hand. "Mary . . ."

She took it, then looked about her. "So? What do you want?"

His smile broadened. "No small talk, huh?"

She looked at him: a clear, cold look. "We're both busy people. Besides, I'm sure you didn't ask me here to discuss my health."

He laughed. "No. Okay . . . I'll come right to the point. I want to know if you'll call off your Eldest Daughter campaign."

"Why?"

He shrugged. "You're making things difficult, that's all. For me . . . and for Michael . . ."

"Michael can speak for himself."

"Sure. Then for me."

She shook her head, surprised at him. "I don't get you, Joseph Kennedy. There was a time when you professed to want change. You said you wanted to help the Lowers. What went wrong?"

He sighed. "I take it that's a no."

"Absolutely." She looked at him a moment, expecting something more, then, "Is that it? No cogent arguments, no

clever reasons why I should give it up? I'm surprised, Joe.
You never used to give in so easily."

"No. Maybe not." He seemed strangely relaxed now, as
if somehow a burden had been lifted from him. "I had to try,
but . . . well, I'm glad. You do what you have to, Mary Lever.
I admire you for it, really I do." He smiled again, but this
time it seemed pained, for some reason much more sincere
than the smiles she was used to from him. "We've never got
on very well, have we? I guess that was my fault. I should
have made more of an effort. But you were right. All those
compromises . . . they're not worth making. The game's not
worth the candle!"

She stared at him, astonished, then laughed. "You're taking
the piss, right?"

He shook his head. "No. And I wish you luck. I really do.
Maybe you'll get done what I failed to do. Oh, and thanks for
the second gift . . . you know, the newspaper. It seems us
Kennedy's don't have much luck, eh?"

She shivered, surprised. "You've made a decision, huh?"

He nodded. "I'm stepping down. I'm going to announce it
tomorrow night. I've booked a slot."

"Ah . . ."

He held his hand out again. "It's goodbye then."

She looked down at it, frowning, then, surprising him, put
out her arms and held him to her a moment.

"Good luck, Joseph Kennedy . . ."

Then, turning away, she left.

He stared at the door a moment, a strange, pained
expression on his face, then, sighing, he looked about him
once again and, seeing nothing there to keep him, followed
her out.

* * *

As the cruiser settled, An Sheng unbuckled himself, nervously looking out through the porthole to his right. Nothing.
He scuttled across to the other side and looked out. Nothing!
Fucking nothing! He hissed with rage, then turned, looking
about him.

378

What if it didn't come? What if . . .

He went to the back of the craft.

"Open it!" he barked. *"Now!"*

The guard hit the release pad. The hatch began to open.

An Sheng stared out as the gap widened. *Come on*, he urged. *Be there!*

But there was nothing. The roof of the City stretched away to the horizon, a flat, dirty-white plain, broken here and there by the up-jutting shape of a ventilation shaft.

He stepped down, chewing at his knuckles. The bastard had *promised* – he'd given his fucking word!

There was a faint noise, carried on the breeze, like the hum of an insect. He turned full circle, shading his eyes, then looked back at the ship. "Where's south?"

The guard pointed past him.

He turned, looking, staring hard for a long time until he finally saw it – *there!* – high up, coming in from the south-west.

It was coming! Thank the gods! Wang Sau-leyan had kept his promise, after all!

He watched it grow larger, the growl of its engines growing all the while. Then, as it settled, he ran across to it, a wave of relief and exultation replacing the heaviness – the *dread* – he'd been feeling all day.

As the hatch hissed open and the ramp unfolded towards him, he glimpsed an honour guard waiting within. Then, as the ramp flattened, a man he recognised as one of Wang Sau-leyan's senior household staff stepped out and bowed low. "Prince An, if you would be our guest . . . ?"

He turned, dismissing his own craft, then climbed up onto the ramp. Africa . . . he would be safe in Africa.

Inside he sat in a chair of soft silk cushions while a girl massaged his neck and a servant brought him wine.

Thank the gods for good wine, he thought, remembering the night with Fifth Brother, when he had first learned of this "rabbit hole". *And thank the gods too for serving girls*, for without serving girls and wine, he would never have unhinged the bastard's tongue.

Yes, and wouldn't the *I Lung* be surprised to see him? That was one reunion he was really looking forward to.

And Wang Sau-leyan? Wang would use him, he was certain of it. How and for what purpose he did not know, but it was better than being dead, and certainly a lot better than bowing to that bastard Li Yuan.

"Is all to your satisfaction, Excellency?"

He smiled and nodded. "Most excellent, thank you." Then, closing his eyes, he let himself relax, the soft pressure of the girl's hands on his chest making him think that exile might not be so bad a thing after all.

* * *

The reporter came across and stood before her, leaning in over the desk in an almost threatening manner. "She's late," he said.

"Yes," Jill answered, looking up at him wearily. "I know. She sometimes is."

"Half an hour late."

She stared back at him. "She'll be here. Okay?"

He turned away, clearly angry. But it wasn't his anger that disturbed her, so much as his nervousness. He seemed quite agitated, unduly concerned at Mary's tardiness. At first she'd put it down to work pressure – no doubt some producer was on his back to deliver something fast – but when she'd asked, he'd muttered something about it going out the next day. And that had struck her as odd. Stations like Downline didn't usually sit on things longer than an hour, let alone all night. But his accreditation was okay and a quick check on the central file showed he'd been working there seven years now. So why the nervousness? Or was it Mary? Was he nervous at meeting Mary?

She looked down again. Maybe that was it. Maybe this was his big chance and he was shit scared he'd fuck it up somehow. Well, if he had any sense he'd simply ask the first question, point the microphone at Mary and let her roll.

The desk com buzzed. She answered it, looking down into the tilted screen. "Yes?"

"It's Michael again . . . he wants to know if she's back yet."

"No. Tell him I'll let him know just as soon as she gets here, okay?"

"Right . . ."

She cut contact and looked up. The reporter was coming back across.

"Was that her?"

Jill hesitated, then nodded. "Sure. She said she'd be here in ten minutes. Okay?"

He nodded, then turned and went back to where he'd been sitting. Getting out a handset, he murmured something into it.

Rehearsing, she thought, then turned, taking the latest print-out from the tray behind her. Twenty-two million, and still they were rolling in. At this rate they would hit their first target by tomorrow lunch-time and could begin the second phase – a full week earlier than they'd anticipated.

She sat back, smiling. All her life she'd been looking for something useful to do – something meaningful – and suddenly, out of the blue, it had been dumped in her lap. She laughed. Like a miracle. And Mary . . . her smile broadened . . . Mary . . . she was like Kuan Yin herself, the Goddess of Mercy, the Bestower of All Gifts.

Mary . . . She looked down, sighing. Why, she was half in love with Mary Lever.

* * *

The guard put out his arm, barring her way.

"I'm sorry, but you can't go down there."

"But I'm Mary Lever. I . . . ."

"I know who you are, Ma'am, but there's been an incident. We've got a squad in, sorting it out."

"An incident?"

"I . . ." He hesitated, conscious of the press of people beyond her, then turned and called to the group of guards beyond him. "Lieutenant!"

The young officer came across and, seeing who it was, bowed low, the light of deep respect in his eyes.

"Madam Lever . . . if you would come through to the office."

She followed him through, then sat the other side of the desk to him, her hands clasped anxiously together.

"Okay. What's been happening?"

"I'm afraid there's been some trouble. Your campaign post was . . . hit, let's say. It looks like the work of three or four men. We're looking at the camera evidence right now. It . . ."

He looked up at her.

"Please, Madam Lever. If you'd sit down again. There's nothing you can do. As I was saying . . ."

"I've got to go there," she said, staring back at him. "Don't you understand? I've got to *see* what's happened."

He swallowed. "There's not much to see, I'm afraid. They . . . well, they didn't leave much."

"What do you mean?"

"I . . . I'll see if the Captain will talk to you. Maybe he'll . . ." He hesitated, then shook his head. "Look, you really don't want to see it, okay? It's . . ."

She leaned across the desk at him. "*You* don't understand, Lieutenant. I have to see it. I have to *know* what my enemies are capable of – what they'll do to stop me. No matter how bad it is, I *have* to see it."

"I . . ." He nodded, then stood, going to the door. "Give me a minute, Madam Lever. I'll speak to the Captain."

Emily waited, a cold, hard certainty at the pit of her stomach. Kennedy. This was *his* work. No wonder he'd made no effort to persuade her. And that was just like him – just like his kind – to keep her out of it to spare Michael's feelings.

She shuddered with indignation and a cold, hard rage. If it was him, she would have him. She would kill him with her own two hands.

They were dead, she knew it. Jill and Anna, Eva and Bess, and all the others who'd stayed on the extra hour, waiting for her to get back. Dead, every one. She closed her eyes, trying to keep the anger uppermost, trying hard not to succumb to the great upswell of grief she felt at the thought of their deaths.

No, she told herself sternly. *You have to be strong, Emily Ascher. Weep later. Right now you must be hard and unyielding, like iron.*

She took a long, deep breath, then went to the door and stood there, waiting for the officer to return.

CHAPTER · 15

<u>HOLOGRAMS</u>

Kennedy knelt before the tiny altar, facing his great-great-grandfather. A scented spill burned in the pot between him and the figure, its smoke curling and drifting through the bright planes of the hologram.

The old man was looking down at his progeny, concerned, one hand extended slightly, as if to comfort him.

"Your problems are grave ones, Joseph, yet you must look within yourself and find the inner strength to cope with them."

Kennedy looked down, his eyes tormented. "It is no use, grandfather. I've tried, yet I can find no peace. Wherever my eyes look there are walls, inside and out. Sleep evades me, and when it comes it is tormented by dreams in which every man's hand is raised against me."

The old man was silent a moment, as if this situation had taxed the limitations of his programming, then he sighed.

"There is only one solution, Joseph. You must retire from public life for a time. Become a sleeping dragon. Yet even as I suggest this I can't help but feel that you're holding something back from me. A man grows tired of the world, certainly, but you are young and at the height of your powers. I cannot understand . . ."

"We live in different times, grandfather. There was more certainty in your age. A man *knew* what was expected of him. But now . . . well, the rules change daily."

The old man shrugged. "If you say so, Joseph – yet I find it strange. If a man is truly himself he is like a rock, and though the waters rise, they will flow about him, and when they recede he will still be there, solid and unmoved, while all else has been swept away."

His eyes dwelt on his great-great-grandson a moment. "You must decide what kind of man you wish to be, Joseph. A leaf or a rock."

Kennedy bowed low, then took the spill from the pot. At once the misted figure vanished, leaving the room feeling cold and empty.

He stood slowly, an ache of tiredness in his limbs, a heaviness in his chest. If he had thought to find answers here he had been wrong. Yet the old man was right in one respect – he had to make a choice, and not merely about his political future. Much more was at stake than that.

As he came out of the room he stopped, surprised to find his wife, Jean, waiting there for him.

"What is it?"

Her voice was quiet, frightened. "There's been an attack. On Mary Lever's headquarters."

"*Aiya* . . . When was this?"

"An hour back. Details are only just coming through. They're not sure who carried it out – no one's claimed it yet – but there are rumours it might have been the Black Hand."

He shivered, then let her lead him through. An hour back . . .

"I must phone Michael . . ."

"Don't you think he'll have enough to worry about . . ."

"No," he shook his head," you don't understand. I was probably the last person to see her. I met her . . . an hour and a half back. I . . . Oh shit! They were probably waiting for her . . ."

She stared at him. "You *met* her? Why?"

"Wu Shih. He wanted me to persuade her. I knew I couldn't, but I met her anyway. I wanted to . . . well, to tell her she was right. To build bridges, I guess. I . . ." He sighed heavily, then went across to the vid-phone and tapped out Michael's private contact number, turning to look back at Jean as he waited to be connected.

"Wu Shih *asked* you?"

He nodded. "He said it was my last chance."

He saw the movement in her face – the realisation of what that meant. Like himself, she and his sons were wired, small control strips inserted in their skulls. If Wu Shih had lost patience he might choose to use those devices to harm or maim them. Kennedy looked away, pained by the thought of it. That threat – that constant shadow – had been with him more than two years now, yet he had never grown used to it. Not for a single moment. Wherever they went – whatever they did – they were never free of it. It made hostages of them all.

As the screen chimed he turned back, looking up into Michael Lever's face.

"Michael . . ."

"Joe! You've heard, then . . ."

"Just now. I . . . Is Mary . . . ?"

"She's fine."

"Thank the gods!" He laughed, relieved. "What happened?"

Michael frowned. "It's not clear yet, but it looks like they were after Mary. The whole thing was set up very carefully . . ."

Kennedy stared at his old friend a moment, then nodded. "I'm sorry. It must be a nightmare. Look, I'll leave you be. If there's anything I can do . . ."

"Sure. Thanks . . ."

He cut connection, then turned. Jean was still watching him.

"What?" he asked, for once unable to read her.

She came across and held him, clinging to him, it seemed, as if afraid to let go. "Let's get away," she said, a real urgency in her voice. "Now. While we still can."

* * *

Wu Shih stared up at the screen, watching as a very angry Mary Lever talked into camera, pouring out all of her hurt and frustration for the viewing billions. Most of the T'ang's senior officials stood behind him in the room. They had gathered at his urgent summons. Now they waited, wondering what he would do.

As the item finished, Wu Shih turned, his own anger on a very short fuse. "Doesn't anyone have *any* information on this?"

Fen Cho-hsien looked about him, then decided to act as spokesman for them all. "First indications, *Chieh Hsia*, are that it's the Black Hand. The ruthlessness of the attack . . ."

". . . could have been carried out by almost anyone," Wu Shih interrupted him. "No, Master Fen, I don't believe it's that simple. Besides, I thought we'd dealt with those bastards. Are you telling me that even after our action against them, they were still able to put a six-man squad into the field at a moment's notice?"

"Maybe we were not as successful as we thought. It was, after all, hard to tell just how much of their organisation we destroyed. This would surely be a perfect way for them to demonstrate that they survived our action."

"And have they *claimed* this outrage?"

Fen Cho-hsien looked down. All there knew the answer. "No, *Chieh Hsia*. But maybe that is because they would not wish to be associated with it publicly. They have as much reason as us to fear what she is doing, yet Mary Lever has won a great deal of support among what they see as their natural constituency. Word has got out down there about what she has been doing and a number of the media channels that serve the Lowers have picked up on the story. The Black Hand would know that and would undoubtedly want to do something about it. Any strengthening of her hand would be a weakening of theirs. The only answer would be to kill her. But to kill her and admit it . . . that would be a different thing."

Wu Shih stroked his beard, considering this, then frowned. "What you say has merit, Master Fen. Even so, I remain unconvinced. I have read General Althaus's reports on the action against the Hand, and I tend to agree with his conclusions. We may not have destroyed their whole network, but we inflicted enough damage on them to make it unlikely, if not perhaps impossible for them to mount an attack like this for some time. Yet if it wasn't them, who was it? Who else would want Mary Lever dead?"

"The Old Men, perhaps, *Chieh Hsia*?"

Wu Shih turned to his Minister of Trade. "Old men? Which old men, Minister Yun?"

"Forgive me, *Chieh Hsia*. I refer to a group of individuals who have formed a covert organisation dedicated to bringing down Michael Lever. These are primarily his major trading rivals, but there are a lot of other interested parties, including a number of Lever's father's former allies."

"I see. And you think it's possible they might have had a hand in this?"

"More than possible, *Chieh Hsia*. To strike at Lever through his wife would be a most effective way of weakening him. It is said that he has relied heavily on her since his accident."

Wu Shih nodded. It was an interesting possibility, and the more he thought about it, the more sense it made. He had known, of course, that Michael Lever had made enemies, but it had not come to his notice that such opposition was organised. If they could *use* that . . .

He went across and stood before his Minister. "Find out what you can about them, Minister Yun and, if necessary, offer them encouragement. But be careful to make sure no trail comes to this door. If they succeed, they alone must be seen to be to blame."

"*Chieh Hsia*!"

"Now go . . . I wish to be alone."

Slowly they filed from the room. Only his Chancellor, Fen Cho-hsien, hung back.

"Yes, Master Fen?"

"Forgive me, *Chieh Hsia*, but one small matter remains."

Wu Shih nodded, understanding without needing to be reminded. He had still to decide what to do about Kennedy.

It was very simple. His attempts to use Kennedy to bridle the North American radicals had failed. The threat to his family had brought some success, but increasingly Kennedy had tugged against the bit. The knife had been held to his throat too long, perhaps and, lacking use, the weapon had lost its edge. Maybe it was time to remind him of its sharpness.

"All right," he said, "I want you to do this . . ."

* * *

Michael heard the front door slam and got up hurriedly from his desk. Crossing to the door, he cursed the harness for slowing him down, yet without a succession of the lightweight exoskeletons he'd never have got close to being mobile again. *Alive*, he reminded himself. *We're both still alive . . . hang on to that!*

He stopped just outside the door, seeing her at the far end of the hallway, talking to the staff who had gathered to greet her. For a moment he gazed at her, relieved simply to see her there, afraid that the image of her he'd seen on the screen had been a lie, then, starting towards her, he called her name.

"Em . . ."

She turned, seeing him, then rushed across and embraced him, burying her head in his chest, her hands gripping his back fiercely.

"Em . . . Em . . ." he murmured, kissing the crown of her head, close to tears suddenly. "Was it awful?"

She looked up at him. "I've got to speak out, Michael. In public . . ."

"I thought you said plenty," he said, beginning to smile, but she put a finger to his lips.

"No. I mean about the old men . . . and Kennedy. All of it. What a stinking mess it all is. I've got to let them know."

He frowned. "Kennedy? Why Kennedy?"

There was a sudden anger in her eyes. "Because he was behind this."

"No . . . You're wrong, Em. Joe . . . he just wouldn't do something like that. It's not . . ."

". . . his style?" She shivered. The tension in her was palpable. "Then why the meeting? It makes no sense. No, not unless he wanted me safely out of the way while his hirelings butchered my people."

Michael stared at her, astonished. "No . . . *No*, Em. He's not like that. Besides, he called me just after the news broke. He seemed really shaken up by it. Concerned for you . . ."

"*Concerned?* Wise up, Michael. What else *would* he do? No, it was a warning. First the meeting, the polite request to back off, and then the attack . . ."

"It was a coincidence, that's all. Shit . . . you being with him, that probably saved your life!"

She stared at him. "*What?*"

"Think, Em. Think hard. Just what would he gain by having you killed?"

"Nothing. But you're not listening to me, Michael. He wasn't trying to kill me, just warn me off."

"But why? I can't see why."

"Maybe because what I'm doing shows up the hollowness of all his posturing. And maybe because he blames me for what happened with you."

He closed his eyes. "*Aiya . . .*"

"It's true, Michael. You just can't see it, that's all!"

"Look, I know you're angry, Em . . . and hurt. But you're not thinking straight. You should calm down. Count to ten . . ."

"No . . ." She pushed away from him, angry with him suddenly. "I could count to a million and this feeling wouldn't go from me. They've got to be *stopped*, Michael, before they kill us all."

"Em . . . Sweetheart . . ."

She put her hands up, fending off his attempt to embrace her again. "No, Michael. Listen to me. My anger . . . it's the only thing I've got. I have to speak out. To say what hasn't been said and show what hasn't been shown. It's my duty . . . can't you *see* that?"

"Sure. I understand. But look . . . you have to step back. This once you just have to. Tomorrow. Do it tomorrow, once you've had time to think things through a little more coolly. Right now . . . well, right now is not the time. Security have promised results . . . and fast. So let them announce the findings of their investigation. Then speak up. I'll back you . . . you know I will. But don't fly at it like this. It'll only rebound on you. And I'd hate to see that."

She stared at him, slowly calming, then gave a tiny nod.

"Good," he said, reaching out and holding her to him again. "Now come through. I think we could both do with a stiff drink."

* * *

Nan Ho sat back, locking his fingers together, and let out a long breath. Tsu Ma's Chancellor, Yang T'ing-hsi had just been on with the latest news from his spies in Wang Sau-leyan's household in Alexandria. They had found the renegades! An Sheng, the *I Lung* and a number of other prominent conspirators were there, guests, it was presumed, of the odious T'ang of Africa.

It did not surprise him. In fact he had half expected to find Wang's fat handprint at the back of all. Yet it did create a problem, and not a small one either. If Wang Sau-leyan *were* the sponsor of this rebellion, then he would have to be deposed. Yet that might prove a lot more difficult than it first seemed.

He was not well liked, either by his subjects or his peers, and yet he *was* a T'ang, a Son of Heaven, and they would need proof positive before they could accuse him publicly. If he denied sheltering the traitors, they would have, perhaps, to take them from him forcibly. And that would be no easy task. No. For once *knowing* was not enough. They had to force his hand somehow . . . or fight him.

Nan Ho stood, then made his way through to where Li Yuan, he knew, was exercising.

As the Captain of the guard announced him, he waited, rehearsing phrases in his head. Yet when Li Yuan came out, towelling himself down, the first thing he said was. "Have you found them, Master Nan?"

"We have, *Chieh Hsia*."

"In Africa?"

He nodded.

"Which of them?"

391

He gave eleven names, An Sheng's last, and saw how, despite himself, Li Yuan was surprised by how high the conspiracy had reached. The young T'ang considered a moment, then nodded.

"And Tsu Ma? What does he say?"

"He wishes to consult with you, *Chieh Hsia.*"

"Of course . . ." He turned, throwing the towel to one of the bare-chested servants who stood, head bowed, just beyond him, then put his arms out as another brought a tunic and fastened it about him. "What do you think, Master Nan? Have we enough to challenge our cousin?"

Nan Ho grimaced. "I . . . do not think so, *Chieh Hsia.* Not publicly."

"No. But privately . . ." He smiled, glad, it seemed, to have something positive to do. "All right. I shall consult Tsu Ma and Wu Shih and see what they have to say. Then I shall speak with our cousin, the T'ang of Africa and find out just what he has to say for himself."

* * *

"Major Kao . . . Chen . . . I wasn't expecting you . . ."

Hannah stood in the doorway to her suite of rooms, a work-smock about her waist. Her hair was tied back, her face and hands smeared with ash. Behind her two servants looked up from their tasks, then carried on.

"I had to come. Find out how you were."

"Ah . . ." She looked down, a momentary tightness in her face. "I'm . . . bearing up. You know what they say. Work hard enough and you can forget anything."

He sighed. "You should be easier on yourself, Hannah. That shoulder . . . you should be resting it. Besides, your father . . ."

She looked back at him, clear-eyed. "I shall grieve my father when I'm ready. Right now . . ." She shrugged. "Well, I guess I'm just not ready yet."

He stared at her a moment, then nodded. "You're staying here then . . . even after what happened?"

She nodded. "This is my home. At least, the nearest to a

392

real home I'll ever have. What happened . . . well, it happened, neh? I can't change that, and I sure as hell won't run away from it. So yes . . . I'll stay here. I'll make some changes, of course. My stepmother's rooms . . ."

She looked down again, swallowing. Chen, watching her, understood. So much had happened that she still couldn't take it all in. All of her family were dead – all, that was, except her stepsister, and she was like a stranger to her. There was nowhere really for her to go. Yet to continue living here, alone . . . it seemed wrong somehow.

"Why don't you come and live with us? Wang Ti wouldn't mind . . . we've room, and . . ."

She smiled. "Look, I'm grateful, Kao Chen. It's a nice thought, and you're a good man, but . . . well, I have to stay here."

"But it's so big. All these rooms . . . Won't you be lonely?"

"No, I . . ." She stopped, as if remembering something, then disappeared through the door. A moment later she returned, holding a silk-paper envelope carefully between the forefinger and thumb of her left hand. Chen took it from her, noting the broken imperial seal on the back of it, and took out the letter.

It was an Edict, a Special Edict granting a pardon to her father. He looked back at her, grinning, delighted for her, then handed it back.

She slipped it into the pocket of her smock. "I've been thinking, Chen. Trying to . . . well, to fit everything into place. My father spent his life in the service of an ideal. A foul ideal, yet I understand why he did it. To have some kind of *focus* for your life . . . we all need that, don't we? So I've decided that I'd use my life. Like that woman in the news. You know, the rich woman, Mary Lever." Her tone was wistful now, her eyes suddenly distant. "I want to be what my father *ought* to have been."

He nodded. "I see that. But you're still only sixteen. It'll be nine years before you come of age. What will happen to you?"

She laughed. "It seems I am to be made an Imperial Ward. Someone will be appointed. Tolonen, perhaps, or, more likely, General Rheinhardt, to make decisions on my behalf. But that doesn't matter. It isn't really that important. What *is* important is that I hold on to what I've learned and put it to good use."

He frowned, not quite seeing what she meant. Yet there was a determination about her that impressed him – that had impressed him from the start.

"And you?"

Her question took him by surprise. "I . . . I've some unfinished business. Wilson . . . all that was a shock to me. To find that the man closest to you is in the Ministry's pay . . ."

"But not the only one, neh? It seems Security was riddled with the *I Lung's* men."

"Yes . . ." He sighed. *Even so . . .*

"Oh," she added, lowering her voice. "The T'ang's special forces – his *Shen T'se* – were in here earlier, poking about. They stripped the place of anything they thought might prove incriminating against the First Dragon."

He narrowed his eyes. "Did they take the File?" The word *Aristotle* had been on the tip of his tongue, but it remained unspoken.

She nodded.

"What did you say?"

"That it was my father's."

"And they accepted that?"

"Why should they doubt it. It was the kind of thing he dealt in, after all."

"Yes . . ." But the thought of it made him go cold. It had all been a very narrow call. "Well . . . I'd better go."

"Good luck," she said, smiling, offering her hand.

He took it, pressing it firmly, then bowed his head. "And you, Shang Han-A. Keep in touch, huh?"

"I shall . . ."

* * *

Wang Sau-leyan turned, facing the camera, his bloated, moon-like face moving forward until it filled the huge screen. "Yes, cousin, how can I help you?"

Li Yuan took a breath, then launched in. "It has come to my attention that certain . . . persons are accepting your hospitality."

"*Persons*, cousin? Come . . . be more specific. I have many guests. Who could you possibly mean?"

Li Yuan controlled his anger, realising that Wang was baiting him. "I mean certain traitors . . . Prince An Sheng and the *I Lung* among them."

"Ah . . ." Wang smiled. "So you've *heard*, eh? But tell me . . . you talk of traitors. Surely there's inconclusive evidence to talk of treachery? Or have my cousins information I've not been privy to?"

Out of sight of the camera, Li Yuan bunched his fists. "There's evidence enough, cousin. Those men are traitors. They plotted to bring down the Seven and murder all our families."

"I see." Wang hesitated, stroking his chins, then smiled. "And our cousins Tsu Ma and Wu Shih, do they agree with you?"

"They do."

"Then there's no question of it, neh?"

"No question," Li Yuan answered firmly, wondering what Wang was up to.

"Well," he said, "as you've *heard*, let me show you."

He moved back slightly, then signalled to the camera. Slowly it turned, looking past him, until it focused on a line of kneeling figures.

"Are these the fellows?"

Li Yuan stared, astonished. All eleven of those named by Nan Ho knelt there. Their hands were bound behind them, their heads shaven. They stared into the camera, hollow-eyed. For a moment he stared at them, wondering why they were so silent . . . then he saw. Their bloodied mouths were empty. Wang Sau-leyan had pulled their teeth and cut out their tongues!

"Those are the men," he said quietly, a shiver of disgust passing through him.

"And these men are known traitors . . . that's what you said, neh?"

Li Yuan let out a breath, then nodded.

"In which case . . ." Wang heaved himself up out of his throne and went across, standing beside An Sheng. He smiled, then signalled to the guard behind him. "Execute the traitor . . ."

"Cousin!" Li Yuan cried out, but it was too late. The guard stepped up and, pulling An Sheng's head back, dragged a knife across his throat.

* * *

Wu Shih was standing in the lower garden when the message came. Pao En-fu bowed low, then came two paces towards him, what looked like a black footstool beneath one arm.

"*Chieh Hsia*, your cousin, the T'ang of Africa, wishes to speak with you."

"Wang Sau-leyan?" Wu Shih laughed with disbelief. "What in the gods' names could that rogue want?"

"He would not say, *Chieh Hsia*, only that it was urgent. I took the liberty of bringing a portable holo-unit."

Wu Shih nodded. "Thank you, Master Pao. Put it down, then leave me."

"*Chieh Hsia*."

Pao En-fu set the portable down, then backed away, moving quickly out of earshot. Wu Shih waited a moment, then gave the voice command. At once the image of his cousin, the T'ang of Africa, materialised in the air. He had his back to Wu Shih.

"Cousin? Are you there?"

"I am here, Wang Sau-leyan. What do you want?"

Wang turned to face the sound. "I hoped to be able to see you, Wu Shih. Where are you? In your garden?"

"I am here," he answered. He was damned if he was going to tell the bastard where he was.

Wang shrugged. "You heard what happened, I take it?"

396

"I heard."

"Then we can sleep safely once more, neh, cousin? Or so one might believe . . ."

Wu Shih stared at the gross shape of his cousin suspiciously. "What do you mean?"

"Only that there are many ways to betray one's fellows . . ." Wang reached into his silks and withdrew a folded slip of paper. "You know, when the *I Lung* first came to me, yesterday evening, he sought to buy my trust. He offered certain papers – things he had unearthed while going about his dark and shadowy business. Among them was this." He tapped the paper against the fingers of his other hand, then smiled. "I am told it is authentic. That this copy was taken direct from the original. But such things are hard to prove, neh? Most things can be copied these days, and seals and documents better than most. Yet I am convinced of the authenticity of this. It . . . rings true, shall we say."

Wu Shih moved slightly to one side, out of the predatory gaze of his bulky cousin.

"What is it?"

Wang turned towards his voice again, untroubled it seemed by the necessity. "It is an agreement. A letter, to be more accurate, written by our cousin Wei Chan Yin to Li Yuan, expressing his loyalty."

"His *loyalty*? How do you mean? Our cousin Wei is a T'ang in his own right. Why, he . . ."

He stopped, understanding. Was *that* why Wei Chan Yin had been so quiet in Council? Was that why he always voted, without hesitation, the way his cousin Yuan voted?

Even so, it still made little sense. Wu Shih shook his head. "It *must* be forged."

Wang nodded. "That is exactly what I thought. Yet even under torture the *I Lung* insisted it was genuine. He said to ask Wei Chan Yin, but . . . well, *he* would not admit to it now, would he?"

"No . . ." Wu Shih turned, beginning to pace to and fro, disturbed by what he'd heard, then turned back. "Show me the document!"

Wang held it up. Wu Shih bent close, studying it. It certainly looked like Wei Chan Yin's hand. Even so . . .

"Would you send me a copy, cousin?"

Wang folded the sheet and slipped it back inside his silks. "Of course. One is already on its way to you. I took the liberty of sending a special messenger. It would not do for such a thing to fall into another's hands."

Wu Shih shuddered. "Cousin, I . . . I am grateful for your confidence. I cannot say how I feel right now, but . . ."

"Of course," Wang said hurriedly. "I understand. This must have come as a great shock to you. If it helps at all, I know exactly how you feel. It . . . well, it *undermines* us, neh?"

Wu Shih stared at his cousin's image, blindly it seemed, then grunted his assent.

"I'll leave you then, cousin Shih."

Wu Shih waved vaguely at the image, forgetting it could not see him, then added. "Oh, and thank you cousin . . ."

"It was but my duty. Until tomorrow . . ."

Slowly the image faded. Slowly the sunlight seemed to return, as if from far away.

Wu Shih turned, looking about him, seeing not the natural harmony, the *greenness* of the garden, but a mess of irregular shapes, a whole vast sea of lengthening shadows.

And if this proves true?

If this were true, then it would be the end of things between them, for such a breach of trust . . .

He shook his head violently and groaned. Untrue. It *had* to be untrue! Li Yuan . . . why, he was like a son to him. He would never have put his name to such a thing.

Never? he asked himself, remembering the wording of the document and how it reminded him of the way Yuan spoke. Never was a long time. And Li Yuan was a young man, and young men were notoriously impatient.

Maybe so . . . yet there was no earthly reason why Wei Chan Yin should submit to Yuan. No reason whatsoever. Whereas Wang . . . Wang could only benefit from this.

Yes, he thought. Yet Wang would never have come up

with something so simple and direct. Not unless it were true. What's more, it rang true that the *I Lung* should have tried to buy his safety with such a tit-bit of information. So maybe . . .

Wu Shih let out a shivering sigh, then turned away, cramp pains making him wince and clutch his side as he made his way down the long path, heading for the palace.

If this proves true . . .

* * *

Jean had stopped crying, but it made it no better. He understood now how futile it had been, how stupid even to think he could outwit Wu Shih. Why, it was like trying to outrun Fate.

So here he was at last, faced by it. His sons were gone – taken while he and Jean sat paralysed.

Yes . . . he understood all right. Understood now what the wires meant – had experienced now that total abnegation of the individual will, that *crushing* of the self. It had been dreadful, the most dreadful thing he had ever suffered. He had ceased to be himself. Had watched, like a prisoner in his own skull, as they bound his darling sons and dragged them screaming from the room. As in a nightmare . . . a nightmare where one could not even feel; where one was reduced to the state of a machine – a thing that watched, dull-eyed and uncaring, all human qualities removed.

Now *nothing* remained.

Kennedy eased back, moving away from his now-sleeping wife, then put his feet to the floor and stood, walking slowly, silently away.

In the doorway he stood a moment, looking back into the darkened room at her, his face creased with pain. Then, knowing there was no choice, he went through into the bathroom and began to prepare himself for the broadcast.

* * *

"Wake up! Come on, you bastard, wake up!"

Cornwell grunted, then turned slowly onto his back. "Wha . . . ?"

Chen poked him hard in the guts. "Up! Now!"

Cornwell's eyes jerked open. "What the . . . ?" Then he saw who it was. "*You!* What the hell are *you* doing in here?"

Chen threw the warrant down onto his chest. "Read it! Then get dressed. I've something I want to show you."

Grunting, Cornwell got up into a sitting position. He glared at Chen, pulling his silks tighter about his bloated stomach. "Have you no manners, Major? Can't you wait outside or something?"

Chen shook his head. "Just read it and shut up!"

Cornwell's eyes flared with rage. His voice hissed from him. "I'll have you for this, you fucker! I'll go to Rheinhardt. He'll have your balls, you chink shit!"

Chen raised an eyebrow. "Just read the warrant, *Shih* Cornwell. Oh, and you might just note whose signature is at the bottom!"

Cornwell picked up the warrant and prised off the seal, then unfolded it and read. "Rheinhardt?" He looked back at Chen suspiciously. "Okay . . . but what the fuck is going on?"

"You'll find out soon enough. Now get dressed. Or do you want to come like that?"

An hour later they sat there, knee to knee in the sedan, having come, it seemed, to a final halt.

"So?" Cornwell asked, leaning towards Chen. "Where are we?"

Cornwell was blindfolded and cuffed, yet he seemed much more relaxed than he'd been at first. He had clearly not expected anyone to come to his Mansion. And the warrant . . . that had certainly dented his self-esteem. But as time had gone by he'd grown in confidence and had begun haranguing Chen again, threatening him with the direst retribution once things were "straightened out". Chen had sat there in silence throughout, content to watch his prisoner, knowing that he was beyond all words, all insults. Why, it was almost funny to hear the big man bluster on. Yet the joke was wearing thin.

"Well?" Cornwell insisted. "Answer me, you dumb, pug-faced chink!"

Chen ignored his question. Instead, he leaned across and undid the cuffs. Cornwell looked up blindly, surprised, then reached up and removed his blindfold. "About fucking time," he said, blinking. "Now what's going on? I demand to know."

"Demand?" Chen laughed humourlessly. "You like demanding, don't you, *Shih* Cornwell?"

"Sure. It gets me what I want. And what I want right now are explanations. You burst into my Mansion, blindfold and cuff me, and bring me fuck knows where, all on the basis of some vague instruction to assist with enquiries. Now . . . if I don't get some answers and soon, then I'm going to make so much trouble that you'll wish you'd never been born."

Chen stared back at him, stone-faced. "I had to make sure you'd come."

"Yeah? Then why all that shit with the cuffs and blindfold?"

"Because I felt like it . . ."

Cornwell stared at him a long moment, then laughed. "You know what . . . I'm beginning to like you, Major Kao. You're not bad for a chink. I can see why they made you Major. You've got balls."

Chen felt himself go cold. To be hated by a bastard like Cornwell was fine and natural, but to be admired by him . . . that was abominable. That was, if it was genuine admiration, and not another of his games.

"Why don't we talk for a bit?" he said, sitting back. "We've a bit of time while things are being set up."

"Set up? What are you talking about?"

"You know how it is, *Shih* Cornwell. We have to prepare things . . ." He smiled coldly. "You must have done a lot of preparation in your time."

Cornwell narrowed his eyes. "What are you angling at, Major? Is this a shakedown? Is *that* what it is?"

"Now why should you think that?"

"Because I know how your lot are. Why, I must have paid more to unofficial 'funds' than you've seen in regular salary. Five, ten times as much!"

Chen nodded, as if impressed. "You must have done a lot

401

of deals like that to get where you are. You've come a long way . . ."

Cornwell leaned forward. "Too fucking right. I didn't have no rich daddy bankrolling me, like some of those bastards. I had nothing. I climbed. And I took care of myself. Not like those soft cunts I had to work with. A pack of weak-kneed bastards they were . . . shit-heads!" He laughed. "You have to be hard in business. You can't afford scruples. You know what I mean, Major?"

"Oh, I know what kind of world it is we live in, *Shih* Cornwell. I was an orphan. Down there, beneath the Net."

Cornwell eyed him with renewed interest. "The Net, eh? So how did you . . . you know, get up here?"

Chen's smile was like acid. "I killed a Minister."

Cornwell stared at him a moment, then roared with laughter. "Killed a Minister . . . I like that. Fucking good! But seriously, what did you do?"

"I was *kwai*. You heard of that?"

Cornwell nodded, impressed despite himself. "You were good, I assume?"

"I survived."

He leaned closer, his perfumed bulk almost touching Chen. "So what was it like?"

"Like?"

"You know, killing men for a living . . . what did that feel like?"

Chen stared back at the man, feeling a revulsion so deep, so intense, that it was like a fire in his veins. He wanted to punch those gross features and keep on punching until they were a bloody mess, yet he kept his face a blank, showing nothing.

"It was a long time ago . . . You forget."

"*Forget*?" Cornwell whistled through his teeth. "I sure as hell wouldn't! Shit! You did it *that* often?"

Chen nodded. "I've seen all kinds of vileness."

"Sure . . . and paid for some, I bet!"

Chen looked down at the hand Cornwell had placed on his knee. Slowly the fat man removed it.

"So?" Cornwell said. "How much do you want?"

"Want? Did I *say* I wanted anything?"

"Come on . . . we're alone here, right? That's why you brought me here." He smiled encouragingly. "So come on . . . what's it worth to get you off my back?"

"What if I said I wasn't interested in your money?"

"Then I'd say you were full of crap, Major Kao! Money, that's all that matters in this world. Without it you're nothing. With it . . . well, you can have anything you want."

"Maybe. But what if I still don't want it."

Cornwell eyed him carefully. "You want on the payroll, then?"

"You have many officers on your books, Shih Cornwell?"

"A few . . . no names. You know how it is."

"And Wilson? Was he one of them?"

Cornwell sighed ostentatiously. "Pity about Wilson. I heard he got snuffed. But yeah . . . he was on my books. Helpful, neh? Sure fucked you up last time out! I thought you had me for a moment, but . . . no evidence, no case, huh?" He smiled. "No hard feelings, though, eh, Major? You and me . . . I reckon we understand each other. I reckon we can work together real well."

"And those workers you sacked . . . the ones your man killed . . . what about them?"

Cornwell frowned. "What the fuck are you still going on about them for? Forget those fuckers . . . what do *they* matter? The question is, do you want in, and if so, at what level?"

Chen stood, then tugged the curtain back. "Out!"

"What?"

"You heard me. Out. There's someone I want you to meet."

Cornwell stared sourly at him a moment, then got up, squeezing out of the sedan. Chen followed.

The place seemed empty, deserted. There was noise – there was *always* noise – but it was distant, muted. Cornwell looked about him, his face wrinkled with disgust at the litter-strewn floor.

"Where the fucking hell are we?"

Chen made no answer, only pushed him forward, shoving him with the heel of his right palm, each shove releasing some of the anger, the tension he was feeling.

"Here," he said finally, stopping in front of an unmarked door. "This is it."

Cornwell turned, glaring at him. "I'll have you, you little fucker. You had your chance, but now . . . well, I'll break you, right? You'll be lucky if you're guarding a shit-pile when I'm finished with you!"

Chen smiled tightly. "Rather apt, wouldn't you say?"

"What . . . ?"

"You . . . how you treat people, the things you do . . . it's shit, that's what it is. You think the world is made in your image . . . that it's all up for grabs and the biggest, fattest maggot gets to eat it all. Well, it isn't like that . . . not for everyone. But you . . ." Chen shook his head, disgusted, then drew his gun, "we might as well all be holograms for all you care. Isn't that right?"

Cornwell's eyes widened. "I don't understand . . ."

"Knock. Go on. Knock on the door."

Cornwell turned, then knocked timidly.

"Louder! Come on, let them know you're there!"

Cornwell looked back at him, fearful now. "Who? Who are you talking about?"

"The scum. You know . . . Or don't you remember?"

The door behind him slid back. A woman stood there, and behind her an elderly Han. Beyond him were a dozen or more others, big men with the look of manual workers. Cornwell turned, staring open-mouthed at them, then turned back, his eyes ablaze with fear.

"No . . ." he said, falling to his knees in front of Chen and grabbing at his tunic. "No, Kao Chen . . . you can't! Whatever you want, just name it. I . . ."

Chen placed the gun to Cornwell's brow, directly between his eyes, and pushed. "Inside. Now."

Slowly Cornwell got to his feet, then turned, facing the doorway. As he did the woman stepped back, as if inviting

404

him in, yet there was something hard and relentless about her face, something unforgiving.

"Deals . . ." Chen said, his voice heavy with disgust. "Why don't you go and make a deal . . ."

And, planting his boot in Cornwell's rump, he pushed, sending him sprawling into the room.

* * *

"It's just starting," Michael said, touching her gently on the shoulder. "Are you coming through?"

"In a moment . . . I just want to finish this . . . You go through."

She sat there, her anger a still and perfect thing within her. Kennedy . . . it all kept coming back to Kennedy.

Michael's voice came again, from the other room this time. "Em . . . ?"

"Okay!"

Damn the man! Damn all his deals and fake deals! And damn him for being the smooth-tongued, charming con-man that he was!

She went through and stood behind where Michael was seated, staring past him at the image on the screen.

"What's he saying?"

"Shhh . . . this is important. He's . . ."

Kennedy looked odd. And then she realised why. He wasn't smiling for once.

"We had such hopes," he was saying. "We wanted to make such changes to our world. But sometimes our hands are tied. Sometimes . . ."

He hesitated, a visible shudder passing through him. "Let me tell you something. This afternoon, the T'ang of North America, Wu Shih, took my children . . . my two boys, Robert and William. They're his hostages now. I say that, but in fact we've all of us been hostages for some time now, Jean, myself, and the boys . . ."

Emily listened, horrified, as he gave the details, understanding slowly coming to her.

"And that's why . . ." he concluded, "I have to do this. To

405

make this small, perhaps futile gesture, to try to put things right somehow. The dream . . ." He sighed heavily. "My good friend Michael Lever was right when he spoke a few days ago. It seems as if the dream died long ago.

"Anyway . . ." Kennedy straightened, facing the camera with something of his old determination. "It's like this. I booked this 'live' slot earlier and recorded this message an hour or so back. What you see, then, is an image of an image . . . a hologram." He gave a faint, pained smile. "The real me, Joseph Kennedy, is dead. Or will be, by the time this goes out."

"What?" Emily put her hand to her mouth. Michael was on his feet.

"Free," he said. "That's all I ever wanted, I guess . . . to be free. And now . . ."

The image shivered, crackled, disappeared, to be replaced a moment later by one of the channel anchor-men. He looked up, bemused, his mouth not working for a moment, then, swallowing, he began to read a news item.

"Aiya . . ." Michael moaned, his face distraught. "No . . . No . . ."

Emily stared at him, bewildered. *Wrong*, she thought. *How could I have been so wrong?*

"Em . . ."

She held him, clinging on, a great weight of sorrow pressing down on her as she imagined how it must have been for him. To have had to live with that every day. And now he was gone . . .

She closed her eyes. Suddenly it all seemed much less substantial than it had been only moments before. Suddenly more . . . *hollow.*

Michael was leaning against her, sobbing. *Comfort me*, he seemed to be saying. *Hold me and take away my hurt.* But this once she could do nothing for him, for the hurt she felt was greater than his own – was as big as the world itself.

"Where now?" she murmured softly, her voice laced with pain and loss. "Oh, gods, where now?"

CHAPTER·16

THE CITY, BURNING

Wu Shih paced to and fro, waiting to be put through to his cousin. He was angry and tired and in no mood for compromise. It had been a long, sleepless night, and the next day or two seemed likely to bring only fresh outbreaks of violence. All attempts to stem the unrest that had followed Kennedy's on-air suicide had failed, even an appeal for calm by Mary Lever . . .

"It's all *his* fault," he muttered, staring at the blank screen irritably. "If only he had not persuaded me to use that abominable wire . . ."

It was true. Deep down he blamed Li Yuan for all of this. If he had only trusted to instinct and used older, more certain methods against Kennedy.

I should have listened to my advisers, he thought. I should have had him killed, then none of this would have happened.

No . . . but then how would I have slept?

There was a soft chime. The screen glowed gold. And then Li Yuan was facing him, concern on his face.

"Cousin Shih . . . how are you?"

"Li Yuan," he answered, coldly, formally. At once the young T'ang's face changed, frowning.

"What is it? What more has happened?"

In answer he held up the letter so that Yuan could see.

"Ah . . ." he said.

The last glimmer of doubt – and hope – died in Wu Shih's breast. "You do not deny it, then?"

Li Yuan shook his head. "I never meant to use it. It was Wei Feng's idea. He had a vision of the times to come. A dark, fearful vision. He had his sons swear to him on his death bed. I tried . . ."

"*Acch* . . ." Wu Shih's face creased with pain and disappointment. "How *could* you, Yuan?"

Li Yuan looked down, for a brief moment like a son being chastised by his father. Yet when he looked up again, his eyes were clear. "I thought it might be necessary. The times . . ."

"The times excuse nothing, Yuan. Good and Evil do not change with the times. Morality is a constant. Besides, T'ang must be T'ang, not the puppets of other men. How else can they rule in confidence and in the fullness of their power?"

Li Yuan stared back at him, saying nothing.

"So . . . it has come to this, eh? When even we cannot trust each other."

"I am still your friend, Wu Shih. Such trust as we had remains."

Wu Shih shook his head, then let the letter fall. "No, Li Yuan. There is no trust between us any more. Nor can we be friends, not after this." A small, shivering sigh escaped him. "You shame your father's memory."

Li Yuan's face was hard, resentful. "No, Wu Shih. I have tried only to keep this great world of ours from slipping into chaos. My father . . . he would have seen the necessity and approved."

"There are other ways . . ."

"There are only those ways which work, and those which fail. You say the times mean nothing, but I disagree. If a man must sometimes do evil to achieve great good, then that is a path he is compelled to follow. The Wiring Project, for instance . . ."

"An abomination!" Wu Shih said angrily. "I should never have agreed. After all, how are men to find merit if the choice between good and ill is denied them?"

"You think there is any longer a choice, cousin? For *any* of us?"

Wu Shih stared at the young T'ang, astonished to find such a thing coming from his lips. "Surely . . . *surely* there is. If I thought . . ."

"You blame me for Kennedy's death, neh?"

Wu Shih hesitated, then nodded.

Li Yuan looked away, coming to terms with that, then looked back at him. "Maybe it's true. Maybe I counselled you unwisely. But were you or I to know how the future would unfold? Would you have guessed, two years ago, that he would take his life?"

"No . . ."

"Nor I. And who's to say that any other means would not have brought the same result. No, Wu Shih. You were riding a tiger . . . I thought you understood that."

"Maybe . . ."

Li Yuan looked down, sighing. "So what now? I suppose you want me to reveal the existence of the letter to my cousins . . ."

"I . . ." Wu Shih nodded. All the fire had gone from him now, all the anger drained into a great soup of despair. The future was ashes.

"By the way . . ." Li Yuan asked quietly. "How *did* you find out?"

He looked up, surprised to find himself experiencing a twinge of shame. "It was our cousin Wang," he answered quietly.

"Ah . . ." Li Yuan smiled sadly. "I should have guessed . . ."

* * *

It fell slowly, almost without warning, the panicked messages of its maintenance crew unheeded at first amidst the general chaos down below, and when finally they were it was already too late. It hit like a giant bomb, impacting at over twenty thousand *ch'i* per second. The results were devastating. The City crumpled beneath it like a paper cup crushed by a fist. More than three hundred stacks disappeared instantly, and for over fifty *li* around the devastation was phenomenal.

How many tens of millions died in that first instant? How many more in the great shockwave and fireball that followed? The unthinkable had happened. An orbital had fallen from the sky and a hole the size of Lake Superior had been punched in City North America.

The City was burning.

* * *

They had gathered about the screen in the main room, Michael, Emily and all of the remaining staff. Many had gone already, leaving to be with their families in this time of crisis, though how many of them would make it home was another matter.

The news was growing worse by the minute. Even before the crash things had been tense, but now it was as if the lid had come off. The City had gone mad. Remotes, sent into the Lowers by the media channels, sent back scenes of awful carnage before they sparked and blacked out.

Emily stared at the screen, chewing a nail and moaning softly as image followed dreadful image. Something had finally snapped in them, or been stripped away. It was like watching animals. Faces driven mad by fear ran past, or came to stare into the lens – grinning gargoyle faces animated by hate and an insane and violent anger. Faces that yapped and bit and howled.

"We must do something," she said for the dozenth time. Sure. But what? How *did* one cope with this kind of thing? Maybe one *could* only watch . . . yes, and pray that something survived once the baying ceased and a more human light returned to those feral eyes.

The City was burning.

"Em . . ."

Michael touched her arm, then drew her aside, talking to her quietly but urgently. "Look, we have to get going. The cruiser's here, up top. We've seats on one of the shuttles. If we go now . . ."

She shook off his arm. "Go? How can we go? Look at it! They need us, Michael . . ."

"*Need* us? You really think we can do anything about all that? No, Em . . . it's gone. Fallen apart. And we've got to get out of here right now or we'll go with it."

410

She stared at him as if staring at a stranger. *Gone?* No, it couldn't have gone. Not that quickly.

She looked back at the screen. Wu Shih was in the picture now, surrounded by his senior Security officers, standing at the edge of the great crater, examining a fallen stack, his face lined with grief, his eyes misted with tears.

"*Gone* . . ." she said, understanding at last. "It *has* all gone, hasn't it?"

"Yes," he said, squeezing her arm. "Look, Em . . . I know you want to help, but there's nothing we can do. Not from here. Europe . . . we'll go to Europe, and then . . . well, maybe we can come back when it's all died down. Maybe we can help rebuild . . ."

She stared at him, taken in by the lie even as she recognised it for what it was. There would be no reconstruction. Not after this.

The City was burning.

* * *

St Louis was gone, and Springfield, and most of the area up to Peoria in the north and Evansville in the west.

Wu Shih stared at the makeshift map that had been laid out on the trestle table and shook his head in disbelief. The crater was marked on the map in black – a huge circle centred on a place called Pana. Beyond it was a band of red, shaped like the yolk of an egg, bulging more to the east and the plantations than to the west, where the City had taken the full force of the explosion. Where they were, in the east stack of Indianapolis, was on the very edge of that outer circle, just beyond the red, more than five hundred *li* from the epicentre, yet even here the damage was phenomenal.

He had flown back over a landscape so changed it seemed like something from a dream. Further in, towards the epicentre, the stacks had melted down and formed strange shapes, like hideous parcels little taller than a man . . . but here they were almost untouched. Untouched, yet eerily silent. Only corpses filled these levels.

He moved away from the table, looking about him at the

huge, gutted shell of the place. In some ways it was worse here than on the edge of the crater. There, at least, the transformation had been so great as to defy the imagination. Here, however, it was only too easy to imagine the suffering. Here everything was scorched and blackened. Ash and debris scrunched underfoot wherever one trod. And the bodies . . .

He shuddered, then closed his eyes, remembering, seeing the two bodies again, as if they were etched on his inner lid. They lay together on their backs, their knees up, their arms in a strange begging position, almost like dogs performing tricks. Looking closer he had noticed how their features had been erased – their faces made anonymous by the heat. Blackened tar covered their grinning skulls.

And the stench . . .

They were flying men in to pile up the dead, but it was a hopeless task. They were piled everywhere one looked, and to burn them . . .

He put his hand up to his face and began to sob. It was like what had happened on Mars. As if it were all happening again.

Punishment . . . this was the punishment of the gods. Destruction . . . endless destruction. And nothing untouched.

General Althaus came across, and bowed. "Am I needed here, *Chieh Hsia*? If not . . ."

He shivered and then looked up, not bothering to wipe his tear-stained face, noticing the ash that stained his hands an unfamiliar black.

"No," he answered wearily. "You'd best go. There's nothing for us here. Let's save what *can* be saved . . ."

* * *

Kemp ran down the corridor, his silks flapping, his breath gasping from him.

He had woken to a violent screaming from downstairs and to the smash of breaking vases. Locking his bedroom door behind him, he had hurried to the House com, flicking through the viewing cameras with mounting panic. There were strangers in the house, roaming his corridors, thin-faced

412

young men in faded one-pieces, *liumang* – punks – by the looks of it. The screaming came from the downstairs scullery where three youths were taking turns to fuck his youngest maid. He watched a moment, his heart thudding in his chest, then switched, looking to the main gate. The guard hut was empty . . .

"*Aiya . . .*" he moaned softly, the bastards had deserted him! Then, knowing he had little time, he went to the door on the far side of the room and, taking the key from his pocket, opened it and slipped through, locking it on the other side.

The bathroom was a big, echoing room. On the far side, high up, was a window. He went across, picked up the bath chair, and set it down beneath the window. Climbing up, he looked out. The gap was narrow – maybe too narrow – and the drop . . . ten, twelve *ch'i* at least, maybe more . . . If he fell he'd break his hips, maybe his back, yet to stay . . .

He sniffed. Fire. They had set fire to the Mansion. He whimpered, then began to pull himself up, the effort almost beyond him. Fear gave him strength however and for a moment he was balanced on the ledge, half in, half out.

Behind him the door-lock rattled. There was a shout of triumph.

"In here! . . . the fucker's in here!"

He cried out, terrified suddenly, and struggled to edge farther out.

Stuck . . . Aiya! I'm stuck!

Behind him the door thudded, as someone threw themselves against it. There was more shouting, and then silence. A moment later a shot rang out. There was the sound of metal clattering across the floor behind him, and then the door burst open.

He couldn't turn. Stuck there, he could only imagine them coming up beneath him. He closed his eyes, expecting another shot, but it didn't come. Instead there was laughter. An awful mocking laughter.

"*Lao jen!*" one of them taunted. "*Lao jen!*"
Old man . . .

He heard the creak of the bath chair as one of them climbed up onto it, then his legs were tugged violently and he fell back, cracking his chin as he fell.

He lay there, stunned, his back numb. As his mouth filled with blood, he looked up through blurred and doubled vision into three young and snarling faces. "*Lao jen . . .*" one of them said gently, almost tenderly, putting a hand behind his neck as if to support him. And then the first blow fell, smashing his nose, blinding him with pain.

"*Lao jen . . .*"

* * *

The imperial cruiser lifted slowly, the two guard ships already in position half a *li* up. Wu Shih, seated inside, looked out through the portal, frowning in stunned disbelief at the infernal scene below. It was hard to imagine that anyone had ever lived there. Hard to believe . . .

As they edged out over the ruins, the cruiser hovered a moment, clearing the out-jutting edge of a fallen stack. As it did, a rocket streaked up from below and hit it near the tail.

The explosion rocked the ship, yet miraculously, when the smoke cleared, it was still there. Slowly, very slowly, it began to spin, a trail of black smoke snaking from its gaping rear. For a moment it lifted, as if it was going to clear the outcrop, then it struck with a sickening crunch and began to fall back to the earth.

Inside, Wu Shih turned, staring back at the jagged hole that had appeared just behind where he was sitting. He was vaguely aware of someone screaming close by, an awful, ragged sound, but it was muted by the ringing in his ears. It was cold suddenly – bitterly cold – though the cabin itself was on fire. Smoke swirled like an ill-focused hologram.

Out, he thought. *I have to get out . . .*

In a haze, he tried to release his belt, but for some reason his fingers were numb and wouldn't work. Looking down he saw blood on his silks, a glint of bone through the bloodied flesh of his left arm.

No, he thought. *Not possible . . .*

On the ground below, soldiers were staring up, mouths agape, as the ship began to descend. A moment later they were scrambling for cover as small arms fire and mortars began raining down on them from nearby vantage points.

"It's the Hand!" someone yelled. "It's the fucking Black Hand!"

There was shouting now and screams, while overhead the two Security cruisers manoeuvred, trying to get into the fight.

The T'ang's ship struck the ground nose first, its reinforced frame buckling.

Trapped in his seat, Wu Shih groaned and closed his eyes. *Alive. I'm still alive.* But the smoke was much thicker now that the ship had come to rest, and the flames . . .

He opened one eye. Two lines of blood lay like sticky threads across his vision, distorting it. He coughed, the sudden pain in his chest like a tiny bomb exploding in his chest.

The flames . . .

He swallowed painfully. His silks were on fire. And his legs . . . both of his legs were crushed.

He groaned. *Help me . . . for the gods' sake help me, I am a Son of Heaven . . .*

Yet even as soldiers ran to assist, there was a small explosion and the whole ship lit up brightly. A mortar had hit it dead centre.

Watching from above, the captain of the second cruiser saw the missile strike and winced, knowing there was no chance anyone would have survived.

"Oh shit . . ." he groaned. "Oh fucking shit! Kuan Yin preserve us now!"

* * *

The hatch was closed, the engines warming up. In an hour they would be in Europe.

Emily sat at the window seat, Michael beside her. In a few minutes the window shields would come down and that would be it. America would be like a dream. Something that had happened in another life.

It was dark now; even so, the sky above the distant City was bright. Rumour had it that Wu Shih was dead . . . shot by an assassin, or murdered in his bed by one of his guards . . . the details were obscure. The only certainty was that it was all up for the great T'ang and his City.

Flames flickered in the thick glass of the portal, like snakes . . .

She had been so close . . . so close to doing something real . . . to *changing* things.

Dreams, she thought. *Nothing but dreams* . . .

She turned, pressing Michael's hand briefly, giving him an encouraging smile. Home . . . for her this was a return home, but for him . . .

For Michael this was a nightmare, a journey into darkness.

As the window shields came down, she ducked her head, catching her last sight of America.

Of America . . . and of the City, burning.

INTERLUDE– SUMMER 2213:

TRUE VIRTUE

---–-–---

"The night is our mother. She comforts us. She tells us who we are. Mother sky is all. We live, we die beneath her. She sees all. Even the darkness deep within us." – Osu folk saying

"You have heard of the knowledge that knows, but you have never heard of the knowledge that does not know. Look into that closed room, the empty chamber where brightness is born! Fortune and blessing gather where there is stillness." – Chuang Tzu, "In the World of Men"

TRUE VIRTUE

Hans Ebert sat on the table rock, perfectly still, like a shape carved from the ancient stone, looking out into the star-filled blackness of the Martian night. Beyond him, squatting among the rocks near the entrance, the boy watched, mimicking the Walker's stillness.

The *ndichie* – the elders – had gathered. Tonight, here before the table rock, they would meet to discuss the way ahead. Right now, however, they slept after their long journeys across the desert. Only the Walker kept vigil, communing with Mother Sky, talking silently with her.

The boy shivered, awed by that still and silent figure. *Tsou Tsai Hei* they called him: "The Walker in the Darkness". And so it was. When the accident had happened and his parents had died, who had come from the darkness to save him? Who had shimmered into being from the air and plucked him from the burning half-track? The Walker . . .

And so he watched, moulding himself, learning all he could, awaiting the time.

"Nza?"

He scuttled across, then settled beside the seated man.

"Yes, Efulefu?"

"Tell me. What do you want?"

Nza hesitated. How many times had he greeted him this way? How many times had they had this single conversation? A hundred? More? He knew the correct answer. *Nothing. I want nothing.* But it wasn't true. And the Walker wanted the truth from him.

"I want to be like you, Efulefu . . ."

There was no movement, no sign that he had heard, only silence. Then, when he had begun to think he would not answer, his answer came.

"You must want nothing. You must learn to row as if the boat was not there."

Nza frowned. Boats . . . He had never understood it, nor had the Walker chosen to explain. Eventually he had gone and asked Aluko, but Aluko had murmured something about earth, and about seas made of water, and he had laughed and told him he must be wrong, because a sea was made of sand . . .

"Nza?"

"Yes, Efulefu?"

"Are you happy, Nza?"

Happy? *Was* he happy?

"I am content, Efulefu."

"Good. Be content with the moment."

Again he did not fully understand. Sometimes, like now, he was content. But there were times when he would wake from dreams of the burning half-track and see the broken visor of his mother's helmet clearly and he would cry out, the pain so deep, so rooted in him . . .

"Nza?"

"Yes, Efulefu?"

"Do you miss your mother?"

* * *

Ebert took off his helmet and hung it on the rack beside his bunk, then turned, facing the tiny square of mirror. His room was tiny, like a cell, but it was enough. He had no need for more.

"Well?" he asked himself.

Two years he'd lived among them now. At least, two years by the measure of his old life back on Chung Kuo. Here on Mars only a single year had passed – one long, cold circuit about the distant sun.

He smiled, then spoke the words that had come to mind. "When the wheel turns, all things become their opposite."

A year back they had sent ships from Chung Kuo to assess the damage. Now more had come, this time with a complement of settlers. They were to rebuild Kang Kua City . . . to start again.

Which was why they met tonight. Why all the *ndichie* of the fifteen tribes had gathered, here at Iapygia where the first settlement had been built.

And what would they decide?

"Efulefu?"

He turned, facing the doorway. The boy stood there, his eyes like two tiny moons in the perfect blackness of his face.

"Yes, Nza, what is it?"

"Chief Echewa wishes to speak with you. In his quarters. He asks . . ."

"Yes?"

He saw how the boy swallowed, his eyes taking a fearful little glance at the black case that lay on his bunk.

"He asks if you would bring it . . . You know, the Machine."

"Ah . . ." He nodded. "Tell him I'll come. And Nza?"

"Yes, Efulefu?"

"You must not be afraid of it. It is but a way of seeing things. The world of men is full of such artificialities. However strange they seem, they are all part of the great Tao."

The boy bobbed his head. "Yes, Efulefu." But Ebert could see that he was far from convinced. For him, as for many among the Osu, the Machine seemed like some kind of powerful sorcery and he was certain that, were he not there, they would have destroyed it at the earliest opportunity.

And yet without it . . .

He turned and picked it up. It was so light. At times it seemed almost weightless.

"Go on, Nza," he said, knowing the boy was still waiting there. "Tell Aluko that I'm coming."

"Yes, Efulefu . . ."

Ebert smiled. Nza – "tiny bird" – was a good boy. In time he might become a Chief, even perhaps *ndichie*. That was, if they had any time. If the new settlers didn't seek – like those before them – to destroy the Osu.

He went out, following the narrow passageway that had been cut from the solid rock until he came to Echewa's quarters.

Aluko was sitting on his bunk, alone in the four-man cell.

"Where are the others?"

"They've gone to eat," the big black man answered. "Besides, I thought it best that we spoke alone."

"Ah . . ." He turned, closing the airtight door, then looked back at his friend. "There's something you want to say that you don't want them to hear, right?"

Echewa nodded. His eyes went to the case. "And then there's that . . ."

Ebert sat, facing him, the case in his lap.

"They'll ask you," Echewa said. "They'll want to use that. You know they will."

"I know."

"So what will you say?"

"That the greatest power . . . *te* . . . can only be grasped by those who do not seek it. That force cannot be used to attain it."

Echewa sighed. "That may be so, my brother. But for once wise words won't do. There is a new threat . . ."

"You've lived with such threats before."

"That's true. Yet things have changed. The tribes expected . . ."

". . . that the Seven would leave them be? To live in peace for ever? No, old friend. It is not in their nature to let things be. They must meddle all the while. And so now."

"Then what will you do?"

"*Me*? I will do nothing. I am not *ndichie*. I cannot decide your fate, Aluko Echewa. You forget. I am Efulefu, the 'Worthless One'."

"Acch . . ." For a moment Echewa's dark face creased with frustration, then, seeing how Ebert was watching him – calmly, a small ironical smile on his lips – he laughed. "Okay? What are you *really* going to say?"

Ebert's smile broadened. "You will have to wait and see, brother Aluko." He patted the case. "You and I both."

* * *

The old Han sat across from Ebert, looking down at the *wei chi* board and stroking his neatly-trimmed beard.

"You are improving," he said without looking up. "Even so, I would place good odds on Nza beating you each time."

Ebert laughed. "That bad, eh?"

Tuan Ti Fo looked up. "Bad? Did I say that was bad? No . . . in fact the boy is very good. He has a natural aptitude for the game. He watches and learns. Have you not noticed how closely he watches?"

Ebert nodded, sobered by the thought. "Yes . . . but I didn't know he played."

"I play him often."

"Really?" Ebert frowned. "You mean . . . *without* the Machine?"

The old man laughed. "You think I live in there?"

"No, I . . ." He looked down. "I don't know where you live."

"Behind it all," Tuan Ti Fo answered, placing a white stone in *Shang*, the South, "among the unnamed."

"Ah . . ."

The old Han's eyes twinkled mischievously. "Sometimes I think you take it all too seriously, Hans Ebert. You have come far these past two years, yet you are still only at the beginning of the path. It is as you said to young Nza. You must learn to row as if the boat was not there. Knowing is but the half of it. Now you must learn to forget. And to laugh. You have forgotten how to laugh."

He stared at the old man a long, long time, then nodded. It was true. He laughed, yes, but it was the laughter of politeness, or surprise, not the full belly-laugh of enjoyment. Darkness . . . all he'd known these past few years was darkness, yet that too was only half of it.

He placed a black stone on the board, in the North, in *Tsu*.

"Ah . . ." Tuan Ti Fo said, chuckling to himself. "Maybe

I'm wrong. Maybe you do have a sense of humour after all."

* * *

It was some while since he had used the Machine other than to talk to the Old Man and for once he felt ill at ease as he spoke to the glowing screen.

"Machine . . . Show me the newcomers. Show me their leader."

At once an image formed. A big, corpulent man – a Han, naturally – looked on as two servants filled an ornate-looking bath. Ebert stared, surprised by the wasteful use of so much water.

"Focus on his face. I want to see . . ."

His voice faded as the Han's fat-jowled face filled the screen. It wasn't a perfect image, for the camera viewpoint was above and to the right, yet it was good enough. He could see, as clearly as if the flesh were labelled, that this was a vain man, a cruel man – one who would not hesitate to carry out his orders, whatever they entailed.

Ebert narrowed his eyes.

"Who is he?"

"His name is Liang Yu and he is *Hsien L'ing*, Chief Magistrate, of the new settlement. Would you like his past record?"

He nodded. At once a summary of Liang Yu's career appeared on the screen.

"Would you like to know his vices?"

He smiled at the Machine's understanding. "No. That's all I need. By the way . . . are you still in touch with Chung Kuo?"

"Chung Kuo, Titan, the Asteroids . . . As long as the satellite links are open I can go where I wish."

"I see." Ebert hesitated; looked away. "The Marshal's daughter . . . did she get back safely?"

"Jelka Tolonen? You wish to see her?"

He looked back at the screen, surprised. "Is that possible?"

There was a moment's delay, and then the image of a young, blonde-haired woman appeared on the screen. The

424

room she was in was almost dark, the only light coming from a small glow-lamp that hovered near where she sat at a desk, writing. He studied her a while, fascinated, his eyes filled with pain and a longing that the years had not purged from him, then, satisfied, he nodded. The Machine, sensing the movement, blanked the screen.

"You want to know what she's been doing?"

"No. I . . . I don't want to pry."

"And the meeting tonight. Will you go to it? Will you take me there?"

Ebert frowned. "Should I?"

"What does the Old Man say?"

"He says be patient."

"Ah . . ." The Machine seemed to pause, as if considering the matter, then spoke again. "Perhaps this once the Old Man is right."

* * *

At the mid-point of the night they gathered beneath the table rock, the Eldest of the *ndichie* standing on the ledge above them, one hand raised, facing the *umunna*, the elders of the Osu.

In their old-fashioned, heavy suits, they seemed like ghosts, or like the crew of some long-abandoned ship, the metallic strips of their helmets glinting in the faint light of two glow-lamps.

"Brothers . . ." the Eldest said, his voice carried on their suit-mikes; a low, gruff voice, heavy with ancient inflections. "They are here. They are back. What are we to do?"

"Destroy them," said one.

"Hide," said another.

"Greet them," said a third.

They turned, looking to the one who had spoken last. It was Ebert.

The Eldest took a step towards him, then beckoned him up onto the rock.

Ebert climbed up, then turned to face the *ndichie*.

"Speak . . ." murmured a dozen, twenty voices.

"What do we fear?" he asked.

"That they will hunt us down," one of the *ndichie* to his left answered. "That they will kill our wives and children. That the Osu will be no more."

"And how might we prevent this?"

"*Destroy* them," the same voice answered.

"Is that the only way? Is *ochu* the only answer the Osu have?"

Ochu . . . Murder. There, he had said it.

"Self-defence," the same voice answered him. "We kill to live."

"Ah . . ." Ebert nodded. "And that is *right*, neh?"

"Not right. But necessary. Us or them."

"And if I could *prevent* them from hunting the Osu?"

There was a low murmur from among the *ndichie*. It was clearly what they had been hoping for.

"Tell us Tsou Tsai Hei," one called to him. "How can this be done?"

"Listen . . ." he said, and as he did, a figure appeared at his side – the figure of an old and wizened Han, his grey hair flowing in the bitter wind, his eyes twinkling in the airless atmosphere.

* * *

Liang Yu, Chief Official of the new settlement, sat up with a start, spilling water over the side of the bath.

"Who the *hell* are you?"

Tuan Ti Fo bowed, a faint smile on his face. "Forgive me, Magistrate Liang. I did not mean to frighten you. But you are such a busy man. You are so seldom alone. I thought . . ."

Liang's face was dark with anger. "Who the fuck let you in?"

"Ah . . ." Tuan Ti Fo turned, looking about him, then shrugged. "I . . . seem to have let myself in. I am told I am good at that."

"A thief! . . . ahh, I understand." Frowning fiercely, Liang sat right forward, gripping the edges of the bath. "So where in the gods' names did you come from? Were you a stowaway?"

426

"Goodness no. I live here."

"Here? What . . . in Kang Kua City? But I thought . . ."

"Oh no. Not *here*. Or rather, here, but not *only* here. On Mars, I mean."

Sticking out his chin, Liang stood and stepped out of the bath, scattering water everywhere. He grabbed a towel and wrapped it round him, then turned, facing Tuan Ti Fo again.

"This is outrageous, *lao jen* . . . Bursting in here without an invitation and . . ."

He stopped, his mouth open. He had put out his hand to prod Tuan Ti Fo in the chest and had seen it pass through the old man.

"*Aiya* . . ." he cried, his voice trembling. "A ghost!"

"Not at all," Tuan Ti Fo said, and, raising his right hand, pushed Liang back firmly with the palm.

Liang Yu stared at where he'd been touched, astonished, then looked up again, his left eye twitching.

"Who *are* you?"

Tuan smiled, then bowed. "Forgive me, Magistrate Liang . . . let me introduce myself. I am Tuan Ti Fo, Citizen of Mars and a friend of the Osu . . ."

* * *

Echewa shook his head in disbelief. "You've *arranged* it . . . What do you mean, you've arranged it?"

"It's done," Ebert answered him, smiling.

"But how do you *know*? Have you *been* to Kang Kua?"

"No. But there will be no trouble. Not now. We shall live in peace from here on, the Han and ourselves. They shall live in the Cities and we on the Plains."

"And the settlers know of this?"

"We have their word."

Echewa shook his head. "Are you *certain* they won't come for us?"

"I am certain, brother Aluko. There will be no trouble now."

When Echewa had gone, the boy slipped back into the room.

427

"Well?" he asked. "Did he believe you?"

Ebert smiled. "Not yet. But he will. As the days pass."

He laughed, imagining how it had been. When Magistrate Liang had switched on his comset to talk to his duty Captain, there had been Tuan Ti Fo. When he had tried to patch-in to the inter-planetary satellite link, there once more was Old Tuan, grinning back at him. Wherever he looked, there would be Tuan, staring back at him.

The new settlement was effectively isolated. Were they to send a message back to Chung Kuo, trying to warn them about what was happening here, it would be intercepted and changed . . . instantly. They could say nothing, *do* nothing, without the Machine knowing. And what the Machine knew, Tuan Ti Fo also knew.

For a time they would be resentful – would feel themselves prisoners, perhaps – yet as time passed and no harm came to them, they would realise that the "ghost" of the old Han was a benevolent spirit and there would come a day when they would step outside their Cities and greet the Osu.

A day of reconciliation.

He turned, looking at the boy, then pointed to the *wei chi* set on the corner shelf.

"Would you like a game, Nza? I'm told you play quite well."

PART 3 – AUTUMN 2213:

THE PATH IN THE TWILIGHT

———•———

"The Southern hills, how mournful!
A ghostly rain sprinkles the empty grass.
In Ch'ang-an, on an autumn midnight,
How many men grow old before the wind?
Dim, dim, the path in the twilight,
Branches curl on the black oaks by the road.
The trees cast upright shadows and the moon at the zenith
Covers the hills with a white dawn.
Darkened torches welcome a new kinsman:
In the most secret tomb these fireflies swarm."

— Li Ho, "Criticisms", 9th century AD

CHAPTER · 17

EMPTY ROOMS

Li Yuan stood at the back of the great study, beside the window, looking out into the Eastern Garden, while his Chancellor, Nan Ho, sat at his desk conducting the meeting.

General Rheinhardt had come, together with Tolonen and the giant, Karr. The big man had just returned from a fifteen-month undercover assignment in the Lowers, collecting information on the state of things down there. Glancing at him, Li Yuan wondered how such a man could ever go "undercover". Eyes were certain to turn wherever such a man went; questions were certain to be asked. And yet his report had been good, the details telling. Now Nan Ho questioned him, looking up from the written copy of Karr's report to meet the man's blue, *Hung Mao* eyes.

"From what you say of this . . . Li Min . . . he seems to have created quite a little empire for himself, neh? You talk of it extending, what? . . . twenty thousand stacks, perhaps more. And fifty levels. Are you quite certain of this, Major Karr?"

Karr, standing there at attention, his hands folded behind his back, bowed his head slightly. "Quite certain, Excellency."

"And you say that, for the most part, this man, Li Min, governs fairly and that there is peace within those areas he controls."

Karr hesitated. "I would not say fairly, Excellency. Harshly is perhaps a better word. His 'officials' as he calls them, are corrupt, their justice arbitrary. His rule is one of fear, not justice."

431

"Even so, there is peace there, neh? Whereas elsewhere in the Lowers there is chaos and clamour for violent change."

"Maybe so, Excellency, but . . ."

Nan Ho raised a hand, silencing the big man. Li Yuan, watching, looked away, hiding his amusement. He had yet to see Nan Ho intimidated by anyone, least of all by their physical presence.

"My point is this, Major Karr. When I had you sent, it was because I feared the very worst. I feared that the situation had deteriorated beyond the point of stability. Yet what you say here reassures me."

Tolonen, silent until now, pushed past Karr and leaned both hands on the front of the desk, facing Nan Ho. "*Reassures* you? But surely this *is* the worst? To find another ruling in the great T'ang's place – is that a *good* thing, Master Nan? Or have I died and woken in a world where all values are inverted? You know what they call the man down there? They call him The White T'ang, and they say that he will one day depose our Master, and extend his rule to every corner of this City. Is that *good*? Or is that not the *very* worst?"

Nan Ho leaned back, smiling tolerantly at the old man. Had any other than Tolonen uttered those words there would have been no smile, just an icy hostility.

"Again, you misunderstand me, Marshal Tolonen. I did not say that things were well, nor that I condone what has happened, merely that – in the context of all else that has been happening – to find such stability in the Lowers is a welcome, indeed a *useful* thing. These are troubled times and it would be unwise to take precipitate action in this matter."

"But what about *these*?" Tolonen said, slamming a flimsy handbill down on the desk – identical to the one Nan Ho had in the file before him. "Is this not a good reason to take action? Or is treason no longer an offence?"

Li Yuan had read the bill earlier and understood the old man's anger. In effect it was a declaration of independence from the rule of the Seven, the setting up of a separate nation within the City Empire. Even so, Nan Ho was right. Mars had fallen, and North America. Now was not the time to take Li Min and his cohorts on. Right now far greater dangers threatened.

Nan Ho had closed the file. He looked up at Tolonen with an unchanged expression, calm, his great authority unruffled.

"It is treason, I agree. And action *will* be taken. But no wars, Marshal Tolonen. We cannot afford another war."

Tolonen straightened up, taking a long, shuddering breath, clearly reluctant to let the matter drop. Then he turned, facing his T'ang.

"Is that your final word, *Chieh Hsia*?"

Li Yuan looked down. Once before – when his elder brother, Han Ch'in had been assassinated – Tolonen had been urged to a course of inaction, of *wuwei*, a course which, it seemed, was against the very fibre of his being. That time he had reacted badly – had marched into the great House at Weimar and killed the man he blamed for the young prince's death. Only quick thinking by his father had prevented war. But times had changed. For Tolonen to act precipitately now would be disastrous. Nan Ho was right. In better times they would have crushed such insolence in the bud, expending whatever force was necessary for the task, but these were evil days. This was but a single threat of many. The great empire of Chung Kuo was under siege, and a single error – one single misjudgement – could bring the whole fragile edifice crashing down.

He looked up. All four men were watching him, waiting to see what he would say; Nan Ho with certainty, the other three, it seemed, hoping he would gainsay his Chancellor. He smiled, knowing how fortunate he was to have such good men serving him.

"It is as Master Nan says. Our hands are tied. We cannot act."

"But *Chieh Hsia* . . . Each day his power grows, and at *our* expense. Why, the drug revenue alone allows him to add a hundred men to his private army every day. Soon the whole of the Lowers will be his, and then . . ."

Li Yuan raised a hand, silencing Tolonen. "That may be so, Knut, but you forget what happened on Mars and in my cousin's City."

"That last was an accident, *Chieh Hsia*."

"Maybe. But an accident waiting to happen, neh?"

Tolonen shook his head, his granite features regretful. "We should have crushed him when we could. After the war between the brotherhoods."

Li Yuan smiled sadly. "I gave the order. Remember? But then the storm hit Nantes." He sighed. "So it is. We cannot deal with every problem as if it were the only one. Things never happen in isolation. Priorities. It is always a question of priorities, and right now our priority is to maintain the peace at all costs."

He paused, looking about him sternly. "However, do not mistake my hesitancy for weakness. I will strike when I must. But not now. As Sun Tzu reminds us, to be cautious can also be a virtue."

* * *

When they were gone, Li Yuan turned to his Chancellor, letting a great sigh of relief escape him.

"They are right, of course. The situation *is* intolerable."

Nan Ho, serious throughout the meeting, allowed himself the luxury of a smile.

"Not *so* intolerable, *Chieh Hsia*. It is not all doom and gloom. My scheme . . ."

". . . is a good one, and before you say another word, I agree to it. Arrange to meet the man and put the deal before him. But first there's another matter I wish you to set in motion."

Nan Ho's brows furrowed. For once he was at a loss. "*Another* matter, *Chieh Hsia*?"

Li Yuan looked about him, gesturing at the silent solemnity of it all. "Empty rooms, Master Nan. I have had my fill of empty rooms. It is time I had a wife again."

* * *

434

Walking down the long corridor that led to his suite of offices, Nan Ho mulled the matter over in his mind. After the death of Li Yuan's wives he had not pressed the matter, knowing just how deeply the young T'ang had been hurt. But lately he had been wondering whether he should raise it again.

To have a single son – that was a dangerous weakness. But to have five or six . . .

As the great doors swung open before him, he clicked his fingers, summoning his Principal Secretary.

"Hu Ch'ang, bring me the Book of Dragon and Phoenix. And send Pi Kung, I need to talk to him at once."

He sat, conscious of all the urgent matters there were to deal with. Since Li Yuan had handed over power to him, he had had little time to himself. He had neglected family matters badly. His wife, his children – he had not seen them in . . . what? A week. He looked about his desk, studying the great piles of official documents, then hauled one bulky folder towards him. It was the application for citizenship he had been looking at before the meeting. He flipped it open, then reached across for his seal, inking the great chop before bringing it down on the bottom of the official form.

He peeled it off the paper and set it back on its stand, then studied the glistening imprint. *There. As simple as that.* Now he had only to arrange the meeting. Quickly he took paper from the drawer, then inked his brush and, with a haste that was uncharacteristic, wrote out the summons.

"Tonight . . ." he murmured to himself as Hu Ch'ang came back into the room.

"I beg pardon, Excellency?" Hu Ch'ang said, stopping half-way across the room, the huge book balanced on his arms.

"Oh, nothing, Hu Ch'ang. I was merely talking to myself."

"Ah . . ." Hu Ch'ang averted his eyes, then came across, waiting as Nan Ho cleared a space for the great book. As Hu Ch'ang set the book down, Nan Ho looked up at him.

"It's been some years, neh? You realise what this means?"

Hu Ch'ang blushed. "That you are taking a second wife, Excellency?"

Nan Ho started forward slightly. "No. I . . ." But the idea

435

wasn't such a bad one. Maybe Nan Tsing would welcome the company of a younger woman? And maybe he could do with the regenerative effects of a new wife in his bed?

He stared at the cover of the book, tracing the dragon and phoenix design inlaid in gold in the blood-red velvet, and nodded. No, not such a bad idea at all.

"It is not I who needs a wife but our Master."

"The great T'ang . . . he is to be *married* again?"

"Yes, Hu Ch'ang. And it is our task, our *sacred* task, to choose him a lifetime's mate. A woman of discretion, demure but strong. Attractive, but not beautiful."

"*Not* beautiful, Excellency? I do not understand . . ."

Nan Ho opened the great book, exposing the first of the many faces within – the faces of all the Minor Family princesses who were eligible to be married – then looked up at Hu Ch'ang again.

"Beauty fades . . . Other qualities . . . well, they grow stronger as the years pass. If the great T'ang wants beauty, we can recruit a dozen maids to keep his bed warm and a smile on his face. But a wife . . . a wife is a different thing." He laughed. "A wife is like a good Chancellor, neh?

* * *

Two hours later it was done, the official invitations sent out to six of the young princesses to attend Nan Ho at the palace. He sat there, satisfied, for once feeling positive about something. Too often these days the burden of governing the great City simply oppressed him. In another age, perhaps, he might have found it a joyful, an *exhilarating* task, but right now it was like being Supervisor of Dams in a time of floods. The most he could do was to contain the damage and save a field or two. Things were bad – worse than he'd ever known them – and in his heart of hearts he felt not the steersman of some great social enterprise but the custodian of decline.

There was a knock. A moment later a tall, slender-looking man in his mid-twenties came into the room. He came forward two paces, then dropped to his knees, placing his forehead to the thickly carpeted floor.

"You sent for me, Excellency?"

"Yes, Pi Kung. I have a job for you. There is a man I want killed. A great man. A very *special* man, so I am told. Is there someone . . . *special* you could find for the task?"

Pi Kung lifted his head and smiled broadly. "Ah, yes, Excellency. I know just the man."

* * *

Karr leaned back in his chair and roared with laughter. Across the kitchen table from him sat Chen, a bowl of *ch'a* at his elbow, an almost inane grin lighting his plain features.

Karr leaned forward again and nodded, his eyes filled with a natural warmth. "Ah, Chen, it's good to see you again. I've missed your company badly. Down there . . . acchh . . . it's hard to say how foul I found it all. That man, Li Min, he's a cold bastard. I met him twice, and to be honest with you, he sent the chills through me."

Chen frowned, his voice taking on a friendly, mocking tone. "The chills? I don't believe it, Gregor. You . . . frightened of another human being?"

"*Frightened?* Did I *say* frightened? No, brother Chen. But there's something about the man that reminds you of Yen Wang, the King of Hells. And his two henchmen, Soucek and Visak . . . Ox-head and Horse-face they are! Niu T'ou and Ma Mien themselves! Yes . . . the chief constables of Hell."

Chen laughed, then grew more serious. "And yet the T'ang does nothing."

Karr shrugged. "What *can* he do? Even if he had the will, it would take all we've got to subdue the Lowers, and what then? Without Li Min there keeping the peace we would have to police the Lowers again – a hundred men a deck, maybe more. And in the meantime our enemies – our real enemies – would take the opportunity to destroy us."

"Our real enemies?"

"Wang Sau-leyan . . ."

"Ah . . ." Chen lifted his bowl, drank deeply from it, then set it down again. "I thought you were *for* dealing firmly with Li Min."

"I am. At least, part of me is. To leave him there . . . well, it's as Tolonen says. He grows stronger daily. And eventually . . . well, eventually there will be war. A far more hideous war, I suspect, than any we've yet seen. And if Li Min triumphs, well . . ." Again he shrugged.

"You say it was peaceful down there."

Karr smiled faintly. "That's the strangest part of it. In some ways it reminded me of how things used to be. Before the Dispersionists. Before the *Ping Tiao*, the *Yu* and all the other factions. It's all very orderly. There's fear, true, but there's also hope. A lot of people down there like living under Li Min. They say it's better than living under Li Yuan. And who's to know the truth. Maybe there is no difference."

"Hold. Careful what you say, old friend. The difference, surely, is in the man. This Li Min . . . you say you've met him. You say he chills you. And Li Yuan? You've met him, neh? Does *he* chill you? Does *he* strike you as the King of Hells?"

"No."

"Then maybe *that's* the difference. Maybe one should look behind the system to the man who governs it."

"You mean Nan Ho?"

Chen laughed. "I mean that orderliness is not everything. Nor is peace a sure sign of happiness. Things are bad, no one denies that, but they could be worse, and if this Li Min were in charge they would be a *lot* worse, neh?"

"Maybe . . . And you, Chen? How have things been? Is Wang Ti . . ." He hesitated. "I mean, is she still as she was?"

For a moment Chen was silent, then a bright, almost impish smile settled on his lips. "Well . . . come and see."

He led Karr through, stopping before the door to the bedroom.

"She's rather weak right now," he whispered, "a virus, the doctors say, but she'll be okay. The other problems . . . well, you'll see."

He slid the door open, then stood there, watching as Karr went across and, kneeling over the bed, reached out, hugging Wang Ti to him.

"Wang Ti . . . how *are* you? It's been ages . . ."

438

Karr moved back slightly, drinking in the sight of Wang Ti smiling up at him. *Thank you*, she mouthed at him, then gave a tiny shiver, a tear trickling down her cheek.

"It's good to see you better," Karr said softly, then leaned towards her again, kissing her cheek. "Marie sends her love. We've a child now, you know . . ."

"A *child*?" Chen said, astonished. "You mean, you've had a child and I didn't hear about it? Why, Wang Ti had only to have fallen for a week and you'd know."

Karr turned, looking back at him, his eyes deadly serious. "It was while I was away. The pregnancy was a bad one and the child was ill at birth. They didn't think it would live. They wanted to call me back, to be with her, but Marie wouldn't let them. She endured it all. For two whole weeks it was in a special incubator. They say they had to revive it more than a dozen times in all. And yet it lived."

"It?" Wang Ti spoke the word softly, her whole face wrinkled with concern.

"A girl," Karr said, turning to her, his face lit with joy. "A beautiful baby girl. May, we've called her, after the month in which she was born. And because she *may* be something special."

Wang Ti stared up at him, her eyes wide with joy, the tears flowing freely once again. But Karr, looking down into her face, found his own joy clouded by the memory of her lost child.

"Does it still hurt?" he asked gently, stroking the back of her hand with his fingers as if to comfort her.

Yes, she mouthed. *But less now. Much less.*

* * *

In the Imperial Palace at Alexandria, Wang Sau-leyan, T'ang of City Africa, lounged on a couch eating strawberries, while in a sunken circle nearby two greybeards, both Masters of the game, faced each other over a *wei chi* board.

The game was near completion, the patterns of black and white stones filling the low, nineteen by nineteen board. The two Masters, their legs crossed beneath them, leaned over the board, their gaze intent. This was a crucial stage of the game and a single stone might win or lose it.

To the side of Wang Sau-leyan a group of richly-dressed courtiers looked on with a jaded indifference, plucking delicacies from the bowls that surrounded their couches, or sipping from silver goblets. Across from them, hunched forward on a low bench, like statues, their chins cradled in their hands, the two other finalists – greybeards, indistinguishable from the two who sat at play – watched with narrowed eyes, knowing that the outcome of this single game would decide it all.

Beyond them, his eyes taking in everything, stood Hung Mien-lo, Chancellor of City Africa. He was busy – more busy than he'd ever been, trying to keep things together – but the T'ang had insisted he be here for this final game, and so here he was, less jaded perhaps than the watching courtiers, but tired all the same. Tired of his Master's whims, his vicious nature, his callous brutality. Tired, more than anything, of being his whipping-boy, his servant.

None of this showed in his face; only a polite interest in the game. But from time to time he would look past the two ancients at the board and watch his Master; see those heavy, gluttonous jowls move up and down as he ate some new delicacy.

As if he could eat it all . . .

There was a sharp click, a little movement backwards by the old Master, Hsu Jung; a smile of satisfaction.

Hung Mien-lo watched, seeing how Hsu's opponent's face wrinkled with dismay as he realised the significance of the play. Then, with a sharp little movement, the man bowed his head, conceding the game. It was over. Hsu Jung had won. Which meant . . .

"Shit!" Hung Mien-lo murmured beneath his breath, then moved out into the circular space.

"Is it finished?" Wang asked, looking up, his chin wet with peach juice. "Have we a champion?"

Hung Mien-lo paused, wondering how to phrase it, then shook his head. "I am afraid . . ."

"You afraid, Hung Mien-lo? And so you should, I guess. Afraid I'll cut off your head, or your balls, or some other part of your anatomy, neh?"

Wang half-sat, laughing, his huge triple belly shaking with it. Beyond him the courtiers, to a man and woman, laughed along with him. But their eyes showed something different. They knew Wang's sudden moods.

"Well?" Wang asked again, fixing Hung Mien-lo in a cold stare. "Have I a champion, or have we all been wasting our time?"

Hung swallowed. "We have a result, *Chieh Hsia*. Unfortunately . . ."

That "unfortunately" made Wang sit forward, his face suddenly hard, uncompromising. "What the fuck are you trying to tell me, man? Have I a champion or haven't I?"

Hung shook his head. "Tradition has it that the four best players must compete to see who is Supreme Champion. Each contestant must play each of the other competitors twice, the winner being the one who has won most games."

Wang tilted his head back, revealing not three but six, maybe seven chins, a huge cascade of flesh that was like the soft rocks at the foot of a waterfall. This last year he had put on weight at an astonishing rate, while in his City rationing had reduced most of his citizens to wraiths – walking skeletons who barely had the strength to protest. But while his body had grown softer, flabbier, his manner hadn't changed. If anything he was harder, crueller than he'd been.

"So?" he asked, the very softness of his voice a warning.

Hung Mien-lo swallowed a second time, then turned, looking across at the four Masters, who now stood together, heads bowed, awaiting their T'ang's pleasure. "So . . . each of them has won three games, and each . . ."

". . . has lost three." Wang finished wearily. He leaned forward, once, twice, a third time, finally freeing himself from the pull of the couch. Slowly he came across, until he was facing Hung Mien-lo. Again, his voice was gentle.

"What you mean to say is that we've spent more than two weeks watching these . . . these *Masters* play out their

441

interminable strategies, only to find ourselves right back at the beginning, neh?"

"Yes, *Chieh Hsia.*"

The change was abrupt. One moment he was smiling, the next he was screaming, his eyes wide, spittle flying from his lips.

"I want a winner! I don't want *four* champions, I want *one*! Can't you understand that, you dolt?"

He lowered his head, not daring to wipe the spittle from his cheeks. "It is tradition, *Chieh Hsia* . . ."

"Well, bugger tradition! You four, here, now!"

The four ancients scuttled across, then prostrated themselves at Wang Sau-leyan's feet.

"Good. Now listen and listen carefully. This once we do things differently. You will draw lots to see who will play who, and the winners of those two games will play each other for the honour of being my champion. Understand me?"

The four answered as one. "Yes, *Chieh Hsia.*"

"Good." Wang turned, walked across and sat again, a strange self-satisfied smile on his lips. "Oh . . . and one more rule. Whoever loses *dies.*"

* * *

Li Yuan was in the stables, watching the groom brush out his favourite horse and braid its mane, when Hu Ch'ang came running from the House.

"*Chieh Hsia,*" the man said breathlessly, stopping just inside the door, then knelt and touched his forehead to the dark earth of the stable floor. "Chancellor Nan bids you come quickly. Your son . . ."

"Kuei Jen?" Li Yuan frowned, his eyes suddenly wide with concern. "Why? What has happened to him?"

"I do not know, *Chieh Hsia.* Only that the boy is unwell, feverish. The doctors have been summoned . . ."

Hu Ch'ang turned, still on his knees, as the T'ang rushed past him, then, not stopping to brush himself down, he climbed to his feet and ran after his Master.

442

The doctors had just arrived as Li Yuan came into his son's bedroom. The curtains were drawn and there was the tart smell of sickness in the air. Kuei Jen's two maids stood on the far side of the bed, looking on anxiously. Li Yuan looked to them, then gestured for the eldest, Welcome Spring, to come to him.

"What happened?" he asked, not looking at her, his eyes never leaving his son, who, pale, his eyes closed, his brow beaded with sweat, moved slowly, feverishly beneath the sheets, oblivious, it seemed, to the hands of the doctor as he examined him.

The girl knelt, her head lowered. "I . . . I am not sure, *Chieh Hsia.* Earlier he was fine. After lunch we played ball in the West Garden, but then he complained of being tired and so we brought him back indoors. He said he would have a nap. I stayed with him, on the chair just there. He slept . . . oh, for an hour or more, and then, suddenly, he sat up, groaning, holding his sides. I asked what was wrong, but before he could answer he was sick. I sent Pale Blossom to fetch Master Nan. The rest you know."

Li Yuan nodded, then made a gesture of dismissal. "Well?" he asked the doctor nearest him. "Do you know what's wrong with him? Is it poison?"

The man looked up, alarmed. "Poison, *Chieh Hsia?*"

"Look at him," Li Yuan demanded. "Just look at the agony he's in."

As if on cue, the four-year-old groaned, bringing a corresponding grimace to his father's face.

"Well? Don't you know?"

"Forgive me, *Chieh Hsia,*" the second doctor answered, turning from the boy, "but a proper diagnosis will take time."

Li Yuan raised himself up, his concern for his son making him tetchy. "The gods help us! If you don't know *say* you don't and get someone here who does!"

There was a rustling behind Li Yuan. He turned to find Nan Ho standing there, his head slightly bowed.

"Thank the gods you're here, Master Nan. These fools know nothing. Where is my surgeon? Where *is* Chang Li?"

"*Chieh Hsia*, please . . . calm yourself. It is nothing serious. If you would come with me a moment."

"And leave my son?"

"*Chieh Hsia* . . . please."

Reluctantly he followed Nan Ho out into the corridor and into one of the tiny ante-rooms, then watched as his Chancellor closed the door behind him.

"Well, Master Nan?"

Nan Ho scratched at his neck, as if what he was about to say were difficult, then, clearing his throat, he began.

"I have made my own investigations, *Chieh Hsia*. They are preliminary, I confess, but I think I have managed to get to the bottom of this little episode."

"And?" Li Yuan said impatiently.

"And Kuei Jen is ill because he ate too much at lunch, *Chieh Hsia*. To put it bluntly, he stuffed himself silly."

"He *what*?"

"It is true, *Chieh Hsia*. He was warned of the consequences, but the boy cannot be told. If he does not get his own way he throws tantrums or smashes things."

Li Yuan laughed. "Are you serious, Master Nan?"

"I am afraid so, *Chieh Hsia*."

"Then why have I not been told of this."

"It has been . . . difficult, *Chieh Hsia*. The boy needs . . . *discipline* sometimes, and yet . . . well, you will not allow him to be punished."

"And rightly so. He is a prince, after all."

"Maybe so, *Chieh Hsia*, and yet you too were a prince, and your father never commanded that *you* were not to be punished. Why, I remember well the time . . ."

"*Enough!*" Li Yuan shuddered, suddenly angry. "Since when was it your place to tell me what I should or shouldn't do?"

"Since you appointed me your Chancellor, *Chieh Hsia*."

"Chancellor, maybe, but Kuei Jen is *my* son and I shall do as I see fit. He is a prince and one day shall be T'ang."

"All the more reason, then, for him to learn self-discipline."

"You speak out of line, Nan Ho."

"I speak as I find, *Chieh Hsia*. To do less would be to fail in my duty. I see a good boy slowly turning bad. Forgive me for saying so, *Chieh Hsia*, but you are over-protective towards the child. Guard him by all means, but do not make a monster of him."

Li Yuan stood there for a long time, simply staring at his Chancellor, astonished. Then he looked down. "I . . . I didn't realise. Maybe you're right, Master Nan. Maybe . . ." He sighed. "Tell me. What would *you* do in my place?"

"There is a man, *Chieh Hsia*. His name is Lo Wen and he is a Master of *Wu Shu*, the martial arts. He is an upstanding and honourable man and would be a fine example to the boy. If I were you I would invite him to the Palace and place him in charge of the boy. That is, if that is what you wish?"

Li Yuan sighed. "But isn't he rather young for this? I mean, he's not yet five."

Nan Ho stared back at him, stern-faced. "It is never too young, *Chieh Hsia*. Why, when you were five you had not one but five instructors, don't you remember?"

"Only too well. I hated it."

"Naturally. When you are too young to understand, you always hate what is good for you. And yet *you* came to respect your instructors, neh? In time you even made one of them your Chancellor."

Li Yuan smiled. "You have no need to remind me, Nan Ho. Even so, I still have doubts. Kuei Jen is so young . . ."

"It is for the best, *Chieh Hsia*. If I felt it would harm the boy I would not have mentioned it. You know that."

"I know . . ." Li Yuan hesitated a moment longer, then nodded. "Go then. Arrange it."

After Nan Ho had gone he stood there a while, taking in what had been said. Nan Ho was his oldest friend, his closest adviser. In all the time he had known him, Master Nan had never failed to do his best by him. And so now. He alone, perhaps, could have said what needed to be said. And there was no doubt – now that his anger had passed – that it *had* been necessary. But how long had Master Nan known and not spoken? Just how bad had it become for him to bring this matter to a head?

A monster, he thought, recollecting Nan Ho's words, then shivered. Was it true? Was it really that bad? And if so, had it been *his* failure? Had he failed as a father? As he walked back through to Kuei Jen's room, the thought nagged at him.

Maybe he had. But it was not too late to start anew. To love without spoiling. To . . .

He stopped in the doorway, looking in. Kuei Jen was sitting up watching him, a mischievous grin lighting his features.

"What's this I hear?" he began, dismissing both the doctors and the maids. "I think it's time we had a little talk."

* * *

Michael Lever was in the shower when the messenger came. The first he knew of it was when Emily rapped on the transparent surround, startling him.

"Hey, what's so urgent?"

"I think it's come. It has the T'ang's seal on it."

He pushed the door open, glanced at the package she held up to him, then ducked back inside, jabbing at the off switch. As he emerged she was holding out a towel for him.

"You want me to dry you?"

He laughed. "Not if I'm in a hurry, I don't!"

Even so, he let her rub him down while he stood there staring at the package where she'd put it on the tall-backed bath-chair, wondering.

"Do you think . . . ?" he asked after a moment.

"Do I think what?" she answered, smiling back up at him from where she was kneeling, dabbing at those delicate areas where the flesh was newest. It was only two months since the last operation and he still complained of soreness, but now that he was out of the harness he was a changed man, as if he'd shed the last memory of the bombing. But it wasn't entirely so. Part of him would remain forever shocked at what had happened to him.

"Do you think he's granted it? I mean, why send a package if the answer's no?"

She stood, watching as he went to the side and began to dress. "You think Nan Ho would say no?"

"Maybe. That's if it ever got as far as Nan Ho. You know what they say – the building has nine floors and each floor has nine doors. There's some truth to that. There *are* eighty-one levels of officialdom, and if you're unlucky you have to pass through every damn one of them."

"Then you don't think Gloria's letter of introduction would have helped?"

He shrugged, then pulled on his tunic. "I don't know. At the time I thought it was a good idea. Now I'm not so sure. I mean, she's in the same position as us. Or was."

That was true, Emily reflected. They and many others who had escaped the fall of North America. And that was the problem, basically. One could do nothing here without citizenship. In particular you could not buy a First Level Mansion. In fact the demand was so great that you couldn't even rent one. Which meant that they, like many others, had spent the months since the Fall as perpetual house-guests, moving from one great Mansion to another, forever beholden, forever dissatisfied, never alone.

As if picking up on her thoughts, Michael looked at her glumly. "That's the worst of it, Em. I own six Companies over here – Companies worth over a billion *yuan* – and *still* I'm classed as a refugee."

"Well, maybe you aren't any longer. Why don't you see?"

He looked past her at the package, then met her eyes again, smiling. "I was like this as a kid. It used to drive my father wild. He'd say, 'Why don't you just *open* it, boy!', but I'd delay and delay. It was like . . . well, the gift itself was nothing. I had lots of things. It was the anticipating. That was the good part."

She smiled, conscious of the hurt that re-emerged whenever he talked of his father. "I know. But this is different, neh? If he says yes, it's a severance from the past – from America and all we did there. And if he says no . . ."

"He can't, surely?"

"Well open it and find out. Or do you want *me* to open it?"

He shook his head.

"Well?" But she understood his hesitancy. It had been the same for her when she had fled from Europe that first time. She still vividly recalled her final moments at the spaceport, staring out for what she thought would be her last glimpse of home. But now she was back. This time it was Michael who was the exile.

He held her briefly, kissing her brow, then went over to the chair and picked up the package. It was heavy and official-looking, the T'ang's seal, its blood-red wax imprinted with his chop, dominating the reverse. He peeled it off and opened the package up.

"What the . . . ?"

She went over and stood beside him, looking down at what he held. It was an expensive-looking menu – the menu for The New Hope, she realised, with a jolt of surprise. The New Hope was an eating place at Weimar, popular with the more radical members of the House.

He opened it, then frowned. Inside was a handwritten note – an invitation to a meal that evening. That in itself was not surprising, they had many invites. Michael was a popular young man and not without influence both inside the House and out, in the greater business world. No, what was surprising was the name at the foot of the invitation – a name which was signed over the imprint of a second blood-red chop.

Nan Ho.

Emily whistled. "What do you think he wants?"

Michael shrugged. "You think we should go, then?"

She stared at him, surprised. "You'd refuse?"

"It's a strange choice, don't you think? To invite us *there*."

"Maybe. But you can't refuse, surely? That would end our chances of citizenship."

"It might. But it might also embarrass the Chancellor if it became public knowledge, don't you think? Questions would be asked. Primarily why Li Yuan's First Minister should be asking an ex-member of the New Republicans to dinner. I mean, it has to be a deal. Li Yuan has to want something from us."

She smiled. "You're beginning to sound like a politician."

He laughed. "Well, I was! And maybe I still am."

She shook her head. "You're wrong. There are lots of political animals, and we seem to have met them all these past few years, but you're different. People respect you because you always think and act as a man not as a politician. Not that you're wrong here. Li Yuan almost certainly wants something of you. It's just . . . well, I'd trust to your instincts. I'd meet him. Hear what he wants. You don't have to agree to anything. After all, he's the one who's put himself out here. If anyone loses face, it's Nan Ho, not you."

"And you? You're invited, too, you know."

She looked at the note again, then gave a small laugh of surprise, for Nan Ho had specifically mentioned her, and by her sobriquet, "the Eldest Daughter".

"Do you think that's meant ironically?" she asked, surprised to find her pulse suddenly racing at the thought.

"Maybe. But we'll find out, neh? Tonight."

"Then we're going?"

Dropping the menu, he put his arm round her, and lifted her face up to his. "Sure. But that's tonight. Right now . . ."

* * *

"What *is* this place?"

Karr stood there at the big ornamental gateway, looking about him uncomfortably. Beside him Chen waited patiently, as if it was something he did regularly.

"This is Shang Mu's Mansion," Chen said quietly.

"Shang Mu's? You mean the same Shang Mu who blew the whistle on what was happening in the Ministry?"

"That's right."

"And we've come to see him?"

Chen shook his head. "Not Shang Mu. He was killed. It's his daughter, Hannah, we've come to see."

Karr frowned. "When you said there was someone I ought to meet, I thought . . ."

"You thought what?" Chen turned, studying his old friend, his dark eyes strangely alive. "A lot happened while you were

449

down-level, Gregor Karr, and not all of it reported on the media. There were moments when I thought it was all up for me. But here we are, you and I. We're alive, neh? And not merely in the flesh."

Karr was about to ask what he meant by that when a camera swivelled overhead and, with a faint clicking, the gate juddered and began to slide back.

Inside, two liveried servants bowed low before them.

"Major Kao," the most senior of them said, then turned slightly, his arm outstretched, inviting them to cross the open space to the main Mansion. "We were not expecting you."

"Forgive me, Steward Tse. If I'd known beforehand I was coming . . ." He paused, remembering his manners. "This, by the way, is Major Karr, of the T'ang's imperial élite."

The Steward bobbed his head lower, then glanced up at Karr, clearly impressed by the big man. "Is this . . . an *official* visit?"

Chen smiled. "No. Not at all. Is *Nu Shi* Shang at home?"

"Of course. She is working just now, but I shall tell her you are here. If you would come through."

While they waited in the marbled entrance hall, Chen staring down into a sunken pool of carp, Karr spoke quickly to him, his voice lowered.

"Well? What's going on?"

Chen turned, smiling. "I'm sorry. I should have warned you. But . . . well, you'll see."

"See what?"

"Something you've probably not seen for some while. Something that's not visible to the common eye."

Karr laughed. "Have you been drinking, Chen? Or have you suffered a bad case of mysticism since I've been away?"

Chen raised one eyebrow. "And if I had? Would that be such a bad thing?"

"A bad thing? Why . . ."

Karr stopped. The Steward had reappeared at the doorway on the far side of the entrance hall.

"*Ch'un tzu*? If you would follow me."

Karr gave Chen one long, hard look, then, shaking his head, followed Chen and the Steward through.

Inside it was cool and shadowed. A long corridor led to a pair of tall doors which opened at their approach. Beyond them was a formal dining room at the centre of which stood a young woman, her long, jet-black hair tied into a single pony-tail, her hands folded before her. She was simply but elegantly dressed, yet what struck Karr immediately was the sheer warmth of her smile on seeing Chen. It was the kind of smile one couldn't feign. As the doors closed behind them, she put out her hands to Chen and came forward, taking his hands and leaning forward to kiss him on both cheeks.

"Chen! How wonderful to see you!" She turned, facing Karr. "And you too, Major Karr. I'm very pleased to meet you at last. Chen's told me a great deal about you."

Karr laughed, his discomfort returning. "He has, has he?"

"Oh, nothing bad. At least, nothing *I'd* take as bad."

Her eyes were shining mischievously as she said this last, and her grip on his hands was unexpectedly strong.

"Come," she said, ushering them through into a smaller, more feminine-looking room furnished in soft pastels. "I'll have the servants bring *ch'a.*" She turned her head, flashing a smile at Karr. "You're quite an expert, I'm told, Major. I hope you'll like our humble brew."

Karr gave a slight bow of his head. "I am sure it will be delightful."

"And if it isn't? Would you tell me?"

Karr looked to Chen, then looked back. "Would you wish that? I mean, some might take it as an impertinence . . . an affront."

She looked to Chen then met Karr's eyes again. "He hasn't said, has he? He's just brought you here, right?"

Karr nodded, a faint smile appearing on his lips.

She turned, wagging a finger at Chen, like a mother-in-law scolding her son's daughter. "Why, Kao Chen, that's very bad of you, to keep Major Karr guessing. You should have prepared him."

Chen laughed. "And spoil my fun? No way!"

She turned back, facing Karr. "Your friend Chen is a remarkable man, Major. I owe him a great deal. My liberty. Certainly my life."

It was an impassioned little speech that made Karr frown and try to reassess just what the relationship between the two was. He had begun to think . . .

"I . . . I don't understand."

"No," she said, smiling again, gesturing towards one of the couches. "But all will be revealed, neh? Now, let me order that *ch'a*, then we can sit and talk."

* * *

The stones swam before the man's eyes, blurring, merging into each other, like a solid line of troops, a great white wall surrounding him. Sweat dripped from his brow onto the board, drip, drip, as if he were being slowly dissolved; as if, before the final stone could be played, there would be nothing of him but a pool of salted water.

He swallowed drily. It was impossible. There was no way out. Master Hsu had a four stone advantage at the very least, and if he lost this group then there was no hope.

His eyes lifted from the board, travelled across the room and rested on the two bodies that lay there in the corner. So still they were. So perfectly, *awfully* still. Such stillness as the great Tuan Ti Fo had once reputedly possessed.

He looked back, trying to concentrate, yet he was close to fainting. The heat . . . It was so hot in here suddenly. As if . . .

He remembered. The game. He *had* to win the game. *Black. I am playing black*, he reminded himself. But it was no use. His concentration had gone. The pressure. The pressure was too much. Last time, when he had realised he'd won, he had felt such relief flood through him. Such happiness! But now . . .

He looked up, meeting Master Hsu's eyes. Nothing. They too were like walls, shutting him out, denying him.

"It's a game," he wanted to scream. "It's only a game!" But the rules had been changed. Then, suddenly he understood.

This is what this game is really about. Life and death. A struggle. And only one survivor. And the loser?

Yes. He understood.

He moved back slightly from the board, wiping his face on the silk of his sleeve. For a moment longer he studied the board, then, drawing himself up, he gave his old friend Hsu the slightest of nods, accepting what the stones had already told him. He had lost. Six, maybe eight stones ago he had lost, and he had known it then. But he had played on, hoping against hope. But for once, hope wasn't enough. For once the game was black and white.

He almost laughed at that. But it was no time for laughter. It was a time for dignity. Dignity . . . and inner strength.

He turned, looking across at the great T'ang. Wang Sau-leyan was looking away, his great jowls chewing on some delicacy. Then, as if sensing something was happening, he turned his head and looked.

"Is it over?"

The man nodded.

"Good." And with the most casual of gestures, Wang waved his guards across.

He turned back, studying the board one final time, realising for the first time just how deeply, how *intimately* he had woven his life into the patterns of the game. He had been a child of four when he'd first been apprenticed, eight when he'd won his first professional competition, twenty-six when he'd first been made a Master. All his life he had struggled for perfection, but until today he had sought it in vain.

He stared at the stones, his mouth open in wonder. No . . . no game had ever been so intense. Not one had ever possessed even a glimpse of such rare and delicate beauty, such clarity . . . such *power*.

He shivered and looked across at Hsu, bowing his head low, honouring the man. If only every game could have been so meaningful. If only he had had a thousand lives to lose. Or maybe not. Maybe that was why.

He felt their rough hands on him, felt them lift him and carry him across, felt . . .

"Messy," Wang Sau-leyan said, and then laughed, his laughter echoed back at him by the watching courtiers. "Still. It worked, neh? I have a champion at last. Someone to represent me at the tournament in two weeks time." He hauled himself up into a sitting position, then swivelled round on his couch and put his feet down on the floor. "Master Hsu, I congratulate you."

The old man bowed his head, maintaining his dignity a moment longer, then was promptly sick all over the board.

"Gods . . ." Wang said, sighing, his face registering his disgust. "Hung . . . take him away and clean him up, will you? Oh . . . and give him ten thousand *yuan*. He was a worthy winner."

Hung raised an eyebrow, surprised that Wang had even noticed how well Hsu Jung had played.

"And the others, *Chieh Hsia*?"

"The *losers*?" Wang smiled, his mouth like a slit in the puffed expanse of his face. "Throw them to the birds."

* * *

The *ch'a* had proved to be a *T'ieh Kuan Yin*, an Iron Goddess Of Mercy, an oolong from Fukien's Wu-I Mountains. Karr had complimented Hannah on its bitter-sweetness, its lingering fragrance, but the *ch'a* had been the least of his delights. An hour into their meeting he found himself enchanted by the young woman, and when, in a break in the conversation, he looked across at Chen, it was to find his friend smiling at him.

"You see?" Chen said. "What did I say?"

"You said nothing, you scoundrel. If I had known . . ."

"If you had known, then you would have spoiled it for both of us. Isn't my Hannah something?"

Karr nodded, then, on a whim, lowered his head to her in respect. In return she beamed back at him.

"But your idea . . ." Chen said suddenly. "You haven't mentioned your idea."

She made to wave it away, but Chen insisted. "No. You must tell Gregor. I think it's a marvellous idea."

Karr looked at her questioningly. "Well?"

454

She looked down, for the first time slightly abashed. "It's just something I've been thinking of doing, that's all. But . . ." She looked up again. "Well, it's all so impractical. I can't see how it could work."

"Well, tell me. Maybe *I* can see a way."

She shrugged, smiled. "All right. It's this. We have the media, neh? It tells us what's happening in our world. Or so we fool ourselves into thinking. In reality it only tells us what it wants us to know. You've seen it for yourself. What's news for First Level isn't news for the Lowers. At each level things are . . . *different*. Not only that, but there are bodies like the *T'ing Wei*, the Superintendency of Trials, responsible for black propaganda, and there's the Ministry, the Thousand Eyes – or what's left of it, now that the Seven have dismantled it. All of them serve to distort the overall picture of events. They're all . . . barriers set up in the path of truth, like screens set up to fend off ghosts. Well, my idea . . . my *big* idea, is to tear down those barriers somehow. Or to get round them. To somehow find a way of letting people know just exactly what's going on. Like the business Chen was telling me about at Kibwezi, or the cover-up over the storm-damage at Nantes, or . . . well, there's a hundred different subjects you might chose. The point is, Chung Kuo needs to have someone outside all the power games. Someone who'll tell it like it really is, without fear or favour. And I want to be that someone."

Karr sat back, blowing out a long, whistling breath. "*Aiya* . . . that's some idea, young woman."

She nodded, but her eyes now were deadly serious. "Well? What do you think, Gregor Karr? I'm not rich like Mary Lever. I've no real influence. Do you think I'm mad to dream of doing such a thing?"

Karr looked down, then reached across and poured more *ch'a* into his bowl. "No. To be frank with you, I've felt the same for some time now. I've felt like I'd burst unless I could tell someone what I've seen and done. I'm . . ." He looked to Chen. "Well, Chen here is the same. I am not happy serving two Masters."

"Two Masters?" She stared at him, not understanding.

"Li Yuan and my own conscience. It feels . . . *unhealthy* somehow. But if there were a way of expressing how I feel – some channel for it – well, maybe I'd feel better."

"So?" Chen prompted.

Karr laughed. "So maybe I know a way. Look . . ." he spread his hands, "it may not work, but it's worth a try, neh?"

She nodded.

"Good. Well . . . it was something I saw years ago. Something the *Ping Tiao* were very good at. Pamphlets. Simple things, hand-printed on flimsy paper. A hundred million they got out one time, passed hand to hand throughout the Lowers. From what I can make out they had ten thousand originals, then left it to others – sympathetic agitators – to print up more from those." He smiled. "Maybe you could do something similar?"

She laughed. "You're teasing me, surely?"

Karr smiled. "Not at all. It might work. You provide the text, Chen and I will get it distributed. Or, at least, we'll try."

Hannah shook her head. "But you're both Majors . . . senior officers in the T'ang's Security service. You can't get involved in something like this!"

"And both special services," Karr said, his smile unwavering. "Who *better* to arrange something like this. This past fifteen months I've made some useful contacts. Contacts we could use to get these things distributed. To spread them far and wide."

He stopped. Chen was staring at him, his eyes narrowed. "Maybe so. But you have a child now, Gregor Karr."

"And you have three. But the risk's worth taking, neh?"

Chen hesitated, then gave a terse nod.

"Good. Then I'll tell you what, young Hannah. You write us something – about what happened at Nantes, perhaps – and we'll take it from there. Agreed?"

He held out his hand, palm open to her. For a moment she simply stared at him, wondering, then, a faint smile beginning to creep into her eyes, she reached out and grasped it firmly.

"Agreed."

* * *

The New Hope was dark when they arrived, only a single lamp above the entrance lit, yet as they approached, two guards stepped from the shadows and unceremoniously pushed them against the wall, searching them for weapons.

"Charming," Emily muttered through clenched teeth as the guard's hand dwelt over-long on her inner thigh, then, with a pat, refrained from taking further liberties.

"Is this *really* necessary?" Michael asked, as he was turned roughly about to face his guard. But the man didn't answer, merely gestured that they should go through.

"Well," Emily said, taking his arm, "there go my last illusions about the civility of these people. Power, that's all they understand."

Michael shrugged, then stopped, peering into the dark interior of the restaurant. As if on cue, a lamp at a table on the far side of the room lit up, revealing the solitary figure of the T'ang's Chancellor, Nan Ho. As they looked, he beckoned them across.

"Representative Lever," he said, standing as they reached the table, then turned, bowing his head to Emily. "Madam Lever . . . Please, take a seat."

Michael helped Emily get seated, then took his own place, facing Nan Ho across the empty table top, the gentle swaying of the lamp above them throwing their faces briefly into shadow.

"What was all that about?" Michael asked, his face set, determined, it seemed, to concede nothing.

"Precautions," Nan Ho answered calmly, then half turned, snapping his fingers. At once a waiter – not one of The New Hope's regulars – appeared at his elbow. He turned back, smiling urbanely at Michael. "Would you like some wine before we eat?"

Michael looked to Emily, who nodded. "Yes," he said. "But that's not what I meant. The need to be cautious, that I understand, but the unnecessary brutality of it. What was *that* meant to demonstrate?"

Nan Ho's smile broadened. "I think you know already. But your question is very interesting. It shows that you've come here with fixed ideas. You think you know what I want. But you haven't heard me yet. That's strange. I expected much more of you, Michael Lever. I expected a certain . . . *subtlety*, let's call it. Something I wouldn't find in another of your . . . kind."

Emily looked down at that, her hands clenched beneath the table. *Your kind*, she thought, the ugliness of the words resonating deep within her. But what did he mean by that? Her *race*? Or did he just mean Michael's faction – the New Republicans?

"I'll listen," Michael said, folding his hands before him on the table. "But I've not come to make deals."

Nan Ho chuckled. *"Deals.* Is that all you think of?"

Michael stared, silent, until Nan Ho shrugged. At that moment the waiter returned with a tray of wine cups and an open bottle. As he set the cups down and poured, Nan Ho looked between them, smiling. Then, as the waiter returned to the shadows, he lifted his cup, toasting them.

"To America's perfect couple!"

Michael fingered the rim of his cup, his eyes narrowed. "So what *do* you want?"

"Me?" Nan Ho sipped at his wine, then sat back slightly, as if this were merely an evening out and he was a regular customer of the restaurant. He looked about him briefly, then fixed his gaze on Michael once more. "I'll tell you. I want peace."

"Peace? That's all?"

Nan Ho nodded. "Yes, but there's a problem with that. You see, the House wants real power, and if it *gets* real power then there won't be peace. So . . ." he sipped again, smiled, "I cannot let it have real power. You see my problem?"

Michael leaned in towards him, his face suddenly bright beneath the lamp. "I see it, but I can't see how you can prevent it. Things are changing. The House *will* attain real power. If not this year, then next."

"That soon?" Nan Ho's face wrinkled momentarily in thought. Then, unexpectedly, he laughed. "Maybe I ought to start packing now, neh?"

Michael stared a moment, then, catching the man's mood, began to smile.

"Better," Nan Ho said, leaning in towards him. "You came here full of hostility towards me. Full of tension and false expectations. That display outside – for which, incidentally, I apologise most profoundly – was meant to pander to them. But we are not like that. We are not simple, abstract forces. We are *people*, and we want what *people* want. When I talk of peace, it is not some vague ideal I seek, it is peace, as you or I would understand the term. Freedom from violence, from tyranny and need. Freedom to marry whom we will and raise a family. Freedom . . ."

"I take your meaning," Emily said rather sharply, interrupting him, "but don't your policies contradict your stated desire?"

"Not at all. The problems we face are many, but the solutions are few. There are too many people, therefore we must limit the number of children we are having. Food supply regularly falls below demand, therefore we must either grow more food – almost an impossibility, I think you'd agree – or, again, limit the number of people. And as for overcrowding . . . well, you take my point, I'm sure. All of our problems have but a single cause – there are too many of us. Many too many. If we want peace – and I'm sure you, as much as I, *want* peace – then we must do something about it."

Michael went to speak, but again Emily was in before him. "Yes, but why limit the statute to the bottom hundred and fifty? Why not make it one law for all. That, surely, is much fairer?"

"Fairer? Maybe. Though not much. Our problem *is* in the lowest hundred and fifty. It's *there* that the population levels are spiralling out of control. But there's another factor involved, which I'm sure you understand, and that's the power of vested interests. And *that* . . ." he paused, looking from one to the other again, "is where you come in."

Emily sat back, eyeing him, not certain yet whether to like this man or not. "What do you mean?"

Nan Ho was watching her now, a look resembling respect in his eyes. "I watched you," he said solemnly. "I saw what you tried to do in America. It was a brave attempt, a genuinely innovative reaction to a difficult situation. And it would have worked, too, given time. You would have changed things, Mary Lever. I'm certain of it. Just as I'm certain that you could do it over here. You and Michael both."

Michael laughed. "We're not even citizens . . ."

Nan Ho turned, snapped his fingers. At once a servant appeared, head bowed, a glossy black folder in his hand. Nan Ho took it from him, then turned back, offering it to Michael.

Michael took it, opened it, showed the sealed documents to Emily.

"A bribe?" he asked, looking back at Nan Ho.

"No. You would have got them anyway. Oh, and before you ask, you get to keep them, whether you do as I suggest or not." He smiled. "Then again, I ask nothing of you but that you do again what you once chose to do freely – to influence people for the good."

"And this?" Emily asked, holding up a sheet of paper which had been inside the folder. "Is this part of the deal?"

Michael took it from her, reading it through. It was a note regarding a Mansion that was for sale. He looked up. "Well?"

Nan Ho smiled, then beckoned a waiter, taking a menu and handing it across to Emily.

"It's not on the market yet, but I understand the asking price is *very* reasonable." The Chancellor's smile was urbane, gentle, yet behind it Emily sensed a steel-trap mind. "You'll need such a place if you are to entertain people. And if you're to influence them, you'll need to entertain them, neh?"

CHAPTER · 18

CITIES OF THE PLAIN

Lo Wen tightened the girth and ran down the stirrups, then looped the reins and placed them in the boy's right hand.

"Are you ready, Kuei Jen?"

The young prince shook his head, a look of keen resentment in his eyes. "I don't want to . . ." he murmured.

Lo Wen straightened, his face on the level of the boy's. "It is not what we want, Prince Kuei, but what we need. If you are to be a good horseman, you must learn the disciplines from an early age. You must become part of the horse."

Kuei Jen wriggled in the saddle, uncomfortable.

"Hold still, Kuei Jen! You will make the horse uneasy."

The young prince looked down, feeling angry and hurt. How dare the man speak to him like that. How *dare* he!

"I won't," he said stubbornly, giving another wriggle and feeling the horse move beneath him. "I don't want to."

"You will and you must. Your father has commanded."

Kuei Jen glared at him, then jutted out his chin and dug his heels hard into the pony's flanks. At once the pony whinnied and began to kick.

"Damn you, boy!" Lo Wen yelled, grabbing the harness while also trying to keep the young prince from falling. "What in the gods' names are you playing at! You could kill yourself!"

"I *won't*!" Kuei Jen shouted back. "I don't *want* to go riding!"

Lo Wen calmed the horse, but his face was dark with anger now. He pulled Kuei Jen down from the saddle and set him aside, then signalled for one of the grooms to take the horse.

Turning, he faced the young prince again.

Kuei Jen stood there, hands on hips, staring back at him defiantly. "I won't," he said again. "I won't."

Lo Wen took a breath, then nodded. "You won't, eh? You would disobey your father, neh?"

Kuei Jen shook his head. "*He* wouldn't make me . . . It's *you.*"

Lo Wen raised his voice, angry now. "You will do as I say, Kuei Jen, or else . . ."

"Or else *what?*"

There was a movement in Lo Wen's eyes, then he moved past the young prince and took a crop down from the wall behind him. "Here," he said, beckoning to him.

But Kuei Jen shook his head and, with one final defiant glare, turned and ran from the stables.

* * *

"Papa! Papa!"

Li Yuan turned in his seat, startled by the sudden intrusion. As Kuei Jen rushed across the room towards him, scattering servants and supplicants alike, Li Yuan stood, frowning deeply.

"Kuei Jen! What *is* this? How many times must I tell you . . ."

He stopped. The new instructor, Lo Wen, stood in the doorway, his shaven head bowed, not wishing to intrude where he had not been invited.

Kuei Jen came round the desk, then clung to his father's side. "Papa! Papa! He wants to punish me!"

Li Yuan took a long, shuddering breath then looked across to where his cousin, Tsu Ma sat in the window seat. Tsu Ma shrugged, yet his expression was eloquent.

Li Yuan turned, pulling his son away from him, and held him out at arm's length. It was hard to do, the boy was not yet five and it felt like a breach of trust, yet he was convinced now of the necessity. Even so, he softened his voice, as if to soften the blow.

"Kuei Jen . . . this will not do. You know how things are. Lo Wen . . . his word is as mine. I have commanded it."

"But Papa," Kuei Jen pleaded, his eyes filling with tears, "I have done nothing wrong. Nothing . . ."

Li Yuan studied his son a moment, then looked across to where the dour-looking Lo Wen waited.

"Lo Wen. Come closer. I wish to talk."

Lo Wen gave a terse nod, then, with what seemed like great reluctance, threaded his way through the attendants until he stood before Li Yuan's desk.

"*Chieh Hsia?*"

"Tell me. Why should my son be punished?"

Lo Wen's head sank almost to his chest. "He was disobedient, *Chieh Hsia*. I asked him to ride, but he refused. When I asked again he made the horse rear. And then, when I made to punish him for that, he ran away."

"I was tired, Papa! He makes me do so much. He never lets me rest. He's always . . ."

"*Quiet*, Kuei Jen. Not another word now or I shall grow angry with you." He looked back at Lo Wen, saw how the man stood there, his face expressionless, his whole demeanour graceful yet tense.

"Is it true, Lo Wen? *Are* you working my son too hard?"

There was the faintest movement of the head. "No, *Chieh Hsia*. He is a healthy boy. A little overweight for his height, perhaps, but sound. What he lacks is muscle tone. If he is to learn to ride and shoot properly, he must develop strength in his calves and upper arms. From such strength comes *ch'i*, the inner strength, the stillness that a great man requires."

"That may be so, Lo Wen, but he is, after all, just a child. Can he not be eased into things?"

Lo Wen looked up, meeting the young T'ang's eyes. "You gave me the boy, *Chieh Hsia*, and said I was to do as I saw fit, that I was to *fashion* him. But how can I do that when he runs to you each time?"

"But if it is too hard for him . . ."

Lo Wen drew himself up slightly. "You recall the tale of Sun Tzu and King Ho-lu's concubines?"

"I do."

It was an old tale and probably apocryphal, but Li Yuan

463

saw the point at once. In the tale the great Sun Tzu, given command of the army by King Ho-lu of Wu, was asked by the King to demonstrate his methods of training. To do so, Sun Tzu had the King's concubines line up with brooms in two groups in the palace yard, appointing the King's two favourite concubines as "commanders". He gave these two orders and told them to pass them on, but all the women did was giggle. Undismayed, Sun Tzu returned to the King and asked if, as his General, he carried his full authority. When the King said yes, Sun Tzu turned about and, after stating that the two "commanders" had failed in their duty, ordered them to be beheaded. King Ho-lu objected, saying they were his favourite concubines, but Sun Tzu out-faced him. *Did you not say I spoke with your full authority?* he asked, and when the King nodded, he proceeded with the executions. After that there was no more giggling. Within the hour the concubines were drilling like old hands.

Li Yuan looked down, then nodded. He wanted to say sorry, to explain to his son why this had to be, but knew that even that was wrong. He had indulged the boy for too long, and indulgence bred a fatal weakness. If he truly loved his son he must make him strong.

"You speak well, Lo Wen. Here, take the boy. Do as you must."

"Papa!" Kuei Jen shrieked, but Li Yuan shook his head.

"You are a *prince*, Kuei Jen, now *act* like a prince!" He turned the child about roughly – too roughly, perhaps – and pushed him towards Lo Wen.

"Do as Lo Wen says. And if you burst in here again, *I* shall punish you, understand me, child?"

Kuei Jen turned, glaring at him, then, with a pride that seemed strange after his previous display, walked slowly from the room, Lo Wen following him.

Li Yuan sat, feeling weak, exhausted emotionally. Then, feeling a vague anger that so many should have witnessed the exchange, he dismissed the waiting servants with a curt, ill-tempered gesture.

"You did well, cousin," Tsu Ma said when they were gone,

standing and coming across to him. "And don't fear. He may hate you now, but he will love you for it when he understands."

"Maybe. But he is all I have. I nearly lost him. To think that he might feel I do not love him . . ." He shivered, then looked up at Tsu Ma again. "Why were we made to *feel* so much? Why can't we who were born to rule have colder, harder natures?"

"Some have," Tsu Ma answered, perching himself on the edge of the desk. "Our cousin Wang, for instance. And by the by, is he coming here tomorrow for the tournament? I hear he's put on weight since we last saw him."

Li Yuan nodded. "We'll see the fat bastard. At least, so his Chancellor informs us."

"Things are bad, neh? They say his City is in chaos."

"Does it surprise you, Ma? He was never born to rule, that one. Why, if he hadn't murdered his brother . . ." Li Yuan stopped, meeting Tsu Ma's eyes. "You've heard the rumours, I assume?"

Tsu Ma leaned in towards his fellow T'ang, his voice suddenly much softer. "The version I'd heard was that he killed them all. Three brothers, his father, two uncles and at least five of his father's wives. Why, it makes Tsao Ch'un seem like benevolence itself!"

Li Yuan smiled, but the smile quickly faded. "And if he falls? If he's deposed and Africa goes the way of Mars and North America?"

"Then we rule what we hold. You, I and Wei Chan Yin. Until the times improve and we can take back what is lost. But let's not think of that now. Let's break for a while. Let's saddle up two of your best horses and go riding for an hour or two. What do you say?"

Li Yuan hesitated, conscious of all the work there was to be done before the morrow. Then, seeing the eagerness in his cousin's face, he relented. "Okay. Let's ride. But we must be back by six, or Nan Ho will be furious with me."

"By six? Why . . . what's happening at six?"

Li Yuan steepled his fingers beneath his chin, then looked back at Tsu Ma. "I'll tell you later, Ma. Over dinner. But now let us go, while the day is still fresh."

* * *

Wang Sau-leyan lay back on the heaped silk cushions of his bed, a wine cup propped against his bloated chest, watching the flickering screen. These were old tapes from the archives, scenes from the time of "The Seeding", from those final days before the City had been built across Africa. The T'ang looked on, unmoved by the unfolding images of suffering, by the misery, the hopelessness the camera revealed in every eye.

"Bankrupt," he said, turning to his Chancellor, who waited in the shadows close by. "They're all morally bankrupt. They forget, Master Hung. Forget the truth of where they came from." He laughed, then shifted his bulk on the cushions, spilling his wine, though he hardly seemed to notice. "*These* were the foundations," he said, pointing a plump, jewel-encrusted hand at the screen. "Eight hundred million they killed in Africa alone. A further two and a half billion elsewhere. And for what? To build a world of walls and levels! A world lacking all decency!"

Hung Mien-lo looked down, conscious of the gross irony of his T'ang's words, yet also disturbed by what he'd seen. "It was the tyrant Tsao Ch'un, *Chieh Hsia*. All that was *his* doing."

Wang Sau-leyan made a noise of disgust and turned to stare at his Chancellor. "So they'd have you believe. But let me tell you, Hung, it wasn't like that. It was our forefathers – our great-great-great-grandfathers – who did this thing. It was they who organised and ran it, they who gave the orders. And all this crap about them overthrowing the tyrant . . . well, they did, but for no great altruistic reasons. The truth is, they wanted power. They were sick with desire for it. And this world of ours is infected with that sickness."

And you? Hung might have asked, but didn't. He never

did. Instead he handed Wang Sau-leyan the list, the latest list of traitors, more than a thousand names this time. Wang took it, scanned it idly, then laughed.

"They hate me, don't they, Hung? That's why they take these risks . . . why they gamble their lives on taking mine. But what's the point in all this plotting and scheming? If it were me, I'd simply wire myself up as a walking bomb and go blow the shit out of my enemy!"

"It would not be so simple, *Chieh Hsia*. One must first be granted an audience. Besides, my guards search all who come here."

Wang stared at him a long time, then nodded. "Yes, Hung. You take good care of me, *neh*?"

There was a strange bitterness in that final word that made Hung Mien-lo look up.

"Give me the brush, Hung. I'll sign it now."

Hung did as he was told, then set the warrant aside. As he turned back, he realised that Wang Sau-leyan was still watching him. Beyond him the screen still flickered with the images of death. The death of the dark continent. Before the Han had come.

"We keep the Oven Man busy, you and I, neh, Hung? We carry on our forefathers' work."

Hung swallowed and looked down, the temptation to say something almost overwhelming.

"Your silence is eloquent, Hung. Oh, I know you hate me too. I'm not a lovable man, neh? But I'm not a hypocrite. I'm not like those bastards my cousins, pretending foul is fair. I *know* what I am. And if honest self-knowledge is a virtue, I am virtuous in that regard if in no other."

He laughed, then rolled back, returning his gaze to the screen.

"It disconcerts you, doesn't it, Hung? All this honesty. You'd rather I were more like them, that I pretended more. Well, I can *pretend* like the best of them, but only for good reason. I never fool myself that I *am* the thing I pretend to be like they do, poor fools."

Hung waited, but there was no more. Wang lay there, his

467

eyes closed, as if he slept. Hung cleared his throat. "And the tournament tomorrow, *Chieh Hsia*. Will you go?"

"Maybe," Wang answered, not opening his eyes. "I'll see how I feel. My champion is there already, I take it?"

"He arrived there yesterday, *Chieh Hsia*."

"Do you think he'll win?"

Hung hesitated. "I'd . . . say it was unlikely, *Chieh Hsia*."

The T'ang chuckled. "Maybe you should have told him he was a dead man unless he did. It certainly brought the best out of him last time, neh?"

"It did, *Chieh Hsia*."

"And now I need my rest. You are dismissed, Hung. Oh, and send the woman. Tell her I've one of my headaches coming on. Tell her . . ." He waved a hand vaguely. "Well, just send her."

"*Chieh Hsia*." Hung bowed his head, then backed away, his face a wall, hiding his innermost thoughts.

*　*　*

The woman stood in the doorway, naked, watching him. She was tall, unnaturally so, and statuesque. Her thick blonde hair hung in four long plaits against the stark whiteness of her flesh, each plait braided intricately with golden thread, while her eyes were so cold and blue that the grey northern sea seemed almost warm by comparison.

As Wang Sau-leyan stared at her a smile slowly formed on her strong, narrow lips. She was beautiful, no doubting it. Coldly, powerfully beautiful. His weakness, his one true indulgence.

She came across and climbed onto the bed, her full and heavy breasts swinging gently above him as he lay there. He watched, mesmerised, as she undid the braids, letting her hair fall like a curtain of fine, golden silk. Then, as her lips brushed against his chest, he closed his eyes again, relaxing.

Afterwards she lay there on the bed beside him, sleeping, strands of her hair fanned out across her pure white shoulders, her firm lips slightly parted, the blueness of her eyes masked by a thin veil of flesh. Light from a lamp across the room picked out her naked form, making her a thing of curves and shadows.

He raised himself on one elbow and studied her, surprised that even now, after eighteen months, he continually saw new aspects of her. She was not like the other *Hung Mao* women he had known – those cheaply perfumed whores masquerading as sophisticates. Nor would she meet their fate. This one was different. She had breeding. Each movement, the smallest nuance of word or gesture, spoke of extreme cultivation. In a strange, almost paradoxical sense, she was *tsu kuo* . . . the motherland he'd always sought.

He shivered, then stood, hauling himself up out of the silken folds of the bed, conscious of the restlessness that affected him whenever he thought of this.

Smiling, he turned and looked at her again, seeing at once how she had turned in her sleep and now lay there, open to him, vulnerable, her left hand curled about her inner thigh, the right hand clenched beside her face. In sleep the child returned. In his mind he could see her, younger and much smaller, all signs of adulthood removed, lying just so upon the sheets, and felt a pang of longing for the reality of the vision.

Pulling on his gown he turned, looking about him. On a table to one side were the three tiny statues he had bought for her. He went across and lifted one from its stand, examining it. It was a white jade swan, its wings stretched back, its long neck craning forward as it launched itself in flight. He shivered, the sight of its perfect, delicate form stirring his memory.

The memory was sharp and clear. He had been thirteen and under-sized for his age. It was the day of his eldest brother Chang Ye's wedding and he had come upon his brothers with their friends – princes all, related to his clan by marriage – in the pavilion by the crescent lake at Tao Yuan. He had made to turn away, when one of them called out to him mockingly.

"Sau-leyan? Is it true you have a taste for *hsueh pai*?"

He had glared at the youngest of the group, his second

brother, Lieh Tsu, and stormed away angrily, humiliated that the thing he had told him in strictest confidence had been so cheaply traded. And as he ran across the grass, the image of his brothers' laughing faces had burned into his mind.

He said the word softly, *"Hsueh pai . . .",* then spoke the anglicised form, "Snow whites . . .", the pet name the boys had for the *Hung Mao* women they met in the Above. Even then he had found them fascinating – had wanted them above the women of his own race.

He pulled his silks tighter about him, suddenly cold, and let his breath hiss between closed lips. The sound of the sea breaking on a northern shore. *And now,* he thought, *their mouths are cold and silent.*

No, not one of them who had laughed at him that day now lived. Not a single one. He had made sure of that.

Wang turned. She was watching him from the bed, her blue eyes tracing the shape of him, as if to make sense of him from how he stood. And when her eyes met his, lips and eyes formed a smile that was rich and warm and loving.

"What were you thinking, Sau-leyan?"

"Hsueh pai," he said, then, seeing that she made nothing of the word, added, "It's nothing. Just a childhood thing. The swans reminded me."

She came across and stood beside him, studying the swans, like an empress even in her nakedness. He stared at her a moment, then placed his hand against her flank, surprised to find her warm. She looked down at his hand and laughed. "Was it not enough for you, my Lord?"

"It is *never* enough. When you come here it's . . ." He shrugged. "Well, it's like I'm home. Like the rest were all a dream, and this here . . ."

She reached up, taking his hands. "I know."

It was a strangely fragile gesture, very different from the strength he normally associated with her. Kneeling, he drew her close and held her to him.

"It will change," he said. "I shall make you my Empress."

She pushed herself back, looking at him sharply. "Impossible."

470

He shook his head. "No. I'll *make* it possible."

She shuddered. "You think the Seven will let you?"

"Those bastards . . . they'll permit me nothing. And yet I am a T'ang. I may do as I wish, surely?"

She was still watching him, her face unchanged. Then, as if she had made a choice, she lowered her eyes and slowly shook her head. "No, Wang Sau-leyan. I'll not let you. You would ruin yourself for my sake, and where would we both be then?"

She touched his cheek, making him look at her again. "Promise me, my Lord. Promise me you'll do nothing rash."

He smiled and kissed her gently. "I promise." But in his mind he was picturing how it would be once the Seven had been honed to One, when, as Son of Heaven, he would take her for his bride, mixing their bloodlines in the start of a great new Dynasty. No one would laugh at him that day. No, he would stand no mockery when he was *Huang Ti*.

"Good," she said, drawing him close, her face buried in the folds of his stomach. "Then come to bed. I need you . . ."

* * *

Nan Ho looked up from his desk, glaring at the man who sat before him. "*Aiya!* Why was I not told of this before now? Why has it had to come to this before I was informed?"

The Minister, chastened by the Chancellor's tone, kept his head low, his eyes averted. "I thought it would blow over, Excellency. I thought . . ."

"You *thought*? More like you *didn't* think. More like you ignored your Junior Minister's memoranda while you pissed away your time in whore houses!"

The Minister's head bobbed up, astonished by the Chancellor's outburst. "Why, Excellency! I protest!"

"*Be quiet, man!*" Nan Ho roared, standing, his face dark with anger. "Don't you realise what's happening, Yang Shao-fu? We have a full-scale epidemic on our hands – something we haven't seen in more than a century – and you've been sitting on your arse for four days, hoping it would 'blow over'! What am I to tell the T'ang? That his Minister *ignored*

471

the facts? That he was so incompetent that nearly thirty thousand people died before he took notice?"

Minister Yang was almost curled into a ball now, his head almost touching his knees as he answered Nan Ho. "It was all so . . . *unprecedented*, Excellency. Such a thing . . ." he swallowed, "as you say, it has not happened in several lifetimes."

"Which is what makes it all the more worrying, *neh*? Why in the gods' names did you not come to me at once?" The Chancellor sighed, exasperated. "And today, of all days, when there is so much else to be done!" He turned away, holding a hand up to his brow. "So . . . what have you done? What measures have been taken?"

"Excellency?"

Nan Ho turned back, astonished to find the Minister staring up at him, his face a blank. "You've *taken* measures, I assume. Quarantine procedures and the like?"

Yang Shao-fu shook his head.

"The gods preserve us!" He took a long breath, then began again, trying hard to keep his patience. "Look. What do we know? Do we know, for instance, where the thing originated?"

"Where it originated? No, Excellency. That we do not know. But we do know where it first came into the City."

"We *know* something! Ahh . . . Well *speak* then, Yang Shao-fu. *Tell* me. *Please*."

"The first cases were reported at the southern ports. At Naples *Hsien* and Marseilles."

Nan Ho sat, understanding at once. His voice was the merest breath. "Africa . . . it's coming in from Africa."

"Of course," Yang rambled on, pleased now that he had something, at least, to report, "we can't be sure of its source, but first indications are . . ."

"Oh, do shut up, man! Let me think!"

Again Yang Shao-fu sat back, his mouth open, staring at the Chancellor in astonishment. In all his years as Minister he had never been treated so rudely, so . . . offhandedly.

"Yes," Nan Ho said thoughtfully, as if talking to himself.

"There's no other way. We'll have to close the ports and ban all traffic between the two Cities. It's a big step, but there's no alternative. As for the epidemic itself, we must take immediate steps to isolate the affected areas."

"Close the ports?" Yang said, his eyes wide. "By whose authority?"

"By the authority invested in me by Li Yuan!" Nan Ho said, leaning across his desk, his whole manner defiant now. "Look, Minister Yang, we have wasted far too much time already. It would not do to waste another hour. I want all the affected areas cordoned off at once and placed under the very tightest security, and all those who've travelled in those areas must be traced and isolated too. Every last one, understand? Oh, and I want you to report to me every hour on the hour, understand me? From now on I want to know *everything* that happens."

The Minister hesitated, then bowed his head.

"Good. Then get going, Yang Shao-fu. *Now!*" Nan Ho stood, shooing him away as if he were the most junior clerk. "Come on, man! Go and redeem yourself . . ." Then, beneath his breath, "If that's possible."

* * *

Emily looked about her at the huge expanse of the Mansion's ballroom, at the great swathes of bunting and coloured silk, and sighed deeply. It was almost done, the last of the preparations finished, three days of solid work complete, but still she wasn't happy. She had never liked these occasions, not that they'd had much chance to throw that many parties back in America, but it wasn't what she had been born to and the pleasure she derived from them never outweighed the discomfort she always felt. In the past she had only gone to them because of Michael. But this time it was her own party and there would be no chance to slip away when things really got her down, no escape from the limelight until the last guest left, some time in the early hours.

She turned, hearing footsteps in the hallway, then broke into a smile.

473

"Gloria! Thank the gods you're here."

Gloria Chung came across, beaming, embracing her friend, then stepped back, surveying the preparations.

"It looks great, Mary. It really does. Who did you use?"

"It's someone Eva recommended. They're very good. I don't know how I'd have coped without them. Mind you, we've had a few problems this morning. Three of her girls reported sick and we had dreadful trouble finding replacements. You wouldn't dream . . ."

Emily stopped. "Gods, listen to me . . ." She turned away, her eyes running over the banners and decorations, checking to see all was well, the habit of the last three days hard to shake. "I don't like it. All the pretence. I . . ."

Abruptly, she turned back. "Look, why don't *you* be hostess?"

"Don't be silly, Em. I couldn't possibly. It's your House, your party. People will expect you to be hostess. No . . . you'll get through, trust me. But I'll be there if you want, at your elbow, to take the pressure off. They can be really quite obnoxious some of these First Level wives. Real Grade A bitches. But we'll cope, neh? We're pretty tough bitches ourselves when it comes down to it. *Am-er-ican* bitches . . ."

Emily laughed. "What *would* I do without you?"

"You'd survive. Now, tell me who's coming. You sent out all the invitations on the list I compiled?"

Emily nodded.

"Okay . . . so who replied?"

"Everyone."

"*Everyone?*" Gloria's eyebrows shot up. "You don't get *everyone* to a party in the Above. Not here, anyway. There are always lots of celebrations going on, especially the night before a tournament. You *always* get apologies."

"Well, *I* didn't. They're all coming. All eight hundred and sixty-four of them."

"Eight hundred and . . ." Gloria gasped. "*Aiya!* You'll never fit them all in . . . And then, well . . . you'll need extra waiters, another five, six cooks at least, more wine. You'll need . . ."

Emily put her hand on her friend's arm. "It's all done. Wine, waiters and an extra dozen cooks!"

Gloria stared at her, her hazel eyes wide with disbelief. "*Everyone?* You're *sure?*"

"Everyone."

"Then the gods help us, Mary Lever, but you're *there*. Base One, first time out. Queen of the Above. Eldest Daughter . . . And tonight . . ." She smiled, her eyes bright with pride, then leaned close and kissed Emily's cheek. "Tonight they come to pay court to you."

* * *

The visit had been unannounced. The first Pei K'ung knew of it was when her father came to her rooms and told her to get dressed, and fast.

"Who is it?" she had asked, and when he'd told her she had stood there several moments in total disbelief. Why should the great T'ang visit her? Her father, certainly, but *her*?

She had dressed simply, modestly, as was her way, then had gone down and presented herself to him, kneeling in the doorway and pressing her forehead once, twice, a third time against the cold marble.

He had come across, standing over her, and told her to get up. Then, for what seemed a long, long time, he had studied her.

"She'll do," he'd said finally, with an abruptness she found strange, then he had turned and walked across to where his Chancellor, Nan Ho was waiting for him.

"Pei Ro-hen," he'd said, addressing her elderly father, "would you leave us for a moment. I have something to say to your daughter."

Her father had bowed low and left, and she had waited, not knowing what to expect. Thirty-eight years old, she had waited. A plain girl, her mother had always said when she was still alive. No wonder she had never married. Not like her sisters, who were – and this was *always* mentioned – pretty girls.

"Look at me," he'd said, in a tone of command that brooked no argument. And she had looked.

He was a handsome man, fifteen years her junior. A powerful man too, of course, and that radiated from him. Strangely, she had found herself smiling.

"Why do you smile?" he asked, his eyes curious.

To be honest, she had not really been sure just why she'd smiled, simply that something in the situation had struck her as absurd.

"I suppose, *Chieh Hsia*, it is because you have come to marry me."

"Have I?" And then he'd laughed. "Well, I guess that much *is* obvious. But we must be clear from the start just what it is I want from you as a wife."

He had paused, putting a gloved hand to his beardless chin as if in thought. "I want no children, Pei K'ung. Indeed it shall be a marriage in name only. There will be no physical side to the relationship. But you will help me, understand? You will share my duties and take some of the ceremonial burden from me. Is that clear?"

For some reason she had frowned.

"Yes?"

"Why me, *Chieh Hsia*? There are a hundred other princesses you might have chosen, all of them far prettier. So why me? Are you punishing yourself, Li Yuan?"

He laughed. "Master Nan said you spoke plainly. I like that. I think we'll get on well. But let me answer you candidly. I chose you because you have no brothers to complicate matters – no scheming hordes of relatives to torment me with requests for favours. And because you are old."

She had smiled at that. "Old, *Chieh Hsia*?"

He blinked. "I mean . . ."

"Oh, I am not hurt by your words, *Chieh Hsia*. I see myself often enough in the mirror to know how I look. And as for your conditions . . . I am agreeable to them. When is it to be?"

"Next week," he'd said, looking to his Chancellor, who had witnessed everything with an expressionless face. "It shall be a private ceremony at Tongjiang. Close family, that's all."

She had waited, as if there was to be more, but that was

it. Li Yuan had called her father back into the room and told him and she had smiled again, more pleased for him than for herself. Yet in truth the matter had intrigued her. *Why is he doing this?* she'd asked herself, and *What does he want from me?*

In time, perhaps, she would know. In time the mystery of it – the sheer absurdity – would give way to a clearer view of things. But just then it had seemed peculiar, like the visit of one of the old immortals to confer a favour.

My life was ended, she told herself as she climbed the stairs to her room again. *An hour ago, there was nothing. And now . . .*

Now her life was about to begin. She paused on the turn and laughed with astonishment, hearing the roar of the imperial cruiser's engines as it lifted from the House pad. Now, at thirty-eight, her life was finally about to begin.

* * *

Chen stopped and turned, facing the young woman. "Well . . . this is it. Are you coming in?"

Hannah tugged at a strand of hair, then made a shrugging movement of her shoulders. "It's late. I really ought to be getting back."

Chen smiled, then patted her shoulder. "Come on. Have some *ch'a*, a bite to eat. Then you can go."

"It's your family, Chen. I'd feel . . . well, like an intruder."

"Nonsense. You'll love Wang Ti. Besides, Karr will be there. He'll want to know how we got on."

She hesitated a moment, reluctance making her purse her lips, then, relenting, she smiled. "All right. Half an hour. And then I *must* get back."

"Okay." He grinned at her, then turned, punching the combination to the door.

They were all in the kitchen. As Chen came through, his youngest, Ch'iang Hsin, rushed at him, throwing her arms about his waist.

"Daddy! You're back!"

He hugged her, then looked about the room. Marie was

477

there, sitting next to Karr, leaning in to him, while in a chair in the corner, a shawl about her shoulders, Wang Ti sat cradling Marie's baby, a big smile lighting her features.

"Isn't she a darling," she said, lifting her face to Chen as he went over to kiss her. He crouched, peering into the bundle of blankets at the tiny baby girl. She had been born premature and grossly underweight, and even now, at six months, she was only half the weight she ought to have been. Chen took a long, heavy breath, then looked across to where his old friend sat, his arm about his wife. It was hard to believe that something so small and delicate had come from their union. If he'd thought of it at all he had pictured some giant of a son, stamped from the same mould as Karr and his mate, not this . . . this tiny miracle.

"She's so pretty," he said, staring at the child once more.

"Isn't she?" Wang Ti said softly, then, looking past him. "So who's this?"

Chen turned, then stood. "Forgive me, this is Hannah. Karr you've met. This is his wife, Marie and their baby, May. And this here is my wife, my dear Wang Ti."

Hannah smiled and came forward. "She's beautiful," she said, homing in on the baby, "and so very like her mother."

"Do you think so?" Karr asked.

"Daddy!" Ch'iang Hsin exclaimed loudly, tugging at Chen's trouser leg. "You didn't introduce *me*!"

"Oh, yes," Chen said, drawing her round in front of him. "And this is *my* little darling, Ch'iang Hsin."

Hannah turned, offering a hand. "I'm Hannah, and I'm *very* pleased to meet you, Ch'iang Hsin."

Ch'iang Hsin beamed, then gave an awkward bow of welcome. "Do you work with daddy?"

"Do I . . . ?" She laughed, then stood. "Kao Chen . . . *do* I work with you?"

"You do indeed," he said, nodding for emphasis. "Hannah, I'd have you know, is a writer. A very good writer, though she's had very little published yet."

Wang Ti looked up, intrigued. "Really? What do you write?"

Hannah looked to Chen, then to Karr. "I . . . I don't know, really. Reports, I guess you'd call them."

"Essays," Chen said authoritatively, then looked meaningfully at his wife. "But come, I'll make some *ch'a*. You must be dry as a bone."

Wang Ti looked to Chen, then looked down, understanding. Leaning forward, she sniffed at the bundle in her arms, then looked across at Marie.

"I may be wrong, but I think May might need changing. I'll take her through if you want to come."

Marie looked to her, then glanced at Karr, who nodded.

"Okay," she said, a wry smile on her lips. "I know when we're not wanted."

"Business to discuss," Karr said, laughing gently and slapping her butt as she squeezed past him. "We'll send some *ch'a* through if you want."

"Oh, don't you go bothering yourselves," Wang Ti said, threading her way between them, "Marie and I will be indulging in something a little bit stronger than *ch'a*, won't we Marie?"

"We most certainly will!"

As the door closed, Hannah turned to Chen. "She's not how I expected her. When you said . . ."

"She's improved a lot," Chen said, cutting in. He turned, smiling, looking at the space his wife had just vacated. "For a long time it was like she was dead. I gave up hope. But now . . ." He laughed. "Well, the baby helps a lot. She loves it now that Marie comes round. It was a brilliant idea, Gregor. I was afraid. I thought . . . well, I thought it would only make her more bitter, but look at her. You'd think May was her own."

"I'm pleased for them both," Karr said, leaning towards them across the table. "Marie hated it where she was. She had nothing in common with those service wives. But here . . . well, it's like she's a different person. They're good for each other. Better than a dozen surgeons."

Chen grinned, nodded.

"So?" Karr said, as Chen busied himself preparing the *ch'a*. "How did it go?"

"It went well," Chen answered. "Those people you knew . . . they were interested. *Very* interested. It seems like we did business."

"That's great. And what about the material itself?" Karr looked to Hannah, smiled. "Any feedback on that?"

Hannah came across and sat, facing him. "There were already rumours – vague things about an accident at Nantes, but nothing certain. The *T'ing Wei* did a good job, but not quite good enough. There are two eye-witnesses, it seems, who escaped the security trawl. But there was no proof, and you know how these things are. The more time that passes, the vaguer things become. However, the very fact that there was a rumour was enough to make people begin to ask questions."

"So what did you say when they asked who'd provided the documentary evidence?"

"I said it was stolen from a senior official's Mansion. Which was true in a way. They liked that. Liked the sense that the leak was . . . well, accidental."

Karr sat back, nodding his satisfaction. "It sounds good. But we'll see, neh? If they do their job, your pamphlet will be all over the Lowers by tomorrow evening. If they don't . . ."

". . . we try again," said Chen, bringing *ch'a* bowls and a plate of soft pastries across. "Until we find someone who can get the things out in the quantities we need."

Karr looked up, meeting his eyes. "Does it still worry you, Chen?"

Chen smiled. "Strangely, no. I feel . . . *freer* somehow than I've felt for years. Happy almost." He turned away, busying himself with the *ch'a*. "In fact, I've decided to resign my commission. We're going to sell up and get out."

"Out?"

Chen returned, placing the steaming *ch'a* pot in the middle of the table. "To the Plantations. I spoke to Wang Ti about it last night. She agreed. In fact, she loves the idea."

"And the children?"

"Ch'iang Hsin and Wu both seem to share her enthusiasm. Jyan . . . well, he's at a difficult age. All of his friends are here. But he'll come round. I plan to take him there. To let him see it for himself. I'm sure he'll . . ."

Chen turned, looking. Jyan was standing in the doorway.

"Dad?"

"Not now, Jyan. We're busy."

"But, Dad, there's something on I think you ought to see. You and Gregor. A newsflash."

They followed Jyan through into his room, then stood there watching the images on the screen over Jyan's bed, while the anchor-man gave the commentary.

"The first outbreaks began, it seems, in the ports of Marseilles and Naples where workers on the big inter-continental freighters were among the first to contract the disease."

"Aiya . . ." Chen said softly, as a picture of a young child – no more than three or four years of age – was flashed onto the screen, his corpse-pale flesh covered in strangely-shaped weals and sores. "Poor little bugger!"

"Something big's happening," Karr said quietly, talking over the commentary. "Look at it. Have you ever seen them screen anything like this before?"

Chen shook his head. "No. The *T'ing Wei* wouldn't let them. It'll cause panic throughout the levels."

"Then why?"

The answer came a moment later, over images of the great port facilities lying idle, visored guards blocking the entrances.

"In these unprecedented and exceptional circumstances, Chancellor Nan has taken the decision to suspend trade with City Africa and isolate the port facilities until the situation has been brought under control. The authorities have asked that anyone suffering any of the preliminary symptoms of the disease should report at once to their deck surgeon. It is stressed that early treatment can prevent loss of life."

"So that's it," Karr said, releasing a long breath. "They've closed the ports. Wang Sau-leyan won't like that. He won't like that one tiny little bit."

"No. But if I were Nan Ho I'd be far more worried about the sickness than the odious Wang. How long is it since something like this happened? A hundred, a hundred and twenty years? And what protections have we got? If this spreads any further, it'll sweep through the levels like . . ."

Chen shook his head, then, remembering suddenly that Jyan was there, turned to his son. Jyan was looking up at him, a naked fear in his face. "Here," he said, opening his arms, hugging him tightly.

"Will it be bad?" Jyan asked, a faint tremor in his voice.

"I don't know," he answered, stroking Jyan's brow. "But we'll be okay. I promise you."

"There's a curfew," Karr said, pointing to the screen. "That makes sense. I imagine they'll close down the transits and most of the inter-stack transportation. It'll be chaos for a day or two."

Hannah, silent until then, spoke up. "It reminds me of something I read in one of my father's books. One of the proscribed texts he kept on his shelves." She paused, recollecting the words, then spoke again.

"Then the Lord rained on Sodom and Gomor'rah brimstone and fire from the Lord out of heaven; and he overthrew those cities, and all the valley, and all the inhabitants of the cities, and what grew on the ground."

She stopped, then, with an embarrassed glance at Chen, looked down.

"Brimstone and fire, eh?" Karr said, his face grim. "Maybe that's not so far from the truth. Well . . . we must look to our own these next few weeks and hope the gods are kind."

From the hallway came the regular buzzing signal of the vid-phone.

"That'll be Bremen," Karr said, meeting Chen's eyes. "You answer it, I'll tell the women. We may be gone some while."

Chen nodded, then, releasing Jyan gently, he went through to answer the call. Wang Ti and Marie had come to the bedroom doorway to see what was happening. Karr ushered them back inside and closed the door. Only then did Chen make the connection.

"Yes?" he said, facing the uniformed figure who appeared. "Major Kao here. What is it, Captain?"

* * *

"Chieh Hsia . . ."

Li Yuan turned from the darkness of the cruiser's window and looked towards his Chancellor.

"Yes, Master Nan?"

"He's on. He wants to talk to you."

He, undoubtedly, was his cousin, Wang. Nor was the reason for his call a mystery. Li Yuan sighed. "All right. I'll come through and speak to him. Give me a moment to compose myself."

Nan Ho bowed, then turned and ducked back through the hatch.

Li Yuan sat back, closing his eyes, saying the *chen yen* for inner peace, but it was no good, the thoughts still filled his head.

Whatever he says, I shall hold my tongue and keep my temper. There is no proof he manufactured this crisis. No proof at all. But I would not put such a thing past him. He would destroy us all, and what better way than this?

He opened his eyes again, nodding to himself, determined not to incite his cousin. Yet he knew how hard it was going to be. Faced by that odious moon-faced creature, something always snapped in him. He stood, brushing himself down, more from an unaccustomed nervousness than need. Then, taking a long, deep breath, he went through.

"Cousin . . ." he said, taking his seat before the screen, Nan Ho to one side of him, out of view of the transmit camera. "How can I help you?"

Wang leaned close to the screen, his grotesque features filling the whole of it. "You might begin, *cousin*, by opening the ports again. And by paying me full recompense for loss of trade and damage on the markets."

"Forgive me, cousin, but it is not so simple. There is an epidemic in my City. And in yours too, I believe, though no certain word of it has come from your Ministers."

483

Wang drew back slightly, anger making his features seem more than usually malicious. "That's scurrilous nonsense, Yuan, and you know it! If there were any sign of this sickness in my City I would know of it! No! This is merely a pretext . . . an excuse to insult me and damage my interests!"

Li Yuan went to speak – to snap back some cutting answer – then checked himself. He took a breath. "It is no pretext, cousin. Nor is any insult meant. The epidemic is real enough and threatens *both* our interests. If it subsequently proves that the disease did not originate in your City I shall, of course, recompense you fully for *any* losses. I would not see my cousin harmed in any way by these . . . *necessary* actions."

Wang stared at him belligerently a moment longer, then, as if mollified somewhat, nodded. "I suppose this means the tournament is off?"

Li Yuan hesitated, realising he hadn't even considered the matter. "No. I . . . I think it would be a good idea if we continued with it. It might be useful to have something to . . . *distract* our citizens. As you might have heard, I have imposed a strict curfew over the whole of my City. It would be good, in the circumstances, to give the people something to take their minds off present troubles."

Wang grunted.

"You will still come, I hope?" Li Yuan asked, after a moment.

"Oh, I shall be there, Li Yuan. You can be certain of it." And, leaning forward, he cut the connection.

*　　*　　*

Less than half the guests had arrived when details of the curfew were announced. Michael had had a big screen set up in the Main Hall and a crowd had gathered beneath it, watching developments anxiously.

Emily, watching with Gloria Chung from the balcony, shuddered as the latest pictures came through. She had never felt so helpless, so impotent. This was *her* City, and it was tearing itself apart.

"It's happening again," she said quietly, seeing the images of riot on the screen as *Hsien* after *Hsien* declared itself for Chaos.

"No . . ." Gloria answered her, "it'll be all right," yet her fingers gripped Emily's arm fearfully.

Down below Michael was going among the crowd of dignitaries trying his best to reassure them and to deal with all their questions, yet it was a hopeless task. A squad of élite guards had been posted at the inter-level transit, but there was no chance that anyone would be allowed to go home, not for some hours yet, if then. From the images on the screen things seemed to be getting worse by the minute, with no sign of the official requests for calm being heeded. Reports had come in in the last hour of First Level Mansions being attacked and burned, and of the murder of several prominent officials.

And of the common people? What of them?

But the First Level media weren't concerned with the fate of the people in the Lowers. What if a million people died? Or five hundred million, as had reputedly been killed when City North America fell? What of it? They were concerned only for themselves; a fortress mentality which had been best exemplified by one of the North European Representatives who, witnessing the carnage on the screen, had raised his wine cup and, in a raised voice, said, "Let's hope they do a good job of it, *neh*?"

Which was why Michael had sent her up here, before she said something she'd regret.

Not that I'd really regret putting some of these bastards in their place!

"Are you all right, Em?"

She let the breath she'd been holding escape her, then nodded. "I'm fine. It's just . . ." She turned, facing her friend. "Achh, it's just that it sickens me. Those people down there in the Lowers . . . they're frightened. This sickness, it's a new thing, and the gods know how it'll all turn out, but these people here . . ." She turned, looking out across the crowd below, conscious of how richly, how elegantly they were dressed –

each costume worth at least a year's salary to a worker in the Lowers. "Well, just look at them, Gloria. All they're worried about is whether their Mansions and their factories will be okay. But when it comes to those people on the screen . . . they don't care if they live or die. It's all the same to them."

"And you? You care?"

She turned back, staring at her friend, surprised she could even ask. But was it so surprising? After all, she had been born to this too. For her it was easy to forget how much things cost. She had never had to think about the value of things. The *real* value of things.

"I've *been* there," she said, trying to contain the anger, the frustration she felt. "I *know* how they must be feeling." She made a sound of disgust and moved away from the balcony. "I was wrong to do this. I knew it. These people . . . at heart they're totally indifferent to all that suffering. As long as they're okay, then things are fine. It can *burn* down there, people can die by the tens of millions, and as long as their little enclave remains untouched, then it's just as if nothing has happened! Isn't that the truth?"

Gloria was staring at her now, shocked. "You don't mean that, Em. There are good people down there in the Hall. Friends of yours. Friends of Michael's. It's not that they don't care . . ."

"*No?* Then why don't they get off their arses and do something? They've got the means. They're rich beyond all need. So why don't they use that wealth to do some good? Why do they use it to buy statues and paintings and other useless shit? Why don't they spend it on *people*? After all, they've got a choice, haven't they?"

"You're being unfair now. Many of them give money to charity."

"*Charity?*" She was openly scornful now, beyond caring whether what she said was hurtful. "What's that but a salve . . . an excuse not to *act*, not to do something *real*."

Gloria shook her head, her face tight now with resentment. "You're a real little revolutionary at heart, aren't you? I thought . . ."

"You thought *what*? That I could be tamed? That I could be made to be the perfect political companion for Michael?" She shook her head. "That's what Kennedy thought too, and look where that led him."

"That's unfair, Em, and you know it."

"*Unfair*? Shit . . . I wasn't the one who was making deals with Wu Shih!"

"He had no choice. Besides, Michael's told me about your meeting with Nan Ho."

She felt herself go still. "He told you? When?"

Gloria shrugged, realising she had said something wrong. "I . . . I can't remember. Last week some time. He tells me these things . . ."

"Tells you . . ." Emily looked away, her lips pursed. "He sees you, then, when I'm not there?"

"It's nothing," Gloria said quickly. "I . . ."

She stopped. Michael was standing in the doorway behind them.

"What's going on? I heard raised voices . . ."

"You'd better ask your wife. I think she'd like to declare war on all of us."

He turned to her. "Em?"

For once she didn't look at him. "It won't work, Michael. I can't *be* Nan Ho's creature, however slack the strings. And this . . . this *farce* . . . gods, it's so *decadent*! There's a sickness here all right, but it isn't just in the Lowers. It's *everywhere*!"

"Em . . . This isn't like you."

"*No?*" She turned on him, anger flashing in her eyes. "Well, you'd best discuss that with your friend here. You seem to discuss everything else."

"Ah . . ." He shook his head. "Look. It's just that I'm used to talking things through with her. We go back years . . ."

But Emily was no longer listening. Abruptly she pushed past him and through the door. Her footsteps hammered on the marble steps leading up to her room and then a door slammed loudly.

"This business . . . it's upset her badly."

"Go after her. She'll listen to you, Michael."

"I don't know . . ." He stared at the empty doorway, frowning. "I've never seen her quite like that. All that *anger*."

"I'm sorry. I shouldn't have mentioned about our meeting Tuesday. She thinks . . ." She laughed. "She thinks we're having an affair."

Michael stared at her, astonished, then turned back to face the doorway once again. "Oh shit! . . . And I thought . . ." He sighed. "I'd better go talk to her, neh?"

"You'd better. And Michael . . ."

He turned back. "Yes?"

She smiled. "If you need me, you know where I am."

CHAPTER · 19

THE MAKER'S MARK

Kuei Jen lay in bed, the covers pulled up tight about his neck, alone in the big, dark room, the familiar shapes of the furniture threatening somehow, changed in the faint, pre-dawn light. He had been crying, but the tears had dried and his eyes were sore where he had rubbed them. There had been noises in the night – shouting, and running footsteps – but when he had called no one had come, as if his section of the palace had been deserted. And then there had been silence – a silence worse than the commotion that had pre-ceded it, for then he really *did* think that they had gone and left him there alone. Left him because he was bad.

He sniffed and felt a shiver pass right through him, wishing, despite the fear he felt, that the darkness would linger in his room a little longer. When it was light the man would come, and it would begin again – all those awful exercises; all those dreadful things he could never manage properly.

Why? he kept asking himself. *Why?* And always the answer was the same. *Because he no longer loves me. Because I've been bad and he no longer loves me.* Again he shuddered, close once more to tears. But if the man came and saw he had been crying there would be trouble. He would be punished for it.

Fighting back his fear he pushed the covers back and slid to the edge of the bed, then ran quickly, fearfully, across the shadowed room to the door, fumbling at the big hexagonal doorknob before it gave and the heavy door creaked back.

Outside, the corridor was empty. There were noises from the left, from the kitchens, but from the right, where his father's suite was, there was nothing. He went that way, running down the broad, dark corridor, his bare feet padding on the cold tiles, his breath coming to him in tiny, shuddering gasps. Outside his father's study he stopped, hearing faint voices from within, remembering what his father had said only the day before about not bursting in. And yet he had to speak to him; had to explain just what he was feeling. If this went on . . .

He squeezed his eyes firmly shut, trying to stop the tears, to be the prince his father wanted him to be, but it was hard. He had had so little practice at it.

Pressing his ear against the door he listened. There were two voices. One was his father's, the other . . . he listened more . . . Tsu Ma's. Yes, even as he recognised it, he heard, more clearly than before, his Uncle Ma's rich laughter. It almost cheered him. But then he remembered that that too was in the past. All joy, all happiness – all that lay in the past now. Today, like every other day from this time on, he would spend with the dour Lo Wen, learning to be a prince.

He reached out, placing his hand against the handle, then stopped, taking in what his father had just said. A wife . . . His father was taking a new wife.

Slowly he backed away, his mouth an "O" of surprise. And then it hit him. *That* was why. A wife! His father was taking a new wife, and there would no longer be room for him in his father's heart. His mouth puckered and a small sound of pain, like the whimper of a wounded animal, escaped him.

He doesn't love me any more. Daddy doesn't love me any more.

"Kuei Jen?"

He turned, his eyes wide with fear. It was the Captain of the guard, Shen Lo-yen. Shen stared back at him, surprised to find him there.

"Are you all right, young Master?"

But Kuei Jen was not all right. With a yelp he turned and ran, straight past his room and on; on through the kitchens and out into the Western Garden, jumping the broad marble steps in twos and threes in his haste, his bare feet stinging, and then on again, down the narrow pathway and through the gate in the wall . . . on until the darkness of the trees embraced him.

* * *

Li Yuan looked up anxiously as his Chancellor entered the room. "Is he found, Master Nan?"

Nan Ho smiled reassuringly. "All is well, *Chieh Hsia*. We found him in the orchard, hiding behind one of the trees. He was a little cold, but no real harm has been done. Your maids are tending to him now."

"Thank the gods!" Li Yuan heaved a huge sigh of relief, then turned to his fellow T'ang. "If Captain Shen hadn't raised the alarm, who knows what might have happened? But *why*? Why should the child run off like that?"

Tsu Ma shrugged. "I'm hardly the person to ask, Yuan. My experience of children is limited, to say the least."

Nan Ho cleared his throat.

"Yes, Master Nan?"

"I think you need to talk to him, *Chieh Hsia*. About your forthcoming marriage. The boy needs . . . *reassuring*. It might also serve if you would let him off his instruction just for today."

"Let him off? But you've been telling me how important it was to keep to his routines."

Nan Ho bowed. "So it is, *Chieh Hsia*. But today is a special day, neh? Besides, it would look well if your son sat beside you on the imperial dais."

Li Yuan smiled. "Must there always be a political reason for doing something, Nan Ho?"

"You are a T'ang, *Chieh Hsia*. Everything you do is political."

"Everything?"

"Well . . . almost everything. I understand the new maid was much to your satisfaction, *Chieh Hsia*."

"And if she wasn't?"

"I would find another who was, *Chieh Hsia*."

"And one for me, I hope," Tsu Ma said, laughing.

Nan Ho turned to him. "If that is the great T'ang's wish?"

Tsu Ma raised an eyebrow at Li Yuan, then laughed again. "I might take you up on that, Master Nan . . . with my cousin's permission, of course."

"Granted."

Again Nan Ho cleared his throat.

"*Yes*, Master Nan? What is it now?"

"Forgive me, *Chieh Hsia*, but the tournament site is ready for your inspection."

"Then lead on."

The sun was still low to their left as they stopped at the top of the steps, looking out across the great Southern Lawn. Directly in front of them, and some half a *li* distant, the newly-built landing strip had been decorated with the banners of the seven Cities, the big silk pennants flapping gustily in the early morning breeze. Closer to hand a dozen big hunting tents had been set up and a trail of servants could be seen going to and fro, ferrying huge silver platters into their interiors. In front of those an area had been cordoned off and a large number of couches had been set up on a semi-circle of elevated platforms for the use of the Twenty-Nine, the Minor Family princes, and their kin.

Directly in front of them was the tournament platform, a huge circular stage decorated like a giant *t'ai chi*, ten thousand tiny black and white tiles forming the interlocking swirls of dark and light, two *wei chi* boards placed at the focal points. While play was in progress, pictures of each board would be captured by floater cameras and transmitted to the huge screens that were displayed prominently in more than a dozen places.

To their left, in front of a huge marquee of golden silk, was the imperial enclosure. Here the five great T'ang would gather while their champions – and the champions of North America and the Australias – would play out their games.

"Excellent," Li Yuan said, nodding his satisfaction. "It will be a marvellous spectacle for the masses, neh?"

"It is to be hoped so, *Chieh Hsia*," Nan Ho answered sombrely.

Li Yuan looked to him, concerned. "Are things still bad, Master Nan?"

"Oh . . ." Nan Ho tugged at his beard, then made a shrugging gesture with his face. "It is much better than it was, *Chieh Hsia*. We have reclaimed most of the areas we lost during the night. But there are still one or two problems. The real test will be tonight. Our forces cannot go forty-eight hours without sleep."

"I see . . ." He huffed out a breath. "Is there nothing else we can do to defuse the situation?"

Nan Ho sighed. "We have done all that is humanly possible, *Chieh Hsia*. Time alone will tell if we have been successful."

"And while we wait, we watch our Champions play games with stones."

"It is the oldest game," Tsu Ma reminded him. "And for myself I cannot think of anything more fitting. There is nothing you or I can do, Yuan. For once things are in the hands of the gods." He smiled. "You know the tale of the woodcutter, Wang Chih?"

Li Yuan frowned. "Remind me."

"Well . . . it is said that Wang Chih went up into the mountains to cut wood, and on his way back he came upon two ancients playing *wei chi* upon a big flat stone. He stayed to watch, not knowing that the ancients were immortals, and when the game was finished he went on his way again. Down in the valley, however, things had changed. His village was not the same as he remembered it and none of his old neighbours was alive. When he looked at his axe he saw that the handle had rotted away, and when he asked what year it was, he was amazed to find that a thousand years had passed."

Li Yuan smiled, amused by the story. "Amazed? Or horrified?"

"Both maybe."

"And the point of your tale, cousin Ma?"

Tsu Ma smiled broadly. "Must a story always have a point?"

"Not always. But yours generally do."

"Then maybe it's this. That of all distractions, none can enchant as much as the game of *wei chi*."

"Unless it's the game of red enters white, hard enters soft . . ."

Tsu Ma roared with laughter, while beside him even Nan Ho allowed himself a smile.

"A maid, cousin Ma. You must have one of my maids."

"And if I tire her out?"

"Then you'll have another, neh?"

And, clapping his cousin on the back, Li Yuan turned and led them back into the palace.

* * *

Chen stopped, looking about him at the burned-out ruin of the main corridor, then waved the first squad through. He was wearing full riot gear, the big standard issue automatic clipped to his chest. They had been on duty now for fifteen hours and had cleared the best part of twenty stacks. Casualties, fortunately, had been light – two dead and six injured – but the night had taken its toll in other ways. What they had seen had changed them. To have had to hurt children, however necessary it had been to restrain them, that was something new, something he did not want to have to do again, nor had he savoured the look of madness he had seen in many of the faces as they threw themselves at his troops.

Chen pulled the visor of the bulky helmet up, then rubbed at his neck. He had been in riot situations before and had seen how otherwise sane men and women could cast off all inhibitions and act like savage animals, but nothing could have prepared him for this past night. It was as if they'd tapped some deeper, darker level – as if Hell itself had emptied out into this mundane world of levels. The Sickness, whatever it was, had unhinged them all, and their fear had led them to excesses beyond the experience of even the most jaded hand among his troops.

Now things were calm again, for a time, and they could assess the full extent of the damage. From what he'd seen it was bad. There was barely a corridor left untouched, and many – like this – were totally gutted. If it were like this across the breadth and width of the City then the cost of this night's work would be unimaginable.

He licked at his lips, wondering how this would affect his plans; whether, after this, he would be able to move his family to the Plantations. Had they been affected? Had this madness spread to the great East European growing areas? If so then there was more trouble to come, for food shortages would feed this tide of chaos. He shuddered, realising for the first time just how fragile a thing the City was.

"Sir!"

He looked up. Two of his men were standing in a doorway half-way down, pale-faced, beckoning to him. He walked across.

"What is it?"

"We think you'd better see, sir!"

He went to go in, but his sergeant stopped him. "You'd best wear your visor down, sir. There are signs of the Sickness."

"Ah . . ." He flipped it down again, clicking it tight, then took two deep breaths, making sure the filter was still working. Then, satisfied, he followed the sergeant through.

"In here, sir."

It was a surgery – he saw that at a glance – but the machinery had been smashed, surgical instruments scattered everywhere.

"In the back room, sir."

He stepped through, then checked himself, seeing what lay on the bare, tiled floor of the operating room.

"*Aiya* . . ." he said softly, both moved and horrified. In a pool of congealed blood lay the dismembered corpses of three young children. He shuddered and then, forcing himself, stepped closer, crouching over them to look. The cuts were clean, like they'd been done with a sharp cleaver: nothing frenzied about them. There were no stab wounds, no sign of slashing as he'd seen elsewhere. No. Heads, arms and legs had been severed carefully from the torsos, the hands from the arms, the feet from the legs, and all had been laid out meticulously, as if in some ghastly ritual.

They were Han, and, looking at them, he could not dissociate himself from the feeling that these were *his* children. For a moment the sense of it was so strong, so overpowering, it made him feel giddy. The eldest was no more than six, the youngest – he let out a low moan of anguish – was only two, three at the most.

"*Why?*" he asked quietly. "Who in the gods' names would do this to young children?"

"Look at the flesh, sir," the sergeant said, something in his voice revealing that he too was having to steel himself to look at the tiny bodies. "Look at the tiny rashes. What does it remind you of."

Chen swallowed and then looked closer. "That's odd." He looked again, then felt a chill run through him. The rash was not a simple blotch of redness but a quite clearly defined mark. A pictogram, endlessly repeated on the flesh. To an untutored eye it looked like an ill-drawn figure nine followed by a small "t", the two linked by a line that rested upon them like the lid of a tomb.

Si, it was. *Death*.

Chen turned, looking up at his sergeant. The man nodded then looked away.

He understood at once. This was no accident, no natural form of retribution. This thing had been *designed*. The rash . . . that was a calling card. But whose?

"Check them for prints and other traces and then burn them," he said, gesturing towards the bodies. "And then I want everyone in this deck held and questioned. We're going to find out just who did this to them."

And then?

He pulled himself up onto his feet again, feeling tired, sickened by all he'd seen. There would be no trials here today, no expulsions and demotions. When he found out who had done this he would take them aside and kill them. That was, if they weren't already dead.

Fear. Fear drove people to do such things. But fear was

496

no excuse. A man did not stop being a man because he was afraid. He was still responsible for his actions.

Chen stepped aside, letting the two men begin their grisly work, then, unclipping his handset from his belt, he tapped out the secure code for General Rheinhardt. It was time he reported in; time the powers that be knew just what was going on.

* * *

They waited as the ship set down, floater-cameras discreetly hovering at a distance from the small group of T'ang who stood there on the lawn below the landing strip.

As the hatch locks clunked open and the door hissed slowly upwards, Li Yuan gestured his secretary forward.

"Go, Tseng-li. Greet your elder brother!"

The young man smiled, bowed in respect, then turned and half walked, half ran towards the craft. As the walkway extended from the interior, he slowed, then stopped, dropping to his knees, his head lowered.

"*Chieh Hsia,*" he said as a figure appeared at the head of the walkway.

Wei Chan Yin strode down the ramp and, lifting his brother to his feet, hugged him tightly. "How have you been, little brother? Have you served my cousin well?"

Tseng-li moved back slightly, then, reluctantly it seemed, though not without warmth, he embraced his brother back. For a moment the two stared into each other's faces, then Tseng-li lowered his gaze again.

"I have tried my best, *Chieh Hsia.*" Then, more softly. "It's good to see you again, Chan Yin. It has been too long."

"Far too long," Wei Chan Yin agreed, squeezing his brother's arms. "But come, let me greet my cousins."

Tseng-li moved back, letting his brother pass, then watched as he went among the tiny group of T'ang, greeting first Li Yuan, then Tsu Ma, and finally Hou Tung-po, the young T'ang of South America.

Wei Chan Yin turned, looking about him. "I thought I would

497

be last here. Where is Wang Sau-leyan? He *is* coming, I take it?"

"So he says," said Li Yuan quietly, his face turned away so that the cameras would not catch what he said.

"I would not have been late," Wei Chan Yin said, his own voice lowered, conscious of the watching floaters, "but something came up. I'll tell you of it later."

"No matter . . ." Li Yuan said. "What we must decide is whether to wait a while longer or whether to begin. It would not do to delay too long. The people will grow restless."

"No," Wei Chan Yin agreed, "yet we should give our cousin the chance to be here at the commencement. Why not send Tseng-li to enquire of Wang's Chancellor?"

Li Yuan turned. "Tseng-li? You heard?"

"And shall obey, *Chieh Hsia*." He turned, bowing to each of the four T'ang in turn. "I shall return as soon as possible."

"Good." Li Yuan smiled and looked about him. "In the meantime, let us spend the time fruitfully, neh?"

He turned, clicking his fingers. At once his Senior Steward ran up and presented himself before him, kneeling, his head pressed almost to his chest.

"Steward Ye . . . tell the Heads of the Families that their T'ang will come among them while we are awaiting our cousin Wang. And Ye . . . do something about those cameras, neh? Until the tournament begins . . ."

* * *

Hung Mien-lo turned from the now vacant screen and looked across his study at the three men who waited, heads bowed, for their instructions.

He breathed deeply, trying to control the muscles of his face; to show nothing of the turmoil within. Five minutes ago it had all been crystal clear, but now things had changed. Wei Tseng-li's enquiry had made him realise what otherwise he would not have known. Wang Sau-leyan was on his way to Tongjiang.

Did he know? Hung wondered, standing and coming round his desk. For last night, when he had specifically asked him, it had been clear that the T'ang had no intention of going to the tournament – not after Li Yuan had insulted him so grossly.

"Let them wait," he had said angrily. "Let them all stand there like stuffed fools before the camera until it dawns on them I am not coming."

But now, it seemed, he had changed his mind and gone.

Unusual, Hung thought, walking across to where the three men waited. For years now Wang Sau-leyan had done nothing without first confiding in him. But suddenly, today . . .

He must know. He has to. What other reason could have made him go?

And yet if he knew, then he, Hung Mien-lo, would have already been killed, these three men with him, their throats cut, their stomachs slit open, exposing the entrails for Wang's carrion to feed upon.

So what then? Why had Wang gone, after all, and not told him?

He stared at the men a moment, then, with an abrupt gesture, dismissed them. *Another time, perhaps.* But the way things were developing events might yet outpace his schemes.

He took a long, shuddering breath.

You are fortunate this once, Wang Sau-leyan. For if you had not gone, my assassins would have found you where you lay – you and that abominable woman.

As it was, there would be no opportunity now for several weeks. The guards he'd bribed would be re-posted shortly, and to bribe new ones would take some time, for it was a careful business, fraught with dangers. Wang's spies . . .

He returned to his desk and reached across, picking up the latest list. Each morning there was a new list; each evening another thousand men and women went to their deaths. And all the while Wang's spies went among the levels like a plague, choosing both innocent and guilty at whim. And Wang Sau-leyan, unconcerned, signed whatever was placed before him.

He leaned against the edge of the desk, his hands

trembling. Step by step he had brought Wang to the edge. Step by step he had made the people fear and hate their odious master, so that when finally he struck it would seem that Ch'eng-huang, the great City God himself, had acted. He had pictured it clearly: had seen himself standing before the cameras, the tyrant's severed head in his hand, as he announced that the Mandate had been broken and a new and better age had come for City Africa. So close he'd been. So very close.

"He must have known. He *must* . . ."

He swallowed, uncertainty eating at him. Maybe it was time to run? To flee to Europe, perhaps, and throw himself upon the mercy of Li Yuan and his Chancellor? Or would that not simply seal his fate? No. He had to be sure. Had to know one way or the other whether Wang suspected him. But how?

The woman. The *hsueh pai*. If he could talk to her, find out what she knew . . .

He shook his head. No. That was too great a risk. It would merely serve to confirm Wang's dark suspicions.

Hung Mien-lo sighed heavily. *Nothing. I can do nothing until his return.* But the bitter disappointment – the frustration of his denied hopes – burned in him like a heated coal, and, gripping the edges of the list he tore it, once, twice, a third time, then scattered the pieces across his desk.

* * *

Li Yuan looked across from where he stood among the Heads of Families as Tseng-li reappeared at the top of the marble steps. He saw the young man look, then, seeing his T'ang, begin to make his way towards him.

"Excuse me, *ch'un tzu*," Li Yuan said, smiling, extricating himself from their midst. "There is some business I must attend to."

They bowed, stepping back out of his way, their own high status eclipsed by his own.

"Well, Tseng-li?" he asked, meeting the young man beside the great platform. "What does my cousin say?"

Tseng-li bowed. "I spoke to his Chancellor, *Chieh Hsia*. He says Wang Sau-leyan's craft will be here in forty minutes."

"Forty minutes . . ." Li Yuan stroked his chin thoughtfully. "That is too long for us to delay. I shall go and speak with my cousins and see if they agree. Meanwhile, prepare refreshments for us in the enclosure. We shall finish here and come across."

Tseng-li bowed and made to turn away, then turned back, remembering something. "Forgive me, *Chieh Hsia*, but Marshal Tolonen and General Rheinhardt have come. They wish to speak to you urgently."

Li Yuan watched him go, then turned and made his way back to where his cousins mingled with the Families.

Tseng-li bowed again and left.

Li Yuan watched him go, then turned and made his way back to where his cousins mingled with the Families.

"Cousins," he said, beckoning them across. "Our cousin Wang will be delayed a further forty minutes. In the circumstances I feel we *must* begin the tournament. There are many games to be played and it would be unfair to our Champions if we were to limit their time any more than we have already."

"He is coming, then?" Tsu Ma said, an ironical smile on his lips. Then, whispering into Li Yuan's ear, he added, "No doubt they had trouble finding a craft big enough to carry the fat bastard!"

Li Yuan suppressed the smile that threatened to break out on his face, then, drawing himself up, addressed his fellow T'ang once more.

"If you would follow me across, cousins, we shall begin. *Ch'un tzu*," he said, speaking to those Heads of Family who stood just beyond the tiny circle of T'ang. "We shall speak again later, at the celebrations. In the meantime, enjoy yourselves. Whatever you want, you have only to ask my servants and they will do their best to satisfy your needs."

There was a murmur of satisfaction as they began to dis-

perse back to their couches. Li Yuan looked to his fellow
T'ang then turned, leading them across.

* * *

Chen stood on the platform of the bell-tower looking out
across Main. Below him, filling the great space, he had gathered together all the inhabitants of this deck. They were
sitting cross-legged, men, women and children, their hands
on their heads, while his men patrolled the perimeters, their
heavy automatics pointed at the floor. From vantage points
on the balconies above, others looked down, their weapons
levelled.

He had called in a special murder squad to go over the
room, at the same time requesting whatever camera evidence existed. It hadn't proved much. Most of the surveillance cameras had been smashed in the first few hours of the
riot. Yet there were one or two interesting snippets, one of
them showing a tall, thin-faced Han brandishing what looked
like a bloody cleaver as he ran along at the front of a mob of
thirty or forty chanting men.

Chen turned, calling to his sergeant. "Okay. Let's get
moving. Issue the hardprint copies of the man's face and have
a dozen men go down the lines checking for him. If he's here
I want him dragged out. We'll beat a confession out of him if
necessary."

"And the prints, sir?"

Inconclusive was the answer. The computer had thrown
up more than twenty likely matches, and not one of them
from this deck.

"Just get going," he answered, then turned back, looking
out across the gathered masses.

More than ever he was determined to give up this occupa-
tion. If he had not known it before, last night would have
taught him what it was to be a servant of the great T'ang.
More than any other, this job dehumanised a man. To be a
part of that great chain of command was to cease to be a
thinking, choosing being; was to become a thing, a tool, less
even than the *kwai* he had once been.

502

Yes, he thought, *but now and then one has the chance to put things right. To use that power to good effect.*

He reached into his pocket and took out the crumpled handbill. They had seen them all over. Found them in the pockets of corpses and scattered in the ruins of empty rooms. WHAT REALLY HAPPENED AT NANTES, it was headed up, and beneath was the picture Hannah had provided.

Hannah's pamphlet. They had distributed it in the first few hours. Had used it to fan the flames.

He shivered, wondering just how many more had died because of it.

It wasn't what we meant . . .

Sure. But just what *had* they meant? To stir things up a little. To make people begin to question what was happening. But the timing had been bad, and what had been written to stir the conscience had been used by others to incite these poor bastards to slit each other's throats and burn each other's homes. And was that *their* fault?

For once he wasn't sure. All he knew was that what he'd seen was hell. And the sooner he and his family were out of it the better.

As his men went out along the lines of seated people, he looked on, tense, expectant. For a time there was nothing, then one of the soldiers turned and called up to him.

"Sir! I think it's him!"

As the soldier turned back, dragging the man to his feet, other soldiers hurried across to help him. Strangely the man didn't struggle, but let himself be led, his head hanging, his whole manner strangely subdued. He was tall and thin, like the man in the surveillance tape, but that didn't necessarily mean it was him.

"Keep on looking!" Chen ordered, seeing how the other soldiers had stopped and were staring up at him. "I'm coming down."

* * *

After the brilliant sunlight of the Southern Lawn, the audience room was cool and dark, the stone flags echoing back his booted footsteps. Dismissing the guards, Li Yuan went across, greeting the two men.

"Marshal Tolonen . . . General Rheinhardt . . ."

"*Chieh Hsia,*" both said as one, bowing their close-shaven heads.

"You have news?"

Tolonen looked to Rheinhardt, then spoke. "There is something you must know, *Chieh Hsia.* Something of vital bearing upon our current troubles."

Li Yuan's eyes lit up. "You've traced it, neh? You've found out where the disease came from!"

Tolonen hesitated, then took a folder from beneath his arm and handed it across.

Li Yuan took it and opened it, then frowned. "What *is* this?"

"It is a photograph, *Chieh Hsia,*" Rheinhardt answered. "A photograph of a section of diseased flesh from one of the victims."

"But this . . ." Li Yuan stared, astonished. "*Si,*" he whispered. "It says *Si.*"

"Yes, *Chieh Hsia,*" Tolonen answered, his granite face even grimmer than usual. "The disease was manufactured."

Li Yuan looked up. "Wang Sau-leyan . . ."

Tolonen swallowed, then shook his head. "I am afraid not, *Chieh Hsia.* For once your cousin's hands are clean. This is one of ours, designed in GenSyn's labs. It . . . got out, I'm afraid. We were shipping it to one of the experimental stations in North Africa . . ."

"*Shipping* it?" He could not believe what he was hearing. "A virulent disease and we were *shipping* it?"

Tolonen looked down, abashed, as if it had been *his* mistake. "It was a clerical error, *Chieh Hsia.* A misunderstanding."

"A clerical error!" Li Yuan exclaimed. "The gods help us! And the clerk? . . . has he been punished for his . . . *misunderstanding?*"

"When he learned what had happened he took his life, *Chieh Hsia.*"

"Ah . . ." Li Yuan looked down thoughtfully. "Does this mean we have an antidote?"

Some of the gloom lifted from Tolonen's face. "We have, *Chieh Hsia*. And I have already implemented immediate vaccination procedures throughout the affected areas."

"Then there is some good news, neh?" he said, unable to keep the bitterness from his voice. He shook his head. Such incompetence! Such criminal idiocy! It was hard to believe *anyone* could be so careless! He heaved a great sigh. "No one must know of this. You understand? If news of this gets out . . ." He hesitated, then met their eyes again, looking from one to the other. "Whatever it takes to keep this secret, *do* it. And have no doubt. The existence of our City depends on it."

* * *

Chen stood across the room from the man, his legs apart, his hands behind his back. The prisoner had been stripped and beaten. Now he rested there, on his knees, his back bent, his hands tied to the pole that had been placed behind his neck, one of Chen's soldiers behind him, holding him up. His face was bloodied and there was a huge welt on the right side of his chest where someone had kicked him very hard. Even so, the man had not talked.

Then again, they had not really begun to question him.

Chen turned his head slightly, looking to the screen on the wall to his left, then pointed to it. As he did, a still from the surveillance tape flashed up – an enhancement of the shot showing the man carrying the cleaver.

"Is that you, Tung Cai?"

The soldier forced Tung's head up, making him look. Tung shook his head.

"That *is* you, Tung. We've had the print computer-enhanced and checked the retinal pattern against the one stored on your file. Surprise, surprise. They match. Now answer me, Tung Cai, is that a cleaver in your hand?"

This time Tung's head came up without prompting. He stared a while, then nodded.

"And this room we're in? You recognise this room? You've been here before? This morning, perhaps?"

Tung looked up, staring at him. A muscle beneath his eye spasmed and then lay still. He shook his head.

"I think you're lying. I think that you and your cleaver were here, Tung Cai. I think . . ."

"It wasn't me!" He blurted out. "I know what you're going to say, but it wasn't me! I told them it was madness! I pleaded with them . . ."

Chen took a long, calming breath. "You know what I'm talking about, then, Tung Cai?"

Tung looked away, then gave the vaguest nod.

"And you know who did it?"

Again there was the slightest movement of his head.

"*Well?*" Chen barked, making Tung start. "I am not a patient man, Tung Cai, and if you don't give me a name soon I shall show you just how impatient I can be."

Tung murmured something, low and incoherent.

"Again, Tung Cai. And much clearer this time so that we can all hear."

"It was the *Wu*," Tung said, looking back at him, real fear in his eyes now. "He said he would curse anyone who spoke about it. He said . . ."

"The *Wu*? What's his name, Tung Cai? I want to know his name."

Tung moaned, like he was in pain. "Old Chang," he said finally.

Chen looked to his Captain who was standing in the doorway. "Go. See if you can find him."

He turned back. "And Old Chang . . . he cut up the children? Just him, on his own?"

Tung shivered, then moaned again, a low, desperate sound. But Chen felt no pity for him. If it had been him, he would have interceded, would have done something to prevent the murders, but this animal . . . well, the image on the wall said it all: Tung Cai had revelled in the orgy of violence. Besides, there was still the matter of the bloodied cleaver.

"So, Tung Cai, let's begin again. Tell me just what happened. And let's start with how you came by that cleaver, neh? Let's start with that."

* * *

"What a beautiful day," Tsu Ma said, leaning back in his chair as a servant came across to top up his wine cup. "Bright sunshine and not a cloud in the sky."

Behind him, in the entrance to the great marquee, the golden banner of the Seven hung limp, the *Ywe Lung* concealed within the furls of silk. On the platform one of the contests had just begun and the two Masters were bowing to each other. Close by the other games went on, the click of stone against wood carried by amplifiers to all parts of the Southern Lawn.

Tsu Ma sipped at the wine, then turned, looking to Wei Chan Yin. "All it needs to make it perfect is a beautiful woman, neh, cousin?"

Wei Chan Yin smiled. "That's true. But I am surprised you never married, cousin Ma. Was there never a woman who stole your heart?"

"Oh, plenty, And many who stole my wallet, too. But a wife! Well . . . one doesn't generally *love* a wife. A wife's . . . well, here comes Li Yuan. Let *him* tell you about choosing wives . . ."

Wei Chan Yin frowned. It was unlike Tsu Ma to be so insensitive. Or had he missed something?

"So, Yuan," Tsu Ma said, turning to him as he came closer, "is everything all right?"

Li Yuan nodded, then settled himself into the chair beside his son, waving away a servant who had stepped forward to offer wine.

"All is well," he said, looking up at the board and studying the state of play. "Nan Ho informs me they have secured the last of the trouble spots and are making inroads into tackling the disease itself. We have a vaccine, it seems."

There was a murmur of delight from all those seated about him.

507

"Why that's excellent news, Yuan!" Wei Chan Yin exclaimed. "We can all rest easier for hearing it!"

Hou Tung-po, who had been studying some of the younger Minor Family Princesses through his field-glasses, lowered them and turned, raising his wine cup in salute. "That was quick work, Yuan. I wish my own people were as efficient."

But Tsu Ma was looking at Yuan strangely. *Later*, Li Yuan mouthed to him, then turned to look back at the screen.

* * *

Chen was standing over the man when his Captain came back into the room. He turned, glaring at him fiercely.

"What is it, Captain Jacobson?"

The Captain looked past Chen at Tung Cai, who cowered at Chen's feet, whimpering. "You'd better come, Major Kao."

Chen wiped his hand against his jacket. "Why?"

"It's the men . . . they won't touch him."

"Won't touch who?"

"The *Wu*. They say it will bring ill fortune."

Chen stared at his Captain, then, without a word, came across, pushing past him roughly.

Coming out into Main he saw what was happening at once. A dozen of his men had formed a wide circle about a seated man. Everyone else had moved away. Chen threaded his way through, ignoring the curious faces, coming out into the empty space surrounding the *Wu*.

Chang was indeed an old man, in his seventies at least, and as Chen stepped out in front of him, the *Wu*'s heavily-lined face broke into a smile.

"Major . . . How can I help you?"

The *Wu* had cast an oracle. The yarrow stalks lay in front of him, like spilt straws. Chen stared at them, then looked back at the *Wu*.

"I'm told you killed those children. Is it true?"

The *Wu*'s smile broadened. "They were dying, Major. They had the Sickness."

"But you killed them?"

The Wu nodded. "Did you not see their flesh? They were

508

cursed, marked by Yen Wang, the King of Hells. They bore his sign."

Chen shuddered. "They were not cursed, old man, they were ill. What's more, we have a cure for the Sickness. A medicine that takes away the rash. We could have saved the children."

He heard the murmur of surprise go out, the low babble of urgent voices as those who had heard his words passed on what he'd said to those further back.

"They were *cursed*," the *Wu* insisted, his smile hardening. "That was no sickness. They had Yen Wang's mark upon them. You saw it for yourself. And look . . . look at the oracle. See what it says! It is *Ku*, Decay. It exhorts us to work on what has been spoiled. And afterwards . . . afterwards there is order."

Chen felt himself go cold with anger. "How *dare* you use the Way to justify what you did! You cockroach! You *evil* fucking bastard!"

He kicked the stalks away, then reached down, hauling the old man to his feet roughly. For a moment he glared at him, then, holding him straight, he slapped him hard, sending him sprawling.

"They were children, you fucker! Sick little children!"

He drew his knife.

"*Kao Chen!*" his sergeant called to him, alarmed. "Think what you're doing!"

But Chen *knew* what he was doing. In his mind's eye he could see those three tiny bodies and knew what he had felt in that first moment he had come upon them – how he would have felt had they been *his*. Stepping over the old man, he reached down and grabbed his hair. Then, tugging his head back savagely, he drew the knife across his throat, ignoring the screams from all around him, holding the kicking man until he lay still.

* * *

"He's here . . ."

The sound of the cruiser's engines echoed across the valley

as it came in towards the landing strip. In the enclosure, the four T'ang got to their feet and began to make their way across.

"So much for forty minutes," Tsu Ma said quietly, glancing up at the big timer-board beside the platform. "More like an hour and a half. Where the hell has the fat bastard been?"

"*Tsu Ma* . . ." Li Yuan said, whispering from the side of his mouth. "Be careful what you say . . . there are floaters everywhere."

"You should have banned them, Yuan," Tsu Ma answered, falling into step beside him. "And you should have banned Wang's Champion while you were at it. He's much too good for our poor fellows. Did you see the way he trounced my man? I've never seen anything like it!"

Li Yuan smiled. "It's true. He plays like one possessed."

"Then let us hope his Master rewards him well. Not that our cousin has been noted for his generosity."

Li Yuan looked down thoughtfully. On the platform, as they passed, the Champions stood hastily, turning to face them, bowing to the waist.

"He cannot help that, cousin. His City is poor."

Tsu Ma leaned in. "Maybe so. But who is to blame for that? His father, Wang Hsien made that City strong – stronger than it had ever been. But that wastrel . . ." He gave a snort of disgust.

Li Yuan smiled, answering Tsu Ma beneath his breath. "The world is watching us, cousin. Let us at least pretend to like him for their sakes."

"For their sakes it would be best if that obese obscenity were dead."

Li Yuan turned towards him. "You mean that, Ma?"

Tsu Ma looked away. "It is only what we all think. Even Hou Tung-po, were he pressed. Think, Yuan. What has the man ever brought us but trouble and dissent?"

It was true. Even so, Tsu Ma's words shocked Li Yuan, especially as he had thought to utter them in so public a manner. All of the camera images were being studied carefully, of course, and their screening delayed a minute. In a

510

control room at the heart of the palace, a team of media experts were busy evaluating what could be transmitted to the people of Chung Kuo and what should be held back, and they had strict instructions not to transmit any word of what passed between the T'ang. Even so, he knew how much could be conveyed by body language alone, and the chance that Tsu Ma's words might get back to Wang Sau-leyan was far from negligible.

Ahead of them, the Heads of the Minor Families, their sons and daughters, their wives and retainers, had risen at their approach and now stood, their heads lowered, as the four T'ang threaded their way between them.

As they came out onto the lawn beneath the hangar, Wang's cruiser was beginning its descent. An honour guard was forming up at the edge of the pad, their Captain barking orders.

Li Yuan made to walk on, but Tsu Ma took his sleeve. "No, Yuan," he said, speaking over the roar of the engines. "The bastard's made us wait. Let *him* come down to *us*."

Li Yuan turned, looking to either side of him at his fellow T'ang, but they, like Tsu Ma, seemed content to stand where they were and await their cousin.

Inwardly he shrugged. *We are like bickering children. But maybe Tsu Ma is right. Maybe it's Wang who made us so. Certainly, I would not weep to hear of his death.*

He watched the craft settle among the other imperial cruisers, the landing struts buckling slightly, like a giant spider's knees, taking the craft's weight. Briefly the engines rose to a crescendo and then the sound cut out. In the silence afterwards he could hear the flapping of the banners.

"Well . . ." Tsu Ma said quietly. "Let's hope they can squeeze him through the door, neh, or we could all be standing here a long, long time."

There was a loud metallic clunk as the door-locks were automatically released and then a long hissing as the hatch began to open upwards.

"Smile, cousin," Li Yuan said, whispering the words to

511

Tsu Ma, who stood directly to his left. "Remember . . . the world is watching us."

"And what will the world see? What kind of advert for the Seven is our obese cousin Wang?"

Li Yuan glanced at Tsu Ma, surprised once more by the bitterness behind his words.

"What is it, cousin?" he asked quietly. "This is most unlike you."

In answer Tsu Ma lifted his chin, indicating the lifting hatch. "It's him. Yuan. He makes a mockery of us all. To think that such a one could be a T'ang."

Li Yuan looked back. The hatch was fully open now, like a single insect's wing folded above the dark body of the cruiser. He strained his eyes, trying to see into the darkness, but it was hard to make out just what was happening within.

"The bastard will keep us waiting," Tsu Ma said. "You can be certain of it. He'll milk it to the last . . ."

Tsu Ma had barely uttered the words when there was a low chunking sound and something flew through the air overhead.

"What the . . ."

The explosion was deafening. The ground shook. Li Yuan turned, horrified. On the far side of the Gardens, where the great marquee had stood, a plume of black smoke was climbing into the still clear air. There was a moment's shocked silence, and then the sound of small arms fire broke out close by.

"*Ko Ming!*" Tsu Ma shouted, pushing Li Yuan down. "Fucking *Ko Ming!*" And then the ground near by exploded.

* * *

Chen sat in the makeshift cell, his hands tightly bound, two guards watching him from the doorway. They had stripped him to his loincloth and cautioned him, then they had left him for an hour while they sought instructions.

The guards were uneasy, he could sense that, but he kept silent and did not look at them, not wishing to make their task any harder than it already was. It was not their fault

512

that he felt the way he did. Not their fault that the system was corrupt and evil.

When Captain Jacobson returned, he stood, facing him. "Well?"

Jacobson looked down, unable to meet Chen's eyes. "We are to take you back to Bremen. General Rheinhardt wants to interview you."

"Rheinhardt . . . Ah . . ." Chen nodded. "Is . . . is all well out there?"

Jacobson glanced at him, then looked away again. "It's quiet now. We've removed the body, but I'm going to keep a double guard posted just in case."

Chen nodded. It was what he himself would have done. "I'm sorry, Captain. I'll say in my report that you had no part in what I did."

Jacobson looked up. "Thank you, sir." Then, awkwardly, he added. "We understand what you did, sir. Many of the men have children. They . . ." He swallowed, then went on. "I guess what I mean to say is that if you want a character reference, sir, I'll speak for you. And there's two dozen others who'll do the same."

Chen looked down, moved by the unexpected offer. In all the time he had led this Banner of the Security forces, he had never once felt really close to his men. But now that he was about to be stripped of his command he felt suddenly . . . related somehow. Tied in to them by way of blood and suffering. Even so, it had taken the death of three children and an old man to do that. Death – *Si* – marked everything, it seemed.

He looked up and smiled. "That's kind of you, Dan Jacobson, but I must fight my own battles. What I did, I did out of choice. And what we choose to do we must pay for, neh? Whatever happens, I was glad to serve with you. You're a fine officer."

Jacobson smiled, saluted, then backed away. "Free the Major's hands and give him back his uniform. Then escort him through. We must be in Bremen two hours from now."

* * *

Li Yuan rolled over and sat up, his ears ringing, then looked about him. Tsu Ma lay at his side, groaning but clearly conscious, his eyes open, staring up at the sky. Near by Hou Tung-po lay dead, his face bloodless, splinters of bloodied metal jutting from his neck, shoulder and upper arm. Beside him Wei Chan Yin lay still and ominously silent.

"*Aiya . . .*" he whispered and took a shuddering breath. The firing had stopped, but there were shouts from somewhere behind him, and from the far side of the landing pad came a fierce crackling as a clutch of burning cruisers sent a thick pall of smoke up into the blue.

Just in front of him, no more then twenty *ch'i* from where he sat, a wide but shallow pit had been blown in the lawn where the frog-hopper mortar had exploded. Another jump and it would have landed in their midst. Earth and debris lay everywhere.

"*Chieh Hsia!*" someone shouted distantly. "*Chieh Hsia!*"

Quickly he examined himself. His silks were ripped at the side but that seemed all. He put his hands up to his neck, then felt his scalp, fearing that numbness had concealed some wound from him. There was a moistness on his cheek, but when he drew his hand back from his cheek and looked it was only earth.

He shivered, then looked back at his fallen cousins. Tsu Ma, he saw now, was in great pain, his face contorted in silent agony. His foot . . . Li Yuan gasped, then swallowed hard. His foot had been blown right off!

"Tsu Ma," he said, leaning over him and touching his cheek gently, trying to reassure him. "Tsu Ma, are you all right?" Then, realising that blood was still pumping from the wound, he pulled off his jacket and wrapped it tightly about the stump, trying to staunch the flow.

"I'll get help," he said, crouching over Tsu Ma again. "Hold on. I won't be long."

He turned, facing the palace. A group of men were running across the grass towards them. He gestured to them, urging them to hurry.

514

"*Come on!*" he yelled. "Quickly now! He's bleeding to death!"

He turned back, then stood, searching the nearby grass with his eyes. *There* . . . he saw it. It lay eight, maybe ten *ch'i* away, like a discarded shoe. He went across and, careful not to touch the damaged flesh, picked it up and carried it back.

Crouching over Tsu Ma again, he looked down into his pain-wracked face, grimacing at him. "You'll be okay, Ma. They'll save it. They're very good."

But Tsu Ma barely seemed to recognise him. He groaned, then closed his eyes, tears forming in his eyes.

Li Yuan shuddered. *The men! Where were those men?*

He turned, ready to yell at them again, but they were upon him.

"It's his foot," he said, pointing to it. "He's lost his foot."

One of them leaned over Tsu Ma's great barrel chest, listening, then looked up, his face ashen, and murmured something to one of his colleagues.

"What's that?" Li Yuan asked, noting the look that passed between them. "What's wrong?"

"*Chieh Hsia,*" one of them said, turning to him. "You must be seen to. We'll look after the T'ang. He is in good hands now."

"What's wrong?" he said again, more insistently.

The man took a breath, then answered him. "It is his chest, *Chieh Hsia*. There's damage to his chest."

Li Yuan frowned. "No. It's his foot. Look!" He held it up.

"*Chieh Hsia,*" a voice said from behind him. "You must do as the surgeon says. You must get help."

He turned. It was Nan Ho.

"Master Nan," he said, relieved to see his Chancellor safe. Then, with a shock, he remembered how the attack had begun.

"*Kuei Jen* . . ." he wailed, standing, the severed foot dropping from his hand, forgotten suddenly. "Where in the gods' names is Kuei Jen?"

* * *

515

Tolonen came in from the north, ordering the young pilot to fly in slow and low over the Palace. Even at a glance he could see that the damage on the Southern Lawn was extensive. The fires were all out, yet the wreckage of at least twenty craft still smouldered on the far side of the landing strip. Elsewhere there was major crater damage and from the number of shrouded figures laid out on the grass beside the burned-out marquee, fatalities were in treble figures.

He sucked in a breath, his worst fears confirmed. Only an élite Security squad could have done so much harm in so short a time.

"Set us down by the East Gate," he said, pointing past the young lieutenant. "And patch Rheinhardt through when you can reach him. I want his input on this straight away."

He patted the boy's arm, then went through, taking up a position by the hatch as the craft slowly settled. They had been half an hour out when the news had come. He had turned the craft at once and flown straight back. Half an hour . . . it was not long, and yet it had seemed a small lifetime, especially when the channels had been jammed most of the time, and what reports they *had* got from Tongjiang had been confusing, contradictory.

As the hatch began to lift, he ducked under it and ran, making his way towards the East Gate. There were guards before the gate. They raised their guns, meaning to stop him, then, seeing who it was, backed away, bowing their heads. He ran through, then, at the top of the marbled walk that bordered the Southern Lawn, he stopped, looking across.

He saw Li Yuan at once and felt relief flood through him. The young T'ang was sitting beside a mobile medical unit, his son nestled in his lap.

"Thank the gods," Tolonen breathed.

Just across from Li Yuan, Tsu Ma was sitting on a camp chair, holding his arm while a medic attended to him. There was a bloodstain at his elbow and the white of bone could be glimpsed through the torn material of his jacket. Not only that, but his right leg was in a portable splint unit, as if he'd broken it. He was talking to Li Yuan, laughing through the obvious pain of his injuries, making jokes to ease the shock of things. But Tolonen, knowing him, knew that there would come a time of anger, and of reckoning.

He ran down the steps and strode across the lawn. Ten *ch'i* from his T'ang he stopped and fell to his knees, his head bowed. "*Chieh Hsia,*" he said breathlessly, his voice trembling with emotion. "I am overjoyed to see you safe and in good health. And the young prince . . . ?"

". . . is well," Li Yuan answered, holding Kuei Jen tighter to him. "When we went to greet our cousin Wang, he got bored and ran off. But for once I am pleased he misbehaved himself. If he had not . . ."

Tolonen turned, seeing for himself the huge crater where the imperial enclosure had been. Then, turning back, he looked about, as if seeking someone else. His eyes met Li Yuan's again.

"And Wei Chan Yin?"

Li Yuan looked down, a cloud falling over his features. "My dear cousin is dead. And Hou Tung-po. They died instantly, in the second explosion."

Tolonen stared at him a moment, horrified. His voice now was a whisper. "And among the Minor Families?"

Tsu Ma answered for Li Yuan. "Nine Minor Family Heads are dead and over forty of the princes. The gods know how many are badly injured!"

Tolonen groaned. Never in their history had there been such a disaster! *Never* had so many fallen in so brief a time.

"But who could have done this, *Chieh Hsia*?"

Li Yuan's voice was cold and hard. "For once there's no need for guesswork. The bastards who did this were from one of Wang Sau-leyan's élite squads – from his *Lan Tian,* his 'Blue Sky' Division."

"The Blue Sky . . ." Tolonen nodded. It all made sense. All, that was, except for a motive.

"Yes," Tsu Ma said, giving a small grunt of laughter that was laced with pain. "Well . . . they certainly came out of the blue sky, today, neh? Like a cloud of devils, they were.

If the honour guard had not fought so bravely we would *all* be dead."

Tolonen stared at him, then looked to Li Yuan. "But if we know . . . ?" He waited, then frowned deeply. "Am I *missing* something, *Chieh Hsia*? If it *was* that bastard Wang, then our course is clear, neh? It must be war." His voice rose, insistent now. "This time it *must*!"

Li Yuan looked at him; a cold, clear look that reminded Tolonen vividly of the T'ang's father, Li Shai Tung. So the old man had looked at him when he had urged action over caution. So the old man had sat, like a rock, when adversity threatened. Chastened, he bowed his head.

"Forgive me, *Chieh Hsia*. I shall await your orders."

"And I will give them. But first Tsu Ma and I must talk. First we must consider how to act."

CHAPTER · 20

BENEATH THE TREE
OF HEAVEN

Li Yuan stood back, watching the medical cruiser lift from the cratered field, then turned, facing Nan Ho and Tolonen.

In the background the Palace was a hive of activity. Two whole battalions had been flown in and were digging in around the perimeter, setting up their batteries to bolster the Palace's own defences. If another attack came they would be ready for it.

"The news is bad," Nan Ho said, without preamble. "Wei Hsi Wang is dead, shot in the back by one of his own guards, and Hou Tung-po's family also. A single bomb took care of them."

Li Yuan swallowed. "Then it is just the three of us now. Tsu Ma, Wei Tseng-li, and I." He half turned as the cruiser banked, then swept overhead. Tsu Ma was on board, being ferried to the special unit in Pei Ch'ing where, it was hoped, they could save his foot.

"And my City?" he asked, looking to Tolonen.

"Rheinhardt is in charge, *Chieh Hsia*. The curfew is in force and – so far, anyway – things are very quiet."

"That is so, *Chieh Hsia*," Nan Ho added, glancing briefly at Tolonen, "but how long will that last? Think of how it must look. The transmissions were cut abruptly and no explanation has been given. They will fear the worst. They will be afraid, *Chieh Hsia*, in shock. They will be wondering what is to happen. We must seize the moment and act, before their shock turns to anger and their anger to revolt."

"And you, Knut? Is this how you feel?"

"It is, *Chieh Hsia*." He sniffed. "However, we must be careful how we act."

"Careful?" Li Yuan was almost amused. "Is this the Marshal Tolonen I know? Are you really counselling caution, Knut? What's brought this on?"

Tolonen gave a gruff laugh. "I know how it must look, *Chieh Hsia*, but hear me out. I have given this matter much thought these past few hours."

"Then speak, but let us make our way back inside, neh? There is something I must see to."

The three turned and began to walk back to the Palace, Tolonen to Li Yuan's left, Nan Ho to his right.

"Tactically things are far from straightforward, *Chieh Hsia*," Tolonen continued. "The Sickness and its aftermath have complicated the matter greatly. Things are unstable and the pressures on our Security forces are great. Indeed, your cousin Wu Shih's City fell under far less pressure. We are stretched thin. Any thinner and we might just melt away."

Li Yuan nodded. "And then there's Li Min . . ." He looked to Nan Ho. "Have we heard anything from our 'loyal subject'?"

"Nothing, *Chieh Hsia*. It seems he bides his time."

"Like a mantis, neh?" He huffed out a sigh. "I should have dealt with him when I could, Nantes or no. I should have reached out and crushed that insect then."

Tolonen, who, he knew, had strong opinions on the subject said nothing, merely lowered his head slightly. "We cannot fight a war on three fronts, *Chieh Hsia*," he said, after a moment, "which is why we must take great care to assess just what action is appropriate. Maybe if we could foster rebellion in his City . . ."

Li Yuan looked to Tolonen, seeing how grim his face was. "And how long would that take?"

"It's hard to say . . . They hate the bastard, certainly, but they also fear him. He has taken ruthless measures to stamp out sedition in his City. I am told he has executed more than fifty thousand these past two months alone."

"So I have heard. None the less, it might be worth a try, neh?"

Nan Ho cleared his throat. "Forgive me, *Chieh Hsia*, but I would counsel most strongly against such action. Revolt is easy to incite, hard to put down. If it should spread to our own City . . . why, our current problems would be as nothing. Besides, there is the matter of whether we wish to keep control of City Africa, or whether we are prepared to let it go the way of North America. Once lost it would be hard to regain. It could be . . . well, generations."

Li Yuan nodded, sobered by Nan Ho's words. They had come to the small lawn in front of the steps. Li Yuan stopped, looking at his Chancellor. "Then what *do* you counsel, Master Nan?"

"War, *Chieh Hsia*. An all-out war against your cousin, Wang."

He laughed, surprised. "It is a strange day, neh? First Knut here counsels caution, and now you, my most cautious Chancellor, tell me to go to war."

"For good reasons, *Chieh Hsia*. As Knut says, we cannot fight a war on three fronts. Then again, perhaps there is no need. If it were to be made widely known what your cousin did today, most men would feel a sense of outrage at the cowardly act. Their instinct would be to hit back against the perpetrator, especially when he is as physically odious as Wang Sau-leyan."

"Maybe so. But can we be so certain that we still hold the sympathies of the masses? Might they not see this as an opportunity to throw off the rule of Seven? I read your reports, Master Nan, and they are not encouraging. Our support is badly eroded in the Lowers and to take such a risk . . ."

"There is risk however we act. Our task is to minimise that risk. But hear me further, *Chieh Hsia*. It is not enough,

I feel, simply to win the people's sympathies. Such winds of feeling are fickle and blow briefly. We must actively involve them in our venture."

"Involve them?" Tolonen frowned deeply. "I do not understand?"

"I mean an army, *Chieh Hsia*. We must recruit an army from the people."

"Impossible!" Tolonen said, offended, it seemed, by the suggestion. "You cannot turn that rabble into an army!"

"Forgive me, Knut, but you miss my point. Our purpose would not be to create an efficient fighting force overnight, but to channel all of the aggression which exists in the Lowers of our City. To focus it *outwards*, rather than against ourselves."

Tolonen grunted. "Even so . . ."

"No, Knut," Li Yuan interrupted. "I like the sound of this. But there are problems, neh, Master Nan? Once such a force exists, who then controls it? And once – should we say *if* – the threat of Wang Sau-leyan is dealt with, where do we focus that aggression next?"

"Against Li Min . . ."

Li Yuan smiled. "Ah . . ."

He turned and began climbing the broad sweep of marbled steps, Tolonen and Nan Ho hurrying to catch up with him.

"Well, *Chieh Hsia*?" Nan Ho asked breathlessly as he reached the top.

Li Yuan turned back, looking out past his Chancellor, his eyes taking in the damage that had been done to the Southern Lawn. "It is a big step, Master Nan. An irrevocable step, it seems to me. It would not do to rush into such a venture."

"Time presses, *Chieh Hsia*."

"I know," he answered solemnly. "And yet I must be clear. When finally I act, it must be without doubts. I must know *how* I am to act and *why*."

He put a hand up to his chin. Then, abruptly it seemed, he laughed. "He almost did it! You realise that? The bastard almost pulled it off!"

He turned, looking directly at his Chancellor. "Master Nan . . . contact Ben Shepherd. Tell him . . . tell him I need to talk."

Nan Ho bowed. "I spoke to him earlier, *Chieh Hsia*. He is on his way."

Li Yuan smiled. "And the war, Master Nan? Do you know also how *that* ends?"

"The war, *Chieh Hsia*? No. Only that it must be."

* * *

Wang Sau-leyan put out a fleshy hand, letting himself be helped up out of the great sunken bath, three of his maids half in the water as they strained to lift him. Nearby, a fourth looked on, a huge pile of golden towels in her arms.

As they steered him up the marble steps, there was an urgent knocking at the door.

"See who it is," he said to one of the maids, waving her across. "But don't let them in. Not until I'm ready."

He sat heavily on the couch, spreading his legs, getting his breath back after the exertion, then looked down at himself. His flesh was almost pink from the heat of the water, fold upon fold of pinkness. He laughed, lifting his arms, letting the maids begin their task of drying him.

"You like what you see?" he said to one of the maids, knowing, as ever, that she would lie to him. For who would tell the truth to a T'ang? Who would dare say, "I find you gross and loathsome"? Not one of these sweet young things, anyway.

"My Master glows like a newborn," she answered, smiling up at him as if she loved him.

A good answer, he thought, *for I feel newborn today*.

He smiled and patted her, then turned, looking across to the doorway where the maid was having a low but urgent conversation.

"Who is it?" he called to her. *And what do they want?* he might have added, but he knew what they wanted. For the past three hours they had wanted nothing more than to talk to him.

523

"It is Chancellor Hung, *Chieh Hsia.* He says he wishes to speak with you."

Wang smiled, then turned back, closing his eyes, enjoying the gentle ministrations of his maids.

"Tell him I'll come. In an hour."

He laughed softly, knowing how Hung Mien-lo would rage inwardly at that. *Maybe he'll even call me names, or try to have me killed . . . again.*

Transparent . . . they were all so transparent.

"Oh, and tell him to meet me in the Great Hall," he added, tilting his head back slightly. "And tell him to dress formally."

* * *

"Sit down, Major Kao. We need to talk."

Chen bowed then sat, facing General Rheinhardt.

The General paused, studying the report, then fixed Chen with a stare. His manner was cold, formal; a side of him Chen had guessed at but never seen. He cleared his throat, then launched in.

"Now, let me say straight off, that the last thing I needed just now was for one of my senior staff officers to go haywire in the Lowers. Apart from the effect it has on the reputation of the service, there's the matter of maintaining discipline throughout the ranks. It's a question of example. If the men see one of their senior officers acting irresponsibly then they begin to ask themselves why they should act responsibly. And when *that* happens . . ."

Rheinhardt shook his head slowly and sat back, looking at Chen as he might look at an errant child with a mixture of sternness and regret.

"You were never the ideal appointee, Kao Chen. Your service record was good, up to a point, but your social record left much to be desired. It's not enough for an officer merely to do his duty, he has to fill a social role. It would have been better for you if you were more like . . ."

Rheinhardt fished for a name.

"Like Hans Ebert, perhaps, sir?"

Rheinhardt bristled. "There is no need to add impertinence

524

to the list of your sins, Major Kao!" He visibly stiffened in his chair. "Now, to the matter at hand. The death of the *Wu* . . . Chang Te Li."

"I spit on his ancestors!"

Rheinhardt looked at Chen, astonished. "You what?"

"He was a bastard, sir. An evil man who terrified those about him. I've no remorse for killing him. What he did to those children . . ."

Rheinhardt raised a hand. At once Chen fell silent, lowering his eyes.

"It seems we have two choices," Rheinhardt said after a moment. "I can either demote you to the rank of Captain, with the ensuing loss of face that such a step would bring, or you can choose to leave the service."

In answer, Chen reached into his tunic pocket and took out a folded note, handing it across. Rheinhardt took it and read it. He nodded, as if satisfied, and was about to put it away in the file when a detail caught his attention.

"But this is dated the day before yesterday, Major Kao." Chen met his eyes. "I had already decided, sir."

Rheinhardt stared at him a moment, his eyes narrowed. "And your decision? Did it affect how you behaved down there?"

Chen thought, then shrugged. "It may have, sir. I don't know. But I've been unhappy in the service a long time now. As for the *Wu*, he was a confessed child murderer and I executed him. It wasn't my job. I know that. But I'll live with the consequences."

Rheinhardt nodded. "I won't be a hypocrite, Kao Chen, and say I'll miss you. You were never one to contribute much to briefings, and your paperwork . . . well, to say it was tardy was an understatement. Even so, I wish you the best. Have you thought about what you'll be doing?"

"I plan to take my family onto the Plantations, sir."

"The Plantations?" Rheinhardt raised an eyebrow. "The gods help us . . . You're sure about this?"

Chen nodded.

"You realise what has been happening?"

"I heard the reports on the way over. I understand the Plantations were relatively untouched."

"That's true. Though I've never fully understood why, when the rest of the City's in total chaos, the Plantations should remain calm. Perhaps it's the kind of people they have there."

Or the kind of life, Chen thought.

Rheinhardt took a long breath. "Well, Kao Chen. That's it, it seems. I'll have the official paperwork drawn up and send it through to you. You'll keep your pension, though at a reduced level, and will be allowed to keep the honorary title of Captain. Otherwise . . . good luck."

Rheinhardt stood, offering his hand. Chen got to his feet, then leaned across the desk, returning the General's firm handclasp. But the smile was formal, a gesture of the lips only. They had never really got on.

"Thank you, sir," Chen said, releasing his hand. He backed away two steps and came to attention, making a formal bow to a superior officer for the very last time. Then, turning about-face, he marched from the office.

* * *

"Mary! *Mary!* You *must* come out of there!"

The door flew open. Emily stood there, facing her husband. She was dressed to go out, her hair neatly combed, a small travel bag in one hand.

"What are you doing?" he said, staring at her.

"I'm going, Michael. I'm leaving."

He made a sound of disbelief. "But you can't. I mean, it was nothing. Gloria and I . . . we're friends, that's all. We've been friends since we were two, three years old. And there's nothing more to it than that, I swear to you, Em. Why, I wouldn't think . . ."

He stopped. It was as if she wasn't listening.

"What's up?" he said more softly. "Why do you have to go?"

She shrugged. "I just have to, that's all."

"But you can't," he said once more. "I won't let you."

"No?"

There was a movement of pained exasperation in his face; an expression that reminded her vividly of his father. "Look . . . can't we talk this through. If you're unhappy . . ."

"*Unhappy?*" She laughed sourly. "You don't *know*, Michael. You just don't know!"

"But I thought . . ." And now there was both pain and bewilderment in his face. He looked down, like a scolded child. "I thought you loved me."

She sighed. "I do. The gods know I do. But . . ."

He met her eyes again, looking for reassurance. "Then why?" he asked. "If you love me, why do you have to go? Why can't we work it through? It was just an argument, that's all. Everyone has them. But it's no reason to go, really it isn't. I love you, Em. And if there's something wrong – if there's something you want to change . . . well, tell me. I'll listen. And I'll try. You know I'll try."

She stared at him, her face softening. Even so, she was determined. "It's not you, Michael. Try and understand that. You're a good man. You've turned out better than your breeding. But . . ." Again she shrugged. "I guess it's me. This life . . . I wasn't born to it."

He frowned. Still he didn't understand. But was that so strange? He didn't know her. And maybe he never would. Not in the way she wanted to be known.

"I still love you, Michael, but it isn't enough any more."

"*Why?*"

She shivered. Was there no way to avoid this? No way he'd simply stand back and let her go? She shook her head. "You don't want to know."

"*What?* How can you say that? How the fuck can you say that?"

It was the first time he had sworn at her. The first time, in fact, he had ever lost his temper with her. He lifted a hand in a gesture of apology. "Look . . . I didn't mean . . ."

"No," she said softly. "Nor I. You want to know why, eh?"

He nodded, his eyes still trying to fathom her.

She let the bag drop, then took a long breath. "It's difficult.

It's . . ." She could feel the pain welling up inside her – could feel how tight the muscles in her face were – but she had come too far now to turn back.

"It started years ago . . ."

She saw his eyes widen and shook her head. "No, Michael. It's not another man."

No, she thought. *Nothing so simple.*

"It's a . . . feeling I have. A belief. It's . . . I guess it's who I really am. Being with you, it was good, Michael. Never doubt that. Better than I'd ever dreamed it could be. But it wasn't enough. All these years . . ." She swallowed, all of the frustration suddenly there in her, focused in the fist she raised and bunched. "I denied myself and denied myself, until I just couldn't do it any more. I'd look in the mirror and wonder who the hell I was. The other night . . ."

She took a breath, controlling all the hurt she felt, all the unsatisfied anger. "The other night it came to a head. I looked out across that hall, then looked at myself and I said, What the fuck are you doing? Who *are* you? Well . . . it's time to find out. Time to take up where I left off." She paused, staring at him, willing him to understand. "I have to go down-level, Michael."

"Down *there*!" He stared at her as if she was mad. "But you can't."

"Why not?" she said, more calmly than she felt. "It's where I came from . . ."

His eyes slowly narrowed. "What are you saying?"

"I'm saying . . . that you don't know me, Michael Lever. I'm saying . . ."

His lips slowly parted. "Who *are* you?"

She stared at him a long time, saying nothing, trying to remember hard what it had been like not to know him. Trying – beyond all else – not to imagine what it would be like without him.

"Emily . . ." she said, the word strange on her lips. "Emily Ascher."

"Em . . ." he said softly, surprised. Then, slowly, his face changed. "Then it's all been a lie. All along."

528

She shook her head, pained by the look of accusation he was giving her. "No. I really *did* love you. I really did try to fit in with your world. But it didn't work, Michael. Your friends . . ."

She stopped, horrified. He was crying. Michael was crying.

She shuddered. *No*, she thought. *Please no.* Then, quickly, before her resolve failed her, she picked up her bag and swept past him, hurrying down the stairs.

* * *

Li Yuan stood beneath the Tree of Heaven, looking out across the wind-feathered surface of the long pool. Near by, embedded in the dark North China earth, was the Family tablet, the huge rectangle of pale cream stone carved with the symbols of his ancestors. He stared at it, trying to comprehend what it represented; to picture all of the hopes and fears, the happiness and sorrow, the hatreds and the passion distilled into each name.

Stone. It all reduced to stone.

It was evening, and in the stillness of the walled garden he found himself thinking back, remembering the sprig of white blossom he had plucked from his brother's fine, dark hair, that day that they had buried him.

And the wind blew. And the haft of the axe rotted . . .

He looked up, into the branches of the tree. The moon was up, speared by the topmost branch.

"Ghosts . . ." he said quietly, offering the word to the darkening sky. "This world is full of ghosts."

Even to be standing there seemed unreal. To be alive at all seemed . . . strange, *unexpected*, as if, at any moment, he would wake from life and find himself within the silent vault, there beside his father and his brother, his body cold and still.

Ghosts . . . tonight they walked this walled enclosure.

As he looked down again, the wooden gate set into the wall on the far side of the garden swung slowly open. A figure stood there briefly in the opening.

"Ben? Is that you?"

Shepherd closed the door and came across. He was taller than Yuan remembered and broader at the shoulder. Moreover he had grown a beard; a short, dark, sailor's beard. It changed him. Yet the eyes were still the same. A vivid green, they burned within the tanned perfection of his face.

"You asked for me, Yuan."

"And if I hadn't?"

"I would have come anyway."

Yuan smiled. "How did you find out?"

"It wasn't difficult. When the screens went black I knew something had happened. I tapped through at once and spoke to Master Nan."

Yuan raised an eyebrow, surprised. "You were watching, then?"

"The game . . . Outside my work it's one of the few things that interest me these days."

"I didn't realise. I would have invited you."

Ben smiled, his eyes never leaving Li Yuan's face. "Then I'm glad you didn't. I understand there's a big hole where the imperial enclosure stood."

Yuan nodded.

"So?" Ben looked away for the first time, his eyes like cameras, taking in everything – the pool, the tree, the tablet and, beyond it, the sealed entrance to the tomb. He looked back. "You want to talk?"

"I want . . . to clarify things."

"Ah . . . *clarity*!" Ben laughed. "How much time have we? A vague muzziness we might just achieve, but clarity?" His smile was roguish. "You've made your decision, haven't you, Yuan? You *know* what you have to do. But you want to feel easier about it. You want me to talk away your last nagging doubts. To make you feel good about it, *neh*?"

That last word – not part of Ben's natural vocabulary – made Yuan turn and look at him again.

"I have to live with myself. Men will die . . ."

"Men will die anyway, Li Yuan. You're not God. You didn't make Mankind. Nor did you fashion them into such nasty, quarrelsome creatures. It's how they are. No, Yuan . . . what you *are* is a King. So let's talk of kings, eh?"

Yuan stared at him, grateful. He hadn't properly understood why he had asked for Ben, but now he knew.

"What do you feel?" Ben asked.

"Relief . . . that Kuei Jen and Tsu Ma survived . . . and Tseng-li."

"And beyond that?"

Yuan hesitated, as if waiting for something, but nothing came. He shrugged.

"No anger, then? No burning desire for revenge?"

He shook his head. Strangely, he felt nothing. People were dead, his Palace had been attacked, and he felt . . . nothing. Now that things had come to a head he seemed *beyond* emotion. Not numb, simply dissociated from events.

Maybe he had suffered too much these past few years, or maybe he had outgrown such feelings – become *inured* to them. Whichever, it was as if a screen had fallen, distancing him from that side of himself.

Ben turned and crouched, putting his hand down to the pool's dark surface. "Master Nan said that you spoke of Wang almost admiringly earlier. That you laughed. He couldn't understand it – how one could laugh after what Wang had tried to do to you. But I told him it was natural. Fear and laughter – they're natural bedfellows."

Yuan watched the ripples spread. "Did you know I am to be married again?"

"*Again?*" Ben raised his eyebrows, then nodded. "That's good, Yuan. A T'ang needs a wife. But not always in his bed . . ."

Yuan smiled. Again Ben read things perfectly.

Ben turned, looking up at him. "Do you miss your wives, Yuan? Do you think of them a lot?"

"I . . . I dream of them."

He had told no one that. No one.

Ben nodded thoughtfully. "Dreams . . . you know, Yuan, sometimes I dream of being you."

"*Me?*"

"Yes . . . In the dream I'm sitting on a throne, a dozen Ministers knelt before me, awaiting my every word. And do you know what I do?"

Yuan stared at him, mesmerised. "No . . ."

Ben stood, then took up a pose, as if seated in a throne, his body suddenly stiff and regal. Yuan laughed.

"'*You!*' I say, pointing to one of them. 'Bring me the imperial pot!' And away he trots to fetch the imperial pot. I turn to another. '*You!*' I say, stepping down to where he's kneeling, 'Unfasten the imperial trousers!'"

Li Yuan laughed. "And?"

"Well . . . as the fellow unbuckles me, his eyes averted, naturally, for to look upon the imperial arse is a crime warranting execution, I stare imperiously about me. Then, when the first one brings back the imperial pot, I squat down on it . . ." Ben made the mime of squatting, his face creasing into the most excruciating grimace, ". . . and squeeze out the most enormous turd."

Li Yuan was giggling now, unable to stop himself.

"Then, as I back away, I command them all to bow down before the imperial turd and, there and then, I appoint it my Chief Minister."

"A turd?" Li Yuan was doubled up in laughter. "And what happens then?"

Ben straightened, his eyes twinkling. "They bow . . . with great dignity, of course, and swear allegiance to the turd, and then . . . then I wake up. And I realise I'm just a man and that my shit . . . well, it's just shit."

Li Yuan took a long breath, then nodded. "I understand . . . and yet . . . well, to be a King . . . it *is* different. What one does – how one behaves – affects a great many besides oneself."

"I do not doubt it, Yuan. Yet kings forget that they are also men. It's when they try and act as gods, forgetting their mortality, that things go wrong. Take you, for instance."

"*Me?*"

"Yes . . . all these years you've been living by a set of

god-like and impractical ideals, thinking the world was somehow awry when in fact it was you all along."

Li Yuan stared at him, astonished.

"I've watched you, Yuan. It's like you've been bound up
inside a tight corset all your life. That whole business with
Fei Yen . . . your belief that there could ever be one perfect,
unflawed love, it's the kind of nonsense only someone who'd
never experienced a mother's love could fall for. Not only
that, but your refusal to believe the worst of people until
your nose is rubbed into the shit . . ." Ben shrugged then
stepped closer, his face shining palely in the moonlight. "Of
themselves these are not bad things. In fact, they're rather
admirable traits . . . in an innocent or a fool, but for a grown
man to hold them is . . . well, to be frank about it, Yuan, it's
pitiful, and for a King . . . why, it's disastrous!"

Li Yuan stared back at him, feeling hurt and resentful, his
face hard. "Is that your counsel, then, Ben Shepherd? That
I should be a bastard like my cousin Wang and make those
close to me hate and despise me?"

Ben looked up, studying the moon's bright face. "Don't
mistake me, Yuan. I say none of this to insult you. You are
a nice man, but niceness is no virtue in a King. You wish to
be a good Confucian – you wish to do what is moral – but
it's been my experience that the moral and the political
are rare bedfellows. If they lie down together it is usually
only a marriage of convenience." He looked back at Yuan,
meeting his eyes. "The world is as it is, Yuan, not as we'd
wish it."

Li Yuan stared back at him a while, then gave the briefest
of nods. "*You* should have been the T'ang, Ben Shepherd,
not I."

"Maybe so, but things are as they are. Wishing them otherwise will not help. *What is* must be the basis of all your policy
from henceforth."

"What ought I to do, then?"

Ben smiled. "You must learn not to fear death. What's
more, you need to embrace the darkness, Li Yuan, to *accept*
it – only then will you see clearly in it."

Li Yuan stared back at him. "You speak like you were well-acquainted with the fellow."

Ben laughed. "Some days I think that's true. You know, I went into the Clay, Yuan. Right inside, into the dust-dry dark. And it was . . . well, it was *incredible*. The rawness . . . the *purity* of things down there!"

Li Yuan nodded, then looked down. Since his wives' deaths he had kept himself separate, distancing himself from the world. But Ben was right. As the world tumbled into darkness, so he must engage himself with it. It was simply not possible to go on as he had.

He sighed. So it was. So it *had* to be. And yet he was afraid – fearfully, dreadfully afraid – of what he might become. The first step seemed so simple. He had but to utter a word or two and it was done. There would be war. And yet . . . once he had set his feet upon that path, where would it lead? Where end? Into what darkness would *his* feet be drawn?

He looked down, staring intently at the moonlit whiteness of the Family Tablet, then shook his head.

Ben was right. Night had already fallen, and he must learn now to embrace the darkness – to see through it with a clearer, colder eye. Necessity must now become his by-word. Even so, he would hold some part of him secure against the dark, *against* the guttering of the light. For there would surely come a time . . .

He looked to Ben once more. "Less of a man and more . . . that's what you'd have me be, neh, Ben Shepherd?"

But Ben said nothing. He simply stood there beneath the tree of heaven, his face pale and shining like the moon, his eyes like doors leading into the darkness . . . and smiled.

* * *

Hung Mien-lo hurried along the vault-like corridor and down the broad steps, his body hunched into his cloak as if he were cold. Four hours the bastard had kept him waiting! Four hours! While all around his City fell apart!

As the guards hastened to pull back the great doors before him, he waved them aside, dispensing with formalities, squeezing through the slowly widening gap and out into the Great Hall. He took two steps, a third . . . and stopped dead, astonished.

On the far side of the Hall, beneath a great array of red silk banners, Wang Sau-leyan stood beside the *Hung Mao* woman, two New Confucian officials murmuring the final words of a familiar ritual.

He stared, aghast, recognising the symbols of dragon and phoenix that decorated the Hall on every side. Seeing, from the bright red silks the couple wore, and from the way Wang stood there, that he was already too late.

"*Chieh Hsia* . . ." he gasped.

Wang half-turned. "Ah, Chancellor Hung, come across. We're almost done."

He walked, slowly, as if in a dream, until he stood beside the couple.

"Well, Hung?" Wang said impatiently. "On your knees before your Empress!"

Hung looked to the priests, who had closed their books and were silent now, but the two men looked away.

Gods, he thought. *The bastard has gone mad!*

Wang turned, lifting his bride's hand, like a bloated spider dancing with a cricket. "Well, man?"

Hung fell to his knees, bowing low before the woman. "Your . . . Highness!"

He raised his head slightly. Wang was looking at his bride, his face lit with a strange intoxication. *Does he* know *how grotesque he looks?* Hung wondered. Then, remembering why he'd come, he hauled himself to his feet again.

"*Chieh Hsia* . . . we have to talk. It's chaos out there . . . absolute chaos!"

Wang smiled at him tolerantly. "In a while, Master Hung. Have you no sense of . . . *propriety*? I am a married man. Will you not congratulate me?"

"Con . . . congratulations," he stammered, more convinced than ever that Wang had gone mad. First the attack, and now this. He would do for them all, see if he didn't!

"Good. Now let us go through and share a cup of wine. It is not every day a great T'ang marries."

Hung backed off, his mind racing. If Wang were mad . . . Then, bowing again, he moved back further, letting the pair pass. He followed, anxiety making him clench his hands. If reports were true, they had already lost control over large parts of the southern City, and the Fifth Banner . . .

"*Chieh Hsia!*" he said, his anxiety finding voice. "You *must* act!"

Wang stopped and turned, his face dark with anger. "*Never* tell me what I should or should not do, Chancellor Hung! Not if you value your life."

Hung stood there a moment, horrified, then threw himself down, pressing his forehead to the floor. "Forgive me, *Chieh Hsia*! I am but a lowly beetle!"

He lifted his head slightly, waiting, then heard the T'ang turn, his tread move slowly away. Letting out a long sigh of relief, he clambered up again, running after his Master, quite certain now that he was mad.

* * *

"Chen? Is that you?"

Wang Ti came out of the kitchen in her dressing-gown and, seeing Chen standing in the doorway, rushed across, holding him to her.

"Chen?" she said, kissing him, then moved back slightly to look at him. "Are you all right?"

"I'm fine," he said, smiling, returning her kiss. "Were you worried?"

"I'd heard . . ." She turned. The children were in the kitchen doorway behind her, looking on. She laughed. "Shoo . . . Leave us alone a moment. There's plenty of time to greet your father."

She turned back, hearing the door pull shut behind her.

"So, Kao Chen . . . what happened?"

"I gave General Rheinhardt the letter," he said. "I've done it, Wang Ti. I've quit the service."

"And what did he say?"

Chen looked away, thoughtful a moment, then looked back. "He wished me good luck . . ."

"Good luck?"

". . . and a reduced pension!"

"Ah . . ." She laughed. "Never mind. We would find it hard to spend all that money where we're going, neh?"

He smiled, then kissed her again, a passionate kiss this time, which she returned. "Shall we . . . ?"

She shook her head, smiling gently at him. "Not now. Later. First see your children. Tell them what you've done. Then . . . well, maybe I'll send them to see their Aunt Marie, neh?"

He laughed and held her tighter. "I'd like that . . . oh, and Wang Ti . . . ?"

"Yes, husband?"

"Have I told you lately that I love you?"

* * *

Wang sat back heavily on his throne then beckoned his Chancellor across.

"Now, Hung, what did you wish to see me for?"

Hung shook his head, unable to believe the T'ang could be so calm. He watched as Wang took a peach from the bowl and, turning it to examine it for blemishes, bit deep into the flesh – to the stone – the juice dribbling down his many chins.

"The attack, *Chieh Hsia* . . . on Li Yuan's estate at Tongjiang."

"What of it?"

What of it? He found himself stammering again. "Y-you kn-know of it?"

"Of course I kn-know of it, you idiot! Who do you think planned it and ordered it?" He bit again, speaking with his mouth half-full of peach. "Well? How did it go? Did I get them all?"

"*Chieh Hsia?*"

"My cousins . . . did I kill them all?"

Hung stood there, his mouth open. "I . . ." He shook his head, trying to keep the conversation rational. "I don't think so, *Chieh Hsia*. There's been little firm news. The media have had a total news blackout the past four hours. But . . . well, I think some of them must have survived."

Wang eyed him curiously. "Why?"

He looked down. Now that he was asked, he didn't know exactly why. Yet it wasn't just a hunch. He had done his job too long not to know the signs. They were alive. Or some of them, at least. Unless it were just Tolonen, holding things together while they tried to salvage something from the ruins. But he didn't think so. In fact, the more he thought of it, the more he was certain.

"I don't know, *Chieh Hsia*," he answered finally, making an effort to control himself. "It's just my judgement."

"Your judgement . . ." Wang spat out the stone, then looked at Hung again. "And your spies, Hung Mien-lo? Can't *they* find out?"

"My spies are dead, *Chieh Hsia*."

"Ah . . ." Wang smiled. "Then we must wait, neh?"

"Wait, *Chieh Hsia*?" The thought of waiting any longer appalled him. He was about to tell Wang he should act, then remembered the last time he had uttered the words and let the thought skitter away from him. "If . . . if we could attend to matters in our own City, *Chieh Hsia*," he began.

"If they're dead," Wang said, speaking over him. "If they *are* actually dead, then I inherit all. Did you know that, Hung?"

"*Chieh Hsia*?"

"It was bold, neh, Hung? *Direct*."

Hung nodded, seeing it suddenly as Wang Sau-leyan saw it.

"*Audacity*, that's what it takes, little Hung. And *Vision*. And *Will*. Three qualities that my cousins do not possess."

And a cold, reptilian nature . . .

Hung hesitated, letting his breathing steady, his thoughts settle.

"And if they *are* alive, *Chieh Hsia*?"

Wang took another peach, examined it, threw it away, then took another. He looked back at Hung Mien-lo, smiling, for that brief moment almost like a friend. "I gambled, Hung. And do you know what? I almost pulled it off. Maybe I have. Who knows?"

"But if they're alive, *Chieh Hsia?*"

Wang smiled, then bit deeply again. He seemed almost to be enjoying himself. "Then we wait . . ." He chewed, swallowed. "Wait to see whether my cousins have the will to fight or not."

"And if they do?"

"Then we have nothing more to lose, neh, Hung?" He smiled, then, with a grunt, hauled himself up onto to his feet. "But come, Hung Mien-lo. Let's go out and speak to our people. Let's *reassure* them. You and I."

He grinned, then put his arm about Hung Mien-lo's shoulders. "You, my most *trusted* man, and I . . ."

* * *

Emily slipped the coin into the lock and pushed the door open. Inside, the cubicle was tolerably clean. Better than some she'd seen, anyway. She closed the door and put her bags down on the slatted bench, then looked about her.

There was a washstand and a half-length mirror. A jug of steaming water stood on the stand beside an empty plastic bowl. On the wall was the usual graffiti, and a few new things she hadn't seen before. She studied them a moment, knowing that this was sometimes the way to get a handle on things down here. "Li Min sucks" read one, and just below it "Don't you wish!" along with the usual freight of pornographic outpourings. But what interested her most was the outline of a black hand – a symbol repeated five, no six times about the walls. Inside were slogans: "Burn Down The Walls!", "Life Is Cheap, Flesh Plentiful!", "Five Fingers To The Seven!", and "Destroy What You Oppose!".

She knew of the Black Hand – they had been active in North America – but she had thought them a local phenomenon. If they were over here . . .

Kicking her shoes off, she got to work. Tipping out the small holdall she rummaged through the second-hand clothes she'd bought, selected some which would make her look fairly anonymous, and put them to one side. Then, with a glance at her old self in the mirror, she began to strip off her expensive, First Level clothes, stuffing them into the empty holdall.

Naked, she went to the mirror and, pouring hot water from the jug into the bowl, she began to wash off her make-up.

Finished, she looked at herself again. *Still me*, she thought. *But not for long.* She went to her travel bag and felt in the inside pocket, removing the electric shaver and a small plastic packet. She put the packet on the side of the wash-stand, beside the jug, then faced the mirror again.

When she was done she turned her head, studying the smooth shape of her head. It was elegant, almost statuesque. *If you could see me now, Michael Lever*, she mused, a slight regret still nagging at her. *If you only knew what I have planned.* But he wouldn't know. He'd never know.

She looked down, sniffing deeply, then continued with her work. The packet was slippery in her hands. She put it down and looked around, then picked up one of the second-hand tunics she'd discarded and wiped her hands on it. Then, turning back, she began again. Taking the lenses from the packet, she set them on the side, then, one at a time, slipped them in carefully under her eyelids.

There, she thought, feeling them slide snugly into place over her pupils. *That's better.*

Her eyes, which had been brown, were now green. She smiled. What's more, examined by a retinal-scanner they would identify her not as Mary Lever but as Rachel DeValerian.

She went to the bag and took out the long, black wig and the special adhesive, then returned to the mirror.

"How many times have you done this in the past?" she asked herself softly. "How many times?"

A dozen, fifteen maybe, she answered herself in the quiet of her skull, feeling the old excitement wash through her like a drug and realising just how much she had missed it.

The wig transformed her. Quickly she dressed, then stood

there, squinting at herself. She turned, looking at herself side
on.

The hair wasn't quite right. She'd need to cut it.
Otherwise . . .

She smiled. "Goodbye, Mary Lever," she whispered, then
turned, facing the black hand on the wall. *And hello Rachel
DeValerian.*

* * *

Nan Ho came to him when Ben had gone, standing there
patiently in the darkness beside the pool, a slender figure in
the moonlight. His voice was solemn, ominous in the stillness
of the walled enclosure.

"Well, *Chieh Hsia*? Have you decided?"

Li Yuan nodded. "Call Marshal Tolonen, and get Tsu Ma
and General Rheinhardt patched in to my study. I shall come
there in a moment."

Nan Ho hesitated, staring at the figure of the young T'ang.
Then, with a bow, he backed away.

Li Yuan watched him go, then sighed, looking about him
one last time. In the moonlight the pool was like a mirror,
and the tablet . . .

He walked out onto the white face of the tablet, looking
down at the names beneath his booted feet. Father and
brother, grandfather and great-grandfather, back eleven generations.

Kneeling, he traced his own name on the whiteness with
his finger, then looked up, feeling a mixture of emotions. Was
this what made him different from the rest? – this perversity
of his, this strange sense of being haunted by the days to
come? Was he the only one to have felt like this? Or was
this morbidity of his a product of the times?

He shivered, partly from cold, partly from the intensity of
what he was feeling at that moment. One day a man would
come and, kneeling upon his cushioned pad, would cut the
name of Li Yuan into the stone, coaxing it from the marble
with a loving care. And what would he be thinking, that man?
Would he be thinking of the death of kings? Or would he,

more like, be thinking of his belly – or of that serving girl he fancied?

He smiled, the thought strangely comforting. Then, pulling himself to his feet, he started across the grass towards the open gate, knowing what he must do.

* * *

Wang Sau-leyan stood out on the balcony looking in, watching her move about the room. Outside it was cool and dark, the half moon high and to the west.

"Come in, my love," she called, smiling, then turning back the silken sheets. "Come in now."

"A moment . . ." he called back to her, savouring the brief perfection of the evening. Soon it would all be gone. Dust on the wind. All things. All memory and vision.

He breathed in, catching the faintest scent of her on the cool night air.

One moment, he thought. *One single moment of perfection, and then* . . . he smiled . . . *nothing.*

He turned and went inside, her perfume like a barrier through which he passed, into a bed-chamber of red and golden silks, of fine lace veils and diaphanous curtains.

"Here, my love," she said from among the heaped pillows, her naked flesh a perfect white against the blood-red silk. *"Here . . ."*

He moved towards her.

There was a thudding, an insistent thudding on the outer doors.

He half-turned, looking towards the sound.

It came again, more urgently.

"My love . . ."

He put a hand up to her. "A while . . . I'll not be long."

He walked through, then stood before the bolted doors. "Who is it?"

"It is I, *Chieh Hsia*! Your Chancellor, Hung Mien-lo!"

Of course . . . He reached out, pulled back the heavy, dragon-headed bolt, then stood back as the doors swung slowly inwards.

542

There were guards and several Ministers, and there, at their head, the Chancellor, his face ashen.

"Well, man, what is it?"

He saw their eyes. Wide, fearful eyes, like the eyes of frightened children.

"Well?"

"We are at war, *Chieh Hsia*! Li Yuan has declared war on us!"

CHAPTER · 21

FLOOD TIDE

The last thing had been packed, the rooms checked one last time to make sure nothing had been overlooked. Now they were ready to go. Chen stood in the main bedroom, looking about him at the strange emptiness of it, remembering all that had happened there.

In some ways it all seemed like a dream. Finished with, it now began to lose its substance, fading into memory. All the joy, the suffering he had experienced in these rooms, where were they now?

He smiled wryly, surprised to find himself suddenly so morbid. A new life beckoned – the life he had planned ever since he'd first glimpsed the Plantations twelve years before – and here he was, musing on the past.

Twelve years . . . He frowned. Why had it taken him so long? Why had he let things drift so far? And yet part of him understood. Life was never as simple as one planned. One's feet were set on a course and it was hard to step from that path and take another. The T'ang's service, his children, the troubles with Wang Ti, all had served to waylay him on the journey.

"Chen . . . ?"

He turned. Wang Ti was in the doorway watching him.

"I was thinking," he answered her unspoken query. "Remembering."

She came across and stood by him, putting her arm about his waist, her head pressed against his shoulder. "Will you miss all this?"

"I don't know. There's so much of us still here. We move

our things, yet something remains of us, neh?" He paused, his rough, peasant's face troubled. "I keep thinking, 'We raised our children here' . . ."

"Yes . . ." He felt a tiny shiver pass through her, but when he looked she was smiling.

He laughed. "What was *that* for?"

"I was thinking of the best of it. The good times." She reached up on tiptoe and kissed him on the nose. "You are a good man, Kao Chen. Not many men would have seen it through the way you did."

He looked back at her, his eyes taking in the sweet familiarity of her features. "I did what I had to. I had no choice."

"No . . ." But he could see she was moved by the thought. For a moment he held her tightly to him, his eyes closed, savouring the warm pressure of her body against his own.

There's no mystery, he thought. *This is why. For this.*

"Are the children ready?" he asked, nuzzling the top of her head.

"Marie's sorted them out."

"Ah . . ."

There was a knock at the outer door.

"That'll be Gregor," she said. "He said he'd try to come."

Chen nodded then released her, letting her go to answer it.

This evening they would be there finally, on the Plantation at Kosaya Gora, the open sky above them, the soft earth beneath their feet, and all of this – this world of walls and levels, would be behind them. He smiled. *Yes, I am looking forward to seeing sunlight and rain once more.*

He went out and greeted Karr, hugging him in a tight embrace. Karr was in full combat uniform. This evening he too would be gone, but to Africa.

"Is it all done?" Karr asked, looking about him at the crates that were piled up in the hallway.

"Finally," Chen said and laughed. "And you? Do you know yet where they're sending you?"

"To the Gold Coast," Karr answered. "I'm told there's been fierce fighting there."

"Ah . . ." Chen answered, nodding, sobered by the thought.

Karr had been appointed to command the first of the "People's Armies", as the media termed them. For the past month he had been drilling the raw recruits in the rudiments of soldiering, but from what he'd already told Chen they were still a good six months from being ready.

"I don't like it, Chen, but needs must, as they say." He smiled. "My T'ang commands."

"You should have come with us, Gregor. You and Marie and little May."

The big man smiled and shook his head. "No, Chen. There's not room for two Supervisors on one Plantation. And what else would I have done? Can you see me hoeing the earth?"

Chen laughed. "No. I guess you're right. But I shall miss you, Gregor Karr. Come and visit us when the fighting's over, neh? We'll show you what you're missing living this way."

Karr grinned back at him, holding his upper arms. "I shall look forward to it."

"And good luck, my oldest friend. Keep safe, neh?"

Karr nodded, then looked past him to where his own wife stood beside Wang Ti in the kitchen doorway, cradling his child. "I shall," he answered softly. "The gods know I have a reason to now."

* * *

General Rheinhardt stood to one side as the huge, makeshift screen was lowered into place. Then, satisfied that the screen was properly positioned, the cameras functioning, he went and joined his officers at the side of the long table.

Near by, facing Rheinhardt across the width of the table, stood Major Dehmel of City Africa's Fifteenth Banner, his staff officers behind him. In the great hall below the platform on which they met, the remains of the Fifteenth Banner – some thirty-eight thousand men in all – were gathered, guarded by a double line of Rheinhardt's troops in full combat gear. They sat there, waiting silently for their fate to be decided, their weapons taken from them, their morale low. For three weeks they had retreated southwards, from Beni Suef to Asyut, fighting a desperate rearguard action, relinquishing stack after stack until, at last, they had been overwhelmed. More than four hundred thousand of their number had fallen or been taken captive. Now it was their turn to sue for peace.

As the great screen lit up, both sets of officers turned to it, bowing low.

Seated upon the dragon throne, the giant figure of Li Yuan, fifty *ch'i* tall and twenty broad, looked down on them.

"General Rheinhardt . . ." he said solemnly. "Major Dehmel . . . Shall we begin?"

"*Chieh Hsia . . .*" Rheinhardt said, then, putting out a hand, indicated that Dehmel and his officers should sit.

The great table had been polished until it gleamed, its dark, wooden veneer clear save for two foolscap documents and a set of inks and brushes. One document was set before Rheinhardt as he sat, the other, a duplicate of the surrender terms, had been placed before the Major.

"Before we commence our business here," Rheinhardt said, sitting up stiff and straight as he addressed the men facing him, "let me say that I have nothing but respect for the men and officers of the Fifteenth Banner. You fought courageously against superior odds. There is no shame in what you do here today."

He saw the nods of satisfaction at that and continued. "So . . . let us begin." He half-turned, looking up at the screen. "*Chieh Hsia*? Do you wish to say anything before we sign?"

Li Yuan nodded, and as he did the camera focused in on his face, which expanded, filling the screen.

"Major Dehmel, *Ch'un tzu . . .* I wish only to endorse what General Rheinhardt said. I have seen how well your Banner conducted itself in the face of enormous and continuous pressure and in spite of quite horrifying losses and the most difficult circumstances. You have discharged your duty to your master well and paid fully the debt of loyalty you

owed him. But now . . . now things have changed. The task
of re-unification and regeneration lies ahead of us, and I have
need of such good and loyal men as you to help me in that
task."

The young T'ang paused, seeming to look out at each and
every man there in the Hall. "In the circumstances, I am
willing to offer a commission to any officer of the Fifteenth
Banner who wishes to serve me in the coming campaign.
Likewise, should any ordinary serving member of the
Banner wish to bear arms on my behalf, they shall have the
opportunity to do so."

There was a murmur of surprise. Li Yuan let it settle. For
a moment he simply looked down on them, his features stern
yet compassionate, powerful and yet benevolent, and then
he spoke again.

"Those who have no stomach for the fight ahead will be
interned for the duration of the campaign on half rations.
Those who *do* and are prepared to swear the oath of allegiance to me here today will be given two weeks leave, will
be placed on full rations immediately, *and . . .*" he paused
significantly, "will have all unpaid back-pay met."

This time the noise from the floor was considerable.

Slowly the T'ang's face receded. Once again the screen
showed him seated on his throne. A cold, slightly distant
figure awaiting their answer.

Rheinhardt looked at Dehmel across the table and saw how
Li Yuan's speech had affected him. He saw how the Major
looked to either side of him, his eyes meeting those of his
fellow officers; how they nodded and then looked down,
silently agreeing something between them.

As Dehmel looked back at him, Rheinhardt found himself
smiling at the man, pleased that, after a month of hard fighting, there was something good to come of it.

Dehmel leaned towards Rheinhardt. "Might I speak to my
men, General?"

"Of course . . ." Rheinhardt stood, his officers getting to
their feet as one.

Dehmel stood. Then, allowing one of his Captains to pull

back his chair, he stepped out from the table and went to the front of the platform.

"Men!" he said, addressing the seated mass, his voice, carried by the lapel-mike he wore, echoing back and forth across the massive space. "You have heard the great T'ang. You have heard his most generous and unexpected offer. You have also heard what fate awaits you should you choose not to fight any longer."

He paused, nodding, a faint smile on his lips. "Now . . . You are great fighters. You have proved that a thousand times, beyond any doubt. What I asked you to do you did, and more . . ." Again he nodded, a fierce pride emanating from him now. "Why, Wu Song himself would have been proud to call each one of you his brother!"

There was laughter at that but also a strong murmur of approval.

"So what do you say? Shall we accept the great T'ang's generous offer? Or shall we skulk like beaten women and lick our wounds?"

There were cries of "No!" at that. Men were on their feet.

"*Well?*" Dehmel said, puffing out his chest. "What *is* the feeling of the Fifteenth?"

It began slowly, only a few voices at first, but within seconds it had been taken up throughout the hall, the two words muffled at first by the sound of the Fifteenth getting to its feet, then emphasised thunderously as thousands of booted feet stamped in time with the chant.

"Li Yuan! . . . Li Yuan! . . . Li Yuan! . . . Li Yuan! . . ."

Dehmel raised both hands. Slowly silence fell. He turned, looking up at the screen, then bowed his head. Behind him thirty-eight thousand men – the last of a once great army – did the same.

"*Chieh Hsia . . .*" Dehmel said, his voice trembling with emotion. "The Fifteenth is yours!"

* * *

Li Yuan stepped down from the dragon throne and gestured towards his Chancellor.

"Master Nan, tell my cousins the good news, then send Tolonen in. I need to speak to him."

Nan Ho bowed. *"Chieh Hsia . . ."*

Li Yuan watched him go, smiling, pleased that the day had gone so well, then walked across to the Great Map.

He was proud of the map. It was something that had occurred to him while sitting at his desk, poring over charts and musing upon the progress of the war. He hated sitting. He liked to walk while he thought. So why not build a huge map that he could walk upon? Nan Ho had acted on his suggestion at once, bringing in craftsman to design and make the thing, adding a few details of his own.

Nestled between the pillars at the far end of the audience chamber, it was a huge thing that was raised up a full man's height above the stone floor. A steeply-sloping ramp followed the contours of the map's edge, allowing access to its surface. Spots lit it from above.

He climbed the ramp and stood there, on its southern edge, looking across to the north, some twenty paces distant.

Africa . . . it was so vast you could pick Europe up and drop it whole into that great northern mass between Dakar in the west and Asmera in the east.

He walked across until he stood above Asyut, his feet planted either side of where the Fifteenth had surrendered to him, then turned, looking about him, studying the map for what seemed like the thousandth time. The surface of the map was translucent, registering those immutable details of geography that Man had failed to alter. Beneath that was a second layer – semi-opaque – that showed the City's boundaries, the growing areas and other details of social importance – sea ports and spaceports, barracks and palaces. Beneath that – and this was Nan Ho's touch – was a constantly updated datastream, showing the placement of troops and supplies, commander details and known movements of the enemy forces. Moreover he had only to press the surface with his toe and the computer would provide him with the latest report from that area. It was a wonderfully helpful tool, and he had spent many nights here, consulting the map, getting clear in his mind what needed to be done before talking with his cousins.

He looked about him. The City itself covered less than twenty-five per cent of that great land mass. In some places, like the Gold Coast, North Africa and the eastern seaboard, it hugged the coast, hemmed in by mountains or desert, in others – in ancient Egypt, the Congo, old Nigeria and in the south – it formed vast blocks, linked by narrow corridors. Another thirty-eight per cent constituted the growing areas, the great Plantations that had been Africa's traditional strength. The rest, just over a third of the total – a higher percentage than for any other City bar Eastern Asia – was desert or mountain.

It was a great City. Or had been until just four weeks back. Now it was effectively six separate Cities.

His own forces controlled a broad corridor from the coast of the Mediterranean at Alexandria a thousand *li* south to Asyut on the Nile – an area constituting half the ancient land of Egypt and a large chunk of what had once been Libya. Added to that he had opened a second front at Freetown, and his forces had liberated that strip of the City that hugged the coast from Dakar in the north to Tiassale in the east, two hundred *li* short of the regional capital of Abidjan. There his Fourth Banner were facing Wang Sau-leyan's Twelfth in a confrontation that was becoming bloodier by the day.

He turned and walked back across. Tsu Ma's forces were in the Congo, Wei Tseng-li's on the Mozambique coast. Neither had met with great success. To hold a hostile City was, they had discovered, much easier in theory than it was in practice. It was like playing *wei chi* in three dimensions. Unless you physically destroyed those areas you had passed through and herded the inhabitants on, the likelihood was that, as soon as you were ten stacks on, the citizens would rise up behind your lines. You could place garrisons, of course, and both Tsu Ma and Wei Tseng-li had taken to doing this, but the cost in additional manpower was enormous and simply added to the already horrendous problems of logistics.

Regular drops onto the roof of the City were not enough, and food and munitions were constantly being depleted to an almost critical point. One bad defeat for either force and they would have to pull out altogether.

The problem was made worse by the fact that, in the south, large parts of the City had already rebelled and thrown off Wang's rule. Two new kingdoms had set themselves up, and though their kings seemed short-lived and their ragged armies posed no direct threat to the Alliance, their example was pernicious. City Africa, seized by the turmoil of the war, had decided it had finished with the rule of Seven, and revolutionary pressures, long suppressed under Wang, had now risen to the surface.

Nor was that the only problem. As when North America had fallen, refugees from the African Above had poured into the other cities. But whereas before there had been room enough – *just* – to cope with the sudden influx, now the position was untenable. Many of those who had fled had been forced to put up with what they considered inferior accommodation, ten, even fifteen levels down. Unrest, something unheard of in the top twenty levels of his City, had spawned some ugly incidents, and he had been forced to intercede to calm things down. Right now things were peaceful, but how long would that last?

The great doors at the far end of the chamber swung open and Tolonen stepped through. The old man looked across, then bowed his head.

"You wanted me, *Chieh Hsia*?"

"Yes, Knut. Join me here. I need to talk."

As Tolonen climbed up onto the map and began to walk across its surface towards his T'ang, Li Yuan saw how his eyes scanned the surface, taking in details.

"You have heard about the Fifteenth Banner?"

Tolonen grinned. "It is most excellent news, *Chieh Hsia*. And with Karr's new force to aid the Fourth at Abidjan, we ought to be hearing good news on that front too, neh?"

Perhaps, he thought, keeping his doubts to himself. But that was not why he had asked Tolonen here. He went across

552

and stood once more above Asyut, then turned, looking directly at the old Marshal.

"Where is he, Knut? Where is the bastard?"

Tolonen shrugged. "Dead, *Chieh Hsia*? It's at least a week since he's been seen in public. So maybe . . ."

But Li Yuan was shaking his head. "If he was dead we would know about it. No, he's alive. The fact that his armies still fight on is proof of that. They would not do so if he were dead."

It was the truth, surprisingly enough. At first he had been shocked by how fiercely Wang's Banners had fought for him. But slowly an understanding of it had come to him. It was not Wang himself they fought for, but for his incarnation as T'ang of City Africa. Such loyalty was deeply ingrained. Without it they would have had no purpose, no real existence as a force, and so they fought – for Africa and their T'ang.

He turned, looking about him, then paced slowly about the map, moving from one of Wang's palaces to the next – Alexandria, Casablanca, Ibadan, Kinshasa, Kimberley, Lusaka . . . he had hit them all. Only Luxor remained. But word was that Luxor had been abandoned.

"If we could find him," he mused, loud enough for Tolonen to hear. "If we could track him down and kill him . . . well, maybe we could end this slaughter."

He looked up, facing Tolonen, almost eye to eye with him.

"Luxor," Tolonen said. "You must hit Luxor next."

"And if he's not there?"

"Then we fight on, *Chieh Hsia*. No one said it would be easy. Such a war as this . . . it could last years."

Li Yuan nodded. That was exactly what he feared. Long years of warfare – what would that do to Chung Kuo? And if, at the end of it Africa were lost, what then for Europe and the other continents? Would it all go into the darkness?

"Luxor, then," he said. "And let us pray this time we find him."

*   *   *

The Hall was echoing silent. Wang Sau-leyan sat on the high throne looking down on the eight prisoners, his bloodshot eyes burning with hatred. Beside him the woman looked away, fear – or was it revulsion? – in her eyes.

The prisoners were kneeling, their heads lowered, more from exhaustion than deference, their hands bound tightly behind their backs – so tightly, in fact, that blood seeped between the cords, darkening them. At their backs a line of imperial guards waited, swords drawn, behind their Captain.

At a gesture from the T'ang the screen behind him lit up, showing the prisoners seated about a dining table, their silks, which now were filthy, brightly clean, their faces, which now were bruised and bloodied, laughing.

Wang leaned forward slightly, his hands gripping the arms of his throne tightly.

"Do you *still* deny it? After all you've seen? After all I've shown you?" He gestured towards the screen without looking. "Are those eight *other* men up there, laughing and talking of my death . . . plotting to kill me?"

He sat back, wiping the spittle from his lips. "You *treacherous* scum! I treat you like my brothers and this is how you pay me back! *This!*"

He shuddered, an expression of pure disgust crossing his face. His arm shot out, pointing at one of the prisoners. "Captain, slit that fucker's throat!"

Several of them looked up. One, finding himself facing Wang's outstretched hand, gave a wail of terror. "No, *Chieh Hsia* . . . you misunderstand . . ."

The Captain grabbed him brutally, locked his head beneath his left arm, then dragged the blade of his knife across his throat. Blood gouted instantly. He let him fall.

"And *that* one!" Wang snarled savagely, pointing at another.

Dutifully, the Captain complied.

The other six were trembling now. There was the smell of faeces in the air.

"You *miserable* little men . . ." Wang snorted, then stood

unsteadily, tottering down three steps before he got his balance. "You . . . *ordure.*"

He came down the remaining steps and, taking the bloodied knife from his Captain, went and stood over one of the remaining six.

"Plead . . ." he said softly, leaning in towards the man. "*Plead* for your miserable life."

The man threw himself down, prostrating himself at Wang's feet. "*Ch-chieh Hs-hsia,*" he stammered. "The gods know . . ."

He grunted, Wang's full weight suddenly on him, forcing the knife down into his back. Wang straightened up. The knife was embedded to the hilt.

"And you?" he asked, turning to another.

The man fainted.

"Boil them," he said, dismissing the guards, then wiped his hands on his silks. "Set up a cauldron and boil them all alive. And do it somewhere close. I want to hear their screams."

He turned, looking up at his wife, seeing how she stared down at her hands, her flesh so pale it was almost translucent. She had not been well these past few days. She was off her food and he had heard her being sick in the night. *Nerves,* he thought, mounting the steps towards her.

"It's okay," he said softly, leaning over her. "I'd never hurt you. You know that. Never."

Then, turning, addressing the backs of his guards as they dragged the prisoners away, he yelled. "Where's Hung Mien-lo? Where's that bastard Hung?"

*　*　*

Hung Mien-lo scampered down the walkway, then strapped himself in again. And not a moment too soon as the tiny, four-man craft lurched to the right, making the course change he had specified.

He looked out, watching the roof of the City come up fast at him, then level out as the craft banked, heading out over the sea. He turned, looking out through the porthole opposite, seeing the great white wall of the City recede slowly, dwindling, dwindling as the craft accelerated.

Hung sat back, feeling the pull of the craft against his body, then closed his eyes, relaxing, knowing, for the first time in over four weeks, that he was safe.

Behind him Africa grew smaller by the moment, like a bad dream fading in the dawn's light. Ahead lay the ruined plains of the Middle East, and beyond them Central Asia and his destination.

He took a long breath, sighing almost, then laughed, wondering what his once-Master would be doing now. *Tending his wife, no doubt*, he thought, and felt a dark tide of satisfaction wash through him.

It had been impossible to poison Wang himself. A dozen tasters had died in various attempts over the years. But his wife . . . Again Hung laughed, his laughter rolling on and on as if it would never stop. It had been easy. Had he spoon-fed her the stuff pure it could not have been easier.

A day he gave her, if that. And Wang himself? Hung Mien-lo heaved a huge sigh, purged by the laughter. Wang Sau-leyan's days were numbered. He had known that from the start: from that moment in Wang's rooms when – in a moment of blinding insight – he had understood that Wang Sau-leyan had murdered his own father. Even so, he had lasted well. A lot longer than he, Hung, had expected. But now the game was up. His Ministers had fled and now his Generals argued openly with him. In a day or two it would be over.

He turned to the window again. Out there, under the bluest of skies, the sea glimmered like a mirror to the horizon. *Perfect*, he thought, recalling for some reason the blue of the woman's eyes. And even as he did he heard the click of the trigger mechanism, the slow whirring of the gears beneath his seat as the bomb's detonator turned a half-circle and engaged.

* * *

The men were dropping from the craft before it settled, scuttling across the roof of the great Palace towards the ventilation shafts.

They had expected defensive fire coming in, but the Palace batteries had been silent, the look-out posts unmanned. Even so, they took positions as rehearsed, going through routines drilled into them a hundred times. There were the dull concussions of grenades and then they were inside, dropping swiftly, silently down the shafts and out into the upper corridor.

At the top of the great stairway the team leader stopped, sniffing the air, then raised a hand, bidding his men be still. There was a strange smell in the air, like the smell of overcooked meat. He listened. Nothing. The place seemed deserted. Then, from way down in the bowels of the palace, they heard a distant groan.

They descended, slower now, checking each room, each intersection before they went on. Down, four flights and then a fifth, until they came to the Great Hall itself and, beyond it, the throne room.

There, in the entrance to the Hall, beneath the faded wedding banners, they found the cauldrons – five of them in a line, the charred remnants of a fire about the base of each. Inside, their pop-eyed inhabitants were flushed a perfect pink, like crabs, the flesh bloated and grotesquely mottled. The surface of the cauldrons was still warm, the water – what was left of it – tepid.

The team leader nodded to himself, then waved his men on. Beyond the throne room was the T'ang's offices and above them . . .

He stopped, hearing the groaning come again, closer now and louder. The great doors to the throne room were partly closed, the view within obscured.

There! he mouthed, signalling to one of his men. At once the man crossed the hall, disappearing behind one of the pillars and reappearing further down.

"Stay where you are!" a voice called out from inside the throne room.

He saw his man freeze, then begin to back away.

A single shot rang out. He heard his man fall, his gun clatter away from him.

He looked back. The doors were beginning to close.

"*Now!*" he yelled, urging his men forward. Then, taking a grenade from his belt, he ran, hurling it towards the ever-narrowing gap.

The explosion threw him back.

Climbing to his feet, he charged again, firing into the smoking ruins of the doors, his men close by, the sound of their guns making his ears ring loudly.

Inside the throne room, just beyond the shattered doors, six bodies lay still, as if asleep, their clothes dishevelled. Coughing, he scrambled over the debris, looking about him. The throne was vacant, the room itself empty save for the corpses.

He turned, issuing orders. "Stewart, Blofeld, secure the stairway to the T'ang's quarters. Edsel, Graham, check the anteroom."

His breath hissed from him. If Wang were here, he was upstairs, in his private rooms. In fact, he was certain of it now. These men – he bent over them, examining their uniforms, making sure – were *Lan Tian*, members of Wang Sau-leyan's élite "Blue Sky" Division, the same that had launched the attack on Tongjiang. They would not have defended the door unless there were a reason for it.

The groaning came again, much louder than before – a ragged, awful sound that tore at one's innards. A death sound.

Upstairs. It came from upstairs.

He picked his way through the wreckage then walked across to the throne, his gun cradled against his chest. At the foot of the steps he stopped, looking down at the three corpses that lay there, the blood congealed in a single, sticky pool about them. This was Wang's work, he had no doubt of it. His face wrinkled with disgust, he turned, beckoning his men across to him, then looked towards the door of the anteroom.

"Clear," Edsel said.

"Good." He waited as they gathered about him, then addressed them quietly. "You know what we have to do. Li Yuan wants his cousin taken alive. He wants him tried for what he did at Tongjiang."

There were grave nods at that, then, at his wave of dismissal, they moved across, taking positions beside the door that led through to Wang's rooms.

He sent four men through to check out the offices. They were clear. Then, with a whispered prayer to Kuan Ti, the God of War, he began to climb the steps, his gun out before him.

* * *

Wang Sau-leyan sat on the edge of the bed, staring at the woman. Her eyes were closed, the lids almost transparent now. Sweat beaded her naked skull, the yellowing flesh stretched tight and flecked with tiny pustules. He watched her, seeing how she writhed in her torment, fascinated by her suffering, and when she groaned again something in him responded to the sound, urging it from her.

Death. This was what death was like. He could feel it. He could actually *feel* it.

He reached across, taking the silver-handled gun from the bedside table, then stood. He could hear them outside. Could hear their whispering and their quiet tread. In a moment they would be here.

Come, he thought, unafraid now that it was upon him. *Death do your worst. I, for one, am not beholden to you. I will not cower at your door. I am a T'ang – a Son of Heaven!*

He laughed, wondering, even as he did, what they made of his laughter. Did they think him mad? Well . . . let them. What did it matter what the *hsiao jen* thought? It was not *their* fate to have their deaths recorded.

He stood before the mirror, studying himself a moment, then turned, hearing the faintest buzzing in the air. At first he couldn't make it out, then he saw it: a remote, the tiny floating camera hugging the tiled ceiling of the room.

It slowed, then stopped, no more than ten *ch'i* from where he stood, its tiny camera eye focused on him.

He smiled, a knowing smile, then returned to the bed, sitting on the end, the gun cradled in his lap.

The first man entered slowly, cautiously, and took up a

kneeling position to the left of the door, beside a standing vase. The second was more nervous. He ducked into the room and scurried to his position to the right. From there the two men covered Wang with their automatics. He watched them, expressionless; saw how they tried to watch him without meeting his eyes, and smiled inwardly. Whatever their orders, when it came to killing a T'ang it went against their deepest instincts.

He stretched his neck, then turned, hearing the woman stir. Her teeth were clenched, almost in a rictus, yet she was still alive. Her breath hissed from her momentarily in tiny gasps, then she relaxed again.

Not long, he thought, and turned as the Captain came into the room.

"*Chieh Hsia* . . ."

Wang Sau-leyan stared at the man a moment, then, with an effort to be regal, hauled himself up off the bed and stood.

"You are not welcome here, Captain. These are my private rooms."

The man's head lowered the slightest degree. He took two paces towards Wang Sau-leyan. "I . . ."

Wang raised the gun, pointing it at him.

The Captain swallowed. "Put the gun down, *Chieh Hsia*. We are not here to hurt you. My orders are . . ."

Wang pulled the trigger.

There was a huge bang and then a moment's shocked silence. The two men by the door were staring at Wang, astonished, yet still they did not fire.

The Captain lay where he had fallen, groaning, clutching his ruined stomach, blood pooling beneath him on the polished tiles.

Wang Sau-leyan looked up into the eye of the remote and smiled. "Well, cousin Yuan? Is *that* what you wanted?"

He looked back at the two men by the door, moving the gun between them. "You? . . . Or *you?*"

He lowered the gun, considering a moment, then, making a show of aiming it again, pointed it at the second guard. "You, I think."

"Husband . . ."

The voice was like a whisper from the other side. Wang turned, looking at the woman. She was sitting up, and her eyes, which bulged from the diseased flesh, stared at him as if from Hell itself.

Husband . . .

The explosion rocked him. It was like he had been jabbed with a red-hot poker. He looked down, seeing at once where the bullet had entered him. Even as he stared the redness spread, and with it a searing pain that was like ice scorching through his veins. The gun fell from his hand. Slowly he sank to his knees.

He turned his head, looking, trying to understand just what had happened. The two guards seemed frozen. Their guns were lowered, their faces shocked. Between them, looking back at him from where he lay, the Captain held a gun. As he watched the faintest trace of smoke lifted from the barrel.

"Ah . . ." he said, smiling through the encroaching blackness. "Ah . . ."

"Chieh Hsia," the man answered him, letting his face fall back into the sticky mess that surrounded him. *"Chieh Hsia . . ."*

EPILOGUE – WINTER 2213:
SUNLIGHT AND RAIN

—— · ——

"To understand others is to be knowledgeable;
To understand yourself is to be wise.
To conquer others is to have strength;
To conquer yourself is to be strong.
To know when you have enough is to be rich.
To go forward with strength is to have ambition.
To not lose your place is to last long.
To die but not be forgotten – that's true long life."

— Lao Tzu, *Te Tao Ching*, Chapter 33

SUNLIGHT AND RAIN

Chen sat on the fence beside the plank bridge, looking back across the fields towards the village. Behind him, at the intersection of the two big irrigation canals, stood the Overseer's House, its three tiers dominating the skyline for ten *li* in every direction.

It was a crisp, clear day, and from where he sat he could see figures moving about in the broad grassy avenue between the blockhouses.

Kosaya Gora was one of the biggest of the Moscow Region plantations and besides the normal dormitories had two dozen big farmhouses, most of them shared by single families – three generations sharing the twelve spacious rooms. As Supervisor, Chen had been allocated one of them. On seeing it, Wang Ti had shaken her head. "All these rooms to keep clean," she'd said, as if scolding him, but her eyes had told a different story. He had seen how she looked about her, wide-eyed, a child again, and Jyan! – even Jyan had smiled when he'd seen what it was like.

"It's so *big*, Dad," he'd said. "The sky . . ." His voice had trailed off in wonder. "I never imagined . . ."

Chen looked down. It had rained that morning and the grass on the embankment was still wet. He jumped down, then crouched, his right palm resting on the dark, soft earth. Plucking a blade he put it to his lips and closed his eyes.

So real, it seemed a dream . . .

He smiled. Twelve years it had taken. Twelve years of exile, from the earth . . . and from himself.

He opened his eyes, staring out across the shining water, then looked closely at the grass blade in his hand. Sunlight and rain, that was all he'd ever wanted. He understood that now. Sunlight and rain.

He stood again, then turned full circle, taking it all in. To the north and east, some two, three *li* distant, were the store-houses – massive covered reservoirs of grain and rice. Closer to hand were the quarters of the Overseer's guards, three one-storey bunkers in a staggered line. South, beyond the block-houses, were the workers' quarters, a dozen long, low huts embedded in the earth.

And the City?

Chen smiled. From Kosaya Gora one could not see the City. One could look forever and see no sign of walls and levels. He laughed, then turned back to face the village.

Two of the figures had broken from the others and were running towards him across the fields. In the late afternoon sunlight he had to squint to make out who it was, then smiled, starting to make his way towards them.

There was a shrill yell of greeting and then a long whooping sound, the last from his twelve-year-old, Wu. But it was his daughter, Ch'iang Hsin, who reached him first.

"Papa!" she yelled breathlessly. "They're going to throw a party! A welcoming party! For *us*!"

He grinned and picked her up, whirling her about. "I know," he said, hugging her tightly. "And there'll be cakes and special drinks!"

As Wu came up, he scooped him up in his other arm, then began to carry them back, laughing, the two children giggling and screeching beneath his arms.

Later, sat at the top of the steps of the blockhouse, Ch'iang Hsin wrapped up and snuggled into his side, Chen looked out, watching the villagers prepare the tables down below. Behind him the door was open, and from the window to his left he could hear Wang Ti singing in the kitchen as she scrubbed the floor.

"Well?" he asked the eight-year-old, putting his arm about her shoulders. "Do you think you'll like it here?"

She nodded silently, but her eyes were filled with the magical strangeness of the place.

He smiled. "It's beautiful, neh? But you should see it in the summer . . ."

He turned, trying to take in once more the overwhelming openness of the place, the unending vastness of the sky. So blue it was, even now, when the snows were only weeks away.

My second life, he thought, and shivered, not from the cold, but from the memory of a summer night twelve years before. He narrowed his eyes, remembering the sound of flute and strings floating enchantingly on the night air beneath a three-quarter moon; the villagers whirling about an open fire, their faces shining, their dark eyes laughing in the fire's light.

And other things. He remembered the stoop-backed youth, Pavel, and all that had happened to him. Dust he was, and yet for that one brief moment he lived again inside Chen's skull, his long face smiling back out of the darkness, his soft-spoken words a haunting echo.

"I thank you, Kao Chen . . . but I think I would die in there. No fields, no open air, no wind. No running water, no sun, no moon, no changing seasons. Nothing. Nothing but walls."

The face receded, the voice fell silent. Dust he was . . .

Chen sat forward a little, holding Ch'iang Hsin tightly to his side. Pavel had been right. There was nothing in the City.

For a moment he held himself still, listening to the sounds of his new life – to the breeze soughing through the fields, to the soft, harmonious voices of the villagers, the hiss and clatter from a dozen kitchens as the women prepared things for the party. But one sound dominated all others – the sound of Wang Ti singing as she worked, like an uncaged bird sat in the branches of a tall tree.

He sighed then kissed the crown of his daughter's head. "We're here," he said softly, as much to himself as to her. "We're really, finally here."

"Yes," she answered quietly, then leaned forward, pointing beyond the rooftops to the west. "Look, papa . . . clouds . . . look at the clouds!"

AUTHOR'S NOTE

The transcription of standard Mandarin into European alphabetical form was first achieved in the seventeenth century by the Italian Matteo Ricci, who founded and ran the first Jesuit Mission in China from 1583 until his death in 1610. Since then several dozen attempts have been made to reduce the original Chinese sounds, represented by some tens of thousands of separate pictograms, into readily understandable phonetics for Western use. For a long time, however, three systems dominated – those used by the three major Western powers vying for influence in the corrupt and crumbling Chinese Empire of the nineteenth century: Great Britain, France, and Germany. These systems were the Wade-Giles (Great Britain and America – sometimes known as the Wade system), the Ecole Française de L'Extrême Orient (France) and the Lessing (Germany).

Since 1958, however, the Chinese themselves have sought to create one single phonetic form, based on the German system, which they termed the *hanyu pinyin fang'an* (Scheme for a Chinese Phonetic Alphabet), known more commonly as *pinyin*, and in all foreign language books published in China since January 1st, 1979 *pinyin* has been used, as well as now being taught in schools along with the standard Chinese characters. For this work, however, I have chosen to use the older and to my mind far more elegant transcription system, the Wade-Giles (in modified form). For those now used to the harder forms of *pinyin*, the following (courtesy of Edgar Snow's *The Other Side of the River*, Gollancz, 1961) may serve as a rough guide to pronunciation.

Chi is pronounced as "Gee", but *Ch'i* sounds like "Chee". *Ch'in* is exactly our "chin".

Chu is roughly like "Jew", as in *Chu Teh* (Jew Duhr), but *Ch'u* equals "chew".

Tsung is "dzung"; *ts'ung* with the "ts" as in "Patsy".

Tai is our word sound "die"; *T'ai* – "tie".

Pai is "buy" and *P'ai* is "pie".

Kung is like "Gung" (a Din); *K'ung* with the "k" as in "kind".

J is the equivalent of r but slur it as rrrun.

H before an s, as in *hsi*, is the equivalent of an aspirate but is often dropped, as in Sian for Hsian.

Vowels in Chinese are generally short or medium, not long and flat. Thus *Tang* sounds like "dong", never like our "tang". *T'ang* is "tong".

a as in f*a*ther

e – r*u*n

eh – h*e*n

i – s*ee*

ih – h*er*

o – l*oo*k

ou – g*o*

u – s*oo*n

The effect of using the Wade-Giles system is, I hope, to render the softer, more poetic side of the original Mandarin, ill-served, I feel, by modern *pinyin*.

This usage, incidentally, accords with many of the major reference sources available in the West: the (planned) sixteen volumes of Denis Twitchett and Michael Loewe's *The Cambridge History of China*; Joseph Needham's mammoth multi-volumed *Science and Civilisation in China*; John Fairbank and Edwin Reischauer's *China, Tradition and Transformation*; Charles Hucker's *China's Imperial Past*; Jacques Gernet's *A History of Chinese Civilisation*; C. P. Fitzgerald's *China: A Short Cultural History*; Laurence Sickman and Alexander

Soper's *The Art and Architecture of China*; William Hinton's classic social studies, *Fanshen* and *Shenfan*; and Derk Bodde's *Essays on Chinese Civilisation*.

The version of the *I Ching* or *Book of Changes* quoted from throughout is the Richard Wilhelm translation, rendered into English by Cary F. Baynes and published by Routledge & Kegan Paul, London, 1951, and all quotations from that text are with their permission.

The quotation used by Marshal Tolonen in the Prologue is from Part II ("Vainamoinen's sowing") of *Kalevala: The Land of the Heroes*, translated by W. F. Kirby, and first published by J. M. Dent in 1907. I would refer the interested reader to the Athlone Press edition of this wonderful work.

The quotations from Lao Tzu are from the *Te Tao Ching* (Chapters 33 and 70 of the new translation based on the recently discovered Ma-wang-tui texts) translated by Robert G. Hendricks and first published by the Bodley Head, London, in 1990. All passages are quoted with permission.

The quotation from Duo Duo's "Death of A Poet" is from his collection *Looking Out From Death*, translated by Gregory Lee and John Cayley, and published by the Bloomsbury Press, 1989. It is used with their kind permission.

The quotation from Confucius, *The Analects*, Book V, is from the D. C. Lau translation, published by Penguin Books, 1979, and used with their permission.

The translation of Li Ho's "Criticisms" is by A. C. Graham from his invaluable and wonderful *Poems of the Late T'ang*, published by Penguin Books, London, 1965, and is used with their kind permission.

The excerpt from Li Po's "We Fought South of the Walls" is from *Li Po and Tu Fu*, translated by Arthur Cooper, and published by Penguin Books, 1973, and is used with their kind permission.

Outlaws of the Marsh (the *Shui Hu Chuan*, or "Marsh Chronicles"), mentioned in Chapter 8, is by Shi Nai'an and Lo Kuan Chung (author of *The Three Kingdoms*) and is available in an abbreviated version from Unwin paperbacks. For those with enough stamina to read a full version, Nobel prize-winning writer Pearl S. Buck's *All Men Are Brothers* (all 1279 pages of it) is recommended. A computer version, "Bandit Kings of Ancient China", is also available.

The Chinese sage, Chuang Tzu, is referred to several times in the text, and a collection of his "Basic Writings" (title *Chuang Tzu: Basic Writings*) can be obtained from the Columbia University Press, translated by Burton Watson [1964]. The quotation used here is from Section 4, "In The World of Men", and is used with the kind permission of the publishers. I strongly recommend this to anyone with more than a passing interest in Taoism, for its delightful wit and charm. The reference to an autumn hair in my text comes from "Discussion on Making All Things Equal" and comes from the belief that strands of animal fur grew particularly fine in autumn, and "the tip of an autumn hair" is thus a Chinese cliché for something very small.

I am heavily indebted to Chinua Achebe, one of our finest twentieth-century writers, for the glossary of Ibo words at the end of his novel *Things Fall Apart*, which I have plundered mercilessly for my Mars sections.

The game of *wei chi* mentioned throughout this volume is, incidentally, more commonly known by its Japanese name of *Go*, and is not merely the world's oldest game but its most elegant.

Finally, for another look at the "tree that died" motif (see Chapter 14) the reader is referred to Philip K. Dick's *The Man Who Japed*, Ace Books, 1956.

David Wingrove, June 1993

ACKNOWLEDGMENTS

Thanks, as ever, go to my editors, for their patience and continuing enthusiasm: to Carolyn Caughey at NEL (for saying "No"), to Jeanne Cavelos at Dell (another fan-turned editor) and to Alyssa Diamond (super-mum and editor!) and John Pearce at Doubleday (Canada). Also to my ex-editors, Brian DeFiore and Nick Sayers, good friends both.

For thoughtful readings of early drafts (and for beer and friendship), I have to thank Vikki Lee France and Steve Jeffery, Andy Sawyer and Mike Cobley.

Thanks also to Sylvie and Nicolas Chapuis, to Michael Iwoleit and all my other translators and to Stewart Robinson, Robert Gillies and Alan Martin – collectively known as Tranceport – for the cut of "A Spring Day At the Edge of the World". I'm looking forward to the album!

To Robert Carter, best of friends, may *Talwar* reap the huge rewards it deserves. And to Andy "the Slut" Muir, thanks for the tapes and see you in the downstairs bar of the Moon on the Green!

To Brian Griffin, first-line critic, a huge *merci* for all you did this time out. Your input was invaluable.

Huge thanks must also go to the players and management of Queens Park Rangers Football Club – Ray, Les, Andy and the boys – for adding hugely to the Tao of my life. See you Saturday!

Writing a multi-volumed novel like this involves a lot of sitting and thinking and what would I do without the background of music. This time out special thanks go to Tangerine Dream, H. P. Zinker, Tranceport and The Guo Brothers.

Finally, to John Patrick Kavanagh, buddy and collaborator, here's a big *Kan pei!* to EMPIRE OF ICE. See you on the shore . . .

GLOSSARY OF MANDARIN TERMS

Most of the Mandarin terms used in the text are explained in context. However, as a few are used more naturally, I've considered it best to provide a brief explanation.

aiya! – common exclamation of surprise or dismay.

ch'a – tea.

chen yen – "true words"; the Chinese equivalent of a mantra.

ch'i – a Chinese foot; approximately 14.4 inches.

ch'i – "inner strength"; one of the two fundamental "entities" from which everything is composed. *Li* is the "form" or "law", or (to cite Joseph Needham) the "principle of organisation" behind things, whereas *ch'i* is the "matter-energy" or "spirit" within material things, equating loosely to the *pneuma* of the Greeks and the *prana* of the ancient Hindus. As the sage Chu Hsi (AD 1130–1200) said, "The *li* is the *Tao* that pertains to 'what is above shapes' and is the source from which all things are produced. The *ch'i* is the material [literally instrument] that pertains to 'what is within shapes', and is the means whereby things are produced . . . Throughout the universe there is no *ch'i* without *li*, nor *li* without *ch'i*."

Chieh Hsia – term meaning "Your Majesty" derived from the expression "Below the Steps". It was the formal way of addressing the Emperor, through his Ministers, who stood "below the steps".

ch'in – a long (120 cm), narrow, lacquered zither with a

smooth top surface and sound holes beneath, seven silk strings and thirteen studs marking the harmonic positions on the strings. Early examples have been unearthed from fifth century BC tombs, but it probably evolved in the fourteenth or thirteenth century BC. It is the most honoured of Chinese instruments and has a lovely mellow tone.

ching – literally "mirror"; here used also to denote a perfect GenSyn copy of a man. Under the Edict of Technological Control, these are limited to copies of the ruling T'ang. However, mirrors were also popularly believed to have certain strange properties, one of which is to make spirits visible. Buddhist priests used special "magic mirrors" to show believers the form into which they would be reborn. Moreover, if a man looks into one of these mirrors and fails to recognise his own face, it is a sign that his own death is not far off.

chung – a porcelain *ch'a* bowl, usually with a lid.

ch'un tzu – an ancient Chinese term from the Warring States period, describing a certain class of noblemen, controlled by a code of chivalry and morality known as the *li* or rites. Here the term is roughly, and sometimes ironically, translated as "gentlemen". The *ch'un tzu* is as much an ideal state of behaviour – as specified by Confucius in his *Analects* – as an actual class in Chung Kuo, though a degree of financial independence and a high standard of education are assumed a prerequisite.

Hei – literally "black"; the Chinese pictogram for this represents a man wearing warpaint and tattoos. Here it refers to the genetically manufactured (GenSyn) half-men used as riot police to quell uprisings in the lower levels.

hsiao jen – "little man/men". In the *Analects*, Book XIV, Confucius writes: "The gentleman gets through to what is up above; the small man gets through to what is down below." This distinction between "gentleman" (*ch'un tzu*) and "little men" (*hsiao jen*), false even in Confucius's time, is no less a matter of social perspective in Chung Kuo.

Hsien – historically an administrative district of variable size. Here the term is used to denote a very specific administrative area: one of ten stacks – each stack composed of thirty decks.

Each deck is a hexagonal living unit of ten levels, two *li*, or approximately one kilometre, in diameter. A stack can be imagined as one honeycomb in the great hive of the City.

Huang Ti – originally Huang Ti was the last of the "Three Sovereigns" and the first of the "Five Emperors" of ancient Chinese tradition. Huang Ti, the Yellow Emperor, was the earliest ruler recognised by the historian Ssu-ma Ch'ien (136–85 BC) in his great historical work, the *Shih Chi*. Traditionally all subsequent rulers (and would-be rulers) of China have claimed descent from the Yellow Emperor, the "Son of Heaven" himself who first brought civilisation to the black-haired people. His name is now synonymous with the term "Emperor".

hua pen – literally "story roots", these were précis guide-books used by the streetcorner storytellers in China for the past two thousand years. The main events of a story were written down in these *hua pen* for the benefit of those storytellers who had not yet mastered their art. During the Yuan or Mongol dynasty (AD 1280–1368) these *hua pen* developed into plays, and later on – during the Ming dynasty (AD 1368–1644) into the form of popular novels, of which the *Shui Hu Chuan*, or "Outlaws of the Marsh", remains one of the most popular.

Hung Mao – literally "redheads", the name the Chinese gave to the Dutch (and later English) seafarers who attempted to trade with China in the seventeenth century. Because of the piratical nature of their endeavours (which often meant plundering Chinese shipping and ports) the name has connotations of piracy.

huojen – literally, "fire men".

kang – the Chinese hearth, serving also as oven and in the cold of winter as a sleeping platform.

Kan pei! – "good health" or "cheers"; a drinking toast.

Ko Ming – "revolutionary". The *T'ien Ming* is the Mandate of Heaven, supposedly handed down from Shang Ti, the Supreme Ancestor, to his earthly counterpart, the Emperor (Huang Ti). This Mandate could be enjoyed only so long as the Emperor was worthy of it, and rebellion against a tyrant – who broke the Mandate through his lack of justice, benevolence and sincerity, was deemed not criminal but a rightful expression of Heaven's anger.

Kuan Yin – the Goddess of Mercy; originally the Buddhist male bodhisattva, Avalokitsevara (translated into Han as "He who listens to the sounds of the world", or *Kuan Yin*). The Chinese mistook the well-developed breasts of the saint for a woman's, and since the ninth century have worshipped Kuan Yin as such. Effigies of Kuan Yin will show her usually as the Eastern Madonna, cradling a child in her arms. She is also sometimes seen as the wife of Kuan Kung, the Chinese God of War.

kwai – an abbreviation of *kwai tao*, a "sharp knife" or "fast knife". It can also mean to be sharp or fast (as a knife). An associated meaning is that of a "clod" or "lump of earth". Here it is used to denote a class of fighters from below the Net, whose ability and self-discipline separate them from the usual run of hired knives.

lao jen – "old man"; normally a term of respect.

li – a Chinese "mile", approximating half a kilometre or one-third of a mile. Until 1949, when metric measures were adopted in China, the *li* could vary from place to place.

liumang – punks.

maotai – a strong sorghum-based liquor.

men hu – literally, "the one standing in the door"; the most common of prostitutes.

mou – a Chinese "acre" of approximately 7260 square feet. There are roughly six *mou* to a Western acre, and a 10,000-*mou* field would approximate to 1666 acres, or just over two and a half square miles.

Nu Shi – an unmarried woman; a term equating to "Miss".

pau – a simple long garment worn by men.

Pien hua – literally "Change".

Ping Tiao – "levelling". To bring down or make flat. Here used also as the name of a terrorist (*Ko Ming*) organisation dedicated to bringing down (levelling) the City.

Shen Ts'e – special élite force, named after the "palace armies" of the late T'ang dynasty.

Shih – "Master". Here used as a term of respect somewhat equivalent to our use of "Mister". The term was originally used for the lowest level of civil servants to distinguish them socially from the run-of-the-mill "misters" (*hsiang sheng*) below them and the gentlemen (*ch'un tzu*) above.

tai – "pockets"; here used to denote Representatives of the House at Weimar who have been bought by (and thus are "in the pocket" of) various power groupings (originally the Seven).

t'ai chi – the Original, or One, from which the duality of all things (*yin* and *yang*) developed, according to Chinese cosmology. We generally associate the *t'ai chi* with the Taoist symbol, that swirling circle of dark and light, supposedly representing an egg (perhaps the Hun Tun), the yolk and white differentiated.

te – "spiritual power", "true virtue" or "virtuality", defined by Alan Watts as "the realisation or expression of the Tao in actual living."

T'ing Wei – the Superintendency of Trials, an institution that dates back to the T'ang dynasty. See Book Three (*The White Mountain*), Part Two, for an instance of how this department of government – responsible for black propaganda – functions.

ti yu – the "earth prison" or underworld of Chinese legend. There are ten main Chinese Hells, the first being the courtroom in which the sinner is sentenced and the last being that place where they are reborn as human beings. In between are a vast number of sub-hells, each with its own Judge and staff of cruel warders. In Hell it is always dark, with no differentiation between night and day.

wei chi – "the surrounding game", known more commonly in the West by its Japanese name of "Go". It is said that the game was invented by the legendary Chinese Emperor Yao in the year 2350 BC to train the mind of his son, Tan Chu, and teach him to think like an Emperor.

Wu – a diviner; traditionally these were "mediums" who claimed to have special psychic powers. *Wu* could be either male or female.

Wu – "non-being"; as Lao Tzu says: "Once the Block is carved, there are names." But the *Tao* is unnameable (*wu-ming*) and before Being (*yu*) is Non-Being (*wu*). Not to have existence, or form, or a name, that is *Wu*.

Wushu – the Chinese word for martial arts, refers to any of several hundred schools. *Kung Fu* is a school within this, meaning "skill that transcends mere surface beauty".

wuwei – non-action; an old Taoist concept. It means keeping harmony with the flow of things – doing nothing to break the flow. As Lao Tzu said, "The Tao does nothing, and yet nothing is left undone."

yang – the "male principle" of Chinese cosmology, which, with its complementary opposite, the female *yin*, forms the *t'ai chi*, derived from the Primeval One. From the union of *yin* and *yang* arise the "five elements" (water, fire, earth, metal, wood) from which the "ten thousand things" (the *wan wu*) are generated. *Yang* signifies Heaven and the South, the Sun and Warmth, Light, Vigour, Maleness, Penetration, odd numbers and the Dragon. Mountains are *yang*.

yin – the "female principle" of Chinese cosmology (see *yang*). *Yin* signifies Earth and the North, the Moon and Cold, Darkness, Quiescence, Femaleness, Absorption, even numbers and the Tiger. The *yin* lies in the shadow of the mountain.

Yu – literally "fish" but because of its phonetic equivalence to the word for "abundance", the fish symbolises wealth. Yet there is also a saying that when the fish swim upriver it is a portent of social unrest and rebellion.

yuan – the basic currency of Chung Kuo (and modern-day China). Colloquially (though not here) it can also be termed *kwai* – "piece" or "lump". One hundred *fen* make up one *yuan*.

Ywe Lung – literally the "Moon Dragon", the great wheel of seven dragons that is the symbol of the ruling Seven throughout Chung Kuo. "At its centre the snouts of the regal beasts met, forming a roselike hub, huge rubies burning fiercely in each eye. Their lithe, powerful bodies curved outward like the spokes of a giant wheel while at the edge their tails were intertwined to form the rim" (from "The Moon Dragon", Chapter Four of *The Middle Kingdom*).